Hearthsraven

Katherine A Smith

Book Three of the Northnest Saga

Available from author Katherine A Smith

<u>The Northnest Saga</u>

Hawkwind's Tale
The Fledging of Hawkwings
Hearthsraven

<u>The Dragonic Voyages</u>

Dragons to Loose
Dragonic Freedom
Dragonic Pride
Dragons to Keep

<u>Children's Books</u>

Otter Twin Magic
Otter Sea Magic*

*Forthcoming

Hearthsraven

Katherine A Smith

Book Three of the Northnest Saga

Kasmith Art and Books
Fort Bragg, CA

For all those on their journey to a healthier, better place,
whether just getting started, in the deepest midst of struggle,
or finally in freedom.

Chapter 1
Northborn Year 0: Winter

The little boy approached her, holding out a fragment of hard yellow fruit in a grubby hand. She could see it was half rotten, but the snow was only now off the ground, new crops hadn't yet come in, and any food was better than none. The skinny kid looked like he desperately needed it too, but warmth was critical for surviving the night: more important than food.

The girl reached out and accepted the fruit. Then the boy handed her a stone, which she took in her other hand. He waited, shivering, as she closed her eyes and concentrated. A minute later she handed it back; the stone was almost hot enough to burn. Without a word of thanks the boy turned and scampered off.

Night was falling. By her count, all the children that lived in the abandoned shack had returned. Most had bought heat stones from her, and she had a little collection of food in payment. It was poor stuff, but it would keep her alive. As silently as possible, she ate everything but the worst of the rot. Hunger more or less assuaged, she crawled into her own corner to sleep in the moldy hay under tattered blankets.

The other children slept together in a ball of unwashed bodies and rags, sharing the warmth of the heat stones. Even though the children survived because she made heat for them, they didn't invite her to join them. She was seen as different, and she didn't give away the heat for free. Making each heat stone took energy. If they wanted one, they could pay or do without. It hadn't earned her their love, but it did mean she didn't have to scrounge for food in winter, and in summer food was easy enough to find.

The girl curled herself up in her corner and spent a few minutes heating up the stone floor she lay on. It would radiate back the heat the rest of the night. That took up most of her remaining energy, and she fell into a heavy sleep.

Northborn Year 1: Summer

Summer was a time of plenty, even for beggar children. They could bathe without freezing and people were more willing to give them food, or even old, threadbare blankets and clothing too worthless to go in the ragbag. Layer enough ragged blankets and actual warmth could be achieved. Likewise, layer enough tattered clothing and it almost equaled a real set of clothes.

The girl who could heat up rocks, however, had put on a growth spurt. She was no longer so cute and helplessly tiny. People were more likely to suspect her of being a thief. They weren't always wrong. She also offered to do work in exchange for food—many of the children did. Because she was older, she sometimes got it, too, but there were other consequences to growing up.

***

The girl awoke in the middle of the night with twisting pain in her insides. That wasn't unusual, considering all the questionable food the beggar children ate, but this felt different: lower and deeper. Then she felt something furry brush past her leg and she kicked out. She heard rats scatter.

Rats were her roommates, but they usually kept their distance, going instead to the refuse piles. Some of the children were even known to catch rats and attempt to eat them, but that was an act of desperation, as eating rats often made a kid sicker than being aching hungry.

The girl sat up and noted sticky wetness on her legs and ragged smock. She touched it, smelled it: blood. Her heartbeat kicked up. Why was there blood? She couldn't feel a wound and didn't remember getting hurt. She would have felt it if the rat had bitten her. Rather she guessed the rat had been attracted to the mysterious blood. Was it related to the pain in her belly? She snatched up the nearest pebble and spelled it for light.

Dim though it was, she could see the blood spots clearly now, staining her smock near her—she gulped. It was all near her groin, and in fact—investigation revealed that it seemed to be coming out of her. She'd never seen anyone get sick like this. Her abdomen clenched, twisted, and she gasped. Her heart beat faster with mounting fear. All she could think was that this was something serious.

"I need a healer," she breathed between clenched jaws.

There was a curfew in the city. No one was allowed outside between dusk and dawn without a permit. Certain people were granted permits—like the lamp fillers and the deliverymen who brought coal to houses in the wee hours of the morning. There were soldiers in the street, patrolling to make sure people without permits stayed inside.

The girl shuddered with unfamiliar pain and stared at the red blood on her fingers. She'd had scrapes and little cuts before, but never something like this: never so much blood. It was like during the war, when people were bleeding, when—

"I'll die," she whispered. "I have to go."

There were a few different sorts of healers in the city. She knew where the one who served the poorest people lived. Sometimes the old woman would treat the beggar children for free, although she wasn't always good at making them well. A few had even died from sicknesses the healer couldn't cure.

It was a long way: a walk of several minutes. The girl would have to try to get there, and hope she didn't encounter any soldiers. There were rumors that drakes watched the streets, too, but she didn't really think that was true. She thought the soldiers just said that to try to make people obey the curfew.

The girl shoved to her feet, trying not to double over with the pain in her belly. She belted her smock tighter, thinking that might help, but it didn't seem to. With the light pebble in a pocket in case she needed it, she staggered to the doorway and slipped between the crossed boards that were supposed to indicate the shack was abandoned and unsafe.

The street looked empty. It was rutted but dried out now in the summer heat, the ridges of mud hardened into tripping hazards not yet beaten down into dust. The healer's house was in the direction of the center of the city—although still nowhere near it. The poor lived around the edges. The poorer the people were, the further from the center they lived.

There were no soldiers in sight, and the nearest lamp was far down the road where it forked. The girl headed that way, bare feet silent on the dirt, until she reached the intersection and turned towards the city center. The houses were crumbling wattle and daub or ramshackle wooden structures half falling over, with more holes than actual walls, draped with worn curtains. She could hear snoring from inside some of them, and an occasional crying baby.

She made it to the next lamp, and the next. The road turned to packed dirt so hard it almost felt like stone, and the ruts were fewer. The houses became straighter, taller, with solid walls that didn't look like the next gust of wind would knock them over. There was a market area ahead where the beggar children often got food.

The girl stepped around the corner, feeling more confident now—the healer's house was close, only a few more turns—and ran right into a patrol of soldiers. She bounced off the lead man. Her head had been down, as she scuttled along bent over and clutching her belly, and she hadn't even seen them.

"Ho, now, what's this?" the man exclaimed. He grabbed her arm in a sharp grip. "You're in violation of curfew."

The girl looked up at him. He was handsome, with thick blonde hair and a wide, strong jaw.

"Please sir," she tried, "I'm sick. I'm trying to get to the healer."

"It's just a street urchin," one of the other soldiers said.

"The law applies to all citizens," the first man affirmed. He shook her a little. "Wandering about looking for something to steal, are you?"

They didn't understand. She plucked at her smock, showing the blood stains and the blood running down her legs.

"Please, I'm bleeding, let me go to the healer," she tried again.

For a second the men seemed confused. Then one, the one that hadn't spoken yet, laughed.

"Blimey, it's a girl," the first man declared. "Or rather, a woman now. You never had a mother to tell you about womanly bleeding?"

What was he talking about? She tried to pull out of his grip. "Please, sir, let me go. I might be dying."

Two of the men laughed.

"You're not dying, little lady," the first man chortled.

He yanked her closer and trapped her in his arms. He swung her around so he faced his two companions.

"Well, a thieving street urchin we would have fed to the drakes for being out past curfew," he said, "but there's another use for a woman."

"Let her go," the third man urged. He had a neat brown beard and wore an expression of concern. "She's not doing any harm."

"Criminals have to pay," the first man argued. "She'll pay me right now."

He grabbed the front of her smock and tore it from her. She yelped with shock.

"She's filthy," the second man, who looked like something had taken a bite out of his nose, winced. "Are you sure?"

"A little blood and dirt never hurt anyone," her captor shrugged.

"Stop it," Brown-beard objected. "The Lords declared, no more messing with the women. We'll get in trouble."

The girl struggled, trying to get loose, but the blonde man's arms were too strong.

"We won't get in trouble unless someone tells," he emphasized.

"No one listens to a street urchin," Bit-nose agreed.

Brown-beard took a step forward, but Bit-nose shoved him back.

"Let him have his fun, and she'll think twice about breaking curfew again," Bit-nose said.

"You want to go second?" the first man asked. "We can all share."

The girl thrashed, tearing at his arms with her grubby nails and trying to kick with her heels. She didn't know what they were talking about, but somehow she knew it was bad.

"Hey, cut that out," her captor ordered.

"Need me to hold her for you?" Bit-nose offered, laughing.

Her heel caught her captor's knee from the side and he stumbled, his grip loosening. She wriggled out, but he still had her arm in a tight grip. As soon as he caught his feet, his free hand came swinging, slapping her hard enough across the face to make her vision go white and then black for a moment.

"Little gutter bitch, learn your place," he growled.

"Stop that," Brown-beard demanded.

"Easy," Bit-nose cajoled, halting Brown-beard with another shove. "He isn't going to hit her anymore, right? And no one's going to know unless you blab about it."

The first soldier snatched at the remains of the girl's smock, ripping it out from under her twine belt and leaving her naked. Still holding her arm with one hand, he fumbled with his own belt with the other.

"This isn't happening," Brown-beard declared.

He tried to push forward again, but Bit-nose countered him, and soon they were struggling with each other. The girl writhed: instinctively fighting to escape. She tried to kick, punch with her free arm, and even tried to bite, which only got her another slap in the face. Against the big man's strength, she had no chance. He twisted her arm up behind her back until she cried with the pain of it and went still, though her heart thundered on.

"That's better," the handsome one grunted, gripping her hip hard enough to bruise.

Her body was immobilized, but something within continued to struggle. It bubbled and boiled up from her core, rose to her skin, barely contained by that thin, taut barrier. The girl could hardly breathe, terrified and battered, but she sucked in a breath and screamed from deep in her belly as the soldier pulled her back against him.

Her talent broke free.

The man shoved her away so she skidded and tumbled across the hard packed dirt, screaming himself almost as high pitched as she had.

"Argh, my privies! She's done roasted my privies, the gutter witch-bitch," he howled.

The girl had landed in a heap, and almost managed to turn over when she felt a hand sink into her matted hair, and she was yanked vertical, scrambling to get her own feet under her.

"She's a witch, a witch," the handsome man was snarling.

He dragged her towards him with one hand still in her matted hair, and drew back his other—fisted. The girl, feeling a chance at fighting back, matched his snarl. As he punched her across the face, she let loose again, this time beyond the surface of her skin: out, out at him.

He lit up like a torch, dropping her to slap at his flaming clothes. Bit-nose rushed over to him, but the girl barely saw it. Her head was swimming and an ache had bloomed inside her skull, and also on her left cheek where he'd punched her. She rolled to her side and vomited what little was in her stomach. Her arms shook as she tried to push herself up, and after a moment gave up.

The burning man was rolling on the ground now, trying to smother the flames. Bit-nose was hovering over him anxiously. Brown-beard, however, had started to draw near the girl. He held her ripped and stained smock out to her, but she couldn't lift a hand to take it.

"I won't touch you," Brown-beard said. "I'm sorry this happened." Carefully, he covered her with the garment, and glanced back at his companions. "At least Gurek got what he deserved."

"I'm dying," the girl told him breathlessly, now more sure of it than ever.

"You were going to a healer? I'll carry you there, if you want."

Bit-nose strode angrily up behind Brown-beard. The girl opened her mouth, wanting to warn him, but he seemed to read her expression, and turned before Bit-nose could strike him. This seemed to put Bit-nose off balance; he'd clearly been expecting an easy hit.

"Gurek's burned bad," Bit-nose glowered. "It's this rat's fault. Take her and let's go back to headquarters."

"I'm taking her to a healer," Brown-beard said. "And Gurek's injuries are his own fault. Maybe it'll teach him not to mess with people, even defenseless children."

Bit-nose bared his teeth. "You're to blame for this, too, Makelat."

"I am," Brown-beard nodded. "I'm to blame for not fighting harder to protect this child from you and Gurek."

The girl huddled under her ruined smock, shivering even as she felt her skin heating again, this time with fever. She hardly reacted as the two men fought briefly but half-heartedly. Bit-nose gave up after only a few swings.

"Fine then," he scoffed. "We'll see how this works out for you."

Bit-nose retreated to pick up the lantern he'd set down at the beginning of the confrontation, and then went to help Gurek up, leaving the girl and Brown-beard in only the faint glow from the nearest lamp. The girl managed to fumble in her pocket and knock out the pebble she'd spelled for light. Brown-beard's eyes widened, but he didn't say anything.

Then came the distant sound of cantering horse hooves. Brown-beard stepped in front of the girl, as if to guard her, and within moments a horse and rider came hurrying down the road, straight towards them. Gurek and Bit-nose were still hobbling off, but the mounted man stuck his hand out at them.

"Halt," he commanded.

He reined in only a few paces away from Brown-beard. The other two men had stopped as though they suddenly couldn't move. The mounted man turned to stare at Brown-beard.

"You. What has happened here?" he demanded. "Speak, man."

Brown-beard drew himself up to attention and recited. The girl listened with only half an ear. Her head hurt so badly she feared it was splitting open, and her belly wasn't much better. She did get a hazy look at the man on the horse. He was lean, with wild, fluffy black hair. He wore more brightly colored clothing than she'd ever seen. Even in the dim light, it almost glowed.

Brown-beard finished his recitation. The mounted man looked over at the two other soldiers, who were still comically frozen in place. After a moment, both the men jerked into motion, almost falling, and hobbled away together out of sight.

"Pick her up," the mounted man ordered.

Brown-beard hesitated. "She'll not hurt me?"

Vaguely, the girl sensed the regard of the mounted man fall over her. Her headache spiked for a moment, like when a bruise got poked, and she whimpered.

"She is too exhausted to do more tonight," the mounted man said, "even if she wanted to."

"She is a witch then?"

"She's a mage," the mounted man corrected, "or will be, with a bit of training. Now fetch her."

"Please pardon me," Brown-beard said as he approached and carefully gathered the girl into his arms.

She could hardly struggle, but since she was dying, supposed it didn't really matter. The man did his best to keep her covered with the smock, and tucked her head against his shoulder so it wouldn't loll and hurt her neck.

"This way," the mounted man gestured.

Brown-beard started walking after the horse, but the girl never saw the journey they took. She fell unconscious long before they reached the destination.

***

The girl awoke some time later, head fuzzy with memories of being bathed and dressed and having some kind of liquid forced down her throat. She was in a softer bed than she could ever recall experiencing, covered with thick blankets, wearing undergarments, and a tunic and skirt that felt whole and gentle against her skin. Her head and belly didn't hurt much anymore. There was no scent of dirt, rot, rat droppings, or unwashed human filth. Curious to know more, she pushed off the blankets and sat halfway up.

Immediately, a little boy sitting in a chair across the room from her straightened from his slouching position, leapt up, and ran off. Daylight trickled through a curtained window, showing a smallish room with just the narrow bed, chair, desk, and a wardrobe. The floor was wood and the walls smooth, bare stone. The girl only had time to make those assessments and recall a bit of the previous night before the door opened again, but it wasn't the boy returning.

"So, awake are you?"

It was the mounted man from before with the fluffy black hair. Now that she saw him in better light, she was able to assess that while he was certainly an adult, he wasn't an old adult. He was lean and tall, as she'd observed, and his clothes were just as brightly dyed as the night before, in shades of vibrant blue: flared trousers and a snowy white shirt under a long, collared tunic. He also wore rings and a necklace of silvery stones. He didn't look friendly, but it did seem that he'd saved her and taken care of her. She dared to venture to speak.

"I'm not dying? Where am I?"

"You're not dying," he confirmed shortly. "You're in the palace. You're mine now, and you have a few choices ahead of you."

The girl swallowed. "Yes, sir," she whispered.

"You're maturing into a woman, as evidenced by the bleeding you're experiencing. It will not kill you. A kind woman named Germaine will explain the finer details of it to you. You have no mother or father?"

A little dazed, she swallowed again and answered. "They died. Father was a soldier. Mother followed him here with me, but she died, too."

"You weren't born here." It wasn't a question.

"In Weldom, sir."

There was a hint of satisfaction in his eyes as he pondered her face. "You understand what those soldiers were trying to do to you?"

She shook her head a little. "Not really, sir."

The man stared at her for a few moments, making her acutely uncomfortable. She looked down at her clean hands and new tunic. It was then she realized her hair had been cut nearly down to the skin. She touched her shorn head nervously.

"Your hair was full of lice and too matted to be saved."

"Yes, sir."

He continued to stare at her. "I could not allow those men to hurt you; you're too valuable. They have been punished."

"Not the good one?" she asked quickly. "The one who helped me?"

"Not him."

A little tension left her. "I'm glad."

"You have mage ability. You're aware of this?"

She twisted her fingers in the warm blanket. "The way I can heat things up?"

"That is but the first sip of the keg if you train your ability."

She didn't know what that meant, but nodded.

"And you're a virgin female, which is almost as rare these days," he went on. "You understand that you owe me your life?"

She frowned. It seemed to her that the soldier with the brown beard was more her savior, but she didn't argue. This man had cleaned her up and taken her off the street, and since her belly and head didn't hurt so much anymore, maybe he had made the sickness—whatever it had been—go away.

"Yes, sir," she whispered.

"You understand that if you ever defy me, I will kill you."

She took a deep breath, and her whole body chilled under the layers of blankets. "Yes, sir," she gulped.

"I have uses for virgin females, but I haven't an apprentice, and am unlikely to find one here." The man leaned back against the doorframe, eyeing her speculatively and caressing his lower lip with a fingertip. "I could train you, if you will learn, how to do far more than blister a man's groin when he tries to rape you."

She stared back at him, still not understanding everything he was saying, but knowing he was deciding her fate—even if he had said it was her choice.

"And I could teach you how, when you decide to spend your virginity, to gain far more magically than you lose mundanely. It would be quite a waste, otherwise, for a mage."

That didn't make much sense to her, either, but she didn't ask for clarification.

"You also have the advantage, being female, of naturally spilling your blood once a month." He spread his fingers in a graceful gesture. "Of course any mage can spill his blood for quick power, but women do it without trauma—without choice as well, but it is what it is; you might as well pick up the power it drops. Thusly do female mages gain their advantage over the male ones."

Now he approached, and the girl felt a shiver of fear, but she dared not

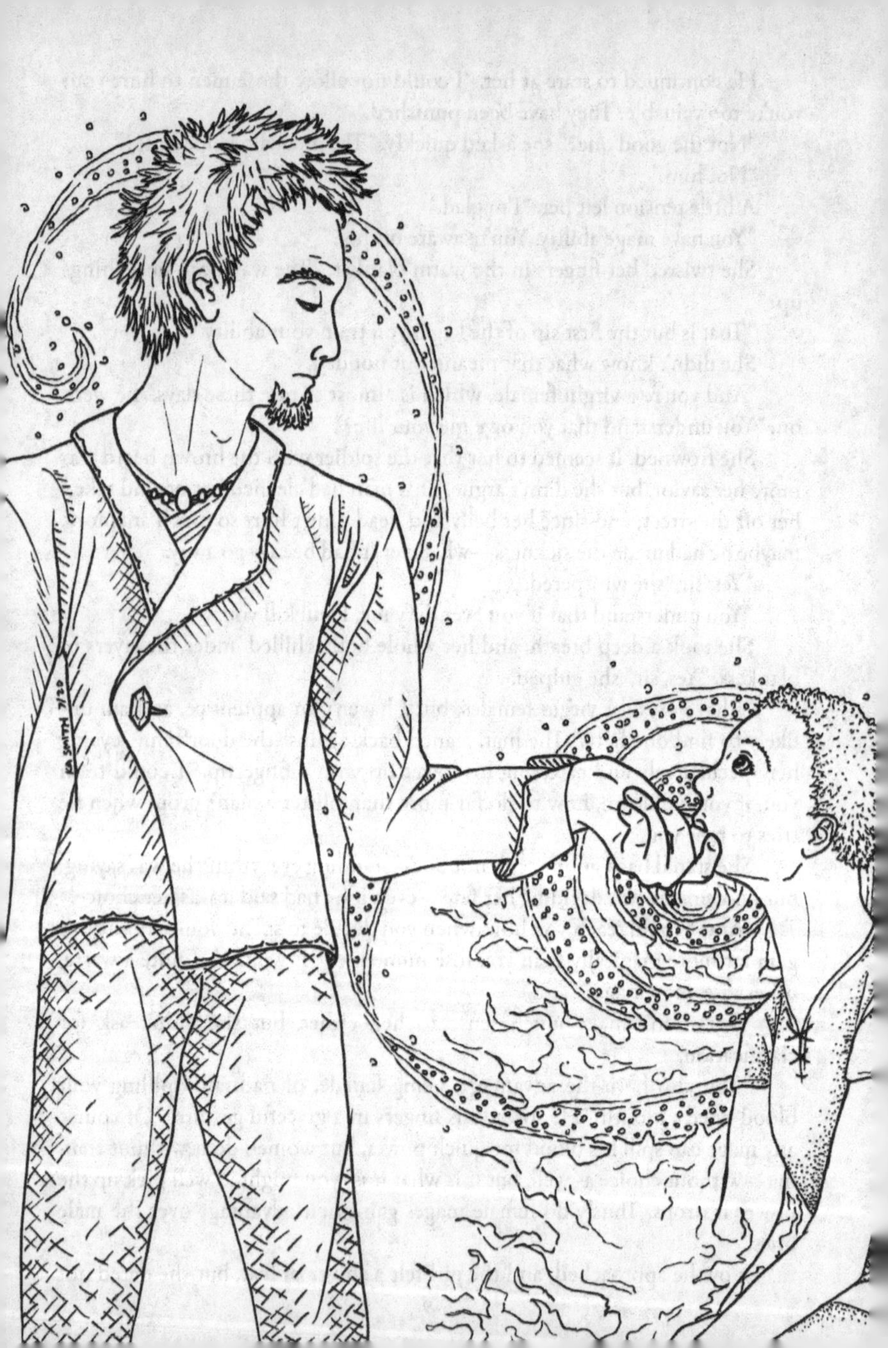

draw away; she sensed that the slightest sign of weakness would incite this snake to strike. He reached out long, slender fingers and brushed her cheek.

"You would never be any threat to me," he purred.

"No, sir," she breathed.

"I am Lord Altare Dhordirh. You will call me Master."

She blinked for a moment, swallowed, as he caught her chin between thumb and forefinger, lifting her face. She realized he was waiting, and must surely feel her jaw trembling. It felt like knowingly stepping into a dangerous part of the city, understanding that there were rogues both young and old with sharp knives watching from the shadows. If she ran, if she showed fear, it would all be over.

"Yes, Master," she murmured.

His mouth curled slightly. "Tell me your name."

"Vor," she answered. "Vor Hearthsraven."

Chapter 2
Northborn Year 1: Summer

A page—a boy little older than Vor, silent and somber—came to fetch her. She followed him to a small square room where her new master was waiting for her. The page left so swiftly and silently it was like he'd vanished. The room was mostly bare, but a heavy table sat against one wall with a couple boxes on it. Altare pointed at a stool in the center of the room.

"Sit," he ordered.

Vor obeyed, tucking her new dark grey skirt around her ankles.

"You are already able to heat up small objects," he said without preamble. "Other than roasting the genitals of that soldier, have you ever heated things to the point of combustion?"

"Combustion, sir?" she whispered.

Altare frowned slightly. "Can you light things on fire? Have you had any schooling? Can you read?"

Vor opened her mouth, not sure which question to address, and then realized the answer to all three was the same. "No, sir."

His frown deepened. "I'll have Germaine teach you. A mage must be literate."

She didn't know what that word meant either, but she nodded. "Yes, Master."

"So," he said, and handed her a stubby candle. "Light it."

Vor stared at the blunt taper and tried to focus. Within moments the wax was getting soft and warm and she was afraid the candle would melt in her hands.

"Stop," Altare directed. "You're too wide. You must concentrate only on the wick." He took the sagging candle away and gave her a fresh one. "Try again."

It took four more candles, although each one got soft more slowly and closer and closer to the tip, before Vor began to get faint wisps of smoke from the wick.

"Breathe," Altare urged. "You're holding your breath. The energy needs to flow, not stagnate."

Vor exhaled, almost feeling like she was breathing fire onto the wick—as it lit complacently. A headache bloomed behind her eyes.

"Excellent," Altare praised.

Vor lifted a hand to her head and almost dropped the candle.

"Ah, you over-stretched a bit," her master chuckled. He plucked the candle from her hand and set it on the table. "Close your eyes for a few moments and calm your energies. The pain should subside."

Vor obeyed, trying to calm her energies—whatever that meant. Into the ensuing silence came the sound of the room's door opening, and she lifted her head to look.

"So," said a strange voice.

A man she hadn't yet met stood in the doorway. He was certainly a few decades older than Altare by appearance, with a graying beard and wrinkles starting to collect around his eyes and mouth.

"This isn't where you usually bring your new toys," the old man observed, eyeing Vor but speaking to Altare.

"She's not a toy," the younger man replied. "Master," he added after a pause.

The two men locked gazes, and Vor suddenly felt like she was back on the streets, watching two feral dogs sizing each other up.

"So," the old man said again, "you think you're ready for an apprentice, do you, my boy?"

Altare did not reply. The old man transferred his gaze to Vor.

"Females are more difficult than males," he grunted, "and it seems she does have a bit of power about her. Won't know how much until it settles, of course." He switched his eyes back to Altare. "You don't know what you're getting into."

"I'm not worried," Altare murmured.

The old man did not immediately reply. Altare turned to Vor.

"Vor, this is my master, Craduticus: Master, my apprentice, Vor Hearthsraven. Bow," he added.

Vor untangled her feet from the rungs of the stool, stood, and made an awkward bow. Craduticus stared at her, seeming to be chewing the inside of his cheek.

"Interesting," he ruminated. "An interesting choice you've made; of course I can see the potential uses for her."

"Vor, you'll address him as Master Craduticus. Understood?"

"Yes, Master," she whispered.

The old man sniffed and glared at Altare again. Altare held his head high and didn't flinch.

"Reckless," Craduticus breathed. "I don't approve."

Altare nodded. "Noted, Master."

The old man's eyes widened. "You shall see what comes of this." It sounded almost like a curse.

"I expect I shall," Altare nodded again.

Without another word, Craduticus turned and left, shutting the door behind him only slightly harder than necessary. Altare turned back to Vor as though nothing had happened.

"Sit," he commanded, handing her another candle. "Do it again."

Northborn Year 1: Autumn

"You have done well," Altare remarked, watching Vor as she manipulated the fire spell. "You learn quickly. Put it out now."

Vor closed her hand, the self-sustaining blaze in the air vanishing. Her master had praised her—and fed her, clothed her, given her warmth and access to bathing and sleeping places. He'd been teaching her magic for two months now. Germaine was teaching her how to read and figure. Her life in his castle was finer than she could ever remember, and if her master occasionally scolded or even slapped her, well, it was a small price to pay.

"Come with me," he ordered, and Vor didn't hesitate to obey.

Her master strode out of the workroom, dispelling the protective shields he'd put over the door with a wave of his hand. He made no effort to shorten his strides. Vor had learned to keep up.

Now, he led her away and down a set of stairs to a narrow door. She'd explored and noted the door before, but it buzzed to her magical senses so she'd known better than to even touch it, much less try to open it. He paused before it.

"You know well, now, how to access your own energy for your magic, but there are many other sources of power," her master explained. "I will introduce them to you, as I see you become ready for them. Some take great levels of control to use, but some are not so difficult."

He unlocked the door with a touch.

"For now, you will only use this power under my supervision. When you're ready, I'll teach you the lock, and you can come here whenever you like, although I do suggest you keep in mind that we are all sharing this power source."

The room beyond was in blackness. Vor detected the metallic scent of blood—not an uncommon smell in the areas of the castle where magic was done. A light sprang up within: just enough to show four pedestals holding what appeared to be large bowls, evenly spaced throughout the wide room.

"When you bleed each month," Altare went on, "your body naturally collects the energy and adds it to your personal store of accessible power. It is, after all, your own energy, and especially since you are a mage, your body will conserve all it can."

He walked in deeper, to the nearest pedestal. Vor followed, and saw that the bowl upon it was carved out of mottled red and green stone. As she peered over the edge, she saw that the inside was coated with thick brown residue and in the bottom was a little puddle of clotting blood. It shone slightly in the light.

"The blood of others provides energy as well," her master murmured. He made a gesture that encompassed the room. "These four pools sit under the four drains in the floor of our good Skire Germaine's laboratory. Her work naturally leads to the spilling of blood, and it collects here, for our use," he explained. "It's not concentrated until it starts to dry out. The Skire washes the blood down with water after her work." He eyed Vor. "You can sense it?"

Vor frowned. "Yes, Master."

It felt different than the energy she was used to using. Her own energy was a leaping, dazzling stream of power: vigorous but obedient to her will. This power was heavy and slow and gradually fading. As she tentatively tried to reach it, it resisted weakly.

"You shall have to apply your will more firmly than usual," Altare instructed, watching her intently. "It is easily captured, just reluctant. It will also fade in time, so it is best collected as soon as possible. The bloodstone bowls help preserve it, but it won't last forever. This here is a bit old; there's not much left. Take it, and store it for later use."

"How?" she asked.

"Make a pocket, pull the power out, and pour it in there. Don't mix it with your own energy." His hand snapped out and snagged her wrist. "This will be something new for you. I can tell you have never manipulated or shaped your own soul before. It is a difficult skill, and the easiest way is for me to show you how. Will you allow that?"

Vor stared up at him, confused.

"I will take control of your magical sight," he explained. "I will direct you to what I want you to observe. I will demonstrate, for you to see, how it is done. Then I will watch you do it."

She chilled, not liking the sound of any of that.

"This is something you must learn if you are to become a mage of more than mediocre power," Altare went on. "A mage of mediocre power is of no use to me."

"Yes, Master," she gulped.

"You consent?"

Her heart was pounding a little wildly, but she nodded. "Yes, Master."

His gaze fixed on hers and he took control of her inner sight, showing her what he wanted her to see: the pocket he'd made in his own soul that held the blood power. In fact, he had dozens of such pockets, she saw, all in different states of fullness, holding different sorts of power she'd never seen before, ringing his soul.

Before her eyes he carved a new one. He redistributed some power from the ones he already had, filling it. Then he sealed the lip, making it into a sort of bubble full of energy, a part of his own soul, and yet keeping the foreign power separate. Altare released her and she nearly staggered.

"I'll teach you about all the different energy types you can store. Your own amount of talent will determine how many you can store at once," he said. "Your talent, as I sense it, is not inconsequential, though we won't know for sure until your powers start to settle in a few years. I expect this will be only the first of many power pockets for you."

Vor swallowed a faint taste of bile in her mouth.

"You will do this, my apprentice," Altare declared. "The first is not easy, but necessary if you wish to be truly powerful."

He'd never asked her what she wished, but she didn't argue. This was her home now, and this man was her master, and if she wanted to remain, she did as he said. He moved around the pool until he stood behind her, leaned down, and whispered instructions into her ear, telling her how to carve out a pocket in her own soul, and then encouraging her as she pulled the reluctant power out of the dying blood and hid it inside it.

She swayed, afterward, clutching the rim of the bowl and trying not to be sick.

"Now back to the workroom, and you will use that power for your studies," he ordered. "Always exhaust your stored power first, before touching your personal power."

Vor turned to follow as he led her from the room, jaw clamped shut.

"This will soon be as easy for you as breathing," he promised.

Northborn Year 2: Winter

She passed her first winter in the castle: a winter of ease like she'd never imagined. Even before the trek into Northborn, winter had brought hardships. After her parents' deaths, winter had nearly killed her. In the castle food remained plentiful—if somewhat bland. Her clothes were plain, but warm. Warm, too, was her bed. Fires roared in the fireplaces, and if she ever was a bit cold, her magic could warm her up to full comfort.

Her lessons continued and were often difficult. Her master was not a gentle man. Vor soon came to realize just how gentle he was not. Demands for perfection she could rise to, and she began learning to hide her fear. The alternative was going back out into that winter—if he would even let her leave.

By the darkest day of the year she was well past the juvenile books set to children, and began studying texts her master assigned her. Reading opened a new world to Vor. She could remember her mother reading to her, and even starting to show her letters, before the war, but now her hunger for words blossomed. Eventually winter loosened its hold, and blossom, too, did the gardens around the castle, with the coming of spring.

Northborn Year 2: Spring

"Altare, come with me, now," Master Craduticus ordered, flinging open the door to the workroom.

The wards reacted, but the old master made a slapping motion and deflected the defensive strike into the walls with a wet thumping sound.

Altare jumped to his feet. "Master, I am in the middle of a lesson."

"Flame it, boy, I need you now," he snarled.

Vor huddled on her stool and wished she could vanish. Silently, she slowed and halted her efforts to draw heat from the bucket of water before her. Altare spun back around.

"Did I tell you to stop?" he growled. "Odd that I do not recall my own words."

"No, Master," she said hurriedly, resuming her work.

She'd been set the task of freezing the water in the bucket. Having mastered the production of heat in various forms of flame, her master was now teaching her the opposite: the removal of heat. It was much like the absorption of any kind of energy, and Vor was finding it tedious but not difficult.

"What is so urgent?" Altare sighed dramatically.

"You'll treat me with some more respect, boy," the old mage warned. "I can still flay your flesh from your bones without working up a sweat."

"I'm sure you can," he said. "And the urgent thing?"

From the corner of her eye, Vor saw Craduticus approach.

"We caught a beast. It's down in the Skire's lair," he explained.

"More fauns?" Altare shrugged. "The females were indeed amusing, but rather devoid of any magical properties. I don't see how they're any more notable than regular humans—"

"Not a faun," Craduticus hissed. "A unicorn."

Altare's pause was distinct. Vor's attention on her task wavered.

"Are you sure?" he asked.

"They can hardly be mistaken for anything else," Craduticus scoffed.

"I want to see it."

"Why do you think I'm summoning you? We need all the help we can get subduing it, and it's only a foal. Our spells are bouncing right off it."

Altare's voice was rising with excitement. "The texts say their bodies have many magical properties—"

"And I assure you, you will have the opportunity to share in every one of them, if you come assist us now. Of course, the Skire wants to dissect it, but we'll have what we need of it first."

Altare spun about. "Practice as you like for the rest of the day, Vor," he ordered. "I'll request a report of what you studied tomorrow."

"Yes, Master," she said.

Without another word the two men left the workroom. Vor continued for a few moments drawing the heat from the water, but gradually stopped.

"A unicorn," she murmured.

She knew what they were; she'd read about them. The texts her master assigned were difficult, but she'd found simpler ones—not for magical study— in the library. One of them had been a bestiary, and had included a few pages on unicorns, along with an illustration. The pages actually hadn't said much. Mostly it had been "some say..." and "legends tell of..." and "rumors have long existed that..."

Still, it had been intriguing. A foal, Craduticus had said. They had a young one. They were going to kill it; Vor had no doubt. Her master had taken her to the butcher that worked between the two rings of castle walls, showing her how the blood and death spilled energy. Those had been meat animals, bred only for food, and killed quickly. A dull pain stirred in her chest. She could imagine in her own mind, the seven wizards standing around a poor, helpless thing, watching as Germaine cut into it, eagerly seeking any magical bits in it. She feared it wouldn't be quick.

Without even realizing what she was doing, Vor slid off her stool and went to the door. Her master hadn't restored the wards when he left, so she didn't have to pause to remove them. She knew the way to the Skire's laboratory, though she'd only been inside a few times. As she approached, she felt the air thicken and crackle with magical overflow.

From outside the door, she could hear exclamations and the ruckus of people moving about, messing with objects that clanked or thumped, and snorts and cries of objection. She touched the door, but it tingled strongly enough to make her snatch her hand away. The layered spells upon it were much more powerful than she was used to working with. Opening the door— or even attempting to open it—would probably knock her across the hallway and crack her skull.

Vor got as close to the door as she could safely, but between the thick door and the muffling of the spells, she couldn't make out individual words. For several minutes the cacophony continued. Then finally came a period of quiet.

"It's over. It's dead," she thought.

Just as she relaxed and turned to go, a scream pierced the door and spells together. Vor clapped her hands over her ears and flinched back against the wall. The next scream was more strangled, but just as agonized.

"They're killing it," she gasped.

Compelled beyond caution, she grabbed the door handle to yank it open, but a shock like lightning stabbed her hand, forcefully knocking her arm away and sending it numb up to her shoulder. She grabbed at her senseless hand with her other and pulled her floppy arm up to her chest, holding it there. Tears streaked down her face.

The screaming went on: awful, throat-tearing screaming.

Ripping her imagination away from thoughts of what they might be doing to it, and choking on a sob of helpless rage, Vor turned and ran.

***

"I wanted to assure you that I haven't forgotten you, my apprentice," Altare smiled.

It was the evening of the day after the capture of the unicorn. Her master had come right to her bedroom door: interrupting her where she was studying a text he'd set to her.

"Leave that for now; I have a treat for you," he grinned.

Unlike other people, she knew it was rarely a good thing when her master smiled. Vor obeyed, following him down the hall and down to the chamber below the Skire's laboratory. She suddenly knew what he was doing.

"Come in, come in," he encouraged. "As you know, Master Craduticus and his hunters brought in a unicorn yesterday. Its body had to be shared among all the mages and I'm afraid they were much too greedy to allow me to save anything for you—especially since it was so small and its horn still tiny. However, we're all full to bursting with energy, even after completing a number of pending works, and this will go to waste if someone else doesn't use it."

The second basin in the room held a small puddle of congealing blood. If she'd expected it to look different because it was unicorn blood, she was disappointed. It was just as red as any other she'd seen. It's energy, however, was of a different measure altogether. It vibrated as rapidly as a hummingbird's wings and to her inner sight glowed a blinding white. It also shrieked of pain.

"This," Altare all but drooled, "is immortal blood. Of course, now that it's been spilled it will gradually fade like any other, but before it does, it should be consumed."

Revulsion gripped Vor in hot talons. Her entire soul revolted at the thought of doing anything with that blood, other than spreading it into the earth. Altare reached into a pocket and extracted an object. It was only after he'd dipped it into the puddle and presented it to her that Vor realized what it was.

"Go ahead," he urged.

She stared at the vial full of clotting blood, and then up at her master.

"It's not as potent as the actual flesh," he said, "but that's long gone now."

He grabbed her hand and pushed the vial into her grip. Some blood smeared on her fingers and she shuddered.

"It will make you stronger," he confided. "We all have felt it. We're not sure yet if the effect is permanent, but it might be. We wonder if it might also have extended our lives. Drink, my apprentice. I want you to be able to partake of the gifts as well."

It hit her. They'd eaten the unicorn foal.

Her imagination—that she'd managed to keep away from pondering the unicorn—now provided her with graphic images of its killing, of the butchering, of why it had screamed like that. She looked up at her master and saw his face and hands bloody: as the same blood now stained her own fingers. Bile rose up and she tried to hold it in, tried to clamp her mouth shut and seal her lips with her free hand, but she couldn't stop it. She choked, and vomit sputtered out between her fingers, spraying down her clothes and out onto the floor.

Altare snatched the vial from her hand before she could drop it, and backhanded her across the face. Vor tumbled into the wall and slid down it into a heap, gagging.

"Ungrateful, filthy child," he snarled. "You are a disappointment."

She looked up in time to see him place the full vial on the lip of the basin. He walked over to her, hefted her up by the front of her shirt, set her on her feet, and slapped her down again.

"You will learn your place," he threatened, "or I'll dispose of you. You show great potential. Why will you not embrace it? If your weakness of mind continues, I shall have to cut my loses."

He pointed back at the basin, his voice rising with every word. "You will drink this: all of it. I would rather you do it eagerly, of your own free will: comprehending the great gift I am providing for you."

His voice returned to a hiss. "But perhaps you are still too young and stupid to understand. So understand this: you are going to drink that unicorn blood. I will force you, if you won't do it on your own. It will not be pleasant. No matter how much you fight me, I will overpower you. So what is your choice? Will you get up, be a good apprentice, and do as I say, or will I have to display my dominance? Hmm?"

A spell of paralysis could prevent her running away, and she had no knowledge of how to block it. Or he might just restrain her physically—she had a sick feeling that he would enjoy that more. How he'd get her to swallow, she didn't know, but she had no doubt he'd find a way. She expected it wouldn't be the first time he'd made someone swallow something. He hadn't yet started her training in making magical potions and powders, but she knew they existed.

Using the wall as support, Vor got back to her feet. She wiped vomit off her face with her sleeve and spat out any still in her mouth. Her knees were skinned from where she'd hit the floor. Both her cheekbones were bruised. An assortment of other scrapes and bruises twinged at her, but she tried to ignore them; her master was waiting for an answer.

"I'll do it," she rasped.

"That's a good girl," he sighed. He patted her head.

The unicorn was dead. This couldn't hurt it any further, she hoped. It might hurt her, somehow, and every bit of her mind, soul, and body knew it was wrong, but there was no point in resisting. As terrifying as drinking the blood was, so too was the thought of what her master might do to her. She was accustomed to occasional slaps and angry words, but there were worse things.

Her cold fingers picked up the vial.

Altare stepped close behind her and put his hands on her shoulders. "Don't worry. It won't taste or feel bad."

Vor fought her revulsion—both for the blood and the man standing behind her. She touched the vial to her lips and stopped, trembling. Her master's hand reached down and cupped hers.

"Part your lips," he murmured.

Vor managed to do as commanded. He moved her hand, tipping up the vial. The slow, thickening blood spilled across her tongue and into the pockets of her cheeks. Altare used two fingers under her jaw to close her mouth.

"Swallow," he said.

It took several attempts. Her master stroked her throat until she managed it.

"Very good."

It tasted like springtime. She had a budding meadow in her mouth and belly, complete with young butterflies and busy bees. The wet rim of the vial touched her lips again. Altare had taken it from her limp fingers and refilled it.

"Open," he encouraged.

She obeyed, and he poured the next volume in. She swallowed.

"See? It's not so bad, is it?" Altare soothed.

He served her a third vial-full, and a fourth. She heard the vial scrape the bottom of the basin. At some point she'd closed her eyes. She was still trembling. When no more vials came to her lips, she cracked her lids open. Altare was wiping the empty basin with his fingers and licking off whatever blood he could get. He took his other hand off her shoulder and stepped away.

"Clean your fingers," he ordered.

Vor looked at her hand where she'd held the vial, dirty with blood. Hesitantly, she sucked on her fingers. They tasted like flowers.

"We're done here," her master announced. "Go see the Skire and have her bandage your scrapes."

In a daze, Vor complied, leaving the room before her master, and went up to the Skire's room above. There she sat on one of the dissection tables while the Skire put salves and wraps on her skinned knees, and chattered on about unicorn anatomy, using terminology that Vor didn't know. Vor glanced around the room, with its curtained cells, and saw not a sign of the unicorn.

***

If the unicorn blood gave Vor any heightened ability, she couldn't tell. For the next few days, she just felt light and peaceful. She didn't see much of her master, and suspected he was doing something with the other masters, related to the dissection of the unicorn and the energy they'd gained from it.

What she did do was go sit in the garden for long periods. After several days of it, the feeling of having a spring meadow within her faded, and her desire to visit the garden faded as well. Somehow, she felt that whatever had been in the blood had moved out of her, and she was relieved.

When her master did resume her lessons, he seemed still to be pleased with her, and made no sign of whether he could detect the essence of unicorn blood in her any more. She gave her all in her studies, demonstrating her ability to remove heat from water—and other liquids, too—and freeze it, so Altare moved her on to mastering the manipulation of air. After her study of air, she learned further manipulation of water, combining with air.

Once a couple months had passed, Vor was almost content again, but as the pattern went, it didn't last.

Chapter 3
Northborn Year 2: Summer

"Open the box," Altare instructed.

Vor had the sense that there was something living inside. In fact, she could detect living vibrations from all the boxes her master had lined up on the worktable. This first smallest one held the weakest energy. To her right, as the boxes grew in size, so did the amount of energy she sensed from them.

Biting her lip, Vor cautiously lifted the lid of the first box, and then pulled her hands away. She didn't snatch her hands back in panic—insects were not something she was unfamiliar with—but nor did she see the need to keep her skin in close proximity if she didn't have to.

"I expect you've seen red roaches before," Altare muttered.

"Yes, Master."

"Competed with them for food, I expect," he goaded.

"Yes, Master," she whispered.

He reached into the box of crimson crawlers and picked one up between thumb and forefinger. Its little legs waved frantically as he held it up inches from his nose. "You can sense the life energy within them."

"Yes, Master."

"There are no red roach mages," he chuckled. "So this energy goes to waste."

Vor's face puckered, but she didn't dare to contradict her master. She suddenly suspected she knew where he was going with this.

"You can make use of the energy, however, if you employ one of two ways to acquire it," Altare explained slowly. "The first is this. Pay attention."

With a wet crunch, he squeezed his thumb to finger. Little internal organs squished out through the cracked exoskeleton, and the waving legs slowed and drooped. Vor watched as the flicker of life energy passed from the bug and into her master, where he tucked it into a pocket in his own energy. He dropped the corpse back into the box. The remaining red roaches ran to it to investigate, and after a moment began eating their former companion.

"Upon death the energy is free for the taking, as you've seen before," Altare went on, "but if your target is not killed by something else for you, then you have the make the effort, and sometimes the energy you expend in that pursuit is nearly as much as the energy you get from the target, which hardly makes it worth it. Death is all around us, however, and there can be many opportunities to pick up the energy that something else has dropped."

He gestured towards the box. "Try it."

Vor stared up at him for a moment with wide eyes. It wasn't that she'd never killed a red roach before. When she'd lived on the street, the little bugs got everywhere, into her clothes, food, and bedding. There wasn't a day went by that she hadn't crushed half a dozen at least. No matter how many she or the other orphans killed, there were always more—an unending plague.

If she'd realized she could steal energy from them when she squished them, maybe her life would have been a little bit easier, but it somehow felt wrong. Looking at the ascending sizes of boxes on the table, she suspected that the life energy harvesting wouldn't stop with bugs.

"Try it," Altare repeated, with a hint of metal behind his teeth.

She knew better—she really did—but she looked up at him with pleading in her face anyway. Her master's stony visage changed not a bit.

"You will learn this skill," he pronounced, "or you will be used for a different purpose and disposed of back to the midden where you came from—if I am feeling generous."

Vor returned her gaze to the box. One intrepid red roach had climbed all the way to the lip and perched there. Its antennae danced about, searching for the next thing to crawl up onto. She plucked it before it could escape, held it up before her, and crushed it.

"Don't let the energy dissipate," Altare scolded. "Draw it in."

She tucked it into one of the pockets she now had in her soul, storing it, and Vor felt she wanted to use it immediately, not carry it around in her own life energy.

"Well done," her master said. "Not difficult at all, was it?"

Vor dropped the corpse back into the box and wiped her fingers on the edge of it. Altare snapped up another red roach and held it out.

"I said two methods. Observe the other. It requires more control and skill, but doesn't require the effort of killing your target. Now, watch carefully. I'll do it slowly."

Vor focused on the bug with its futilely waving legs. Over a few seconds, the vigor of its limbs decreased, and it was clear to her magical senses what was happening. Altare was pulling the energy out of it without killing it first.

"With this method," he instructed conversationally, "you can take a little or a lot, or all of it. Of course, if you take all the target's energy, it will die."

The red roach went still finally, and Altare dropped it.

"Any living creature can sense the theft and will try to escape. You have to restrain your target, which could take more effort than killing it. Harvesting energy this way is all a matter of analyzing how to get the most profit. It's not a tool for every situation."

Vor glanced at him.

"Yes, your turn," he smiled. "You might find it a challenge, as it does take skill. Red roaches shouldn't present too much difficulty, but mammals, and especially humans, can resist strongly. Now, pick up another one."

Vor obeyed. There were only a few left.

"You observed how I did it. Try to mimic it."

The bug's energy existed like a dense cloud within it, filling every bit of its body. Yet it was surprisingly tenacious, sticking to itself and refusing to do more than swirl as she tugged at it.

Altare put a hard hand on her shoulder, his fingertips digging in. "Keep trying."

She felt him insinuate his will, prodding her into the right technique. As she finally got a hold of the red roach's life force and began pulling it out, she sensed acute distress from the creature. She wasn't causing it physical pain, but rather a soul-deep anguish that even such a tiny insect could feel.

"Good," her master praised. "Draw it out and take it into yourself."

Vor hesitated, disturbed by the bug's distress. Altare's fingers pinched tighter.

"Keep going, all of it."

She closed her eyes, unable to watch as the red roach's struggles slowed and stopped, but she couldn't numb herself to its death. Its milky energies joined that of its fellow, tucked into a soul-pocket.

Altare clapped her on the shoulder. "Excellent. You've got the talent for it. Let's move on."

He released her, placed the lid back on the red roach box, and opened the next one. Inside in a bowl of water were a couple crayfish like the cooks sometimes boiled for dinner: each a few inches long with blackish, segmented bodies and several legs. Altare plucked one out, avoiding its little pincers.

"Here," he grinned, handing it over to Vor. "Show me what you can do."

***

Five boxes had been opened. From crayfish, they'd moved to newts, then lizards, then rats. The rats had been a bit of a shock. It was only because rats had been a threat on the street that Vor had been able to take one up and suck it dry of energy. She'd competed with rats for food even more than with red roaches. They bit and clawed and left droppings everywhere. They were nasty, filthy animals to her mind. The two in the box were wild gutter rats, flea-ridden and fierce, just like the ones she'd lived with.

All she'd had to do was think of the time she'd crawled into her pile of rag blankets, surprising a rat that had taken shelter there and getting bitten several times before she'd managed to shake it out. With that episode in mind, she was able to stop thinking of the rat as a warm, furry, living creature. She could almost imagine that it was that very rat that had bitten her, and had dropped its drained body back into the box with only a deep and ignored twinge of remorse.

Altare lifted the lid of the sixth box. Inside was a pigeon. He had to grab it immediately before it flew. Frantically it struggled and flapped, but soon enough he had its wings trapped under his hands and it accepted the futility of its position. Pigeons were street animals, too. They fed wherever they could and left droppings all over, just like rats, but they weren't aggressive. There had been times Vor had sat and watched them, and even thought they were sort of pretty.

"Flying creatures," Altare said, "have a different energy than crawling ones, just as you've seen that water creatures are different, too. How would you describe the difference?"

She furrowed her brow. He was going to make her kill it.

"Vor," he ordered after a moment, "answer."

"Hotter," she murmured, "wilder, faster, brighter."

"I suppose you could say so. Not stronger, though: mammals have stronger energy than birds. You may find bird energy difficult to catch, but not hard to master once you have it."

He held out the pigeon caught in his hands. "Give it a try."

Vor allowed him to transfer the bird to her grip. Her hands were smaller and she held it against her chest. It was a surprising mix of soft feathers and hard bony points. It cooed, with its little head twitching about curiously, but she stared straight ahead, not looking at it.

Altare let her hold it for a minute, just waiting, arms folded.

"Take some," he commanded eventually.

"Do I have to kill it?" she found herself whispering.

He didn't throw his hands up, but a slight roll of his shoulders with a lifted eyebrow gave the impression of it.

"Why would you not?"

Now she looked down at it.

"You would waste the energy?" Altare all but scoffed.

Vor's brows pinched.

"Do it," he ordered.

She looked at him, and his face brooked no argument. Her fingers tightened on the bird, slipping under some of its dingy feathers.

Slower, firmer, he repeated: "do it."

Vor shut her eyes. Maybe if she weren't looking at it, it would be easier. Through her sense that revealed magical energy to her inner sight, the bird swirled with vibrant green light, densest in its head and guts, but present in every bit of its living tissue.

Taking just a little wouldn't kill it. Jaw clenched, Vor siphoned away a few wisps and the bird pushed against her hands and chest, trying to get away.

"That's the idea," Altare said sounding long-suffering.

Vor squinted up at him. "Alright?" She started to extend her arms to place the bird back in its box.

"Finish it," her master growled. "You wouldn't waste food. Why would you waste energy?"

She couldn't articulate that leaving the bird with its own energy—and life—intact did not feel like wasting it.

"If you won't," he threatened, "I will. Now hurry up. You're turning a simple exercise into a trial for both of us."

Vor tucked the pigeon back against her chest. She sucked away a little more of its life and felt it start to relax, its struggles ceasing. She was killing it.

She stopped.

"Do it," Altare commanded.

She couldn't.

"Vor Hearthsraven," he hissed, voice starting to rise, "you will obey me. Do as you are told."

She squeezed her eyes shut and drew away some more energy. The bird was motionless now, but she could still feel its rapid pulse.

"Finish it," he ordered when she paused again. "Finish it now."

Tears squeezed out of the corners of her eyes. "I'm sorry," she whispered to the pigeon, and with a final sip sucked out the last of its life. The bird's pulse died away. To her inner eyes the body had only the slightest residual glow. Even that faded to blackness after another few moments.

Altare heaved a sigh. "Impossible child."

Vor fought to stop herself from sobbing, to remain still and silent, like the dead pigeon.

"Put the filthy thing back in the box," her master grumbled. "They're riddled with diseases and parasites."

Vision slightly blurry from tears, Vor did as ordered, setting the bird as reverently as possible back in the box.

"Go wash yourself, and put those clothes in the laundry," Altare commanded. "You're dismissed."

Vor turned blindly towards the door, but before she got it open she felt a pat on her head and arrested her movement in shock.

"And well done," her master praised, "you've taken vital steps today in your magical development."

Without replying, Vor stepped out from under his hand, fumbled open the door, and ran down the hallway.

Northborn Year 3: Summer

Her master didn't ask her to draw living energy from animals again soon, for which she was grateful. Summer passed again into autumn, and she enjoyed her second winter in the castle, until spring came again. Lessons continued for Vor mostly in the line of technique. Altare introduced her to most of the elements, although he kept her mainly working with fire, and a bit of air and water, leaving earth for later, since he said it was more stubborn. Basic light and dark spells she mastered easily, but her master told her there was much more that could be done with them than turning the lights on and off—especially with dark. He taught her also simple magical locks, wards, and shields, and permitted her free access to the blood room below the lab.

With the passing seasons, and no new orders to kill or steal life energy, Vor began to relax again, to hope that maybe her master would not regularly demand such methods from her. Outside of lessons, she began studying herbs and flowers, minerals and crystals, and the meanings and uses of runes used in magic circles. These she practiced drawing over and over with a chalk and slate until she saw them in her dreams.

Then one day Vor showed up for her afternoon lesson to find her master waiting impatiently, but without any magical tools or teaching items on the workbench or on the workroom floor. He was also frowning slightly, and she immediately hesitated.

"I'm not going to hit you," he growled. "Come with me. We're going to the Skire's lab."

Vor followed as he left the room, leading her downstairs. When they reached it, Altare paused outside the closed door and faced his apprentice.

"You've been here two years now," he said.

"Yes, Master," she concurred.

"When you came, I assured you that the man who assaulted you would be punished. He has been, somewhat. I had him imprisoned. He's been there since the event: two years. Every day that you walked here in freedom, ate wholesome food, was clothed, warm, able to bathe whenever you wished, given a generous room with a soft bed, given education, mental stimulation, and useful tasks, he has rotted in a stone cell with nothing but old straw to sleep in, a bucket for his waste, another for water, and the crudest of food, with no clean clothes, no sight of the outer world, and no knowledge of when he might be released."

Vor swallowed and looked down. She hadn't known the man would be punished so severely, and she began to feel guilty.

"I have done this to him, not you," Altare emphasized, "for attacking my apprentice."

She nodded, feeling some easing of the guilt.

"Today, you will take your own revenge."

Her head snapped back up. What did he mean?

"Come inside."

Altare opened the door and Vor went through. The laboratory was well lit with a half dozen lamps. Skire Germaine was there, bustling about fetching items and arranging her workspace. She paused only long enough to nod at Altare and aim a sniff in Vor's direction. The Skire was polite to Vor, and had been a capable teacher of reading and writing, but had never shown her affection. The disapproving sniff didn't seem to indicate that the Skire disliked Vor, but more that she disliked whatever situation Altare had set up and brought Vor into.

"This way," her master urged.

She saw that there was something on a table, something large and pink-brown. Her brain knew what it was. Her mind refused to acknowledge it, and she started to turn away.

"No, no," Altare chided.

His hand between her shoulder blades propelled her close, but she squeezed her eyes shut.

"You've never seen a naked man before?" her master chuckled. "Get used to it. Only children are taught about modesty. Adults know well what naked human bodies look like, even if we don't show them in public, or to children. It's rather silly, isn't it?"

He slapped the back of her head. "Open your eyes and look."

Wincing, Vor obeyed. It was indeed the handsome blonde man who had accosted her two years ago when she ran through the streets at night trying to get to a healer, mistakenly thinking she was dying. He had been tall and strong then, with bright eyes and lustrous hair. Now he was filthy. He stank of rats and privies. His skin was nearly hidden under grime, though Vor could see hints of burns scars through the grunge—scars she'd put there. His hair was longer, matted, and dull, mixing with his uncut beard. His limbs were wasted and all his bones showed. His face, when he turned it towards Vor, was the face of a man who had long ago given up.

"I'm sorry, little girl," he rasped, "for what I did to you."

Vor put her fingers over her mouth and turned to her master. "Let him go, please."

"Let him go?" Altare echoed. "So he can do what he tried to do to you to someone else, to someone without the ability to stop him? No. Besides, that would ruin my lesson plan."

"But he's sorry," Vor protested.

"No, he's not. He's saying that to try to get released."

She firmed her stance. "I think he's really sorry."

"Why are you forgiving this chunk of dung?" Altare rounded on her. "He attacked you. He tried to rape you."

Vor's forehead puckered with confusion.

"Do you still not know what rape is?" her master demanded.

She bit her lip and didn't answer.

"You know what sex is? You must have seen dogs on the street mounting each other, if nothing else. You know how babies are made? The Skire told you?"

"Yes," Vor admitted in a small voice.

"Well, rape is when a man has sex with a woman, without her consent. He was going to do that to you. You intend to forgive him, let him go? What if he does that to some other woman? Then it would be your fault."

Vor's clasped hands tightened and she stole another look at the man's face. He'd shut his eyes. "But I think he knows better now," she explained.

Altare looked down at her as though she'd deeply disappointed him. "Perhaps I should have left you on the street, and let you be executed for being a witch."

Vor couldn't reply.

"People don't change," he told her. "Useless people like this, that cause problems, need to be eliminated. They drag down the rest of us."

Altare moved swiftly to the man's head. The prisoner opened his eyes, looking up in tremulous hope, but Altare put a hand on his forehead, and Vor felt magic moving. It was too complex for her to follow what Altare did, but the prisoner went quietly still.

"I've paralyzed him," her master explained clinically. "Today I'm showing you another source of power." He went to a bucket and washed off his hand that had touched the prisoner's dirty forehead. "You've seen how death releases energy, and how life energy can be harvested from the living. These techniques provide a certain amount of power: that which the body contains in its current state. You know you have more power available to you when you bleed each month. It should be no mental feat for you to understand then, that the letting of blood releases energy."

The Skire brought over a book and set it on the next table, beside her inkwells and quills. Altare snapped his fingers to regain Vor's attention.

"Bloodletting a subject will release more energy than outright killing it," her master explained. "Terror and pain release energy as well, so a conscious subject will give you more power on top of that."

He drew from his belt the short knife he always carried. Its blade was no more than six inches long, but the edge shined sharply.

"I will understand this time if you do not wish to participate," Altare allowed, "although I had hoped you might want to get some of your own back against this criminal." He leaned over the table a fraction. "The burn scars you gave him are rather significant, though. Perhaps you've gotten all the revenge you need?"

With a quick slash, her master opened a shallow cut on the man's thigh.

Blood welled forth, and Vor felt as well the spurt of energy that accompanied it.

"You sense it?" Altare checked.

"Yes, Master," Vor confirmed. "Now, will you let him go?"

"This is not just about you," Skire Germaine suddenly declared. "My studies of the pancreas and spleen are not complete. I'm hoping to get a good sample from this specimen of at least one of those, and if I could see the digestive system at work—"

"Hush, Skire," Altare said gently. "You will have your specimens."

He put a second cut beside the first.

"Not if you bleed him to death first," the Skire protested. "He must be alive for me to see the action of the intestine and glands."

"Oh, very well."

Altare drew a long line of red down the prisoner's body, from sternum to below his navel. The man's wasted muscles quivered, but he made not a sound or movement.

"Do you feel, Vor," her master murmured, "the fear and despair that flavors the energy? It gives it a little extra frisson of power, more than if he were unconscious during this. In fact having him conscious but paralyzed I find to add even more energy than if he were free to scream and struggle. The energy that would have been expelled physically, instead—having that outlet blocked—comes out with the blood energy."

Vor had backed away until her back hit the table that held the Skire's book.

"Stay," her master encouraged her. "Watch. You need not help, but opportunities to see within the body under such controlled situations are not excessively common. And take as much of the energy as you like."

Altare dug the cut deeper. Blood pooled on the man's belly. The next knife pass prompted a surge of energy laced with despair.

"Yes, see, there's the abdominal wall," Skire Germaine gushed. "Now please don't cut the organs."

Altare gestured towards her tray of implements. "I won't step on your toes, Skire. Go ahead and continue as you like."

The woman went quickly for a blade: a small, narrow tool unlike the knives Vor was used to seeing. She took over the belly cut with slow, careful precision. Altare went to the prisoner's untouched thigh and began carving runes in it, just deep enough to get a little blood to flow.

"Come look, Vor," he ordered.

Timidly, she obeyed, stepping around the table to hover back of his left elbow.

"I use these runes commonly to amplify blood energy," Altare instructed. He handed her his knife. She took it gingerly. "Carving them into the body increases how much energy we can get. Copy them."

"Master," Vor protested softly.

"Copy them," he repeated.

Blood had gotten on the knife handle and smeared on her fingers. The unbroken skin of the man's bare hip quivered before her eyes. She hesitated.

"Compared to what the Skire is doing to him, he won't even feel these little scratches," Altare growled. "Now copy the runes."

Indeed, the Skire had the man's belly opened now, having used a few cuts perpendicular to the first one. She had some metal hooks attached to the table, holding back the flaps of skin and muscle. His internal organs glistened and pulsed like gigantic worms, swimming in blood. The prisoner still did not move, and his breathing seemed labored, but his mouth had fallen open somehow and his eyes stared straight up at the ceiling. Germaine reached in to search among his organs.

"Master, I don't like this," Vor begged.

He slapped the back of her head. "It's not about liking or not liking," he declared. "You think your likes and dislikes have a place in magic? It's about power: where to get it, and how to use it."

"I don't like what the Skire is doing," she whispered.

"Skire Germaine does useful research," Altare scolded. "The Skires help us understand the living world."

"But," Vor protested, even softer, "he's in pain. It's not right."

"You silly girl," her master sneered. "Very well."

Altare moved around to the prisoner's head and placed a bloody hand over the man's face. Vor sensed the magic moving again, and a few second later, the prisoner's tight muscles relaxed. The visible thumping of his heart calmed.

"Thank you, Lord Altare," the Skire grumped from where she was making notes and sketches in a journal. "He'll last longer that way."

"There," he huffed. "Now the man feels no pain. I have done as you wished; now you will do as I wish. Practice those runes. Cutting them into skin is far different from writing with chalk on stone."

Vor lifted the knife. The first cut was the hardest, but the knife was sharp and parted the skin with only a little pressure.

"The curves will be the most difficult," Altare instructed, "and if you dig deeper you'll encounter layers of muscle, which will also obstruct your path."

She tried to forget that she was working on a living, dying man. She tried to pretend the mangy skin was just paper, and the knife just a quill with red ink.

"Ah yes," the Skire said, breaking her concentration. "There is a good spleen here. Its full function is still unknown, you know, but I have several theories. What's needed is experimentation, but it's so difficult to implement."

The woman reached in with a blade and began sawing motions. Vor had to look away, fighting the urge to throw up, cry, or scream. The body shuddered under her knife, a convulsion.

"Have I done enough?" she breathlessly asked her master.

He was frowning at her, but finally nodded. She put his knife down on the edge of the table.

"May I go?" she pled.

"No, you'll stay," he said, "until the end."

Vor backed away from the table, holding her sticky hands clasped out in front of her. The Skire dropped a small, bloody organ onto a plate and reached back in.

"The pancreas is somewhat diminished," the woman grumbled on.

Altare bent to put his mouth close to Vor's ear. "Can you sense the death coming?" he breathed. "Watch the energy."

It was swirling, bucking within the emaciated man, and dripping off in globs that went floating away. Vor could see her master gathering them in and storing them. Blood was running now off the edge of the table, finding the nearest grate in the floor, to dribble away to the basins below.

"Have you gotten what you need, Skire?" Altare asked.

"Well enough," she griped.

"Excellent."

The master mage picked up his knife, went to the end of the table, and flayed open the bottom of the prisoner's foot. Vor recoiled, spun away, and almost vomited. She didn't see what else her master was doing until he moved into her peripheral vision a few minutes later, near the man's head.

"The human body can take a great deal of damage, and yet live," he commented.

The Skire had stepped away now and was washing blood off the two organs she'd extracted, ignoring her victim and whatever Altare was doing to him.

"Remember this, Vor," he said.

He began cutting out one of the man's eyes.

"There can be much pain before death," he went on conversationally. "Much suffering. Death can be delayed over days, even weeks, if the damage done is not too severe. Imagine existing in such a state, while your body tries to repair what has been done to it, while you know that there is no hope, that the end is only death—whenever it is granted to you."

He held up his prize, impaled on the tip of his knife.

Vor clapped her hands to her mouth and ran crying from the room.

Chapter 4
Northborn Year 3: Summer

Her master didn't call for her for the next few days, and never scolded her for fleeing when he'd said she would stay until the end. Vor spent most of the time in the garden, staring at the blossoming flowers and the industrious bees. It was the only thing that calmed her. When she tried to sleep, she woke from bloody nightmares, and huddled in her bed with a lamp lit, waiting for dawn when she could go out to the garden. There, she could lie on the grass and nap without seeing the blonde man's face.

She had not a thought for her neglected studies. When she thought of anything, it was of how she might escape, and where she might go: back to the streets? Could her fledgling mage powers keep her fed and warm somehow? She couldn't come up with a sure way, thinking of dozens of different wild ideas and discarding them just as quickly. It made her head spin, until she just went back to watching flowers.

That was how her master found her.

"I won't do that to you," he told her by way of greeting.

Slowly, Vor forced herself to look up at his impassive face.

"Not unless you've truly earned it," he added.

A shiver passed over her, despite the sunny day. She realized that he didn't know that it wasn't just that she feared him doing such a thing to her; what also disturbed her was that he did such things to anyone.

"There are many difficult steps in becoming a mage," Altare went on. "You are my apprentice. I will teach you. All I ask is that you learn. Do as I ask, and I'll have no cause to discipline or dispose of you. Do you understand?"

Vor licked her lips, and managed to whisper, "yes, Master."

Altare set a hand on her head.

"Then come inside. I have some new magic to show you."

She obeyed, and for the next several months he taught her nothing but technique. They spoke no more of the man in the laboratory. Now, though, Vor knew what the energy of human pain, blood, and death looked like. She sensed it in her master from time to time. It made him powerful: power that

Vor envied. She didn't ask to be included in the bloodletting sessions, but she began to visit the butcher her master had shown her months ago. There, life energy was dropping all the time. At first, it made her queasy, picking it up and storing it, but gradually she got used to it, until it became just another way to make her strong.

Northborn Year 4: Winter

Six months had passed since Altare and the Skire had cut up Vor's childhood attacker. Her nightmares of it had started to fade. With the energy she got from the butcher, she'd made quick advances in her studies, and her master had expressed his approval. Now winter gripped the castle again, but inside was warm and safe, and Vor awaited her next lesson.

"There is another energy source that is easily available," her master murmured as she sat obediently on her knees in the center of the workroom. "You might choose not to make use of it yet, but it is important that I begin training you in it, so that you will be ready when the time comes."

"Yes, Master," Vor said.

"I will have you observe me, so that you become aware of the process of collection."

"Gladly, Master."

He came to stand over her. She stared at the floor.

"Innocent that you are—or mostly innocent—it may be shocking, but it is best to just get it over with. Come with me."

Altare strode from the room and Vor hurried to follow. He led her down hallways and up a flight of stairs she wasn't familiar with, in an area of the palace she'd not been introduced into before. They passed through a door that Altare unlocked by placing his hand on it. Vor could sense the magic moving, but again he used a technique that was too advanced for her.

"You will never come here without being escorted by me," he commanded.

"Yes, Master."

"My private quarters and other rooms that belong exclusively to me are beyond this door. You are a temporary guest."

"I am honored, Master."

He paused in the middle of the hallway and turned to face her. "While you are here, you will not speak." Gently, he set a fingertip against her throat. "You will not be able to speak."

The magic slipped into her so softly, Vor hardly felt it, but she opened her mouth to consent—and nothing came out. She couldn't make a sound.

"Excellent," Altare grunted. "I'll remove the spell when we're done here."

He continued on, and Vor followed him, but there wasn't far to go. He turned into a room furnished mainly with a large bed in a heavy frame, with thick posts at each corner. Altare pointed to a wall.

"You will stand there," he instructed.

Vor obeyed, relieved. For a moment she feared he was intending to bed her, as men do with women. Since the soldier that had tried to rape her, and Skire Germaine's explanations, she now knew a fair bit academically about the process of procreation, but it wasn't something she wanted to try, especially not with her master.

"You will not move." Altare set his hand just lightly on her head.

Stillness dropped onto her like a blanket. It wasn't that she couldn't shift her weight to keep her balance, or blink her eyes, but if she tried more than that it felt like a heavy weight held her down. It was too much effort to lift a hand or take a step. Silenced and paralyzed, all she could do was watch and listen.

Her master stepped out of the room. A minute later he returned leading a naked woman. Her drew her forward by a long, fine chain attached to her only garment: a silk collar around her neck. The woman walked gracefully, without a hint of reluctance, a small pleasant smile on her face. She didn't seem to notice Vor; she had eyes only for Altare.

Without bidding she went straight to the bed, turned, and sat coyly on the foot of it. Altare had gone to shut the door. Vor heard the sound of a lock. Then he returned to the woman, unhooked the chain from her collar, and began to undress.

Vor's paralysis did not prevent the blood vessels in her face from dilating. Seeing a stranger naked was one thing, but seeing her master suddenly disrobing was something else entirely. Of course, he'd seen her almost completely naked when he'd rescued her from the soldiers, but that was different. It hadn't been voluntary, and it hadn't been in preparation for sex—as it seemed obvious that was what was about to happen. She could look away with her eyes, but not turn her head, and she tried not to look too closely.

"I hope you're watching the magical currents," Altare scolded. "This is part of your training."

Vor returned her attention to the bed, face still burning with a blush. Her master had the compliant woman on her back now. Vor tried not to watch, but to observe the patterns of energy, as she'd been instructed. Indeed, there was a lot of activity. As Altare continued with the process that Vor was trying not to look at, more and more energy was generated. It crackled and burned, swelling and pulsing, until the silent woman finally gave voice and there were two crescendos—one small from her, one larger from him.

Altare neatly gathered in every drop of erupting power and stored it all away in yet another pocket in his soul. The woman lay listless on the bed as Altare stood and began gathering his clothes, pausing to reattach the chain to her collar. He locked the other end to a ring set into a bedpost.

"And that," he said calmly, "is your average, mundane, ordinary dose of sexual magical energy. You can get that from any consensual encounter, more or less of it depending on how excited you and the other become."

He was putting his jacket back on, and walked over to Vor, tapping her to take the paralysis off.

"Let's go," he said, pointing her out of the room. "If you don't gather the released energy as I did," he went on as they walked, "some of it will dissipate, totally wasted. The participants will reabsorb some of it, and some of it will actually transfer between participants. In the woman's case it plays a necessary role in eliciting conception. I took all of it though, so she can't conceive this time and is exhausted now because she didn't get any back, but she'll recover. It's much better to gather it and put it to use—unless you need offspring for something. That's another whole process, and I don't permit you to engage in it."

Vor couldn't ask any of the questions in her head as her master took her back out of his private quarters. Only when they returned to the workroom did he take the silence spell off her.

"Who is she?" she asked first.

Altare frowned as though the question displeased him. "She is none of your concern: one of several, content and happy here. Now come ask me an intelligent question."

Vor forced herself to obey. "You said ordinary, mundane?"

"You'll understand better once you start harvesting energy from sex yourself," he answered. "There is simple sex, and more involved sex, group sex, and nonconsensual sex, as well as sex with a virgin, of course. Each kind will give you different types and amounts of energy."

He leveled a finger at her. "Don't go trying it until you're fully trained. Your first time will release considerable amounts of energy and it would be a ghastly shame for it to be wasted. I intend for you to be able to gather it. A former master took mine from me, and it was one of the most inconsiderate things he did to me. I killed him later, and got back more than what he took from me, but still. It was appallingly unfair."

"It wasn't Master Craduticus?" Vor ventured.

Altare frowned more deeply at her. "He is alive, now, isn't he? So it wouldn't have been him. You are more stupid than usual today."

Vow bowed her head. "Please forgive me, Master."

She heard a disapproving grunt. "Perhaps witnessing your first sexual act is to blame. You will get used to it. Go practice whatever it was I recently ordered you to practice."

She fled, while trying not to look like she was fleeing.

***

"Today will be your next lesson in gathering energy from sex," Altare announced as he led Vor again towards his private quarters. "You have seen mundane sex. I want you to compare that to what you'll witness today: virgin sex."

Vor's brown crinkled with confusion. "I thought you said your master took yours from you?"

Altare rounded on her. "Not mine," he scoffed. "I will not be the virgin involved, idiot girl. Why did I ever take you as an apprentice?"

He turned back to his quest. Vor hurried to catch up.

"When a virgin has sex, be it male or female, a great deal more energy is released, and there is a permanent shift in the energy patterns of the virgin, an alteration in the soul that allows for the production and the consumption of sexual energy. As a mage, whether you or your partner or both of you are virgins, you can collect this energy. Because there is so much, it is best to plan the event for directly before a major magical work."

He paused as if thinking. "Actually, I've never witnessed two virgins having sex where one is a mage. I wonder if the mage would be able to collect both volumes of released energy? It would be quite a lot."

He eyed Vor. "Perhaps I should find a male virgin for you, so I can see if it's possible. They're not easy to find, though."

Vor felt a surge of stomach acid into her throat, but tried to keep her face flat. The more he talked about it, the less and less interest she had in ever trying it.

"You'll be silent again for this," Altare announced, stopping to touch her throat.

He took her through the locked door and back to the same room where she'd watched him bed the magically compliant woman. He directed her to stand in the same spot, and put the spell of paralysis over her again. Vor waited while Altare left the room. It took several minutes for him to return. All she could think while he was gone was how stupid this was. She didn't care about sex—and didn't want to see any more of it.

39

When Altare came back he led a girl in by the hand, smiling at her with all of his charm, which he was able to turn on when he wished. The girl, who looked not much older than Vor herself, was dressed like a peasant except for a diamond pendant strung around her neck. She didn't seem to notice Vor, and walked as though in a dream, all her focus on Altare.

Her skin was already flushed pink, and she kept herself close to the master mage. He paused with her in the middle of the room to kiss her deeply. Vor turned her eyes away. She tried not to look as Altare edged her closer and closer to the bed. She tried to close her ears to the mage's seductive suggestions and the girl's awkward replies, and then to her gasps and cries.

It took longer to finish this time, and the girl was clearly not enslaved as heavily as the other woman had been. Vor was certain to observe the energy patterns, and they were far more dynamic than the first example, especially coming off the girl. When Altare achieved the union there was a huge spike as well as alteration in the form of the girl's soul.

Altare seized all the energy, even managing to suck some extra from the girl that hadn't been naturally released. When he finished after his own lesser spike of energy—which he gathered right back in—he stepped away from her unconscious body, brimming with power and panting with exertion.

"That," he heaved as he snatched up his clothes, "is how it's done."

He freed Vor from her paralysis and shoved her out the doorway ahead of him, leaving the girl where she lay on the bed. He locked the door behind them and propelled Vor further out of his private wing so swiftly that she stumbled. Once beyond the outer door, he tapped Vor's throat to release the silence spell.

"Save your questions for later," he ordered. "I have work to do with this power. I'll summon you when I want you."

Altare turned without waiting for a reply and vanished back inside his chambers. Vor rubbed her throat and stared at the shut door.

"My only question is," she whispered to the silence, "is it always like that?"

***

Vor had some days to herself. What her master was off doing, he almost never told her. When he did tell her, she had to hide her revulsion. There was nothing she could do to control or stop him, so all she could do was learn not to think about it. In time, the things he told her about ceased to shock her, or get any reaction from her. On her free days, she was able to pursue her own interests, once she'd practiced her set lessons enough.

Ever since being assigned the books of herbs and flowers, she'd become fascinated with plants and their properties. She took her books out into the garden. Spring had shaken off winter and greenery was growing again. She began trying to identify what she saw: cobweb flower, chamomile, and columbine: belladonna, bisby, and bleeding-heart: fox glove, fairy's blush, and forget-me-not. The gardeners made the land flourish and blossom, and though most of the plants in the garden off the royal wing were not for eating, Vor's books told her of other uses for many of them. This one sped the heart; that one clotted the blood; this other cooled fevers.

Touching each lightly, reading over their qualities, and searching out the next one: that was how the palace castellan found her. Vor jumped to her feet and stood facing the woman, torn between showing a defiant face and an avoidant one.

"What are you doing, Vor?" the woman asked.

Her tone was kindly, curious, as one might speak to a wary animal. Vor knew her name was Amlee. Her master had explained that the woman was the mistress of the servants, and though Vor was only an apprentice mage, that she was superior to the woman. Amlee had approached her soon after she came to the castle. She'd offered smiles and words as warm and soft as fresh baked bread.

Vor's own uneasiness and a firm order from Altare had sent the woman away. Since then, Vor had seen her again many times, and even exchanged some words with her, but her uneasiness remained. Amlee asked questions. Vor's master and the Skire did not ask questions. Amlee invited answers, thoughts, and opinions. Altare and Germaine demanded obedience.

"It's nice to see you enjoying the spring weather. So often our lord keeps you deep in the palace. Are you studying herbs?"

Vor didn't reply, but her open book on the bench was evidence enough.

"There are herbs in the kitchen garden, though they are young yet this year. Come with me and I'll show them to you, if you like?"

Amlee smiled, turned to walk away, glancing back over her shoulder. Woodenly, Vor started to move to follow her. She didn't want anything from anyone, but she did want to expand her knowledge, and there were no culinary herbs in the royal garden. The bait was too tempting.

Across the courtyard Vor had seen from the windows but rarely ventured into, they came into another garden—the kitchen garden. Here was only efficiency and practicality. The beds were long and rectangular with narrow paths between them. Many beds were already turned and fertilized. Others still lay fallow. Some held the last of the plants that did survive, and even thrive, throughout the winter. Amlee paused at one where dozens of tiny little sprigs were sprouting out of the soil.

"This will be the herb bed this year," she said clearly, although Vor had stopped, still some feet away. "You may take a little, once the plants are grown, but if you want a lot, please ask me or the cook, Marklin. Of course, feel free to look and examine them as much as you like."

Vor said nothing. Amlee glanced at her smiling, and then curtsied and left her. After a few moments waiting for something else to happen, or someone else to come out and confront her, Vor came up to the bed. She knelt, put her book on the stone path, and began to identify the herbs.

***

"I don't know that you're ready for this," Altare grunted, "but an opportunity has presented itself. That can wait. Come with me."

Vor rose from where she'd been grinding dried beetles to powder as a step in making a simple potion, and followed her master. He seemed both excited and apprehensive.

"In the past months you've shown growing signs of maturity and wisdom," he said as they walked. "This encourages me. I hope your childhood tantrums are behind you now. You are coming to understand the ways of magic and all its aspects, are you not?"

What was she supposed to say? "I am trying, Master."

"That is good. That is very good."

They stopped before the door of the room Altare had taken her to before, where twice now he'd shown her the collection of energy from sex. It had been a few months since the last time, and she'd hoped that would be the last. She hid her disgust. Hadn't he shown her enough of this?

"There is just one more basic variable in sex magic," he said. "From there you find only combinations of variables to create variety. You have seen in the other two examples, only passion. What is passion's opposite?"

"Disgust," Vor provided.

"Revulsion, rejection, disgust, as you say, are also powerful emotions integral to the human condition."

With that he pushed the door open and pointed Vor to the spot she'd occupied before. The room was otherwise empty but for them and the bedroom furniture. Resisting a sigh, or indeed any expression, Vor took her spot. Altare tapped her and placed the paralysis and silence spells upon her again.

"This may be difficult for you," her master announced, "but I urge you to observe academically. I am, after all, trying to teach you something. Now, there are many things one can do to a man to cause him to suffer. You have seen some. There are certain parts of his body that are extremely sensitive to pain, of course, but there is also mental suffering. Force him to compromise his strongest beliefs. Force him to submit to someone he does not respect. Slander his good name and cause others to lose all respect for him. Force him to hurt the people he loves and protects. Violate his women in front of his eyes, while holding him helpless to interfere. Slaughter his children."

Altare had removed his gloves and now carelessly threw them onto a side table.

"All of these things work—to a lesser or greater degree—on women, too. Men and women are not all that different, but there is one thing that is particularly effective in making women suffer, without necessarily hurting them much at all, compared to, say, breaking off fingers and toes or smashing joints with hammers."

He walked over to stand right in front of Vor. Quite deliberately, he reached out and petted her cheek, and then her neck, and then drifted his hand down her chest. Vor tried to recoil, couldn't because of the spell, but something of her distress must have shown in subtle ways on her face. Altare smiled and removed the offending hand.

"Have her touched by a man she doesn't want," he murmured. "It was so repulsive to you that you set a man on fire to get him to stop, with your pure, untrained magical will. I felt the ripples of it way up here in my lonely tower; it was that strong. You didn't understand his intentions, but it distressed you in the most primal way possible, and brought forth great power from you."

He walked away from her again and Vor felt a huge sense of relief.

"Don't worry," he called back over his shoulder, now unlacing his tunic. "I'm well aware that you don't want me, and it is not you whom I'll take today."

Her breath caught in her throat. Altare removed tunic and shirt and loosened his trousers. He couldn't be serious. He was going to—?

"I'll be right back. Stay there." He chuckled. "Of course you'll stay there; you can't move a muscle."

Her master exited back out the door, leaving Vor half panicked. She knew her master was cruel. She knew he killed both animals and people, often torturing them in the process. She knew perfectly well that he had several mentally broken sex slaves for his own exclusive use, and switched them out with new ones on a regular basis. But the idea of him committing such a violent act right there in front of her—for academic purposes, to try to teach her something— filled her with futile fury. He'd punished a man with years of imprisonment, followed by torture and death, for only attempting the act on Vor that he was about to perform in full on someone else.

When he came back in, dragging a bound and gagged young woman, Vor was seething with rage—and still unable to move or speak. He bodily threw the woman onto the bed and turned to Vor.

"I have made some concession to your delicate sensibilities," he panted from the struggle. "She is not a child, but a woman grown, although finding an adult virgin was about as difficult as finding a flying ox."

Altare made a gesture towards the door, and it slammed shut, locking both magically and mechanically. The bound woman was frantically writhing, but she was tightly tied hand and foot. She wiggled around and saw Vor standing there immobile. Her terrified eyes widened and she cried out something muffled by the gag, but Vor did not have the ability to make any response.

"No matter how much this upsets you, kindly show some professionalism and pay attention to the flow of magical energies," Altare drawled. "I assure you, she will not be damaged permanently."

Instinctively, Vor knew that wasn't true. Altare meant physical damage, but there were other kinds. He walked to the bed and dragged the woman closer by her feet. Vor could do nothing to stop him. Nor, it seemed, could his victim. Vor didn't see him use any magical methods of restraint, and though the woman fought as much as she was able, Altare was able to overpower her. Vor had never observed her master using purely physical strength; she hadn't known he was so strong.

Once he had her contained, he went to work on her clothing. She continued screaming through her gag, until Altare leaned down, stroking her heaving, futilely thrashing body in a grotesque parody of sensuality.

"Shh," he ordered. "The girl is incapable of moving or speaking, so there is no point in calling out to her. Your screaming does nothing but exhaust you."

Vor's jaw muscles bunched as much as they were able. Her master didn't want his victim expending energy he might harvest. Despite whatever energy was getting used by her screaming, however, Vor could observe her life energy surging and twisting like a pinned snake. It didn't actually have a visible color, but the combined rage, fear, and despair seemed to stain it indigo and crimson to her mage senses.

She averted her eyes. She could do nothing to halt the violence—or could she? Her master had said that revulsion and disgust generated power. Those feelings were pulsing in her as well. Furious, she harnessed her own energy. He'd paralyzed her body, but not her magical powers. In a rage, she threw force against the paralysis spell, once, again, and again. Faintly, she thought she sensed it shudder.

Her master suddenly stopped in the midst of his exploit, whipping his gaze towards her so that flecks of sweat went flying.

"Vor," he rumbled warningly.

She tried again, altering her attack to try to burn the confining spell away.

"Vor," Altare repeated, more strongly, "what do you think you could do if you broke out?"

If burning didn't work, perhaps freezing the spell until it cracked. Her master raised a hand, and struck the bound woman almost hard enough to break the skin. It did break Vor's concentration.

"If you break free," he hissed, "I'll kill her and take you in her place, right here on the bloody sheets, beside her corpse."

The raw threat in his voice made Vor quail. Her attempt at breaking the paralysis spell wavered.

"Good girl," he grunted, his attention returning to his sobbing captive. "Now observe closely."

How could she? Vor squeezed her eyes shut, but couldn't block her magical senses. She detected the sharp spike of power from the helpless woman, laced through with pain and anguish. Altare sucked it up like a thirsty warrior after a heavy arms practice. Her master's growing aura impinged on her senses, making her wince. At last it boiled over, bloating him with magical strength.

Vor watched him sort and store it away in the pockets in his soul. The woman's energy faded and ebbed low as he sucked up more and more of it, but didn't vanish entirely, so he wasn't intending to kill her, at least not yet.

It was over.

Sudden pain bloomed across Vor's face, but she couldn't move, and the impact of the strike bounced through her body. Her eyes flashed open. Altare stood before her, still completely nude, lips pulled back from his teeth in a snarl.

"You shut your eyes, didn't you?" he accused.

Vor didn't reply; couldn't reply. Altare pivoted on his heel, throwing up his hands.

"Shall I have to find another virgin and show you again?" he demanded.

Vor looked over at the beaten woman on the bed. She lay limply now, all the fight gone out of her, clothing torn away and hair a tangled mess. Her hands were still bound, but it seemed that Altare had freed her ankles. She made no effort to stand or flee. Her sides moved slowly: she breathed at least.

Her master snatched Vor up by her shirtfront. The silence and paralysis spells dissolved and Vor clutched at his hands, eyes gone wide with fear.

"I shall have to show you personally, won't I?" he seethed.

"I saw," she babbled. "I saw all the energies, and how they differ from—"

He threw her, not at the bed, but to slam into the door. She crumpled at the threshold, ears ringing, as Altare strode over to her, still wearing not a stitch. She curled into a ball in terror, certain he was about to grab her up and begin the torture, but instead she felt a weakening sensation.

Vor lifted her head. Altare stood over her, hand out and almost touching her back. He grinned.

"Mm, such delicious energy you have now, my apprentice," he purred. "Such fear, such revulsion."

Her throat went dry. She tried to pull back her aura, distance herself from him, and keep him from taking her power.

"Ah, terror, but where is the rage?" her master murmured. "Aren't you going to set me on fire, like you did to that soldier?"

"Please," she begged, feeling her energy draining from her like blood. "Please, Master, stop."

After a moment, he lowered his hand. The drawing slowed and ceased. Tears streaked down Vor's face and she started to tremble.

"Perhaps there are some things females can't learn," he said flatly. "Perhaps you are not strong enough to overcome the fragility of your sex and appreciate all sources of power. A pity."

Behind her, Vor sensed and heard the door unlock.

"Go," Altare ordered. "I have things to do here. You would only get in the way."

Vor struggled out the door, shut it behind her, and staggered off down the corridor. Chilled and sick, she made it to her room, crawled under the blankets of her bed, cried herself hoarse, and fell into a shallow, restless sleep.

***

Her master was cold to her. He didn't praise her, gave her rough, terse commands, and hardly watched what she did in lessons. He didn't even bother scolding her or slapping her for her failures. Was he that upset with her? Vor doubled her efforts: pushing herself to the verge of debilitating headaches trying to excel in the tasks she was set. It didn't seem to make a difference whether she performed well or poorly.

Without his words and blows, she struggled to maintain her motivation, and yet as she relaxed, she absorbed more deeply what her magical texts were saying. Vor started taking notes in a blank book the Skire let her have. It had been water damaged, so the pages were rippled, but she managed. Gradually, she made connections and conclusions and generated ideas beyond what her master was teaching her.

Cautiously, she tried out some of her theories, using a workroom when she knew Altare was busy elsewhere. Many of her obscure notions failed, but when she had even a glimmer of results, excitement swelled in her. When she invented a glowing water light from liquid in a clear flask—again borrowed from the Skire—the biggest smile she could remember having in a long time bloomed on her face.

Vor sat with the water light in her hands, its inconstant light dappling the room around her. She didn't expect she was the first mage to come up with the idea of merging elements to get water to hold and produce light, but it hadn't been something her master taught her. She'd made it all on her own. Her master didn't think much of light magic anyway, except as a way to illuminate rooms when there was no other handy method.

Were there other things he didn't know? There must be. Vor petted the bottle for a few minutes, and then withdrew the energy it was holding back into herself. The light faded and went out. She drank the water and returned the flask to the Skire. Then she went back to her magical texts and her notebook.

There would be other magical inventions to create, if she just thought hard enough.

Chapter 5
Northborn Year 4: Spring

Vor snapped awake in bed as a rumble shook her room. The building was stone and unimaginably heavy, but she quickly realized that the shaking was not from a physical source, but a magical one. Another wave of vibration swept over her and she tasted in it the power signature of her master.

Her feet hit the floor but even as she stood, she wondered what she would do. The surges were powerful—far more powerful than anything she could produce. It was late evening, early night, and she hadn't been sleeping long. It was probably just her master working on something: but without shields or wards, in such strength that it was spilling over everywhere?

"Not likely," Vor breathed.

Another wave swept through, and this one was different. After a moment, she realized it had Master Craduticus' power signature woven through it. A surge from her master followed immediately upon its heels, and then another, and then one of Craduticus' again. As wild and unlikely an idea as it was, she could only think one thing: her master and Craduticus were fighting.

Vor staggered as the magical shaking and pulsing increased in tempo. She flinched at a loud but distant bang. A moment later came a whoosh and a sizzle echoing down the corridors. Her skin started tingling unpleasantly. Her head buzzed, and she started to fear for her own safety. These kinds of conflicting powerful surges could throw her own energies into chaos.

The floor seemed to buck below her feet as Vor made for the door to her room. Bouncing off the hallway walls she fought her way down a couple floors to the lowest workroom she had permission to be in. The wards recognized her and parted for her when she gave the signal at the door.

She practically fell across the threshold, but as soon as she did it was like stepping in out of a raging typhoon. The waves of power and crashing sounds still reached her, but only faintly. Vor shut the door and fetched some chalk. She drew a quick circle around herself, inscribing runes—mostly for earth, which was the most stable—around the inside. With that completed, she felt even safer, and the magical assault couldn't reach her, unless it reached cataclysmic levels, at which point the castle as a whole would probably collapse.

If the masters were fighting, one would win. She couldn't know what had set this off, but she'd always seen tension between them. They worked together sometimes, too, but the rivalry was obvious. Craduticus had taught her master ever since he'd killed his first master, but Altare was getting older, asserting his strength. Even she could see that. Master Craduticus would have seen it as a challenge to his position, or so she assumed.

Vor pulled up her knees and rested her head on them. If her master didn't win, she didn't know what Craduticus would do with her. The thought that Craduticus might kill her master elicited an upwelling of a mixture of emotions. On one hand, she wouldn't be angry, only relieved. On the other, it would make her future—and even her safety—unsteady indeed. Craduticus might just throw her out, but as her own master had reminded her many times, there were other uses for her.

Vor remained where she was, huddling in on herself and sensing the progress of the battle, if that was indeed what it was. Craduticus' surges of power were lessening both in frequency and strength. Several more minutes passed, with Altare's strikes beating harder and faster. Then came a huge surge from Craduticus—and then everything faded.

Silence descended, but the air energy retained a lingering vibration from all the magic that had flown through it. Vor stayed in her circle. Had that last surge been Craduticus' killing blow? Or perhaps one was running, the other in pursuit, and battle would be rejoined as soon as they met again. Perhaps half an hour passed while Vor waited, wondering if she should go back to her room.

Then the wards to the room parted, and Altare—singed, panting, with hair and clothes disheveled—stuck his head into the room.

"Vor," he huffed, "you're safe."

He slumped through the door, almost collapsing, managing instead to lower himself to his knees with some semblance of control. He put his forehead into his palms, body still heaving.

"Clever girl," he laughed. "You got yourself down here and into a circle. Well done."

"What happened?" she ventured to ask.

Altare shook his head. "It came to the cusp. Words became blows. My former master slapped me across the face, like he used to." He lifted his head enough to eye Vor. "Like I do to you," he murmured.

After a moment while Vor sat prickling with perplexity, Altare went on, lowering his head back into his hands.

"I wasn't going to take that anymore, and told him so. There's a time when a master has to acknowledge a grown pupil as his fellow, not his menial. If he can't, if he won't, there will come a point when the former pupil, well," he threw up a hand. "This happens."

Altare let out a breath in a heavy gust. "But Craduticus had been going odd for months, now. I think perhaps his mind was being touched with senility. It's unfortunate. He was a brilliant man."

"Did you kill him?" Vor asked softly.

"No. No, he ran off," he growled. "He managed to entrap me and make his escape before I could break loose. He won't get far, frail as he is. I'll send shadow-dogs after him, as soon as I gather more energy."

Vor nodded but didn't speak.

"You can go back to bed," Altare concluded. "It's safe now."

"Yes, Master," she whispered.

He lurched back to his feet. "I'll be busy tomorrow. Conduct your own practicing."

"Yes, Master."

"And well done, again, on getting yourself safe during that. He would have killed me. I couldn't spare anything to try to protect you."

Altare stumbled back out the door without another word. With careful deliberation, Vor erased the runes in the right order, broke the circle, and left the workroom, putting the wards back up as she went. She went back to her room along hallways that no longer seemed as though they were trying to buck her into the ceiling, and crawled back into her cold bed. She wrapped the blankets tightly around her.

So someday a moment might come like that between her and her master, and if they weren't both ready for it to happen, they might fight. Then her master would kill her, or she'd kill him, or one of them might escape for a while. That day was still years off, but Vor wondered if she'd ever attain enough power to equal him, or surpass him. If she didn't and it came to a fight, the outcome was inevitable.

Northborn Year 9: Winter

Years passed. Vor came into her full height and form. Her magical abilities, too, matured, until she lived in the magic as much as she lived in air, drawing it in with every breath. Altare had completed the bulk of her magical education. Magic was mainly about energy and redirecting it to perform tasks that ordinary physics forbade. Vor could gather energy from many sources now, store it in herself, and change and apply it as needed. She could blend types together as well to perform more complex tasks.

She'd memorized a wide breadth of runes used mainly in conjunction with magic circles, to give her more control over her work by soliciting attention and essences of elemental magical powers. Exactly how and why the runes worked, she didn't know—and she wondered if any mage truly knew—but because they were so useful, she'd drilled herself in memorizing more than she thought even her master knew.

In addition, she could now summon lesser sprites of every element, and he'd shown her the summoning of other, more powerful elemental creatures—and what they could do. Those lessons hadn't been pleasant. The creatures were fierce, dangerous, and somewhat unpredictable. Worse than that, her master's idea of how to show her what they were capable of centered on using them to execute prisoners in excruciating manners.

As Altare came to have less and less to teach her, he began setting her to magical works that needed doing for the good of the castle or kingdom, or inviting her to pursue her own works—approved by him, of course. Vor found some of her deepest interests lay in devising new recipes for potions, powders, and salves, whether infused with magic or efficacious due simply to the natural qualities of the ingredients. Her master was dismissive of that line of magic and paid little attention to her work in the stillroom, which suited Vor just fine.

And if she preferred not to use blood magic, he never criticized, as long as she didn't flinch from it when it was necessary. She learned well not to flinch. Objecting never changed the end result. Her master was still the master, and

even if there were fewer lessons now, he was still in command. There was one area of her education, however, that she knew he had not ceased thinking of.

Pages were usually young boys, around the ages of seven to twelve, used to carry messages or make simple deliveries, fetch items or do easy cleaning tasks. Vor noticed that as she reached her mid-teens and then approached twenty, the pages got markedly older and were switched out every few months with different physical types—all of them attractive in face and physique.

Altare found excuses to summon her frequently—using the teenage pages instead of magical summons—or send her messages—again using pages. The young men were also quite solicitous, unlike most boy pages who had been taught not to speak, not even to smile, and to always keep their eyes down.

Vor sat in the stillroom, working on a difficult potion, and sliced up belladonna roots with vicious but exacting precision. She'd had her space repeatedly invaded—did they not know of personal space? She'd turned down over a dozen when they'd invited her to walk in the garden. Several had tried to touch her hand, arm, back, or face—they'd been given one verbal warning each, then slapped if they persisted. She hadn't used her mage powers on them; she figured that just wasn't fair.

The little bits of belladonna root went into a solution to steep. She moved on to measuring out arrowroot powder, silently snarling at the inoffensive ingredient. Of course the teenage pages had also said things to her—and she knew exactly what they were trying to do: had been instructed to do. If Altare had wanted her innocent, he shouldn't have forced her to watch sex in action.

Some had sounded so sweet. Others had been coy. Quite a few had been brash and even vulgar. She'd received so many compliments on various parts of her anatomy she could have wallpapered her whole suite with them and had extra for carpet. A few had tried coercion. A number of them apparently thought they were being seductive.

A measure of arrowroot powder safely balanced on a scale, Vor put the jar of it away and fetched the next ingredient on her way back down the ladder: pumpkin seeds. She had no interest in having sex with any of the pages. There had even been some that she found quite handsome, and perhaps if they hadn't been given explicit instructions to bed her by her master, and she'd met them as a normal person without any manipulation on the situation, she might have considered it. Just the fact that Altare was trying to get her to behave a certain way made her completely cold.

A short while later she was putting the final touches on her potion. It was actually a cream for the castle soldiers who had achy joints. Vor smiled a little; not everything had to be for some high magical purpose. She hardly put more than a touch of magic into it, but the soldiers thought it a miraculous medicine from a mage-witch. Whatever the reason, it worked better than medicines the palace healer and midwife, Jesine, made for the guards. Vor's talent had incidentally made Jesine her enemy, but the woman obsessed so over her trauma from the invasion that it colored everything she did and said, leaving Vor with little but feelings of aversion. The inclination seemed to be mutual. Jesine had her own, smaller stillroom in the servants' quarters, so Vor rarely had to encounter her.

Now though came a knock on the doorframe and she slanted her gaze over. Beyond the open door was one of those good-looking teenage pages. This one was fairly new, and had apparently taken the track of being polite and smiling. He had a good smile, she had to admit, and a charming face—but they all did in one way or another.

"Yes, what is it?" she asked.

"Master Altare requests your presence," the young man said with a little bow.

"Fine. Where is he?"

"He requested that I convey your ladyship to him."

Vor hid a sigh. "Of course he did. Lead on."

He bowed again and turned. Vor followed him upstairs, down halls, and she realized they were approaching her master's personal quarters. She didn't take that as a good sign. The main door was unlocked. Altare met them in a hallway two turns in where he'd clearly been waiting.

"Ah, Vor. So good of you to come," he greeted. "This way."

She walked on, passing the page, but then a moment later noticed he was still following them. She was about to comment on it when Altare led her into a room, the page still right on her heels.

"Master, this boy—," she started.

"Yes, yes," Altare interrupted, quickly shutting the door.

Vor glanced around. The room was dim, but her master touched a globe of yellow stone hung off a wall mount and lit it up. Then she saw. There were thick rugs, tapestries, a set of dressers and a chest—and dominating it all, a massive bed topped with a mound of satiny pillows.

"I've had this room set up just for you, my apprentice," he went on. "I even had you moved into your new suite in the royal wing, in the hopes that the accommodations would be, well, more accommodating, but since you are so reluctant to act on your own initiative, I thought I'd push you along a bit."

"What," she hissed, biting off the word, "are you talking about?"

His smile faltered and turned into a stern but kindly countenance. "You'll stay here in this room with this young man, Ferghus, until you've harvested the energy released from two people losing their virginities at once. I'll expect a thorough report, as I am quite curious."

"I will not," Vor declared.

Altare's benevolent expression slipped some more. "What is your objection? He is quite healthy, untouched, and willing. The bed is ideal—not too soft—and plentifully wide. There are intimate garments in the dresser, and a variety of items in the chest. You can easily adjust the room's lighting to suit your level of modesty." His voice rose. "I've made numerous concessions to your squeamishness, Vor. You can't ask for a better setting than this. You're nearly twenty years of age. What in the world are you waiting for?"

She felt her cheeks grow warm, but her resolve did not abandon her.

Altare grit his teeth. "Were you an ordinary girl, you would have wedded not long after you first started bleeding. By now, you'd probably have two or three brats of your own." He waved a hand. "As you know, harvesting the energy from the act will prevent conception. There should be no reason for you to hesitate."

"I don't want him," she said clearly.

"What's wrong with him? I'll fetch you another, to whatever specifications you have. Virgin men are hard to find, but I'll get as close to what you'd like as I can."

"Nothing's wrong with him," she ground out, "I just don't want him."

Altare took a sudden step back. "You," he uttered, "you would prefer another woman? I'll admit I hadn't considered that."

"That's not it," she burst out.

"How am I to continue your education in—"

"I don't want this kind of education," she spat.

He took another baffled step back. "Why ever not?"

Vor let out an exasperated sigh. "I'm just not interested."

Her master stood a few moments. His expression of confusion warring with some instinctive urge to make her do what he wanted was almost comical to watch.

"You won't just try, a little?" he asked. "Perhaps you will find it easier than you fear. Ferghus has been educated what to do."

Vor considered it for about half a second, but her visceral reaction told her. She shook her head. "No, Master. This isn't something I want."

His expression hardened. "You realize you're cutting yourself off from a source of power?"

She nodded.

"You won't do it on your own sometime without telling me about the results? I'll be able to tell if you've done it."

She almost gagged. "There is honestly nothing appealing to me about it."

He stared at her as though he'd never seen her before. "That's odd. You know that it feels good, at least, even excluding the benefit of power to be gained?"

"What I have observed," she said carefully, "has never looked enjoyable to me."

Altare stared at her a few moments longer. "Perhaps the teaching techniques I used were not the best," he allowed softly. "They worked when my former master used them with me, but you are a female, not that you act much like one. Perhaps I misjudged."

She didn't have a reply to that.

"As you wish," he said at length, turning to open the door. "Be gone, back to whatever you were working on. But should you change your mind, the slightest word can make whatever or whomever you wish available to you. Understand?"

"I understand, Master."

He stopped, hand on the latch, and then slowly looked back at her. It was a different expression, one of calculation and consideration. A chill crept over her. She was suddenly afraid that he'd changed his mind—and that he might force her. It was completely within his power to restrain her while Ferghus did as instructed. He'd get to see the energy from it released at short range. Plus, and she writhed inside with revulsion—he'd probably enjoy it.

"No," Vor said, staring directly into her master's eyes. "Let me out."

Still, he hesitated, and she wondered what he was thinking.

"You killed your master for what he did to you," she said. "Would you do the same to me?"

"Not the same," he grunted. "You could keep the energy."

"He took something from you that you could never get back. It's the same thing."

Altare's brows lowered as though he didn't fully agree, or understand, but he swung the door open. Vor didn't wait for further permission. She didn't know what would become of Ferghus, or what had become of the other young men her master had paraded past her. All she wanted was to get far away, and keep herself at least safe; she'd realized years ago that it was hard enough protecting herself, and she'd decided she came first.

Neither of the men followed her, but she didn't feel safe in her own suite—especially now that she knew why her master had moved her into it—

the stillroom, or anywhere else she often went. Impulsively, she turned her feet towards the Skire's lab. Reaching the door a minute later, she knocked politely.

"It's Vor," she called out.

"Come in, come in," the Skire's voice called back.

Vor turned the handle and went inside. The room reeked of death and blood—it always did—but there was no current specimen under dissection at the moment. The last fawn had escaped years ago; Vor could hardly remember the event, and she'd never even seen the creature, just heard something about it. The unicorn foal was likewise long gone, as were the last of the griffins the Skire had been allowed: none of which she'd seen. Since then it had been mostly humans she'd cut up, although every now and then hunting parties brought in something odd from the forest.

Vor knew her master sometimes worked closely with the Skire on projects that Vor wasn't invited to. She'd tried to close her ears to any mention of them, but knew they involved the young women Altare collected, and magic, and rituals. Sometimes Vor thought she heard babies screaming, but if that was the case, she'd never seen any come out of the laboratory.

The blood bowls below the room were often empty lately, as reflected by the Skire's empty tables and cells. Vor wondered how much that frustrated the woman, to have no specimens to examine. The woman in question was seated at her desk with four books open in front of her, writing in a fifth. Three lamps spilled bright puddles of light across the paper.

"Vor," Germaine said, smiling a little. "It's nice to see you. All is well?"

It was a stock question; Vor knew well that the Skire didn't really care about her one way or the other. She folded her arms self-consciously and walked into the darkness of the lab.

"Our lord wants me to lie with a man," she said bluntly. "I don't want to."

In the dark, she could see the Skire, illuminated by light, but the woman's light-dazzled eyes wouldn't be able to see her as well. Germaine frowned.

"You shall be a person of importance," the Skire said. "You shouldn't throw away your mating urges on anyone other than your husband."

"I don't have mating urges," Vor clarified.

The Skire shrugged. "Mating urges are perfectly natural, and come to most all creatures, including humans."

"I don't," Vor repeated, "have mating urges."

The Skire eyed her. "You should. Your body is mature. The glands should be producing the correct fluids for them to arise."

"This isn't about me or my body," Vor growled. "It's about stopping my master from forcing me to have sex."

Germaine sniffed and went back to her book. "He should know better. I thought he would treat his apprentice, another mage, a learned woman with a bright future, better than that."

"It's because of the magic. Sex releases magic energy," Vor explained.

"Does it?" the Skire uttered, now writing again.

Vor gave up. Although Skire Germaine had observed feats of magic many times, she'd repeatedly stated that she could find no mechanism of magical production in the human body. Vor thought that maybe she doubted magic existed, despite the evidence of mage powers having tangible effects on the world.

Vor sat for a few minutes anyway, listening to the scratching of the Skire's pen, interspersed with the metal-on-glass sound of her dipping it for ink. When the Skire was engaged in her work, it was hard to get conversation from her. Vor supposed she couldn't blame her. It was like someone interrupting Vor in the midst of a magical task, or the concoction of a potion; she wouldn't want to talk to them, either.

So it seemed the Skire would have her save sex for marriage, while her master wanted her to start engaging in it regularly with whomever she wanted. Curious, Vor extended a gentle magical probe towards the Skire, and observed her aura. Not being a mage, the Skire couldn't feel it. After a moment, Vor retracted it and considered what she'd sensed. The Skire wasn't a virgin, and she wasn't married. She never showed any sign of interest in anyone Vor had seen. There was not a hint of a lover, ever.

"Why aren't you married?" Vor asked.

Germaine jerked her head up, blotting her page. "What a question. I'll have you know it's none of your affair," she said firmly.

"Don't you have mating urges, too? Being mature and such? With glands?"

The Skire's mouth crinkled at the mockery. "The work is more important."

Vor shrugged. "Maybe that's how I feel, too."

"Valid," Germaine allowed. "It was nice of you to visit, Vor."

She knew a dismissal when she heard one, and she wasn't enjoying the conversation anyway. Vor slipped off the table and exited, pausing outside the shut door. If it hadn't been winter, she might have gone to the gardens to sit; her master very rarely came there. She was almost tempted to go there anyway and risk the frostbite, just to feel safer.

No, if she would suffer in the cold, so were the guards along the walls suffering. It made their arthritis worse. Vor turned her feet back to her stillroom. She had the joint salve to finish, and then she could make a delivery. Hearing the thanks of the guards and knowing she would make their patrols a little easier would be the best medicine to overcome the distaste of what her master had tried to do to her.

Chapter 6
Northborn Year 10: Spring

"Vor," Altare summoned, "come with me."

She was at her desk in her sitting room, trying to memorize the cantrip to summon a greater air sprite. Air-type summons depended heavily on tone and rhythm, making them almost like a song, and Vor struggled with them.

Her master looked out of breath, his clothes and hair a little mussed.

"What has happened, Master?" she enquired, standing at once.

"I'd like to show you a griffin," he grinned.

"A griffin?" she echoed.

"There's one in the Skire's lab. Come on."

Vor followed him out and down the hall. "From the mines? One of them got hurt?"

She knew there were griffin slaves in the mines below and around the castle. A few times she'd been called to go down there for one task or another, but she'd only seen the griffins as shadowy shapes in the dark: chained and shackled and laboring wearily. When there had been griffins in the Skire's lab, years ago, she'd never been invited to get close, although her master had brought back enormous feathers from them.

"A wild one," her master corrected.

"You captured it?"

"It came walking into the lab," he chortled. "The Skire called me and I helped her contain it."

By his tone of voice, Vor knew he meant magically called. The Skire possessed an amulet enchanted to allow her to scream for Altare and provide him a link to teleport to her, wherever she was. Vor had never heard of her actually using it before, and it put a huge magical burden on her master. Teleportation was a skill he hadn't taught to Vor yet, and to do it spontaneously, without a magic circle to help, was tremendously expensive in terms of power. That much she knew. It explained his fatigue.

"That seems exceedingly odd," Vor commented.

"It was following a girl," Altare explained. "She tried to hit me so I banished her, but I caught the griffin."

So he'd used a second teleportation spell, following right after the first, also without any preparation or a supporting circle? Then he must have done something to subdue the griffin, too. Vor was surprised her master was still standing. Where did he get that kind of energy? He must have engaged in a lot of blood and bed lately.

"Here," Altare panted, having reached the door to the lab.

He followed her inside. A huge heap of grey fur and feathers was strapped down to the largest table. Vor heard the shiny sound of shears; the Skire was cutting off the griffin's feathers, but looked up as the two mages entered. The whole area was painfully bright with a dozen lit lanterns.

"Vor, look at this," the Skire gushed. "It's a griffin, a female griffin, and she's pregnant."

Vor approached slowly.

"Not to worry, she's completely unconscious," the Skire went on, "and fully restrained."

The griffin's foreclaws and hindclaws were encased in strips of leather, bound into fists, and her bill was strapped closed. Her eyes were shut.

"I have some hoods somewhere in storage," the Skire babbled, "but this works for now."

It was a gorgeous creature. Vor had to hide a wince as the Skire picked up her shears again. Long, grey, black-tipped primary feathers dropped to the floor with the crunching of severed rachides as thick as Vor's fingers. The griffin's tail feathers were already cut off, down to sharp little nubs. It looked more pathetic the more feathers came off.

"What are you going to do with it?" Vor caught herself asking.

The Skire looked at her like she'd grown a second head. "She's pregnant," she repeated. "I'm going to continue my investigation of embryonic development. I have a fair bit of research on cats and dogs, far more than I ever wanted on pigs, and even some on horses and humans, but precious little on griffins."

She stroked down the beast's chest. "They are the most fascinating creatures. They are feathered like birds, but give live birth. They have fur like mammals, but no mammary glands, so they feed their offspring meat. No other mammal has feathers. All birds lay eggs. Do you not realize what a unique opportunity it is to investigate the growth of the fetus? Someday perhaps I will complete a theory on how the creature came to be like this in the first place. Nothing happens without a reason, you know."

"You can do that?" Vor asked timidly. "You can look at the fetus as it develops?"

The Skire shrugged. "Well, look at it, no. If I open the womb to actually see it, the pregnancy terminates. I've never had any success with repairing such an incision; the female will invariably miscarry. I can, however, feel through the walls of the womb to detect shape and form. It's imperfect, but the best I can do. If I had a few dozen pregnant griffins, I could go ahead and remove the fetus at different stages of growth, to get complete information."

She glared at Altare, who had taken her seat behind her desk. He had his head leaned into the support of the chair and his eyes were closed.

"Someone won't agree to breeding the slaves," Germaine accused. "Then I could have all the research specimens I need."

"It doesn't work that way," Altare slurred. "I've told you and your own data supports it. Even if we could get them to breed, there would only ever be a few females pregnant at once, not all of them."

"Over time that would be enough," the Skire argued back, "and we could artificially inseminate if they won't do it on their own. I've never observed a copulation, but I'm sure with some trial and error—"

"Enough, Skire," Altare ordered.

"What's inseminate?" Vor asked timidly, not sure she wanted to know.

"Seed a female in estrus with gametes taken from a male," Germaine snapped.

Vor just raised her eyebrows and kept her mouth shut. There were two more words she didn't know, but she figured it out by context. Gently, she touched the silvery feather-fur of the captive griffin's neck. So the Skire was going to be cutting this one open. Nothing Vor said could stop it, but it was just an animal, and her master or one of the other masters would magically anesthetize it each time, so it wouldn't feel pain. It wouldn't even know what was happening to it.

"Take a good look, Vor," Altare urged. "This might be the only one you ever see."

She walked around the table. The Skire eagerly kept pace with her, pointing out features of its anatomy in a constant stream of data. The examination confirmed her first impression: it was a beautiful creature. As she left the lab with her master, all she could think was that it was a shame it was going to be cut up, but it was none of her business, and she had no power to prevent it.

***

"Vor, come with me."

This time she was in the middle of trying out the air sprite summons, but her concentration burst like a bubble at her master's order. She didn't bother to sigh.

"Yes, Master. How can I serve?" she said.

"I need your skills. This way," he replied.

Vor followed him to one of his private workrooms, a small one. There was already a circle drawn on the floor, with three associated smaller circles of blood. Runes of for the elements of dark and blood were everywhere. It was not a pretty working, but not unlike others she'd seen him do.

"Here," he pointed her to a bare section of floor beside a bowl full of water. "I need more information on what my shadow-beasts have been observing. You remember my former master Craduticus?"

"Yes, Master."

"You remember how he evaded me, years ago?"

Vor hesitated. "I was too much a child to understand the situation," she tried, hoping to avoid implying she thought her master weak.

Altare didn't seem to care what she'd said. "He's on the move, and there's a girl with him, the same one I banished the day I caught the griffin."

Vor looked at him with concern.

"Yes," Altare murmured. "I think he means to challenge me. I think he's coming here. I nearly had him a few nights ago, but he destroyed my shadow-beasts somehow."

"How can I help, Master?" Vor asked. "You are far more powerful than I."

"I want you to look through the eyes of some animals around the cabin where they're staying. I can't do it right now. I tried, but I have too much blood energy in me and the animals sense it and reject my intrusion." He gave her a little sneer. "You're so pure, they ought to allow you."

It was true that Vor hadn't taken up any blood energy for several days, while her master was steeped in it almost continually. Long distance scrying through animal eyes was not an easy skill, but she could do it.

"I'll do my best, Master."

"Of course you will."

He held out a piece of chalk to her and she knelt and started drawing her circle of runes: life and air runes, mainly, with a touch of water. Altare watched over her impatiently. At last, she handed the chalk back, and settled herself to enter a meditative trance.

"Here," he said, holding out a small bowl of congealed blood. "You can use this for the location. It's from the sacrifice I used to summon the shadow-beast. Just follow it to where the beast was. It shouldn't be enough to make the host animals reject you."

Vor focused on it. The blood had no energy left in it, but it did have direction: a link back to where the shadow-beast had last been before sunlight destroyed it. She'd never summoned a shadow-beast herself, but she knew the theory. The more powerful the blood used, the more powerful the summoned beast would be. The sacrifice of a more intelligent animal would make the shadow-beast more intelligent, likewise the stronger and bigger a sacrifice, the stronger and bigger the shadow-beast. This blood felt bovine in origin.

She took in the direction and followed it on wings of magic for several days ride to a small house in the mountain foothills. She could only see vague shapes, which appeared obediently in the bowl of scrying water. That would have been as far as her master could have gotten. Locking the location in her mind, she cast out for the little flicking energies of living creatures. Immediately, a bright torch of energy appeared, and she flinched away from it.

"There's a person there," she reported softly, trying not to break her own concentration.

Her master kept silent. Vor drew back a little from the human and looked for something smaller. The only other things around were birds. She tried to find the one with the biggest brain—locating a jay—and softly insinuated herself into it, trying to see through its eyes.

A more complete picture began to form in the bowl. There was the cottage: old but still sound, with thatch that needed replacing, crowded around by overgrown weeds. A young woman was moving through those weeds, heading behind the house where a small orchard grew.

"Yes," Altare muttered, "that is the girl. Look for Craduticus."

"He'll sense me," Vor murmured back.

"He was never good at subtlety," her master denied.

Vor urged the jay to fly closer, around the house, but the old man was nowhere to be seen. She let the bird settle near where the young woman was knocking down mumfruit from a tree.

"Unfortunate," Altare sighed. "I'd hoped to get a look at him, see how strong he seems. The girl is good enough looking, though. I'm rather glad I didn't manage to kill her after all. Perhaps once I've done away with the old man, I can bring her back here: spoils of war."

Her master was hopelessly predictable when it came to comely females. He was probably already thinking about how he'd seduce or overpower her, and the girl would have no chance at stopping him. Vor's emotions surged, the jay fluttered and scolded, and the young woman in the scrying bowl startled, standing up and looking around.

"She sensed something," Altare warned. "End it, Vor."

Vor let the vision dissolve, releasing the jay, and relaxed. Her master was stroking his tidy little beard.

"I didn't sense any magical ability in her," he said. "She attacked me with a club, not magery. Perhaps she's just more perceptive than most. Thank you, my apprentice. You may go now."

Vor stood up, stepping over the circles and heading for the door.

"May I ask what you're going to do about Master Craduticus?" she wondered.

Altare barked a laugh. "I'm going to teleport there and kill him tomorrow morning. Leave me now, I have a lot of energy to collect, unless you want to help with that."

Absolutely not. "No, Master. I have work to do."

"Go on, then."

Vor headed back to her workroom and tried to concentrate on the summoning for the greater air sprite, but her tongue seemed to stick to her teeth and her throat was too tight. She couldn't quite manage it.

***

Vor was in the midst of simmering a potion, waiting for her master to return from his venture to eliminate his former master. A sudden, wrenching compulsion drove her to her feet, staggering towards the door. She was barely able to reach out and take the potion off the fire, before yanking the door open and sprinting down the hall. It wasn't her choice. She could have tried fighting it, but there was too much of her master's magic in her body, and it was he who called—demanding her presence like he never had before. It was as if he were screaming in her ear, shaking her back and forth, shoving and ramming her body onward.

She hadn't even known he was back. His pull directed her, led her to the door into his private wing. She fetched up against it, locked. After a breath, she sensed the lock release and she was able to push it open. Altare had opened it remotely. She raced down the darkened hallways, running deeper into his realm than she'd ever ventured before.

Closed doors carved and painted with larger than life flowers sped past her. The summons dragged her onward to the terminus off the hall where another door stopped her. It was made of a dark, dull red wood bound with stained grey metal. She set her hands on it. They tingled with magic and she snatched them back. That single touch had been enough to tell her that the most complex magical lock she'd ever encountered was laid on this door: more intricate than even the one she'd felt on the door of the Skire's laboratory when the baby unicorn was being vivisected.

She could also sense her master behind the door, and still his summons burned in her veins.

"Help me, Master," she shouted. "I dare not try the lock."

Something clicked to her mage senses, and another click, followed by a silent hiss, and the menace of the magical lock vanished. Breathless, she pulled on the handle and the heavy door swung open.

Inside, a blackened corpse lay on the floor in the middle of a smudged chalk circle with three rings of runes—more complex than she had ever drawn. Mainly there were air runes, but also life, and several blood runes: written in blood. Behind the circle, against the far wall, a table held a lumpy silver-grey rock caged in several hoops of different metals. It glowed slightly but made no aggressive movement. Vor recoiled at the stink of burned flesh. Then the corpse moved, and she gasped in horror. Its magical aura—depleted down nearly to nothing though it was—was her master's.

"Vor."

It was less than a voice, as if a fire bellows had tried to speak. The charred fingers on the nearest outstretched hand twitched, scraping at the floor. All his skin was gone. His flesh was charcoaled. It must have been magic alone keeping him alive in such a state. Hardly able to draw breath, Altare hovered on the knife-edge of death.

He was completely helpless.

Vor stared down at him for a moment that felt like an hour. Her hand twitched. She had at her belt her utility knife. Normally used for harvesting woody herbs, cutting twine, or any other number of mundane but necessary tasks, it would also cut flesh. One swipe would open her master's neck. One stab would sink it between his ribs to pierce the back of his laboring heart.

Surely he could not survive that. She could be free of him.

"Vor," he repeated, somehow conveying menace.

With surprising strength he shot his hand forward and caught her ankle. Immediately he sucked at her energies like a man dying of thirst, and she shuddered and tried to resist, offering up stored energy instead of her personal soul-energy. He managed to lift his head. His eyes were clearly blind, but he pointed his face unerringly towards her.

"You will bring me the girl from the chrysanthemum room," he rasped out.

She could easily guess what he would do with her.

"Bring her," he growled, "or I will take you instead."

His grip on her ankle was strengthening. In a moment, it would be too strong for her to break. Vor wrenched away and his hand groped after her.

"Bring her, Vor," he ordered again.

She backed away. There might still be time. In just a few moments he'd grown dramatically stronger from the stolen energy, but she could probably still overpower him. Altare wheezed, and then again, convulsively, and Vor came to realize that he was laughing. His jaw opened, showing white teeth in a lipless mouth.

"You can't kill me, Vor," he declared. "Bring me the girl, or you will die, if not right now, then shortly, and I will make it hurt."

Altare made no idle threats, but—she cried out in pain as spikes of agony racked her guts. It faded after only a breath, but she was left shaking and stunned.

"You've let my magic into you too many times, Apprentice," Altare whispered. "I will kill you, and it will hurt." He lifted his head higher and screeched at her. "Bring me the girl!"

Vor turned, tripping over the doorjamb, and hurried down the hall. She found the door carved with chrysanthemums. There was a simple magical lock. She knew the spell, and solved it with only a moment of concentration. Pulling the door open wide, she braced herself for what she might see.

The room was small, with a narrow bed and a few pieces of other furniture, all worn but serviceable. It had a window, although it was barred and at any rate the room was a few stories up. A teenage girl sat in a silken wrap, watching and listening to a caged songbird singing. She looked over only slowly at Vor. Her skin was pasty pale from lack of sunlight, and her long black hair clean but dull.

She wore a silk collar. Vor found the length of fine chain on a hook by the door, took it, and approached the girl, who made little response. Her face seemed fixed in a mild expression of ignorant peace. Below the neck of her robe, Vor could see two diamond pendants hanging against her clavicles. Vor attached the chain to the collar.

"Come with me, please," she told the girl.

After a moment, the girl stood, still with the same contented smile. Vor didn't need to pull on the chain—the girl followed her obediently. Once in the hallway, Vor stopped. How could she lead this girl to her master?

But then, agonizing compulsion gripped her. Vor set her feet against it, but there was no hope. Her master demanded, and she could not resist the summons. Panting and sweating, Vor returned to the room with her master's blackened body, the chrysanthemum girl right behind her and showing no sign of revulsion.

"Yes," Altare gasped out. "Here, bring her here."

Vor entered the room. Altare snatched at the dragging chain, and with a furious yank pulled the girl down onto her hands and knees. The girl almost landed on him, but made no objection to the rough treatment. Altare gripped her nearest wrist and groaned. The crisp burned flesh of his body started looking redder. He reached up with his other claw-like hand and yanked down her wrap, denuding her.

"Knife," he commanded.

"What?" Vor uttered, backing away again.

"Your knife." His voice was stronger now. "The one you were going to kill me with: give it to me."

She put her hand on it, and backed away another step, shaking her head mutely. Altare snarled but didn't insist. Instead, his head darted at the trembling girl. She whimpered as he sunk his teeth into her thigh. Blood splattered to the floor and the girl screamed as he began tearing into her flesh.

He was starting to get to his knees, charred arms closing around the girl's shaking body, when Vor turned and fled. The girl's throat-ripping screams chased her down the hall. She didn't know where she was going until she found herself running for the castle gates with nothing but the clothes on her back. She'd almost reached them when, like a dog reaching the end of its rope, she was jerked to a stop. She all but fell to the ground, barely managing to catch herself on hands and knees.

Almost as real as though he were standing beside her, whispering, she heard her master's voice: "you're not going anywhere. You are mine."

Vor stood back up, recovering her breath, mind replaying the image of her master ripping skin and muscle out of the chrysanthemum girl's leg with his teeth, and the blood splattering. She couldn't hear her screams from here, but she could only imagine the girl was dead by now. Violence and blood letting would get more energy from her than just sucking her soul-energy dry. She doubted that her master would prolong the harvest much though; he needed energy desperately to begin repairing his body before the damage actually did kill him.

He would probably get enough strength from the chrysanthemum girl to fetch the next girl himself. Energy couldn't be directly converted to healthy tissue. Having extra would help his body heal rapidly and recover from otherwise fatal wounds, but he wasn't going to be whole again overnight. It would probably take him weeks. Still, it was too late now to try to kill him. Altare would eventually return to his former glory.

When he did, Vor would suffer the consequences of her actions. Vor had helped him, but he'd also known she considered killing him, and she'd disobeyed about the knife. He might still be angry with her. He would probably punish her once he was strong enough. His everyday punishments were words and blows, but she wondered what he might do in this case.

After a few more minutes, Vor was able to turn her feet back towards the palace. There was nowhere else she could go, so she would regain his good graces to try to mitigate her punishment. Back in the stillroom, she fetched the herbs and other ingredients she needed. It didn't take her long to make up a pot of soothing burn-balm. There was another person who could help, too. Not Jesine: the healer midwife wasn't allowed anywhere near Altare's private quarters; he didn't seem to like her.

Vor hurried down to the laboratory.

"Skire," she called politely. "Our lord needs your help."

The woman was bent over her notes, writing in her tight, precise handwriting, but gave her attention to Vor immediately.

"He has been burned," Vor told her. "Do you have bandages, and anything else that could help him?"

Skire Germaine was not a healer—quite the opposite—but she did try to make her living specimens last, and that meant keeping them in relatively good health until she killed them.

"Of course, of course, right away," the Skire babbled.

Vor helped her load a carpetbag with supplies. Vor didn't suppose the Skire was allowed in her master's private residence, but then neither was she. It was too late for that now.

The doors were still unlocked. Vor led the way. The stench of burned flesh was mixed now with blood as the pair approached the door at the end of the hall. There were blood smears in the hallway, and another of the carved flower doors was open. The Skire wouldn't be troubled by the sight or smell of dead bodies, but Vor made a slight gesture, encouraging her to hang back, as she approached the terminal room alone.

Her master knelt in what had been the chalk circle. He'd redrawn it in blood. The remains of the first girl had been pushed to the side. She no longer had all her body parts attached, and it seemed she'd been partly disemboweled. The second girl—Vor looked away. She wasn't dead yet, but it didn't look like it would be long. A bowl under the table she lay on caught her blood. Altare was dipping his hands in it and painting it on his crisped body.

He sensed or heard Vor's approach and looked over at her, although his eyes still looked blind.

"Vor," he murmured.

His voice sounded more natural, but still raspy.

"Master, the Skire and I have brought bandages and burn-balm," she said softly.

He chuckled. "You seek to regain my favor."

"I seek to help you heal."

"Do not," he snarled, "lie to me."

Startling her considerably, he stood. Blood dripping from his cracked flesh, he took a few unsteady steps towards the edge of the circle.

"Fetch me two of our prisoners," he instructed. "I shall allow you to choose which ones. I'll not waste more of my little darlings on this. Leave the balm and bandages; the Skire can help wrap me. Then leave me alone. Tomorrow, I will have a task for you, and a chance for you to redeem yourself. And if you do well, I shall even reward you."

"Yes, Master," Vor consented.

He waved a bloody hand, sending flecks flying about the room. "And send me a pair of pages with bags and buckets, to clean up this mess. Have them give the remains to the griffin. It's so befuddled with spells it won't know what it's eating, and why waste beef or pork on it?"

Chapter 7
The Fetching of the Princess 

Vor awaited the summons from her master all morning. She finished the potions she'd been working on the previous day, attended to some neglected reading, did her daily martial practicing, and cleaned herself up afterwards. It wasn't until late afternoon that she finally felt the call from Altare.

Following it, she found him in his largest private workroom. It seemed the bodies had already been cleared away and the floor mopped of any resulting blood pools. There was, however, a circle with several rings of runes and symbols inscribed around it in blood, in the middle of which sat her master. He was wrapped head to toe in bandages and wore a robe over all.

"Ah, Vor, I can almost see you," he murmured when she entered and came to a stop outside the circle.

His eyes today were still glossed over with scar tissue, but he followed her with them as well as he had before. His voice was stronger, too.

"I can forgive you for contemplating killing me," he went on at once. "I would have been surprised if you hadn't. Had you accomplished it, I suppose I would have deserved it," it was difficult to tell but she thought he frowned, "for being weak."

"Master, what happened to you, if this humble servant may ask?" Vor enquired.

"Much occurred. There is not time for a blow-by-blow account of the battle, for I must send you off all but immediately on a mission."

Her eyebrows flew up. They'd gone places together before, but he'd never sent her out alone.

"Alas, I must ask you to attempt something I could not do, but thanks to my efforts, you should encounter little opposition. I will tell you briefly what happened, as it may be useful. You know I set out to confront Craduticus and end him. We know he paired up with the girl I banished from the Skire's laboratory, when the griffin was captured. I even detected him attempting to scry the griffin a few days ago, and almost caught him. Well, I found him, and the girl, alone, and made my attack. I would have defeated him."

"What happened?" Vor dared to ask, genuinely curious.

Altare's hands balled into fists. "He had help. Two griffin mages and a third griffin, a fighter, appeared in the sky and counterattacked. The fighter disposed of two of my shadow-beasts. The smaller griffin engaged me directly, while the larger protected the old man and the girl. Against those two mages, with my minions destroyed, it shames me to say that they got the better of me. I was also," he grunted, "distracted."

"Distracted?" Vor echoed.

"The girl," his voice changed, suddenly dripping with desire, "is the missing princess of Northnest: Jessika."

Vor shook her head. "I don't understand. I thought they were all dead. I remember the ceremony, when the caskets were put in the tomb. There was one for the younger princess."

"That was what everyone was supposed to think, but the youngest royal's body was never found. Sure, it's possible a drake ate it, but they were fairly well trained not to eat until directed. The smallest coffin in the tomb holds an imposter body. Jessika's was missing."

"How do you know this girl is the princess?"

He turned a warning glare onto her. "Do not doubt me."

"Forgive me, Master."

"One of my minions shredded her clothes and her skin, and I saw the tattoo. She's the right age and complexion as well." The unconcealed lust returned to his voice. "I want her. Go fetch her for me, Vor."

Vor's mouth dropped open but she shut it quickly. "And the griffin mages, and Master Craduticus—?"

"The old man I sent away to wander in darkness. His mind might eventually return to his body, but not for a long while. The smaller griffin mage will be dead by now. The larger might present a challenge, and likewise the fighter griffin might present some trouble. I will send a troop of soldiers with you.

They should be able to neutralize any resistance long enough for you to get the princess and get away. Place a cloaking spell on the wagon so it can't be magically traced. I don't think that's beyond your ability."

"No, Master," she affirmed. "I can do that."

"My minion tore up the princess' back considerably, I'm afraid. You'll have to spend some time removing the dark magic taint before she'll heal. I only hope she doesn't bleed to death before you collect her."

"Yes, Master."

"She's a bit of a fighter. Watch her carefully for escape attempts and have her guarded. She's also a virgin so don't let her alone with a man. There are some who'd take advantage of a crippled woman."

"Yes, Master," Vor said again, keeping her expression flat.

She imagined that the only reason Altare wanted her virginity protected was so that he could take it himself, and the only way he'd know of it in the first place was if he'd probed her aura, or even stolen some of her energy for a taste. Vor wished again that she'd killed him when she had the chance.

"There, on the table," Altare went on. "I've marked the location of the cabin and the best route to it. Go as quickly as you can, getting there, but do not overtire yourself on your return. Cleansing her back will take considerable amounts of energy."

Vor fetched the map, seeing that he'd marked it in blood. Typical.

"What of her companions, Master?" she asked. "Finish them?"

"I want the griffins," he hissed. "I will take care of them myself, if the opportunity arises. The old man is no threat anymore. His powers have waned. If he ever awakens and confronts me again, it will be entertaining to rub him out. Don't bother with them any more than you have to. With the support of the soldiers, they should present no threat. Just get the girl, and bring her."

"I see," she agreed, privately relieved that he was not commanding her to kill everything that moved.

"The scroll there, by the map, will give you the authority to requisition anything you need. Complete this task for me, and not only will I forgive your thoughts of murder, I will reward you."

Vor took the scroll of paper, knowing it would be a document with not only Altare's but also the King's seals. Using it, she could get a wagon and driver, draught beasts, supplies, and soldiers and horses. Her martial instructor could point her towards the most reliable men—ones who would obey her even though she was a twenty-year old woman. Being a mage also helped with that.

"Prepare your task force tonight and leave in the morning," Altare commanded.

"Yes, Master." Vor bowed. "Is there anything else I can do for you before I go?"

"I am recovered enough that I can see to all my needs now," he answered. Then he chuckled. "I just won't be pretty again for a while."

"I will bring you the princess," Vor promised. "Until then, may your recovery be swift, my master."

***

She had brought him the princess, just as ordered. Amlee and Edgard were currently showing the young woman to her rooms. Vor was on her way to report to her master. She didn't rush. Even after more than a week with the princess, she hadn't gathered what she wanted to say to her master about her, and needed the delay of a slow walk.

The princess, Jessika, was both more and less than she'd expected. She was less pampered, less snooty, and less beautiful than Vor had always thought princesses were supposed to be. She was also stronger, in a number of ways, than Vor had anticipated. She hadn't seen the woman cry. She hadn't whined, although a few times she'd thought the princess was exaggerating her injuries.

Vor had been glad to remove the contamination from her back, that she might heal, but her now-ingrained expectation of treachery and need to have a hidden advantage had led her to insinuate some of her own power into the girl's flesh. There it would remain for weeks—forever if she could have the chance to renew it periodically. She'd had to give away knowledge of it sooner than she'd liked, when the princess tried to escape and the incompetent guards had failed to detain the injured, weaker, smaller woman.

She'd also felt guilty about it; using magic on non-mages was unfair, or so Vor felt. Not that her master had the slightest compunctions about it. He would bend all the magic he wanted upon Jessika; Vor had no doubt. He'd mentally enslave the woman, leaving her in a state somewhere between his broken-minded playthings and the psychically barricaded king. Vor disliked what he'd done to all of them, but the consequence of trying to stop him was likely becoming one of them, once her master defeated her attempts at resisting.

He was going to do it to Jessika. Vor wondered if there was any way to stop him without serious consequence to her own person. She'd always wanted to stop him but—She grimaced to herself. She hadn't. Could she have stopped him? No, probably not, but she hadn't tried. It was like she'd given him permission, even approval.

No one was around, so Vor could let her face twist into a snarl without anyone seeing. That righteous, naïve girl had said things, things that made Vor think things she had been successfully avoiding thinking for years. Jessika certainly did not have a complete picture of how the world operated—at least not the world Vor lived in, a world that now she would be thrust into. Still, she said things Vor knew were true: knew but did not want to acknowledge.

It had made her defensive, made her cruel, like her master. Now it left her only conflicted, troubled. Vor shoved those feelings down; she was good at that. She had a task to perform. That was much easier than thinking those thoughts that cut at her like shards of glass.

"Ah, Vor, you've returned," Altare greeted eagerly when she knocked and entered the workroom, though he must have sensed her approach long before. "The princess? She's here?"

"Being shown to her rooms," Vor confirmed.

"You've healed her?"

"Yes, all the dark energy is gone from her back and she is—"

"Excellent."

Altare was up, striding around strongly, wringing his bandaged hands with vigor that Vor would have thought painful. He wore a robe that concealed most of him, but everything exposed was still bandaged.

"I can't go to her yet. I still look like this," he griped.

"She's not going anywhere," Vor reminded him.

"She'll try to get the griffin. You must watch her, Vor."

"I'll put wards on the doors and halls approaching the lab, to alert me if she comes near."

"See to it," Altare agreed.

He stopped at a table full of pots of burn-salve, bundles of fresh bandages, and a bowl full of bloody ones. There he leaned himself, staring down at the tabletop.

"I marked all the clothing in her rooms," he muttered. "She won't be able to go anywhere without me sensing it."

He hadn't asked about the journey, how Vor had captured the girl, if she or any of her men had been injured, or what the princess's mood or personality was like. It didn't much surprise her. Most of Altare's focus was on himself, what he wanted, and what he could get with whatever techniques existed. She decided she wouldn't bring up any of those topics he didn't ask after.

Altare was heaving with eager breaths. "Once I have her in my hands, she'll be all mine. I just need another week or so. Distract her. Become her friend. Introduce her to the Skire and see if she can't be talked around on the griffin thing."

It wasn't in Vor's habit to roll her eyes, but she had the desire to. "I think that highly improbable; she is excessively fixated on her quest to retrieve the griffin."

"Do as I say," he growled.

Vor bowed. "Yes, Master. How else can I be of service?"

"Leave me," he ordered. "Just keep her safe until I'm ready for her."

"As you wish."

He'd said before that he'd reward her for a job well done. It seemed he'd forgotten about that, but Vor was unsurprised.

***

And so she left her master to his plotting and planning and went to follow his orders—but become friends with Jessika? Make Jessika and the Skire friends? Convince her to forget the griffin? From what Vor had heard her say, the girl considered the griffins to be family. Her master asked an impossible task, as evidenced by the disaster of the dinner for the three of them.

Vor stalked back to her room afterwards, scrubbed herself in her own little bathing chamber and tried to throw herself into her studies. After a quarter hour of rereading the same page over and over she gave it up and took herself down to her stillroom. She knew she was too flustered to make anything complicated, but potion components needed chopping, crushing, distilling, and that would occupy her hands at least, without her brain needing to get much involved.

"I knew the dinner would be a disaster," she whispered to herself after some time.

More than that, she'd allowed it to be a disaster. She'd introduced the Skire too soon. It should have been just Vor and Jessika, but—

"He wants me to be her friend," she hissed. "Me. Me who has no friends. Me who can't remember the last time she had a friend."

No, Vor decided. She would have to be a different person to ever be friends with Jessika. The younger woman was distinctly too—too—Vor sighed. She was everything Vor wasn't; that was what was bothering her. Jessika was bold, defiant, and stalwart. Yes, she was also ignorant, emotional, and stubborn, but those qualities might be overcome with time and experience.

Jessika had passion. And Vor? The most Vor ever felt was fear, frustration, disgust, maybe some anger, but there was nothing that would make her eyes flash with courage, nothing that would bring her to confront an enemy on hostile ground, when the odds were completely against her, and taunt and vow and call for a fight.

Yes, that behavior was stupid, Vor knew perfectly well. That was another reason why she would never do such a thing, but when Jessika did it in the dining hall, Vor had felt ashamed of herself—and impressed. Yes, she'd also been impressed.

A little voice whispered to Vor, reminding her of her own admirable qualities, but Vor usually gagged that voice. Yes, she knew she was methodical, observant, and rather quick with the book learning, but those didn't stack up, weren't good enough, weren't enough in any sense. Jessika would not appreciate that about her. The princess saw a devoted servant of a cruel man. Jessika couldn't understand that, and rejected it as evil.

"And maybe," Vor murmured, carefully capping a vial of distilled oil, "maybe she is right."

***

"What?"

Vor couldn't stop herself from shaking.

"What did you say?" her master repeated, although she knew he'd heard her perfectly well.

Altare stepped closer, hands slowly opening and closing as though he longed to grab her and throw her to the floor. He wore only loose trousers that he slept in, hair tousled, having just been awakened by Vor's frantic attempts at summoning him. They stood in the hallway in front of the main door to his complex of rooms in the dark middle of the night. The glowing crystals they each carried were the only source of light.

"Repeat that for me, my dear, loyal apprentice," Altare coaxed.

"The princess has escaped, my lord," she managed to say.

"This is a story I must hear," he went on, dangerously calm. "Tell me more."

Vor's mouth and throat were both dry. Her heart pounded.

"Two men came into the palace, went to the princess' room," she croaked out. "They gave her new clothes, and removed your amulet."

"I felt nothing of it," he snapped. "I still feel nothing of it."

Vor explained quickly. "It's wrapped in a handkerchief imbued with spells, on her bed. I didn't touch it."

"I see. Continue."

"They gave her a new necklace, enchanted to liberate her mind, and led her to the roof of the old griffin barracks."

"How do you know this?" he demanded.

Vor shut her eyes in fear. "I left magic in her back, my magic, when she let me cleanse—"

"I am well aware. I allowed it to remain."

Vor skipped ahead. "I chased after her, to the roof, and fought to reclaim her. There were three griffins waiting there. One was a mage. I saw her before, at the cottage when I captured the princess."

Altare nodded tightly. "She defeated you."

Vor bit the insides of her cheeks in shame. "I tried, but she threw me off the roof. It was all I could do to land without harm."

"You should have died."

Her eyes snapped open and she stared at her master. His visage did not soften.

"You should have died for your failure, Vor," he reiterated, voice as cold and flat as black ice.

She could only stare, certain now that he was going to kill her.

"Why did you not summon me as soon as you sensed her unusual behavior?"

"I didn't think there was time," she said weakly.

Altare tilted his head and gazed into her eyes. "Liar."

"I wanted to recapture her," she blurted. "I wanted to show you that I could."

"Pride," he scoffed. "Your pride has cost me the princess. I hope you're happy."

Vor was far from happy, but her master's acceptance of her second excuse lifted a small measure of terror from her. She had wanted to be the one to confront the princess. She wasn't sure, however, how much she'd really wanted to recapture her. She'd wanted something though: wanted to show some kind of strength, some kind of—something.

What she hadn't wanted was her master to unleash his fury on the girl or her rescuers. Vor hadn't wanted to kill any of them either. The one man falling off the roof hadn't been intentional. At least, she hadn't planned to throw anyone off. The dark spears she'd cast were not of the same caliber as the one Altare had used on that other griffin mage. They would have hurt, if they'd hit, but would have only disabled the victims for a little while. If Vor had managed to recapture the princess and scare off the would-be heroes, she wasn't sure what she would have done with the girl then. She would have had to come back, but—

"You will be punished."

The words jolted Vor from her conflicted musing. Altare leaned close.

"I am going to punish you, Vor," he repeated softly, sinister as a serpent, "for letting the princess escape."

He touched her cheek with one cold finger and she tried not to recoil.

"You've taken something very important from me," he murmured. "I will think of an appropriate consequence."

"I have failed you," Vor accepted. "I should be punished."

He nodded slowly, eyes searching her face. "Well said. Do you have a suggestion? How should I punish you?"

She didn't doubt that he would choose to do opposite of whatever she said. Then again, he might think she'd think that, expect her to give a clever answer thinking he wouldn't do it, and then do just as she suggested.

"My master, being far wiser than this foolish servant, knows best what I deserve."

Altare slid his entire hand onto the side of her face.

"Yes," he said. "I will think of something appropriate." He stood up straight again, drawing his hand slowly off her cheek. "Go back to bed, Vor, and dream of your fate."

"Yes, Master," she said, bowing deeply.

"Just one more thing."

She glanced up. His right fist slammed into her left side, knocking her off her feet to bounce off a wall and stagger down the corridor, where she landed heavily on her hip. Vor gasped and grabbed for her ribs, feeling sharp jabs with every shallow breath. She hadn't been at all prepared for a physical attack. Her master stood calmly, looking down at her from several feet away.

"That's not all," he assured her. "Your punishment is just beginning."

Altare turned about and retreated back into his rooms. The magical door shut and locked securely behind him. Vor stayed on the floor for a few minutes, fighting back tears of pain. She figured some of her ribs must be cracked. Feeling over her side with her fingertips, she didn't detect anything that felt obviously like a break. She supposed she should be grateful he hadn't hit lower. He could have bruised her gut or maybe even caused internal bleeding—she wasn't sure how much of an impact that would take.

Vor couldn't draw a normal breath without piercing pain. Panting, she used a wall to help herself stand and began her cautious way back to her room. For a moment she considered going to the Skire for help, but the woman was not a healer, and what could anyone do for cracked ribs? They couldn't be set. They couldn't be stitched, or splinted. No, her best resources for dealing with the injury were her own.

She went down to the stillroom. As quickly, but still carefully, as she could she mixed both a potion she could drink to dull the pain, and a salve she could put over her ribs to keep down the inflammation and help lessen the bruising. By the time she got back up to her room, applied the salve under wraps of bandages, drank the potion, and crawled into bed, it was the deepest, darkest pit of night before morning.

Vor didn't think she'd be able to sleep, but the potion she'd mixed included herbs of soothing. Despite the pain in her side, she sank into uneasy slumber. She didn't wake up until a few hours after sunrise, when her master woke her with violent and insistent magical summons.

***

Altare howled and erupted in random flashes of lightning and fire. Vor stood amidst the maelstrom and tried not to flinch—or run from the room. She didn't know what was wrong yet—other than the princess being gone, as she'd told him hours ago. Her master had summoned her with a furious mental yank, without explanation, and she'd come to the workroom to this.

At least he'd chosen to throw his tantrum here. The bolts of fire and lightning hit the heavily shielded and reinforced walls and were absorbed, showering sparks but doing no damage. The walls should be able to hold against the onslaught for a while yet, hopefully until Altare's immediate stores of power were exhausted or he regained control of himself.

Still— "Master," she begged, "tell your unworthy servant what more has transpired."

With an obvious exertion of control, the mage sucked in a breath and with it held his next flurry of strikes. His clothing writhed and popped with a life of its own from the magical overflow.

"Dead," he groaned. "Skire Germaine is dead."

Vor's hands flew to her gaping mouth, and then she forced her usual calm mask back into place. The Skire was a strange, deranged woman, but she'd been the only other female in the capital that Vor had ever willingly communicated with: not a friend, but a compatriot, an everyday fixture of Vor's life.

"How?" Vor uttered.

Now she did flinch as Altare's furious gaze fell on her.

"Griffins," he breathed. "They have fetched the Skire's griffin specimen and fled, killing the Skire, as she was in the laboratory at the time, late last night, or very early this morning."

"But, the wards, the detection spells," Vor stuttered. "I didn't sense—" Of course, she'd drugged herself into slumber, but hadn't slept so deeply that the triggering of one of her wards wouldn't have alerted her.

77

Altare waved away her words. "They came neither through the tunnels nor down the stairs. Those wards are still up, and unbroken."

"Then how?"

Her master idly put his clothing back in order, and rubbed his forehead in an unusual show of dismay.

"They must have opened the ballroom floor," he said. "It's been years, but that was how we used to lower large creatures into the lab. I didn't expect an attacker would know of them, and I didn't think to ward them."

"There are doors in the floor of the ballroom?" Vor clarified.

He shrugged, settling his jacket. "We discovered them shortly after taking the castle. It seemed an ideal situation. The Skire needed a laboratory. The room was there, already almost perfectly appointed, with a feasible, if not easy, way to get large creatures in."

"I wonder what it was used for before that," Vor mused.

"We thought it might actually have been a surgery room for the griffins—intended for healing them, of course, but no matter. The Skire is dead, throat ripped to shreds. Her blood mingles in the pools with that griffin's."

Vor fought to keep her composure as it began sinking in. Her hands balled into fists. She tried not to breathe too deeply and set off the pain in her cracked ribs.

"Can we strike back, at the griffin, at least, with its blood?" she asked.

Altare waved a hand in the negative. "I tried. It is shielded by something I cannot crack. That revenge is beyond us, for now."

Vor seethed. How could this have happened? The same night the princess escapes, Skire Germaine is killed and the griffin captive stolen.

"I salvaged the energy from the blood," Altare growled, "and it will be the last we get from the pools, unless we have the butcher move into the room or we do it ourselves."

Vor didn't think that was much of a loss. She hated using blood energy; it made her skin and soul both crawl with disgust. She wasn't about to vocalize that thought, however.

"They came in under our noses," Altare snarled. "They will pay. Griffins: I will see them all cut into fried chicken, especially any that dare to be mages. We will have them," he murmured. "I will burn out their talents and burn them alive when we catch them."

"Who were they?" Vor asked. "Other than being griffins, how will we find them?"

"Whom do you think?" he scoffed. "Who was trying ever so hard and hopelessly to retrieve that griffin?"

Vor's eyebrows danced up. "The princess?"

"Of course the princess." His lash of power barely missed her and left the smell of ozone in the air. In flinching away from it, she'd twisted her torso a little, and her side seared with pain.

Altare tugged at his goatee in frustration. "They rescued her, flew off with her, waited for us to relax, and came right back. It's been too long since I've had an enemy. I've gotten clumsy. It won't happen again."

The master mage strode around the room as he often did to stimulate his thoughts. Vor resisted the urge to rub her bruised ribs, and waited.

"It is worse now than before the princess came," he snarled. "Now the people think she is here. They will expect to see her."

He continued pacing, which was a good sign as far as Vor was concerned. He'd gone from anger to planning. Unless she said something stupid, he was unlikely to strike out at her now. Her own emotions were settling, too. The Skire being killed was indeed awful, and it was almost Vor's own fault. She'd failed to stop the princess from escaping, and if it was indeed the princess's people who had broken in, killed the Skire, and took back the griffin, indirect blame could be laid at Vor's feet.

She wasn't about to point that out to her master; she felt scared enough as it was. If her master made the connection and felt vindictive, he could deal out punishment on Vor that might leave her within an inch of her life. She was already due punishment from allowing the princess to escape; she wouldn't say anything that might increase her coming reprimand.

"I shall have to create a decoy until we get her back." Altare came to an abrupt halt and his head snapped over to Vor. "And I believe you shall provide the energy for it: your punishment and a temporary solution in one stroke."

"Yes, Master," Vor agreed, hiding her dread.

"Not now," he smiled. "I shall let you anticipate it for a while. Do have some rest. I'm sure you need it after your pursuit of the princess and your fight on the rooftop with the invincible griffin mage. I'll summon you when I'm ready for you."

"Yes, Master," Vor bowed. "I look forward to it."

Altare swept out of the room and Vor took a different exit. She could prepare for the power drain, and indeed, she felt she had earned it.

Chapter 8
The False Princess

The girl looked somewhat like the princess. From a distance, the people wouldn't be able to tell the difference. Altare was waving away a bulging man in a leather vest. His arms were patterned with tattoos in black and blue ink. On the table, the girl was nude, lying on her belly. The leather-vested man hefted his bag, swiped once more at the seeping blood on the girl's back, nodded politely to Altare, and left.

"I hope you are prepared," Altare murmured.

The girl didn't respond. He was speaking to his apprentice.

"Yes, Master," Vor said.

"No record could be found of what the royals used for their golden tattoos," he grunted, poking at the girl's back. "This was the closest we could come, but it doesn't shine right, in the light. We'll have to hope they don't notice." He eyed Vor. "Or rather, you'll have to hope they don't notice."

She kept her countenance calm.

Altare's lip curled, as though angry that she didn't look scared. He grabbed the prone girl's shoulder and flipped her to her back. Then he yanked her up into a sitting position. Three diamond pendants dangled against her sternum. She made no objection to the rough treatment.

Vor recognized her. She was one of the girls Altare had kept around for a long time. She'd never shown any ounce of personality in Vor's presence. Long practice had made Vor an expert at keeping a neutral face in all but extreme situations, but she wanted to wince and look away. These girls were the most pathetic creatures. Vor only hoped that, whatever the state of their minds and consciousness might be, they did not suffer.

"She's as broken I can make her without a major working," Altare grumbled. "But now that you're here to supply the energy, I'll be able to rework her enough that she'll believe she's the princess for at least a year or two. After that, the spells will need to be renewed."

"Then perhaps there was no need to capture the princess in the first place?" Vor postulated.

Altare didn't strike her, but the expression on his face suggested that he wanted to. "Your idiocy knows no bounds."

Vor made no reaction. How was she wrong? If he could make a living human doll that would fool everyone into thinking it was the princess, why did they need the real one?

"We only need this one because you lost the real one and people will wonder."

She still thought there was a flaw in that argument somewhere, but her master gave her no time to explore the idea further.

"Besides, these kind of spells break down the mind with time. Eventually they'll turn her into an invalid, incapable of speaking, walking, or caring for herself. After a couple renewals of the spells, she'll begin to degrade to the point that the falsehood will be revealed. Or perhaps I can say that the princess is hopelessly ill and wasting away. That would preserve the fiction. Now, come here," he ordered, and Vor obeyed, stepping up beside him.

"So what will happen to her then?" Vor dared to ask.

"There will be no more use for her except, of course, the final use," he muttered. "If you hadn't lost the princess, there would be no need to use her up like this."

"Yes, Master."

It was her fault, wasn't it? She'd let the princess escape. Now this girl—though she was already mind-broken and next to lifeless—would be warped and destroyed as a consequence to Vor's actions. Though, if Altare had never ordered the capture of the princess in the first place, none of this would have happened.

Altare's magical aura was surging with power. He'd obviously charged himself up as much as he possibly could, using every method available to him. Vor hadn't done the same, but she'd husbanded her resources and gone to visit the butcher. It still turned her stomach—and put meat off the menu for her for a long while—but the energy was going to get spilled anyway. She didn't see the harm in picking it up, at least compared to wanton killing, forced bloodletting, energy theft, or orgies with broken-minded slaves.

Her master reached out and put a hand atop the girl's head. He interlaced the fingers of his other hand with Vor's.

"Be silent," he said. "This kind of mind magic is perhaps the most complex working there is."

He hadn't ordered her to observe, and Vor found that she didn't want to watch. Her master was fully focused on the brain of the naked girl anyway, and he wasn't paying attention to where Vor's focus was. Vor closed her eyes and tried not to look closely at the magic.

After an hour or so, when her master apparently exhausted all of his own energy that he was willing to spend on the working, Vor felt him start to tug on hers. She let it down, feeling it sucked from her like blood. She allowed him the stored blood-energy first, and then her reserves, but he exhausted all that and kept drawing.

Vor's entire being flinched away, but her master did not release his grip. She would ruin the working if she broke away, and his fury might very well cause her permanent fall from his grace, or even her death—but she didn't want to allow it. If Altare sensed any of her fear or revulsion, he gave no sign.

Any instinctual resistance she might have had, he brushed right aside, burrowing into her personal energies and sucking away as much as he needed. Vor staggered, catching herself on the table edge. Her legs started to go weak. Altare gripped her hand hard enough to make her bones grind together, preventing any escape.

One leg buckled and Vor went down to one knee. She rested her forehead against the table. Still he pulled from her. Tingling numbness invaded her limbs and her head swam. Just as she thought she might lose consciousness altogether, he released her hand.

Vor slumped to the floor, muscles twitching. She found an iota of energy and lifted her heavy eyelids to look up at her master. He was bowing over the girl's hand. With her other, the girl tried to cover her nakedness, blushing and stammering. Altare swept off his half cloak and tied it around her shoulders.

"You are lovely as you are, Your Highness," he purred, "but let us find you a gown. We would not want to startle the servants."

As he guided the false princess down from her perch on the table, he gave one glance to Vor. His expression said it clearly: "this is your punishment. Do not resist me, or next time I will take all your energy."

Vor closed her eyes. She had not the strength to speak or nod in acceptance, and hoped her master would take it as surrender, but as he led the false princess from the room, Vor wondered. Perhaps Jessika had something right. Perhaps it would be better to resist, even if it did mean defeat and death, than to ever let him do this to her again.

***

Altare had few magical allies remaining at the palace. Aside from Vor, there were three knotty old men, and no other women. There had been two others, besides Craduticus, when Vor came to the castle nearly a decade ago, but both of them had died. Vor had never known them well; her master had kept her apart from the other master mages. They hadn't been old, and their sudden deaths had been accidents: obscure, unlikely accidents.

So the five remaining mages sat down in Altare's less magical study—the one he didn't keep his magic-related texts in—to discuss their next moves after the princess' escape and the Skire's death. The three old mages were next to useless, easily cowed by Altare's power and dominance, but having them was more useful than not having them, her master had told her.

"We are under assault," Altare was saying. "The signs are just beginning, but they will increase, until we have an actual war on our hands. The threat comes from the princess and her griffin allies. She may have more allies as well.

She will try to destroy us and take back this kingdom for herself."

One old man was chewing on his mustache and didn't seem to be listening. The other sitting beside him elbowed him and he startled.

The third lifted a trembling hand. A little lizard ran up from his sleeve and coiled around his fingers. Vor identified it as a very minor earth elemental, not a real lizard at all. "Information," he wheezed. "Scouts should be sent."

"Of course," Altare agreed. "You'll see to it. Vor, provide Master Chirolen with clothing samples from the princess' chambers, or better yet hair from her hairbrush, if there is any."

"Yes, Master," Vor said.

"Master Eriducus," Altare went on, and the elbowing wizard tried and failed to sit up straighter. "Go into the archives. Find me everything about griffins, especially griffin territories or sightings outside the borders of Northborn."

"Yes, Master Altare," the man agreed.

"And Master Ulver," Altare continued, raising his voice.

The mustache-chewing man blinked and focused on him. "Yes, my lord?"

"The mines are still producing?"

"Very well, very well," Master Ulver nodded, head bobbing.

"Are they really?"

"Well, no," he revised. "Steady drop, lately, always a steady drop: veins petering out, you see."

"Is there enough work still for the slaves?" Altare enquired, sounding only mildly interested.

"Enough, enough," Ulver nodded some more.

"For how much longer?"

Ulver scratched his balding head and chewed again on his mustache for a moment. "Another year, perhaps?"

Altare sat back. Vor watched him as subtly as she could, knowing he knew she was watching him, but practicing on being as subtle as possible about it nonetheless. He appreciated little efforts from her like that.

"Our hold over the land is nearly complete," he murmured, and Ulver leaned in, obviously not able to hear. "We have everything we came for," he rephrased, louder this time. "It would have been nice to legitimately take over ruling. If I could have retained the princess I would have wedded and bedded her within the year, and had a half dozen brats by her in the next dozen, making me king after our current king's unfortunate but not unexpected death from old age."

He slowly turned his gaze onto Vor. "That sadly is no longer possible."

"The princess can be recaptured," Vor spoke up.

"We shall see, but I won't plan on it. Even if it were to happen, who is to say that my apprentice would not release her again?"

Vor gritted her teeth and remained silent. Altare tapped his fingers on the desk.

"The people so far have accepted the imposter princess. I wonder if they would continue to believe if I wedded her and spawned an offspring with her. She might die tragically in childbirth, but then would it be tolerated for me to rule as regent for the child? A civil war is hardly a tidy thing."

For a few more moments he mused in silence. "Is this country worth keeping?" he muttered.

Vor couldn't hide her surprise. The other wizards—those who could hear him anyway—seemed shocked.

"Give up power?" Eriducus wheezed.

"We took this country with blood and steel," declared Chirolen, fist clenched, startling his little lizard pet.

"Once all the mage-stone is mined, what use is it?" Altare countered.

"It is ours," Chirolen hissed.

Altare glared at the men, and Vor guessed he was probably thinking how it wouldn't be theirs much longer. She hadn't thought it at the time, but she'd come to suspect that the deaths of the other two masters had probably not been accidents, and that her master had been involved. If Chirolen, Eriducus, or Ulver became too problematic, they'd probably have accidents, too.

"I agree our lives are comfortable here," Altare allowed. "Others are in power back in Weldom and beyond. Fighting for a place there would be troublesome, but once the supply of mage-stone stops, we'll be of no more use to them."

The old mages seemed to actually consider that. Their ability to think, at least a little, without having enough power to threaten Altare, was why Altare left them alive, Vor thought. The master mage sat back, pondering again and stroking his beard. Old master Ulver scratched at his scalp.

"We'll need drakes," he creaked. "You always need drakes if you're to fight griffins."

Altare raised his gaze to him. "You think Weldom will give us back our drake swarms for this, when the mage-stone is about to run out?"

"Don't tell them?" Ulver shrugged.

Altare just blinked at him, slowly, like a housecat. "That thought did occur to me." He stood suddenly and started pacing. "I'll have my revenge on those griffins," he growled. "I'll have them sliced and burned and plucked and

broken with hammers. Drakes would bring them to me."

"They are mages," Vor reminded him softly.

Altare threw a hand up in dismissal. "Throw enough drakes at a mage and even the strongest will fall. Even should he take down twenty, the twenty-first will defeat him."

"Will Weldom send us that many?" Vor queried, making her voice light and curious.

"We're their source of mage-stone," Chirolen contributed, "their only source since their own mines dried up."

Altare was nodding. "I'll draft the documents and send them to the High Ministers, but I don't expect a speedy reply: bureaucracy. Vor, detail crews to repair the old Feathyr barracks. We'll put the drakes in there. Give me an estimate of how many will fit. Master Ulver, assist her. Vor has little knowledge of drakes."

"Are we prepared to feed them?" Ulver croaked out.

"Assess the situation and tell me," Altare ordered. "Don't forget to count the prisoners as a food source, and the slaves, once the mines run out."

Vor chilled. True, the prisoners and slaves had—or would have—no other immediate use, but they were thinking beings, and could potentially be put to other productive tasks no one else wanted to do, especially if there was to be battle.

"This generation of drakes will have no experience fighting griffins," Altare was going on. "The drakes can test themselves against the griffin slaves."

Vor held her tongue. The griffin slaves hadn't fought or flown for a decade. What kind of a test would that be? It would be a slaughter.

"Dismissed," Altare ordered.

Vor bowed and turned to go take up her assignment. Rebuilding the barracks would take many months, but if her master was right about Weldom's bureaucracy, it might take that long for the drake swarms to show up—if Weldom cared enough to send them, if Weldom cared at all.

Northborn Year 11: Summer

Vor smoothed her face into an expressionless mask as she strode down the hallway and into the study. She saw her master through the open doorway, with Edgard, the palace steward, standing like a flagpole to one side. As soon as she stepped inside she understood the reason for the summoning.

"You may go," Altare said to Edgard.

The man bowed and left without a word. Vor took her spot beside and slightly behind her master and looked across the desk at the young man who faced them. She recognized him immediately.

"Your name, then?" Altare invited.

"Karolan Freyaliv," the young man answered.

"Edgard tells me you're from Lackland."

"Correct, sir."

Altare went on, asking mundane questions of little import, while Vor watched the young man from behind her mask of impassivity. His nose still looked a bit crooked from when she'd broken it: smashing her palm into it while kidnapping the princess Jessika from the cottage in the woods. He'd cut his blonde hair short and attempted to grow a beard since then, and it looked like he'd gotten at least a foot taller, but none of those changes could disguise him.

Even if they could have, his magical aura was unmistakable; he was doing nothing to try to hide or obscure it. She'd seen him throwing fireballs with some amount of skill. She'd even been forced to expend some energy snuffing the magical flames before they started a wildfire. She knew him. He was an ally of the princess and the griffins. What was he doing here and how could he possibly think she wouldn't remember him?

"I need a teacher," he was saying. "Mine can no longer keep up with me."

Altare lifted an eyebrow. "You are that skilled are you?"

The young man, Karolan, stuttered, "well, no, not really, it's just, he's not really well anymore. He's gotten old."

Altare went on interrogating him, now asking about what sort of magic he was comfortable working. Vor went on staring at him, wondering why she did not reveal his identity to her master. She should, of course. This man—boy even, he could hardly be sixteen—was an enemy. He had fought against her and her soldiers. His allies had, presumably, killed Skire Germaine.

It was her duty to hand that information over to her master, but she did not say a word.

"You are clearly lacking education in critical areas," Altare sneered, "yet in others you sound competent, if you are reporting truthfully your abilities. You understand that I already have an apprentice." He made the slightest gesture towards Vor. "She, too, is woefully lacking in certain areas."

Vor struggled to retain her expression of bland indifference.

"I doubt I have the time or energy to spend on trying to make decent mages out of two who need so much work."

"I will happily await my turn," Karolan said. "Set me your most menial tasks, the most loathsome, the most disliked, in return for a little food and a place to sleep, and I will await your leisure."

"A little food," Altare scoffed. "Growing boys do not eat only a little food."

Despite his negativity, Vor could tell that her master was intrigued. It was evidenced by the fact that he had consented to the interview in the first place and not thrown the boy out on his ear after the first minute. Altare suddenly swung his head to look at Vor. She nearly startled.

"Then again, perhaps a little competition is what my wayward apprentice needs?" he mused.

"This boy is no kind of competition, Master," Vor murmured.

Altare laughed aloud. "This could prove to be quite interesting." He looked back at Karolan. "You might serve more than one purpose."

"As many as I may, sir," the boy said with a short bow.

Altare waved a hand. "Enough of that 'sir' business. You will call me 'Master.'"

***

Vor trailed as her master led the interloper down the hall towards the most external magical workroom. He said he was going to see what the boy was made of. Vor figured she could discover that easily—with a nice, sharp blade—but why bother? He was made of blood and bone and guts like every other creature.

She tried to glare a hole in Altare's back. How dare her master take on a second apprentice? It was a bigger slap in the face than any he'd given her physically. Yet, a part of her was relieved, too. Perhaps now he'd leave her more to her own studies, and wear out his need for dominance on someone else.

"Come in, Vor," he ordered when she lingered outside the workroom doorway, about to go off on her own.

She hesitated.

"In," he pronounced.

She didn't dare disobey when he gave her that look. Vor stepped through the disarmed magical barriers and took a place in one corner of the room.

"No, no," Altare went on, beckoning her closer.

She complied, while anxiety began to twist her belly. With a brush of his hand he positioned her facing the newcomer. She didn't like what this looked like.

"No kind of competition, is he?" Altare hummed. "Let's see. If you kill him, you won't have to share my attention, now will you?"

Karolan glanced briefly towards the master mage, and then firmly flicked his eyes back to front. In that glance Vor thought she saw a moment of fear, but she didn't react to it. Altare, walking to the corner Vor had only moments ago occupied, didn't notice it.

"Should you kill her, young Karolan, I will be most impressed, and not hesitate to take you as my new apprentice," he went on.

"A mage duel, to the death?" Vor clarified, unable to believe it and yet—somehow not surprised.

Altare made half a shrug. "I hope you've been saving up energy."

She looked back at Karolan, trying to keep her face neutral even as her heart rate kicked up. His expression was cracking just a bit, but he hadn't collapsed in terror or run for the door. Vor felt Altare put the room's shields up. She wasn't sure this room could contain the power necessary for killing blows; it wasn't that sort of workroom.

Vor reached for energy, making ready all she had. It wasn't much. She'd spent the morning practicing and was partly depleted. She would have to be careful and smart. Maybe she could end the fight quickly, before he wore her down. She didn't—or couldn't—sense the young man gathering his powers. Either he was so good he could do it subtly, or he thought he didn't need to, or he didn't know he needed to.

She'd seen him fling fireballs, but that wasn't particularly advanced magic. Vor narrowed her eyes. Perhaps he wasn't much of a mage at all, and had no experience in mage duels. Altare was staying safely in the corner, putting up his own personal shields as protection from stray—or intentional—strikes.

"Whenever you like, have at," he invited with a flippant wave of his hand.

Vor clenched her jaw. Fine then. Not able to tell if her opponent was ready or not, she tightened a fist and made a sharp punching gesture. An invisible wave of force rushed across the room.

Karolan's eyes widened as he sensed it coming, but instead of trying to block it or take the blow stoically, he twisted his body to the side, using just enough energy to deflect it. He still staggered, but most of the power hit the wall behind him, fragmenting and bouncing away.

Vor gave him no time to put together a counter attack. She reached a hand up and yanked down. A lightning bolt followed her gesture, striking her opponent and knocking him off his feet. It hadn't been very powerful—that required building up the blow slowly. His shorn hair stood on end, and he twitched a few times, but his own shields had taken most of the hit. Still, it couldn't have been comfortable.

Now, he turned a snarl onto Vor, and she heard Altare chuckle. Karolan rolled to all fours and slapped a hand down on the floor. The stone rippled and bounced as though it were a bag full of water. The wave travelled quickly although its intensity lessened the further it went from its source. Still, Vor found her footing unsteady, and she stumbled, barely keeping her feet as the floor buckled.

This time, Karolan gave her no time to catch her focus. He sent a fireball just like the ones she'd seen him throw before, directly at her. With no time for a clever counter, Vor crossed her arms in front of her face and threw power to her shields. The fireball smacked in and burst in flames all around her, scarring her shield, but she remained unscathed: just a little hotter.

In the time she'd taken to block the strike, he'd gotten back to his feet, but he was breathing heavy, as if it was an effort to produce such strikes. It seemed he had a good few tricks, and Vor's energy was low, too. If she didn't have enough energy to strike at him herself, perhaps there was another way to get the power to defeat him.

Vor flung out a hand and sent a bright spark zipping across the room at him. He dodged, and she sent another, and another. There was virtually no power behind the strikes. Even had they connected with bare skin, all they would have done was sting a little, but they were flashy and looked far more dangerous than they were.

All she needed was a few seconds. She could keep producing the sparks while chanting under her breath, calling on an elemental servant. Across the room, Karolan missed a dodge and a spark impacted harmlessly against his shields. Just as she finished the cantrip, he seemed to realize that the sparks were a distraction, but it was too late.

Vor hissed out the final word, and directly before her a flame sprang to life. She didn't have the energy left to call upon a major elemental, much less one of the dreaded greater varieties, but a lesser salamander would be sufficient, she hoped, to get the young man to surrender. The flame flashed and morphed into a slender creature of flame as long as her hand. It looked back at Vor with obedient but mischievous white-hot eyes.

She couldn't help but quirk a smile. Salamanders were not powerful, especially not the lesser salamander she'd called, but even a little fire that wouldn't go out was sufficient to dismay most enemies. Being of fire, they could writhe through most magical shields. They had enough intelligence to understand simple commands, and she only had to gift it with a little bit of energy to convince the playful creature to do as she asked.

She flicked a finger towards Karolan. "Burn off his clothes," she murmured, just loud enough for the salamander to hear.

It rippled with pleasure and streaked through the air in a zigzagging path. Vor didn't need to direct it any further. If it finished its task it would return

to her for more direction—and more energy—or to be dispelled. If Karolan did figure out how to defeat it, the creature would only be banished back to its own plane, not actually killed, but Vor doubted he'd encountered salamanders before.

Karolan's reaction seemed to uphold her surmise. The salamander went straight for his feet, dove through whatever weak shields he had up, and in a quick figure-eight pattern lit the cuffs of his trouser legs on fire. Karolan yelped and danced about, trying to escape the little beastie, but it was much too fast for him. He could have disintegrated it with a forceful blast of power, if he'd first caught it in a spell of holding, or he could have summoned a water sprite to fight it, if he'd known how.

Instead, the salamander flitted about, unconcerned with the young man's exclamations or flailing hands. His trousers burned up to his knees while the elemental got his shirtsleeves smoldering. Vor relaxed, sure of her victory. She glanced at her master. He nodded, but gave her a disappointed look.

"You've won, but you didn't do it yourself," he grunted, making no move to save Karolan from the tricky—and dangerous—elemental.

"I spent months learning the cantrip and developing the strength of will to command salamanders, Master," Vor retorted. "Even longer to learn to summon one while casting other magic."

He shrugged and waved a hand. "Dismiss the creature, before the boy is denuded, unless of course that's what you wanted to see?"

Vor growled, but did as bid. "Return," she ordered, sending a pulse of her will along with the word.

The elemental zoomed back to her side, rippling with sparkly giggles, but seeming a bit reluctant to leave off its play.

Vor spoke the words to dismiss it, and it twirled as it vanished into smoke. Meanwhile, Altare had gone to Karolan, and with a gesture extinguished the magical flames. The young man collapsed, his clothing considerably damaged and his skin red and shiny with burns, but he didn't seem seriously hurt.

"There's salve for your injuries," Altare was saying. "I'll have Vor bring you some. Come this way to your rooms."

Vor's mouth dropped open as her master urged Karolan to his feet.

"I won," she declared. "I could have killed him."

"I wasn't going to allow that, once I saw him merge water and earth magic so expertly," her master answered smoothly. "He has talent. He wants to learn. This may be a good thing. You need some motivation, and he may have other uses."

Vor buttoned her lips. Fine. Then she wouldn't tell him that the boy had been with the princess and the griffins. She supposed, if she did, he would get rid of the boy, or use him as bait, or at least interrogate him. That would prevent him from becoming Altare's apprentice, which was what she wanted. So then, why didn't she want to tell her master?

As Karolan limped across the room, Vor frowned, trying to guess the best course of action. She certainly didn't want the boy here, did she? She had the knowledge necessary to get her master to reject him. Her fingernails bit into her palms as she tried to pummel her brain into telling her why she didn't want to use that knowledge.

Altare and the boy were striding ahead. Her master was giving him a quick introduction to the palace and the rules he expected him to live by. Vor glared at their backs, wanting to call back the salamander and send it—and several of its friends—at the both of them. She was angry with her master. That was it. She wanted to defy him. She even wanted this boy to cause trouble for him.

"I was here first," she growled under her breath.

Even as she said it, she knew it was childish, and she didn't care. Now he had her trailing around behind him like a scolded puppy. He would probably be grimly satisfied if she ran off and moped. Silently and obediently following him would be more challenging, so she tagged along, edging closer so she could hear what the men were saying.

If her master were about to discard her, she wouldn't make it easy for him.

Chapter 9
The Schooling of Hawkrain

Vor could have slammed the pot of salve down in a petulant sulk. Instead, she merely looked blankly at the boy when he answered the door, as though he were of no importance.

"For your burns," she said mildly.

Her disinterested attitude seemed to give him pause. Cautiously, he reached out and took the pot from her flat palm. He'd put on a new pair of trousers, but still smelled a bit like burned hair and clothes.

"You're called Vor?" he asked.

"I am." Her neutral expression did not waver. "You may call me Mistress Vor."

He seemed on the verge of saying something, caught himself, revised, thought for a few moments, and opened his mouth again. He glanced at the pot of salve as if for rescue.

"Do you require assistance applying it?" she snapped at him.

"No," he stuttered.

Without another word, she turned to go.

"Mistress Vor?"

She stopped and looked back over her shoulder, wordlessly.

"I," he hesitated, "look forward to working with you."

She narrowed her eyes. "Do you?"

He seemed struck without words.

"We shall see," she told him softly.

She departed, feeling a surprising stir of interest. A grin threatened, but she fought it down. The boy was no magical threat. She could play with him—toy with him. Of course there was also potential to investigate him. If he were plotting some deeper game on behalf of the princess and her griffins, perhaps Vor could discover it, reveal it to her master in a critical moment, and gain his favor.

The grin was winning, but there was no one around to see, so she let a hint of it surface on her face. As long as she could keep her skills ahead of his, there was no real danger, and every potential for amusement.

***

The next few days she hardly saw her master. He didn't summon her. She didn't see the new boy either. It was obvious that Altare was putting him through his paces somewhere, testing him, and finding out the limits of his knowledge and abilities. It was relieving to have all her time to herself—but she couldn't stop thinking about the two men off together engaged in magery, and her excluded. It also deprived her of chances to try tormenting the boy, and gradually her excitement over the idea dwindled.

Vor was in the main library, returning a few volumes after having made the notes she needed from them in her own journals. She restrained herself from slamming down the books she'd borrowed; one did not treat books that way. She had to stop and take a few calming breaths. She knew perfectly well that her master did works with the other mages he kept. That never bothered her. So why did this?

"I am not jealous," she hissed to herself. "After all, I hate him, both of them."

She carefully shelved one book, and went back for the next, when a noise at the door made her look over.

"Oh," the interloper said, "I beg your pardon. This is the main palace library?"

"It is," she told him.

Karolan took a few steps into the room. He looked a little pale, and weary. There was a bruise on his cheekbone. So her master wasn't going lightly on him.

"I was told I should fetch a couple books for study."

"Go ahead," Vor said flatly, resuming her shelving and turning her back on him. "The library is free for all to make use of. Sign them out on the logbook by the door."

She heard him walking about, pausing to look at shelves, then moving again.

"I'm sorry, but do you know where the geology books are?"

Vor straightened and pivoted to face him. She stuck an arm out straight, pointing unerringly.

"Thank you."

He seemed to find what he was after. She was down to her last book when she suddenly whirled, sensing him approach.

"What?" she snapped.

"I think this is the botany section?"

Oh. "It is."

"There should be one on identifying flowering plants?"

Her master had set her to memorizing that book, too—when she was twelve years old. Was this boy's education truly so woefully incomplete? Vor turned and reached for the rolling ladder; the book was shelved just beyond her reach.

"Ah, I see it." Karolan nabbed it before she could.

She hadn't even gotten the ladder into place yet. He flipped open the cover, just standing there right beside her. This close, she had to look up at him. She'd seen he was tall, but hadn't realized he was so tall. He'd been her height or shorter when she'd broken his nose less than a year ago. She had to look up at her master, and now she had to look up at this boy. A strange discomfort oozed through her and she took a step back.

"You're enjoying your lessons?" she challenged.

Karolan shut the book, adding it to the other one he'd selected, and looked at her. "Yes," he said after only a slight hesitation.

She let a faint smirk onto her face. "Are you really?"

"Master Altare is so talented. I'm lucky to have the chance to learn from him."

"Indeed you are." It was on the tip of her tongue to tell him that she knew who he was, but he didn't give her the chance.

"We could practice together sometime," the boy went on. "You're more skilled than I am, too. I think I could learn a lot from you, Mistress Vor."

She raised an eyebrow.

He gave a little shrug. "Maybe there's even something you could learn from me."

That made her pause. Was she imagining that he'd put a hint of double meaning into that sentence? Or was he only talking about magic? He had to have a hidden motivation for being here. What could he possibly be about, wanting to practice with her?

"I have important things to do," she told him. "Besides, I know all my flowers and crystals already."

As briskly as she could, she shelved her final book and swept out of the library. She didn't look back. Somehow, despite her conviction to torment the boy, she found herself wondering who had won that exchange: her or him.

***

Well, she hadn't wanted to be excluded. Her master had unknowingly granted her wish. Vor stood even with the new boy, Karolan the mysterious. Altare had been working them both on merging air and fire magic. Air and fire combined the most easily of all the elements. Although it took a lot of energy to keep the fire going, when the air was mixed with it and feeding it, it was not technically difficult.

Its only use was to rapidly dry things out. Vor could see the potential application of drying laundry in the winter, when the sun was not available. She supposed, with an experienced touch, it could be used for baking—but why bother when ovens did it so well already? Sometimes magic was not the best solution for everything. The other application was combative. A swirling tower of superheated air dropped over an enemy would suck the breath from his lungs and burn him inside and out.

"Well done, Vor," her master said. "You've caught on quickly."

She narrowed her eyes at Karolan, but he ignored her—or was so unobservant he didn't notice. It seemed he'd known the technique from the start. So her master was catching her up to what this younger, weaker, inferior boy had already learned.

"Once again."

Altare extracted two more soaking wet towels from a bucket and tossed them one at a time into the air. Vor took the first one, air keeping it aloft and untangling it as fire feathered in around it, beginning to make it steam, without burning it.

"Let us all have dinner together."

It took a moment for her to understand what her master had said.

"Like a family," he continued. "We haven't dined together since the Skire's demise."

Vor lost her spell, the energy popping and dissipating. The damp towel splatted onto the floor. Her master tsked.

"Control, Vor. You can't let a little thing like words disrupt you. So, dinner, in one hour, the second dinning room: be there. Clean up first."

He swept out as silently as he'd appeared, leaving Vor scowling behind him and Karolan looking baffled.

"I am clean," she gritted out.

She kept her clothes in impeccable order. After her youth living in filth on the streets, she prided herself on having hygienic and tidy clothing. Her hair was always clean, brushed, and tied back neatly. Her hands did get dirty when making potions and salves, and she did get sweaty when she practiced her martial training, but she washed up after, and she wasn't dirty now. Whatever was he talking about?

Although she wanted to kick the dripping pile of towels and throw the bucket of water at Karolan, she took proper care of each. Her irritation simmered silently inside. Karolan had been with them for over a week. Now her master was not only giving them classes together, he was making them all eat together, and telling her to clean up. She sneered. He was trying to get her in bed with Karolan. Well, that wasn't happening.

"I can take that," the boy offered weakly, reaching for the pile of magic-dried towels she'd just picked up.

Jaw clenched so hard it hurt, she pushed the bundle into his hands and strode from the room.

"Never," she swore under her breath. "That duplicitous princess-loving beanpole can go bed his own self, the bitches in the kennels, the mares in the stalls, the soldiers in the barracks, and my master, too, for all I care, but he's not getting me."

She did go wash her face, though, and hands, and put on her least worn set of clothing. Altare would have to be satisfied with that. Vor marched herself off to the public wing of the palace, cool mask carefully in place. The servants got out of her way, usually with a bow or a subservient bob of the head. She had always supposed they didn't know she came from the gutter, a consequence of the war that ate her parents, but she was their superior now.

As she entered the dining room, her master was settling the false princess into a seat at the head of the table. He was holding her hand, smiling his most charming smile. As Vor watched, he bent over her hand and sensually kissed the back of it. The false princess blushed and smiled, leaning in closer.

Before Altare could do anything else, he noticed Vor and straightened up. His gaze travelled down and back up her body with clear disapproval.

"What?" she spat.

"Manners, my apprentice," he berated calmly.

"These are the best clothes I own," she clarified, "Master."

"You may soon need formal garments for court," he remarked.

"These will do," she argued. "They are perfectly presentable, clean, well-fitted, and of quality fabric."

He sighed—rather dramatically, Vor thought. "You will insist on wearing nothing but grey, and only suits, with trousers."

She couldn't believe it. He was really going to stand there and criticize her clothing? He'd never before made any comment on it. She was saved from having to make a reply by Karolan's arrival.

"Ah, my new apprentice," Altare welcomed. "Come here."

Karolan gave only a quick glance and a nod to Vor before obeying.

"Your Highness, may I present my new apprentice Karolan Freyaliv," Altare introduced. "Karolan, her Royal Highness Princess Jessika."

The young man missed only half a step, but Vor was watching for it, and noticed. She wondered if her master did.

"Your Highness," Karolan said, dropping gracefully to one knee and bowing his head. "I am honored to meet you. Let this humble servant be ever at your call, ready to answer your every need."

"Rise," the false princess murmured, "and be at ease."

"Let us sit and dine together," Altare interjected.

He took the chair at the false princess' right hand, pointing Vor to the seat across from him, and Karolan to the seat beside that. Vor complied, and managed not to snarl at Karolan when he pulled the chair out for her. She was accustomed to pulling out and pushing in her own chairs.

She sat with uneasy grace, and Karolan sat beside her, although he put a little extra space between them. As soon as all four bums had settled on their seats, the servants began coming in, placing dishes and serving the first course. Of course Amlee was there: ever the field general giving orders. Kari was the teenage girl who seemed to be Amlee's second-in-command now. She did a good job of not drawing attention to herself, but Vor was a little surprised that Altare hadn't collected her yet. Comely maids tended to vanish, leaving behind vague letters expressing their unhappiness and intent to return to their families—or something like that.

Vor recognized a couple of the menservants, too. They were two of the teenage pages her master had tried to tempt her with a couple years ago, but not Ferghus. They seemed to know their roles now, serving Altare and Karolan, while Amlee served the false princess and Kari served Vor. Kari anticipated all of Vor's needs and remained silent. Vor reciprocated by pretending she didn't exist, in the hopes that might help prevent Altare's attention from being drawn to her.

Her master raised his glass. "Isn't this nice? A big happy family," he smiled. "Soon to be more of a family in truth. I can announce that in two weeks a celebration will be held. Our precious Princess Jessika has taken pity on this poor, simple mage and agreed to accept my hand in matrimony."

From her angle, Vor saw Amlee's lips part in surprise or dismay, just for a moment, before she brought an expression of joy onto her face.

"Congratulations to you both," Karolan praised.

Altare reached out, and the false princess put her hand immediately into his. She smiled with what looked like true happiness. Vor supposed that Karolan had no idea the girl's brain had been retrained to make her think she was the princess and fall in love with Altare—but he had to know that this wasn't the real princess. Except that Altare wouldn't know that he knew, or that Vor knew he knew.

"Congratulations," she said simply. "What a celebration it will be."

"Only the announcement of the engagement," Altare clarified. "The wedding shall be next month, as it will require more time for planning."

"Naturally," Karolan nodded. "You must tell me how I can be of assistance."

"There will be much to do, fear not."

"A toast then," Vor drawled, lifting her glass, "to true love."

Altare's eyes flickered at her for an instant, but he followed suit, raising his goblet.

"To the princess and her groom," Karolan added, "and a long life of happiness together."

The four of them clinked their glasses and drank. It was only a cold fruit juice tea, not wine—which was most customary for toasting—since any kind of alcohol muddied mage senses. Altare eyed Vor once more over the rim of his goblet. She gave him an innocent little smile.

"Let us partake," her master said.

They fell to, but she felt his eyes run over her frequently throughout the meal. Karolan did most of the talking, making easy enquiries about the upcoming celebrations. Altare replied. The princess seemed incapable of much speech. Vor answered shortly when spoken to.

It seemed to take forever for the four courses to be finished. At last the dessert plates were cleared away and a strong mint tea was served to end the meal. The false princess was visibly wilting, and Altare ordered Amlee to see her to her rooms. He dismissed the other servants with an idle wave of his hand and Kari hurried to assist Amlee.

"How nice to sit and take a meal together," her master commented. "It has been a while, hasn't it, Vor?"

"Since Skire Germaine's passing," Vor answered.

"Yes. Skire Germaine was a student of biology, the study of living bodies and systems," Altare explained for Karolan. "She often worked with us mages in our endeavors, but she was murdered last summer."

"Murdered?" Karolan echoed. "By whom?"

Vor could have commented that she expected he knew all about it, but held her words. What a performance he was giving; she couldn't bring herself to ruin it.

"We have had some trouble with griffins," Altare said carefully. "It seems one broke into her laboratory and killed her. It was a baffling crime. We never caught the beast."

"That's horrible," Karolan grimaced. "Are none of us safe behind stone walls?"

"I keep wards and shields in place now to detect aerial approach. It can be exhausting, but I do what I must to protect the palace. It's one task I hope the two of you may be able to take turns at soon."

"Yes, Master, of course," Vor said. She wondered: would he really be so eager to have Karolan help with protecting the castle if he knew the boy was an ally of Germaine's murderer? She hid a smile in her teacup. It was amusing.

"I will do my best," Karolan agreed, "though I have never set such large wards before."

"I will teach you," Altare waved the comment away. "With enough power anything is possible." He took a swallow of tea. "Speaking of power, Vor, Karolan needs a knife."

"A knife, Master?" she asked blankly.

"Like yours," he told her with a trace of impatience. "Like mine. Like what any mage carries."

Ah. "Of course, Master." She used her knife for utility purposes, but it was also meant for bloodletting and power collection thereby.

"Commission the blade from the blacksmith tomorrow," Altare ordered.

Vor glanced towards Karolan and made a weak gesture. "Shouldn't he—?"

"You know what is needed," her master interrupted. "You will go place the order."

"Of course, Master."

"I could go with her," Karolan offered.

She did not want him with her.

"You will have lessons tomorrow," Altare denied.

Vor was relieved.

The boy subsided. "Yes, Master."

Altare finished his tea and stood up. "This has been nice. We must do it again, regularly perhaps. Good night, my apprentices."

He strode swiftly from the room, leaving Vor and Karolan alone.

***

Vor sipped her tea, slowly, eyes straight ahead. Beside her, Karolan took a large swallow and almost choked. She held back a grin. So, he was nervous around her? Good: he should be.

"I'm sorry you have to go run an errand for me," he said.

"It is no matter," she replied evenly. "Have you memorized your flowers?"

"What? Oh, right, the book, um, sort of. There are quite a lot of them."

"There are far more than that book contains, but those are the most common and most useful in this region. There are additional rare ones of even more importance when it comes to potion making. Do you know anything of powders, potions, or salves?"

"Only a little," he said. "I know a few recipes for poultices, for injuries."

"I suppose that is something," she muttered, and drank the last of her tea. Vor stood to go.

"Wait," Karolan blurted. "I wanted to ask, what was Skire Germaine like?"

Vor's eyebrows rose a trifle.

He pressed on. "You knew her?"

"I did, somewhat," she answered after a moment. "She often possessed useful information, but I didn't have any particular feelings towards her."

"Oh, so, it must have been sad for you when she died, somewhat?"

"It was a shock," Vor allowed.

Karolan took a moment.

"If there is nothing else," Vor began.

"Was she evil?" he asked.

Vor stared at him. He knew his allies had killed her; he had to know. She wondered if he had been present. From the wounds on the corpse, it was obvious a griffin had killed her, but—no, hadn't he been using a crutch? He'd been injured so he couldn't walk. Probably he hadn't been able to participate in the raid.

"Evil? That depends," Vor replied, "on how you assign value to intangibles like knowledge, human progress, and liberty."

"And life?" he added. "And pain?"

"None of the specimens felt pain," Vor explained, which she knew well was only partly true.

He cleared his throat a little. "At least, not physical pain," he clarified.

"Any other type of pain is a person's own fault," Vor told him.

His brow crinkled.

Vor explained slowly. "Physical pain is a message of harm to the body, and for the most part that is beyond our control. Other reactions to our world that cause mental or emotional distress are all within our power to change. We choose to feel sad or angry or distraught, and we can stop any time. Only those who are mentally weak are prey to such afflictions as emotional suffering."

Karolan just stared at her, brow lowering further.

"If any of the specimens inflicted that kind of suffering on themselves, it was wholly their own choice," Vor went on stubbornly. "Besides, many of them were just animals, without the brain-based ability to feel such complex emotions, according to the Skire."

He leaned forward eagerly. "According to the Skire," he parroted. "How do you know she was right? She was just making that up so she wouldn't feel so bad about hurting all those people."

Vor stared right back at him. The echoes of baby unicorn screams bounced through her head. She kept her face an impassive mask, but guilt and anguish welled in her chest. He was saying things like what Jessika had said, and it was starting to challenge her in the same way.

"You don't actually know, do you?" he pressed, more intent than she'd yet seen him be, and her eyes widened a trifle. "That's what she told you, that those people were animals who didn't feel anything as long as their bodies were numbed."

Vor tried to gather herself. "You seem to know a lot about it," she observed with thinly veiled threat.

Karolan straightened, sitting tall in his chair. Their gazes locked, and she knew then that he knew she knew who he was—or so she suspected. The question was: would he confront her now, or—

"You're right," he demurred, looking away. "I don't know much about it. I got worked up. Please pardon me, Mistress Vor."

She also looked away. "You're also right," she allowed. "I only know what she told me. I don't know her research techniques or what data she collected to support her statements."

Karolan cautiously lifted his eyes. Such genuine spirit shone from them that Vor suddenly felt stained. Her desire to toy with him melted even further. He was naïve, yes, but with an honest heart, with convictions that hadn't yet been compromised—as hers had.

"I will tell you this, however," Vor went on, more softly. "If you intend to remain a student of my master, you might want to keep such opinions to yourself."

Before she could step any deeper into it, she pivoted and strode from the room, leaving Karolan alone at the table. She clenched her jaw. It suddenly felt like she'd discovered a hanging thread on a garment. If she didn't stitch it up, the whole thing would start to unravel with just a tug.

***

"Master blacksmith."

"Mistress Vor," the man bowed deeply.

"I have a commiss—" She broke off abruptly as movement caught her eye. There was another man in the shop, sitting back at a table. He was carving what seemed to be a helve, but he'd stopped as soon as she'd stepped into sight, and now watched her with the wariness of an ice-lion spotting a rival. She knew him. Like Karolan, he'd been at the cottage where she'd captured the princess. Then he'd been with the group that had rescued her from the palace. She'd almost thrown him off the roof.

It was an invasion. This was an outright invasion; her master was right. They were moving on the castle with plans for a coup. From his posture and expression, she knew he recognized her, but he wasn't doing or saying anything. She could call him out, like his ally Karolan—or not.

The blacksmith, Rikan she knew he was called, followed her gaze and turned.

"My son, Rikah, a simple boy but a good hand for carving," Rikan explained. "Bow to the lady, boy."

Rikah got to his feet and bowed as deeply as his father had. Vor gave him no response and returned her focus to the blacksmith, but she remained aware of his son in her peripheral vision. From her belt she pulled her utility knife.

"I have a commission," she completed. "Another one like this, please, for the lord's new apprentice, Karolan Freyaliv."

She hadn't needed to give his name, but she'd wanted to see how his probable ally would react. Rikah had returned to carefully shaving bits of wood from the axe handle, and made no response at all to the name.

"Young lord Karolan will have my best work, Mistress," the blacksmith assured her. "I beg a moment of your time to take measurements."

"Of course. His hands are larger than mine, so perhaps a bit longer and thicker in the handle."

"Excellent, Mistress. It shall be as you say."

The blacksmith fetched a scrap of paper, a charcoal stick, and a measuring tool. He rapidly sketched the shape of the blade and noted its dimensions before returning it with another bow to Vor.

"Do you have preference for the wood of the handle? The same as yours? Pine?"

She hadn't thought to ask Karolan before she came, but the wood it was made from did make a difference. When she'd learned that she would need a knife for her studies, she'd researched the magical properties of various local woods. Eyes staring at nothing, she turned her knife over in her hands, allowing her impressions of Karolan to guide her to intuit a suitable wood.

"Cedar," she said at last. "Do you have cedar?"

The blacksmith nodded. "I have some fine cedar."

"Cedar, please."

"As you wish, Mistress. It will be ready in three days."

"I shall return then."

Rikah was giving all his attention to his knife and helve as Vor walked away.

Chapter 10
Karloan's Intentions

For the intervening three days, she saw neither her master nor Karolan. Having her own time let her to catch up on her backlog of stillroom work while allowing her personal energies to recharge. By the third day she even found her spirits light enough that she looked up from a completed bottle of digestive tonic with a faint but genuine smile of satisfaction.

Vor located a page to deliver the bottle to Master Ulver, who had mentioned indigestion, and took herself towards the blacksmith to pick up Karolan's knife. It was lunchtime but she knew well that Rikan took his lunches at his shop. The short walk brought her down to the ring between the inner and outer castle walls, where the artisans had their shops and livestock was quartered.

She came up to the shop, but there was no sound of metal on metal, and no sign of Rikan. The double sliding doors were both wide open, however, and sitting at the same table was Rikah, carving on a block of wood that didn't look like anything in particular yet. Vor stopped in the opening and Rikah noticed her at once, setting down his block.

"Mistress Vor," he said.

She suppressed a smirk. He hadn't liked saying the "mistress" part, she could tell.

"I have your order. My father stepped away for a few minutes."

He got up and fetched a small sack from a shelf. Almost hesitantly, he approached and held it out to her. Vor reached out, displaying no threat, and took it. She opened the sack and the short, sheathed knife fell into her palm. She pulled off the sheath and examined the blade: simple but elegant, as she'd come to expect from Rikan's work, and wickedly sharp. There was also a fold of paper in the sack: the bill.

"Edgard will come to settle the balance," Vor commented.

"My father informed me," Rikah nodded.

She eyed him. "You carved the handle?"

"I did, Mistress."

"Fine work."

"Thank you, Mistress."

She returned it to its sheath and dropped it back in the bag.

"If I might ask," Rikah began hesitantly, "what will the lord's apprentice be using the blade for?"

"Magery," Vor said shortly. "I don't expect a blacksmith's boy to have any knowledge of the art."

Her words were deliberately provoking, and she knew it. Rikah's jaw firmed. Vor allowed herself the tiniest hint of a smile. How tempting it was to prod him further. The young man was tall, taller than her or Altare, though shorter than Karolan, and much broader. He had skin that had seen sun and a body that had seen work. His eyes were guileless and honest brown. With no magical ability of his own, he was practically no threat: an easy target.

Vor pocketed the sack.

"Thank you for your work. Please extend my thanks to your father," she said instead of another sally.

Rikah seemed slightly surprised. "I shall," he answered.

"Good day."

Vor left.

Karolan was difficult to find. Vor had to ask four different pages before one was able to give her a hesitant clue. He had seen the young man from a distance, sitting in the most secluded corner of the private gardens. Afternoon was waning as Vor was finally able to seek him out.

"Karolan," she announced herself as she approached from behind him.

He swiped at his face and his head whipped around to look at her. The skin around his green eyes was a little puffy. He visibly fought to smooth his expression. Vor pursed her lips. It was as she'd expected. Methodically, she picked her way over to him. He was sitting at one end of a stone bench, looking down at a small pond covered with lily pads. Willows encircled the little nook, blocking off most of the view from beyond their hanging branches.

Vor came up beside him and held out the sack with the knife. "For you, forged by the master blacksmith Rikan, and handle carved by his son Rikah."

She'd intentionally given the names, dropping the hint of his ally to see the boy's reaction. Karolan reached out for the sack while a subdued delight replaced the distress on his face. That was evidence enough that the two young men knew each other. Vor let it go into his hands and he pulled the knife out, running his fingers first over the smooth, short handle, before briefly examining the blade itself.

"I didn't have a chance to ask you what wood you wanted," Vor confessed. "I chose cedar for you. It has protective qualities."

There was much more to it than that, but Karolan could look up the wood himself if he was curious. A number of different woods had crossed her mind for him, but cedar had stuck. It was just for the handle of his utility knife, not an actual element of a magical working, but cedar carried always with him would encourage Karolan's inner strength, and help him to resist Altare's influences. Vor had no doubt that he didn't come here because he wanted to learn from her master.

Karolan was holding the knife handle tightly, almost like a lucky charm. His jaw trembled. Feeling as though someone else had suddenly taken control of her body, Vor found herself sitting down next to him. Her own action stunned her, but what came out of her mouth next nearly terrified her.

"What did he make you do?" she whispered.

Karolan's gaze snapped over to her. He looked away, opened his mouth, swallowed, and tried again.

"Energy theft," he rasped, "from animals, until it killed them."

"Ah, yes," Vor nodded. "I had that lesson when I was thirteen, I think."

His eyes danced back to her, but she was looking out over the pond.

"And you did it?" he breathed.

"Of course. Didn't you?"

"Yes," he said after a moment. "I didn't want to."

"Neither did I."

"Then why did you?"

She shrugged a little. "I chose to. I didn't like the consequences if I didn't."

He breathed out and joined her in her supervision of the pond. "Yeah, I didn't like them either."

"It's not going to get any easier, you know," she told him, still keeping her voice low. "There will be worse things."

"Why," he asked, barely audible, "why are you working with him?"

"You think I have a choice?"

"He—you're enslaved? Magically?"

"No," she replied, but then revised to a more honest answer. "No, well, a little, but I am bound here by much stronger chains."

"What chains?"

He was looking at her face in profile again. He was so damned sincere and vulnerable.

"You wouldn't understand," she said.

"I'd like to," Karolan replied, quietest yet.

A purely internal shiver of alarm went through her. "No, you wouldn't," Vor retorted immediately. "You definitely do not want to understand this."

She stood and looked down at him. His innocent green eyes, now bare of subterfuge, looked back up at her, almost pleading.

"You should leave," she advised.

He shook his head. "I can't."

"You're going to get hurt, in more ways than one. I'm not threatening you. I'm just telling you what you can expect."

He nodded and looked back out at the pond again. "I knew that when I agreed to come," he whispered.

"Karolan," she ordered through gritted teeth, and he looked up at her. "You should leave. This is not the place for you."

He held her gaze until it started to become uncomfortable, and Vor suddenly felt like the vulnerable one. At last, she looked away first.

"It's not the place for you, either," he breathed, so quietly she wasn't even sure she'd heard him.

His words stabbed into her, into some unshielded soft spot. She had to catch her breath; she hadn't known there was still someplace that she could be hurt, and why did his words do it? He wasn't right; there was no other place for her. He must be doing that thing Amlee did sometimes—giving her sympathy and showing concern for her. Vor wanted none of it. With a mental thrust, she hardened her emotions.

"Don't say I didn't warn you," she hissed at him.

She spun about and strode back to her stillroom. There were still a couple more orders she could work on, but even isolated from Karolan, hands busy with a task, his words hung with her. How could there be any other place for her? Who else would value her? How else could she survive? Even if there were solutions to those problems, her master would never let her go. He would kill her sooner than free her, and the only way around that—led her to thoughts that made her hands shake, and risked the completion of the potion she was working on. Vor banished the thoughts.

She'd tried once and failed. No, there was no way to leave her master.

***

Vor followed the page her master had sent to fetch her. The boy led her to one of the general workrooms that Vor didn't use very often, but which her master used frequently. The page gave her an inexpert bow and departed. She checked for active wards on the door, found none, and went inside without knocking. Her master and Karolan were standing at a table in the corner, looking over a diagram.

"Ah, Vor, finally. Come here," Altare summoned.

Karolan looked up at her and gave her a little nod. She didn't return it.

"As I mentioned, I want you two to start taking over some of the general palace wards," her master went on. "I've increased their number and strength since the threat of griffin attack. I have the other masters handling a few, but that still leaves me with rather more than I'd like. I'm keeping the most critical ones, but there are several you'll now be in charge of renewing."

"Of course, Master," Vor said.

She kept her face smooth. Altare was worried about a griffin invasion, so he was keeping wards on the castle, and he was unknowingly about to put one of the griffins' allies in charge of some of the defenses. It was delightful, but Vor preferred to enjoy the irony alone, without informing him.

Altare pointed out three shapes on one side of the castle diagram, and three on the other. "Vor, handle these, and Karolan, these. Vor, yours are a bit bigger, but you have more experience with wards."

She examined the plan. Altare had set up a double dome of shields over the palace: an outer dome based off the outer wall and mountain cliffs behind, and an inner dome based off the inner wall. Before this, she didn't think he'd been shielding much at all. They had all felt safe enough with human guards on the walls, using their normal human senses to watch and listen for anything approaching.

The diagram divided the domes into arching pie-shaped pieces, with different mages' names noted on different pieces. It looked like Altare was still powering all the pie slices that covered doors through the walls: some half dozen of them. The other master mages were powering the rest of the inner dome. Several slices in the outer dome, however, had recently been reassigned to Vor and Karolan.

Both of their sets covered portions of the outer wall where there weren't doors or many windows. If those wards were weak or absent, they wouldn't directly expose a point of entry into the castle, but a griffin could still fly in through the hole, land on the wall, drop over it to the ring between the walls, and then make its way to an inner wall door. Of course, there would be human guards on the doors in the inner wall, and Altare's wards over them. It would get the invaders halfway to their goal of the palace, however, and that was nothing to dismiss.

Altare had indeed given Vor larger sections. Hers stretched up higher, covering the renovated Feathyr barracks, where the new rainbow drake swarms—provided they arrived—would be housed. Karolan's sections were opposite, on the other side of the main door to the inner wall, over the private wing of the palace.

"I'm going to show you my process for renewing them. You'll have to pick a power source," he warned. "These are energetically expensive, but you'll only need to renew them once a week. Now, I'll renew one section. Then you'll do the rest. I hope you have some energy to spare."

Altare stepped to a bare spot of floor, took a piece of chalk, and started drawing a simple circle with a few runes of air. Renewing a ward was not that difficult—Vor had done it many times before. These were quite large, though, so the circle would provide some extra support. She engaged her inner sight as Karolan stepped up near her, and she sensed him do the same. Energy ran from her master's many pockets of power, and in only a few minutes he was done.

"There," Altare concluded. "Not too difficult, is it."

"No, Master," Karolan said.

"Well, then. Let's see you both do it."

Vor might have asked a clarifying question or two, but thanks to her fellow student's confidence she had to try the task right away. She cast a glare at him, but he didn't seem to notice. They each took chalk, knocked out a quick circle—although Karolan took a bit longer to write the runes—and set to the assignment.

Vor faced the direction of the Feathyr barracks and let her eyes unfocus, extending her senses to examine the wall of wards. She was inside both the inner and outer wards, so she'd have to work the magic through the inner ward. That added a complication, but it was Master Ulver's work between her and her area of responsibility, and she knew his magic well enough to thread her energy through it without too much trouble.

She had to draw on more of her personal power than she wanted to, since she didn't have much stored up. As she finished, she wondered where Karolan was getting his extra mage energy. Without the Skire regularly dissecting specimens, the blood bowls were long empty. Vor usually got hers from the butcher, and had found she could gather some from a walk in the garden, or some bouts with the hanging bag in the salle, but she hadn't run into the boy gathering power in any of those locations yet.

Task completed, she cleaned up her chalk circle, but before she could exit, her master gestured her over. Her thoughts of the previous day echoed in her head along with a little fear. She was accustomed to being frightened of Altare, but she'd gotten fairly good at appeasing him. Still, no amount of appeasement would allow her to leave. Karolan could, and should, but she—

"He's not bad," Altare muttered to her.

She just lifted an eyebrow in her master's direction and said nothing.

"He's got a lot of careful control, and good husbanding of his resources, but had no power storage ability at all when he came, and gaping holes in his knowledge of some magical elements."

He paused, as if waiting for her to contribute to the conversation, but she again said nothing.

"He's able to pull off some magic without any preparation: rather remarkable evocations," Altare went on. "So what do you think of him?"

"He's a distraction neither of us need," she said. "A waste of your time: you should show him the door."

Her master chuckled. "I think he'll make a fine mage. He just needs some work. He's made of harder stuff than you, but that means he'll endure better, once he's properly shaped."

Vor shot a glance at Altare. "What do you mean by harder stuff?"

"You were easy," he grinned, and then tipped his head, smile fading, "in most areas: damnably stubborn in others."

Vor clenched her jaw, trying not to express the sudden surge in anger she felt. Easy, was she?

"This boy has an unbending core. It's a challenge to mold him, but he'll be great once finished."

Karolan dropped his hands, which he'd been holding up while he worked as if pressing the wards into place. He stepped back out of his circle.

"I'm finished, Master," he announced.

"Fine work, both of you. I expect nothing less," Altare said. "Monitor your sections and be certain to renew them before they fail. I will be checking."

"Yes, Master," they both murmured.

"That's all for now," he dismissed them with a little wave. "Go enjoy yourselves, children."

Vor marched straight out the door. Her idea of enjoyment did not include either of the men.

***

A week passed with Vor spending most of her time alone. It seemed to be the new pattern; her master was devoting all his energy to warping his new acquisition. The idea of that troubled her deeply. Karolan hadn't come to be warped and shaped into a dark mage—or at least she didn't think so. Exactly why he'd come, she still wasn't certain, except that it must have to do with a coming invasion.

The idea of her master contaminating the boy made her wince. Karolan didn't have to be here—not like her. He didn't have to be exposing himself to Altare. She knew he had a sort of family, with the princess and Rikah the blacksmith's son, and the griffins. He could be with them. He had options, yet he was here anyway, wading into the cesspool that was her master's domain.

The other idea, the idea of not being with her master, of leaving—somehow—lingered as well, resurfacing time and time again as she continued with her independent study and her work in the stillroom. Again and again she fetched up against the same barriers to it: Altare would never let her leave; he'd be furious; she'd have to fight him; he would kill her, or perhaps defeat her but leave her alive, and exact punishment on her for her betrayal in tiny, painful steps for however long he chose to keep her alive.

That thought was enough to banish the idea temporarily, each time it occurred. Vor hadn't seen Karolan in that week since the lesson on renewing the wards, but as Altare had said, the wards ran down in about a week. Hers were due for renewal. She checked Karolan's side out of curiosity, and saw that his were low, too. Her evening was free; she turned her feet toward the room where she'd renewed the wards the first time.

She could only hope that—no, no such luck. Karolan was already in the workroom when Vor arrived. She narrowed her eyes at him for a moment, but then chose to ignore him, going straight to a spare bit of floor and fetching chalk from a box on a shelf.

"Vor," Karolan began, "I want to talk to you."

She stopped and eyed him. "There's nothing to say, and nothing that should be said where others might be listening. Our master's spells are all over these walls."

"Oh." She watched him look around. "Yeah, you're right. Well, what if I did this?"

He came over to her, alarmingly within arm's reach. His fingers seemed to knead the air, and she felt magic moving.

"What are you doing?" she worried.

"I cast a spell of silence."

He didn't have to look so smug about it.

"How?" she demanded. "And on what, the air? You didn't even draw a circle."

"My first masters never drew circles, so I learned to do a lot of magic without them," he said, turning to look at her with a superior smile. "That seems to be a human thing."

"You're human," she pointed out ruthlessly.

Karolan shrugged, still amused. "Yes, well, I guess so, mostly."

"Mostly?"

His mirth faded. "No one can hear what we say now."

It was true. The slightest investigation showed his spell to be solid and sure. Not even Altare would hear through it. He'd have to step within it or actually crack it, and either would be notable enough to give plenty of warning to stop talking.

"I never really learned to use circles," Karolan continued, "until I came here. I see their uses. Without them, you have to hold all the structure in your conscious intent."

Vor did not remove her gaze from him. His masters must have been those griffin mages. Now, here he was, bold and brazen, telling her about them. What was he thinking? Didn't he know she was his enemy? He stood there, smiling that self-satisfied smile, as if he had no fear of her at all.

It made her want to snarl; she held it in. How dare he? How dare he be so relaxed? How dare he take lessons with her blood-soaked master with hardly a sign of distress? What vast confidence was he drawing upon? How could he possibly be so calm and secure? The desire rose in her to disrupt it, to throw him off balance. She took a floor-eating step closer.

"I know who you are," she hissed.

He just blinked at her, slowly, and smiled a little more. "I know you do."

That wasn't the reaction she'd hoped for, but she tried to rally. "I figured you must. You did nothing to hide your aura, and you don't look that different, just taller."

"So why haven't you told on me?"

"Weren't you afraid I would?" she demanded. "I still could."

Karolan took a step closer, too, and she had to tip her head up farther. How impertinent of him to be younger than her by five years but nearly a foot taller.

"You didn't answer my question. As Thornwing would say, I asked first," he grinned.

Now he was throwing around the actual names of his griffin allies, or so she guessed. "Insolent," she vocalized finally.

"I am, a bit," he agreed, but then his smile melted into a more serious expression. "You even got me a cedar handle for the knife. You could have saddled me with elm or vine, even yew, but you wanted me to resist your master. Why did you do that?"

She swallowed, unable to answer.

"You can tell me," he assured her. "No one will hear. I won't tell."

"Why are you here?" she demanded.

He shrugged. "You don't know? I'm here to kill Altare."

Vor's breath caught and her heart pounded. He didn't seem to notice. The audacity of it astounded her, but she found she had not a whit of fear for her master's safety. Was that because she knew Karolan had no hope of succeeding, or because she didn't care if he did?

Karolan sought her gaze. "Tell me why you're helping me."

"I am not helping you," she denied immediately.

He grimaced for a moment. "Yes, you are. A word to your master would ruin everything. Why haven't you said anything?"

Her extremities were tingling with alarm. This situation was out of control. She couldn't be here. She couldn't be saying these things, or hearing these things. She should tell her master. Of course, then Altare would—

"I don't know," she heard herself say. "I just don't want to tell him."

Karolan nodded, accepting that inadequate answer. "But if he found out who I am, and that you knew and didn't say anything, you'd get in trouble."

"Maybe," she muttered. It would be more than getting in trouble; he would consider it betrayal.

When she said nothing more, he went on. "And you're right; I was afraid you would tell him, but I thought there was a chance you wouldn't."

"Why?" she needed to know.

"Because of some of the things Jessika said about you."

"I did cruel things to her," Vor said. "I hurt her. I was standing by while Altare turned her into one of his mindless toys. I can't imagine that she said anything good about me."

"She said she didn't think you were evil, not completely," Karolan murmured. "She thinks maybe the reason you didn't call your master when she was trying to escape, was because you wanted her to get away, so she wouldn't become a mindless toy, as you put it. She thought there was more to you than what she could see. She thought maybe you'd let me see it."

Vor's eyes widened.

"I wish I knew why," Karolan went on.

"Why?" she retorted.

"Why you're doing all this."

She found it hard to swallow. "All what?"

"Staying here as Altare's apprentice," he said, "helping him do such awful things, like killing people and hurting people. You're even doing things like that yourself."

Vor stared off into the dark, breaking away from his green eyes.

"Sometimes you have no options," she said.

"There are always options."

"And each comes with consequences," Vor retorted. "Sometimes the consequences are so severe, the options are not worth considering."

She heard Karolan take a breath. "Altare will kill you?"

"He will do that and worse," she assured him. "I cannot defy him."

Karolan took longer to speak this time. "Would you like to be free of him?"

Vor furrowed her brow. "It's impossible."

"What if it weren't? Just try to imagine it."

"I have tried to imagine it. I'd be lost, alone," she stuttered, unable to articulate the feeling inside her—that of being a fish in a pond full of fish, but everywhere she swam, the other fish turning away, and not knowing where to go, what to do, being angry, afraid, just like she was now. "You think that would change anything?"

"It would present the chance to change at least, and to control your own future. If he's what you're afraid of, removing him would free you."

She shook her head. "He can't be removed. He's too powerful. Even if it could somehow be done, he'd take me down with him. He'd burn me out before he died himself."

Karolan moved back into her line of sight, his eyes oddly intent. "What if he didn't? What if he were gone and you were free?"

Altare meant pain and threat of more, but he was also the reason she hadn't died on the streets. He continued to provide her with a place in the world. Without him, what would happen to her? How would she survive?

"I don't know what I'd do," she admitted. "I don't know where I'd go or how I'd eat or—"

"Say those things were taken care of," Karolan said, stepping closer still. "How would you live your life? What would you do with your power?"

She looked up at him. "I don't know. You think I'd be any different? He made me what I am. He's left his maker's mark upon me."

"I think you can be whatever you want to be," he murmured.

"No," she denied. "I can't."

"Why not?"

Had he moved closer yet again?

"Do you know the things I've done?" she whispered. "I broke your nose, left you and your companions to die, kidnapped the princess and hurt her repeatedly. I even tried to kill one of the men who came to rescue her—I mean, I wasn't intending to kill him. I was just trying to get her back, and he was in the way, but he would have died if that griffin hadn't saved him. I attacked the others with her, too, and would have hurt them. Those are just the things involving you and her. You don't know all the things I've done with my master, and things I've let him do, when," she fisted her hands, "I should have stopped him. The things he's done, and things I've helped him do," her teeth were bared now, but she could fight down the self-revulsion that swelled in her. "People are dead now who would be alive if it hadn't been for me."

"But you've done other things, too. The soldiers tell me you make them an ointment for their sore knees."

She ignored that. "I could have killed my master," she confessed. "I had a chance, when he came back burned nearly to death."

"Maybe you'll get another chance, and this time you'll take it."

Vor grabbed his shirt in an angry hand. "Or maybe I'm just as evil as he is."

Karolan put his hand over hers, trapping it, before she could push him away. "You're not."

"Maybe you can't tell anymore. He's going to get you, too. He's trying."

"He won't get me."

How could those green eyes be so confident? They filled all her vision and she couldn't seem to look away. He had such long blonde lashes. Karolan's fingers moved against hers, rubbing gently. He was leaning in.

"He will," she confirmed. "He gets what he wants. He'll use every tool at his disposal. He's even using me. I'm corrupting you. You must know it," she whispered.

He bent lower. "No, you're not," he breathed back.

Somehow, she didn't see it coming. His mouth claimed hers, rough and little off center, but she arched into him as though struck by lightning. Her eyes closed without conscious consent—and Vor broke away with a gasp.

"I am not doing this," she declared, whipping away.

Karolan held her wrist, not tight enough to hurt, but enough to halt her bid for freedom, and stepped in to face her again. He bent his head down once more, and without thought her free hand went to touch his cheek, and this time it didn't shock her into escape. This was good. It felt good.

That couldn't be right.

She broke the kiss again but didn't pull away this time. "I am not," she panted.

"I know," Karolan interrupted. "I know. You're not doing this."

"I'm not," she insisted. "Let me go."

His arms went around her and they met again. He pulled her in hard against him and she only struggled for a moment. He tasted good. He was so warm. Heat bloomed inside her with the voracious hunger of a wind-fueled wildfire—and then hard on its heels came all-consuming fear.

Vor shoved him off, drew back, and slapped him hard across the face.

Karolan rocked back, just slightly, but took the hit with hardly a flinch. Vor tried to catch her breath, staring at him in horror, offending hand curled against her chest.

"I," she uttered, "I said I'm not doing this."

Karolan's eyes smoldered at her.

With a throttled cry, Vor turned and ran.

Chapter 11
Secret Plots

Vor knew basic self-defense, but her mage studies took too much time for her to be able to devote herself to becoming an expertly skilled fighter. Still, she tried to practice regularly, and one of the arms masters gave her intermittent instruction. There was no reason for the highly trained soldiers of the capital to fear her in a physical fight, but they all got out of her way as she strode to the salle where both she and they trained.

The defenseless hanging practice bag took the full force of her fury. Punches, palm thrusts, elbow and knee strikes, and the occasional kick thudded into the sawdust with bruising force. Vor kept a firm hand on her mage powers. If she let loose with them, with her emotions so riled, she might level the salle. Instead, blow after blow landed, until her knuckles were scraped and bleeding and she'd strained a couple muscles in her back and legs.

The fury ran out along with her energy. She fell against the bag, glanced around, and saw that she'd cleared the salle. No one wanted to be in range of an angry mage. Alone, she slid down the bag to the floor, landing on her sore knees. With the departure of her rage, tears suddenly swelled like a bud about to flower. She cranked down on them; she would not cry. Between her early life of suffering on the street, and her years of enduring her master's cruelty, she'd learned well not to cry, so she told herself that the little drips of liquid hitting the floor below her face were drops of sweat.

***

How was she supposed to sleep? Vor hadn't gone back to the workroom. She'd finished renewing her share of the castle wards from her own bedroom. It took more energy, but somehow her agitated state meant she had plenty to spare. Quietly seething, she bathed after, but skipped dinner. She ate a few handfuls from her stash of nuts and dried fruits in her room.

Unable to sleep, she sat up and tried to read, keeping the light as low as she could. She didn't know if Karolan knew where her room was, but she didn't want light leakage around the door to encourage anyone to disturb her. Reading wasn't working either; her eyes kept skating over the same sentences without taking them in.

All she could think about was her critical error in the workroom. She should never have answered any of his questions, never engaged in any kind of conversation, never told him she knew who he was—and definitely never kissed him. She supposed she shouldn't have slapped him either.

Vor rubbed her eyes. This wasn't happening.

"Well, it happened," she spat at herself. "I screwed up. I just have to make sure it doesn't happen again."

Besides, he was a boy, five years her junior. How was it that he had controlled the conversation so well? He'd gotten things out of her she should never had uttered, even to a blank wall in an empty room, much less to an adversary. He was her adversary, right? Vor pressed her palms to her face. How was it that she didn't know anymore? Furious, she surged to her feet and started pacing.

"Damn the boy," she hissed.

After a few moments she threw herself back in bed and turned out the light, but as she lay there in sleepless darkness, all she could see were his sincere green eyes. They followed her down into her dreams.

***

She spent the next day closed up in her room, reading and studying, but then the summons came: another stupid dinner. She couldn't easily refuse, however, and a quiet part of her whispered that it would be a convenient and legitimate way to see Karolan. Another part of her yelled at the first part to shut its idiot mouth: she did not care at all about seeing him.

The energy change was tangible when Vor walked into the room. She felt it like a splash of hot water. Karolan was there already—she ripped her gaze off of him as quickly as she could. Her master, also present and helping his fiancé to take a seat, looked between the two of them at once.

"What happened between you two?" he asked with the first hint of a grin.

Karolan brushed the back of his knuckles over his cheek.

"I hit him," Vor said flatly.

Altare practically leered. "Did you?" Vor recoiled as he extended his energy in the lightest brush against hers, taking a tiny taste. He huffed a laugh. "No real progress, but nice to see you getting along: if I just leave the two of you alone for a little while, it should all work out, shouldn't it?"

Vor snarled soundlessly at him.

"Finally found one you like, did you?" Altare taunted.

"Hitting a person does not indicate positive regard. I want him gone," Vor demanded.

"He stays."

Vor advanced two steps on her master before thinking better of it. Her hand shot out to point. "He doesn't belong here. Get him gone."

Altare fixed her with a firm glare. "I am the master here, and soon to be king. You are just an apprentice. I say who stays and goes."

"I will not always be your apprentice," Vor hissed.

It had slipped out before she could stop it, and now she felt like the recipient of a splash of ice water. Her master's energy roused and she suddenly had his full attention. He advanced on her now, slowly, bringing her to within arm's reach. She didn't retreat, even though a large portion of her was screaming at her to do so.

119

"If you are not my apprentice, you become my rival," he murmured. "Is that what you want?"

Behind him, Vor could see Karolan having gone still and carefully alert. He was anticipating a fight, but Vor knew well that now was not the time.

"No, Master," she told Altare. She bowed her head the bare minimum needed to indicate her submission. "Please pardon my hasty words. I forgot myself."

His baleful expression slowly softened. "Well said," he praised. "I still have use for you, Vor, my precious, loyal apprentice."

He turned slowly, leaving his eyes on her as long as possible, and graced the whole room with a sunny smile.

"Let us eat." Then he spun back. "Vor, begin Karolan's stillroom training tomorrow."

"Excuse me?" she snapped.

"Vor," he warned again, and then shrugged. "He knows nothing. You can certainly teach him the basics; you're quite accomplished at powders and potions, and I can't be bothered to waste my time on it. Besides," he leered again. "It will give you some alone time. Remember, I want a full report."

Vor showed him her teeth, and gritted out, "yes, Master."

"Good girl." He turned and kissed his fiancé's hand.

Vor went to her seat. Karolan didn't look her way, but he pulled out and pushed in her chair for her, as was his habit now, apparently. Altare led the conversation this time. Karolan replied to his questions. Vor glared silently at everything, but at the same time was embarrassingly conscious of Karolan beside her. Now she would have to teach him, alone together in the stillroom?

Her idiot emotions jumped up and down with puppy-like excitement, trying to get her to imagine what was going to happen. Her better sense ruthlessly slapped them down and they went with a whimper. She wouldn't let anything happen. It was what Altare wanted, and she wouldn't give him what he wanted. Besides, it wasn't what she wanted, either.

When dinner was over and the final tea served, she didn't linger behind: swallowing down the hot tea in just a few gulps and fleeing the dining room. She felt her master's delighted gaze following her out every step of the way—and wanted to slap it off his face.

***

Vor knew how to prevent having to teach Karolan about stillroom work: not be in the stillroom. She could go hide like a frightened child somewhere, so when he came for lessons, she wouldn't be there. Of course he might report

120

that to Altare—he'd have to eventually.

No, she could be brave. After all the challenges she'd faced, she could certainly face this without a flinch. Vor spent the first hours of the morning picking out some simple powder recipes to teach him. She'd do a good job at the teaching, and keep the relationship purely that of teacher and student.

When Karolan knocked on the doorframe and she looked up at him, that resolution started to melt like snow in spring. He had an excellent moody glower, except that behind it glinted mischief. As he locked gazes with her, the memory of what had happened in the workroom assaulted her. She forced herself not to look at his mouth.

Vor ripped her gaze away and slapped down a book of basic powders.

"Come in," she ordered. "This is a stillroom and has some basic rules. Have you ever been in one before?"

Karolan stepped in and turned to shut the door behind him. "No," he said.

"Then you wouldn't know to always leave that door open," Vor growled.

He raised his eyebrows at her, door half shut.

"Especially in a magical stillroom, a great number of poisonous ingredients are used," Vor explained. "Fresh air circulation is vital to protect your lungs. Further, there is no eating or drinking in the stillroom. Some ingredients can be caustic or absorbed through the skin. Don't touch your face or rub your eyes, and you should wash your hands frequently, especially when you're finished and ready to leave. Are you listening?"

Karolan was just watching her, door still held half shut. He kneaded the air, and Vor sensed his silence spell fall into place again.

"Karolan Freyaliv," she hissed, "whatever you think is going to happen is not going to happen."

He quirked a smile at her, "well, that puts some power in my hands, doesn't it. If I don't think of it—"

"Open that door," she commanded.

He obeyed, and then came further into the room.

"Listen to me," she requested softly. "I'm going to be blunt. My master has been trying for years to get me to start harvesting energy from sex. He threw attractive young men at me for several months a couple years back, hoping I'd pick one of them. I didn't."

Karolan nodded. "He told me."

Vor gaped. "He told you?"

"And he told me what I should do with you if I could manage it, in detail."

She scowled at him. "Well, I am not going to have sex with you."

"Right," he nodded again. "I mean: I don't want to do anything he's trying to make me do, so I don't think we should, at least not yet."

Vor's jaw dropped further. "Not yet?" she enunciated. "Not ever."

His glower and mischief both faded, leaving only sincerity. "Vor," he sighed.

"No, don't," she ordered, pointing her finger in his face. "Don't you," somehow she found it hard to catch her breath, "don't you try that on me. I've had everything tried on me, and it won't work."

A bit of his mischief glimmered back. "Something worked a couple days ago."

Suddenly her face was hot and she pivoted away in shame. She sensed and heard him step closer.

"You can hit me again, if you want," he offered.

"I shouldn't have done that," Vor blurted. "I'm sorry."

"I know why you did it."

"I won't do it again."

Karolan didn't reply, but then she felt him touch her hand. She didn't pull away, but squeezed her eyes shut and felt him move closer. His breath brushed her ear.

"I'm going to take you out of here, Vor," he whispered, "but first I need your help."

"What?" she retorted. "With what?"

It was a few moments before he replied, and Vor thought he might be steeling himself. Then came his words even softer than before.

"Other than teaching me how to make potions and powders," he murmured, "I want you to betray your master and help me kill him."

***

Vor's mouth and throat went completely dry.

"You can't kill him," she croaked. "No one can. I saw him burned to a blackened corpse by your griffin mage. He recovered."

"Yes," Karolan said, mouth still by her ear. "His master, Craduticus, told me why he's so resilient."

"Craduticus is alive?"

"Yes. He helped me plan this—he and several others. I'm just one part of it. We didn't know where you'd fall in it, but if you're with me, it will make it much easier."

Ah, so was that the reason for all this? Vor licked her lips and tried to get some spit flowing again. "What if I betray you instead of him, now that I know your plan?"

For a few breaths, Karolan neither moved nor spoke, but then he bent his head and rested his forehead on her shoulder. "I trust you."

Vor stood, heart pounding, Karolan's hand still on hers. Several moments passed.

"Do you know about the mines under the castle?" he asked.

"Yes. I've been in them."

"You know what's being dug out?"

"Mage-stone," she said. "I suppose Craduticus told you about it."

"Yes: able to bolster certain spells, act as a reservoir for energy and a foundation for magical works, and also prevents the birth of mage-talented babies by proximity during pregnancy."

"That's why Northnest had no mages," Vor supplied, "and so was easy to conquer with enough drakes."

"He has some, a large node of it," Karolan said. "Craduticus told me. Altare's put fail-safe spells into it. He can't be killed while it exists, at least not easily."

Memory flashed.

"I've seen it," Vor hissed, "once, when he warped back from the fight and nearly died of the burns. He called me to the room, to help him recover. It was there."

Karolan's hand tightened on hers. "Where?"

"Deep in his personal chambers, behind locked doors." She shook her head. "We'd never get to it."

"We'll find a way," he promised. "Now we know our target. First, the node, and then him."

"You make it sound so simple," she grunted.

"I have a tendency to over-simplify things," he smiled. "I've been told."

"I've sensed the magical locks on those doors. They're nothing I could solve."

"If we can't pick them, perhaps we can blow them up."

Vor scoffed.

Karolan lifted his head and Vor turned hers. He sought her gaze, eyes again fully serious. "Will you help me? If you won't, will you at least not get in my way?"

She stared at him but wasn't really seeing him. To kill her master—everything would change if it happened. Her life would be broken. She might have to run. Where would she go? There was nowhere: no one else who could protect her. For a breath it terrified her, and she felt she could not, must not let that happen. And yet, she hated him, despised him, and feared him. The emotions knotted inside her, a hopeless mess.

"It doesn't matter. If we raise a hand against him, we're both going to die," she promised.

"Maybe not. You said you wouldn't always be his apprentice. What were you planning when that day comes? If you don't intend to be his full partner in his crimes," he let the rest trail off.

He was right. She could try to join Altare as an equal, gain his full trust, and sink with him into villainy, or she could try to break away. Breaking away would mean a fight; he'd never just let her escape. If she didn't want to be like him—and she didn't—it was inevitable. Someday he would push her too far. Someday she would be strong enough and old enough to resent it beyond suppression—she was nearly there as it was. How much longer could she tolerate him?

"I never wanted to make this choice," Vor breathed.

"But you know you have to," Karolan urged.

"He'll kill me. He said he would, if I ever turned against him."

"Do you think you can live the rest of your life, never turning against him?"

She shook her head.

"You're strong, Vor, and I'll help you. We'll do it together. I'll tell you true, I don't think I can do it without you."

She frowned a little. Was he trying to guilt her into it? Or flatter her into it? She closed her eyes, trying to calm her emotions and use her brain. She had no doubt Altare deserved to die, and she had no reservations about doing the deed herself. In fact, part of her surged up with primal desire to do it herself. So what held her back from agreeing to Karolan? She couldn't deny that answer: fear. She was afraid, if she tried, he'd kill her or worse. She was also afraid of what would happen if someone, anyone, she or another, did kill him. What would become of her? It would be like being cut adrift. How would she survive?

"No matter what," Vor whispered, "whether I don't help you, whether I kill him, or whether he defeats me, I will be afraid." She winced, feeling the agony of decision drain away. "It is all the same, then, and only one of the three possibilities gives me any chance of escaping him, even if it scares me, too."

Her heart thudded along, steady and strong. She knew her answer, had always known it deep inside.

"I'm with you," she told him.

She was plotting to kill her master.

After that, Karolan said no more about it. He just tucked his head closer, kissed her cheek, and drew away. Vor stood a few moments longer, letting her resolution settle inside her. She sensed him dismiss the silence spell.

"Are there other rules for the stillroom?" he asked conversationally.

"Yes," Vor answered, and turned about, impassive mask back in place. "Contamination: it is essential that ingredients remain pure. To ensure that, there are several different handling techniques."

She went on to show him with bottles of plain, colored water, and little jars of colored sand, how to prevent accidental mixing by using different spoons, by setting down the lids upside down—all sorts of minor but essential techniques. Karolan listened, watched, practiced as she directed, and made not a single intimate gesture. The only exception was whenever their eyes met, and his expression would heat and intensify, and she would look away.

In the midst of this, both Vor and Karolan tensed and turned, sensing the presence of their master, and Altare appeared in the doorway so suddenly it was as if he'd teleported himself there. Since teleportation—of oneself or others—was so expensive energetically, Vor doubted he would have used it just to create some drama. Besides that, he didn't look out of breath. He did look a little disappointed, as though he'd hoped to surprise them while they were engaging in acts of lusty passion.

It was only that which convinced Vor that he hadn't been using some kind of mental magic to distract them from noticing his presence, from where he could have been watching them during their preliminary plotting of his demise. Karolan's silence spell was tight, and would have prevented him hearing, but their actions had been subtle, not the carnal desire Vor expected he was wishing for.

Still, Vor hoped her darker skin hid the slight blush that stole upon her. Somehow, Karolan was not blushing. Instead, he grinned and winked at Altare. Vor almost thought he was serious for a second, and that was enough to give the expression of disgust she hung on her face verisimilitude.

"I see you are hard at work, my apprentices," Altare smirked.

"He's hopeless," Vor grunted.

"My teacher is as lovely as she is patient," Karolan simpered.

He reached up to pet her head and Vor jerked away.

"I will cut his hands off if he doesn't stop that, and then how will he do magic," she seethed.

"You couldn't have a better partner," Altare told her seriously. "Consider it. Well, I'll leave you to it. Karolan, I'll have some practice for you this afternoon, if you're not otherwise occupied."

Her master's grin made obvious what he meant.

"If I don't maim or kill him first," Vor threatened.

Apparently unimpressed, Altare turned on his toe and vanished out of sight down the hallway. Neither Vor nor Karolan made any other comment about their master's words. Vor went on to guide him in mixing a few little batches of powder that the dog handlers used from time to time in their hounds' food, for various medicinal or behavioral purposes. Karolan did a decent job of it. A couple hours had passed by the time Vor decided she'd shown him enough for one day—and she'd run out of lesson plan. She directed him in helping to clean up, until everything was stowed and the workbench was bare.

Vor was about to praise him and invite him back tomorrow, when it seemed he turned around and was about to leave.

"Karolan—" she uttered.

But he closed the stillroom door instead of leaving, and faced her again.

"Everything's put away, so the door can be shut now, right?" he asked.

Vor was caught without an answer as he approached. She straightened up imperiously. He kneaded the air again.

"I renewed the silence spell."

"You're quite good at that one," she offered indifferently.

"I thought I might need it, so Starbright taught me," he shrugged. "It's one of her specialties."

"A griffin, I presume?"

He nodded. "I'm told you called her 'mage of light' when you faced each other on the rooftop."

"Ah," Vor understood. "She tried to kill me, after I attacked her."

Karolan shifted his weight. "I didn't," he made an awkward gesture towards the closed door, "want to talk about Starbright."

"Oh?" she asked coolly. "What are your intentions, then?"

He lifted his gaze to hers, warmth coloring his cheeks, eyes uncertain, and he suddenly showed every one of his meager sixteen years. Vor kept her face carefully neutral, but behind her sternum her heart was fluttering like a trapped moth. Now that the lesson was over, and they again stood under the silence spell, her earlier resolution to betray her master came back to her. She couldn't yet predict all the challenges to defeating him, but at least she wasn't alone in it; Karolan was with her—and now they stood alone together.

"I thought," he swallowed, "or, I hoped—"

He stopped before her, bare inches away, and she again had to tip her

head up to look at him. She raised her eyebrows, but her mild attempt at intimidation failed with him looming over her. He licked his lips and Vor felt like the temperature of the room must have jumped up dramatically.

"You can call me Karo, when we're alone," he offered in a murmur, "or Rain, if you want."

"Rain?" she murmured back.

He was still blushing. "It's kind of my realer name, short for Hawkrain. Only family and close friends use the short version, I mean, among griffins. I'd like it, if you want to."

Vor nodded a little. She reached for him, needing some kind of bolstering, her hands landing indecisively on his chest. He put his arms around her and they stayed that way for some time, before having to go back out into the world as custodians of their secret pact. And if he pressed on her a bit more than an embrace, this time she didn't hit him for it.

Chapter 12
Preparations

Vor and Karolan fetched their lunch together. The mages didn't eat on a schedule, so Altare ordered cold foods be left out in one of the small dining rooms for the couple of hours before and after noon. The mages went and got some whenever it was convenient—or didn't, if they were too deep in a magical work to bother.

Vor sliced up some fruit and took an egg sandwich.

"I notice you don't eat much meat," Karolan mumbled.

She shook her head. "Not in my line of work: I see too much flesh and blood as it is."

There was no silence spell in place, and so they held back most of what they might otherwise have said. They sat at the same table, but Karolan had his glower back in place, and Vor had put on her expressionless mask, which she had perfected over the years.

"You'll go to your afternoon lesson?" Vor muttered.

"Yes," he confirmed. "What are your plans?"

"I've been instructed to help fit the princess for her engagement celebration gown."

"That's soon, is it?"

"In two days," she said. "My master might give you duties, too. I don't see why I need to be involved in the gowns, though. The servants know far more about it than I do."

"What are you plans for the evening?" Karolan murmured to his lunch, almost too quiet to hear.

Vor took a moment. So, he wanted to spend the evening with her? They hadn't made any concrete plans about how to destroy the mage-stone node and kill Altare. Other things had occupied the rest of their time in the stillroom. Perhaps he wanted to talk about it—or perhaps he wanted more of the other things he'd gotten in the stillroom. As exciting as these new feelings were, Vor didn't think it was wise. Or maybe, she thought to herself, she was just afraid. Or maybe again, she knew she shouldn't be doing the things Karolan was making her do.

"I'll be in the mage library, studying," she said.

"That sounds like a good idea. May I join you?"

Well, it was far safer than having him in her room.

"Fine," she grunted.

***

Amlee was polite as always. Vor was polite right back. She had established long ago that she wasn't going to cling to the older woman as a mother figure and didn't appreciate gestures of affection or sympathy. Amlee seemed to respect that, and Altare had chased Amlee away from Vor whenever she tried to get close, so there hadn't been much chance to develop any kind of bond.

The false princess was sitting on the foot of her bed, her gaze unfocused and staring into space.

"Your Highness," Amlee said. "It is time to try on your gown."

The enchanted girl looked up aimlessly.

"For your engagement celebration, to Lord Altare," Amlee went on.

That seemed to get the girl's attention. She smiled and stood. Vor kept her thoughts to herself, but she wondered if the fake princess would last much beyond the wedding before going out of her mind. Amlee had gone right along with the swap, even though Vor knew perfectly well that the castellan would have noticed the difference, even had she not been involved with the true princess's escape.

Vor let Amlee and Kari do most of the work, instead standing back and supervising—not that either of the servant women needed any direction. It was a long, dull afternoon. Dresses had to be one of the most boring things, and Vor had to stand there and watch one get argued about and adjusted. At least Amlee and Kari were straightforward, and as efficient as they could be. It gave her time to ponder the servants' position in this whole jumble of kings, mages, and princesses both fake and real—and what might happen to them as

128

she and Karolan tried to kill Altare.

She knew that both the women had helped Jessika escape, but Vor hadn't fingered them as accomplices. She wondered if they knew she knew. They'd hidden their involvement well enough, but the path the rescuers had taken could hardly have been achieved without the complicity of the servants, and nothing happened in the servants' quarters that Amlee at least did not know of.

A year had passed now since the escape. If Vor had said anything to Altare about it, she expected the women would have been collected and disposed of—at least Kari; good castellans that tolerated the mages' activities were hard to find. Amlee seemed simple, but was adept at walking the knife-edge of un-involvement with, while having knowledge of, what Altare was and did. The other old mages got up to mischief, too, although less of it as they aged, and much less depraved than Altare's activities.

Vor didn't want anyone else to get entangled in the attempt to remove the lord of the castle. Amlee was particularly observant. She only hoped the woman would keep to her usual duties, keep her mouth shut, and keep the other servants equally out of the way. If anything brought them to Altare's attention, he would think to use them—as a power source, as hostages.

Amlee looked up, as if sensing Vor's gaze, and caught her looking at her.

"Is the train long enough, Mistress Vor?" Amlee asked.

Vor had instructions from Altare for what he wanted, in basic terms. Altare wasn't particularly skilled or interested in gowns either, but he still had a sense of style he wanted displayed. Vor went closer to look and measure, replied, and the fitting continued. When it was done, after a few hours of work, other servants took the partially finished gown away and Kari started helping the wearied false princess get dressed again. Vor gave a nod and headed for the door to the suite. Amlee followed her out and curtsied behind her.

"Thank you for your help, Mistress," the woman said, "as now and always."

Vor turned to eye her. Had Amlee put an extra inflection on her words to add another meaning? Amlee had been particularly solicitous to her since the escape last summer, but Vor didn't want any thanks, or any change in behavior towards her. Her master was far too astute in picking up on little variations, and asking why they existed.

"Say nothing of it," Vor told her.

Amlee's eyes flashed up, and Vor thought her point hit home. Amlee bowed her head again.

"Yes, Mistress," she murmured.

Vor gave the woman no more attention. She left the suite, going to grab some dinner and bathe before her evening appointment.

Vor pulled down a book. The mage library was not overly large—only a single, single-story room about the size of a modest bedchamber—and definitely not open to the public. Altare had granted her full use of it, however, a few years ago, and removed the last of the mage locks on the most dangerous books, which had been there for her protection during her youth, or so he said. Vor was pretty certain that he had other books not in the library—the most advanced and deadly ones—kept in his own quarters.

She went to one of the two small tables, touched the clear crystal hanging from the ceiling to create light, and sat down. She'd selected a book on locks. She knew a dozen basic mage locks, but had little need to use them. There were dozens more written down, and she expected that the ones Altare used for his own doors were modified from the most difficult recorded ones or used in combination to add security.

The door opened some minutes later and Karolan stuck his head in, saw her, and entered, shutting the door behind him. He smiled as brightly as the light crystal. Vor kept her face smooth, held up the book to show him the title, and went back to reading. He looked a little disappointed at her lackluster greeting, but she ignored him. She wouldn't write anything down; on the off chance her master searched her room, which he had done a few times in the past, she didn't want him finding anything incriminating. Instead, she committed the book to near-perfect memory.

Karolan searched the shelves for a few minutes before fetching a book of his own and sitting down at the other table. He showed her the spine; it was about mage-stone.

"Have you ever seen any?" Vor asked quietly.

He shook his head.

She nodded. "Later."

They both read in silence as the sun set. At last, after a couple hours, Vor finished the volume on magical locks, head full to bursting with new knowledge about them. When she looked up, Karolan had his head down on his table, asleep. He'd only turned a few pages into his book.

"A lot of help you are," she grumbled under her breath.

Vor shelved her book and went to poke her companion awake. He sat up with a grunt, squinting his eyes, and then seemed to realize where he was and whom he was with, and smiled again.

"Get up," she ordered. "It's late."

He did, stretched, and put the book away.

"I don't suppose you learned anything," she remarked.

His sheepish grin was answer enough.

"Follow me," Vor said.

The castle was quiet, but the mages kept odd hours sometimes, and there was no guarantee that Altare was asleep or in his rooms. It wasn't forbidden, what Vor was about to do, but she wasn't sure if her master wanted Karolan knowing about mage-stone and the mines yet. If so, that was too bad, because Vor was going to show him at least a little. Perhaps not all of it: perhaps not the griffin slaves; she didn't think he'd respond well to that.

Vor took a crystal from her pocket and conjured a light, and led him down to the hallway that also connected to the stairs that led to the late Skire's laboratory. From that hall, a few other passages branched off. A few traveled elsewhere, but others were old, and led to dead end vaults where the country's treasury resided. Beyond those passages, however, was a new tunnel. It was warded, but Vor had permission to pass through and knowledge of the key to the ward. She took the ward down, led Karolan through, and put it back up behind them.

"The former rulers of Northnest," she said softly, "seem not to have known that their castle was on a lode of mage-stone. There are thin veins of it extending throughout much of the country, like roots. There are even granules of it in the dirt and sand."

"Or maybe they did know, and that's why the castle is where it is," Karolan suggested.

"It prevents mages from being born," Vor argued. "Why would they want that?"

"Who knows?" he shrugged.

"At any rate," Vor went on, "this tunnel was dug after the castle was taken. It goes down to the mines. The vaults, back there on those other hallways, are full of mage-stone that's been dug up. It's sent periodically back to Weldom."

"To Weldom?" Karolan puzzled.

"Yes," she confirmed. "That's where the invaders came from. The mage-stone is why they took Northnest. We supply Weldom with mage-stone."

"Oh," he subsided. "Right."

"I can't show you the mage-stone in the vaults," Vor said. "Only my master and Master Ulver know the mage locks and have keys."

"I haven't really met the other masters here," Karolan commented, "although I've seen some a couple times."

"There are only three besides my master and us, and they're old and mostly useless. My master killed the others."

Karolan's eyes popped wide. "He killed them?"

"No," Vor replied. "They died accidentally and tragically, on the official record, but he really killed them."

"I see."

"Here, come this way."

The tunnel widened before a set of stairs, leaving a landing, above which was mounted a pulley system. On one side of the landing was a barrel on a rolling dolly. Vor peered into it, but it was empty.

"We'll have to go down to see the stone. They haven't loaded any up here recently."

She led the way down the stairs. Warm, faint light was coming from below, accompanying a breath of rank air laced with sharp earth and metal smells.

"The veins are running out," Vor told Karolan. "My master is worried what will become of us when we're no longer useful to Weldom. There were other, much smaller mines in other parts of the country, shortly after the take-over, but they've all been exhausted."

They reached the bottom of the stairs, and there in buckets were pebbles, nodules, and nuggets of shiny grey stone. Vor knelt by the nearest and picked up a handful, letting the rough, unfinished rocks trickle through her fingers. Karolan went to another bucket and picked up a lump the size of an egg.

"That's a good one," Vor remarked. "Five years ago, pieces of that size were common. Now they're rare."

"And what can you do with it?"

"You can put spells in it, and they'll keep running. It's like extra storage."

"You can put spells in anything," Karolan frowned.

"Yes, for a while," Vor allowed. "Put a light spell on an ordinary stone and it will last a few days maybe. Spell one of these to glow, and it will last for months, even years, if the stone is big enough. You can also store energy in mage-stone for years, and then pull it back out when you need it. Nothing holds spells or energy as well as this does."

"And the thing about no mages being born?" he prompted.

Vor frowned. "I don't know how the mage-stone does it, but pregnant women in close proximity to it have ordinary babies."

"Why is that useful to Weldom?"

"Mages have power. People in power want to have all the power. People in power use their power to gain wealth, which causes oppression when they take wealth from others. They don't want the poor to have the power to fight back.

In Weldom they melt mage-stone and mix it into the metal used for commoner's tools, kitchen utensils, even building materials, like door hinges and wall hooks. They force the price down on anything made of metal with mage-stone in it. To get pure, undiluted metal, you have to pay more. Sometimes jewelers will even polish pieces of the stone and sell it as cheap pendants and charms. Of course, the poor don't know what the shiny rocks are, or what they do, or that it's in the cheap metal items they buy. Even if they did, they can't afford pure metal items."

She looked over at Karolan, dropping the last of the rocks into the bucket. "It means only the rich can birth babies with mage potential. Poor women are exposed to mage-stone all the time, and don't even know it, so their babies are untalented. It keeps the power among the rich."

Karolan stood, dusting off his hands on his trousers. "Where are you from, Vor?"

She gave him a wry smile. "From Weldom."

"So your family was rich?"

She shook her head, hesitating. Well, what was the harm in telling him? "My mother was born into the nobility, yes, but she wasn't a mage. She had a comfortable life and was going to be married off to some other wealthy person, but then she made a terrible mistake."

"What?"

Vor snorted and leaned back against the wall, crossing her arms. "She fell in love, with an ordinary soldier. What's more, she bedded him, resulting in me. She wanted to keep me, and marry my father. When she told her parents, they disowned her, but I guess I was far enough along that my mage potential had already set in, and subsequent exposure to mage-stone with my father's family—where she ended up living—didn't extinguish it. Of course, I didn't know I was a mage until I was eleven, and my master took me in."

"But how did you end up in Northnest?"

She lifted a hand. "The invasion happened and my father was deployed. I was only nine, or thereabouts, but my mother insisted on following him, taking me along. Stupid. Well, he got killed, and then she died not long after."

"Leaving you alone," Karolan concluded for her.

"There you have it."

She'd left out the details of her mother's death. It hadn't been a gentle thing, and she didn't want to talk about it. Luckily, Karolan didn't ask. They stood in silence for a while, staring at the buckets of stone.

"My parents died, too," Karolan offered.

"You're from Lackland you said?"

"Yes. I came to Northnest with my uncle."

"What killed your parents?" Vor asked.

"They were fisher-folk. They died at sea, not unusual," Karolan shrugged. "I hardly remember them."

"Your uncle wasn't a fisherman, too?"

He shook his head. "He hated the sea, but he followed his big brother to it because he didn't know what else to do with himself. He didn't know what to do with me, either, but there was no one else for me to go to. He took us both out of Lackland as soon as my parents' deaths could be confirmed, and came up here. He found work as a laborer from time to time, but he was probably dead drunk when the invasion happened. I doubt he felt a thing. I'm only alive because an old woman saw me wandering around and brought me to the palace nursery, and then of course I was rescued."

He looked over at Vor, smiling. "I've got a great mom now," he confided. He waved his hands in the air a little, and she realized he was miming wings.

Vor glared at him, shaking her head. "Don't," she urged. "We shouldn't even be talking like this."

Karolan nodded in acceptance, then jerked his head towards the tunnel down. "What's that way, the mines?"

"That's right. I don't think we should go down. They know me, but you haven't been given permission to be down here."

"I guess we should go back then."

She was relieved he didn't press her. One sight of enslaved griffins, and she had no idea what he'd do. Of course, there were enslaved humans, too, but somehow she thought this young man would be more distressed over the griffins than he would over others of his own species being chained.

"Take that piece of mage-stone," Vor suggested. "We might need it to practice on. I don't know how to destroy mage-stone."

Karolan pocketed the egg-sized nodule he'd picked up before, and Vor took him back up the stairs and down the tunnel, opening and replacing the ward as she went. As they approached the exit, she had the sudden fear that Altare might be waiting for them, that he somehow knew they were plotting to kill him. There was no evidence of it, but sometimes Vor thought he could actually read her mind. She didn't want to have to fight him; she had no doubt that she'd lose. Maybe if his magic weren't in her she'd have a chance—

Vor took a deep breath and stopped.

"What is it?" Karolan asked.

She made the kneading motion he used when he cast his silence spell, and he complied.

"Do you remember how I put my magic in Jessika's back?" she said bluntly.

He frowned a little "Starbright told me about it, and Cray told me it could be done," he answered.

"Did he teach you how to remove it?"

"He did. He thought it might be useful for me, coming here, to know how, just, in case."

"My master has put his magic in me. Before we fight him, I need you to remove it."

"You can't do it?"

"Not from within. I've tried, believe me."

Karolan nodded without hesitation. "I'll do it." He took her hand and squeezed it.

"Thank you, but not right now. I don't want him to detect it."

"Alright."

"Take down the spell."

He did, and they kept moving. Vor pulled her hand out of his grasp. He made no reaction, but she wondered if it made him feel rejected. This attraction they had troubled her almost more than it made her happy—or rather, his attraction to her: she still couldn't figure out if she really was attracted to him.

Altare was not waiting for them when they exited into the private wing. Vor stopped and turned deliberately to Karolan.

"Good night," she told him.

"More stillroom lessons tomorrow?" he asked.

"I'll show you some simple salves."

"No potions?"

"Potions usually require boiling and or distillation. That's advanced work."

"Alright."

"Good night," she said again, firmly, and turned to go.

Karolan caught her wrist. "Vor," he breathed, pulling on her.

He stepped into her. For a moment she stood against him, his hand tipping her head up and his mouth hot and strong on hers, but then she broke away and he let her.

"No," she mumbled, "not here. Not," she couldn't articulate it. "I'm not doing this right now. Good night."

She couldn't look at him, and started to walk away.

"At least you didn't hit me," he murmured good-naturedly.

Vor paused, wanting to respond, but thinking better of it, just in case they were being overheard. She kept walking, finding her way back to her rooms and shutting the main door. It had no physical lock, but as she stood within, she felt the need to keep everyone out. She fetched a piece of chalk and drew a circle on the back of the closed door. She wrote in a few runes and exerted her power to set the spell, one she'd just read about in the library.

The door was mage-locked now: a simple one, but it would at least give her warning if someone were trying to get in. Nobody would be able to sneak in; they'd have to stop and work on the spell, and she'd sense the magic moving enough to wake her. Her master would surely be able to solve it with a minute or two of work, but that would still give her a minute or two not to be sleeping and defenseless.

Exhausted in too many ways, Vor changed clothes and got in bed. She snuggled herself down and wrapped her body around her pillow, imagining it was her annoying, duplicitous, charming fellow apprentice—and then felt disgusted with herself and rolled over, forcing herself down into sleep.

***

They didn't get to have the stillroom class the next day. Altare immediately recruited them both for engagement party preparations. Masters Eriducus, Ulver, and Chirolen were about as well, being sent here and there to put up or take down enchantments. The public would be let into the courtyard again, as at the coronation ceremony last year, and there would be a banquet in the biggest dining hall for all the notable people of the capital.

Altare ruled with the king, with his three master mages giving advice, but there were the generals of the small standing army and notable rich lords that took interest in the politics of the country. All those people, with their spouses if they had them, would be attending the banquet, but there were still plenty of places Altare wanted them not to be able to go. A few mage locked doors would keep the guests from snooping.

Vor, predictably, was sent to be the false princess's shadow, to do the final check of the gown, have her thoroughly bathed by a half dozen maids, watch as the girl's hair was styled and her face painted, and rehearse her in what she had to say and do for the balcony ceremony and the banquet. Mainly, she just had to smile, nod, and demure, but Altare suspected some practice at it would help her. Since the poor magically warped girl now had a brain like a sieve, Vor agreed.

What Altare sent Karolan to do she didn't know. She didn't get to see him until they ran into each other at dinner, grabbing quick food from the small dining room where lunch was also set out.

"Are you done?" he muttered to her.

She nodded. Amlee and Kari were putting the false princess to bed, and she wasn't needed any longer.

"Library?" Karolan breathed in question.

She gave another brief nod. They parted, each going to eat alone. Master Eriducus came into the room next, hunched and limping a little and grumbling under his breath, and she was glad he hadn't caught her so close to Karolan.

Chapter 13
Before the Banquet

This time Karolan beat her to the library. He was trying to read the mage-stone book again. He looked up and smiled when she came in.

"Shall we look at this together?" he offered.

"If someone else comes in, I don't want us seen that close together," Vor said.

"Just slap my head and call me a hopeless idiot," he suggested, "or whatever other insults come to mind. Then go to the other table. Put a book out so it looks like you were studying before I asked you a question."

Vor stifled a sigh and complied. It would be a thin fiction, but might fool one of the old masters. It probably wouldn't fool Altare, but then, he wanted them engaging in mating behavior, so it didn't matter. They read together, discussing the content in whispers and murmurs. Mage-stone, it turned out, was tough stuff. Dense, hard, and non-metallic, with a high melting point, it seemed fairly indestructible.

"Maybe it's brittle," Karolan suggested, "and we could drop it off the roof of the Feathyr barracks to shatter it."

"Not a bad idea," Vor muttered, "if we could carry it that far. It was quite a large lump and might be really heavy."

"We could make a harness and carry it between the two of us. Or maybe we could crack it apart with hammers."

"We might not even be able to remove it from the room," Vor worried. "We might have to find a way to do whatever we're going to do there. Or, we'll have to unweave a lot of complicated spells to free it."

They read on, learning whatever they could, picking up and examining the filched nodule from time to time, until the night deepened, and eventually both were yawning fit to split their heads open. Vor reached over and shut the book.

"We should get some sleep," she said.

He caught her hand. "Do you want to sleep in my room?"

The words seemed to have burst from him without his consent, but he didn't immediately try to take them back. Vor pulled her hand from his grasp.

"No, I don't think that's a good idea," she replied.

"Why not? I think it's a great idea."

He would. "Rain," she said softly, "have you thought about where we're going to get the power needed to break through locked doors, destroy that mage-stone, and then fight my master?"

"Not really," he admitted, blinking at what must seem to him a return to an academic topic when he'd had primitive urges in mind. "Griffins work magic with personal power."

Vor shook her head. "Personal power will not be enough," she denied. "You know how to store now, right?"

He squirmed a little. "Yes, but it's disgusting."

"It's not that bad. It doesn't hurt you and it's incredibly useful. Comfort depends on what kind of energy you store."

"I suppose you're used to it." His voice had turned a trifle dark.

"I am," she confirmed, forcing herself not to bristle at his tone. "I've been doing it for years. I visit the butcher, stand outside, and pick up the blood and life energy the animals drop when they die. A good workout gives me some extra energy, too, or sitting in the garden for a while. I also get energy each month when I bleed."

"When you—? Oh." His face turned pink.

"But none of that fills me to capacity, unless I abstain from magic for days and purposefully build it up with all those techniques. I'm not sure we'll have the luxury for that, and there's a quicker way."

She eyed him until he became visibly uncomfortable.

"What?" he muttered.

"What my master wants us to do," she said grimly. "We're both virgins and virgin sex releases huge amounts of power, even when it's only one virgin with someone who's not. If both of us trigger that energy at once, it should fill us up."

It seemed she'd shocked him. Karolan stared, aghast, and then his face wrinkled in distaste.

"A minute ago you sounded like you wanted to do that with me," Vor accused.

"I, I do." He blushed deeper. "Just, not that way."

Vor folded her arms. "If we're going to do it, it might as well accomplish something."

Karolan raised a hand in protest. "It's not meant to accomplish any-thing," he blurted. "It's just supposed to be fun, and make us feel good, and," he blushed even redder and his pale skin hid it not at all, "and make us feel close to each other."

Vor narrowed her eyes at him. "I was unaware of those purposes."

"What else is there? Use it for making babies? Or use it for energy pro-duction, like you say?"

"Well, I don't want a baby," she grunted.

"We should probably think about that, I mean, how not to make one."

She flicked a hand. "Don't worry about that. If we pick up all the energy produced there will be none left to start one."

"Um," he winced, still as red as a radish, "it's something else that makes babies."

She grit her teeth at him. "Yes, I know about the physiological part."

"The what part?"

"What kind of energy do you think is getting released in sex? It's energy of creation, of life. It takes more to get a new life started than just some bodily fluids, and if we suck up the energy there won't be any to do it."

He ducked his head. "If you say so."

Vor huffed out a breath. "The point is, I think we're going to need that energy, so we shouldn't waste it by doing it before the right time. Otherwise, we could blood let and slowly kill someone, or a few someones, or a bunch of animals, and I know neither of us want to do that. So, are you willing?"

He looked pained. "Is that the only way," he murmured, "that you would lie with me?"

Now it was her turn to be perplexed. "I, I don't know."

Karolan turned away from her and shelved the mage-stone book. Then he stood for a few breaths, back towards her, and Vor wondered what he was thinking. When he turned back around, he still looked sad.

"Alright," he agreed. "I'll do it."

Then he approached her, deliberately and inexorably. Vor retreated two short steps until she fetched up against one wall's bookcase with a muffled thump. Karolan kept moving until he was right against her, and reached up to hold her face in his hands. She stiffened; she could guess what he would do next.

"Vor, why are we doing this?" he asked her.

"Doing—? You're here to kill—"

"No," he cut her off gently. "This."

Karolan bent down to take her mouth. Vor resisted, but not as strongly as she could have, letting him conclude the kiss when he was done.

"Not here," she scolded. "Someone could come in and see."

"No one will care," he smiled a little. "Did you like that?"

Her face suddenly flamed with heat. "I—"

"Because you know what that is a prelude to?" He gave a sheepish wince. "How is it that I grew up with griffin parents but know more about human courtship than you do?"

She couldn't answer, and stared at his chest, avoiding his eyes.

"You've been letting me do this to you," he muttered. "I thought it was because you liked it."

She pushed a little against his chest. "Let me go."

"Will you stay and listen to me if I let you go?" he asked. "Or will you run away?"

Vor closed her eyes and stopped pushing on him. She would indeed have run away.

"I can't imagine what growing up here was like," Karolan murmured to her. "I don't suppose you ever had a good example of two people who cared for each other, like a husband and wife?"

She shook her head mutely. Somehow this younger man was making her feel like a foolish child, a stupid, foolish child. She figured that wasn't his intent—his words were gentle—but she felt ashamed.

"But you must know something," he went on. "You used the L-word yesterday."

"L-word?" she echoed disdainfully.

"Love."

Her brow furrowed. Had she?

"When you spoke about your mother, falling in love with your father," Karolan prompted. "You even said she bedded him because of it." He tried to nuzzle her face, but she was keeping her chin down and he was too tall for the angle at such close proximity. "I'll bet they kissed first, like we've been doing."

Her face burned, and it was somehow spreading, down her neck, through her chest and into her back, and lower into her belly, making her knees turn to water. She took handfuls of Karolan's shirt. Her arms trembled and her hands felt weak.

As if he knew, he put an arm around her, hugging her so she leaned on him and tucking his head down atop hers. She felt his heartbeat under her hands; it terrified her. She wouldn't think about what he was saying. She wouldn't accept what she was feeling. She was vulnerable—she knew it. She was becoming weak. This couldn't be allowed.

Karolan just hugged her. Vor didn't try to get away, but she knew she had to. She couldn't bring herself to pull away. Her hands released his shirt, slid down, and awkwardly went around his waist. As if touching some foreign beast's hide, afraid it might jump up and snap at her, Vor tremulously set her hands against Karolan's back.

A measure of tension left his body, and he released a sigh: replete with satisfaction, even victory. He shifted his arms more tightly around her—and her fear leapt up and overcame any other sensation.

"No, no, no," she panicked, pushing, struggling free of his arms.

He let her go, but pursued her closely with a hand on her shoulder: not trying to confine her, but perhaps an attempt to maintain the intimacy.

"Vor, it's alright," he tried to soothe. "Don't run away. Talk to me."

She went for the door but he held it shut. Vor spun about, putting her back against the door and facing him.

"When I was eleven a soldier tried to rape me and I set him on fire," she stated, words tumbling in a rush. "My master has forced me to watch him collect energy from sex both willing and unwilling, and has threatened to do it to me. He paraded young men past me trying to get me to pick one and was about to lock me in a room with one until I did what he wanted. You have to forgive me if—" as if to complete the set of emotions she'd experienced that evening, a hard lump rose in her throat "—if I'm scared and I don't know what to do, or what I want."

Some hint of understanding spread across Karolan's face. "I'm sorry," he whispered. "I don't want to hurt you."

She shut her eyes, mortally ashamed when a tear ran down. "I know. Let me go?"

"You could blast me away if you really wanted to," he muttered. "You're a much better mage than I am."

Karolan took his hand off the door and Vor managed to open her eyes and stand up on her own. She turned to unlatch the door, and he darted out a hand and caught one of hers. She startled, but didn't pull away.

"Vor," he said hoarsely, "I like you."

Her throat felt sealed shut; she couldn't speak. Wordlessly, she pulled open the door, pulled out of his grip, and fled.

***

"Here, put this on," Altare ordered, holding out a bundle of cloth.

It was the morning of the engagement announcement celebration and the mages had just finished breakfast together. There hadn't been much conversation. Vor had kept her head down, hiding her eyes red-rimmed from lack of sleep. She especially avoided looking at Karolan, but now she had everyone's attention. Vor took the bundle in shock and let it fall open.

"A gown?" she declared.

"It's grey, the color you like," her master said. "I had the tailor make it to your most recent sizes, no frills, no ruffles. It's simple, and elegant."

Vor couldn't seem to close her mouth.

"I'm wearing mage robes," Altare explained, "he's wearing mage robes," he pointed at Karolan. "All the other mages are wearing mage robes. You're not going out there in ordinary day wear."

"Then why can't I wear mage robes?" Vor demanded. "I'm a mage."

Her master's brows lowered dangerously. "You're a woman. You'll look good in it. I need my apprentices to look good, confident, and powerful. All the generals and local lords will be there. I'll not have you skulking around like a gutter-trash hoyden." He snatched the knit cap off her head and shook it in her face. "And you're not wearing this."

"It keeps my hair out my eyes," she protested.

"Amlee will come do your hair, so it stays out of your eyes."

Vor still couldn't close her outraged mouth. Do her hair? What did that even mean? How did a person do hair? Brush it, yes. Wash it, yes, but do it? Altare leaned in and poked a finger in her face.

"Wear it," he threatened.

"Or what?" she growled back.

"You know what," he told her, even quieter, and started to turn away.

"Over a dress?" she scoffed.

He spun back, pointing his finger like a dagger at her again. "Ask yourself that question, Vor. Why all this drama over a dress?"

She finally buttoned her lips. Maybe he was right. What harm was it, really, except in her mind? What did she care what other people thought if they saw her in it? Altare was pacing away now. The other old mages were following him like little fishies behind a big fishy, hoping to snap up scraps. Karolan sent a cautious glance her way.

"It might look good on you," he offered.

"Shut your mouth."

***

Vor put on the dress. Kari had to help with the lacing, even though it was indeed much simpler than the confection that the false princess was wearing, or the coronation gown Vor had seen the real princess laced into. Her usual

142

suits—she had several identical copies—were well tailored so they fit her perfectly. So did this dress, but there was somehow a big difference.

She felt almost naked in the dress, even though it covered most of her skin. It even had long sleeves and the hem fell all the way to within an inch of the floor. It didn't expose her back or much of her chest—but still. She wanted to hide.

"A fine fit, Mistress Vor," Kari said. "Would you like to see in the mirror?"

"No," she refused.

A knock came at the door. They were in the main room of the false princess's suite. Amlee and the other servants were dressing the princess in her bedroom. Kari went to the door and opened it a crack.

"My lord," she greeted. "The women are dressing."

"That's fine," Vor heard Altare say. "Take these, for Vor."

Kari accepted a bag and shut the door with a curtsy. She returned and brought out the contents of the bag. There was a pair of decorative rather than utilitarian shoes and another small sack. Within that was a necklace made of polished mage-stone.

Vor frowned at it, feeling a tickle of unease. Kari helped her step into the shoes while she focused on the necklace. Accepting jewelry from Altare had a long, bad history behind it. It was his habit to put spells in diamonds, crystals, all kinds of gems, and use them to control people—especially his captive girls.

"May I help you with the clasp, Mistress?" Kari asked.

"No. I'm not wearing it," Vor replied.

Besides Altare's usual habits, the fact that it was a mage-stone necklace he'd sent unnerved her. Did he know that she and Karolan were plotting to destroy his fail-safe node stone? Was he trying to taunt her? Or had he just picked it because it was silvery, like the dress? She put the necklace back in the sack and tucked it in her pocket. At least the rotten dress had pockets.

"May I arrange your hair, Mistress?" Kari suggested.

"Fine," Vor gave in. "Please do something to keep it from getting in my face."

Amlee and three other maids younger than Kari led out the false princess then. Two little girls were carrying the train. The false princess had her hair twirled and curled and twisted into a precariously balanced masterpiece accented with jeweled hairpins. Amlee immediately came over to help Kari with Vor's: removing the bands she used to hold it up, so it fell in a long wavy black mass. Kari let out a soft sound of longing.

"You really should leave it down, Mistress Vor," Kari urged gently. "It's so pretty."

"Tie it up," Vor ordered, "securely, please."

"Perhaps you should just keep it cut short then," Amlee suggested bluntly, but her nimble fingers went to work.

In a few minutes, the two women had Vor's hair all bundled up again, but this time elegantly, and secured with two long stilettos.

"Time?" Vor requested.

Someone told her.

"We have several minutes. Take your ease," she instructed.

A maid went and fetched beverages, so everyone could have a drink of something. Vor went over to a table, found where her chalk had gotten to, and drew a small circle. She marked out some quick air and water runes around it and dropped the mage-stone necklace in the middle.

Amlee came over and peeked nervously.

"It's just chalk," Vor said. "It will wash off."

The woman nodded. "May I ask what you're doing?"

"Checking for spells," Vor answered, voice low. "It's from our lord. He intends me to wear it."

Understanding flared in Amlee's eyes. She remained silent while Vor held a hand over the necklace and focused. There was no guarantee she could detect her master's most subtle spells—and if he truly intended for her to be enchanted, he would have used his most subtle, surely knowing that she would check. Vor had to wonder though, why he'd bother. If he wanted her as a mage, as his apprentice, doing his work, and showing a powerful face to the visitors, enchanting her would only compromise all those things.

She was also, she thought, sometimes a bit subtler than her master lately. Vor checked the necklace inch by inch. If there was any kind of embedded spell, she should feel the vibration of it, even if she couldn't unravel it or tell what kind of enchantment it was. She could find nothing, but there was one other thing she could do.

"Is the fire still burning in the princess's chamber?" Vor asked.

"It's dying now, but yes," Amlee answered.

Vor snatched up the necklace and went to the bedroom fireplace. Fire cleansed and unworked spells. The entire necklace was metal or stone, not cord, so it wouldn't burn up. Vor stirred the fire with the poker until some flames were dancing again. Then she hung the necklace on the end of the poker, squatted out of range of soot, and dangled the necklace into the flames.

As the fire flickered over the chain links and polished stones, enlightenment came, and Vor sat for a moment, mouth gaping and eyes wide. Then she pulled the necklace out of the flames. Amlee promptly provided a hand towel from the bathing room, and Vor took the hot necklace up with it.

She turned, unseeing, idly rubbing the soot off the stones, and started to pace. They didn't have to destroy her master's mage-stone node. They just had to undo the spells in it. They could do that by immersing it in fire. All they had to do was provide the fire—a very hot, very large one. They'd probably burn down the castle if they lit the room on fire, but that magnitude of fire was what it would take. Vor didn't remember there being a fireplace, and the node was so big it might not fit in an average fireplace.

"It is alright now?" Amlee wondered.

"Yes," Vor replied absently.

"I'll put it on for you?"

Vor held out the still warm necklace and Amlee took it. She put it around Vor's neck, latched it, and Vor felt no hint of enchantment—not that she would have noticed if the spell were good: at least, if she were an ordinary human. Enchanting another mage was particularly difficult. Vor felt confident now that, even if he'd put a spell on the necklace, she'd removed it. Fire resistance could be woven into spells, but even the highest resistance could not protect the spell from extended contact with fire, only brief.

Altare's node would surely have layers of resistances and protections, but with a hot enough fire and enough time, even those would be overcome. She wanted to go tell Karolan about the idea right away. Why hadn't they thought of it sooner? It was so simple. She supposed, sometimes when people expected something to be extremely difficult, they could only think of complicated solutions, and the obvious one would be overlooked. It was a lesson she hoped she'd remember for future problems.

"Mistress Vor, it is time," Amlee informed her.

"Good, let's go."

***

Like the revealing of the return of the princess months ago, the announcement of the engagement to the people happened from the high balcony over the courtyard. Vor guided the false princess and her entourage. There was no queen of course, but the king took the center and made the announcement himself. Altare must have programmed into him the lines to say.

Vor stood on the side of the women, as the false princess's main attendant, beside Amlee in her role of castellan. Karolan stood opposite her, behind Altare, with Edgard at his side. The king held out his hands for Altare and the false princess, and brought their hands together.

The people cheered, and to Vor it sounded mostly genuine. The false princess was smiling widely and seemed to have eyes for no one but Altare. Vor wondered if perhaps the people really were happy. Maybe they saw this as a positive turn in their country's future. There hadn't been a royal family for over a decade. Perhaps they would take whatever they could get, even if it included one of the men who had been a part of the invasion.

Of course, Altare had been twenty when the invasion happened, younger than Vor was now, and had not been in charge. Maybe they didn't know that he was just as bad as the master wizards who had led the drakes in for the attack. Ulver, Chirolen, and Eriducus had been among those wizards, and so were kept out of sight for the most part, at least from the commoners. Craduticus of course was fled, and the other two leading mages who had remained after the takeover was complete were dead.

The group on the balcony stood for several minutes, waving, tossing coins, and letting the people cheer before retreating back inside, out of the light. Down in the courtyard, the celebration went on, with food, drink, music, and dancing. The door in the inner walls, to the palace courtyard, would remain open until sunset, though the doors through the arches into the kitchen and pleasure gardens and the palace itself were firmly shut and barred. It was a rare chance for opportunistic merchants to set up temporary stalls and hopeful minstrels to plunk tunes in sight and sound of the palace itself—all hoping to come away richer. Vor turned away from the cacophony with relief. She had no desire to mingle among the merrymakers and they'd be making no money off her. Besides, she had other tasks to attend to.

"Take her to rest before the banquet," Altare instructed.

Vor obeyed, leading off the false princess although she was much more eager to get to talk to Karolan about her realization that fire could be the answer to their problems. The false princess did indeed seem to be wilting, though, so with Amlee and Kari and the help of the other maids, they brought her to her rooms and helped her to rest on a divan with fortifying tea and light snacks.

"Mistress Vor," Amlee murmured, as they stood back, letting Kari take the lead. "May I speak with you?"

That was surprising, but Vor complied and they went into a separate room. Amlee shut the door.

"Will she be well?" the castellan asked softly.

"Well?" Vor echoed incredulously. "You think she might get well?"

Amlee folded her hands, bowing her head. Vor approached the older, taller woman.

"Castellan," she began. "I think you know."

Amlee made a helpless gesture, starting to open her mouth.

"We shouldn't talk about this," Vor forestalled her.

Amlee sighed and turned pained eyes onto Vor.

"Yes, and it's going to get worse," the mage told her quietly. "You can guess."

"You allow all this, Mistress?" Amlee whispered.

Vor clenched her jaw. She wasn't going to reveal that she and Karolan were plotting Altare's demise.

"If I take the diamonds off," Amlee went on breathlessly, "and put them in the fire like you did—"

"Do not take them off," Vor ordered. "That would probably kill her, or render her comatose."

Amlee's gaze was still soft, but steady. "Perhaps that would be a better fate."

Vor did not deny it. "But you would take yourself down with her, and he would just make another. And you would no longer be here to protect those girls." She meant the maid servants: all of whom Amlee watched over like a mother hen, trying to keep Altare from taking interest and snatching them away like a fox after tasty morsels.

"Vor," Amlee breathed, suddenly taking one of her hands.

Alarmed, she pulled her hand out of Amlee's. The castellan looked slightly hurt.

"We hope," she whispered, "sometimes, that you might—"

"You don't know what I've done," Vor declared into her face. "I am just as corrupt as he is."

Amlee had swayed back a bit, but didn't relent. "No, you're not. We have hope for you."

"You're foolish," Vor refuted. "I cannot even save myself."

"Sometimes," Amlee murmured, stepping closer again, "the first ones you save are not yourself."

Vor raised a finger threateningly. "You need to stop talking like this. You're going to get yourself into trouble."

"I agree to take the trouble onto me, if it will keep the trouble off of others," Amlee smiled.

Vor snarled soundlessly and strode from the room.

Chapter 14
Guests at the Banquet

Vor and Karolan both had seats at the high table for the banquet. It was going to be several courses and last probably a few hours. The king was there, too, with his hood pulled up and an ornate crown atop it to hold it in place, hiding the gruesome magical device that was implanted into his skull to control him. His false daughter sat to his right, with Altare beside her. The rest of the table to Altare's right held the three old master mages, and then Vor, and then Karolan at the end. To the king's left came the highest generals of the army and the superintendent of the peacekeepers, with their wives if they had one. A lower table held the lords of the city and the guild masters with their spouses.

Master Ulver, who was considerably hard of hearing, sat to Vor's left. She was hopeful that once the banquet got going it might be loud enough for her and Karolan to talk a little without being overheard. The king stood to open the banquet with a short speech remarkably similar to what he'd given on the balcony. The servants and pages were out in full force and had already filled the many goblets, so everyone was able to stand and toast the future bride and groom. It was wine, not what Vor would have chosen, but she didn't dare refuse, taking the tiniest sip only.

After that, the food started coming out of the kitchen and the feasting began. Amlee was attending to the false princess, as was only proper. Vor knew that Marklin the cook would be fully in control of the kitchen orchestration. The first course was a vegetable soup. Vor stared down at it, trying to resign herself to enduring the coming ordeal; this was just the beginning.

Karolan's knee nudged hers under the table. She didn't react. The tablecloths went all the way down to the floor, so no one would be able to see, but it still somehow felt like a bad idea. After a few more spoonfuls of soup, as conversation got going, she peered at him from the corner of her eye. He peered back and a smile started creeping onto his face. Vor gave him the slightest shake of her head and he managed to control his expression.

She went back to her soup.

"You look good," he muttered.

Vor avoided choking, and cautiously eyed him. "So do you."

All the other mages were in robes, which in Vor's opinion were impractical for wear during actual work, but looked dramatic, although Karolan had pushed his trailing sleeves up to his elbows so they didn't get in his soup. He'd shaved off his attempt at a beard, which made him look tidier, and the muted greens in the robes brought out the color in his eyes. He glanced at her throat.

"Is that mage-stone?" he asked.

"Yes," Vor confirmed.

Servants swarmed the tables and swept away soup bowls, to be replaced with plates of steamed fish and vegetables. Fish wasn't common in Northborn, but there were a few freshwater rivers and lakes that could provide. Vor noted rather a higher percentage of vegetables than fish. Still, it was tasty and a nice change from her usual fare.

"Where did you get it?" Karolan resumed as they ate.

"My master gave it to me."

His eyebrows twitched a little. "Is it safe?"

"I tested it and ran it through fire."

"Fire?"

"Fire cleanses and clears spells. It gave me an idea."

She let him think for a while, but she had no doubt he'd come to the same conclusion she had.

"You think it will work?" he mumbled.

"I think it's our best hope, actually."

They ate deep in thought for a while, until cheers greeted the emergence of a whole roasted wild boar on a platter. The fish dishes were cleared by one crew of servants, while another began slicing into the boar and plating out the choicest pieces for the king, the false princess, and Altare.

The smell of pork permeated the dining hall and turned Vor's stomach, but she forced herself to eat what she was given. She'd seen, heard, and felt so many pigs slaughtered that eating their flesh had long ago lost its appeal. At least there were roast vegetables with it, and some kind of boiled and spiced grain.

"We'll need a lot of fire," Vor murmured.

Beside her, Karolan nodded. "We can cast it?"

"We might burn down the castle."

He made a slight shrug. She silently agreed. Burning down the castle—at least the wooden bits, as a lot of it was made of stone—wouldn't be the end of the world if it allowed them to eliminate Altare. Plates were gradually emptied as the cooked boar was transformed to a boar skeleton. Servants carried the remains away and began preparations for the second half of the meal. Goblets were refilled, used plates swapped for clean ones, utensils replenished, and fresh napkins distributed. Vor managed to request a beverage other than wine and to her relief got fruit juice tea.

Abruptly, Altare stood, and the attention of all the guests turned onto him.

"I wish to thank you all for honoring my future bride and me with your presence here tonight," he spoke out. "I am humbled by my lady's choice and feel only such joy that our princess has been found and brought back to her father the king, where she belongs. I hope you will all join us again next month for the wedding."

"To the bride and groom," one of the army generals called out.

The entire room took up the cry and goblets were lifted. Vor and Karolan followed along. Everyone drank, the mages only sipping, except Vor, who could now take a refreshing swallow.

"My thanks again to you all," Altare said, bowing a little. "And now, some entertainment as the next course is readied: my apprentice, Mistress Vor Hearthsraven."

For a few seconds, Vor didn't realize what had just happened, but the room went silent, and all eyes shifted onto her. Her skin chilled and her eyes locked onto her master's. He stared back at her with a merciless smile. What was he trying to do to her? Why hadn't he warned her he was going to do this? Did he mean to embarrass her? Would that not embarrass him as well? He'd said he wanted his apprentices to appear strong.

Woodenly, she started to stand. Karolan jumped to his feet and pulled her chair out for her. For once, she was grateful. He stepped back, not retaking his seat, but standing a few paces behind her. It felt comforting to know he was there, and some of the attention transferred to him.

What to do? Entertainment? Her master surely meant a display of magery. Calling lightning or setting things on fire would not be appropriate. Nor would any of the simple practical tasks that could be accomplished with magic; they weren't flashy enough. Plus, she wasn't fully charged; she hadn't been able to visit the butcher, garden, or salle for a few days what with all the preparations for the celebration.

Well, perhaps then—

All those hours of practicing, of singing until her voice got hoarse, until she'd mastered the summons, would come in useful now. Vor lifted a hand palm up, and concentrated a morsel of power there. Then she opened her mouth and began to sing to her hand, stringing the words together with her will, keeping the feeling light and gentle.

After a few phrases she could feel the power moving; it was going to work, and a bit of her anxiety faded. It didn't take a lot of energy, just energy applied with careful and practiced focus. With the last word—in some old language she knew only by rote—she blew into her palm. There sprang a burst of color, and not just once, but twice, thrice.

Transparent and ever shifting in shape, three winged creatures—now like butterflies, now like birds, now like dragonflies, or tiny winged humanoids—blossomed into view. They lifted off, dancing before her, each with a wingspan as wide as her spread hand. Murmurs of surprise and interest came from the gathering, but she wasn't done yet. The air sprites were awaiting their orders; Vor fought back a grin.

All the different elemental sprites she'd learned to summon were playful to some degree. The air sprites, or sylphs, while lacking the destructive potential of salamanders, the limitation of undines that must always be in water, or the single-minded focus of the various earth sprites, were the most playful of all. Since she'd gotten three instead of one, she wondered if the party had been attractive to them.

They could only take simple commands, for they weren't bright, but Vor knew the command that would have the most spectacular effects. It was what they did, their place in the order of the elements.

"Play," she whispered to them, more with her will than with words. "Freshen the air."

With beats of their wings the three sprites gave off little bursts of wind that brushed her face, but then Vor felt a streak of magic pass by her right ear. It struck the sprites directly, but did them no harm. Rather, they suddenly bloomed with light, sparkling like crystals and sending refracted rainbows all over the room. This seemed to delight them even more, and this time their giggles were almost audible to ordinary human ears, somewhere between the buzzing of bees and chirping of birds.

One shot up towards the ceiling in the guise of a dragonfly with wings shedding glittering scales. It circled the room in a rapid ring of light and Vor felt the accumulated muggy heat from so many people, lanterns, and candles disperse. The second sprite zipped off among the guests, turning figure eights and spirals among them like a luminous turquoise bird with a streaming tail.

Women reached for their elaborately coifed hair in a mix of concern and delight. Some of the men made to catch the creature, but it was congealed from air and wind itself, and slipped right through their fingers. Where it passed, the odors of food and drink diminished, cleaning the olfactory palates of the guests.

The third sylph however, took on the form of a butterfly as golden as honey. In a much more leisurely manner it flew up to Vor and circled her. The scents of spring flowers and the sighing of new leaves surrounded her. With her at the center, it made an ever-widening spiral just above the reach of the diners. Vor watched as the quiet bliss of spring settled on them as well.

Their task complete, the three headed back towards Vor, and she breathed one more command to them, gifting them some more energy as payment. They complied and descended in a trio onto the false princess. She raised her hands in delight, and the dragonfly and bird-shaped ones appeared to land on her palms. The golden butterfly grew long tails off its hindwings and settled on her head like a tiara.

For a few moments, they sat there, until Vor silently banished them. The false princess seemed to look around her with more awareness than before, and her gaze touched on Vor for a moment. Vor gave her a little bow.

Then the room erupted in applause. Vor looked at her master. He was slowly clapping with a sardonic look on his face. She couldn't tell if he was pleased or not. She sensed Karolan behind her with her chair, and she sank gratefully down into it. He sat down beside her and clasped her hand under the table.

"Thank you," she whispered.

"What were those?" he asked.

"Sylphs, air sprites, similar to the salamander I set on you the first day you came."

"Very pretty."

She gave him a quick look. "Thanks for the light spell; that made them even prettier."

"You're welcome," he smiled.

The meal was resuming, with servants bringing out little bowls of a sweet orange paste over a nugget of pastry, with mint leaves and curls of lemon rind adorning it.

"That song was how you summon them?" Karolan went on.

"Yes. They're very particular and it has to be just right."

For a few minutes they nibbled at the sticky dessert in silence.

"You know, you really impress me," Karolan murmured.

Vor felt the start of a blush and attempted to refocus to stop it.

"Hush about that," she tried to scold.

She thought he almost laughed. Servants took the dishes of citrus sauce remnants away and began bringing out what seemed like an army of platters. Vor counted one with half a dozen chickens, one with three geese, and various parts of a beef on several different salvers. They paraded past the high table before the servants began distributing pieces to the guests along with more roasted vegetables and potatoes.

Vor began to wonder how much more her stomach could hold. The guests however praised the feast highly. Marklin had indeed stepped up and turned out all he could. Vor wondered how he would top it for the wedding feast next month. The consumption of the chickens, geese, and beef took some time, but then it was swept away, and the servants brought out bowls overflowing with leafy greens sprinkled with nut oils and flavorful vinegars.

This was more Vor's style and she filled whatever room she had left in her belly with greenery. Hard on its heels came little plates of cookies and tiny cakes, to which guests helped themselves as they wished.

"I think this means we're almost done," Vor said in an undertone to Karolan.

"I'm really not used to this," he mumbled back. "Griffins just rip their food to shreds and swallow it down raw."

She shushed him. "You can't talk like that."

"Oh, right, sorry."

"You will be sorry when my master rips you to shreds—and he might even swallow some of you down raw."

But then the musicians trooped in and arranged themselves at the far end of the room, beyond an empty space of floor. Wine was refilled and other liquors began appearing, like mead, beer, and brandy. Couples started standing and moving onto the floor as the musicians began to play. Vor and Karolan both looked on in strangled horror.

"I don't know how to dance," Karolan whispered.

"Neither do I," Vor concurred.

"A hole in your education," said a voice from behind them.

Both turned; Altare stood there, casually swirling a glass of brandy in one hand, apparently despite that alcohol muddied mage senses.

"Alas that I have not the time to rectify it tonight," he went on, "but it will be rectified." He shifted his regard exclusively to Vor and a hint of a smile crept onto his face. "Well done. Of course I expected no less. You two are certainly working well together."

Vor wasn't sure if that last statement showed approval or not.

"He has his uses," she commented levelly.

Altare raised an eyebrow. "Indeed he does. I am glad to see you taking such an interest in them."

He passed them, headed down towards the dancing.

"Do you think he suspects?" Karolan muttered, almost silently.

Vor had to take a few moments to think about it. "I don't know," she said at last. "It's only going to get more dangerous. If he catches us, we're dead, or worse."

"Can we leave yet?"

"I don't think so," she grunted.

"You know, these are good."

"Did you empty that whole plate?"

"Well, they're good."

Vor felt herself smile a little.

Then, with a rush of air that made every flame flicker, the main doors to the dining hall swung open and banged against the walls. The musicians halted with a squawk and the dancers spun to a stop. Conversation died instantly.

In the open doorway stood three people: two men and a woman, all in elaborate mage robes. Vor had never seen them before. The man in the lead was tall, and older but not yet elderly. He had short grey-freckled brown hair but a bald spot on top, and a clean-shaven face. His posture and form suggested he had not let a scholarly life make him soft. He wore a somber, imperious expression.

The other man, standing to the leader's right in the triangle formation, was younger—perhaps only a handful of years older than Vor, and close to her height. He had long, straight deep brown hair braided back from his face, and skin a shade or two lighter than Vor's. His eyes were darting agilely around. The woman was petite but also no child—younger than the leader and older than the other man—with black curly hair pulled back in a tail and pale skin tending to pink, with what was either burn scars or a large birthmark on the lower half of one side of her face. She looked about as deadly as a dagger.

The three moved forward in perfectly measured strides.

Vor almost gasped as she felt her master's summons jerk violently on her and she obeyed, getting to her feet and hurrying with as much decorum as she could manage to come up behind him, on his right. Karolan seemed to have gotten the idea and followed quickly, mirroring her position on Altare's left.

The dinner guests parted, separating to the walls as the wedge of new come mages advanced. Altare moved swiftly to meet them, trailing Vor and Karolan in a reflection of their triangle formation. More slowly, the other three old masters hobbled down as well, making a third row to their triangle, behind Vor and Karolan. The two groups came to a halt facing each other. Altare bowed, and his entourage followed suit. The newcomers gave brief but formal nods.

"Altare Dhordirh," the lead man said in a ringing voice that spoke only of youth, despite his apparent age.

"I am he," Altare replied.

"We come from Weldom to congratulate you on the eve of your engagement," the man went on, although without a smile.

Vor felt a measure of tension leave the room, but none of the mages relaxed.

"You honor me too greatly," Altare declared.

"I am State Wizard Colby Srawn. My associates are Wizard Milsa Thauket," indicating the woman, "and Wizard Giri Holstor," indicating the young man.

Altare bowed again. "You are all welcome."

From behind, Vor detected the tightening of her master's neck muscles. He extended a hand back towards her.

"My apprentices: Vor Hearthsraven," he extended his other hand, "and Karolan Freyaliv. Also, advisors and retired master mages Eriducus, Ulver, and Chirolen."

The regard of the newcomers fell over Vor and the others. She felt herself instinctively pull in her energies and form protective shields. The neutral expressions on their faces did not change, and Vor did her best to match them.

Altare plowed on. "Will you join our feast, and allow me to show you what meager hospitality this humble country can muster?"

"We shall," the wizard stated "Lead on."

Altare pivoted as Colby led his group closer, taking up a position at Colby's side. They passed between Vor and Karolan, and as Colby's associates came in range, Vor and Karolan pivoted as well. This put Vor beside the pale woman Milsa, and Karolan by the dark man Giri. Altare's old mage advisors peeled to one side, bowing low as the others passed.

The musicians began their song again. In the time it took for the nine mages to return to the high table, the servants had flown in, in a flurry, clearing and resetting places where Altare's five mages had been sitting. Now Altare brought the State Wizard to sit at his right. Beside him sat Wizard Giri, then Milsa, and Vor retook her former seat, with Karolan again at the end. That left the old mages, Eriducus and the others, seat-less, but they vanished off somewhere anyway.

Servants brought the newcomers clean plates and several different dishes of food to choose from—apparently scavenged from the remains of the previous courses. They indicated their preferences and were served, or served themselves. Altare immediately engaged Wizard Colby in conversation. Wizard Giri appeared to be paying close attention but not contributing.

Wizard Milsa gazed slowly around the room, and then settled her eyes on Vor, who matched her dispassionate expression as well as she could. For a moment, the two stared. Then Milsa relented with a confident smile.

"Come, let us be friends," she said silkily. "I am Milsa."

"And I Vor."

"You have been your master's apprentice for some time?"

"Since childhood."

"And who is your gentleman?"

"Him?" Vor glanced at Karolan. "My master's other apprentice," she put a hint of disdain into her voice, "a recent arrival, Karolan Freyaliv, of little consequence."

Vor had the feeling that this woman would eat Karolan whole if she got any bit of him into her hands, and had already made up her mind to keep Milsa's attention on herself.

"Indeed. And how many years have you, Vor?"

"Twenty-one."

"Yet you are still an apprentice. Your master must have been your age when he took you on."

Vor took a slow drink of her juice tea, mind racing to try to decide how to respond. She settled on humility.

"I still have much to learn," she demurred.

Milsa showed her teeth in a smile. "So modest you are."

Vor bowed her head.

"I am glad to see that Weldom's customs hold here as well, somewhat at least. We do not leave our apprenticeships until middle age. I myself am a few years still away from becoming a master. And you, boy, how many years have you?"

"Sixteen, Mistress," Karolan answered evenly.

"A delicious age," Milsa purred.

"If you like the taste of sour milk," Vor interjected.

Milsa eyed her. "I take it you do not." Her gaze shifted back to Karolan. "I find I don't mind it."

Stinking rat dung. Vor tried to think of something to get Milsa's attention off him.

"Nor does my master," Karolan contributed with a little smile.

Vor might have choked but she took swift control of her throat and face. Milsa sat back a fraction of an inch. It would do Altare no good if the rumor got around, but only she and Milsa had heard, and perhaps Milsa would take it no further. Or perhaps Milsa would eventually realize the lie, and then there would be consequences all around if she acted on it.

"You will miss him then, when he is gone," the lady wizard remarked.

"When he is gone?" Vor echoed.

"We come to invite him to visit Weldom, to report on the situation here. He won't be gone but a few days."

Vor hid her excitement. "We will have difficulty managing without him," she said.

"I'm sure you'll find a way. It will, after all, only be a short time. I worried his bride might miss him the most, but perhaps that is not the case."

Milsa had turned slightly to rest her gaze on the false princess. She would know the girl was enchanted, just by looking at her. She would know the king was under magical control as well. Vor doubted those things bothered her. After all, it had been wizards from Weldom who had set up both situations. Even if she knew the princess was a fake, she probably didn't care.

Kari had taken Amlee's position behind the false princess. Vor expected Amlee must be running about now with a task force of tiring servants, preparing three suites of rooms for the new arrivals. Vor wondered if the wizards had travelled overland to get here, or if they'd teleported in. None of them looked particularly exhausted, but she hadn't been brave enough to probe any of their auras. They might be powerful enough to have done it without signs of serious fatigue. If they were, they were stronger than Altare, and much stronger than either Vor or Karolan.

Wizard Milsa made no more attempts at conversation, but listened in on what her associates and Altare were saying in-between bites of food, or let her gaze wander over the room, occasionally touching on Karolan. The party was still boisterous, with plenty of dancing. Servants had brought out trays of fruit and cheese, and the musicians looked nowhere near to stopping.

Amlee returned however, and subtly made sure Altare had noticed her. Moments later, the wilting false princess was rising, to be led away. Altare rose, too, to kiss her hand with all the gallantry he could display. Amlee guided her off and Altare sat for few more minutes, until Wizard Colby and Altare got up together. Milsa and Giri followed suit, so Vor and Karolan did, too.

The two master mages led the group from the room. This time, Vor found herself walking beside Giri, which put Karolan and Milsa together behind her, but she dared not look back. Karolan would have to fend for himself. Beside her, Giri gave her a smile that might have been genuine.

"You must be from the western side of Weldom," he said, "like me, in the mountains?"

"Mount Brasson," Vor admitted with mild surprise.

"Ah, Mount Brasson, a beautiful area," Giri nodded. "The black maple trees are particularly lovely in autumn. I've had occasion to visit a few times."

"You might know better than I, then. I came to Northborn when quite young, so I remember little."

"You came with your master?" Giri asked with a hint of hesitancy and a quiet glance towards Altare who was several steps ahead and talking with Wizard Colby.

Vor shook her head a little, and after a moment explained, "My father was a soldier."

"For the invasion? I can only imagine that must have been difficult."

Vor did not reply.

"I am from Croun, farther to the south," Giri said after a few moments.

"I have heard of it, but never had the pleasure of visiting."

He waved a hand to indicate it was no matter. "No trees as lovely as yours, but wildflowers that carpet the slopes in spring in every color of the rainbow and some others besides."

Up ahead, Altare began giving the wizards a tour, and Giri fell silent, relieving Vor of the need to figure out how she should keep replying. Altare pointed out the critical areas like privy and bathing chamber, as well as the library and dining rooms. Upstairs he indicated a set of three adjoining suites. Vor noted through the open doors that they all had lighted lamps and inviting little fires in the fireplaces of their sitting rooms. Amlee had indeed been quick. Edgard with two older pages and a maidservant—not Kari, who must have been attending the false princess—stood ready to attend the guests.

"Can I interest you in another drink?" Altare invited the three wizards.

"The journey has been fatiguing," Colby declined, "but I look forward to more conversation tomorrow."

"As do I," Altare assured him.

The two men went on with a few other pleasantries. Meanwhile, Milsa had moved towards the room given to her, and the maidservant came to curtsy before her and hold the door open. Milsa went in without a backward glance. Karolan remained where he was: seeming reluctant to approach any closer. Giri, however, stepped near to Vor, and she had to throttle down her instinctive urge to backpedal. He smiled warmly.

"Would you like to hear some more of Croun?" he enquired. "I would hear of your childhood in Brasson as well."

Vor's words caught in her throat. How polite was she supposed to be to these people? Altare and Colby were still talking. She noticed Colby glance her way, and then ask something of her master. Altare looked over, too, coolly met her gaze for a moment, and then nodded to the State Wizard, giving a reply Vor couldn't hear. Colby glanced over and exchanged a look with Giri.

Altare and Colby bowed to each other, Colby went into his room, and Altare vanished into the darkness down the hall, so there was no help there.

Giri was still smiling at her. It seemed like an authentic smile—but how could she be certain? These people might be as duplicitous as her master.

"You won't do me the honor of your company this evening?" the young wizard went on.

He reached out and took her hand, applying the slightest of tugs. Was he suggesting what she thought he was suggesting? Karolan, several feet down the hall, shifted his weight, and Giri's eyes snapped to him instantly.

"Ah," the wizard uttered, not seeming displeased or surprised. "Of course, you are both welcome."

Vor's mind raced. She did not give in to Giri's pull on her hand. She did not return his smile, but nor did she want to offend him, so she didn't snatch herself away or scowl. This arrival of wizards from Weldom could be critically bad—or maybe somehow good? It would cause a dramatic change in the dynamics of her betray-and-kill-Altare plan, but Vor couldn't yet know what way those dynamics would swing, or how she could influence them by her actions. So how indeed should she respond?

Giri was watching her appraisingly.

"You do not," he said gradually, "replenish your energy in company? Not even in the company of fellow mages?"

Vor managed to swallow, but couldn't resolve how to respond. Giri considered her for another moment. Then he nodded down the hall after Altare's retreat. "It seems your master would wish you to take your ease with us, after our difficult journey, but I'd not accept that which is not willingly given."

Vor paled and felt her back straighten in alarm. Giri's eyes widened with what appeared to be true concern. Then, she felt the faintest, most delicate and unobtrusive touch of his aura on hers, and the concern in his eyes matured into quiet alarm. She knew what he'd touched her to sense, and her energies flinched, even though she held her body stiff and still to prevent visible offense.

"I see," he whispered. "Curious." His gaze switched to Karolan, who twitched after a moment. Giri looked back at Vor, brow knit with thought. "Very curious."

Vor's throat was paralyzed such that she couldn't speak, only stare, trying to keep her expression impassive while dread clamored within. Her silence didn't seem to bother Giri; he gave her a gentler smile. Emboldened by signs of his restraint, and the example he'd set of touching her aura and Karolan's without permission, Vor extended the tiniest, lightest probe of her own that she could. She couldn't match Giri's skill, but she focused so hard trying she almost gave herself a headache. As lightly as she could, she touched at the edges of his energies.

Surprise and pleasure bloomed on Giri's face—surely indicating that he'd felt it; as skilled as he was, how could he not have? Vor withdrew her touch immediately, for she'd sensed what she'd wanted to sense. He was seriously depleted. She had no idea how he was even still on his feet and behaving normally. He needed rest and if possible an energy source to draw from. That explained the hushed conversation between Altare and Colby, and Giri's interest. It seemed there was the thought of her being that energy source.

Typical of her master to offer her up when he must have known she wouldn't like it, but Colby and Giri couldn't have known that. Vor's jaw clenched and she tried not to let her face cloud with too much conflicted anger. Giri gave a little nod.

"Some other time then." He bent over her hand and kissed the back. Some of his long hair slipped over his shoulder and brushed her wrist. He stood back up after a few moments. "I confess myself pleased to have been assigned here. Investigating your master's operations looks as though it will prove quite entertaining. May you have a pleasant evening, Vor Hearthsraven."

"And you, sir," Vor did her best to reply, although her voice was close to a croak.

His eyes glimmered. "Thank you. I shall."

Without another word he released her hand, turned, and led his page into his rooms. The page shut the door behind him. Vor pivoted and walked quickly to Karolan. Without speaking they descended, and took the back passageways between the public and private wings. The wards were keyed to let them pass. She only hoped the wards would stop the new come wizards if they tried to follow.

Once in the near complete darkness of the secret hall, Karolan pulled her into a hug. Vor held him tightly in return, but ended the embrace after only a moment, too uncomfortable to let it go on.

"This will change things," she whispered.

"I know."

"We must be very careful."

She half expected they would run into Altare, or be summoned, but there was no sign of him. They climbed the stairs towards their rooms. No one was about. They stopped in front of Karolan's door, which they reached first.

"I'm," Karolan breathed, "a little scared."

"Me, too."

"What should we do?"

Vor shook her head. "Nothing will happen tonight."

"You're sure?"

"These are not impulsive people, and they've had a difficult journey," she whispered. "I think whatever is going to happen, will be tomorrow, after they rest and meet again with my master."

In the dark, Karolan took her hand, and rubbed the spot the wizard Giri had kissed with his thumb.

"Was he saying your master had given him permission to lie with you?" Karolan asked.

"And with you: that's what it sounded like. That Milsa was practically drooling over you at dinner. I'll bet they teleported at least part of the way here. Giri at least was seriously depleted; I looked at his aura. It would have helped them renew their energies," Vor gritted out, "considerably."

A sound rather like a growl emanated from Karolan.

She took a deep breath. "But he didn't know at first that we don't do that, that we've never done that. I think it confused him: that my master would say we'd join them, when we clearly aren't in the habit of it. Never mind it now. Save up energy," Vor advised, her voice barely audible. "I think if these people come after us, we won't stand much of a chance, but if they mean to attack, they will go after my master first. We might have an opportunity to escape during the fight."

"And if they catch us?"

"They might not kill us, but it won't be good. If they judge my master," she shivered, "we are his apprentices."

She felt Karolan's breath against her hair as he moved close. His hands were cold.

"Put wards on your door, so at least you'll have the chance to be on your feet if they do come," she suggested.

"Alright."

Karolan pulled her in for another hug.

"I won't let him touch you," Karolan told her.

She doubted he'd be able to stop Giri and his associates if they made a concerted effort, but she appreciated the sentiment. It had all left her feeling uncomfortable in her own skin, and she disengaged from Karolan as quickly but gently as she could.

"Or her you," she promised. "Go to bed."

"Alright, good night."

"Good night."

Vor's room was around a corner and a few doors down. She scanned for magical anomalies before she went in, found it clear, and shut the door behind her, putting up her wards. Only then did she realize she had no one to help her out of the dratted dress. She had to break one of the ties behind her back, but she didn't plan on wearing it again anyway.

It was difficult to sleep, but she was tired due to her previous sleepless night, and knew she might need the rest in the most critical way. Eventually, she managed to struggle down into slumber.

Chapter 15
The Inspection

Her master's summons woke her just before dawn. Vor struggled out of bed and into her clothing, tucked her mane of hair under a cap, and obeyed, following the magical call to one of her master's major workrooms. She tried to appear alert, but she hadn't slept well and the uneasiness of the previous evening had landed back on her full force.

"I am here, Master," she announced.

Altare was pacing, arms folded, wearing some of his more formal and opulent garb in green and gold.

"Where's the boy?" he demanded without looking at her.

"In his rooms, I expect," Vor replied. "Shall I fetch him?"

He growled with a frustrated clawing gesture. "I haven't gotten any magic in him yet to call him. I figured he'd be with you."

Altare stopped pacing to regard her, and spat a curse.

"I don't even need to touch your aura. You refused the wizards, didn't you?"

"Wizard Giri said he would not accept that which is not freely given," Vor quoted.

"So you freely give," he snarled at her. "Are you still an idiot girl? These people are from Weldom, our patrons."

"Then they are allies," Vor asserted.

He scoffed. "Well, they are not enemies, yet. I sent a missive, explaining why we need the return of a drake swarm. I've been long in waiting for a reply, but I did not expect them to send wizards—and a State Wizard, too."

"What is that, Master, if a humble servant may ask?"

"There are lots of wizards," Altare explained. "To gain the title of wizard in Weldom, one must be so appointed by five other wizards. Being recognized as a wizard helps with employment and gives you certain privileges, but it comes with responsibilities, too: some might go so far as to say obligations. State Wizards are wizards in direct service of the High Ministers that run the country, under the command of the High Wizard, who implements commands. Ordinary wizards may also be employed by the government, but it's rather like they are infantry in the army and a State Wizard is a general."

"How many State Wizards are there?" Vor asked.

"There's usually one to two dozen. They are the ones that handle anything serious involving magery."

Vor nodded in understanding. "It seems Weldom is taking your missive seriously then, Master."

"And you insulted them," he hissed, "the same as if we'd denied them food, or warmth, or shelter."

Vor looked at the floor. "Wizard Giri did not seem insulted."

"He took it well because he is a mature man who realized he was facing a disobedient child," Altare growled. "You have lowered my prestige in their eyes."

"Please forgive me, Master."

He approached her and seized the front of her jacket. "I grow woefully tired of your lack of maturity, of your squeamishness, of your incompetence, Vor." His voice dropped as he glared down at her. "I find myself more and more considering how I might be rid of you. It is upon you to convince me not to."

Altare released her, which was surprising. She'd been internally bracing for a slap at the least.

"Go to the kitchens and oversee their breakfasts," Altare ordered. "As soon as they ring, go with the servants and greet them. Bring them to the blue dining hall. I'll go get the boy and meet them there."

"Yes, Master," Vor nodded.

"Be gone."

***

The kitchens were abustle with activity. Despite what must have been an exhausting night for the cooks and servants, they were up and orchestrated like a well-trained battalion of troops. When Vor stepped through the doorway, several people took the time to nod or bow and smoothly resumed whatever they'd been about.

"All is well, Mistress," Marklin called to her, arms full of a tray of pastries. "Our best breakfasts will be ready shortly."

Vor nodded to him and looked around for Amlee, catching sight of the back of her head just outside the door to the courtyard gardens. She headed that way, stepping aside for each hurrying kitchen helper, so as not to upset their missions. As she neared the door, she saw that Amlee was talking closely with a maidservant.

"No, you'll not be dismissed, Pella," Amlee was assuring the girl. "And you're not hurt?"

The young woman shook her head in a shy negative. She startled like a wary cat when Vor reached the door, and her face blushed a painful red. Vor's brows rose in unwilling surprise when she recognized that the girl had been the maidservant assigned to Wizard Milsa the previous evening. Vor had never heard her name. She was in her late teens, but sturdier than her master liked—he preferred sweet-looking, skinny, helpless girls—with astute eyes that had probably kept her out of trouble: until now, it seemed.

"Go on, then," Amlee dismissed her, and the girl practically bolted, grabbing up a basket and heading into the rows of garden. "All is in order, Mistress," the castellan said.

"Is she alright?" Vor asked softly, already guessing what had happened.

Amlee winced. "As long as she doesn't kindle," the older woman whispered.

Vor shook her head. "She won't." When Amlee looked dubious, she elaborated. "Mages have ways of preventing such things."

Some of the anxiety departed Amlee's face, but she still didn't look pleased. "I don't care for these guests, Mistress."

"Yet they are kinder than my master," Vor reminded her with an ironically arched eyebrow. "She walks free, unhurt, and unencumbered by enchantments."

Amlee grimaced, but wiped it off her face quickly. "You may be right at that," she murmured, "and Pella says she wasn't forced, but I'm not sure of it. I've just about had my fill of mages."

"Present company included," Vor quipped.

Amlee jerked and pressed a hand to her chest. "Mistress," she gaped, "I didn't mean—"

Vor half-smiled at her. "I did."

Amlee relaxed a fraction. "In another time I would rejoice at hearing you banter so, Mistress, but this is hardly the proper atmosphere."

"You're right," she allowed. "I expect considerable changes coming soon, but whether for good or ill, that I cannot say. Do what you can to look to your own, and keep your people safe."

The two women went back into the kitchen, Amlee joining in with the preparations as smoothly as a bird joining its airborne flock. Vor just tried to find a place to stand where she would be out of the way.

The ringing of the bells put everyone into faster motion, and Vor went immediately for the hallway with a half dozen servants trailing after her. On the second floor, at the three doors for the visiting wizards' rooms, the servants peeled off two by two—women for Milsa and men for Giri and Colby—and entered after a knock to begin preparing their charges for the day.

Vor waited in the hallway. After some minutes, State Wizard Colby emerged, spotted her, and came unerringly over to her with purposeful steps. He took her hand, bowed over it, but did not kiss it. She bowed, too, managing to prevent a head to head collision.

"Good morning to you, sir," Vor greeted. "I hope you were able to find some rest in our primitive accommodations."

"Rest in plenty, good apprentice," he smiled back at her.

After his continually somber expressions of the previous evening, the warm greeting surprised her.

"I apologize for my apprentice's forwardness," he went on.

Ah, he meant Wizard Giri's offer of the previous evening.

"Not at all," Vor replied. The man's sudden forthrightness encouraged her. She hadn't spoken with him directly last night, but she hadn't expected such courtesy. "I must apologize as well. It seems you were misinformed," she said softly.

He raised a brow just slightly and understanding flashed between them. "So it would seem."

Giri and Milsa emerged then, both looking renewed but somewhat tense. It was then that Vor noticed they were all wearing fresh mage robes.

"Our luggage arrived last night," Colby explained with a hint of smugness, as though she'd asked aloud.

"How fortuitous," Vor managed.

"Isn't it?" the wizard agreed. "I assume breakfast is waiting."

"Of course," she rushed, "yes, please, this way."

***

Altare had somehow timed it perfectly to seem as though he and Karolan had just arrived when Vor led in the three wizards. Colby's smile was gone as though it had never been there. Giri and Milsa also seemed reserved and self-possessed. The servants were bringing out the first dishes. Altare made obeisant noises at Colby and the others, gesturing for them to be seated, and the whole group set to the food.

"Weldom has received your word and knows of your need," the State

Wizard said to the room at large as the meal was coming to a close. "We are here to assess that need for ourselves, and look forward to inspecting the whole of the situation."

"You will surely find the truth of my words," Altare assured him.

"I would spend some time hearing those words afresh from your mouth," Colby replied. "During that time, Milsa will tour the mines. Your other mages will accompany her. Giri will observe the state of your armed forces. You will provide a suitable guide: one of the generals perhaps."

"Of course," Altare declared.

Without needing prompting, Edgard removed himself from the room. Vor thought he was probably going to fetch the most loyal—and nearest—of the army generals. Altare's gaze ran rapidly over his mages. She could almost see his spinning thoughts, trying to pick whom to send into the mines with Milsa. Ulver was nearly deaf, even though he was the one technically in charge of the mage-stone mining, and wasn't exactly the brightest gem in the box—but perhaps that was for the best.

"Vor, Master Ulver, won't you show Wizard Milsa our vast enterprise," he ordered.

"Yes, Master," Vor nodded.

"Eh?" Ulver croaked.

Vor was sitting next to Ulver and put a gentle hand on his arm. He leaned close. "A tour," she said, loudly and clearly, "of the mines."

"Oh, excellent, excellent," Ulver bobbed his head.

"Send your other apprentice as well," Colby ordered.

A flicker of unease crossed Altare's face, but he nodded at Karolan. "You, too, boy."

"Yes, Master," he agreed.

"Perhaps Masters Eriducus and Chirolen could lend some perspective to Wizard Giri," Altare said quickly, before Colby could get another demand in. "They have been here since the beginning, and can recount all the history of our military and peace keeping efforts."

Colby unfurled his fingers as though he cared not. Then he shoved to his feet. Only Giri and Milsa were prepared for it, standing as soon as he did. The others hurried to do the same. As the group reached the door, Colby and Altare leading, a tall, hefty man in uniform intercepted them. Edgard had indeed been swift. Vor recognized the man as General Krant, although she'd rarely exchanged words with him. He was older but still hale, with short graying hair, cut in military tidiness and equally neat mustaches.

"Ah, excellent," Altare purred, as though he'd expected him. "State

Wizard Colby, may I present General Krant."

The General bowed deeply. "An honor."

Altare gestured towards Giri, who had come up beside them. "Kindly show Wizard Giri our forces and answer any questions he may have. Masters Chirolen and Eriducus will accompany you."

"Gladly, sirs," Krant nodded with precision. "If you will come this way?"

The four men moved off together, Krant already beginning to expound. Altare turned to Vor and Ulver. Karolan stood uncertainly behind them, with Milsa at her master's side.

"The State Wizard and I shall be in my private office," he said. "Master Ulver, Vor, Karolan, please show Wizard Milsa all she wishes to see."

They bowed, although Ulver lagged by half a breath. Vor faced Milsa.

"Madam, if you would accompany us to the mines?" she invited.

Milsa gave a smile that stretched the scarring on her face. "I'd be delighted."

***

Ulver might have been old and deaf, but he handled the wards on the tunnels and vaults with a practiced hand. They were lucky that the next outgoing shipment of mage-stone was due to depart shortly, so the vaults were relatively full, although less full than they would have been in the past, when the mines were fresh and the veins still thick.

Milsa nodded at the contents without comment, and they led her on deeper. Vor let Ulver do the talking whenever possible, and Milsa soon learned that she had to raise her voice and speak clearly when she had questions. Karolan walked behind Vor and kept his mouth buttoned, too.

They reached the stairs and wide landing where the loads of stone from below were stashed before being moved to the vaults. A half a dozen human slaves with an overseer in lazy attendance were just starting to haul the loads up the incline on the pulleys. When Ulver and the others came into view, the overseer snapped to attention. The slaves continued their work with bowed heads.

"So you still use slaves for the mine work?" Milsa observed as they passed the group. "They seem well-cared for."

Ulver was in charge of dictating everything about how the mage-stone was mined, including the slaves. The men—there were no female human slaves—all wore magical collars that prevented them from going beyond certain boundaries, so there was no chance of them escaping. Even had they attacked the overseers and overpowered them, they would not have been able to leave the mines, making the effort meaningless, for it took a mage to remove the collars.

The overseers were instructed not to use gratuitous beatings, but nor were the slaves allowed to speak while working, or rest for more than a few minutes at a time. They were given enough food that they could work hard, and enough comfort that they did not become ill.

Vor listened as Ulver rambled on about it to Milsa, emphasizing that it made the mining more effective, to have slaves that were not abused. Vor hid her surprise when she heard Milsa praise and agree with his tactics. Somehow, knowing how brutal Altare was, and based on the slaughter during the invasion, she'd expected that Weldom—and its officials—would be equally callous and cruel.

Vor didn't generally agree with slavery, but if there had to be slaves—and from her reading of history, she knew it was not uncommon—it sat easier with her when the slaves were not mistreated. Still, these ones were mostly political prisoners, not violent criminals, who had resisted the takeover by Weldom or spoken out against it. They were here until they died. Vor didn't think their crime deserved this punishment, but she had not the power to free them. Only Altare and Ulver, and possibly the other two old masters, knew how to remove the collars.

The group had passed the long stairs with the pulleys and now paralleled a wide path where donkeys pulled carts of readied mage-stone along. Vor knew there were only four donkeys assigned to the mines now, since the flow of mage-stone had lessened, and while they walked, only one poor beast plodded past with a partially full cart. Milsa glanced in and raised an eyebrow. Ulver cast one helpless look back at Vor, but neither of them could think of anything to obscure the shortfall.

They came to the main cavern where the excavated stone was brought to be sorted and loaded. Natural light came in through a grate high up on one wall—far beyond the height that anyone could have leapt to, and the holes were only big enough to stick an arm through, not enough to crawl out through. Nor was anything other than a distant wall visible through it. Additional lanterns supplemented the daylight.

Along one side of the cavern were the cells where the human slaves slept. They were barred, but inside could be seen proper beds, small tables, and stools, shelves with a few meager possessions, with hooks on the walls where clothing could be hung. There was also a larger cell that served as a washing area, with spigots and tubs and shelves of worn towels. One man was currently using it, washing a tub of clothing. Another man, also a slave, was in the kitchen area cleaning up after breakfast.

In the middle of the room, a dozen humans stood at tables sorting through bins of rocks. With little hammers and picks they knocked off common dirt and minerals until they had clean lumps or pebbles of mage-stone. These they put into buckets. They worked steadily with another overseer sitting on a tall stool, watching over them. Milsa stood nodding, observing the operation with what appeared to be approval.

Then a griffin walked in from one of the work tunnels that led away into the mines.

"What is that?" the woman demanded. "Is that, is that a griffin?"

Ulver bobbed his head in confirmation. "The griffins are stronger and have better vision in the dark than humans do. We use them for most of the mining."

Karolan took a step up beside Vor. A covert glance at him showed his eyes wide, his mouth dropping open. She grabbed the back of his shirt and tugged. He flicked his eyes at her and seemed to catch himself, settling back on his heels and composing his expression.

"How many do you have?" Milsa asked.

"Twenty four," Ulver answered promptly.

"And where did they come from?"

"They were here when we came," the old mage shrugged, "as defenders of the country, I mean, of course. We repurposed them," he beamed proudly.

"Waste not," Milsa murmured, but it didn't seem that Ulver heard. "They don't try to harm anyone?" she asked more loudly.

"They know their place."

The approaching griffin came to the tables and dumped the contents of a sack hung from a harness on its side into one of the bins. The nearest human nodded at it. It nodded back, and turned to retrace its steps. Unlike the humans, the griffin had its feet shackled wrist to wrist and ankle-to-ankle, with a central chain running front to back between them. They were political prisoners, too, but they had also been violent and possessed the physical characteristics that made them potentially dangerous.

Their wings were snugly bound with a fine mesh sheath. Once a year, Ulver would magically knock each one unconscious, the sheath would be removed, the new grown flight feathers cut off, and the sheath replaced. During working hours, a muzzle with an attached light stone covered their powerful bills. Each morning they had to put it on. If they didn't, they weren't freed from their cells, and they weren't fed at the end of the day. If they were caught removing it while working, they were beaten until they replaced it.

Ulver explained all of this to an attentive Milsa. Vor kept her face impassive, but while she thought the humans were not treated that badly, she wondered about the griffins sometimes.

"Would you like to see closer?" Ulver invited.

Milsa assented, and the group came forward to the square of tables where the human slaves were working. The slaves kept their eyes down on their work. Milsa spent some time peering into bins and buckets.

"Let's see some of the tunnels," she requested at last, straightening.

"Of course, of course," Ulver agreed, turning to lead them off. "The nearest veins have of course been exhausted, but there are more deeper into the mines. It may be farther than madam wishes to walk."

"I have nothing wrong with my legs," Milsa said archly.

The woman muttered a word and her clothing started giving off a glow, making it easier to see. Ulver also touched a crystal he wore as a pendant, and it lighted up, too. They went down one of the largest tunnels, with the flattest floor, and Ulver pointed out all the old seams they passed, which had been depleted. After several minutes and as many turns and branches, they came to a place where seven griffins were hard at work along a short section of tunnel. A human overseer was leaning against a wall when the mages arrived, but quickly straightened up.

Between the overseer and Ulver, they pointed out how the creatures used a variety of tools to break the stone, including pick axes and shovels, as humans would, although sized to their larger bodies. They also had special picks that they could hold to punch and chip at the rock with. They clawed at the walls sometimes, but only to remove loose rock, as their natural claws were suited for ripping into prey, not stone.

All seven griffins had noticed the four mages arrive, but they put their heads down right away, continuing their work. Ulver walked right in among them, Milsa at his side, the overseer hovering attentively, but Vor and Karolan halted before the crowd. She nudged him again, for he was gazing around at the slaves with a pained look on his face. He leaned over to whisper into her ear.

"I didn't know there were still griffins down here," he hissed. "Cray told me he thought they would have been killed by now."

Vor said nothing, but gave him a look telling him to be silent. The nearest griffin, a particularly small one, hesitated, as if it had heard, or maybe it was just pondering how to attack the next bit of rock.

"That one is practically a fledgling," Karolan muttered. "It can't be much older than Day and Night."

This time the little griffin definitely paused. Its head turned slightly towards Karolan.

"Shut up," Vor breathed.

Up ahead at the end of the tunnel where the vein they were following would presumably be as yet untouched and thickest, Ulver and Milsa had pushed aside one of the griffins. Milsa was looking closely at where it had been digging. The overseer was pointing out features of the wall. After a few moments, Milsa straightened up and pivoted, walking back towards where Vor and Karolan waited. Her face was blank. The vein was small, Vor knew. If Milsa knew about mining mage-stone, she knew it, too.

Ulver hurried eagerly past. "This way to the next, a new hit on a fine lode."

"Do show me," Milsa encouraged.

Vor and Karolan stood back against the tunnel wall to allow them to pass. The overseer followed them out eagerly, thanking them for coming. Ulver babbled on vigorously about how promising the new lode was, with supporting commentary from the overseer. As Vor began to step into place behind them, she noticed Karolan suddenly bend over, aiming for the little griffin he'd pointed out.

Alarm froze Vor in place, her body shielding Karolan's from view for the two moments it took him to reach out and grab the griffin's magical collar. The creature halted in place. Vor aimed a reprimanding kick behind at Karolan, and it glanced off him. If Ulver or Milsa turned to see what was keeping them, or if the overseer finished his kowtowing and returned, they'd be in trouble—or would at least have to make up a story to answer what they were doing.

Karolan ignored her. Then, in horror, Vor heard him whisper to the griffin.

"Hawkwind is free. She is coming."

***

Vor and Karolan caught up to Ulver and Milsa quickly, but not before she'd snarled at him, "what do you think you were doing?"

He leaned over to mutter to her, "I was deactivating its collar and warning it to be ready."

"What?" Vor gasped as silently as she could.

"Cray taught me how, in case there were any left."

They had to stop talking as they came up on the other two mages, who were just turning down another tunnel. Neither Ulver nor Milsa gave any indication that they'd missed them. A short walk brought the four to a circular room where six griffins were all working in the center at chipping out rock from the floor. Another overseer, this one less obsequious, was also in attendance. Milsa circled the group, so Vor and Karolan were always in her line of sight. Vor was relieved when Karolan didn't try anything stupid.

Minutes later, as Milsa and Ulver left the room in the lead, Karolan looked longingly at the cluster of griffins, but Vor prodded him along with glares of warning. This overseer was watching them. The four visited the other three locations where digging continued, and Vor managed to keep Karolan from causing any trouble.

At last, the group began returning towards the surface. Milsa seemed satisfied but gave nothing else away. Karolan looked mildly distressed. Vor worried but tried not to show it. If Ulver—or worse, her master—came to check the collars, there would be questions. And what good did it do, anyway, for Karolan to deactivate one? The griffin was still shackled. Even if that one did escape somehow, what would it accomplish? Its companions would still be prisoners.

***

It was late for lunch, but Ulver returned them to the dining hall for food. Two pages waited by the open doors, and a couple servants stood ready within. Giri, the other two old masters, and General Krant had already returned and had the remains of their lunches before them. Giri and Krant were chatting benevolently. The servants immediately began filling glasses, and the four new come mages took seats.

"Ah, Milsa," Giri welcomed, "and how were the mines?"

"Mine-like," she answered deflectingly.

"Likewise the army," Giri smiled, "being army-like, I mean, not mine-like."

Milsa answered his smile with just a hint of her own. Vor caught herself a bit amused by Giri's banter as well. Their eyes caught on each other for just a second as Vor glanced his way, and she wrenched her attention back to her plate. She reminded herself what had happened to Pella, and all amusement faded.

"Once you've eaten I think we should report to Colby," Giri suggested mildly.

Milsa nodded. The General stood.

"I will take my leave then, sir and madam wizards," the man bowed.

"Have a wonderful day, thank you," Giri replied, and the General left.

Vor and Karolan ate silently, although Vor thought she felt Giri's gaze fall over them from time to time. She felt relief when the two wizards finally set down their napkins.

"I'm sure we'll see you all at dinner," Giri said to the room at large, indicating that none of them should come along. He gestured at the pages. "We're ready now."

The two wizards and two pages departed, leaving Vor and Karolan with the three old mages. Silence fell at once, and Vor snuck a glance at the masters. They glanced back at her. For a moment, she hesitated, but then reminded herself that they couldn't possibly know about her planned betrayal of her master. It would be natural for her to be concerned for other reasons, were she still loyal, so she spoke.

"All went well?"

"Eh?" Ulver grunted, but the other two nodded cautiously.

Eriducus made a gesture at the servants, and both immediately left.

"What do you think?" Vor murmured.

Chirolen shook his head slowly. A little earth-lizard poked its head out of his left sleeve, and he idly stroked its spiny crown with his opposite hand. "Can't know what Weldom is thinking."

"We've got nothing left for them," Eriducus muttered, "but that's no reason to let go territory. We still have our hold on the country, but the young master declaring himself king?"

"Over reaching himself, he is," Chirolen worried as his pet crawled fully into his right hand and appeared to snuggle there.

"What are you all whispering about?" Ulver asked loudly. "Speak up."

"I'll tell you later," Eriducus enunciated to Ulver.

The mages fell silent again. Vor and Karolan finished their lunch and the former eyed the latter.

"Master Altare assigned me to teach you the ways of potions and powders, and the lessons have been much delayed," Vor said clearly. "Let me take this opportunity to get one in."

Karolan gave a sigh. "Potions are boring," he grunted, stabbing at his last bit of potato.

"Get you up," Vor threatened.

He obeyed and Vor marched him out of the room. Once they were out of sight, Vor quirked a bit of a grin at him. He winked back, but her mirth faded as quickly as it had come when she thought about what he'd done in the mines.

Chapter 16
The Wizards Depart

Karolan enacted his usual silence spell as Vor set about showing him how to mix salves, so they could mutter at each other with impunity. Even though Altare and the Wizards were supposedly in conference, and the old master mages gone off somewhere to do whatever, Vor felt like taking no chances.

"Why didn't you tell me there were still griffins in the mines?" Karolan asked. "You know I live with griffins. Didn't you think I'd care?"

Vor scowled. "I couldn't take you down there or the overseers would have stopped us, or reported it. If I'd told you about them, you would have gone sneaking down there yourself, wouldn't you?"

He mashed harder at his mortar full of herbs. "Yeah, I might have."

Vor gave a tight nod. "Or you would have pressured me to take you. I don't know if you could have gotten through the wards. If we'd alerted my master somehow, the questions would have been uncomfortable, at the least."

"Have you ever spoken to them?" Karolan asked next.

"I don't speak to the slaves, human or griffin," Vor answered. "I'm not supposed to."

"Do you know their names?"

"No. I don't think anyone has bothered to ask. That's enough; dump those out into the water."

Karolan followed her directions. "This is going to be a salve for burns, you said?"

"Since we're going to try to roast the mage-stone node, I figured we might end up needing it. Now scrape all the flesh out of these pieces of aloe vera."

"How can we free the griffins?"

Vor huffed. "You don't give up."

"Not about this."

"I'm not sure," she confessed. "My master has plans for them. If he can get Weldom to send a drake swarm, and since the mines are almost played out, he intends to let the drakes learn how to fight griffins by practicing on the slaves."

Karolan dropped a piece of aloe. "We can't let that happen."

"Pick that up; it's getting dirty. I don't want to see that happen, either. I don't know yet how to avoid it. You think deactivating the collar on that one little griffin did it any good?"

"I need to deactivate them all," Karolan bemoaned, now picking bits of grit off the aloe.

Vor ground methodically at her own mortar. "I'm glad you know how; I don't. If we get a chance, we could lead them out, and maybe send them into the forest. Their wings are cut, so they can't fly."

"There will be other griffins coming," Karolan whispered, "when it's time."

"Hawkwind: the name you told that little griffin?"

"She's my mom," Karolan explained. "She got me out during the invasion, with the three other kids, including Jessika. She was a Feathyr. If those griffins were Feathyrs, too, some of them might recognize her name. It might raise their morale."

Vor pondered that for a while. "It might, but I hope the overseers don't notice. The other two kids, one was Rikah, right, that blacksmith's son?"

"That's right," he confirmed.

"Who is the other?"

The rhythm of his mixing broke. "A girl: Kassandra." His voice caressed her name.

"Ah," Vor murmured.

Karolan said nothing more for a few minutes, but stared fixedly into his bowl, blending the crushed herbs, aloe goo, water, and some arrowroot powder.

"What happened to her?" Vor asked at length.

"What do you mean?" he asked too quickly.

She took some time to reply. "She wasn't at the cottage when I attacked with the soldiers, was she?"

"No, she doesn't fight."

"Not everyone need fight," Vor soothed.

"She's peaceful," he said, glowering at his mixture. "She's a child of the forest. She sort of left us, us other three. She's different. It's hard to explain."

Vor didn't press.

"She's like my sister," Karolan added.

Right, a sister: Vor suspected there was more to his feelings than that. She didn't expect anything useful could come from making him talk more about it, though. Dropping the topic, she directed him in finishing off the salve and jarring it.

"Down here," she said, pulling up a hatch in one corner of the stillroom. "The salve won't keep for long, but this cellar is cooler."

It wasn't much of a cellar, being only a couple feet deep and about as wide, but it was big enough for temporarily storing items that needed to be kept cold to retain their potency or prevent spoilage. They put their two new pots of salve into it and Vor closed it again.

"Here, next I'll show you a numbing salve," Vor went on. "It can be used to stop itching from bites or skin rashes, or to soothe pain from any superficial injury."

She walked him through the steps, and an hour later stashed two new jars of the medicine in the tiny cellar beside the burn salve. As they were cleaning up she felt the unmistakable tug of Altare summoning her.

"Leave that," she said, already going for the doorway. "My master is calling us, or well, me, but you should probably come, too."

She saw Karolan's hand make the wiggle that meant the sound barrier was down, and then he was on her heels as she followed the direction of the magical pull. It led her to her master's public office: the same one where she'd first encountered Karolan when he'd come to the palace.

Everyone else was already there. The three old master mages were crammed in shoulder to shoulder along one set of bookcases. Altare and Colby were both sitting behind the desk, and beside the desk stood Giri and Milsa. Once Vor and Karolan came in, standing between the door and desk for lack of anywhere else, the room was cozily crowded.

State Wizard Colby stood, twitching his robes into hanging straight as he did.

"Excellent, we are all here," he said flatly.

Vor glanced at her master. His expression was carefully closed to reveal nothing, but from long experience of reading him, she thought he was angry and—could it be—scared?

"It is clear that there is no point in having the king or princess here for this," Colby went on, "as the real power that runs Northborn is in the room already."

He made a gentle unfurling gesture towards Altare. No one disputed it.

"Not that there is anything wrong with that," the Wizard said with a little quirk of his lips. "Weldom has been pleased with the results of the conquest. Northborn has been a useful and loyal appendage to the home country. Situations change and evolve, however, and it is high time for an official assessment of Northborn's needs and responsibilities. My associates and I have gathered much data here, but we have not the power to make executive decisions. For that, we must return to Weldom and bring our findings before the High Ministers."

The three elderly master mages were nodding and muttering along in apparent agreement. Altare had made no move. Vor and Karolan likewise waited with bated breaths to hear more.

"We will depart tomorrow morning," Wizard Colby said. "We will be depriving you of your leader's presence for a few days at least." He glanced down at Altare with a smile. "But I assure you he will be returned in good time and good health."

Vor smacked down her excitement with a stick. There would never be a better opportunity to break into his rooms and fry his mage-stone lode—there was no way he could take it with him. Beside her, Karolan made a soft sound of protest.

"Focus on your potion-making skills until I return," Altare told him immediately. "It will not be long and I will resume your lessons."

"You can depend on us," Master Eriducus pronounced. "We will stay the course until your return."

"Good man," Colby praised.

Master Chirolen waved a hand. "You'll not leave one of your associates to help, until Altare's return?"

Vor wanted to slap the man silent.

"I think it unnecessary," Colby remarked. "It will be a short time, and despite some concerns about marauding griffins, I've seen your shielding and your military seems competent."

"Vor," Altare murmured, and she met his gaze. "I will depend on you to keep the rest of the palace wards running while I'm gone."

"Yes, Master," she said, although not without a wince of trepidation.

He nodded. "It's a lot of work, and will require more energy, but I trust you can handle it. I will renew everything tonight. With a little luck, I will return before they need another recharge. I will leave orders with the guards to post extra sentries in addition. There is nothing else I will require of you in my absence, except your usual duties. Keep the mines on schedule. If any administrative problems arise, Masters Chirolen, Eriducus, and Ulver will handle them."

The three mages bowed their heads in agreement.

That was all he would require of her? Vor thought of Altare's enslaved girls, trapped in their tiny rooms behind doors carved with flowers. How would they eat? Perhaps he meant to put them into a sleep of hibernation, wherein their bodies could survive for days without food or water. Or maybe he had some other plan for them. She hoped he didn't intend to let them die of thirst. No, he wouldn't waste the energy resource like that. Vor hoped he wasn't planning instead to kill them all tonight—however many he currently had; she didn't know the count.

"I have faith that Northborn's needs will be answered appropriately and timely," Wizard Colby resumed.

"As do I," Altare concurred firmly.

Colby smiled tightly. "That is all. I expect the evening meal will be ready soon?"

Altare stood. "Momentarily," he affirmed.

"I think we know the way now," Colby said. "We shall see you all there."

***

The three Weldom wizards left the room together, but Altare swiftly made a negating gesture before anyone else could speak. "Not here," he muttered. "Vor, Karolan, with me."

They left the three old mages behind, Altare striding swiftly, almost running, to one of his workrooms. He threw the shields back up once they were inside and spun to face his apprentices.

"Will you come back, Master?" Vor asked immediately.

"I fully intend to, but—"

"They're not going to hurt you?" Karolan blurted.

"Don't interrupt me, boy," Altare growled. "I think they suspect us of planning to secede from Weldom. That is, of course, not our intention and I have tried to reassure them of it, but they see me marrying the princess and eventually becoming king as a threat. I shall have to convince the High Ministers that we intend to remain an obedient tributary state."

"Do you think they will agree with that?" Vor asked.

Altare shook his head. "I think they want to bring us fully into the fold, abolish Northborn as it stands, and make it just another prefecture of Weldom, under the direct governing of the High Ministers."

"Would that be bad for us?" Karolan asked.

The master mage shrugged. "We'd no longer be in power. I don't think they'd kill us. There might be places for us among the wizards employed by the government. Our lives would change dramatically, I expect, but that is life: change."

Despite his confident words, he looked shaken, and not at all pleased by the prospects. Altare took a deep breath and ran his hand over his face.

"There's a chance they might leave the former royalty as a sort of figurehead, without any actual power," he added. "Whether they'll allow me to wed the so-called princess is a different question."

Vor lowered her voice. "They must realize the princess is an imposter?"

"They know," her master muttered. "I recounted the acquisition of the real princess and the loss of her in my missive. I had to tell them where this one came from, and they can see she's enchanted." He shrugged. "That doesn't bother them, at least not that they've told me."

"The princess is fake?" Karolan gaped convincingly.

"I never told you?" Altare grunted. "Yes, a fake. I had the real one for a while. My apprentice allowed her to escape."

The glare he turned on Vor was of considerably reduced fervor from the usual; her master had larger concerns on his mind.

"Have you told them about the signs of hostility from the true princess and griffins unknown?" Vor pressed.

"Yes. I had to explain why we want a drake swarm. They don't seem to be taking the danger seriously, however." He slapped a fist into his other palm. "Do they think I would turn them back against Weldom? They have dozens of swarms. What would one be able to do against their might? I can't quite figure out what they are planning, or what they think will happen."

"Perhaps they don't know," Karolan offered tentatively. "That's why they want you to go talk to the High Ministers?"

Altare stood, tugging at his goatee. "They hide much of what they do and don't know," he grumbled. "They evade my questions and turn them around on me." His eyes darted back to his apprentices. "As long as the griffins don't attack while I'm gone, I expect you should be able to handle everything. The country is largely self-running, at least for a matter of days. If there is an attack," he grimaced, "you may be in trouble. Those three old mages aren't worth much. The army is strong, however. As the dead and dying start piling up, there will be plenty of free energy around. Use it. Send it back into the teeth of the attackers."

"Yes, Master," Vor said quickly. "Master, what if you do not return?"

He gazed at her seriously. "If they decide to kill me, they might purge above and below. That's the tradition. That means they'll go after my masters and my apprentices—root and branch."

Vor did not have to fake the shiver that went through her. Where could she hide from wizards as powerful as Colby and his fellows? Trying to fight them was out of the question. It would be like a worm trying to fight the bird that plucked it from the grass.

"Of course they might not, and I don't think I have done anything so disloyal that they would have cause," Altare was swift to point out. "However, it's possible I won't return because they choose to keep me there. Cooperate with whomever they send back here, and it will all work out."

Vor didn't think he sounded confident, but she wasn't going to say it aloud.

"Do you have any further questions?" he asked. "I have much to do to-night, and we should get to dinner now."

"No, Master," Vor and Karolan murmured.

"Let's go then."

***

The dinner was quiet. Since the wizards had announced their decision, there seemed little point in talking further. Vor, seated between her master and Karolan, said nothing. Eriducus quizzed the wizards with names of other wizards he'd known back in Weldom, ten years ago, asking after their statuses. Colby was able to answer some of his enquiries.

Milsa and Giri muttered together a little, but to Vor it didn't seem like they were getting along very well. After some particularly sharp but still inaudible exchange they both glanced at Vor, and she had the urge to retort that she hadn't done anything to either of them. After that, however, her master gave her a glare, too, and she had to fight the instinct to snarl at him. His eyes narrowed, suggesting he would have slapped her had they not been in company.

Vor turned back to her food. She was heartily sick of him and couldn't wait for him to leave so she could start undermining him in preparation for killing him. Beside her, Karolan was chatting with Chirolen, trying to find out what plans he and the other two masters had for the next day. Vor hid a wince and thought he was being too obvious. She kicked him under the table and he stopped.

As the meal concluded, Altare again invited Colby for a drink, and this time the State Wizard agreed.

"Perhaps we all could use such a diversion," Milsa spoke up, "after such a long day."

The lady wizard flicked a glance at Karolan and Vor. Altare opened his mouth to reply, but Giri cut him off.

"I actually, was hoping I might make use of your training salle," he announced. "I find myself with an excess of physical energy."

There were a few raised eyebrows, and Milsa narrowed her eyes at him.

"I would need a guide, however," Giri added.

"Vor," her master snapped. "See to Wizard Giri's needs."

She seethed inside, almost trembling from it. "Yes, Master."

"Karolan," Altare went on, "join us. Masters, will you come, too?"

"Eh?" Ulver croaked.

"Come along," Eriducus sighed, prodding his fellow.

180

A slight glance passed between Colby and Giri. Vor would have missed it if she hadn't been watching the latter. Her anxiety mounted, but so did her perturbation. She and Karolan were being split up—him going where Milsa went, and her being assigned to Giri. Everyone stood, putting down their napkins or taking final sips of their tea. Then the larger group moved off, leaving Vor with her unexpected and unwanted after-dinner task.

"Your master has a way with words," Giri remarked once they were alone.

Vor held her tongue.

"Don't worry," he said softly. "I won't invite you to share my company again, not unless you've changed your mind."

Now she was practically biting her tongue. There was an invitation right there, the infuriating man.

"Would you show me to the salle?"

"You went on a tour of our military facilities with General Krant today," she said narrowly. "You know perfectly well where it is."

He didn't react to her combative tone, except to smile a little. "Of course I do. Would you show me to it?"

Confusion bubbled in her chest. He just waited for her.

"Fine," she spat at last. "This way."

Giri kept up with her easily, able to match her pace with no trouble since they were about the same height. She tried to be quick, but without expressing that she wanted this duty done with as rapidly as possible. From the dinning room, down the hall, two turns, out the side door into the main courtyard—

"You enjoy being a mage?" he asked suddenly from slightly behind her, as the darkness of the evening closed in around them.

"I do," she replied without hesitation.

"You're learning much from your master?"

A little snort escaped her. "Yes."

If Giri detected the many layers of that one word, he made no indication. "How long have you been with him?"

"Since I was eleven."

"That's young. In Weldom we are generally not apprenticed until a few years older than that. I've been with Colby since I was fifteen, when my family brought me to the capital to begin my training."

"He took me off the street," she admitted.

Giri walked in silence for a few moments and was able to catch up with her as her stride faltered a little. "Then this is your home, and he is like your father."

Vor reacted before she thought better of it, darting a look at the wizard, and said nothing. In the dark, his face lit only by distant lamplight, it was hard to see his expression, but she had the sudden suspicion he was fishing for something.

"He's not my father," she muttered.

"I'm sorry we'll have to take him away for a while."

This time, she kept her gaze straight ahead. "It is no trouble."

"Hm, well, good then."

They reached the side door to the salle, and Vor stopped. Lights still shone from within, out through the big unglazed windows, and she could see her companion clearly again.

"As you requested," she said archly.

His delighted smile, like when she'd probed his energies the night before, surprised her. For a few moments he stood facing her, and her sense of unease swelled.

"I wish we didn't make you so uncomfortable," he offered. "You know we mean you no harm?"

She narrowed her eyes again. "I don't know that."

He seemed to deflate a little. "Your master won't be harmed either, while he's away."

Vor blinked at him, and finally settled on, "good."

"I'm sure you'll take care of things so you're ready for his return."

His gaze locked on hers and the air was suddenly charged. He seemed to be waiting for something—her reply, of course.

Vor managed to nod. "Naturally," she demurred. "I'll be ready for his return."

A smile started to creep onto Giri's face, but then it was swept off.

"Thank you for your assistance in guiding me, Mistress Vor," he said.

"I trust you can find your own way back."

"Yes."

"May you have a pleasant evening then," she farewelled stiffly, thinking of what he'd done the previous evening.

"It will be as it is," he shrugged. "I wish only for some solitude with my thoughts. I hope your evening is pleasant as well."

Did that mean he wasn't going to be bedding one of the servants again? Why not? Was that not his habit then, and the previous night had been some kind of exception? Or this night was an exception? He was indeed perplexing. Vor realized suddenly that she'd been standing there in silence for several breaths, scrutinizing him. Giri hadn't made comment, and did not seem upset by it. On the contrary, he seemed to have some kind of delight hidden just under his skin.

She scolded herself silently. What did any of it matter to her anyway? Vor gave a tight nod and turned to go. "Goodnight."

His soft voice seemed to follow her back into the darkness. "Goodnight."

***

It was morning. Wizard Giri was drawing a big circle on the pavement of the courtyard, with three rows of complex runes around it. Milsa and Colby already stood within it, explaining to Altare the teleportation spell they intended to use. They had their luggage with them, too. It seemed that on their arrival they had just transported themselves and then later on worked together with a distant mage in Weldom to send the bags over. This time, they'd be taking them along, since none of the Northborn mages were trained in communicating over such long distances magically or in teleporting objects across whole countries.

Giri finished the last of the runes for the circle and came to hand the fat stick of chalk back to Vor, looking only a little worn from all the work done on his hands and knees on the hard paving stones. Worn or not, she envied him his ability to participate in such a magical work.

"I'd like to learn the teleportation spell, too, sir," she told him. "Perhaps I could send your luggage to you."

"And I'd love to teach it to you, but there is not the time," the wizard told her with a smile. He took her free hand, bent over it, and kissed it as he'd done before. "Teleportation is a challenging skill. Another day, Mistress Vor Hearthsraven, for I am sure we'll meet again."

Somehow, this time his gallantry didn't bother her so much. That they would meet again, however, she wondered about. He didn't know of her plot against her master, and after that was completed, she might very well need to flee. Giri suddenly leaned in, mouth nearly touching her ear, and Vor started to pull away.

"No," he whispered, "listen. Pretend I am telling you something funny."

Heart pounding, Vor managed an awkward smile, but her master wasn't looking their way anyway.

Giri's breath rose gooseflesh on her skin. "We know you plot against your master. Keep smiling."

Her expression nearly faltered, and panic bubbled up inside her. Giri continued.

"He doesn't know. He can't see what's in front of his face with all his other troubles flying about his head. We approve, and have seen enough to know

183

it is inevitable between you two. Do your best, or perhaps, your worst." He chuckled. "But know this: when he returns, he will not come alone. An attack against him may be misconstrued as an attack against those who accompany him. Be ready, for nor does Weldom care much if you fail and he kills you—although I would prefer to see you the victor. You have more to offer Weldom."

He touched her shoulder lightly. "Now smile and wish me good journey."

Giri straightened up.

Vor smiled. "May you have a safe journey," she said clearly.

His grin widened, and he transferred his gaze to Karolan, who stood a few feet away, glowering at him. "Do find something productive to do with your free time," he winked.

At last, Giri released Vor's hand—only at which point did she realize she'd been holding onto his in return. She stared at it for a moment as her fingers cooled, feeling as though it had disobeyed her, but somehow not angry at it. Giri went to join his fellow wizards and Altare. The latter were brimming with energy, which they had obviously acquired the night before. Only Giri wasn't shining with magical overflow. The others had arrived at breakfast so powered up they almost floated.

It was an interesting observation to Vor; it seemed Giri had not made use of Pella—or any other servant girl—to renew his energy, as she had suspected from their conversation. Perhaps he really had been going to the salle to try to recharge, and not just as a ploy to get Vor alone and talk to her. For she was certain that his announcement to her that they knew her plans had only come about because he'd inferred meaning from what she'd told him the night before. On the one hand, she berated herself for not having tighter control. On the other, she found she actually didn't mind that he knew. Perhaps that was why she hadn't had tighter control; some part of her had wanted to tell him. Some part of her trusted him. Why? It was so confusing it made her lightheaded.

"I believe we are prepared," Wizard Colby announced as Giri joined him.

Vor took Karolan's wrist and encouraged him to step back from the edge of the circle.

"A full report," Altare ordered before they moved out of speaking range.

She didn't bother to reply, not even with an extra scowl. Colby had already begun the spell and the other three quickly cottoned on, taking hands and focusing. Vor could sense massive amounts of energy moving, but there wasn't much to see visually: just a little breeze that lifted their hair and clothing. Then, as though they'd been painted on a bed sheet that was suddenly snatched away by a storm, they and their luggage were gone.

Beside her, Karolan let out a breath. "What did he say?"

"Not now."

The three old master mages had come to see them off, too. Now, they began to move, grumbling and muttering, back towards the door into the public wing. As they departed, Amlee came out with three pages trailing her, burdened with buckets and mops. She stopped beside Vor.

"May we clean up, Mistress?" she asked diffidently.

"Yes, go ahead," Vor nodded.

Amlee made a gesture, and the three pages went to work on the chalked circle with their mops.

"Is there any cause for worry, Mistress?" Amlee asked.

Vor wasn't sure how to answer. "I don't think so," she said at last. "Not for you or the servants, at least."

"For you?" Amlee lowered her voice with concern.

"Don't worry about me," Vor ordered shortly. "Thanks for cleaning up."

Karolan paced her eagerly as she turned towards the private wing, passing through the pleasure garden on the way. The day was turning out to be a bright one. Every flower in the garden seemed to be in bloom, so they moved through a cloud of floral perfume on their way to the door. Vor clenched and unclenched her hands, eyes darting around anxiously.

He was really gone. Altare was gone, leaving her alone for the first time in—well, she'd been alone when she'd gone to fetch the princess, but other than that—how long, she couldn't remember. The ominous threat of him being around, that at any moment he might stick his head through the doorway of whatever room she was in, might summon her at any time, had abruptly lifted. She couldn't quite enjoy it yet; some part of her couldn't believe it was true.

"We have a lot to do," Karolan muttered as they passed through the door into the wing, blocking out the sunlight and leaving the scent of flowers behind them.

"Yes," she agreed shortly.

"We should get to it as quick as we can. Who knows when he'll come back?"

"Yes," she repeated. "We need to get his magic out of me, and then gather energy to go break into his rooms and destroy his mage-stone, and then go do it."

"And I need to send a message to my people."

Vor stopped walking. "What?"

Karolan stopped, too, a few steps ahead, and looked back at her. "I need to tell them it's time."

"Time for what?" She walked up to him, incredulous. "Are you really talking about an invasion, an attack to take back the country? You heard what he said; the army is strong. You'd better have an army of your own, even without the drake swarm here."

"The plan isn't to fight the army," he said quickly.

She folded her arms. "And how do you intend to avoid them?"

"Sneak in," he shrugged.

"And do what?"

"Well, now that Weldom and those wizards are involved, it changes things," he winced. "But the plan was to get the king out, and any griffin slaves, and anyone else who wants to come—and this is all assuming Altare is dead—and then see what the army would do. We'd send emissaries, and see if they're reasonable about restructuring the government."

Vor stared at him for a few moments, and finally shrugged. "You know, I don't really care what you do with the kingdom."

She began striding past him, and Karolan reached out and caught her arm, stopping her. "What do you want, Vor? What do you care about?"

"I want him gone," she said after a moment of thought. "Then I want a place I can study, a place I can learn, and have quiet, and do simple things that accomplish some useful purpose."

Karolan blinked at her as though that wasn't what he'd expected her to say.

"Let's go," she urged. "If you want to send a message, fine. We'll do that, too: all the more reason not to dally. The day is already too short."

She headed towards the workrooms deep behind the common area of the private wing.

"What will you need to send the message?" she asked.

"Well," he prevaricated, "I was hoping you would help."

"I'll help," she agreed. "I presume you'll be sending it to that griffin mage?"

"No, actually, um, Vor, stop?"

She halted and looked back. He was several feet behind her now.

Karolan pointed vaguely back the way they'd come. "It's not a magical message. It's verbal. I couldn't risk bringing a contact stone or something here. I was afraid he'd sense it."

"Verbal?" she echoed.

"I was going to ask Amlee to do it, but since we're working together now, I want to let them know that, so I think you should do it, and I don't want to arouse suspicion from the guards or anything, which might happen if I go do it—"

Vor planted her hands on her hips. "Just tell me. What do you need me to do?"

Karolan pulled out his knife.

Chapter 17
The Cat's Away

Yes, Rikah was there and Rikan was busy: perfect. Vor continued her approach. Her nerves danced a little.

"Master blacksmith," she greeted as she came within easy hailing distance of the forge.

Rikan was in the midst of working on something. The forge was hot and Vor felt its heat even from a distance. Still, he put down his hammer and started to go to her, bowing as he came.

"My apologies for the interruption," she said. "I have a small repair to ask for."

She held up Karolan's knife, showing the bent tip.

Rikan nodded. "Aye, Mistress. I can fix that."

"Please, continue with your work. I'll leave it and come back tomorrow."

"As milady wishes. Rikah, take the lady's order," Rikan said.

With another bow he went back to his forge, clearly eager to strike while the iron was hot. Rikah set down his current carving project and stood, brushing curls of wood from his apron. Vor moved deeper into the shop to meet him, hiding her relief that it was all working just right. She put the knife down on the table, luring Rikah to come close enough to pick it up.

"What happened to it?" he asked, sounding a trifle shocked.

Vor huffed through her nose. "He got it stuck in a man's backbone while blood letting for power," she lied outrageously.

Rikah's gaze snapped back up to hers, his expression showing clearly that he didn't know whether to believe her or not. Vor stared firmly into his eyes.

"Interesting weather we're having lately," she muttered.

The skin around his eyes whitened. It wasn't interesting weather. It was ordinary summer weather.

"Indeed," he replied, after swallowing. "What do you think of it?"

He'd given the reply, word for word what Karolan had told her it should be. She found herself having trouble swallowing, too, and told herself it was the heat off the forge making her sweat. Still, she did not break her gaze from Rikah's.

"Looks like rain," she whispered.

He seemed to have difficulty taking a breath, and she saw a smile trying to fight its way onto his face. Vor grit her teeth and shook her head just slightly in warning. He finally inhaled, and nodded, keeping his countenance neutral.

"Two days," he said. "I think we'll have rain in two days."

"Two days," she repeated. "I'll be back tomorrow for the knife."

Rikah bowed, deeply. "Yes, Mistress."

***

"Two days," Vor reported to Karolan.

"That's quicker than I'd hoped. Hawkwind and the others must already be prepared. They have high hopes for me."

"I just hope my master doesn't return before then," she worried.

"We should do it tomorrow," he suggested. "I'll get his mark out of you today. Now."

It was sudden, but Vor had to agree; they could not afford to tarry.

"Let's go to a workroom."

She led the way. Karolan wouldn't be working explosive magic: subtle magic, rather. They didn't need a powerful workroom, and Vor took him to one that she used a lot, and not one frequented by her master. Vor bent to drawing a circle.

"I have to go get a piece of wood, to transfer the contamination into. I'll be back, soon, I hope," Karolan said.

Vor nodded and continued with the circle. She was nervous and her hands shook a little. Would Karolan actually be able to do it? He was younger and less powerful than she was, but if Craduticus had really shown him how, then maybe it would work. Vor herself had put magic into Jessika, but she'd never intended to remove it, and it would have faded in time without renewal. Her master's mark in her was everlasting—or he was renewing it without her noticing—and she'd never been able to track it down, but she knew it was there.

"Do you know where in your body he has his magic?" Karolan asked as he reentered and shut the door.

"No. When he's exerted himself to summon or restrain me, it seems to affect me everywhere. You'll have to check every inch."

Karolan set down a lump of wood as big as his head. He must have raided the palace woodpile. He joined her with another piece of chalk but looked impatient. "I don't think we need the circle. The technique Cray showed me was simple, just delicate."

188

Vor shook her head. "I don't know if my master will be able to feel it. I'm making a shielding circle, to cut us off from him. Draw more fire runes."

"But when I'm done and you emerge—"

"If you've done a thorough job, when I emerge he won't be able to sense me at all, although of course I don't know if he can right now or not. If he can sense me now, as soon as this circle is active and I go in it, I should vanish to him. He won't know what happened to me, if I died, or what. When I step back out, it will be the same, with his magic gone from my body I'll still be undetectable." She drew one last rune with a bit of a flourish. "However, if he can sense me right now, and you start removing the magic bit by bit, he will sense that, and know what's happening, and be alerted. If I just vanish behind these shields and never reappear, he should be more confused."

"I think maybe I understand," Karolan muttered, going to stand inside the circle.

Vor stepped in, too, and then knelt from inside to hold her hands out near the chalked circle.

"I'm putting up the shields," she informed.

Karolan stayed quiet for the next couple minutes, letting her work. Vor wasn't certain how exactly her master connected to her. She only hoped Karolan could root it all out. Likewise, she wasn't sure what sort of shields would cut the connection. Barriers to the mind relied on life and air energy. Fire shields made the best barriers to magic, since it would absorb and disperse it. She put up several layered shields, hoping it was enough.

"I'll feel rather silly if he actually can't sense me at all from this distance," she remarked, "going to all this trouble."

Vor turned to face Karolan. He'd taken a seat to wait for her.

"This might take a while," he said. "You should probably just lie down."

She complied, lying stretched out on her back: now wishing she'd brought a pillow. Karolan moved around to her feet.

"I need you to relax and take down as many of your personal shields as you can," he told her. "It's harder to work this through shields."

That was like a knight removing his armor during battle, but Karolan wasn't an enemy—not anymore. Vor closed her eyes and began the silent, internal techniques that would dismiss her shields. She had a few layers. The outer ones were easy, but the deepest one, closest to her skin, was near instinctual now, after having it in place for nearly a decade. She tried. She truly did, but she didn't have the ability to bring it down.

She had to stop and take several deep breaths, putting herself into a deeper trance. Karolan waited patiently for her. She tried again, but it was no good. She already felt psychically naked with the others gone. Even with her eyes shut, not focusing on him, Karolan's aura shone with brilliance. He was beautiful, but she feared if her innermost shield did come down, his nearness would give her magical sunburn.

"I can't," she confessed.

He probed her a little with his own energies. "That's alright. I think I can manage."

"I'm sorry," she muttered. "I can try to thin it temporarily in the area you're working."

"That might be enough. I'm going to start."

Vor kept her eyes shut, and he didn't touch her, but she felt his attention like the heat from a fire, starting on her right foot. It stayed there long enough that it started to hurt, just as if she'd been too close to a real fire. She tried to bear it.

"This is insidious," Karolan murmured.

The heat began slowly moving up her ankle. Her toes thankfully cooled.

"There's nothing overt," he went on. "He's left these tiny little traces, like little bits of thread, so tiny, but lots of them, everywhere. It's different from what you did to Jessika. You left obvious hooks that Starbright had little trouble removing, but these—"

She tried not to shiver. "How can you be sure you're finding them all?"

"They light up," he said grimly. "Your own energies respond to the touch of mine in a certain way, but those little threads do not. Then I make a sort of net that passes through you and sweeps up them."

"I see," Vor grunted, feeling helpless.

The heat had moved to her shin, approaching her knee.

"It's not your fault he did this to you, Vor," Karolan murmured, "and not your fault that you can't remove it yourself. It's like a horse can't seek out and remove its own ticks, but someone else can."

But she still felt like it was her fault. Vor struggled to keep her face expressionless. Karolan's ministrations reached her thigh.

"He's also got them feeding off your own energy," he went on softly, "so he doesn't have to renew them. You'll be more powerful once they're all gone."

"Get them all," she whispered.

"I will."

Once he came to her hip, he left off her right leg and went over to her left foot, to begin again.

"He probably snuck them into you one at a time," Karolan postulated. "It wouldn't take much. He might not have even needed to touch you. Over years, even at the rate of one a day, it would explain having this many, and with this many, it would be enough to control you."

"He asked my permission," Vor said, "once, shortly after I came here."

"He asked you if he could leave magic in you?" Karolan asked incredulously.

"Not exactly," she clarified. "He asked my permission to take control of my inner sight, to show me what he wanted me to see. I consented. I think that was the first time."

"You willfully accepted the touch of his power," Karolan caught on.

"After that, there was no longer an instinctual resistance."

"So he could slip a bit of contamination into you here and there without you consciously noticing."

Vor nodded. "I had to do the same with Jessika. I had to ask her permission to use my magic on her, to cleanse her back. She gave it, and then I had access to her, not only to heal her, but allowing me to leave residue in her skin, too. Of course it was easier since she's not a mage."

Karolan had reached her left hip now. He moved to her left hand and started working towards her shoulder.

"I'm doing the easiest parts first," he explained. "These threads are clustered more commonly around your nerves. Your torso, and of course your head, have bigger, denser nerves and probably more threads. That may take longer."

"Take as long as you need," Vor said. "You can borrow my energy, if you get low."

With her shields so thin, she sensed his smile with some measure of shock. She didn't have to open her eyes to confirm it.

"I'm doing fine," he murmured.

He reached her left shoulder, got up, switched to her other side, and started on her right hand. For a while, he worked in silence, and Vor tried not to wallow in self-recrimination for letting her master do this to her.

"You know," she mused as Karolan neared her right shoulder, "maybe I need to check you for the same thing."

"No," he replied. "He hasn't gotten any into me."

"He said something like that, a few days ago, that he couldn't summon you yet, but it's still possible—"

Karolan chuckled a little. "He's been trying, but I've never given my verbal consent, or nonverbal."

"Nonverbal?"

"Of course," he said. "Cray told me some about it. For most people, giving verbal permission will make the soul comply, usually, but it doesn't have to be verbal."

Vor pondered that in silence for a few moments.

"After all," Karolan said softly, as he reached her right shoulder and relented, the magical heat fading. "You never gave me verbal permission to touch your energies this closely, yet I can."

"I asked you to do this," she reminded him.

"Yes, but," he paused, and Vor opened her eyes to look at him, sitting on his knees with a little pink touching his cheeks. "You gave me nonverbal permission—and likewise I to you—long before that."

"What are you talking about?"

He rubbed his forehead, hiding his face behind his palm. "When people touch, souls touch, if it's consensual, without needing verbal permission."

He glanced at her, at her uncomprehending eyes, and turned pinker.

"When we kissed, the first time," he fumbled, "our energies touched. You didn't notice?"

"I hit you," she gritted out. "I resisted. I told you I wouldn't do that with you."

"Your soul had other ideas, and it didn't resist. I know; I felt it. You would have, too, if your mind hadn't gotten in the way. That's why I didn't care that you hit me. I knew what you really wanted."

Had she really wanted that? Vor turned her head away and closed her eyes again, feeling her face heat up. Karolan went on, his voice a susurration as soft as the wind.

"I knew you only hit me because you were scared at what you were feeling. That's all you knew, all that your master ever taught you: to attack anything that frightens you, anything beyond your control. That's why he hits you."

"Please, just continue with the cleansing," she asked.

The heat of his magical attention appeared by her right hip and began spreading into her core. For a little while, he was silent, and Vor started to relax again.

"I think that's how your master knew," Karolan muttered then, breaking her light trance, "the next time he saw us together. He could tell we'd given each other permission and our souls touched freely."

The cleansing heat soaked into her low belly, and between the location of his working and the topic of conversation, the encounter was suddenly turning intimate. Without most of her shields, she could even feel her soul responding to his—extending curiously in his direction to touch—just as he'd said it did.

"Vor," he grunted, "can you calm down a little? Think about latrines or something: not about me. It's making it hard to focus."

She almost grunted, too. It hurt to do it, somehow, but she forced her mind to consider the dumping and scrubbing of chamber pots, shaking rat droppings out of her meager bedding when she'd been living on the streets, or cleaning up blood and offal after a magical sacrifice.

"That's better, but it's making you tense. Don't bring your shields back up," Karolan requested.

She hissed through her teeth and summoned up the vision of sitting at peace in the garden, alone, watching birds. After a few moments, she thought she felt her energies calm. Karolan's focus had moved up to her waist by then.

"This is going well," he offered, "but there's still a lot left."

"Take your time," Vor said.

Concentrating on staying serene, she nearly drifted off to sleep as the magical heat permeated her core, up her torso, out to join the cleared area of her shoulders, and then into her throat and neck. She was in an actual trance by the time she sensed Karolan move and come to sit behind her head, a knee by each of her ears. He set his hands lightly on her forehead.

"This will be the hardest," he whispered, "but you're doing great. Stay like this."

Vor focused in that soft way that was not quite focusing to keep herself low in the self-imposed trance. Seeing nothing but the flowers of the garden, her thoughts were nearly silent as Karolan delicately insinuated his search among them. There were a few times her energies flinched, as he pushed through a bit too abruptly, but each time he would slow in response, trying to be gentler.

How much time passed Vor didn't know. When at last Karolan drew his hands off her head, she let her eyes flicker open. As she surfaced from her trace state, she found her body stiff and aching from the hard floor. Karolan moved away, and she turned her head to track him. She could see the exhaustion in his face.

"It's done," he whispered. "You're clear."

He touched the block of wood he'd set down earlier, and Vor saw fresh stains spread across it to join others. They discolored what had been an ordinary piece of light-colored wood, with irregular rings of white and black, like spreading mold or water damage. Karolan saw her looking.

"It's hawthorn," he explained. "I've been putting all the little threads into it. They had to go somewhere."

"A good choice: hawthorn will degrade them."

Karolan finished the transfer and wearily stretched out beside her on the floor. "Yes. It will just take a little while," he grunted.

"We could also burn it," she suggested.

"That would be quicker," he agreed.

His shoulder and hip touched hers, and he found her cool fingers, interlacing his with hers. After a moment, she frowned.

"You're dropping your shields," she observed.

"Just like you did."

"Why?"

Karolan rolled to his side, put his free arm around her, and nuzzled his face into her neck. "Do you feel it this time?" he mumbled, "or is your mind still in the way?"

Vor didn't answer aloud, but she let him pull her against him and the floor no longer felt so hard. Kisses led to caresses, and soon Vor had to slide her hand into Karolan's hair and pull his hungry mouth off her skin, while trying to fend off his roaming hands with her other.

"Not now," she said. "We're not ready for it."

"I'm ready for it," he countered.

There could be no doubt of that, but she tried to soften her rejection.

"We need a different circle, I haven't gathered what I need to try the doors, we have to get rid of the piece of hawthorn, and you're exhausted—"

"I'm not that tired," he refuted at once.

"Rain," she soothed, "please."

With a stifled growl, Karolan shoved to his feet.

"Tomorrow," Vor asserted.

"It's not fair," he accused, back towards her, tugging his clothing into place. "We want each other now."

Vor clenched her jaw. "Stand back. I'm going to incinerate the wood."

He waved a hand to indicate consent and walked to the far edge of the circle, still not looking at her. Vor focused, extended a few fingers, but didn't dare touch the contaminated hawthorn. Moments later the edges began to smoke and darken, and then licks of fire sprang up around it. It was shortly burning merrily, and while she watched, she methodically restored her shields. After a few minutes, the wood dissolved into a pile of cinders.

"You can break the circle now," Vor announced.

"And we may see if I really found every little bit of the stuff, or if he can sense you."

Karolan smudged the chalk with his foot, making the shields pop and dissipate. Vor waited with bated breath. She didn't know what might happen if Altare was able to tell, far away in Weldom, that she wasn't infested by his little residues of power anymore. After several breaths, there was no sign of any response from her absent master.

"I think you did it," she said. "Thank you."

"Right," Karolan grunted, and began walking to the door.

"Rain," she called, getting to her feet herself. "I'm sorry."

He stopped.

"You're right," she admitted. "It is unfair."

Karolan finally looked back over his shoulder at her. "I wish we were just ordinary people," he said. "What's going to happen when this is all over?"

"When what's over?"

"When we've destroyed the mage-stone and he's dead, and the country resettles itself or whatever, and we're free to pick our next path," he explained. "Are we going to pick the same path, you and I, and walk it together?"

"I don't know," Vor admitted, honestly.

"Do you want to pick the same path?"

She hesitated.

Karolan chose not to wait for her. He yanked open the door, exited, and slammed it behind him. Vor sat staring at it, still not sure what her answer would have been. Her mind couldn't get past this task that felt insurmountable. A large portion of her still thought it couldn't be done, that Altare could not be defeated. It was worth trying, but she seriously wondered if they would fail, and she would be killed, or tortured and enslaved like her master's flower girls. She couldn't imagine succeeding. She couldn't imagine a future path—either alone or with Karolan.

It was late afternoon. Vor cleaned up the circle and the cinders. Karolan wasn't in the kitchen when she went to get food. He didn't answer her knock when she went to his door—though whether he was inside or not, she didn't know. What she would have said to him had he answered, she didn't know either. She just knew she felt bad and wanted get rid of the feeling by getting his forgiveness.

Vor went to fetch the book on magical locks out of the mage library. Those books were supposed to stay there, but without Altare around, she didn't bother to follow the rule. She took it back to her room for refreshing her memory, and once she finished it, selected a few items she thought might be useful when they tackled the locked doors and the mage-stone node the next day. She tried not to think about what they were going to do to get the energy for it. When she went to bed she felt cold and alone.

A bath was the first order of the day. She also put on her best suit, because why not. Betrayal and conquest called for looking as good as possible—within the bounds of practicality. She asked the kitchen for a heartier breakfast than usual, including meat. When she carried it back to the dining room, she nearly collided with Karolan.

"Ah, hi," he said.

"Good morning," she replied. "Get some food," she added, before she could let any of her anxiety show.

Vor set to thoroughly devour her meal. Karolan joined her a few minutes later with approximately twice the amount of food she'd gotten: growing young men, just as Altare had implied. No one else was around.

"The master mages are probably sleeping late," she muttered.

He shrugged. "I would have, too, but I woke up with the dawn and figured it was probably best to get an early start."

"Breaking through those doors might take a while," Vor agreed.

"And destroying the mage-stone."

"Yes, and that. We might have to try several techniques. I'm still not sure how to do it, except to try fire."

"I know some fire spells," Karolan offered. "They just might burn down the palace."

"We'll figure it out."

"And hopefully he won't sense what we're doing and come back to stop us."

Vor swallowed a lump of fried potato and made an understatement. "Yes, that would be bad."

"So," Karolan murmured after a few minutes of silence. "What needs to happen first?"

Vor was soaking up the last of her eggs with a bit of bread, but eyed him sharply from under her brows. He met her gaze for a breath and then looked back to his rapidly emptying plate.

"I guess we'll need the power," she confirmed.

His eyes snapped back up.

"Finish your food," she admonished softly.

He swallowed down the last of his rashers so quickly she thought he might choke.

"I'm done," he announced.

"Let's go then," she murmured.

They left their dishes for the servants to clean up and rose from the table. Karolan followed intently. She led him to her room and as soon as they crossed the threshold he went to grab her, but she pushed him off.

"Not here. I just need to get a couple things," she explained.

He fidgeted, but she gave him no more attention. Vor grabbed a couple hand towels from her little bathroom—far inferior to the main bathing chamber downstairs that she'd made use of that morning—and pulled the top blankets off her bed.

"Hold these," she ordered, shoving the bundle into Karolan's arms. She picked up the book on mage locks and her bag of a few other items she thought might be useful. "Come on."

She made another stop at the stillroom—prompting Karolan to sigh impatiently. She fetched the little tubs of burn and pain salves they'd so recently made and added them to her bag. Now she headed for a workroom. If they were going to do this, she was going to ensure they got every drop of power, and a workroom with shields and a circle on the floor would make a big difference. She chose the biggest room, with some of the strongest shields, normally used for major works.

"Put them down in the middle," she instructed once they entered.

She set down her bag in a corner and went for the box of chalk. Karolan did as bade, not only dropping the blankets, but straightening and folding them into a thick pad. He put the two towels beside the blanket pad. Vor could hardly hold the chalk; her hands were shaking. She couldn't believe she was going to do this. Her body felt alternately cold and hot, as though it was confused as well.

"Here," she croaked, holding out a piece of chalk for Karolan to take. "As many containing and amplifying life runes as you know, and add in some others—air, water, earth, fire—just not light or dark. I don't think they'll help."

Karolan again obeyed silently. They worked their way around the circle, checking each other's runes and adding in duplicates in any empty space. Vor started to wonder if they were both putting it off. At last Vor sat back on her heels. They'd written three rings of runes, far more than was necessary for something like this—simple energy containment and amplification.

Vor plucked the chalk from Karolan's nerveless fingers and resolutely put it away, before kicking off her shoes, returning to the circle, and stepping inside. She held out a hand to him. Karolan looked around nervously, as if displeased by the setting, but he stepped out of his own shoes, took her hand, and stepped across the circle. His hands were cold. Vor brought them both to her chest and pressed them against her sternum.

"Rain," she said, and his gaze snapped onto hers. "It's alright."

He swallowed hard. "I didn't really want it like this," he muttered.

"We need all the power," Vor reminded him. "Don't forget to pick it up when it drops. I guess you haven't observed it before but—"

"I've seen what happens," he interrupted. "I shared a house with Jessika and Koki for several months. It was hard to miss, even from a different room."

"Jessika and," she stuttered.

"Koki, the man you knocked off the roof," Karolan explained. "He's a faun, it turns out, but I guess she likes him, so they've been," he trailed off.

"You saw the energy released when one or the other did it for the first time?" Vor persisted.

"No, but—"

"It's a lot, and we're both doing this for the first time," Vor plowed on. "You're not as accustomed to storing power like I am, but try to pick up as much as you can."

He nodded, looking down and away.

"Rain," she summoned.

He looked over at her through his long blonde lashes. His cheeks were coloring, but he didn't move. Vor stepped in closer. She tipped up her chin.

"Rain, kiss me," she requested.

Still he hesitated. Vor let go his hands and put hers on his chest. He licked his lips, but didn't otherwise react. After a moment, she ran one hand up to his neck, and one down, low, until he gasped. Vor pressed up onto her toes and he dove for her mouth.

There. Now she had him.

Chapter 18
Breaching the Barriers

Vor stood up, slowly, in stages. Karolan lay panting, although he hadn't done much work, so it couldn't have been from physical exertion. She winced, fetched the towels, and tossed one onto his belly. Her skin tingled and felt stretched tight—but not from the physical act, from all the energy she'd had to pick up and store away.

"Lot of good you are," she muttered under her breath.

She'd been stunned by the first double-explosion of power, far more than by the pinch of pain. Karolan apparently had been, too, but she'd still managed to suck in the energies, filling her depleted reservoirs with the dancing, shimmering stuff. She thought maybe he'd grabbed a bit, but if so it had been a handful compared to the bushels she contained. Just as she'd gotten it all handled, had come a second pulse, from Karolan—which she'd also had to find some empty storage space for—and then it had been over.

So much for that: as she'd expected, it hadn't felt good at all.

"Get up," she commanded. "Get dressed. We have locks to bust and a stone to destroy."

Vor walked across the circle; it didn't matter if it got smudged now. She cleaned up with her towel as best she could, fetched her clothes and began pulling them back on.

"Vor?" Karolan whimpered.

"What?" she snapped back.

"Come here," he begged, holding out his arms from where he still lay on his back atop the rumpled blankets.

Something twisted inside her chest. It hurt more than the pain in her groin, more than a lot of things she could remember.

"I'm holding my share of all this energy, plus most of yours," she gritted out. "I'm going to explode if I have to hold it much longer so I am going to go break through some doors. You can come help if you want."

She stepped back into her shoes. Karolan was slowly getting up, but he sat and put his head in his hands.

"Do you know where the first door into his rooms are?" she asked as she put some chalk in her pockets, fetched her bag and book, and checked that she still had her knife.

"Yes," Karolan grunted.

"I'll meet you there."

As Vor strode from the room, he lifted his head, watching her, but she didn't look back.

***

She tried to solve the door first, instead of blowing it up. It was a complicated mage-lock, but she wanted to save most of the power for the final door and the destruction of the mage-stone. After several minutes, her studying paid off. She sensed the series of clicks followed by the final dispersal of the power, and let her held breath go.

The door was now unlocked. It could physically be opened, but there was still a series of wards on it that had to be taken down. Altare had never intended anyone but him to touch them; if she went to grab the door handle, they would trigger: burning, freezing, blasting, or shocking her with lightning. Each one would have to be carefully defused before she opened the door.

Vor spun as she sensed someone approaching, but it was only Karolan:

dressed and determined, but also despondent.

"Good," she said. "I got the door lock, but I need help with the wards. Come here. Do you see how they're layered? I have to remove them one at a time, but touching the first one triggers the others. Can you insulate them as I go?"

He stood beside her and wordlessly raised a hand palm out. Vor sensed him set to work, doing as she'd asked. Defusing them was harder than distracting them and having them just target somewhere else as they went off, but she didn't want any of the other masters attracted to the ruckus. One by one, over the next half an hour, with Karolan running interference, she took down the layered wards.

"Now we can go inside," she said.

Vor led the way. She could remember vaguely where the heart of her master's domain was, and she only took one wrong turn. They had to keep stopping however, to remove what appeared to be random wards strung at varying intervals along the hallways. Vor had almost walked right into the first one before Karolan had grabbed her arm and pulled her back. Finally, they reached the hallway with the flower-carved doors, but with the delay to defuse the random hallway wards it had taken them an hour to get that far.

"What's in these?" Karolan asked, the first words he'd spoken, as they passed the decorated doors.

"My master's mind-broken sex slaves," Vor answered bluntly. "He uses them for power generation," she shrugged, "and probably for enjoyment, of some kind."

Karolan grimaced. "Shouldn't we let them out?"

"Not now. They're safer in there until we have the castle under control and he's dead. Besides, they wouldn't know to escape; they don't act without orders. Here, this is the door."

It was unchanged from the one time she'd seen it before: dark, dull red wood bound with stained grey metal. It was wide enough for her and Karolan to stand side-by-side before it, and taller than Karolan's height. They stood looking it over, testing it lightly with their mage senses. The longer they examined it, the more Vor's spirits sank.

"That's impossible," Karolan muttered.

"It's a right mess of a lock," Vor agreed. "I might have to try to blow it up, but the backlash will be immense, especially considering that the wards will go off at the same time."

"How do you want to approach it then?"

"Here." She handed him a chalk from her pocket. "Start drawing us a protective circle."

Karolan fell to work making a partial circle whose ends abutted the door-frame, while Vor reached out a hand to the door, not quite touching it. The lock itself was complicated, and it interlaced with at least a dozen wards. Her master definitely did not want anyone getting into this room. He must have put additional defenses on it before he left for Weldom. She couldn't imagine him taking all this stuff down and putting it all back up every time he wanted to use the room. Had he suspected someone would try to get in? Or was he just being overcautious?

Vor's mage senses suddenly shrilled alarm and she spun about just as Karolan cursed and did the same. She readied a bolt of power.

"No, no, Mistress Vor," Master Ulver pled, raising his age-spotted hands and showing empty palms.

The three old master mages had appeared at the end of the flower hallway. They all lifted their hands in pacification.

"We're here to help," Ulver insisted.

Karolan and Vor exchanged dubious glances.

"You're trying to defeat him, aren't you?" Master Chirolen spoke up. "That's what we want, too."

"That's what we've wanted for years," Master Eriducus concurred. "We always hoped you'd try it. You're stronger than even the three of us together, Mistress Vor."

"We never were overburdened with power," Ulver bemoaned.

"Just good at controlling the drakes," Chirolen nodded.

"But that's why he never killed us," Eriducus shrugged.

"Enough," Vor ordered. "Why should I trust you?"

"Have we ever hurt you?" Ulver asked.

She took a moment to think. "No," she admitted.

"You did conquer Northnest and kill a lot of people," Karolan interjected.

They bowed their heads. "We did," Eriducus agreed. "We were younger, and drunk with power."

"When Craduticus broke away," Ulver contributed, "he wanted us to help. He thought we could take down the crakrat together. We were too scared, but we did listen, and we've been thinking on it all for a long time now."

Vor frowned at them.

"Crakrat?" Karolan muttered to her, perplexed.

"A nasty little beast," Ulver explained. "It looks something like a rat, but to call it a rat is an insult to true rats. It has less fur and more muscles, will fight or eat absolutely anything, and carries all kinds of nasty diseases. The males are known to overpower and mate with any female crakrat they can find, and both sexes will eat their offspring if there's not enough food around."

He glanced at his fellow mages with a rough chuckle. "We thought it a good name for the wretched little upstart, and call him that in private."

Vor suddenly realized that the old mage had been speaking and responding perfectly during the whole conversation. He'd even heard Karolan's mutter from a few yards down the hallway.

"You're not going deaf, are you?" she accused.

He smiled, showing yellowed but not rotten teeth. "Better for him to underestimate me. How can we prove to you that we are with you?"

Karolan came abreast of Vor. "You know Craduticus is alive?" he confirmed.

"We know the crakrat has been trying to eliminate him, yes," Ulver said. "But old Cray almost killed him a while back, it seems."

"That was actually a different mage, but yes, Craduticus was with that party," Karolan nodded. "Craduticus, with others, has sent me here."

From back down the hall Eriducus wheezed a chuckle and elbowed Chirolen beside him. "Told you I smelled old Cray on the boy."

"The crakrat never noticed," Chirolen coughed back. "Too confident, too certain that he was all powerful." He shook a finger. "He stopped paying attention: a fatal mistake."

"How can we prove that we're with you?" Ulver asked again, over his chortling colleagues. "Would you like to take our wands and have us stand defenseless between you and the wards you're about to tackle?"

"And what would be the point of that?" Vor dismissed. "I need help, not meat-shields."

"I'd say you could bleed us for power," he squinted, "but you already seem to be brimming."

"Found a use for the boy," Eriducus winked.

Vor couldn't help but scowl. "Do you know this lock or these wards?" she asked.

"We haven't been back here in years," Ulver declared. "From what I sense, the wards and lock are all different. He's keeping a mage-stone in there, isn't he?"

"Yes," Vor replied, a little surprised that the old mage knew.

Ulver shook his head. "I thought so. It would explain his strength, and that I never saw that big lodestone go out to Weldom. It was pure and solid and heavier than a mounted knight in armor, including the horse: took a dozen men to carry it out. The High Wizard would have been delighted by it.

Instead it went to a bloody butcher."

"We have to destroy it," Vor said.

Ulver raised his hands. "Of course, of course you do. It won't do anyone else any good now: far too contaminated with his spells and energies."

"Well?" demanded Chirolen from behind. "Are we going in there or not? Where do you want us, Vor?"

Karolan took a step forward. "Listen. Cray and more mages, and warriors, are coming, whether we're able to destroy the mage-stone or not. If you—"

Ulver stepped up boldly in the face of Karolan's bluster and patted his shoulder. "Yes, yes, boy, we haven't a chance of standing up to old Cray and a bunch of his allies."

Eriducus and Chirolen came close to stand with him. Vor didn't say anything to try to dissuade them.

"We're not much long for this world anyway," Chirolen smiled. "One way or another, at the hands of the crakrat, at the hands of Weldom, we figure our ends approach."

"We've got a chance now, though," Eriducus contributed, "to do something useful for a change: something that might help some folks."

"Before we go," Chirolen concluded.

"I see," Vor grunted.

"Or who knows?" Ulver beamed. "Maybe it'll all work out, we'll end up on the winning side, and you and Cray and all will take some pity on us, let us live out our natural days helping to grow turnips or teaching some children reading and figuring?"

"Lot better chance of that by helping you than just staying shut up in our rooms while the excitement happens without us," Chirolan grumbled.

Vor looked them over for another few moments. Her gut was telling her to trust them. Her brain was still scared, but after a moment of struggle she gave in with a sigh.

"Alright then, come into the circle," she invited. "Do any of you think you're better than me at mage locks?"

"Simple ones," Eriducus said, but the other two immediately disclaimed.

Vor nodded. "Master Eriducus with me then. Everyone else had better watch the wards and keep them from going off if I trigger them."

"Almost ready with the circle," Karolan announced, having gone back to scrawling runes.

"Here, no, put more earth runes," Chirolen wheezed. "They'll help ground out anything that hits us."

The old mages couldn't get their stiff bodies down on the floor to help with the writing, but they took up chalk and started tracing earth runes on the wall on either side of the door. Vor hadn't thought of that, but she could soon observe some weakening of the wards thanks to them.

"Grounding it all out," Chirolen commented, nodding. "The crakrat never did like working with earth: too slow and stubborn for him. He's never understood that you can get greater results by investing greater time. He always liked the flashy, quick stuff."

Vor pulled a jar from her bag and opened it, releasing a crisp green scent. Beside her, Eriducus looked down at it.

"Cattail and poppy," she explained.

"Ah, yes," he approved, reaching over to take a scoop with his fingers. "That should help relax the spells."

Vor did likewise, and they raised their hands, holding them inches from the door, moving them slowly, feeling for the nexus points: where the spells were anchored or overlapped. When they found one, they smeared on some of the paste. It wouldn't unwork the spells, but it might loosen the bindings, making it easier for Vor to unravel them. When at last everyone was done writing runes and smearing paste, she put the jar away and together faced the door with the other four mages.

"I'm going to enter the locking spells," she announced. "Eriducus will advise and shadow me. Everyone else, watch where I'm working and keep the wards from going off. Unwork them if you can. This might take a while, so sit down if that's easier."

No one moved or disputed her orders. She glanced briefly at each of them, and they nodded or just stared resolutely back at her.

"Alright, I'll begin."

Vor moved close, standing with her nose nearly brushing the wood of the door. She let her eyes unfocus, and began observing the lock with her magical senses. It was more than a tangle of thread, more than a heavy portcullis, more than a maze, but all portions of those. Different types of energy had to be applied at different places, in combination or alone, in the correct order. If any step was done incorrectly, a ward would flare that would, at best, knock her away, forcing her to start over, or worse, attack her with energy that had been stored and coded to react a certain way—such as fire or lightning, just like the previous door.

With the support of the others, she could probably make some mistakes and survive them, since the other mages would deflect, absorb, or distract the wards, but no shield could last forever, and some attacks could be so strong that they could go right through or around a shield. Besides, they might all need their energy for destroying the mage-stone, so Vor didn't want to depend on her companions' strength yet. She wanted to solve the lock without making any mistakes.

Hunched and withered Eriducus leaned close to her. "Vor, here is what I suggest. Think of your master. What kind of lock would he put on the door?"

"Nothing elegant," she murmured after a moment of thought.

"Indeed, but not random, either, for he intends to return and open this door again, and he won't want to have to guess."

"So there will be a pattern," she surmised.

"So I expect. I have known Altare far longer than you, and I have never seen him do a creative thing in all his life. He only knows how to copy. He is skilled. He is powerful, but he does not invent."

"He won't have used something straight out of the book, though," she refuted.

Eriducus agreed. "No, not a pattern from the lock book—he's too suspicious for that—only techniques. The pattern will have come from somewhere else, some other book, or something else he's been working on recently that's at the top of his mind."

"The palace shields," Vor blurted.

"Hm, a good possibility," Eriducus concurred, "considering how concerned he is with the possibility of an invasion."

"And he would have strengthened them all last night, right before or after building this lock. They would have been on his mind. If I'm right, two domes," she muttered, "one inside the other, divided up like pie pieces, with gateways." She lifted a hand idly to point. "Then the door is a map, and up is north, down is south, here west, here east. So the gateways are here: this nexus, and this, and this. Yes, the strongest wards run through them."

"And in them you will find the locking points, just as though they were gates and portcullises," Eriducus said.

"Linked into the whole dome, the whole circle of power-lines, touching other wards," Vor muttered.

"The structure supports the theory," he whispered. "Let's try it."

"So I must come through the main gate, in the outer wall. That's here."

She had a starting point and her focus moved to it. To open it, the right sort of power was needed. Vor took a careful taste of the magic and grimaced. Unsurprisingly, it was blood magic. She reached for the blade at her belt and lifted it to her other palm, but Eriducus was following her path and put his hand between her palm and blade.

"No, no," he said, turning over his wrinkled hand in hers. "Bleed me."

Vor hesitated.

"Let me be of some use, child," he scolded gently. He took the knife from her and ran it along the flesh below his thumb so blood welled. "There. Take it."

Vor obeyed, pulling on the freed, fresh energy and applying it directly to the first nexus, the first gate. It released at once, but half a dozen wards glowed in response. Karolan, Chirolen, and Ulver stirred, each moving in his own way to try to diminish the wards before they triggered.

"No, no, it's wrong," Vor breathed. She cast her gaze around seeking the nexus that would disarm them. "The guard towers, of course."

There was more than one guard tower around the outer wall, and she felt instinctively that they would have to be released synchronously. She spread her hands in a kinesthetic aid to her mind, seeking out the alerted locks. There were four, she expected, just like in the real outer wall. The wards glowed ever brighter.

"They're on a timer," Eriducus growled. "Hurry."

She didn't have time to taste every nexus. She had to choose. Four: four what?

"Earth, air, fire, water," she guessed, but which element for which nexus?

She recalled the lore she'd learned of the elements. Air to the north, where it was so cold that water was still and covered the earth, and fire was reluctant to go. Earth to the south where water was driven away by the sun, which baked the earth from which fire had long ago burned the trees, leaving no fuel to support it. Fire in the east where the sun rose. Leaving water in the west, from where the rainstorms came.

Rapidly, she dug into her bag, as Karolan made a grunt of urgency. A bit of dirt she smeared on her knee. She dipped her left fingers in a jar of water and took up a fragment of wood in her right hand. The wood she ignited though the fire burned her skin, but then she touched the fire and water to the east and west nexuses as she lifted her dirty knee to rest on the southern one, and leaned in to blow firmly onto the northern one.

It wasn't the only way to do it. If she'd known it was coming, she could have been ready with a bit of actual magic energy of each sort, but using the physical elements with some magic behind them worked just as well. The four nexuses took in the power, and unlocked. The wards calmed. Everyone let go their held breaths, except Vor, who had just exhaled hers onto the northern nexus. She extinguished the burning wood and put it away.

Eriducus patted her shoulder gingerly. "Well done."

"The inner wall's gate," she muttered.

"There are windows, too, and more guard towers," the old mage reminded her.

She could see the nexus that corresponded to the inner gate pulsing like a heartbeat, but which of the other remaining nexuses would light up when she opened it? There could be dozens this time, between all the windows and guard towers.

"Remember, we know the pattern now," Eriducus encouraged. "Altare won't have wanted something hopelessly complex. He will have assumed no one would get that far, and if they did, they wouldn't guess the pattern like you did."

Vor nodded, but the old mage's words didn't get her any closer to the solution. She stared first at the inner gate. Its pulsing was nearly hypnotic, and though it was indeed rhythmic, its energy moved like a dancer hitting a different pose on each beat: regular yet full of variety. She'd never seen anything magical behave like that.

"What is this?" she asked Eriducus.

"Hmm," he grunted. "Have you seen the patterns of energy flow repeat?"

"Not yet. They're all different."

"Nothing does that by itself," he declared. "This behavior requires a mind. Chiro?"

Chirolen scooted over next to Vor's other side.

"Mm, yes, yes, well, my goodness," he observed. "This is more than I'd expected from him and yet sadly just his style."

"What is it?" Vor asked.

"Poor creature," he sighed. "The crakrat has woven a lesser fire sprite into that lock nexus."

"But," she nearly spluttered, "they're useless, nearly mindless."

"But not completely," he countered.

"Excuse me," Karolan interrupted, "but what's a fire sprite? Is it what you set on me that first day, when we fought?"

"That was a lesser salamander, a creature that can think, and can take commands," Vor explained. "Fire sprites live in fire, any fire, every fire. They don't need to be summoned, and they can't be commanded."

"Some might venture to say that not only do they live in fire," Chirolen lectured, "but they are the fire, itself. The distinction of where fire ends and fire sprites begin has never been fully understood by any mage, according to my research." He sighed. "Oh, too many mysteries yet to be solved. No, truly, I mustn't die yet." He patted Vor on the shoulder. "You'll look kindly on us for helping you, won't you? And leave us alive after the fight is over?"

She hunched her shoulders. "Yes, fine. I have no intention of killing any of you. Just tell me what to do with the fire sprite."

"Well, I'm sure it doesn't want to be trapped in there," Chirolen blustered. "At least, provided it's capable of wanting things. Throw some water at the door. That'll get rid of it."

"That will kill it," Vor objected.

Chirolen scratched his stubbled chin. "That's provided it's alive," he offered.

"If they live in fire," Karolan pointed out, "then they must be being born and dying all the time. No fire burns forever."

"The boy has a point," Eriducus nodded with approval.

Vor didn't care. Enough creatures had died because of her master. If there was any chance it was alive—and Eriducus had said it wouldn't be behaving the way it was if it didn't have a mind—she would save it. The question was how. Removing it would release that nexus point, but she couldn't command a fire sprite to move, and she couldn't just rip it out or she'd shred it. Her master must have captured the little creature, shoved it into the spell, and then shoved the strands of the lock into its body, fusing them. To open the lock, her master would no doubt have simply ripped the sprite apart, and then dealt with whatever wards that triggered.

"You think they die when their fire goes out?" Vor queried.

"That's one theory," Chirolen shrugged.

"And other theories?" she prompted.

"That they both come from and return to wherever it is that fire lives when it is not here," he said. "It would be the same place that salamanders and other creatures of flame come from when we summon them."

Vor gave him a sharp look. "So they would be allies?"

"Who?"

"These sprites, and other beings of flame?"

He looked perplexed, his face wrinkling like a winter apple. "I, hm, well, yes, I have observed such behavior before among creatures of the same element, at least behavior that looked as though they were allies. One can never truly know, of course."

"Of course," Vor concurred quickly. "Alright, when I release this lock I think there will be a whole bunch of smaller lock nexuses that light up." She waved a hand hopelessly. "I'll have to deal with them then, because I don't know which ones they are. Just, try to keep everything calm as long as possible."

"What are you going to do?" Eriducus pressed.

"I'm going to get the sprite out."

"Yes, but how—?"

Vor shook her head. "Quiet, I'm working."

It would take less power if she did it aloud. Softly, she began the cantrip. The other mages—except Karolan—all recognized it and straightened with interest. None of them tried to stop her. She knew it well, and shortly the being she'd summoned came to her, turning slowly in the air before her: a salamander, just an ordinary lesser one.

She offered it some energy, more than she needed to, but it wiggled with delight, absorbing it all with movements that suggested it was bathing in it like an otter in a stream. Fed, it looked to her, waiting for its command. This was the difficult part. Lesser salamanders were not very bright, and her request might be too complex for it. Usually they were just commanded to burn things.

Vor materialized an extra glob of energy on her finger, and moved it. The salamander's gaze tracked it, as if still hungry. Thusly, she brought its attention to the fire sprite trapped in the spell. It was such a little thing compared to the sleek and splendid salamander, like a mouse to a human. The salamander seemed to look at it, and then turned its head back to Vor, tilted as though enquiring.

"Free it," she told the salamander.

Its flaming tail flicked, and it stared at her for another few moments.

"Take it with you," Vor added.

A ripple went the length of its body.

"Save the sprite," she commanded.

This time it gave a complete undulation and spun about. As quick as a flash of flame it dashed directly into the door, vanishing, but Vor and the other mages could see it entering the spells, weaving among them. There was no doubt, the dancing flicker of the sprite responded to the presence of the salamander: not trying to flee, but stretching and yearning towards it.

The salamander wrapped around the tiny creature, and fled out of the door, back into the visible world. It was now ablaze with brighter flame. It sped directly at Vor and then circled around her in a stream of gold and scarlet, not touching her.

"Be gone," she told it.

With another upward run towards the ceiling, it fluttered and vanished.

Then the lock spell came apart.

Chapter 19
Altare's Inner Sanctum

The wall shuddered and all five mages instinctively put out their hands as if to stop it from falling on them. To Vor's inner sight new nexuses were pulsing now. In a ring that she thought was a representation of the inner wall, energy surged from one minor nexus to the next. It started small where the ring had been broken by the removal of the fire sprite, and grew as it passed each nexus in turn, until it splashed onto the final one in the broken ring, at the other side of the opened fire sprite nexus.

Then it repeated, and the surges were speeding up.

"Stop it, stop it," Ulver begged.

Vor could see the wards shuddering, perhaps trying to trigger, but the other mages were holding them down with brute magical force.

"I don't know what this is, Vor," Eriducus confessed. "Can you solve the nexuses one at a time?"

They were small, simple, but the pulsing power kept sweeping over them, foiling her attempts to insinuate her own power. Besides that, something about the ever increasing surges and the building power of each orbit was feeling familiar, like something else she'd observed just recently, something she'd sensed without really paying attention.

The other mages were resisting it, but the surges didn't feel malicious to her. In fact, she suddenly had the thought that stopping the surges was the wrong thing to do. Stopping them would trigger the wards. She was sure of it the more she observed the growing pulses.

"Blow it up," Chirolen panted. "We have to."

"No," Vor declared. "It needs, it needs something: completion. It's building towards something."

Then it hit her. If she hadn't just that morning done what she'd done with Karolan, she wouldn't have recognized it. Well, she had plenty of that sort of energy left over. With a wry but humorless grin, she began feeding it, building the circling pulses even faster.

"What are you doing?" Ulver cried out.

"I'm unlocking it," she shouted back. "Hold on."

The splash of energy as each surge hit the end of the broken ring grew until the door started getting hot from the overflow, and still she fed it. Someone was making inarticulate cries of distress, but she ignored him. The wards were shuddering even harder, but Vor sensed the end was near. In a final blast that made them all stagger, the last set of nexuses flared up, overheated, and died.

They all heard clearly the sound of the door unlocking.

***

Now there were just the wards to deal with. These the three relieved old masters tackled without hesitation. Ulver grabbed Karolan's upper arm, and started muttering to him, pointing out what he was doing, and getting the young man to help. Chirolen and Eriducus teamed up, too. When unraveling someone else's wards, it was always a good idea to have a partner to watch the back trail.

Vor sat herself down on the floor, feeling exhausted from the energy drain. She still had power left—her own plus the remains of what she'd collected that morning—but she'd spent a lot to get through the two doors. If the three old mages hadn't shown up, she wondered how she and Karolan would have managed. She closed her eyes and tried to get into a trance, to settle her energies.

A half an hour later, or maybe even an hour, Ulver was shaking her shoulder.

"We're done," he said. "It's time to open the door."

Vor climbed to her feet and checked the door and wall anyway, but detected no signs remaining of the many wards.

"Good work," she mumbled.

She started to reach for the handle, but then Ulver knocked her hand away. Vor stared, stunned, until he explained.

"In case we missed anything," he said. "Better let someone less talented open the door."

He meant, less valuable. "Alright," Vor agreed, although Karolan threw her a dubious look.

Ulver seemed to brace himself. He touched the handle with a fingertip, then grabbed on, twisted, and pulled the door open.

Nothing happened.

"Thank goodness," Ulver sighed. "I didn't really want to die yet."

Vor started to step forward.

"No," Ulver objected again, grabbing her arm. "Check the threshold." His eyes darted around the room. "Check everywhere, for more wards and shields."

The five mages all tried to crowd into the doorway, each gazing about with their magical senses in slightly different ways, looking for traps. Vor found herself nearly blinded by the radiance of the mage-stone, however, and

212

had trouble seeing past it.

"That thing is swamping me out," Chirolen grumbled. "I can't see a blast-ed thing."

The others mumbled laments of similar content. Ulver grumbled inar-ticulately under his breath.

"Well, nothing else for it," he announced—and stepped across the threshold.

Stunned at his temerity, Vor nonetheless managed to throw a shield of energy up, swooping it around him powered by the speed of wind magic. It was the only thing that saved his life.

A bolt of lightning struck, hitting him directly, but the shield caught most of it, burning away under the onslaught with a visible shower of sparks. Ulver staggered back, his legs collapsing out from under him and his wispy hair standing on end. The other four mages caught him and dragged him back out of the doorway. They sat him in a corner. Chirolen and Eriducus imme-diately knelt on either side of him, despite the popping and cracking of their knee and ankle joints.

"You old fool," Chirolen scolded.

"It was," Ulver wheezed, "the quickest way."

"And what if our Vor had not been quite so quick with tossing up shields, hm?" Eriducus jabbed. "You'd be dead."

"There could still be more traps, too," Karolan rued.

Ulver managed a shaky chuckle. "Toss me in again."

"Moron," Chirolen scoffed. Then he leaned closer, adding his free hand to the top of Ulver's where he held it. His voice dropped to a whisper. "Dying recklessly, even in the attempt to kill the crakrat, will not absolve you of your guilt or debts. Only service to others will do that."

"This is service to others," Ulver retorted, making no attempt to keep his voice down. The other two old mages sat back a bit, as if reprimanded.

Ulver's bloodshot gaze shifted to Vor. "Oh, I am sorry, child. I'm sorry. I never did anything to try to protect you from him."

Tears suddenly dripped down his cheeks to soak into his beard.

"He's addled," Eriducus huffed.

"Lightning will do that to a man," Chirolen nodded sagely.

The two old mages stood up, holding onto each other for balance, and leaving Ulver sitting limply. They turned back towards the threshold.

"Now, about this room," Eriducus grunted with an attempt at cheer.

After an uncomfortable glance, Karolan moved to join them, but Vor went and knelt down in front of Ulver. Like his fellows had, she picked up his hand.

"Will you be alright, Master Ulver?" she asked softly.

"I've got things to do," he rasped out. "I can't die now." Weakly, he lifted his free hand and patted hers. "I'll be alright. Just let me rest a bit."

Vor nodded, almost stood, but then made herself stop. "You don't have to apologize," she told him. "We are all prisoners here, in various ways. I know you couldn't help me without endangering us both. I was never afraid when I was with you, and that was gift enough."

He smiled, making several river deltas of wrinkles appear on his face. "You're a good girl."

She winced. "No, not really."

"You might not be perfect," he clarified, "but you're good."

"Thank you," she allowed. "So are you."

Slowly, his eyes blinked shut and his hand went limp in hers. Suddenly afraid, Vor put her palm over his thin chest, but felt the limping throb of his aged heart go on unabated. She looked at his spirit, his life energy, and it continued its deep and constant glow. He was not dead, at least not yet, but unconscious.

Gently, she set his hands into his lap and wished she had a blanket to wrap around him. As she stood, Chirolen stepped back over to her, shucking off his outer layer of robes. He handed it to her as the more agile one, and she bent down to tuck it around Ulver. Chirolen patted her shoulder when she straightened up.

"He'll be alright," the old master confided to her. "We three have been together so long, it's like we share one soul. I don't think one of us can die without the other two of us going at the same time."

She raised her eyebrows at him.

"Well," he revised, "maybe not, but let's not test it. Now, about this threshold."

Karolan was on his knees, head down nearly to the floor. Eriducus had his eyes closed, hands up, fingers twitching occasionally. After a moment, he relaxed.

"I think maybe Ulver got it all," he said. "I can't sense anything else, but that stone is so bright I could be missing things."

"Give me a rock or something," Karolan requested, sitting back onto his knees and holding his hand up.

"Hang on," Vor said, going to her sack.

She did have a few rocks—along with the vials of water, bit of dirt, and fragments of wood she'd brought. She fished one out and handed it to

Karolan. With her inner sight she watched as he packed as much life energy into the stone as it could hold.

"Put up some shields," he cautioned, "just in case."

Vor tossed another shield in front of the group, and then he threw the stone into the room. Before it even hit the floor, a bolt of pure power shot out of empty air, smacking the rock so hard it flew straight to the right and impacted the wall hard enough to shatter it. Everyone startled, and Karolan held up his hand again.

"Another," he requested.

Vor gave him her next one. When he tossed it in a few moments later it made it all the way to the floor, bouncing a little before coming to rest. It sat there, and they all stared at it, waiting for something to happen.

"It's safe?" Vor murmured.

Karolan moved slightly forward, but then Chirolen put a restraining hand on his back.

"Wait," he ordered. "There is something."

They waited, and after a minute, a glimmer on the floor caught Vor's eye.

"There," Chirolen pointed. "Do you see it?"

It was hard to make out its form, but whatever it was moved slowly along the floor, only an inch or two high.

"He'll have a bowl of earth soaked with blood somewhere in here," Chirolen explained. "That's a crystal snake, born of earth and blood magic. Your idea was a good one, young Karolan. Crystal snakes are blind, slow, and cannot travel far from bloody earth, but they'll seek out life energy."

"They're venomous?" Vor supposed.

"In a way," Chirolen shrugged. "They're difficult to study, for they can't be handled or commanded, only released, but I know a little. They don't bite like a real snake. They will wrap themselves around their prey, embedding their sharp edges into the prey's life energy. Something seeps out of them, contaminating the energy with a magical substance that acts like a poison, but not to the body. It spreads and multiplies, altering the host's life energy so that the prey can no longer use it. Shortly the prey falls."

"And the crystal snake eats the altered energy?" Vor guessed.

"I don't think so," Chirolen said uncertainly. "But the corrupted energy follows the snake back to its bloody earth den and soaks into the dirt. Give the snake enough prey, and soon more than one will emerge from the earth. I think it uses the energy to make more of itself, but I'm not certain."

There was a little glimmering ball now, directly around the rock. As Vor watched she could see the clean energy Karolan had put in the stone turning a muddy, grainy brown.

"That is bizarre," she commented.

"We definitely need to kill it," Chirolen pointed out.

"How do we do that?"

"They are quite indestructible," he said, "but it will dematerialize if we destroy its home. Does anyone see a bowl? It will have to be on the floor; crystal snakes are poor climbers."

"I saw it," Karolan said at once. "It's under that table, way at the back."

"Ah, well then, a simple blast of fire ought to burn all the life out of the blood and earth."

"And set the room on fire," Vor added.

"We might have to do that anyway," Karolan shrugged, "to destroy the mage-stone."

"I would suggest putting the fire out as soon as it's done its work," Eriducus interjected. "We'll address the mage-stone after."

"I can do it," Karolan declared, and looked around at the others as if daring anyone to disagree.

"Fine, have at," Vor concurred.

Karolan bent back down, and she saw him gather power. He made a flicking gesture with one hand, and a stream of fire shot out, hitting the bowl dead on. Immediately, the ball of glimmering snake twitched and writhed. The bloody earth in the bowl burned, charring the underside of the table. After a few moments of it, the crystal snake vanished. Karolan held out his hand, face tense with concentration, and the fire died.

"Well done," Chirolen praised. "I certainly hope that's the last of it."

Vor sighed. "I've had enough. I'm going in."

She wove layers of shields around herself as the others watched nervously, but did not object. Only Karolan caught her eye and murmured, "be careful."

She couldn't say she would be, but she set foot into the room with the best shields she could make without a much more involved process requiring a workroom and a rune-heavy circle. Her master had definitely gone to a lot of effort to protect the mage-stone, but he'd been full power that morning, and all of the locks, wards, and set spells must have cost him considerably the night before. She couldn't imagine that he'd had enough energy to do much more than she'd already encountered. Where would he have gotten the power to fill himself more than twice in such a short time?

Vor walked to the center of the room, only a few feet from the big node of stone, and nothing happened. No spells triggered. No wards came crashing down. No other elemental creatures rushed out to attack her. She turned about to look back at her companions.

"I think it's safe," she told them.

Karolan came in next, having put up his best shields around himself, too. Eriducus and Chirolen exchanged glances and stayed outside the threshold.

"Forgive us if we don't have the same confidence in our shields," Eriducus grimaced. "Perhaps we can advise just as well from here?"

"That's fine," Vor nodded, turning back to the mage-stone. "Now, how do we destroy it?"

The node pulsed with power, more even than an average human contained, and much of it tainted with pain or lust. She could also sense spells embedded into it, as though carved into its surface but visible only to magical inner sight. It didn't have any shields of its own, though. To function as Altare's power source and work the fail-safe spells he had in it, it couldn't have shields, or they would at least impair if not totally cut him off from it.

"You thought of fire?" Eriducus piped up.

"You'll not be unweaving it," Chirolen agreed. "The crakrat has spent the past decade engraving his spells into that rock. It won't be unworked in an afternoon—if ever. Better to burn them out."

"Yes, we thought of that," Vor agreed, "but how to get it hot enough, for long enough, without incinerating us as well?"

Chirolen chuckled a little. "Don't use mundane fire."

"Mundane fire?" she echoed.

"You can summon lesser salamanders, I have observed," the old mage went on. "Can you summon a greater salamander?"

Vor's eyes widened at him. "I, I never have," she stuttered. "Can you?"

"I did once," he said, now all serious as he matched her gaze.

"Can you do it again?"

He shook his head. "I was much stronger then, full of the power of the blood of others. If I were to try it now, I've no doubt the beast would kill me, if it would even come."

"And you think I could do it?" she challenged.

"Do you know the cantrip?"

Vor swallowed, mouth gone dry. "I do."

He gave a twitchy shrug. "You've never tried it?"

"I watched my master do it once," she said. "It demanded much of him."

"Yes," Chirolen nodded gravely. "The greater salamanders are not to be trifled with, but one could obliterate that mage-stone, without burning anything else in the room."

Eriducus was looking nervously between Chirolen and Vor. "If it comes, but demands more than Vor can give, it could eat her and us, too," he uttered.

Chirolen frowned and held up a finger. "I wasn't going to suggest it," he said, "except that just a short while ago, you did something remarkable. You summoned a salamander to save one of its fellow fire beings."

"The sprite?" Vor confirmed.

"The sprite," he nodded, now rubbing his chin. "I've spent most of my life studying the little creatures we can bring across from wherever they live. Your interaction with the salamander was notable. I must say I haven't observed such behavior from one before. I think, if you try for a greater salamander, it will come."

Vor stared at him. "And what of its payment?"

Chirolen stared right back. "How much do you want the crakrat gone from this world, from your life?"

"You know what is likely to happen to you, if you grow much older and stronger," Eriducus added. "He's not going to tolerate you much longer. He will break you, corrupt you, or kill you."

"Unless you fight back," Chirolen concurred, knobby hands fisted, "with everything you have."

Karolan was watching her with concern painted in broad stripes across his face. Vor hesitated to make an answer, but there was no point to it. She knew the old mages were right, and in her deepest soul she had already decided to do it. She was sure she couldn't call a greater salamander silently, so she could safely run the cantrip through her mind, making sure of the words, before saying them aloud.

"Vor," Karolan murmured, catching her wrist. "Is this going to hurt you?"

"You saw how I had to pay the lesser salamander with energy," she said.

"Yes."

"A little dog requires a little food. A big dog requires more food."

His grip tightened. "How much does a greater salamander eat?"

She met his gaze, but could not keep the truth from him. "A lot," she breathed, "probably most of what I have left."

"Your personal energy, too?"

"Yes."

Immediately, she felt magical inflow from him. Their souls were used to each other by now so she absorbed it automatically.

"Enough," she objected, pulling away.

"It's not a bad idea," Chirolen remarked. "If it's not fed well enough, it will refuse the task and turn on us all."

Karolan caught her arm again and pulled her towards the two old mages.

They added their touch beside Karolan's. Vor winced away, but she couldn't deny the truth of it, and didn't fight the flow of power they donated to her.

"Don't jeopardize yourselves," she urged. "And get behind a shield. Alright, stop, that's enough."

All three of the men had grown pale, their energies thinned. Vor extricated herself, giving Karolan a push to make him join the other two behind the threshold. She wasn't completely full, but considerably replenished. It would have to be enough. She shed her jacket and left it outside the room. She rolled up her shirtsleeves past her elbows. Behind her, she sensed Karolan erecting a shield in the doorway.

Vor knelt down, taking chalk from her pocket, and drew a circle. She ringed it with the strongest fire runes she knew. Even just that made the air around her warmer. In front of her the mage-stone throbbed like a malignant tumor. Fire enjoyed destruction. She could only hope the greater salamander—if it came—would be well disposed to the task she asked of it.

The three mages were silent behind her, offering no further advice. She stood alone in the room and took deep breaths, putting herself into a light and focused mental state. She brought to mind images of fire. If she could have, she'd have lit a fire in a fireplace, to make the setting more welcoming, but it turned out the room didn't have one. She would be courteous if she provided some source to be a portal for the creature, however.

"There's a candle in my bag," she said. "Roll it out to me?"

A moment later it came trundling along the floor and she stooped to fetch it, lit it with a flick of magic, and affixed it to the floor in front of her with a bit of its own wax. Anxiety threatened and she tried to melt it away. She'd need all her concentration. At last, when she felt as calm and focused as she thought she'd get, she began the chant. This one, too, was in some old language she didn't know except by rote.

From the first sound that left her mouth, she felt sudden pressure in the air, and knew that something was going to happen. It built as she worked her way through the long and complicated cantrip. Greater salamanders apparently required much more coaxing than lessers, for the summoning cantrip was about ten times as long. As she neared the end, she felt a hot breath of wind. She smelled sulfur and smoke.

Then she almost fled as the little candle flame before her suddenly roared up. A circle of flame erupted out from its base, but didn't burn the floor. It even washed over her feet with nothing more than a tickle of warmth. The roaring candle flame did not subside, although it wasn't consuming the candle any faster than a normal candle flame. It twisted and bulged, darkened to deep red, and then burst into orange and sun-yellow.

Out of the flaring flame came a shape of fire: nose, head, and then shoulders, one foot, another, a long body and two more feet, concluding with an extensive tail. It moved out of the flame, away from Vor, between her and the mage-stone, completely wreathed in burning fire. The one she'd seen her master call had appeared in much the same way, except that it had crawled out of a fireplace. Its forefeet hit the floor, followed by its belly, then hind legs, and the lengthy weight of its tail. With disconcerting speed, it curved its body around into an arc, so both nose and tail tip pointed towards Vor.

She knew what to expect, so wasn't confused when the flame that it seemed to be made of began to subside. Lesser salamanders had always looked to her like pure fire that was simply shaped to resemble the little soft-skinned amphibians she found near the ponds in the garden. Greater salamanders, however, except for having a head, four feet, and a tail, did not much resemble the cute little water newts.

This one was larger than the one that had come to her master. It lifted a head that looked like nothing more than a lizard's—except that it was as long as her forearm and crowned by two back-curving horns. A forked tongue of flame flickered in and out of its closed mouth, through the tiny gap at the front of its lips. The fire that had wreathed it all but died, revealing its black-scaled body. Between the scales, where one might glimpse a hint of skin on a real lizard, the fire continued to glow red and orange, as though its insides were a raging inferno trapped within a shell of scales.

Hints of smoke rose from it. Its eyes were so yellow they nearly looked white-hot. A row of hooked spines ran down its backbone from the base of its skull to the tip of its tail. Each long toe ended with a sharply curved claw as black as its pointed scales. It rested its tail and belly all along the floor, but Vor had no doubt that it could still move faster than she could run. Its ponderous steps as it inched closer to her were methodical, not labored.

Then she startled as two more wisps of flame burst from her candle. They flew out with the speed of diving falcons and spun all about the greater salamander. It twitched its tail as though annoyed, but didn't snap at them. They came to stillness, hovering in front of Vor's face. She saw that they were both lesser salamanders, although one was the standard size she was used to—about as long as her hand—and the other barely bigger than her thumb.

The little one quivered and jerked, and then darted at her, spinning orbits around her head and shoulders and then zipping over to the greater salamander and repeating the behavior. The big beast took a few heavy steps closer, and the tiny salamander retreated to its companion. The pair backed off, closer to the candle flame.

The greater salamander lifted its head up towards Vor. Its shoulders came as high as her knees and it was able to lift its nose to her belly button level. It was close enough now that she could have reached out and touched it, but she didn't dare. This was no domesticated dog or cat. It might be friendly; it might agree to a bargain; but it was not tame. Besides that, although it could choose whether or not to burn its surroundings with physical flame, she doubted that touching its cinder-like scales would leave her unscathed.

It looked deliberately down at the two lesser salamanders. Vor followed its gaze. Then it lifted its head to look directly at her. There was some sort of meaning there, but she wasn't sure what exactly. It gave her a slow nod, and its tail made a languid lash across the floor. It looked behind itself with a flexibility she didn't think real lizards possessed, to stare at the mage-stone. Then it returned its gaze to her, and gave another deliberate nod.

Vor couldn't stop herself from trembling, but she knew what she had to do now. It was acting ready to do what she'd called it for—as though it already knew what she would ask. Years ago when her master had demonstrated summoning a greater salamander, it was because he'd wanted it to slowly burn to death two prisoners—and to impress his apprentice. That salamander had been much more violent than this one, snapping, lashing, biting her master several times as it sucked his energy in payment. She'd been terrified of it, even though she'd known she was in no danger; she wasn't the summoner then. As long as it was sufficiently paid, the salamander would not have hurt her unless her master had commanded it to, so really, it was her master she should have been afraid of. Now, Vor, too, had to give this one its payment, before the task. Elementals were always paid first.

She held out a shaking hand toward it, her left one. It didn't move until her fingers were nearly touching its nose. It nodded once more, and then, quick but not brutal, it opened its mouth and bit down firmly onto her forearm.

Vor flinched, and heard muffled words and movement from the door, but she could only guess that Chirolen and Eriducus were holding Karolan back. She supposed she could have told him what the greater salamander's price included, but then he probably would have tried to stop her.

The beast gave a little growl of satisfaction and began to drink the energy it wanted out of her. Vor offered up her reserves first, the gifted energies from Karolan and the other mages, and what she had left over from the morning's activities. It resettled its bite once, making her grimace anew. It burned, and it did have teeth, although they were small, dense, and sharp, not big fangs, so it did not do deep damage. Her master had healed his injuries later with stolen life-energy from his victims, but Vor had never done such a thing—although she had rarely endured any major injuries—and assumed she would carry whatever scars the beast left on her for life.

It drained her further and further, soon sucking on her personal energies and making her lightheaded. Blood, too, began sizzling and any that didn't burn up ran down her hand to drip off her fingers. She staggered, and went down to her knees before she fell. The best lowered its head as she did, not releasing her yet.

She thought she heard Karolan objecting, calling her name, but her senses were being overwhelmed with the sound and sight of fire. She stared into the salamander's white-hot eyes. She felt the flames in her body, under her skin. The pain in her arm had moved beyond the ordinary and only her tightly clamped jaw prevented her from screaming aloud. Her whole arm felt on fire. Tears dried below her eyes before they could fall.

And yet she was not afraid. She knew the salamander would not kill her.

A voice that was the roar of flame spoke in her mind: "peace, summoner," it rumbled. "I know of your task. It will take much power, that I must take from you."

Vor nodded wordlessly.

"The pain, too, is my price."

She fought not to howl as it bit her again in a slightly new spot, a few inches closer to her elbow. Her head swam on the verge of unconsciousness.

"It is an honor to serve a mage such as you," the beast told her. "You who saved my littlest sibling, when it was more effort for you to do so, for no extra gain."

Then it released her, and she fell to strike her arms against the floor, barely keeping her forehead from striking there, too.

Still clinging to consciousness, she saw its feet shifting, turning its body in rhythmic motion until the arc of it circled the small square table that held the mage-stone, its tail tip reaching between its front feet. Shaking, Vor raised her head as much as she could to watch what her power had purchased.

The greater salamander opened its jaws, revealing a throat lit from within by flame as yellow as dandelions. The fire emerged as though the beast were vomiting it up, splattering across the stone, dripping onto the table, and spreading like a living thing. It brightened from yellow into green and blue, soon becoming so sharp that it drove new tears from Vor's eyes and she had to squint, and then look away.

Heat washed over her and she thought she should try to back up. Although the fire didn't seem to be catching anything other than the stone

and its table, she could see the wood of the floor warping, and soot was blackening the ceiling. Her skin tightened painfully from the heat. Her arms trembled as she tried to move. The blood on the bitten one, also smeared on the floor, was already dry and brown.

She couldn't find the strength—and then two tiny flames, by comparison, were hovering in front of her. It was the lesser salamander and the much lesser little one. They stood there, between her and the conflagration that had been the mage-stone, and the heat lessened until it was only that of a hot day in summer. The burning mage-stone brightened like a sun until she had to squeeze her eyes shut. It roared and hissed and spattered in her ears.

Vor put her head down behind her arms and waited, until some several minutes later the heat and sound began to subside.

***

The mage-stone was gone, or rather, reduced to such wreckage that it would never serve any function other than a few dozen ugly, cracked paperweights. Vor managed to sit up. Her two shielding lesser salamanders flitted over to the exhausted greater salamander, making orbits around its head. This time it did snap at them, but so weakly there was no chance of it actually catching one.

They relented, but there was no candle flame for them to return to now—the candle had melted and the wax completely evaporated in the heat—so they stayed near to their larger sibling's shoulders, as it made ponderous steps back towards Vor. She had not the strength to stand, much less fight it off if it had any quarrel with her, but it merely stopped before her, and gave another nod.

"Thank you," she croaked.

It moved its head closer and she was afraid it might bite her again, but instead its tongue of flame licked her on the cheek, not painful at all, just a little hot. She lifted a hand and petted its neck lightly, although it burned her fingers. One bit of mage-stone was still smoldering. The greater salamander turned to it, and just as it had arrived, sheathed itself in flames and walked back into the fire, losing shape and form until it returned to whatever body it held back in its own world. The two lesser salamanders went with it.

***

Vor jerked awake. Karolan was spreading burn balm and pain dulling salve onto her bitten arm.

"What happened?" she demanded, glancing around.

She was on her back in the flower hallway, not far from where Ulver was still propped up in the corner, but he was awake now, and smiling.

"The crakrat is sure to be furious," the old mage cackled.

Karolan began wrapping her arm with a bandage.

"You passed out. The mage-stone is destroyed," he told her. "Chirolen and Eriducus are collecting the remains in buckets. We'll put them in an ordinary fire for a while, just to be sure, but most of it burned away somehow."

"Young Karolan dragged you out of there as soon as the salamander vanished," Chirolen said, coming to stand over Vor, also with a smile. "That was the most magnificent summoning I've ever witnessed. Well done."

She almost managed a smile. "I'm not doing it again."

"Oh, no, I wouldn't recommend it," he agreed. "Greater elementals like that shouldn't be called on a whim."

Vor frowned, thinking of the one her master had summoned. It certainly had been angry, much different than the one who had come to her. Now she suspected that it had not liked the task he'd demanded of it. No element—not even darkness—was inherently evil.

"I only wish it were over," Karolan lamented, "but we still have to deal with him, when he comes back."

"The crakrat will be much diminished," Ulver said. "He'll still be a fearsome enemy, but now he can be killed."

Karolan finished the wrapping of Vor's arm and sat back.

"I should tell everyone, since we're all on the same side now," he began. "There's going to be some folks arriving here, griffins, and others, tomorrow."

All three old mages seemed surprised but not dismayed.

"Well, that will be fun," Eriducus smiled. "You'll ask them not to eat us?"

"They don't eat humans, whatever you might have been told when you came here with drakes," Karolan scowled. "We need to free the griffin prisoners, though, in the mines, or they'll be angry."

"Indeed," Chirolen agreed. "I think it's time all the mine slaves be released."

"I can do it," Ulver volunteered.

"I think we'd best go together," Karolan said, "and explain the situation."

"Except for our Vor," Eriducus interjected. "I think she needs some food and bed rest. Karolan, put your young muscles to use and haul out these buckets. Chiro and I will get Ulver and Vor out of here."

Chapter 20
Falconsong's Vengeance

Falconsong had discovered that she could remove her collar. When that strange man had touched it, when he had uttered those words—Hawkwind is free; she is coming—she had felt clearly the constant warmth from the collar fade away. Now it was just a ring of metal, one that had left a ring around her neck calloused and bare of feather-fur. The latch behind her head could be flicked open. The hinge below her throat could be flexed. She sat in her darkened cell with the open collar in her hands.

The question was: what to do about it?

It was deepest night. She'd waited until she could be sure everyone was asleep—especially the humans across the cavern, who could look directly into the griffin cells—before removing it, in the hopes that no one would see and make a fuss. Hurriedly, she put the collar back on. The chains still bound her legs, and of course her atrophied wings were still tightly strapped down, but she could walk out. She could find someone to help remove her other bonds. She could rip every one of her captors to pieces, to shreds, and leave them as nothing but a bloody stain on the stone.

Her muscles clenched, her feathers rose, and she held back a furious cry of rage. She would be out, and they would be dead, and soon. If Hawkwind—she didn't know who that was—was indeed coming to help, all the better. It was a griffin name; of that she was sure. There were other Hawks among the prisoners. Could this Hawkwind be a Feathyr who escaped? She'd never heard the name mentioned before, but it was nearly impossible to talk, because they would be beaten, so no one would have wasted words speaking of a griffin assumed to be dead, not escaped.

The dream of escape was one they all shared, and now, she was free, or nearly. She had to free her fellows, too. How would she do that? Their collars weren't unlocked, or so she assumed. That strange man had only touched hers. Her fantasies had never included how she would be freed, only what she'd do after she was free. She had no idea how to free anyone.

Should she tell the others? Falconsong gathered up her chains as silently as she could, and scooted on three legs to one side of her cell. She knew her two neighbors the best of all the captive griffins, for she sometimes shared whispered conversations with them at night. To her right was a much older male, Snowdark, and to her left a poor, tormented female in the midst of her life, Cloudglow.

There would be no point in trying to talk to Cloudglow now. Falconsong figured she must be awake, for she was the only female Cloud in the mines, and she was again in her monthly estrus, so she would be huddled silently in her ragged nest, aching and needing, unable to get what her body demanded—and practically out of her mind because of it.

Instead, Falconsong went to her right. Snowdark might be awake, too. The males slept poorly when a female was in heat. There were only four females that happened to, but with four of them having it once a month, that was still on average one or two nights a week that they and the males had difficulty sleeping. Falconsong tried not to let the anticipation scare her too much, but she knew she was approaching maturity, and there were no other Falcon females. In a few years, it would start happening to her, too.

She scratched slightly against the stone wall of her cell. It was a signal everyone knew. She heard the muffled clanking of chains and nearly silent three legged hopping. Then Snowdark scratched back. She pushed her bill through the bars, head right against the wall. She saw and felt his bill touch lightly against hers as he did the same.

There was no luxury for wasting words. If anyone reported a conversation, or if the night overseer who slept in a cot near the exit happened to hear, all the prisoners would suffer beatings.

"My collar is open," she whispered.

"How?" Snowdark breathed back.

"A strange man, today, touched it."

Snowdark could figure out on his own that it must have been the young male human they'd never seen before who had come in with the old man mage and the young dark female mage: both of whom they all recognized. There had been a strange new female mage, too, also younger than the old mage. So that young man must also be a mage, if he had unlocked Falconsong's collar.

There was one more thing. "He said: Hawkwind is free. She is coming."

Snowdark said nothing else. He scratched twice to indicate he was leaving. A few moments later, Falconsong heard a more distant scratch—he was calling the griffin who lived on his other side, another male, this one called Icetalon. No doubt he was unable to sleep, too. Unable to think of anything else she could do, Falconsong went back to her own nest of scraps and straw, curled up, and tried to sleep.

***

The next day, most of the griffins were oddly silent. They were always silent, but this was a strange, pregnant hush. The news had been passed in the night. They glanced at each other, and knowledge shone from their eyes. Many of them looked even more piercingly at Falconsong. It was not with distrust, as though they thought she was making things up. No one lied here in the mines. Although they could hardly communicate with each other, they all felt a powerful bond of fellowship, and all had seen the strangers. The other griffins working in the same location as Falconsong had probably noticed when the strange man stopped to touch her. They had no reason at all to doubt her words.

The overseers didn't notice anything different. They shoved the griffins about with the ends of clubs as they usually did, and the griffins had learned it was best to just comply. They were ordered into work groups without any sort of plan by the overseers, so griffins could usually arrange to be in the same group by standing close to each other as the men waded through them to prod them in one direction or another. They didn't care which griffins they were overseeing; all the griffins were equally placid.

Falconsong didn't even think the overseers knew which of them were male and which female. They didn't know any of their names, and indeed the griffins couldn't have spoken to share their names because of the contraptions they wore that kept their bills shut during the day.

She found herself herded into a group of four with Snowdark, Icetalon, and Cloudglow. The latter had tried to join a group of five other females, but apparently that group had been full, and no matter how much she'd jostled and other females from the group had tried to move over to take her place in Falconsong's group, the clubs had come down, and Cloudglow had given in under the beating, moving over to join the other three.

Falconsong ground her bill. It would make the day terribly difficult for Glow and the two males, to be working in such proximity while she was in estrus. Falconsong put herself between Glow and the males, as if that would help, and the group moved out with an overseer in front. When they reached their work area, Glow put herself as far away from the others as she could manage.

Falconsong went to work, but her mind was on escape. Perhaps if one of the human mages came back down to the mines today, she could overpower him, and force him on pain of death to release the others. Of course, she knew that mages had ways of defending themselves, and the overseers would surely descend upon her with their clubs—or worse; there were spears, too, but hardly ever used. Perhaps the other griffins, and even the human slaves, would join in the revolt, once they saw her act. Or perhaps they would be too scared of punishment, and leave her to the consequences of her actions.

The mages came rarely to the mines, however. Falconsong thought it unlikely that any would return the day after they'd just been there. That strange man, though, the one that had unlocked her collar—he must be an ally. He must want them to be free. Why else would he undo the magic? Perhaps he would return. If he did, she must be ready to leap to his aid at the first sign.

"Back to work," the overseer grunted, breaking Falconsong out of her contemplations.

He wasn't talking to her; she'd been working automatically while her mind wandered. No, Cloudglow had paused, trembling. The larger female looked up at the man, an expression of pleading in her eyes and the lay of her feathers, but there was no way the human would read it there.

Different overseers treated the slaves differently. Some were quite lax, not offering a blow, or even a word, unless the griffins were clearly shirking. A few would even tolerate quiet talking from time to time. Falconsong recognized this one, though. He was stocky and dark, with thick brown hair and overgrown stubble, and known for sometimes hammering nails through his club.

Glow did not submit at once; estrus made females bold and combative. The overseer lashed out, thwacking his club into her hip. Cloudglow staggered only slightly, and her hackles rose. He hit her again. Now he had the attention of every griffin in the cave, but none of them moved. Any moment now, Glow would put her head back down, would go back to work—that was how it always went.

Falconsong felt her own hackles rise. She gurgled in her chest, unable to speak, although she wanted to order the man to stop, that if he just left them alone, they would do the work. He hit Cloudglow a third time, harder, with what looked like all his strength, and the griffin warbled in her chest as she stumbled. That was the end, surely. Glow would submit now.

But the big female did not. She lifted her head higher, her pleading expression turning to one of anger. Falconsong felt her body tensing and moving back into a crouch. The man lifted the club up with both hands now, prepared to bring it down in a huge overhead strike that might even break bones.

Falconsong's thoughts raced and time seemed to slow for a moment. Her collar didn't work anymore. They couldn't do things to her with it. If they came after her, it would have to be with physical means. She would go through them all, and up to find that strange man. She'd bring him back to free her fellows. The blow was about to fall. It was time.

With one furious wrench, Falconsong pulled the muzzle from her head. In the next instant, she launched at the overseer. Her chains hindered her somewhat, but she'd gotten used to their limitations over her life of wearing them, and they did not stop her from slamming into the man and knocking him off his feet, onto his back.

No rational thought remained then. He was prey. She was predator. Her hooked bill fastened onto his throat before he could cry out. She twisted and ripped, and it was over. The taste of his blood filled her mouth. His body shook, twitched, and shortly subsided. Still she stood on him, foreclaws sunk into his pudgy body.

"Falconsong."

Some sense returned, and she looked up. Snowdark approached, having removed his own muzzle and hooked it to his harness. He shook his head.

"What have you done," he uttered, but not with any feeling of shock or horror: only dread.

"I'm going to escape," she said.

"How?"

"I don't know yet."

"You're going to be caught and killed, and probably us, too," he predicted.

Icetalon and Cloudglow both removed their muzzles as well, and approached.

"Song," the other female murmured. "You didn't have to do this for me."

"What were you going to do?" she shot back. "You were about to attack him, too."

"I don't know what I was going to do," Glow babbled back, claws flexing.

"Are you badly hurt?" Snowdark asked.

At his words, as if recalling to her that he was there, Cloudglow's eyes fixed on him with naked hunger, and then switched rapidly to Icetalon, blazing with single focus. She strode swiftly up to the younger male, and Snowdark shoved Falconsong, getting her to fumble a few steps down the tunnel from where the overseer's body lay.

"Come on," he whispered, nudging her firmly.

"Don't you want—?" she stuttered.

"No," he said decisively, and then stammered, "I mean, well, yes, of course, and in another time, absolutely, if she wanted me, too, but she likes Talon more, and we have things to do."

"What? You're coming with me?"

"No. We're going to remove the other overseers."

Falconsong stumbled to a halt and stared at him. "You're serious?"

"Completely, but we're not going to kill them, understand? We overpower them, gag and bind them. Wait, stay here."

They stood in the long tunnel between the cave they'd been working and the sorting tables, and no one had seen them yet. Snowdark turned back, and Falconsong waited, trying to shake the blood out of her bill. The big male returned shortly with one of their mining tools and Falconsong's muzzle. He handed the latter to her, so she could hook it to her harness like his, and still make use of the light from its glowing stone

"Help me with this," he said. "I've been filing my chains slowly, for years, hoping I could one day break them. Now is the time."

Looking closely, she could see what he'd done. The loop that held each shackle to the chain was already the weakest part, and he'd worn them all down. He required Falconsong's help to line up the pickaxe, and it took both their strengths to strike the shackles just right. The ringing sound of metal on metal was different from metal on rock, but they could only hope it wouldn't echo too far, and even if it did, the other overseers wouldn't leave their posts to come investigate.

After several blows, the first loop broke. They got quicker as they went to the others, and soon Snowdark was able to discard his chains. Then, they used the pickaxe to pry the C-shaped shackles open. He discarded those, too.

"I don't think we'll be able to do yours so easily," Snowdark lamented, "unless you've worn them down?"

"I haven't," she confessed. "I was afraid of the noise."

"Alright. You can come with me to a certain point. Then I'll go down to the next work area, silently, and jump the overseer. Once he's subdued, I'll come get you and we'll head to the next. There are five work groups today, but we should be able to access all of them without going through the main cavern. Icerock has been filing his chains, too, so we should be able to free him, and maybe others."

Snowdark moved off along the tunnel and Falconsong followed, carrying the pickaxe and her chains. When they reached a split, he took the right side, heading for the next work area. He raised a hand to tell her to stop, and moved forward on his own. She fidgeted with impatience until he returned a few minutes later.

"He surrendered quickly," Snowdark whispered. "He looked relieved, even."

They moved on, and repeated the pattern until the male brought another older male up with him, Icerock. They used the pickaxe to remove his shackles, too. Now the three of them continued, hitting the last two work groups.

"Now for the main cavern," Snowdark growled. "There will be a few overseers there."

"There will be no more need for stealth," Falconsong contributed. "I can't run as fast, chained, but if you two go for the most distant ones, I can get the closer ones."

"All the others are massing in the tunnels as close to the main cavern as possible," Snowdark informed. "They'll be ready to attack, too, but they're staging themselves slowly, so as not to make too much noise."

"Then we'll go for the exit and block it," Icerock declared.

"Hopefully the human slaves will understand and aid us. I don't want to kill them," Snowdark nodded.

The trio approached the main cavern. No one seemed to have noticed anything out of the ordinary. The human slaves stood at their sorting tables, working on piles left over from the previous day. There were four overseers, but none were near the exit, and the first cart of the day was not yet full, so no one had ventured out to dump it yet.

Snowdark and Icerock shared a silent glance and nod. They unhooked their muzzles with the glowing stones from their harnesses, leaving them behind, and ran in as quietly as possible. The sorting table area was well lit, so no one saw them coming at first. Falconsong waited until they were noticed before beginning her own stumbling run. The overseers did not stand to face the charging griffins. Two backed up, arms out as if to keep them off. One ran for the exit. The fourth threw down his club, dropped to his knees, and called out for mercy.

Snowdark reached the running one and slapped him down, claws retracted. Swiftly, he covered the man's mouth with a hand to keep him from shouting. Icerock faced the two fearfully retreating ones, but did not attack.

"Surrender quietly," he said, "and we won't hurt you."

The two raised their shaking arms, nodding, mouths shut. Falconsong skidded to a halt before the one who had dropped to his knees.

"Hush," she scolded. "Cry out again and I'll claw you."

He whimpered, and a puddle of urine began to spread out from under him.

"I won't hurt you if you just stay still and quiet," she told him grudgingly.

Forehead on the ground, the man nodded. She stood guard over him just in case. The human slaves had gathered together in the center of the sorting tables, staring around warily. The rest of the griffins, except for Cloudglow and Icetalon, emerged from the tunnels now. They'd all removed their muzzles. Some were hugging and preening each other with an almost frantic urgency; for so long they'd been isolated from each other.

Falconsong saw Eaglegrace snuggling Eaglebold, who was her daughter. Although they'd seen each other every day, they probably hadn't been able to do more than a quick secret touch for years. Chortles, chirps, and babbled words filled the cavern, until Falconsong spun about.

"Quiet," she hissed as loudly as she could.

The gathered griffins looked over at her almost as one, with a few stragglers.

"We mustn't let them know what we've done," she went on.

"They'll find out," one human commented. "We'll all be punished."

She rounded on the group of them, and they flinched. "We're not going to hurt you," she promised. "Look at this."

Falconsong reached behind her head and unlatched her collar. With a tug, it fell clanging to the floor. The humans gasped, but the griffins had all already been informed of her unlocked collar via whispers in the night.

"Barricade yourselves down here and wait," she said. "I'm going up to find the man who took the magic out of my collar. I'll get him and bring him down to free all the rest of us."

Everyone started talking at once, including a few who argued against her going, but she walked right past everyone to find Snowdark. The humans fanned out, gathering up the overseers, binding them, taking anything they had in their pockets—like keys—and placing them into cells. The ones that tended to hit the slaves more often might have gotten a bit roughed up, but no one else was killed.

"I need my chains off," she told Snowdark once she had his attention.

"We'll do it," he agreed. "Let's get some tools. Everyone needs to have their shackles removed."

The humans helped, too, and soon enough the best technique was discovered. The chains had been forged on, not meant to ever be removed, so there was no lock. They had to be broken. One by one the griffins were unshackled and stretching their legs. The group even figured out how to remove the dense mesh that pinned down their wings, and then the griffins were cautiously stretching those, too. By the time Falconsong was fully freed the day had moved on into afternoon.

Icetalon and Cloudglow had even come to join the group and have their chains and mesh removed. Shortly after that was done, however, Cloudglow vanished back down a tunnel with Hawkdive, another male. She would be too distracted to participate in the escape for the rest of the day, but Falconsong probably wouldn't be back for at least a few hours anyway. She had no memory of the world beyond the mines, and no idea what she would encounter or how she would find that blonde human male.

Falconsong stood at the exit with Snowdark.

"I wish I could come with you, to help," he said.

"Not until your collar's off," she grunted back.

He walked his back legs in and sat. "You must be very careful. There could still be drakes up there. You never saw them, but I did. They gave me all these scars. Often I've wished they'd killed me. If they're still there, collars or not, going up means we'll die, most if not all of us. We can't fly anymore so—"

"Enough," Falconsong snarled.

She was only a juvenile, and he nearly old enough to be considered an Elder—had they actually been living in proper Lines—but he obeyed.

"We will escape," she asserted, starting off down the hallway. "I'll be back."

Snowdark didn't call after her, and she didn't look back. On a couple occasions she'd come a short way down this hall, where the donkeys pulled up the carts of stone, but not often. The little beasts were easily startled by the griffins, and it was the job of the human slaves to guide them along anyway. Lamps in the hall kept it bright, and Falconsong moved along with little hesitancy; this was her path to freedom.

She reached the stairs, where the donkeys would stop for the carts to be emptied into barrels. There were a few such barrels sitting empty, waiting for the first load of the day, below the hook and pulley. Falconsong set her feet to the stairs and started up. At the top was another barrel, this one on a rolling dolly, also empty. The hallway continued out ahead of her: darker than the one she'd just come through.

A bit of fear tempered her hunger for escape, and she set her feet more carefully. It felt strange to walk without the shackles and chains. It was so quiet, and she kept readjusting her stride for her greater range of movement. She must have been brought down this hall as a fledgling, but she didn't remember it. Her first memories were of the cells, the chains, and the collar. She remembered the sores on her wrists, ankles, and neck and the pain they caused for weeks and weeks until the callous built up. She remembered huddling alone in her pile of straw and old blankets, sobbing and missing warmth and protection. She supposed now that she'd been missing her mother. Her mother was not among the slaves. The Skire must have killed her after Falconsong had been taken away from her.

Falconsong's fear had started to ebb, thinking of those early memories, of her missing, presumed dead, mother, and she walked faster, ready to strike out at the first sign of movement in the hall. She saw nothing but more dim hallway, however, and so she was completely stunned when she hit some invis-

Snowdark,
Cloudglow, Icetalon
and Falconsong

ible barrier that not only blocked her way but also knocked her back and off her feet with a bill-rattling shock of power.

She bit down on a cry of pain and protest, and struggled back to her shaking feet.

"What was that?" she hissed to herself.

Examining the hall again, she still saw nothing and no one. Nothing on the floor, nothing on the walls, or the ceiling: no sign of what she'd hit. Falconsong edged forward an inch at a time. She wasn't sure exactly where she'd been when it had happened. A few minutes into her investigation, her fur stood on end, and she leapt back.

Again she crept up to the spot. Again she felt the alarm and her skin prickled, but this time she didn't jump back. She reached out carefully to lightly touch—and something invisible knocked her hand away with the strength of an overseer's club.

Falconsong hissed with the pain and tested her fingers, which seemed undamaged, only achy. Back again, testing and detecting, along the floor, up the walls, all the way to the ceiling, which she could only reach by balancing on her back legs: the barrier was perfect. There was no week spot, no gap, no way around.

"Confound it," she growled. "My collar is off. I should be able to leave."

Having never heard of magical wards, she had no idea what she'd found, or that it was immune to anything mundane she might try. So back to the main cavern she went, to fetch rocks and clubs to throw at it, to beat upon it. The inanimate objects passed right through the ward, but whenever Falconsong touched it herself, it knocked back her hand with as much strength as ever.

She threw water and a burning torch at it, too, but they also passed right through it. As evening came, in desperation she took a running start and threw herself at it as fast as she could. The shocking rebound cast her several yards back down the hallway, twitching and smelling of burnt fur and feathers.

Defeated, she returned to the mine.

"I can't get through," she bemoaned to Snowdark.

"Eat something," he said simply. "We've been working on another idea."

The meat for the griffins was dropped in once a day through the metal grate high in the wall that also let in light. There was a hatch in it big enough for chunks of animals to be shoveled through, but even if the griffins could have reached it, it was too small even for Falconsong to get out through. A human might have wriggled through it, but they all still wore their collars.

"When the meat arrived, we pretended we were working, like normal," Snowdark explained. "We weren't sure if we could trust those people who bring the meat. It gave us an idea, though. Look."

Falconsong followed him. The slaves were building scaffolding with whatever materials they could scavenge or repurpose.

"Soon it will be tall enough to reach the grate," Snowdark said. "Once it is, we'll use all our tools to break through the stone around the grate, pull it out, and then you can escape that way."

"They'll hear us," Falconsong worried. "This place is always silent at night."

"We'll try to be quiet, but you're right. We might be able to finish the scaffolding tonight, but the work on the grate might have to wait until morning."

"And the more time that passes, the more likely we'll be discovered before all our collars are off."

Snowdark shook his head. "It's a risk, all of this, and yet, I feel better than I've felt in years. Even if I do end up dead, I'm glad we're trying. I'm glad we're fighting."

***

By morning, all the sorting tables had been repurposed as scaffolding. The griffins had dragged their old, musty nests out of their cells and crammed them together where the tables had once stood. They'd slept in a warm huddle to get the comfort and affection they'd been long deprived off. Even Cloudglow had returned with her last paramour to join them. The humans, too, although they were all unrelated males, had dragged their beds out of their cells and lined them up on the floor side by side.

No overseer woke them, but they were so accustomed to rising with first light that the slaves were up and moving at dawn. The scaffolding was not completely solid, and if the griffins fell, they wouldn't be able to glide to a safe landing since their wing feathers were cut and their flight muscles atrophied besides, but the nests were all pushed into a pile below the scaffold, in case anyone did fall, and the work on the grate began.

Falconsong, too, climbed up the swaying structure, pickaxe in hand, to begin chipping at the stone around the metal. It quickly became apparent, however, that the grate was deeply sunk into the stone and the removal process would not be quick. The morning stretched into noon, and as some griffins wearied of the precarious perch and awkward work, others took their places. There was only so much weight the scaffolding could take, and only so much space around the grate.

The slaves not employed in the grate work, especially the humans, had meanwhile been raiding all the locked supply cabinets in the main cavern.

They'd set to work finding or modifying items into weapons. Others were taking turns in the bathing area or making larger meals than they ever were allowed in the kitchen.

The griffins had started trying to preen themselves clean, particularly under where the mesh holding their wings had been. Many of them had ingrown feathers. A few humans even began helping with trimming or clipping problem areas and cleaning sores with soap and water. None of the griffins had enjoyed a bath of any kind since their capture. There wasn't enough water available to wash a couple dozen griffins, but they did what they could to start getting cleaner than they'd been in years.

Falconsong could only take so much of it, though. Soon enough, she was pacing, waiting for another turn on the grate. Frustrated, she went back to the hallway, trotting up to the spot where her thrown rocks, clubs, and extinguished torch marked the invisible barrier.

It was darker now in the hall. The two distant lamps that lit the area had run out of oil and hadn't been replenished. She wondered if the overseers had been missed. Most of them left the mines each night, although one or two stayed in cots along the donkey hallway. It occurred to her then that they might know how to get through the invisible barrier—but what if they could get through and she couldn't? Then they would run away and tell someone that the slaves were rebelling.

"I'll tie a rope to them," she uttered, "so they can't get away."

As before, Falconsong cautiously tested the barrier, but it was still there. After several minutes of frustration, she turned with a hiss to go back to the main cavern. Maybe it was her turn on the grate again, or maybe they'd even gotten it open by now. Or maybe she'd interrogate the overseers, or try bringing a bound one up to the impassable point. Maybe Snowdark would help her.

Then she caught a hint of light, moving light, coming from the far exit to the hall.

Falconsong ran, feet as silent as she could make them, until she reached a turn in the corridor. She dashed around the corner and hid. She wanted to see who was coming, and if they could pass through the barrier. It was a good many yards away from her, but she worried they'd notice if she stuck her head around the corner.

"What's all this?" a voice wondered.

"Someone has been trying to get through the ward," another voice answered.

That second voice was of the old human male who came to the mines sometimes. He was a mage, and would knock each griffin unconscious once a year for their feathers to be cut off.

"I freed one of the griffins."

That was the voice of the young man. Falconsong's excitement began to rise as he continued.

"I don't know if it was a male or female, but he or she might have been trying to escape."

"You turned off its collar?" the old man asked.

"Yes."

"Even with the collar off, it wouldn't be able to get through the ward, but if it has come this far and been throwing things through the ward, it must have freedom of movement now, suggesting that the slaves have overthrown the overseers."

"So we might be walking into a dangerous situation," the man who had spoken first said.

"Let me go first then," the young man's voice replied. "I bet they won't hurt me, since they know I can free them, and since I freed one secretly."

"Won't do us any good to get ripped to pieces before we can assure them we're here to help," the old man she recognized agreed. "Now let me get the ward down."

Heart pounding, Falconsong stepped out into the hallway.

"Wait, what's that?" the third voice exclaimed.

She had their attention now. There were three of them: two old men and one young.

"Don't hurt me," she said, "and I won't hurt you."

The young man stepped in front of the two others. "We won't hurt you. We're here to set you all free."

Falconsong approached nervously along the corridor. "You unlocked my collar," she said. "You said Hawkwind is coming."

"Yes. She should be here tomorrow, she and others."

"She's a griffin?" Falconsong confirmed.

"Yes, she's my mother—oh, uh, well, sort of my mother. She raised me. She was a Feathyr here. She got me out during the invasion and escaped."

The young griffin came within a few yards of the barrier, still wary.

"I'm Hawkrain," the man said. "Hawkwind became the Hawkmother and adopted me into her Line. What's your name?"

Falconsong didn't know what to think. Her crest feathers alternately fluffed and lowered. She eyed the two old mages. She didn't trust them. The young one might be all right, but those two had been her captors. Even though she didn't recognize one of them, he was dressed like his companion, so she figured he was an enemy, too.

"We've freed ourselves of our chains," she said, "all of us. Only this invisible barrier is protecting you from us. If you cross it, we could kill you. If you try to hurt us, we will kill you."

"I'll come down alone, if you want," the young man who claimed to be called Hawkrain said. He gestured over his shoulder. "I can understand if you don't trust them."

One of the old men gave a little sigh and nodded.

"Did you kill the overseers?" the other old man asked.

Falconsong stepped back. "One of them," she admitted. "He was beating one of us. I did it."

"Then he had it coming," the young man said, but the older two turned a little pale.

"You stay there," Falconsong ordered. "I'm going to bring some others, and you'll turn off their collars, and then you can come through, but you stay there for now. Understand? You stay there."

"We'll stay here," Hawkrain agreed.

Falconsong turned and ran off down the hall.

Chapter 21
<u>The Last Feathyrs</u>

She was back just a few minutes later with Snowdark and Icerock. Several other griffins had come part way along the hall, but were hiding beyond the corner. The old man she knew raised a hand.

"Don't come closer," he warned. "This ward will react to the collars and hurt you badly."

The griffins stopped.

"All right, just you, Hawkrain," Falconsong called out.

"Hawkrain?" Snowdark muttered.

"That's what he says he's called," she told him.

After a few gestures from the old man, the young one stepped forward, past the point that had stopped Falconsong. He kept his hands open and out to his sides and moved slowly until he stood in front of the trio of griffins.

"You are the one that claimed Hawkwind is coming," Snowdark commented.

"Yes, I am. She raised me after she escaped with me, during the invasion," the human replied.

"I remember her," the male griffin went on. "She had spirit."

"She still does," Hawkrain smiled. "She became Hawkmother and had six chicks."

Snowdark's feathers fluffed up. "Who else escaped?"

"No other Feathyrs we know of. We found a home with the wild griffins, in an Aerie called South-scree."

Falconsong sat silent, watching the exchange.

"Did she kill the Skire?" Icerock asked next.

"No, it was one of the Aerie griffins who accompanied her. His name is Waterleap."

Snowdark nodded. "Someday I would like to hear her tale." He took a step forward and lowered his forequarters. "Hawkrain, would you release me?"

"Gladly," the man declared.

He set a hand on the lock of the collar, and a moment later flicked it open.

"You can take it off now," he announced.

Snowdark straightened and did just that, letting the collar clank to the floor. His fur and feathers lifted and his body quivered.

"I never thought I would be free of that thing," he whispered. "My thanks, Hawkrain, my thanks."

"Let's get you all freed," the man urged.

He turned to Icerock, who stood on Falconsong's other side. He stepped forward as well, and in another few moments, his collar hit the floor to join Snowdark's.

"There are more," he said. "Please, won't you come?"

"It's why I'm here," Hawkrain replied. "Let's go."

***

Falconsong had remained silent and in the background as the two males agreed to let in the other human mages, and soon the three humans were moving through the crowds of slaves, touching collars. They piled the collars with the chains and shackles, and then everyone gathered around.

"Listen," the young one called Hawkrain explained. "We are freeing you in secret. There are no drakes here now, but the wizards from Weldom may soon bring some back."

"I knew it was Weldom," one former slave muttered, and others echoed the comment.

"We can lead you out through the tunnels under the castle. We can't go out through the main gate, for the army is not with us, at least not yet. All you men, we can provide you with new clothes and shoes, and supplies for a journey, and you can try to make your way back to your homes or families, if you want."

"Or?" someone asked.

"Or you can stay with us. The lord of the castle, Altare, is away right now, but he will be back, along with more wizards from Weldom, and probably a drake swarm."

"You intend to fight them?" another asked.

Hawkrain raised his palms. "Our reinforcements will be here tomorrow. We're going to feel out the army. If the army decides to be with us, we will fight. Otherwise, we're going to take the king and run."

Every griffin but Falconsong roused his or her feathers, and Icerock uttered: "The king?"

"Princess Jessika was also saved by Hawkwind," Hawkrain explained. "I grew up with her. The king has been enchanted by magic to serve Altare. She wants to save him."

A human slave called out: "And where will you all go?"

"There's a place for the few of us in the forest, but it can't hold all of you, humans and griffins," he confessed.

"We humans can try to vanish into the towns and cities if we must," another former slave said, "but our griffin friends here will find that impossible."

"And it will be a month before we can fly," Snowdark confirmed. "That puts us at a disadvantage if we were to stay to try to fight the drakes, but we are pledged to defend the royal family of Northnest. If any yet live, we must be with them, drakes or no drakes."

"This time we know they're coming," Hawkrain said.

"And," one of the old men spoke up, "this time there are mages on your side."

Muttering ran around the room.

"Tell us this," Snowdark said. "Do you think the army will come to stand against Weldom and their drakes and wizards? They're from Weldom, originally, aren't they?"

"Many of them are," the old man replied, "especially the commanders. Others were born here, survivors of the invasion, who joined up for a livelihood."

"And how many griffins are coming with Hawkwind?"

They looked to Hawkrain.

"A handful," he had to confess. "The wild griffins don't much want to be involved with this."

"And I can't blame them," Snowdark sighed. "Will they take us in and let us join them, with the king and princess?"

"Possibly," Hawkrain winced. "There is some precedent for that now."

Snowdark looked around. "I think we Feathyrs should run to wherever the king and princess run. The humans should melt back into the populace, going as far as they need to for anonymity, and we griffins must throw ourselves on the mercy of our wild cousins."

There came a few objections from the crowd. Falconsong, too, felt her hackles rise. She wanted to hit back at these people who had killed her mother and stolen her chickhood, not run away beaten.

"Look at us," Snowdark raised his voice. "We can't fly. We're weak and worn. Our best chance is to run. Most of you remember the drakes. They'll kill us as we are now. If we can escape and get stronger, perhaps we can come back and fight, and reclaim our home for ourselves and our royals, but if we try it now, we'd die for nothing."

"Hawkwind and Princess Jessika should arrive tomorrow," Hawkrain spoke up again. "Before you run, you should speak with them."

"We certainly will," Snowdark declared. "Hawkwind is one of us, and Jessika our commander. We shall have to hear what they ask of us."

The old mage that Falconsong recognized shrugged his shoulders. "For now, it's getting near evening. Do you want to come up? You could see the sky, and sleep in the old Feathyr barracks, if you want. They've been cleaned up recently in expectation of the drakes, but for tonight at least they could be yours again."

Before any of the griffins could respond, one of the human slaves stood up from where he'd been sitting. "I think we'd like to get out of here," he grunted, gesturing around at his fellows.

"I'm sure we can find you beds tonight," the other old mage said.

The man just gave a vague nod in reply, and the humans began standing, going to bundle up whatever few possessions they had, some of them taking one of the handful of spears the overseers had held in reserve for controlling the griffins—not that the weapons had been any use in stopping their overthrow. The old mage who'd made the offer of beds stood up.

"I'll see to them," he told his companions.

He went to join the crowd of men, leading them towards the exit hallway as soon as they were ready. The familiar old mage stood up next.

"Why don't you lead the griffins to the barracks," he suggested to Hawkrain. "You know where they are? I'll see to the overseers once they're gone."

Hawkrain stood as well. "If you're ready," he said to the griffins, "we can go now."

Falconsong let the others go first, out the hallway, up the stairs, past where the invisible barrier had been. The griffins took nothing with them; they had nothing to take. As they went, they had to squeeze through some doorways just wide enough for the largest of them. Falconsong found herself walking on soft floors—some kind of thick fabric under her feet. The walls were colorful and the light bright. All of it served to dizzy and bewilder her.

Then they came out of the building.

Falconsong crouched down at the edge of the last doorway. Above her was an endless, roofless dome of darkening blue. To one side the dome was turning red. She stared, unable to move, limbs shaking, and seized with the desire to run back down to her cell in the mines. She knew it was absurd, but her fear of this strangeness was not reasonable.

After a few moments she felt someone nudge her and managed to look over. It was Cloudglow. The older female nibbled her cheek feathers.

"The sky won't hurt you, little one," she crooned. "Soon you will fly up into it. You will embrace what you were born to do."

Falconsong whimpered, ashamed of her panic but still unable to budge. Cloudglow hid the view with a ragged wing and trilled the way she would have to a scared fledgling, continuing to preen Falconsong's head feathers.

"Stay with me, and I will protect you," Cloudglow promised, "just as you protected me yesterday. Don't look at the sky. Just look at the ground, and come right beside me. We will soon be into the barracks and you'll feel better."

With Cloudglow's stream of encouragement murmured into her ears, Falconsong was able to get her limbs straightened and her feet moving. She tried not to look around her too much. As she moved further out, and nothing terrible happened, she gained a little more confidence.

When the long string of griffins encountered other humans, both parties startled and recoiled in shock, although the griffins less so. There was no keeping the secret of them now. They crossed the outside courtyards where men up on high walls were staring and pointing. No one took any aggressive action, but they were clearly agitated, and Falconsong began to think this was a bad idea. They should have escaped straight into the forest and not shown themselves, but how could she have known?

When they reached a set of double doors, Snowdark and Icerock took the lead, pushing them open. The rest of the griffins gathered nervously around them.

"We will be fine from here," Snowdark told Hawkrain.

The young man fished in his pocket for something, held whatever it was tight in his hand for a moment, and then handed it over to Snowdark.

"Take this. I put some magic into it," he explained. "If I detect any sign of danger, like drakes approaching, I will make it glow, and you all will have to try to escape, or whatever. Otherwise, perhaps we can talk again in the morning. Do you need food? I can see about making the people who brought the meat to the mines bring it here instead."

"That would be good of you," Snowdark agreed, taking the stone.

"Here, I'll make a few light stones, too. What else do you need?"

"We will be fine for tonight. Let us speak tomorrow, as you say."

The parade of griffins began moving into the building, past Snowdark and Hawkrain. Falconsong let Cloudglow guide her in, and indeed she felt better once she was within walls again and the sky was hidden.

"There was one Line per floor, before," Cloudglow murmured, "but perhaps we should all just stay on this first floor tonight. We are so very few."

The other griffins seemed to feel the same. They filtered in among the rooms, picking whatever spot they liked to sit. Snowdark walked about, leaving glowing stones on the floors of each room. Some of the griffins started to sort themselves by Line. Falconsong selected a corner not far from where Cloudglow now sat, surrounded by the three other Clouds, all males.

There were three other Falcons as well, also all males, and all older than Falconsong—her big half-brothers and uncles. As the griffins began settling down, all three of them came quietly to sit around her. If she'd grown up in a normal time, they would have been the ones who fed her tidbits when she was just a demanding downy ball in a nest. They would have provided themselves as big, gentle, moving targets for her to chase around and practice her first pounces on. Maybe one or more of them would have shown her flight muscle exercises and helped her to take her first flight.

They hadn't been able to do any of those things for her. Her mother had raised her, alone, in the cell in the Skire's laboratory, until her first set of juvenile feathers replaced her down. Then she'd been put in the mine to work, knowing little but her own name, which her mother had crooned to her over and over. She had learned of the other Falcons. She'd been told about the Lines, about the roles the Linemembers played. She'd been told she would be the Falconmother—someday, if the slavery ever ended, if they ever were freed or escaped.

Now her three Linemembers gathered around her, unsure and still scared, but there.

"Song," the oldest, Falcondream, murmured. "We are with you. Will we stay together?"

She looked around at them: Dream, the oldest but not yet old enough to be an Elder, in white and dark gray; Strong, just a bit younger than Dream, in brown with black in his clipped wings and crest; and Flash, who had been young when the invasion happened, now a full adult, looking like a smaller version of Dream but with more white in his fur. Falconsong was dark gray: almost black, the smallest, not even an adult yet. She thought she must look like a shadow hiding in the corner.

"Our Line will die without you," Falconstrong added. "We will protect you with our lives, if you will have us."

"Please," Falconflash added in a bare whisper.

Dream glared at him briefly, and then took a step closer. "Whatever it takes," he said. "We'll all work together, to find ourselves a home, if that's what you want."

"I'm sorry we couldn't protect you before," Strong said. "Can we start again?"

Falconsong looked between them, at their eyes—golden, yellow, and orange—starting to glow in the fading light. She nodded.

"Yes," she confirmed. "Let us stay together."

Her Linemembers huddled around her, keeping her warm in the center of their clustered bodies. Tomorrow was unknown, but for the moment all was better than it had been in many years.

***

Hawkwind pulled up, turning in a tight circle and trying to keep close to Thornfire. The other griffins in the group did the same, waiting for word of how to approach the castle.

"This way," the mage announced at last. "There are wards everywhere, but there's a hole here. Rain must have made it for us. Stay right behind me."

It was early morning, barely dawn, and they were flying out of the rising sun. Besides that, Starmother—formerly called Starbright—had made charms for each of them that blurred their appearance. She couldn't make them invisible, but she could make them hard to focus on as light bent around them in odd ways, especially from a distance. It made it uncomfortable to look at each other, but Hawkwind considered that a small price to pay for making it harder for enemies to hit them with arrows.

Thornfire led the way down. Unfortunately, Starmother hadn't been able to join them, since she was much too important to risk now. Besides, this venture was all Hawkwind's business and the Aerie at large hadn't wanted to get

involved. She could hardly blame them. She felt lucky Thornfire, Thornwing, Thornsoft, and Thornspike had volunteered. The first three were her oldest friends among the Aerie griffins—two of them were sires of her chicks—and Thornspike had come along simply because she liked mayhem, and wanted to get back at some of the ones who had hurt her so badly a year ago.

Hawkwind had expected attack as they approached the castle, and she saw much running about on the battlements—confirming her fear. A bell began tolling. Hawkrain's message had been to come now, but perhaps he'd acted in error; this didn't look safe. The people running about weren't yet attacking, however. Mostly they were pointing and exclaiming to each other as the griffins approached the outer walls.

Then Hawkwind heard a cry, a griffin contact cry, from ahead. Her hearing pinpointed it immediately, and morning light flashed off of tattered feathers: umber and sepia much like her own. There was a griffin on top of the old Feathyr barracks. Hawkwind swerved. She was unburdened; Jessika was riding on Thornwing at the back of the flock. She zipped in after Thornfire, who was circling for a landing in the main courtyard, and banked to buzz the barracks.

The griffin on the roof cried out again, lifting both cut wings.

"No," Hawkwind breathed. "It isn't."

She looped the building again. The rest of her group was landing, and she thought Jessika might have called her name, but Hawkwind wasn't listening. She dipped and spread her tail, flaring her wings open to brake, and dropped onto the crest of the roof where the other griffin stood. She didn't even manage to fold her wings; they drooped onto the roof tiles. Her jaw sagged open, too.

"No," she moaned, "no."

The other stared at her, trembling. Hawkwind felt her legs go numb. They splayed out to her sides and she fell to the roof on her belly. Nausea rose in her throat so she thought she might vomit.

"No," she repeated.

A sobbing, anguished, ugly cry broke from her.

"Wind," the other said softly.

"No," Hawkwind denied.

Her wings shook like a gale. Her throat tried to close and she gasped after her breath. She stared at the thick, shiny fur on her forearms as tears soaked her cheek feathers. Her clean, preened primaries scraped against the slate. She clenched her unchipped, unbroken claws. Her tears blinded her.

"I," she choked out, "I didn't come get you."

"No, Wind, hush, easy," the other crooned.

"I didn't come get you," she mourned.

"You couldn't. You didn't know I was here."

The other griffin had a ring of thick, calloused skin around her neck, and similar ones around her wrists and ankles. Her fur was ragged and thin, and she was so skinny; her keel jutted out sharply without plump flight muscles to round out her form. Her flight feathers were all cut away, and her wing edges had more bare, raw spots.

"Call," Hawkwind sobbed.

The other approached, bending down, and nibbled her neck feathers. Another moan broke from Hawkwind.

"I should have been with you," she wept. "I should have leapt when you leapt."

"Who would have saved those children then?"

Hawkwind shook her head.

"I'm free now because you obeyed when told to pull back. I made my choice."

Hawkwind tried to control her breathing. That was what Icefeather had said, that Hawkcall and Eagleye had made their choice.

"It's not your fault," Hawkcall went on. "Because you escaped, that young man you saved, Hawkrain, was able to return. It's thanks to him, thanks to you, that I am free now."

"I should have come sooner," Hawkwind refuted. "I spent years in comfort in my own Line, with my favorite males, having chicks and raising them, not wanting for anything, while you suffered here."

"I was here," she agreed, "but I did not suffer. I had pain sometimes, yes, and I awakened, too, so that has been difficult, but I chose not to suffer. Every moment, I chose not to suffer. Even when I thought I could not endure, I chose not to suffer."

"I don't understand," Hawkwind exclaimed.

At last she looked up at her sister, her full sister, for they shared the same sire as well as mother. Hawkcall was only one year older.

"You are allowing yourself to suffer now," Hawkcall said, "instead of simply being joyful that I am alive, that we are together again: instead of accepting that yes, this is difficult, has been difficult, but asking now how can it be made better?"

Hawkwind stared.

"The past is done," Hawkcall continued. "Now we have a bright future to look forward to. You choose to allow thoughts of suffering to contaminate this moment, this moment when we reunite?"

Something of what she was saying got through. Hawkwind set her feet and pushed, getting herself back to standing. She folded her wings.

"How are you so wise?" she asked humbly.

"Pain is a good teacher," Hawkcall said simply.

At last they both began to smile.

"I would hug you," Hawkcall apologized, "but I think I have mange, and I don't want you to get it."

"We'll get you clean and healthy," Hawkwind declared. "You'll join my Line in South-scree?"

Now tears sprang to Hawkcall's eyes. "Yes. Yes, I'd like that. There are three others, too: Dive, Winter, and Gold. I'm sure they'll come, too."

"I remember them."

Dimly: Gold was an older female, her mother's age, who had never awakened; Winter was also older, a male, and nearly pure white; and Dive, a young male with similar coloration to herself and Call, only a few years older than them. Hawkwind had wondered if Dive was their full sibling, too. Their mother, Hawkbright, had been well known to favor one male in particular. Of course, nothing had ever been said aloud, but she'd always suspected.

"Is—" Hawkwind began hesitantly.

"Yes," Hawkcall said at once. "He's alive."

***

Hawkwind rejoined her group in the courtyard. The former slave griffins were pouring out of the barracks now. Hawkcall of course had to come down all the way from the roof via the internal stairs, so she wasn't out yet. Karolan had come running out of the palace, and behind him came three old men, moving cautiously with both age and anxiety. Behind those elders, hanging back in the doorway they'd come through, were a dozen apprehensive men. Half of them carried spears, but they weren't making any aggressive moves.

Rikah ran up to Hawkwind and the others, too, coming in through the main gate without regard for the indecisive soldiers standing there. A handful of servants had also gathered, watching from a distance. Hawkwind saw many more faces peeping through windows, behind curtains. Jessika got down off Thornwing and went to embrace her Hawksibs—and then was surrounded by curious former Feathyrs. Hawkwind joined the Thorn griffins in eyeing the gate soldiers that were taking such interest in them.

"We should get what we came for and get out of here, fast," Thornfire was saying.

"I agree," Hawkwind nodded.

"Who are they?"

"They were mine slaves, it seems," she explained. "Before that, they were Feathyrs. I lived among them before the invasion. They survived the attack and were imprisoned."

"We freed them yesterday," Karolan added, coming up to her now to hug her neck.

"I'm glad you're safe, Rain," she said, hugging him back with one arm.

"A lot has happened."

"Indeed, my apprentice," Thornfire interrupted archly.

"Master," Karolan grinned, going to give him a hug, too.

Thornfire grunted. "You are much too strong; let me go. But I am happy to see your smile," he added.

Karolan released him and stepped back, said smile fading.

"There's lots to do, too," he grimaced.

By that time, Cray had gotten himself down off Thornsoft's back, and Hawkwind observed with amusement as the three old mages from the palace greeted him. Karolan pointed each of the men out, giving their names to Hawkwind and the others.

"You're flying on a griffin," one accused, hand out and pointing imperiously.

"Good to see you, too, Chiro, old man," Cray grinned.

"Old man?" the other retorted. "Observe who doth speak!"

The four converged on each other with much backslapping and cheerful insulting.

"You won't believe it—"

"Called a greater salamander, she did."

"Burned that stone right up."

"The crakrat's going to be in a right fit when he gets back."

"No, not sure when that will be, but he might be bringing wizards with him."

"And a drake swarm, don't forget the drake swarm."

"Our Vor, couldn't be prouder of her—"

"That boy did help a bit."

"Well," Cray said at last, "it sounds like we have a number of tasks ahead of us, and no telling how much time we have."

"It's good you got here when you did," one agreed.

Another of the old men was looking with worry toward the main gate; soldiers were gathering there. More soldiers were emerging from the salle and barracks, all of them armed, but though they were starting to form up, they were still conversing with each other. It seemed the griffins did concern them, but the lack of violence and apparent welcome by the master mages was perplexing them. Was this an attack or not?

"Let's get out of sight; we're causing a ruckus," the old man urged. "Will your feathered friends come inside?"

"Pardon me," another voice, strong and female spoke up, loudly enough to get most everyone's attention.

A woman, older but not old, had stepped forward from the group of servants. She gave a little curtsy. Hawkwind nodded back along with several others.

"Amlee," Jessika exclaimed from where she'd been talking with the freed griffins, Rikah at her side, and ran to give the woman a hug.

"I believe the throne room would hold you all," the servant woman announced. "Please come inside."

Chapter 22
The Escape

It did hold them all. Hawkwind, Jessika, Thornfire, Cray, and Karolan took to the dais at the far end. The three other old mages and Amlee with a tall stately man stood nearby. The griffins filtered in around them all, and the dozen or so men—some with spears—who had lingered behind the old mages also followed the group into the throne room.

"They're former mine slaves, too," Karolan explained. "Some have gone out on their own, but these ones say they have no home or family left to return to. They want to come with us."

Hawkwind frowned at that. "We don't really have places for all these griffins, much less extra humans."

She said no more at that time, but the issue would have to be addressed eventually. The gathering began to settle down, with everyone looking to the people on the dais for direction.

"Go fetch Mistress Vor," Amlee whispered to a young woman in the dress of a maidservant, who ran off through the griffin crowd.

Shortly after the young woman had gone, there came a disturbance near the entrance. The griffins parted and bristled defensively as a tall man in uniform came striding through with eight soldiers around him, all well armed. One of the old mages—despite Karolan's help, Hawkwind couldn't yet keep straight who was who—stepped forward to face the man.

"General Krant," he greeted.

"And what's all this?" the general demanded.

Cray stepped up beside his fellow mage. "You might call it a rebellion," he said with a wide smile.

General Krant raised his eyebrows. "A rebellion?"

The remaining two old mages joined their fellows, one shrugging: "we've decided we don't like Lord Altare anymore, not that we ever did."

The four of them laughed.

"So we're leaving," Cray went on, "and we're taking this lot plus the king with us."

"He's my father and he's been enchanted and I want to free him," Jessika declared in a burst. A few Feathyrs nodded firmly, and several moved between the princess and the soldiers, shielding her.

General Krant narrowed his eyes. "Your father? You don't look like the princess. I've seen her up close."

"The one you've seen around lately is a fake," one of the old mages explained. "Altare enchanted her after he lost this one, the real one."

"Yes, we'll be taking her, too," Karolan piped up, "the false princess I mean, so we can try to disenchant her."

"And these griffins and men, too? Mine slaves, aren't they? That's a lot of people you plan to take," the general grunted. "Technically, I believe I'm supposed to stop you."

"That's where it gets complicated," a different one of the old mages said. "You see, Altare will be returning sometime soon, with some wizards from Weldom, and probably a drake swarm, too."

The general seemed to snap to tighter attention. "So you're telling me all the bulls are about to break loose? All the chickens coming home to roost? All the cows— ?"

"Yes, yes, all the livestock and then some," Cray confirmed.

Everyone was quiet for a few moments. Into that quiet, the woman Hawkwind had seen once, on the rooftop of the old Feathyr barracks, at night, trying to reclaim Jessika, walked into the room. Jessika had told her the woman's name was Vor; that she'd kidnapped Jessika, hurt Karolan, and cast sleeping spells on the others; that soldiers with her had nearly killed Waterleap, Thornwing, and Thornspike; that she'd put magic in Jessika's back that had allowed her to physically jerk her around and paralyze her; and that she was Altare's apprentice and to all appearances a mage that walked the dark path.

However, she'd also cleansed Jessika's wounds of the dark energy left there by the attack of one of Altare's shadow-beasts, had not called her master when

Jessika was escaping the castle; and had been the one who'd delivered Karolan's coded message to Rikah that it was time for the rescue team to invade. Jessika had said there might be something more to Vor than met the eye of the casual observer. Hawkwind scrutinized the woman now, wondering whose side she was on, and what game she might be playing.

It wasn't just Hawkwind watching her. Everyone's eyes turned to her, the way their eyes might turn to moonlight shining through dark branches. She wore a trim gray suit, with a pile of black hair bundled up and tucked under a knit cap on her head. Beyond her tidy but ordinary appearance, she wore an invisible mantle of power; the same sort that Thornfire wore. She walked with her back as straight as a poker, without a sign of fear, eyes slowly sweeping the room, catching only for an extra second on Karolan.

The general turned to her. "Mistress Vor, what have you to say about all this?"

She looked blandly back at him. "You don't want to fight Weldom. That will just get all your men killed. On the other hand," she actually winced a bit, "I can't allow you to hinder these people."

He frowned. "I see."

"So, I ordered you to let them go."

His frown deepened. "Is that what happened."

"That's what happened."

"And you think that will be good enough?"

"It will be good enough for Weldom."

He was chewing his lip now. "And for Lord Altare?"

"I'm going to kill him."

He rocked back and forth on his feet a little, as a few people gasped and griffins flicked their crests.

"Ah. I see. Going to kill him, are you."

"Does that bother you?"

Krant tapped his chin for a moment. "He is my lord," he muttered.

"Only because he killed his superiors," Vor stated, "and made it look like an accident."

Krant raised his eyebrows and tapped his chin a few more times. "Ambition, I admire. Cleverness, guile, even deception: these, too, have their places." Then he frowned. "But cowardice is bad form."

Vor's gaze did not waver. "I will face him when I kill him, and all will know he died by my hand."

Krant nodded once. "I know, also, some of what our lord does. He has wrongfully punished my men, taken them for his own purposes, even those who have done no wrong, and he turns his power onto innocents, onto those with no chance of fighting back, like orphaned, beggar girls."

Vor looked slightly curious.

"I know some of your story, Mistress. I know how it began. It was my men who wronged you, leading to our lord's attention falling upon you."

Everyone in the room had gone quiet, but neither Krant nor Vor seemed bothered that everyone was watching.

"And one of your men who defended me," Vor said softly.

"I sent him away, far away, to keep him from our lord's attention."

"Thank you. My master killed the blonde one, Gurek, I think he was called. He and the Skire," Vor's voice trailed off. "It was not the death he deserved, and I'm sorry."

Krant nodded again, but more deeply. "And these wizards you say are coming, they will not stop you?"

"Weldom won't care as long as no one attacks them. They consider him a nuisance."

He waved a hand. "They won't care that all these griffin and human prisoners, the fake princess, the old king, the old mages, are all gone?"

Vor almost smiled. "No. That will just make it easier for them."

"Easier for them to do what?" Jessika demanded from the dais.

Vor turned her head to regard the younger woman. "To take direct control of Northborn, of course."

"No," Jessika declared, and the Feathyrs stirred with a ruffle of feathers.

"The mines are nearly drained," Vor went on in a harder voice, "so they won't really care that the slaves are gone. The three old mages are so weak they are of no consequence. The king and fake princess would be annoying to get rid of without angering the people, so just as well that they've run off on their own—a story which everyone here will put forward as the truth it is. Altare is the only one causing them a problem, because he has some power and wants to keep it. The only way through this is to give Northborn to Weldom—and in fact deliver it to them freshly laundered with a bow on it, free of problems. Otherwise, Weldom will destroy us all, and easily."

Hawkwind took a moment to think about it, and she couldn't disagree. Jessika, however, strode down towards Vor, who didn't even blink.

"This is my kingdom," she declared as a few Feathyrs bristled.

"An accident of birth is the only thing that gives you any right to it," Vor argued back, showing a hint of anger for the first time. "Your family was defeated and your troops devastated. It is only by luck you survived. Unless you can take it back with strength—and you can't—you should accept your change in fortunes with good grace and make what you can of your life. We all must give up things we wanted."

Jessika fisted her hands in frustration, and Hawkwind hoped she wasn't about to start an actual fight. "But what's going to happen to it?"

"Weldom does not unduly oppress its people," Vor replied. "No more so than any other country. They will probably manage it better than an inexperienced girl like you could."

Jessika seemed to swell. If she were a griffin her feathers would have been prickling, much like a few of the Feathyrs' were, although most seemed by their posture to be in agreement with Vor, and uninterested in a fight—especially against the drakes of Weldom.

Jessika's teeth showed. "I—"

"You can't go back," Vor raised her voice. "None of us can get back what we've lost. Go forward. You have a family of people, human and griffin—and even faun, I hear—who love you."

That seemed to arrest Jessika's imminent explosion, but clearly did not satisfy her. Hawkwind, however, found herself giving a slow nod. That was similar to what Hawkcall had said. She was beginning to see the wisdom of it. The woman in grey stepped back from Jessika and looked around at the gathering.

"Get yourselves gone before my master returns, all of you," Vor ordered.

Cray stumbled down the steps. "No, Vor, you can't fight him alone. Come with us and lure him out. Then Weldom will see that he is aggressor, not you."

"He's right, Vor," one of the other old mages nodded urgently. "If you attack him, the other wizards may move to defend him, and you'll be defeated."

"That puts everyone else at risk," Vor rejected.

"We'll send the vulnerable ones someplace safe," Hawkwind suggested. "We can hide them where he can't find them. We've done it before."

Cray put a tentative hand on Vor's shoulder. She looked at it pointedly and after a moment he removed it.

"He'll come after you," the old mage said. "I hear you destroyed his magestone. He'll definitely come after you."

"He mustn't have time to think," Vor said emphatically. "He mustn't have time to organize or see reason or make a plan. I need him wild and reckless, or I won't have a chance."

Hawkwind raised her wings to get attention, and got it. "Let's move out the non-fighters now. Whatever else is decided on, they must get to safety." She pointed a wing at Jessika. "Fetch your father."

Cray turned away from Vor to gather up Jessika. "I'll help you. Let's go."

"I'll come, too," one of the other old human mages volunteered.

"Bring him back here," Hawkwind continued. "Rain, go get that false princess you mentioned, if she must be brought."

The woman Jessika had called Amlee stepped forward. "I can help with her."

Rikah raised a hand. "I should go instead of Rain. He's a mage; you might need him here."

It was shortly sorted out, with several people dashing off to various places. After a few more quiet words between Vor and General Krant, the man turned and led his soldiers back out of the throne room. Then the lady mage approached the dais.

"Come this way," she said. "I'll make you an exit."

Hawkwind lifted her crest in surprise. "Make us an exit?"

Without answering, Vor passed the throne to the back wall where hung floor to ceiling curtains and tapestries. Hawkwind followed closely, watching as Vor lifted aside one drape, revealing a blank wall. The woman held a hand out, nearly touching the stonework, and a few moments later the outline of a door large enough for a griffin appeared.

Hawkwind furrowed her brow, thinking back.

"That's right," she realized. "There was a door behind the throne, but it was never invisible before."

"We made it invisible," Vor said shortly. "I just now revealed it and unlocked it."

She gave it a firm push and it swung into a dark hall.

"So, do you know the back ways?" Vor asked Hawkwind.

"I do, I think," the griffin nodded, "but it's a bit of a walk to a bolt hole exit from here."

"I could blow out the side of the castle," Vor shrugged, "if you like."

"Let's not do that," Thornfire spoke up firmly, eyeing Vor. He gave her a nod of respect. "Quite a bit of power you've got around you. How about you save it for killing your master?"

Vor's visage darkened. "I wish I did not have to," she told the griffin mage, "but he is going to try to kill me."

"Then you should return the favor," Thornwing butted in. "Say, Hawkwind, so all these other griffins were Feathyrs, right? So they should all know the way out, too, right?"

The crowd of freed slaves was listening eagerly to every word, and muttered with confirmation. One griffin nudged to the front of the group. Hawkwind's gaze fixed on him at once, recognizing his coloration—so similar to her own—although he was rather ratty and much older than when she'd last watched him from a distance, before the invasion. She was now into her full size, too, which made her a bit bigger than him. He smiled up at her.

"I can lead them through, Hawkwind," he said. "I remember the way well."

She stared into his amber eyes, knowing the lay of her feathers was betraying her feelings but unable to prevent it. Her mother and her grandmother were both gone, but he was alive, and she thought—she hoped; fresh tears began to bud. The male leaned in and nibbled her cheek feathers.

Bill by her ear, he murmured. "I thought you were dead with your mother, until I heard your name whispered in the dark three nights ago. I'm so happy. You look so well. All three of the chicks I sired yet live."

Tears streamed and she couldn't stop them. It was true, as she'd always suspected. Hawkwind returned the preening, although his fur and feathers were ragged and dirty.

"You have grandchicks," she told him softly. "You'll meet them soon."

They both drew back and Hawkwind saw that his cheek feathers were wet now, too.

"Thank you, Snowdark," she said aloud. "If you could lead everyone, that would be a big help."

"There's a chance there will be magical traps," Vor interjected. "I think my master has been placing some down there, in case of attack."

The two old human mages who had remained behind spoke up. "We'll be going with you all. We're sorry, Vor, but against the crakrat we'd just be a liability for you. You'd spend all your energy trying to protect us."

"Understood," she nodded, "but you can detect traps and protect this group."

"Yes, we can. We just can't move all that fast."

"Ride us," Snowdark invited. "With our legs strengthened from years of mining, your weight will be little burden."

The two old men broke out in grins. "Hee hee," one chuckled. "Not only old Cray gets to ride griffins."

"What are you saying about me?"

The two jerked, turning about to regard Cray as he limped over to them. Behind him came Jessika, guiding her bemused father by one arm. He was looking around at everything with a faint smile.

Hawkwind frowned. "Will he be able to hold onto a griffin's back?" she worried.

Cray shrugged. "I can make him, and we can tie him down."

"I'll fetch some rope," the tall, stately servant man said, and dashed from the room.

As he exited, Amlee and Rikah returned, guiding a young woman. She too, looked around as though in a dream, smiling slightly.

"I wish we had a cart for them," Hawkwind rued. "You'd better walk beside her, Dare. She'll be riding a griffin, the king, too. Can you make sure they don't fall off?"

"I will," Rikah agreed at once.

"We'll help, too," spoke up one of the group of men who'd been identified as former mine slaves. "We'll go with the griffins and help anyone who needs a hand."

"Thank you," Hawkwind told the group at large.

One of the griffins from the crowd stepped forward, apparently selecting herself to carry the vacant-eyed girl. Hawkwind recognized Eaglegrace, a former matriarch and the mother of her lost friend Eagleye. Hawkwind looked over the escapees, identifying all she could, but Eagleye was not among them. Eaglegrace cautiously brought herself in front of the girl, likely expecting fear, but instead the girl's face lit up.

"Pretty," she crooned, reaching out to touch the old matriarch's cheeks.

"I'll take the king, if you like," Snowdark volunteered.

The tall man returned with a coil of what looked like silk cord, much gentler on the skin than actual rope.

"Get going," Vor urged. "There's no reason to delay."

Karolan stepped up beside her, putting a hand on her arm, and Hawkwind noted that Vor did not shake it off.

"Your master's flower girls," he murmured.

Vor frowned. "We can leave them. They're unremarkable, and I don't think they'll be hurt."

"You don't think so?" he emphasized.

"Their doors will all be mage-locked, which will take time and energy to open, and you'll have enough trouble looking after an invalid king and one mindless girl, much less half a dozen," she growled. "I want you all gone from here sooner rather than later. Leave them. At the least, my master will no longer be around to hurt them, and that's bound to be an improvement in their lives."

Vor pulled away from Karolan and walked off, as if to stand back and watch the loading of the griffins from a distance. Hawkwind thought she saw an expression of hurt flicker across Karolan's face, but he shook it off and went to assist. The king, fake princess, and three old mages were getting situated on their mounts. Shortly, the first of the griffins—those bearing the three mages—began exiting through the door at the back of the throne room. Hawkwind saw each of them off, recognizing most of them, and exchanging greetings with them.

"I don't remember you," she said gently to a small dark griffin who approached, bracketed by Falcondream ahead and Falconstrong behind.

"I'm Falconsong," the young one said. "I was born in the Skire's laboratory."

"Falcon?" Hawkwind murmured.

She did a quick mental evaluation. The Falcon Line had not been present in Snow-in-lee. Nor did any of the Aeries she knew have the Line. She glanced over the remaining former slaves, and did not see any other Falcon females she knew.

"You are the last," she said to Falconsong, "the only hope for the future of your Line."

"I know that," the juvenile said back. "I will make my Line strong again."

The three Falcon males accompanying her all mantled with pride.

"I'm sure you will," Hawkwind agreed.

The four Falcons went one by one through the door. Next came four Clouds, and Hawkwind noted again that they were also three males and one female, but this female was mature and awake.

"Cloudglow," Hawkwind said. "You are Cloudglow?"

"I am," she nodded. "Hawkwind. We used to play sometimes, as fledglings."

They smiled at each other, and Cloudglow too made her way into the tunnels. Hawkwind felt her heart acutely. Her people were alive. There was only a fragment, only twenty-four of the few hundred that had once lived at Northnest—twenty-five if she counted herself. There had been more Feathyrs stationed at other towns and outposts. She supposed they hadn't survived the invasion, but maybe they'd flown off somewhere. She would probably never know.

The human slaves, walking, had interspersed themselves along the line. Rikah had gone into the tunnel also, accompanying the false princess, and Jessika had gone to keep an eye on her father. Thornwing and Thornsoft had mixed in with the leaders, to act as guides or aerial scouts once they emerged. Thornspike took up the tail end of the line, grumbling that she hadn't gotten to fight anything yet. As her tail feathers slipped from sight, Hawkwind was left standing with Thornfire, Karolan, and Cray, plus Vor and the small cluster of castle servants.

***

"You won't go, too?" Vor asked, turning her eyes onto Amlee. "You should, you know."

The older woman just smiled. "You are already overburdened with humans, and what would we do wherever you're going?"

Vor didn't have an answer for her; she didn't even know where it was they were going. Not that she was necessarily going where Karolan's people were going anyway.

Amlee stepped close and embraced her, effectively paralyzing Vor. "It's you who needs to get away, Mistress. Those Weldom wizards won't bother good servants who keep their mouths shut and do their work, but you they'll have interest in."

Amlee released her and Vor tired not to look shaken.

"Win," the castellan whispered. "When he comes, you must win."

"I know," Vor uttered in reply.

She was already nervous enough, thinking of the coming confrontation. Her energies had barely recovered from summoning the greater salamander the day before. She'd spent the previous afternoon asleep and hadn't had time to do much more than some quick meditation to renew her power. Now there was a mage duel on the horizon for her and she was woefully unprepared.

"We'll be with you, Vor," Cray said bracingly.

She eyed him. "He defeated you last time. You think this time will be different?"

"And you are far younger and more inexperienced than I, and you think you have a chance of defeating him?" Cray countered. "You've never once traded blows with him, have you?"

"There are four of us this time," Karolan spoke up, looking around at Vor, Thornfire, and Cray. "And he is minus his mage-stone power source."

"If the Weldom wizards throw in on his side, we'll be in trouble," Vor pointed out, "but Wizard Giri implied they wouldn't if they weren't attacked, so make sure anything you do goes only at him, and only after he's made the first move against us, not before."

"Understood," Cray agreed. "And we should be going, shouldn't we?"

He gestured towards the open door. Vor shook her head.

"I don't know where is better to face him, here or in the forest," she confessed.

"In the forest, undoubtedly," Cray declared. "That is a place of life, of light—things my former apprentice knows little of. Here, he might pull in military allies. He knows the layout of the castle. He's worked magic here and

261

might yet still be able to pull power from reservoirs you know nothing of. He'll be at a greater disadvantage in the forest, and we might find other allies there."

"Fine," Vor capitulated.

"Do you need to fetch anything before we go?" Cray asked.

"I'm ready."

She already had a satchel of a few critical items. She didn't know if she'd be coming back to the castle, but hadn't wanted to be burdened by a heavy load. For better or worse, she would make do with what she had.

"Go ahead," she said. "I'll close the door behind us, and with luck he'll never know how we got out."

"I'd better put the wards over the castle back up," Karolan muttered. "Just a minute."

Karolan stepped away to focus. The big griffin called Hawkwind ducked her head and passed into the hidden hallway. The smaller griffin, the mage, went next, and Cray followed him as quickly as he could. Most of the servants had dispersed now, probably going to clean up all sign of their passing. Only Amlee, Kari, and Edgard lingered.

"Be careful," Vor told them. "I hope this all passes over and around you."

"You as well, take care, Mistress," Amlee said, the other two nodding behind her.

"There's nothing that makes me your mistress," she found herself saying. "Only my master put me where I am, and I'm about to destroy all that."

Amlee just smiled. "Then be safe, Vor."

"I'm ready," Karolan announced.

"In you go," Vor ordered, and he vanished into the dark hallway.

"It may be we'll meet again," Amlee said hopefully, "but if not, thank you for everything, and best of luck to you."

"And to you," Vor replied.

Then she turned to follow Karolan, closed the door from within, and restored the invisibility spell upon it—which was really just fusing a bit of the stone outer edge with a bit of the stone frame so the outline of it couldn't be seen. Setting her mage-stone necklace to glow—she figured she might as well make use of it—Vor walked into the darkness.

***

Vor had just passed through the bolthole exit where the other three mages and Hawkwind were waiting, when she felt it. The rippling waves of energy from a massive teleportation spell knocked her to her knees. Beside her, Karolan exclaimed and grabbed his head, while the griffin mage hissed and Craduticus fell all the way to his rump.

"What is it?" Hawkwind demanded.

"A spell," Craduticus croaked out, "a big one."

"Teleportation," Vor confirmed as her vision cleared. "They're back. It must be the Weldom wizards, and I'll bet my master has returned with them."

"Then he'll be searching for us any minute," Karolan supposed.

"Likely, yes," Craduticus agreed.

"That was a huge spell," Vor groaned, "I didn't feel that when they left a few days ago, when it was just four people and some luggage. I hope they didn't bring drakes."

"Drakes? Then let's get moving," Hawkwind urged. "Cray, the going will be rough; you should probably ride me. We'll stay on the ground, though, so we won't be seen."

"A good idea," the old mage nodded.

In moments the mages had shaken off the impact of the spell waves and the group was moving through the undergrowth. Hawkwind went first bearing Craduticus, followed by Thornfire, with Karolan and Vor at the back. The griffins served to break the trail somewhat, making the way easier for the humans. It was all up hill, though, which made lungs and hearts work all the harder, and there was no spare breath for talking.

It took them less than an hour to catch up to the other group, where the humans and griffins had stopped to take a rest in a hollow in the forest. The trees stretched up tall here, fighting each other for sunlight, and the forest floor was in twilight, leaving only minimal undergrowth. A fern-shrouded stream ran through the area and a few griffins were still drinking at it.

"Ah, there they are," Eriducus called out as the five arrived.

"Did you feel it?" Craduticus replied.

"The energy echoes?" Chirolen confirmed. "Yes, just a bit. That's someone coming back, isn't it? A lot of someones?"

"I expect so," Vor agreed. "I don't know yet if it's my master. It could be they kept him in Weldom."

"Even if it's not, they'll be surprised to find us all gone," Ulver observed.

"Definitely, but they might not come after us right away."

Jessika came up to them then, with Rikah in tow.

"Break off and head to the ruins," Hawkwind instructed. "We should keep moving."

Then Vor's skin prickled and every hair on her body tried to stand up straight. Impulsively, she threw power to her shields and crossed her arms over her chest in a vain attempt at defense. The ominous certainty of doom fell over her, and she realized what was happening with a gasp.

"What is it?" Craduticus demanded.

"He's scrying me," she blurted.

Craduticus cursed. "Of course he is. Get the non-fighters out of here right now."

Vor squeezed her eyes shut, trying to erect more shields.

"Did you cleanse her?" she heard Craduticus demand.

"I did." That was Karolan. "Head to toe, I got it all. I'm sure of it."

She felt his arms go around her and she didn't resist. A few moments later, additional shields were bolstering hers and the sensation faded. She opened her eyes, seeing Craduticus and the griffin mage, Thornfire, also gathered within touching distance. Karolan was warm against her. She didn't push him off, but he slowly drew away and turned his gaze elsewhere.

"It's not surprising," the griffin mage rumbled. "He surely has your hair and blood. Those are difficult ties to break."

"But if Karolan did remove all magical contamination from you, then he won't be able to hurt or control you," Craduticus encouraged.

Vor looked around at the griffin gathering and saw that at least half the griffins had departed, no doubt following their king and princess. Masters Ulver, Eriducus, and Chirolen were gone, as were Jessika and Rikah and some of the human mine slaves. Other griffins had remained, however, and so had five men bearing spears.

"This isn't the best place for a fight," Thornfire said.

Everyone jumped when another human suddenly popped up, practically right between Hawkwind and Thornfire. She was petite, with alabaster skin and a bundle of curly black hair held back by vines and tendrils. Then Vor realized she was clothed in vines, too, along with a small personal forest of leaves and flowers. Her feet and lower legs were not shod, but coated with what seemed to be bark, as though it was her skin. Her eyes were like pools of summer skies.

"There's a nice clearing that way," the young woman said, pointing.

"Kassie," Karolan gasped in surprise at her sudden appearance.

"Hawksky," Hawkwind declared. "There's going to be mage fighting; this isn't a safe place for you."

The young woman gave a little smile. "The clearing is that way," she repeated. "Come on."

Chapter 23
Master Versus Apprentice

Griffins bounded over, inviting the humans onto their backs, and the group moved out after the strange woman. Vor found herself riding a charcoal grey griffin with black markings. Their guide danced nimbly through the forest ahead of the crowd, as agile as a doe. She was odd indeed: strange and beautiful, and Vor didn't miss how Karolan's gaze was fixed on her. So, this was the fourth child that Hawkwind had saved, who Karolan called sister.

Vor pulled her mind away and focused on keeping her seat. Her mount was not one of the slave griffins, but one that had come with Hawkwind. She hadn't asked its name and didn't even know whether it was a male or a female. Only rarely had she ridden horses, and this was far beyond those tame experiences. For one thing, she wasn't giving any directions to her mount, and never knew which way it was about to run or leap, although largely it was following the griffin in front of it. It had a harness on, which she held to tightly.

After several minutes, the group burst into a clearing, just as the plant-girl had said. The sun was now high overhead, minimizing shadows. The griffins were gathering in the meadow, their riders dismounting.

"Thank you," Vor said to her mount as she got down.

The griffin nodded in reply, and made a hand gesture. Not knowing what that meant, Vor just nodded back.

"Go into the trees," she told the group. "Get out of sight. Physical attack might be our best chance against Altare, and that will work best if it's a surprise."

Griffins and humans both began obeying. Thornfire, Craduticus, Hawkwind, and Karolan remained in the center of the clearing with Vor.

"Move under the edge of the trees, too. I think it's best if he doesn't see any of you," Vor told them. "Let him think I ran away alone."

"He'll guess we did this together," Karolan said. "I'm not at the castle anymore either, so he'll expect me to be with you."

"Is there any sort of plan?" Hawkwind asked.

"I don't really know," Vor confessed. She found herself looking to Craduticus.

The old man nodded slowly. "There's no telling when he'll show up, or what he'll bring with him. He might bring magical constructs like those shadow-beasts he's so fond of. I'm afraid the first confrontation will need to be between him and Vor. We'll see how he reacts to her and what he unleashes."

"We must let him strike first," Vor concurred. "If he has any wizards from Weldom with him, we must not attack them," she emphasized. "I hope I will have time to announce that my quarrel is only with my master."

"Do that," Craduticus agreed.

"Once the fight begins," she went on, "we just have to throw everything at him that we have. Non-mages should be careful, though. They will have no defense against any of the magic we'll be using. If they get in the way, they could get hit by us, not just attacked by him."

"I'll pass the word," Hawkwind murmured. "Anything else?"

The four mages looked at each other, but no one had any more words to offer.

"Let's wait then," Craduticus suggested. "If he's as angry as I expect, he won't be long in striking at us. If we are lucky, he'll be so angry he rushes here without preparation or plan."

Hawkwind moved off. Thornfire found a spot between a couple trees to lie down. He shut his eyes: perhaps meditating, or just napping. Karolan followed the plant-girl—Kassandra, Hawksky—to a spot a few trees away, where they stood and spoke quietly.

"Sit with me, Vor?" Craduticus invited from his seat on a fallen log.

She ripped her gaze away from the pair under the boughs and regarded the old master mage.

"It's been a while," he went on. "When I left, you were just a girl. I wish I could have taken you with me, but I could no longer match my apprentice in power." He shook his head. "I could barely get myself and Breeka out."

"Breeka?" Vor asked idly.

"A bat-cat, I suppose," he shrugged. "That's what I started calling it anyway. I don't suppose you ever got to see it; there were many things my apprentice didn't involve you with. I managed to leave it behind for this venture, though it didn't like that at all."

He was staring at the grass between his feet now. Vor moved over to sit on the log, a couple feet away from the old mage, and tried to open herself to the life energy of the place, letting it recharge her. Craduticus shifted his attention back onto her.

"You've grown up," he remarked, "and come into your power. I'm proud of you."

"How so?" she retorted. "You hardly know me."

"I observed you more than you knew. I'm proud of you for not letting him corrupt you."

Vor frowned. "Who says I'm not corrupted? You don't know the things

I've done."

His chuckle made her push down a snarl.

"I can see the living breath of the forest flowing freely into you, Vor, and you're not even tugging on it. It wouldn't do that with anyone tarnished beyond redemption."

She didn't reply. It didn't matter what he thought. She was what she was, and intending to shortly murder her own master. There was no way not to see herself as checkered at best.

"You like the boy?" Craduticus asked then. "Hawkrain."

Vor stiffened. Did she? She shut her eyes as though that would quiet the jumble of emotions within.

"Young men are foolish, but they can't help it," Craduticus said. "Suddenly their bodies wake up and start telling their brains what to do, and it gives them trouble. It must be something like when these griffin females wake up and go into heat for a day or two, and spend the whole time with as many different males as they want, only to return to being their normal selves afterwards. Only for young men it doesn't go away after a couple days. They're like that all the time, and most of them don't get a crowd of willing young women—or even one willing woman—to help them deal with it."

She didn't need to be distracted by this now. Vor focused on her meditation, trying to fill her energy reservoirs, trying not to think about Karolan. They had hardly spoken since yesterday, when they'd—she swallowed—done all that stuff. The memory was like a sore tooth: sometimes it felt good to bite down on it, but mostly she wished it would go away.

"Meanwhile, young women," Craduticus went on, "well, how can I comment on young women? I've never been one. You'd know better than I, but I can't imagine it's easy. You're trying to figure yourself out, too, and that young man is feeling things and wanting things and half the time doesn't know what he's feeling and really wants. It can't be easy."

Vor sighed and opened her eyes. "Nothing is easy."

"Well, you might be right," Craduticus agreed. "At least, nothing good is easy. What Altare does, that's easy, since he has the power, but it's not good. He's done a lot of things, hurt a lot of people, and killed a lot of people, for his own greed. It's time he gets what's coming around to him."

"I just want to be free of him," Vor said.

"Is that why you're helping the boy, and so helping the rest of us?"

"I would have had to confront him eventually," she deflected.

Craduticus was silent for a few moments. "Give the boy some time. He'll grow into himself."

"He doesn't want me," she whispered. "He's just frustrated that he can't have what he really wants."

"Is that so?"

"What is she?"

"A nymph, according to a faun I know," Craduticus answered without needing clarification. "I'm afraid I don't know much more than that, but you're right. Even if he wants her, he can't have her anymore. She is something beyond his reach."

"A forest spirit, a guardian of trees, known to associate with unicorns," Vor recited after recalling for a moment. "That's all I ever read about them."

"Yes, unicorns," Craduticus rumbled. "We all have our burdens to bear."

They sat for a while in silence. The day was lovely, too lovely for a fight to the death. The meadow was perfect: abounding with red clover, long grass, and bees and butterflies. It was too perfect to become a battlefield.

"And what do you want, Vor?" Craduticus asked by and by.

"I don't know that, either," she was able to reply at once. "I wish people would stop asking me."

She could have said more, but then came the sound—still distant, but chilling nonetheless—that Vor didn't know she still remembered until she heard it: raspy but thunderous growling. It overtook the buzzing of bees and singing of birds with deep rumblings. Craduticus got to his feet as quickly as a man of his age could, and Vor was right up beside him.

They weren't the only ones to recognize the sound.

"Drakes."

The hushed exclamations ran around the clearing, followed swiftly by admonitions of quiet. Karolan rushed back to Vor's side. The plant-girl, too, crouched nearby, watching the sky. Thornfire was on his feet now, raptorial eyes focused into the distance.

"Here they come," he announced.

"How many?" Craduticus asked. "A swarm is fourteen."

The griffin turned his gaze onto them. "In that case, I would say, two swarms."

Vor's courage plummeted. "Then Weldom gave him at least two swarms, and he's brought them both against us."

***

The swarms arrived in precise formation. In front, sixteen of the drakes were arranged into groups of four. Each quartet was strapped into a set of harnesses and suspended from the center of their diamond formation was a basket. All four quartets set down at the far end of the clearing. From each basket stepped a person. The remaining drakes stayed airborne, circling the clearing on easy updrafts.

Vor and Karolan were ready. They waited inside circles drawn into the earth. Karolan was on his knees in some kind of trance. Vor had two salamanders at her side. She'd called earth elementals, too, but they were hidden under the dirt, ready to spring a surprise attack when she called for them. No one else from the extended party was visible.

The first person out of a carry basket was Altare, his wand pointed directly at Vor. She opened her mouth to call out, but he gave her no chance to speak. A lance of fire went shooting directly towards her. It impacted her shields, burning away the first layer, but she drew up more power to replace it.

"Vor," Altare thundered, "I'll kill you."

She caught a glimpse of the three other occupants from the flying baskets. It was Wizards Colby, Giri, and Milsa. They had made no move to attack. In fact, they'd stepped back together nearly shoulder-to-shoulder, and Vor thought they might have put up shields. So they were just going to observe?

Altare was shouting again. "You burned my mage-stone, Vor. You think that gives you a chance? I will punish you, and then I'll kill you."

Altare made a throwing gesture, and several dark stones trailing smoke went flying. They passed right over Vor and Karolan to land in the untouched meadow behind them. Vor stole a glance over her shoulder just in time to see three of the stones erupt into flashing, snarling beasts of shadow.

"I see your friends," Altare taunted.

And the shadow-beasts leapt not at Vor, but into the trees, which immediately triggered a ruckus. Someone must have accidentally shown themselves, or Altare had spent power sniffing out the presence of large concentrations of life energy. Vor could not take her attention off Altare. The men and griffins under the trees would have to fend for themselves.

"Do you see me?" Craduticus shouted.

From Altare's right, a silver jet of power came shining. The mage deflected it with a slash of his wand and it dug a furrow into the ground.

Altare laughed. "Old man? You came back from where I sent you? Let me send you back again."

A blue flash flew at Craduticus, but he was ready with his own staff, knocking it harmlessly aside.

"It's over, my boy," he declared. "You cannot reign forever as you've done."

Altare laughed louder. "But I have all the power of Weldom on my side."

He sent another lance of flame at Vor, and another, and another, and she had to buckle down to replace her shields over and over. Meanwhile, Craduticus sent more silver jets at Altare, but the latter darted his wand around, alternating between his attacks on Vor and deflecting Craduticus's on him.

"You have no chance," Altare gloated when both he and the old mage paused for breath. "The Wizards of Weldom are with me. Against their power and mine you cannot win."

He looked back at the trio of wizards, but they had made no move. The drakes, too, sat obediently where they'd landed or maintained their circling pattern above.

State Wizard Colby spread his hands slightly. "We said we would accompany you," the man enunciated. "We did not say we'd help you kill your apprentices, or your former master. As they have done nothing against us, that is a personal matter you had best settle on your own."

Some of the color ran out of Altare's face, but he rallied in an instant. "I don't need your help. Witness my power."

Vor gritted her teeth in an eager smile. So they weren't going to get involved. That made the battle a bit less suicidal. She flicked both her hands out.

"Go," she whispered to her salamanders. "Burn off his clothes and then his skin. Distract him. Make him dance."

The two impatient creatures went zipping away, zigzagging to present a moving target as they closed on Altare. The mage pivoted, apparently choosing to focus on one, knowing he couldn't hit them both. He sent out a wave of power, blasting one of the salamanders into smoke, but the other had reached his shields and began burrowing through them.

"Pest," he growled.

Craduticus called lightning down on him. It splattered against his shields, fragmenting into the ground around him. He hadn't carved himself a circle into the dirt, so his shields weren't anchored, and thus were weaker. With enough firepower against them, they would come down. Vor made a lance of her own fire and sent it shooting at her master. Assaulted on three fronts, Altare had no time for making attacks of his own.

Then a griffin came tumbling out of the trees with a shadow-beast on its back, raking dark talons into its flesh. Vor redirected her next lance to blast into the beast, dislodging it. Another griffin leapt out and pounced on it. The sight of griffins made the drakes stir and attracted the attention of the wizards.

"Only Altare," Vor shouted to her allies. "Leave the drakes and the others. Don't attack them."

If the drakes got into it, the griffins would be hard pressed. They were well outnumbered and weak from all their years in the mines. A third griffin joined the two trying to shred the shadow-beast, but they were all bearing injuries already. The fighting under the trees continued—no doubt more griffins were taking damage there.

Another lightning bolt hit Altare's eroding shields, but in the time Vor had been distracted, he'd blown away her other salamander. Then he suddenly stumbled, as though he couldn't get his footing. His feet sunk into the ground up to his ankles, and then deeper.

"Yes," Karolan grunted, and Vor flashed a look at him.

"You brought up water," she guessed.

"He'll be in a swamp shortly," he confirmed, wiping sweat from his brow. "Took a while, I'm just glad he didn't walk away from that spot. If he stays there, the swamp will suck him down."

But then Altare laughed again, bringing everyone's attention back onto him. He plunged his hands into the sloppy soil and began chanting.

"Hit him now," Craduticus ordered.

Karolan sent a fireball, and Vor more fire lances. Craduticus produced additional lightning bolts, but Vor knew he couldn't keep that up forever. He was generating them out of the clear sky, without bringing in thunderclouds to help—which would have taken much more time but would have made each bolt less energetically expensive and more powerful. Altare shrugged off the attacks, even when bits of them got through his shields to mar his clothes and skin, his concentration unbroken. A spear came sailing out of the trees to the mage's left, but it missed him entirely and sunk into the ground several feet away, shaft quivering.

Vor whispered a command to her hidden earth elementals, but they popped out of the ground not near her target, but behind her, within her own circle. The creatures—resembling lean toads but with mouths full of teeth and horny protrusions all over their bodies—shrank back in obvious fear.

Then the creature—Vor assumed it must be a greater elemental of some kind—Altare had summoned burst from the swampy ground.

Everyone around recoiled, hands going over mouth and nose, for the thing stank of rot. Vor stared, unable to identify it; her master had never demonstrated calling this creature before. It had six legs, all long, covered with spiky green fur and tipped with attenuated clawed feet. Its shoulders hulked up huge, supporting a massive head that looked something like a cross between a turtle and drawings of a bird Vor had seen labeled as a parrot. It had a huge bill like the parrot in the drawing that looked strong enough to sever whatever it got a hold of.

Its midsection and hindquarters tapered down but were still muscular, ready to propel the front portion. Its long tail was lined with spikes, and its back and head were armored with thick bony plates. The whole creature from bill to tail tip was longer than any two griffins and as tall at the shoulder as a tall man. The drakes flinched back from it, but calmed after a moment.

"What is that?" Karolan gasped from beside her. Vor could only shake her head.

Its beady eye fixed on Altare. He gestured broadly towards Vor and her end of the clearing.

"Food," he told it. "Eat."

Was that its payment, not the summoner's own energy? The six-limbed-parrot-beast launched with upsetting speed, crossing the clearing in an instant. Vor jerked back as it hit her shields, but even though it looked and felt solid, it was from an alternate plane, and magic shields impaired it. She noticed Craduticus resuming his attacks on Altare, but had no spare attention to watch. The beast was clawing at her shields with two limbs and they were shredding under it with showers of sparks. Meanwhile two more of its limbs began clawing at Karolan's shields just a few feet away, and his face was a reflection of Vor's dismay.

Then a blast of fire smacked the creature head on. Vor looked up to see Thornfire in the air, wreathed in flames himself. He hit the creature again and again with each sweep of his wings, but the fire seemed to be rolling right off. The beast shook its head and opened its bill as though to bite the griffin out of the air—though Thornfire was well out of its range—and its claws continued their work on Vor and Karolan's shields.

Hawkwind hit the creature next. From a running start out of the trees she slammed into its back, raking with her own claws, and then leapt away. Immediately, another griffin hit the beast, but it happened so fast, Vor hardly saw it—just a streak of white and black spearing down from the sky like lightning, and then shooting off and away almost as fast.

The six-limbed-parrot-beast squalled its fury, but the strikes didn't distract it much. Vor hit it with her own fire, repeatedly, right in the chest, until it heaved its body off her crumbling shields, and just in time; they'd been about to fail. Then its spiked tail came slashing around, shattering Karolan's barriers and making him jump back out of range, before barely being deflected by the remains of Vor's.

Thornfire hit the creature repeatedly with more shots of fire, keeping it occupied enough not to go after Karolan, but just barely. By then, Hawkwind seemed to have organized an attack group. Several griffins darted out of the surrounding trees and assaulted the beast, leaping on its back or standing cautiously close and taking swipes at its legs, but all they seemed to do was distract it. Karolan ran for the trees in turn, and then frantically backpedalled to escape a pouncing shadow-beast. Another griffin followed it, harrying the smoky creature, and Karolan managed to dodge out of range.

Vor took the chance to look for Craduticus and Altare. The two men were deeply engaged: exchanging blasts and bolts and angry words.

"Now," she whispered to the two earth toads still cowering behind her. "Go. Bite."

She wasn't sure they'd obey, but the six-limbed-parrot-beast that so upset them was in the other direction now from where Altare was. They swam into the dirt and vanished on their mission. Vor set to reconstructing her shields. If they'd been completely ruined, as Karolan's were, she'd have to abandon her circle or have an unbroken minute to begin building up their foundation again. She could fight without a circle, of course—as Altare was doing—but her position was much stronger with one.

As she finished, she was dismayed to see Craduticus being driven to his knees by alternating blasts of force and flashes of blue. Altare had devoted all his attention to his former master, and the old man was weakening—but then Karolan ran out of the forest to stand beside him, weaving new unanchored shields to protect him at least temporarily. And then Altare made a capering leap and his attacks faltered.

Vor chuckled. Her earth toads had reached him and, as ordered, were biting at his feet. Her mirth was short lived, for the six-limbed-parrot-beast's tail whacked her reinforced shield wall with shuddering strength and a blast of light. Nearly a dozen griffins were harrying the creature now, but none of them seemed to be doing any damage to it. It whirled again, smacking her shields another powerful tail blow.

Fire hadn't had any effect on it yet; she needed a new tactic. Vor looked up at the cloudless sky and fisted her hands. One she put straight up, and began feeding power into the atmosphere, building up an imbalance that could only be resolved one way. Her other hand she pointed towards the six-limbed-parrot-beast, giving it the opposite charge—that which would restore the balance. For several seconds she built the two opposing energies.

"Get away," she screamed at the griffins as she felt the balance tip.

They darted back just as a piercing stab of lightning struck the creature, dancing across its bony plates and spikes. It gave a squawk of outrage, quivering from the electricity, and staggered, dropping its chest to the ground. As soon as the play of lightning ceased, the griffins leapt in, clawing and biting

with greater vigor, and prompting another angry squawk.

It was back on its feet far faster than Vor liked, and apparently even angrier than it had been before. Its summoner had promised it food, but the food was proving too agile to eat. Perhaps, Vor hoped, if they could keep it unsatisfied long enough, it would turn back on Altare and demand payment out of his own flesh. Of course, even if it managed to eat him before he destroyed it, that might not sate it, and it could still come after anything else that moved.

The griffins were coordinating their attacks, but obviously tiring. One caught a slap from the six-limbed-parrot-beast's tail and fled into the trees, bloodied across its face and neck. Another had been trying to get under the creature's belly but got stomped on by one of its six legs, and had to limp out of the fight with one back leg no longer supporting its weight. No one wanted to get in range of the monstrous beak, but the six-limbed-parrot-beast kept trying to snag its enemies and drag them close. Most of the griffins had bloody tears and gashes from wriggling out of its claws. They couldn't last much longer.

Hawkwind, that black and white griffin that struck at such great speeds, and Thornfire kept hitting the creature aerially, but Thornfire's flame attacks hadn't had an impact, and the beast even seemed to shake off the physical assaults of the other two. A pair of humans ran out from the trees now with spears, and Vor winced. She didn't expect them to be able to keep up with the creature's speed the way the quick griffins could. They rushed in boldly, putting their weight behind their spear attacks, trying to drive the sharp points through the beast's thick skin.

They must have made an impression, for the six-limbed-parrot-beast squalled again and turned in a flash, yanking the imbedded spear shafts out of their hands. One man ducked, taking only a glancing blow and rolled under the beast's belly to escape, but the beast caught the other with one clawed hand and yanked him in. Three griffins leapt up at the beast's head, clawing for its eyes, but it ducked its head down between its first pair of legs.

There was no time to call another lightning strike. Vor hit the creature with a blast of fire, trying to avoid hitting any of the men or griffins, although one griffin did dash away, startled or singed. The black and white skydiving griffin executed a precision strike on the beast's second pelvis, staggering its hind legs but not seeming to upset it much. Thornfire hit it with a golden beam of light that didn't seem to do anything but make it squint.

Then came the wet crunch, the scream, and the squirts of arterial blood as the six-limbed-parrot-beast bit into the captured man. Secure in its beak and no longer having to hold the man down, the beast slashed up, grabbing two of the griffins on its head and pinning them to the dirt. It pressed down and

Vor heard bones snap as the beast tossed its head to help swallow the partially severed, still struggling man.

Several people cried out in denial. Vor gathered a substantial portion of her remaining power between her hands, as though holding a ball before her. When her hands started shaking, unable to contain any more, she drew back, and launched it—a globe of pure kinetic energy.

"Look out," she warned, as the power left her.

It struck the six-limbed-parrot-beast square in the side of the head. The partially masticated man went flying out of its bill in a mess of flesh and blood. The sheer force of the blow knocked the creature up and off its feet, staggering to the side, off of the two broken griffins. Other griffins dashed over to pull them away, into the dubious safety of the trees. The man who hadn't been bitten into pieces also scrambled away. Without the support of the main bulk of griffins, Vor thought it a wise course.

Now only two griffins remained circling the six-limbed-parrot-beast on the ground, and those two were keeping their distance. The three aerial griffins continued their attacks, but they, too, seemed at a loss for how to hurt the beast. The creature took little time regaining its stance, and seemed to look eagerly about for its next target.

A lance of fire hit Vor's shields, and she flinched.

"Are you ready for me, Vor?" Altare demanded.

At a glance, she saw charred earth and smoldering trees where Craduticus and Karolan had been standing a short while ago. There was no sign of either of them. Vor could only assume they'd either been incinerated or had been forced to pull back completely into the safety of the forest.

"Your allies are falling," her master taunted. "You'll soon be mine."

He sent another lance of flame with a twitch of his wand, and Vor tried altering her shields to deflect it, instead of taking it head on and losing her outer layer.

Altare took a step closer. "How would you like to die?" he grinned.

The six-limbed-parrot-beast slammed into her shields, only to recoil and turn when Thornfire hit it with lightning. Altare's next fire lance impacted her shields directly, and she felt them waver. Digging into her personal energies, she reinforced them.

"You're almost out of time," her master went on mercilessly, "and out of power."

A griffin cried out and Vor darted her gaze over. The six-limbed-parrot-beast had caught one of the two remaining ground-bound griffins under its foreclaws.

"I see you bedded the boy," Altare added. "He's not dead yet, just wounded. If you give me your report, I might consider some mercy for him."

Thornfire was pouring blasts of power onto the six-limbed-parrot-beast, but it was only delaying the inevitable, and the griffin mage must surely have been nearly depleted. The fire he wreathed himself in was fading, too. As Vor watched, a pure bolt of power sailed up at the griffin. He dodged, but not quickly enough, and the bolt caught his wing, burning off a few flight feathers. Thornfire fluttered and flapped, but could not stay airborne. He managed a controlled crash at the back of the clearing, behind Vor.

"Roast chicken for dinner," Altare gloated.

Hawkwind attacked the six-limbed-parrot-beast again, landing on its back and trying to sink in her claws and bill. The beast thrashed, keeping its griffin prey pinned, but attempting to shake off this new pest on its back. Hawkwind dug her bill in, and the beast screeched in pain.

"I don't think so," Altare declared.

Vor was already moving power. She threw a wind-borne shield between Hawkwind and the bolt her master threw. The bolt shattered against it, but destroyed the shield as well. Altare's focus snapped back to her.

"Worry about yourself," her master goaded.

His next energy bolt came straight at her. Vor tried to deflect it as she'd done the fire, and was partly successful, but the effort nearly drove her to her knees. Then a shadow-beast came running out of the trees, leapt, and caught Hawkwind. It dug its claws into her, having much better success than she was having against the parrot-beast. Her fur and feathers flew as it tore at her, and she tumbled from the six-limbed-parrot-beast's back to fall heavily to the ground under its feet.

Spying new defenseless prey, the parrot-beast's free forefoot came down on Hawkwind with crushing force. The shadow-beast had rolled free, saw the lone remaining mobile griffin, and pounced for it. The griffin evaded, and spun to face it, beginning to exchange claw swipes and snarls. Another bolt crashed into Vor's shields and they quivered on the verge of collapse. In the distance, back with the carry baskets, she thought she saw movement where the wizards were gathered, but nothing came of it.

"It's over, Vor," Altare grinned.

But then it wasn't.

As the six-limbed-parrot-beast was regarding its two prey items, it opened its massive bill for a fatal bite. Out dashed a small figure—lean, graceful, and clothed only in leaves.

Kassandra skidded to a halt next to the stinking six-limbed-parrot-beast and stuck her hands into the torn up soil. Up burst long, snaking vines that darted unerringly for the creature's head, between it and the trapped griffins. The beast tried to bite, but hit unyielding fibrous vines. They lashed around its neck, over and under its bill, and it tried to retreat, taking its feet off Hawkwind and the other griffin.

"No," Altare denied. "No you won't."

He sent a blast of force, but Vor had a shield in place, though generating it had almost made her pass out. Her master was starting to look tired, too, and now his behemoth swamp elemental, or whatever it was, was facing a threat it couldn't conquer. Kassandra hadn't moved, and all her focus was on producing more and more vines to bind the immense creature.

"A nymph," Vor heard Altare exclaim.

She dropped to one knee, fighting for balance and consciousness both, and tried to pull in more energy from anywhere she could. There was spilled blood. It made her queasy, but she drew up the energy of it. As the closest mage to it, she had first grab at it, and it began to renew her.

"I'll have you," her master declared.

Now he sent a whiplash of power. Vor hadn't enough energy yet to do anything to stop it, and when she did get a deflecting shield out, it was too late, bouncing off the magical lash. It wrapped Kassandra's slender white neck and the young woman immediately grabbed for it, leaving off her vine growing. Altare yanked and she toppled into the dirt, desperately pulling at the cord choking her. Already her pale skin was bruised blue and abraded.

"No," Vor pled, but another voice was stronger.

Karolan's roar of rage broke through the clearing, and he ran out, barely able to keep his feet. His clothing was half charred off him and his skin shiny with burns. He limped on one leg and had a bloody head wound that had plastered his hair to his face. He scrambled right past Vor and her shaking shield to seize Altare's lash. It shocked his hands as he touched it, but after a flinch he held on gamely and began tearing at it.

"Idiot boy," Altare growled. "Get out of my way and I may let you live."

"No," he cried back. "You can't have her."

Karolan lifted a hand to blast a fireball—though his aura looked so weak, Vor truly wondered where he'd find the power for it.

He never even got the spell off. Altare lifted his own hand and another blast of energy issued forth. Vor threw out the best shield she could manage, but it only stopped part of the strike. Karolan took the rest in the face. It knocked him back so he lost his grip on the lash. He fell onto his back directly in front of Kassandra, who was still on her knees. Now blood ran from his nose to drip down his face.

"Rain," Vor winced.

Karolan shook his head, rotated, and put his arms around the young woman behind him. With feeble hands he tried to untangle the lash from her neck, but it was wrapped tight. The six-limbed-parrot-beast was immobile now, bound in thick vines, but how long they would hold it Vor couldn't guess. There was no sign of any more shadow-beasts. Thornfire, still smoking from his burned feathers, stepped up behind Karolan and Kassandra.

Altare stared hate at the group. "Griffins that dare to be mages," he hissed.

"Surrender," Thornfire ordered. "You'll not harm anyone further."

"I'll kill you this time," he promised.

The master mage's face twisted in rage. With a brutal yank he wrenched back the whiplash—and as it came, it sliced deep into Kassandra's neck and throat.

Karolan screamed, beyond words, as the young woman's eyes widened. Her lips parted, she coughed, and blood ran from the corner of her mouth. The tide of scarlet below the lacerations coated her skin and the leaves she wore like clothing. Karolan tried to stem the flow, but it ran between his fingers and overflowed his hands.

Vor stared, unable to breathe, appalled.

"She's first," Altare snarled. He pointed his wand at Karolan. "You're next."

Vor had no memory of moving. All she knew was that she was suddenly between Karolan and Altare, having abandoned her protective circle, arms crossed out in front of her chest, building a new shield. Altare's fireball impacted her, breaking all around, but it only toasted her a little.

She took a step towards him.

Spikes of living darkness came at her next. They rocked her back and blurred her vision, but none of them got through.

She took another step.

Altare threw punches of pure power at her, making her stagger. She felt the ache of each one in her bones, but she ignored the feeling and threw more power to her shield. Blood trickled out of her nose and she tasted it in her mouth.

She stepped closer again.

"What do you think you can do, Vor?" Altare dared her. "You're weak. You're out of energy; I can see it."

Lances of fire at short range blasted against her shield, eroding it to a thin wisp and making her skin tighten with heat, and making the edges of her clothes smolder, too.

"Come back to me," he invited. "I'll let them go, and I won't kill you, not right away."

Vor took yet another step. She could have reached out and brushed his chest with her fingertips, but her shield was faltering. Again she thought she saw the wizards in the back shift, but no one did anything. She stood, panting, the taste of her own blood on her tongue, legs trembling with the threat of collapse, and stared at her master.

"How about this?" he coaxed. "I'll block your memories of all this unpleasantness. You can be one of my flower girls. I'll slice away your mind, bit by bit. You'll forget it all. You'll be at peace."

Now. She had to hit him now, but with what?

"Do you know," he went on, "before I came here today, I bled them all out so I'd have the power to kill you?"

Vor felt a moment of horror at his words, but she had not the luxury to be distracted. She didn't have enough energy left for a killing blow, not even if she suicided, using every bit she had, leaving nothing for herself. All that would do was wound him, and she'd be dead.

"It's fitting that you replace them. What do you say, Vor? I'll let these others go. You have my word." His smile was half sneer and he licked his sweaty lips.

Her eyes darted around, looking for inspiration. In the distance the wizards were clustered up, as if in heated debate, but there was no help from them. What could she do? There was nothing, nothing left—there. There was a spear on the ground, mostly hidden under the muck.

"I'll take you back to Weldom with me. Perhaps I could sire a son on you. The child of two strong mages like us would be a strong mage, too. I could mold him, shape him to follow in his father's footsteps."

Now.

Vor dropped to her hands and knees as though exhausted, or capitulating. She let her shield go. Someone shouted: maybe several someones. Her fingers dug into the mud, closing around the spear shaft. She sensed her master leaning over her, reaching down to her—

She came up to one knee, spear point snapping up and leading. Her other hand went to the butt of it and she anchored it against her hip. Vor had trained very little with weapons, focusing mainly on hand-to-hand self-defense, but she didn't let that worry her. She knew the pointy end was the part to stick into the enemy.

The spear bit into Altare's pectoral, just left of his breastbone. He re-coiled, but Vor went with him, surging to both feet with effort that made her lightheaded, pushing as hard as she could. Her master spent little time learning to fight, either, so he had few martial skills to aid him now. He slipped in the swampy dirt, and she pressed. He tried to turn, to get out of the way of that driving point, but Vor pushed faster than he could evade. She kicked out, hooking one of his feet out from under him, and he fell on his rump in the mud, back on his elbows. He tried to scoot back from the spear. With one hand he grabbed the shaft, near the head, but now Vor was in a lunge above him, her body weight behind the strike.

Altare fell to his back, writhing, trying to get away. Vor straddled his body, spear almost straight down now, both hands on the butt, shaft hugged to her chest.

"Vor," he babbled, "stop. Stop!"

She gritted her teeth and glared down at him. "No."

"I'll let you go. I'll let you all go. You're free to go!"

"No."

The spear wasn't going in any deeper, and after a moment, she realized she had the flattened head perpendicular to his ribs. She rotated it. It slipped in.

Altare drew a great gasp of air, eyes and mouth gone huge, both hands now pulling and yanking at the spear shaft. His feet beat frantically against the ground, digging up gouts of dirt and mud.

"Vor, Vor," he begged.

"No," she breathed.

The spear point bit deeper. Then she felt Altare pull at her remaining life energy as desperately as a drowning man pulls on his rescuer. Vor tried to keep it away, wall it off, but he pulled and pulled and she felt the grip of her hands start to weaken. She mustn't stop; the wound wasn't mortal yet.

Vor's gritted teeth turned into a snarl. With magical hands of her own, she plunged into her master's power. Voraciously, she took, and took. Her hands strengthened again. She leaned into the spear.

Altare twisted below her like a spiked and dying animal, grunting and snarling. She drew out his life energy like water from a well—more and more and more. His attempts at pulling on her power could not keep up as his blood began to run from him, as fear of death took him. He stared into his apprentice's visage and saw no mercy there.

"Vor," he rasped out, "Vor."

Below the point of the spear, his heart throbbed. Vor drove the spear into it.

Altare thrashed, kicking, bucking, but there was no escape. The muscles of his heart attempted a while longer to beat, but with the blade of steel through its center, it was no use. The blood backed up and spilled out. As his heart stilled, as his blood and body started to cool, he wondered if his own first master had felt what he was feeling: looking up into the vindictive face of his traitorous apprentice.

It was his last thought. Then Altare Dhordirh died.

***

Vor pushed on the spear until it emerged from the back of her master's body and pinned him to the ground. Her hands were oddly cool and calm as she released the butt of the spear. She stepped back, watching as the color of his life energy faded and dispersed into the dirt and air. She still had a large measure of his energy in her—that she'd stolen from him to hasten his death. With a grimace she expelled his filthy power in a burst, although it left her with only the dregs of her own, and she almost fell to her knees.

Then she was able to hear the ruckus behind her.

Several people were calling Kassandra's name. When Vor turned she saw them gathered around the young woman. Vor stumbled over with the intent to join them, but her legs couldn't keep up. She lost her footing and tumbled to all fours before she made it, staring at what she saw. Kassandra was coated in her own blood. Altare's magical lash had severed the vessels of her neck beyond repair. Wherever she wasn't covered in blood, the girl was pale blue now, and dying.

The six-limbed-parrot-beast struggled still against the vines restraining it. No one was attempting to fight it and Altare's death had not dismissed it. Vor glanced back at the Weldom wizards. They were speaking rapidly with each other and frequently looking over, but had not moved either to attack or assist yet.

Then a scream came out of the forest.

Vor clapped her hands over her ears but the sound pierced right through

283

them. She recognized the scream—for she had heard ones very like it several years ago, outside the door to Skire Germaine's lab. A blinding light burst from between the trees, scattering branches and leaves like a windstorm. The light leapt over the six-limbed-parrot-beast with a grace that transcended the most agile deer, and as it passed, the beast's skin began to split between its armored plates, across its head, and down its limbs. It shrieked and writhed, but there seemed no escape for it.

The bright light landed on four legs, gray but glowing from within like a thundercloud filled with heat lightning. On its brow was a dark spike of dusk. Its mane and tail streamed star-filled midnight. It lashed its head and screamed again and Vor feared her head would split.

Then it lowered its head and charged, slashing right and left with its spear of evening, driving back the humans and griffins that supported Kassandra. Even Karolan was knocked flat on his back, leaving the nymph trembling on her knees. Vor hadn't been close enough to take a hit, and was still able to gaze upon her. The bark-like texture she'd seen before on the young woman's feet had moved up to her knees, and moved higher even as Vor watched, growing up her thighs, hips, to her waist. The leaves and flowers she wore withered and fell from her.

The bright light came and stood over the girl, so that Vor couldn't bear to look at her any longer. The last image she had before turning her head was of Kassandra lifting her shaking hands up to touch the unicorn's face.

A second scream, deeper, came from the other side of the forest, and forth burst another bright light—this one blazing like a winter sun and crackling with blue fire. No one had been hurt when the first unicorn knocked them away; this second one trampled among the fallen, but again did not strike them, only rushed through until it, too, stood over Kassandra.

With the double light of two unicorns, Vor had to close her eyes. She heard Karolan sobbing roughly, and there was some kind of singing, or humming, just beyond the reach of her ears, but it filled her head nevertheless. She could do nothing but bear it and wait.

When it finally began to fade, Vor lifted her head and squinted around. The two unicorns were walking slowly away, back to the trees, shoulder to shoulder, heads deeply bowed. Their brightness had diminished and the breeze seemed to pull it away from them as it pulled at their manes and tails, like smoke from a blown out candle. They looked more like old, weary mules now than like immortal creatures with magic beyond anything a human could claim. Even their colors were washed out nearly to white.

As they vanished into the trees, Vor turned to where Kassandra had been.

Had been—for she wasn't there anymore. In her place stood a small, slender tree, but by its shape Vor could recognize faintly that it had once been the plant-covered young woman. The bark had grown up over her chest and crept along her arms, that still held the position Vor had last seen, of reaching up to the gray unicorn's face. The arms were branches now, with other twigs sprouting off them, all festooned with leaves.

The bark had also mercifully covered the gaping slashes in Kassandra's throat. Covered, too, was her face, and from her head grew up and spread more branches, forming the tree's full crown. Where she'd been kneeling, the trunk bulged and curved around to follow the shape of her legs before spreading into roots that plunged into the torn up soil in the center of the clearing. With no other trees around to shade it and steal its sun, the new tree would grow strong and tall. Even as she gazed upon it, Vor saw a bird flit over and dart into the canopy.

"Kassie."

It was Karolan, crawling towards the tree. He lifted a shaking hand but didn't touch the trunk. Her blood still coated him up to his elbows.

"No," he moaned. "No."

Vor flinched away from his howl of denial. Others went to him, trying to hold and comfort him, but his screaming went on. Vor wanted to put her hands over her ears again, but bit her cheeks instead, letting his soul-deep grief crash against her. Kassandra had paid the price of this—Kassandra and that man who'd been bitten in half, and others who might be dead under the trees, and others who were injured, maybe maimed.

Gradually, Karolan's screaming turned into sobbing.

***

"Mistress Vor."

She raised her head from where she was sitting, barely able to keep herself from sprawling. Wizard Giri was standing near. When she made no hostile move, he crouched down to be closer to her level. His gentle eyes settled on hers.

"This isn't your fault," he offered softly.

"It is no one's but mine," she snarled back, too exhausted to be polite.

He made an exasperated sound. "Don't be so arrogant. Karolan and his companions were planning to kill Altare months ago, long before you made the conscious choice to betray him. Weren't they? They used you to achieve their ends."

The sense of his words penetrated, and Vor let her grimace fade.

Giri went on. "The nymph chose to step into the fight without anyone's bidding—much less yours. Altare murdered her when all she was doing was trying to protect her friends. She didn't lift a single attack against him directly. This is not your fault."

Karolan's weeping had become soft and hoarse. Vor looked over at him. He was sobbing into Thornfire's arms. As if sensing her gaze, the griffin lifted his head to regard her. He gave a slow bow of his head.

"That griffin doesn't blame you, either," Giri observed.

"Karolan will never forgive me," Vor whispered.

"Karolan will never forgive himself," Giri corrected. "He will have much greater ease in forgiving you."

There were others gathering around the tree now: Hawkwind, the black and white griffin that had been doing aerial strikes, a brown and rust colored griffin, and the gray griffin Vor had ridden. They were all bloody and Hawkwind was limping badly, but heedless of wounds they leaned on each other, warbling, crying: mourning.

"Here, drink," Giri prodded, holding out a skin.

"What is it?" Vor asked.

His face fell a little at her distrust. "It's a tea, very dilute, but it will help you," he assured her. "You need some fluids."

He was probably right. Vor accepted it and took a swallow. The cool liquid bathed her insides and she felt a little stronger. A whoosh of fire distracted her, and she looked over. State Wizard Colby was standing by Altare's corpse. He'd ignited it. Black smoke started to rise. She looked next to where the six-limbed-parrot-beast had been, but its flesh had split open and decayed. Even its bones were melting as Vor watched: little bits falling off the top edges to plop into the mud as stinking vapors rose.

"It was a demon, not an elemental. It couldn't stand up to the presence of the unicorns, and it'll be gone soon enough," Giri remarked. "Will you come back to the castle with us?"

Karolan and his companions were ignoring her completely now. Was there any point in staying with them, or in just wandering off alone? She was exhausted and hurt. Vor didn't have much wild land experience, but she could guess that being alone in the forest in her current state would not be a good idea. Should she try to join Karolan and the griffins? She could try, but she felt immediately that she did not belong there.

Giri's presence, however, was glowing beside her. After the battle, when she was bruised down to her bones, limping on her last dregs of power, and stained with her master's blood, it was the wizards who had come to her, not the ones she'd helped. Realizing that, something shifted in her mind.

"I suppose so," she sighed. "But I'm not sure I'll stay there. Not for long, I mean."

"Will you return to Weldom?"

"I don't know yet."

Giri didn't press her, and for a moment, just sat with her as she took another drink.

"Master Craduticus," she realized, "the old man who was fighting from—"

"We know who he is," Giri assured her. "He's one of us, even if he's been away a long time. Look there."

Over in the blackened area, Wizard Milsa was kneeling next to a huddled form, brushing dirt and charred branches off him.

"Is he dead?" Vor asked.

Giri offered her his hand. "Let's go see."

She accepted, needing his help to get to her feet. Pure stubbornness kept her standing and allowed her to walk over without having to lean on him. Milsa had her hands on Craduticus, giving him some energy. The old man was whole, but his hair and most of his clothes were burned off. His exposed skin was red and blistered. Blood ran from his nose, mouth, and ears. On a man so old, such injuries could indicate fatal consequences. Vor dropped to her knees.

"Master Craduticus," she called. "Altare is dead. I killed him."

She thought maybe there was a slight response, a twitch of an eyelid.

"There are still students who need your teaching," Vor continued. "If you still wish to live, we still wish to have you."

The man shuddered and groaned. Giri quirked half a smile and shrugged out of his outer robes.

"Let's get him on this," he suggested, "and send him back to the castle. We can tend him better there."

"There's a healer," Vor informed. "Her name's Jesine. She can probably help. She'll at least be better than nothing."

"Vor?" Craduticus rasped. "You won?"

"I won," she confirmed, "with help. With your help."

He tried to smile and coughed. "Good girl."

Then he quieted, and fear clutched at Vor. She grabbed for his wrist, but Giri caught her hand.

"No, it's alright. He's just resting now. He'll recover," he assured her.

Vor tried to help roll Craduticus onto Giri's robes, but she was so weak she couldn't manage much except sitting still. Giri and Milsa together were able to carry the old mage away and set him in one of the drake baskets. They strapped him in, and then Milsa went to another, got in, and at some unspoken signal the two quartets of drakes powered into the air, taking Craduticus and Milsa with them. Half of the circling drakes departed, too, providing an escort.

Vor got up on her own this time, before Giri could return to her, and they went to join Wizard Colby. At his feet was a pile of charred bone fragments and ash, still smoking. Vor looked down at it, at all that remained of her master Altare.

"That's that problem taken care of," Colby was saying. Then he looked up and grinned at Vor. "Ah, the winner."

"I had a lot of help, sir," Vor demurred.

Giri smiled at her, but said nothing.

"You'll join us back at the castle?" Colby asked.

"For now," she confirmed. "What are Weldom's intentions, sir?"

"Right to the point," he chuckled.

"You might consider speaking with the remaining royals of Northnest," Vor mentioned, though every word cost her energy. "The king, I am sure you're aware, is in poor condition, but his daughter—not the one you saw before, she was an imposter—is alive, and eager to have some part in the kingdom of her birth."

"And where is this princess?"

"She's in hiding at the moment, along with Ulver, Eriducus, and Chirolen," Vor explained.

"She's wise to be wary of Weldom," Colby grunted.

"I told her to stay away," she said, trying not to sway with another bout of lightheadedness. "If you grant her safe passage, however, she would probably consent to speak with you. I think Master Craduticus knows her fairly well. He would have more thoughts on it."

Colby folded his arms, watching the ash from Altare's body dance in a light breeze.

"You know, I have little say in anything," he commented. "I am only a servant, a messenger. I cannot make decisions on behalf of the Ministers, but I would be willing to speak with the woman."

"She doesn't have any military might," Vor mentioned weakly. "I don't see how she could be a threat to Weldom."

"Ah," he countered, "but if she is a royal of Northnest, and the people are behind her, then there could be a problem."

Vor shrugged a little. At this point, she just wanted out of it. The griffins and remaining men were crawling out of the trees, gathering behind the

Kassandra-tree. Someone had done the grisly job of collecting the slain man's body parts and bringing them—as much as possible—back together, but there was no resurrecting him. The other wounded had begun lining up on the far edge of the clearing, where the ground was less mangled. The more able bodied were starting to move among them, staunching wounds and setting broken bones.

"May we help them?" Giri asked softly.

Colby frowned. Vor took an unsteady step towards the triage area.

"I can help them," she said. "I should at least tell them that they can expect no hostility from us—you—right?"

She looked between Giri and Colby for confirmation. After a sigh, Colby nodded.

"If they make no aggressive moves against us, we'll make no attack on them," he allowed. "We have no orders to attack random groups of people outside of Northborn's borders, where I believe we are now."

"Master," Giri said, "permission to assist with the wounded?"

Colby heaved a deeper sigh. "Oh fine, very well." He made a shooing gesture. "Just don't exhaust yourself."

The State Wizard turned to go back to the waiting double quartet of drakes. Giri looked to Vor and gave an encouraging smile.

"After you," he said.

***

Vor first sought out Hawkwind. The big female was with another griffin that looked similar in size and coloration but had hacked off flight feathers and shackle scars. They were examining each other's wounds. Although coated with plenty of blood, neither were missing body parts or currently hemorrhaging. Hawkwind was clearly favoring her left hind leg, but it didn't look deformed, as it would have had it been badly broken.

"Hawkwind?" Vor called timidly.

"Vor," the griffin replied.

She started to get to her feet, but Vor waved her down, wanting to collapse herself.

"Rest, warrior," she said. "We mean no harm. We wanted to let you know that Weldom holds the castle now, but there won't be any attacks or retaliation, or anything like that, not unless they're attacked first."

Vor couldn't tell what the griffin was thinking. Her face seemed impassive and serious.

"What of Jessika?" Hawkwind asked.

Giri took a step closer and the griffin's sharp gaze flicked to him immediately.

"I'm Wizard Giri Holstor, from Weldom," he introduced. "We who have come are acting on orders from above, so we can't make critical decisions, but we're happy to talk with the princess—and her father, if he is able. In fact, if you want to bring him back to the castle—I know you just removed him and would be sorry to make you carry him all the way back again—we could probably assess what can be done about the device Altare and the other mages have used on him. The false princess, too, that Altare has bewitched we might be able to help. I can make no promises of anything, but at the minimum we don't want conflict or bloodshed."

She listened politely to his speech. "You've certainly allowed it here," Hawkwind growled.

Giri tilted his head. "This was a private matter between Altare, his apprentices, and former master. It did not interact with our orders to secure the capital, not unless someone had attacked us." A hint of steel came into his voice. "Luckily, no one did, or the outcome would have been dramatically different."

"I see," the griffin replied, just as cool.

Giri's expression was completely unapologetic.

"I will carry your words to Princess Jessika," Hawkwind said after a moment. "It may be she will wish to make a visit. I was once a Feathyr, and so were several of these other griffins. They were imprisoned as slaves. We all saw our friends and families slaughtered in the invasion. You can understand if we do not have positive feelings for Weldom."

"Indeed, I can," Giri answered sincerely, but without any hint in his voice of either guilt or sympathy.

"How can we be assured that our visit will not be misinterpreted by the drakes or their masters as an attack?" Hawkwind queried.

"I might suggest an arrival by land, not air," Giri offered, "through the gates, properly announced, as any polite person might make a visit. I will instruct my fellows to be on the lookout for such a house call."

Hawkwind gave a tight nod.

"In the meantime, might I be allowed to help with the wounded?" Giri asked with every inch of courtesy.

The griffin's gaze flicked over to Vor. "You trust this man?" she rumbled.

"You ask me that?" Vor retorted in surprise. "Do you even trust me? I have been your enemy."

"Yes," Hawkwind concurred. "An honest enemy, and now an ally."

Vor felt her lips start to curl back from her teeth. "We shall see, but for what it's worth, yes, I trust him to help, not hurt, at least here, at least now."

Giri glanced at her, half his mouth quirked at all the qualifications she put on her statement of trust, Vor guessed, but another slight hint of disappointment at her distrust lingered in his eyes.

"Very well then," the griffin consented.

Giri bowed and started away for the most injured. Vor took two steps to follow and lost sensation in her legs, falling to her hands and knees. He was back beside her immediately, a warm hand on her back; she didn't have the strength to shake it off. She felt him assess her energy with a brush of his, and couldn't stop him from doing that, either.

"Rest, Vor," he urged. "You have nothing left."

She started to protest, and then changed her mind to nod agreement, and then the dirt and grass was suddenly rushing at her face, and then there was darkness.

Chapter 25
The Shifting of Power

Vor awoke in her own bed, back in her room at Northborn castle. She opened her eyes to look up at her familiar ceiling, like she had a thousand times.

"He's dead," she breathed.

She remembered the battle. She remembered driving the spear into her master's breast, through his heart. She remembered watching him die. Now he was gone. Wizard Colby had burned his body to ashes. And the swamp demon had bitten a man in half. And the nymph-girl Kassandra had died, and the unicorns had come screaming, and Karolan had screamed like he was dying, too.

The castle felt empty, like some multi-limbed tentacular monster that had filled every room and corridor with its bulk had pulled in its appendages and flowed back through whatever portal that had brought it, away into some other world from which it could not return. In its place now was a scatter of new little bright lights, noisy and random and imperfect, but human, and a lot of empty space.

Afternoon sunshine snuck around the edges of the window curtains. She was clean and the burn-bite wound on her arm had been freshly dressed. She could feel a few other bandages, too, covering wounds she hadn't noticed getting during the fight. Even her hair had been washed. Someone had obviously tended to her in her unconscious state and put her to bed in one of her sleeping shifts.

She hoped it hadn't been Wizard Giri.

Then she blushed.

Then she paled with horror and shoved to a sitting position. Vor covered her face with her hands and rubbed her forehead.

"No, I have no interest in Wizard Giri," she scolded herself.

She recalled the warmth of his hand on her back, and the brush of his aura, just before she'd collapsed on the battlefield. She didn't know how she'd gotten back to the palace or how she'd gotten clean, or who had done any of it. Logically, the wizards had carried her back with one of those drake baskets, and turned her over to Amlee and Kari at the palace. Maybe the healer-midwife Jesine had come in to dress her wounds.

Her stomach, realizing she was awake, rumbled and pinched with hunger. Her mouth was dry and her thirst hit her a moment later. Vor almost never used the bell pull to summon a servant, but she thought this situation qualified. She swung her trembling legs out of bed to step over to it—and tripped a magical ward on the floor. The simple trap went off with a tiny snap, and with no harm whatsoever.

"Well, now they know I'm awake," Vor groused.

She hadn't even thought to scan for wards. Someone had the audacity to place a trap right by her own bed, in her own, private room. Perhaps there was no need to summon a servant now; the mage who set the ward would have sensed its activation. Vor figured she'd probably have a guest or guests of some kind in a few minutes. She tried to taste the residue of power to sense who had set it, but it was fast fading and she got nothing useful.

A robe much heavier than her sleeping shift had been tossed over the foot of the bed. She managed to reach it without passing out, and ran a quick magical scan over it, but detected nothing out of the ordinary. She pulled it on: wincing at aches in her back and arms. She checked her own energy level and found it on the low side of normal—instead of nearly nonexistent. Rest had helped renew her. Food and drink and a walk in the garden would complete the cure.

As she'd expected, a knock came at the main door to the suite.

"Come," Vor called.

The guests came into her bedroom a moment later. It was Amlee and Kari, carrying a tray and a jug and both smiling cautiously. Vor made a helpless wave.

"As you like," she grunted.

The women put down their burdens on the table by the window and came over to either side of her. Vor let them help her up and guide her to the table.

"I'm fine," she protested grumpily as they reached their destination.

Kari backed off, but Amlee was not so easily deflected. The castellan helped unite bum with chair and took the lid off the tray. Kari poured her rosehip water. The food was light and bland, suitable for someone who was recovering from bed rest and had a totally empty stomach. It would do for now.

Vor dug in. Amlee and Kari hovered annoyingly. At last Vor arched an eyebrow up at them. The castellan smiled more broadly and dismissed Kari with a gesture. The maid curtsied and turned to go, but before she exited she looked back over her shoulder.

"We're glad you're back, Mistress," she smiled.

"Kari," Amlee warned.

The young woman bobbed her head and left, shutting the door behind her. Amlee turned back to Vor still with a hint of a smile.

"Are the wizards giving you trouble?" Vor asked.

"Not at all," Amlee said, "unless you count Pella's infatuation with a certain one of them."

"Really?" Vor asked in some surprise, recalling the maidservant who had been assigned to Wizard Milsa the first night they'd been in residence at the castle some days ago. She'd assumed one or more of the wizards—honestly, she assumed Giri—had bedded the young woman, and the evidence supported something like that.

"It will pass," Amlee assured her. "Pella knows better. Her good sense will return before long. It's not often that a maidservant who attracts the attention of a lord has a good first experience and is treated kindly after—especially not in this castle."

"Are they continuing to make free with the servants?" Vor enquired darkly.

"No," Amlee said. "There's seven of them now, but they keep to themselves. Pella's fantasies go unrealized."

"Good," Vor decided.

"Yes. Masters Eriducus, Ulver, and Chirolen have returned; I wanted to tell you. They have been accepted here without retribution."

"Weldom is being generous, I sense," Vor commented.

"That may be. They also bore a message that Princess Jessika and an entourage will be arriving in two days."

"That will be exciting," she said, only a little dryly.

Amlee didn't reply, but let Vor eat in silence for some minutes. She felt much better for having the food and drink. At last she'd eaten all she could and nudged the tray away.

"Young Master Karolan has not returned," Amlee offered softly as she approached to cover the tray.

That hit a soft spot, not deeply, but there nonetheless. Vor let go her breath.

"I don't know if he will," she said. "He might come with the entourage, if he's recovered some. He lost a loved one in the fighting."

"I've heard the recounting of the battle," Amlee murmured.

"How is Master Craduticus?"

"Recovering," the castellan answered, "but still abed. He is an old man and his injuries are considerable. I hope he will be well again in time."

"Thank you."

Vor said no more, and Amlee gathered up the remains of the meal, managing to juggle both pitcher and tray.

"I am told to inform you that you're invited to dinner with the rest of the mages and wizards," the castellan said, "at seven. It is already after five, but—"

"I'll be there," Vor told her at once, and then took a second to try to figure out why she'd agreed so automatically.

She frowned, and couldn't come up with anything concrete, except that she thought she needed to be there. She owed the wizards something, and it was her castle, sort of, and she wanted to get a look at them, and thank some of them. She shook her head a little: something like that. Then another thought occurred to her, and she surrendered to it. If she was going at all, she might as well—

"Last week for the engagement party I had a dress. I had to break the ties to—"

"It's been repaired. I'll be here at a quarter 'til to help you with it, Mistress."

Vor nodded mutely. Amlee left.

***

This time, Vor let Kari and Amlee leave most of her hair down, just instructing them to braid back the front, so it wouldn't get in her face or fall in her food. She showed them a braiding pattern used commonly in the western mountains, where she'd been born. She remembered her mother used to braid her hair with it, and wore such braids herself. Giri had his hair braided with it, too.

Vor was almost late for dinner, but not everyone had sat down yet, so it wasn't a shameful entrance. Edgard and several other servants she recognized—not Pella—were there getting ready to set out the first dishes. Giri smiled at her, and Milsa and Colby, too, wore pleasant expressions at her appearance. There were a few more wizards besides them, turning to look at her. Chirolen, Ulver, and Eriducus all leapt to greet her.

"Well again at last."

"Such a fight I hear."

"That's our Vor, beat the crakrat just as he deserved."

She couldn't help smiling at them, but urged them to sit down and stop making a fuss. They directed her to a seat next to Ulver, right at a corner of the table, so there was no one else directly beside her, and everyone except Wizard Colby sat.

"Some brief introductions," he said. "Everyone, this is Vor Hearthsraven, former apprentice of the late Altare Dhordirh and his conqueror, daughter of Juleena Mrandis, of House Mrandis in Lenali, on Mount Brasson."

Vor's breath caught and she tried too late to stop her eyes widening in horror.

They knew who her mother was.

Vor had her father's surname because her mother had been disowned from her ancestral House. Her father had been a common soldier and the surname Hearthsraven should not have attracted any attention. Although he had officially married her mother in peasant fashion, before the heads of the village, it hadn't been sanctioned by her mother's House, which technically made it illegitimate, and likewise made Vor a bastard. Any records regarding her would have been sketchy at best, and couldn't have been easy to track down.

Someone had made an effort.

Vor felt herself pale and flush. She'd never wanted her parentage acknowledged. Telling Karolan some about it had been one thing—he wasn't from Weldom and had been raised by griffins besides—but these people were likely nobility. They would know of House Mrandis, at least by name. They might know of the disgraced daughter of the House. If Colby had told them any more than he'd just announced, they would clearly know she was the daughter of said disgraced lady and a peasant man. Even mentioning only her mother's name was a hint that her father was common or—worse—unknown.

"Mistress Hearthsraven, four new come wizards from Weldom: Strafa Morne, Ylanzo Elssev, Rossilla Omistri, and Lissian Trekel."

"A pleasure to meet you all," Vor said, clawing back her poise. "I hope your stay here, however long it may be, is a comfortable and rewarding one."

Colby went on to mention a little more about each of them, including that indeed they were all from Noble Houses, although mostly minor ones.

The newcomers were two men and two women, one of each being older and one of each being younger, but all were older than Vor. The older woman Strafa showed the dark skin and hair of western Weldom, like Vor and Giri, although she was darker than either of them. The older man Ylanzo was nearly a match for Ulver and the other two Northborn mages in appearance, with thin white hair and a thick beard. The younger woman Rossilla—who probably had three decades and change—was also somewhat dark with a sweet face. The younger man Lissian of barely three decades if that, was pale and freckled, with surprisingly red hair.

None of them made comment on Vor's heritage, and Giri gave her another smile from across the table as the group of eleven set to the dinner. Was there a hint of apology in that smile? Vor couldn't decide how to respond to it. She was still mostly full from her earlier meal and ate little, instead listening and watching the conversation while staying largely out of it. The wizards were talking of plans for Northborn. At this point it mattered little to Vor what became of the country, which was a good thing, because it was clear that Weldom was planning to annex and absorb it entirely.

***

Vor managed to get in a quick walk in the garden after the meal. The wizards had broken up into groups, going off to various destinations. It seemed there were already some set friendships among them, and Ulver and the other two mages were fitting in well. They, too, had gone off somewhere. Vor thought she was alone, standing at the pond and staring at the sunset reflected in the water, but then she sensed a brush of gentle energy. Its owner was making no effort to disguise himself.

Giri had found her.

"Mistress Hearthsraven, may I join you?"

The request was diffident, polite.

"As you like," she murmured neutrally in reply.

He stepped up to the bank of the pond, not too close to her. "You're recovered, I see."

Vor sighed and didn't try to hide it. "Oh, stop with the small talk."

She sensed rather than saw his smile. "How do you like them?"

"The wizards? They seem fine."

"Do you want to stay with us? You're welcome, you know."

"I have not decided."

"Where else would you go? You're from Weldom."

"I'm a bastard from Weldom," she corrected. "And State Wizard Colby just told everyone all about it."

"I wish he hadn't said that, but believe me, they don't care," he said firmly. "All that matters is power. Yours is settling and it's not inconsequential. You'll soon see just how powerful you can become."

Vor turned to walk back to her rooms. The sunset was fading into night. The summer insects started to sing and Giri was becoming just a dark shape on the water's edge. It was warm still; she could have stayed out without a chill, but she found herself wanting her solitary space in her room. It wasn't that she didn't like Giri, but—

"I've had enough talk of power," she said as she moved away.

"Vor," he called out, and she paused. "Don't be afraid of us," he said then, almost plaintively.

She turned and caught his gaze in the twilight. "Goodnight, Giri," she said.

"Will you consider it? Will you talk with me about it again? Ask me anything you like?"

Realistically, it was a good option: she knew that. It was just that there was more to ponder as well, and something about it made her a little nervous—not scared, just uncertain.

"I will consider it," she promised.

"Tomorrow, the masters want you to brief them on the princess and her companions."

Vor huffed. "I know little."

"You know much more than they do."

She nodded. "I will talk with them."

"Thank you."

"Goodnight, Giri," she said again.

This time he didn't call her back, although he looked like he wanted to.

"Goodnight, Vor."

***

"You're certain she is the daughter of the old king?" Ylanzo asked yet again.

Vor's lips thinned. "As certain as I can be without having watched the king bed the queen and then waited until the queen swelled up and witnessed the birth and—"

"Enough, Mistress Vor," Colby interrupted with a hint of reproof. "We understand that you believe she is the rightful princess."

Giri however, was chuckling behind his hand, and Ulver and company

299

looked amused, too. Craduticus still wasn't with them, but Vor thought he might have laughed as well, had he been there.

"And she wants to rule the kingdom, does she?" Strafa mused.

"She has no idea what running a country is like," Vor said. "She was stolen away during the invasion and raised by griffins. As I understand it, she didn't return to human society until last year, and since being rescued from this castle again by griffins, hasn't been back in human society. I was told she's been living with a faun, in the woods I presume."

Colby shook his head. "She certainly can't be given any power, at least not immediately, but we can find out if the Ministers would allow her a presence among the council here."

"It might make the people happy," Rossilla contributed, "more accepting of this transition, especially if she publically endorses it."

Colby shrugged.

"And what of these griffins?" Ylanzo pressed. "They were Feathyrs?"

"Some were, and made into mine slaves, but others are wild, and only involved because they are friends of the princess," Vor explained.

"You don't think they present any threat to us," Colby surmised.

Vor frowned. "It's hard to say. I've almost exchanged more blows than words with them, so I don't know them well. I don't think the wild ones will want anything to do with us. Some of the mine slaves—former Feathyrs— might be angry, and want some kind of revenge, but they are few. There is only one, called Hawkwind, who might want to talk, who might come with the princess, I think."

"You've exchanged blows with them?" Strafa clarified with a trace of alarm.

Vor almost smiled. "The wild ones have mages, good ones. A couple times there were disagreements as to the disposition of the princess."

"But you say they won't get involved," Ylanzo pointed out.

"I don't think they will," she repeated, "unless we do something aggressive."

"Or have another disagreement about the princess." Colby sat back and crossed his arms. "This Hawkwind, what's he like?"

"I think it's a female," Vor corrected. "She seemed stalwart, brave, and fierce in battle, and protective of her people."

They all digested that.

"I've never met a griffin," Lissian murmured.

"Glorious creatures," Chirolen offered unexpectedly. "I saw them fight during the invasion." He shook his old head. "Brave and fierce are two good words for them. I could tell by watching them that they were much like us.

They banded together, reinforced weak points, and leapt to the defense of the wounded, yet they fought like the wildest human warriors: smart and vicious."

He rubbed his brow with a hand. "They fought to their last breaths and died the most honorable deaths warriors could hope for. It was then that I knew what we were doing was wrong."

The room fell into complete silence. Eriducus put a hand on Chirolen's shoulder, his eyes also downcast. Ulver had winced at almost every word, and was chewing his mustache.

"That is in the past now," Colby offered eventually, "and can't be changed. Vor, you think this Hawkwind will come with the princess?"

"I think she might," Vor allowed.

"And they might bring back the king and the false princess that Altare enchanted," Giri put in.

"And who invited them to do that?" Colby grumped. "I suppose we can do something about them."

"Karolan Freyaliv, and another escapee called Rikah might also come," Vor said.

They enquired about those two for a bit and Vor told them what she knew—only the relevant facts. The wizards might know she'd had some kind of personal involvement with Karolan, but she omitted any mention of it. She wasn't much looking forward to the visit by Jessika and whomever she brought with her. If she could have, she would have hidden in her room or the stillroom, but the wizards had already expressed that they wanted her present.

She did manage to escape to the stillroom once the wizards were done interrogating her. A few hours spent making potions and powders for the needs and ailments of the various people in and around the castle restored her serenity. Hand delivering those goods afterwards, as dinnertime approached, renewed her contentment. The smiles and thanks of her recipients always did that for her.

Vor took her evening meal in her room, avoiding any company. After that, she turned out all the lights except the one by her desk, and continued her studies. Now without a master, she would have to make her own way. Not knowing how long she would remain at the castle, she had to get through as many of the magic books in the library as she could and commit them to memory and into her journal in shorthand notes.

Someone knocked on her door around dusk, but she ignored it. She suspected it was Giri, and refused to think about what they might speak of, or worse what they might do, if she let him in. She recognized that she was particularly aware of him; she just wasn't certain why, or what it might lead to if she allowed it to develop. After one more try, the knocker—whoever it was—went away. When fatigue found her, she retreated to her bed with a book. When the candle burned out, she lay in the dark until she fell asleep.

***

As expected, Vor was summoned to be present when the delegation lead by Princess Jessika reached the castle the next morning. She put on her best remaining suit, and fixed an impassive expression on her face. Entering the throne room she saw that a collection of chairs, as well as a few couches, had been brought in and put in a roughly circular arrangement—a good indication of equality and that this was to be a discussion, not a lecture. There were small end tables dotted among them as well.

Vor was pleased to see Craduticus finally up and about. He was the only one sitting just yet, and he had a particularly comfortable chair that was slightly reclined. The other wizards were gathered near the door to greet the delegation. Vor went to stand beside Craduticus, and he gave her a weak grin.

Then Amlee lead the group into the room.

The two young men, Karolan and Rikah, came first, looking around warily as if expecting a trap. Karolan seemed to recognize Colby, Giri, and Milsa, and bowed stiffly. His eyes flicked over the rest of the group, including Vor, without pausing. Introductions began, and Jessika came in behind the two men, looking tidy and clean at least, but hardly like royalty in simple trousers and shirt.

Then came the griffins. First was Hawkwind, limping only slightly on one hind leg. With her was the other griffin that looked quite similar in coloration and size, but had the scars of collar and shackles from the mines, cut feathers, and several wounds that had been shaved and stitched. But there were more griffins, eight more: six with the marks of mine slaves, and two fully feathered and presumably from the wild. Vor strained her ears to hear the introductions.

Hawkcall: the one that looked like Hawkwind. Thornfire: yes, Vor recognized him. Thornwing: a brown and rust colored griffin that had also fought the six-limbed-parrot-beast. Then the six former Feathyrs, former mine slaves: Snowdark, Eaglegrace, Cloudmoon, Icerock, Falcondream, and Falconsong. The last one, Falconsong, was the juvenile Karolan had freed down in the mines. Falcondream seemed to be staying protectively close to her, but she glared around with fierce eyes.

The griffins—most bearing some amount of injuries from the battle against Altare and his minions—arranged themselves in a semicircle beyond the edge of the circle of chairs: opposite from where Vor was standing

302

by Craduticus. After the crowd of griffins came four men who also looked to be former mine slaves. They were guiding the old king and the false princess with gentle hands. Amlee immediately took charge of the false princess, who seemed to recognize her with pleasure.

Introductions concluded: everyone took a seat. The griffins sat directly on the floor. Even Colby relinquished the opportunity of having a position of dominance by sitting down. Vor took a chair beside and slightly back from Craduticus. Ulver was on her other side. Jessika had taken a central seat, with Rikah and Karolan flanking her. Hawkwind had found a spot clear enough for her to sit near Jessika, too.

The griffins and Northnest citizens stared across the circle at the wizards from Weldom and a tense silence fell. Amlee led some servants in, and they began handing around tea, even to the griffins—who accepted but then seemed puzzled as to how they might drink from the tiny, delicate cups. The silence deepened as a few people sipped but no one spoke.

Vor wished she weren't there. Anywhere would have been better. She resolved to keep her mouth shut. What happened to Northborn, or Northnest, really was none of her affair. She wasn't planning to stay. She didn't know where she'd go, but she didn't see herself living in the castle much longer, so it didn't matter what happened to it. She wasn't about to be the one to break the silence.

One of the griffins cleared its throat. "Well." It was Thornfire. "As a neutral party, perhaps I can help to get things going," he offered.

"Neutral party?" Colby echoed.

"Indeed." He set his teacup down on a side table and stepped over and around chairs, pushing a few empty ones aside, until he'd made a space for himself in the inner circle. "I'm only here to observe," he explained. "I'm not from Northnest or Weldom. I need only report the results of this discussion to my people, so we are aware of whatever you all decide on."

"Your people?" Colby prompted.

"You humans tend to call us the 'wild griffins,' although we consider ourselves quite civilized."

"But you are friends with Princess Jessika then," Wizard Strafa pointed out.

"So are others on your side of the circle," Thornfire observed.

The wizards glanced at each other. A few looked at Vor. She glared right back.

"That would be me," Craduticus announced, raising a hand. "I vowed to spend my remaining life protecting her."

Several of the wizards looked stunned by that admission.

"Perhaps you should switch sides," Ylanzo suggested narrowly.

"Ah, but I'm quite comfortable here, resting these weary bones of mine," Craduticus grinned back. "I was thinking that perhaps we should start by discussing how we might all clean up the last of my misguided apprentice's messes."

He gestured towards the innocently idle king and false princess.

"Hmm," Chirolen grunted. "The crakrat killed old masters Bellara and Mikin. They were deeply involved in making that nasty cap on the king's head. We three didn't have much role in it."

"But I did," Craduticus said. "I will do what I can, with the help of anyone else who is willing, to undo what the cap does, as much as is possible at this point."

Jessika spoke up for the first time. "Will you be able to take it off?"

"Ah, child," Craduticus winced. "I think it unlikely, but I hope we may at least be able to remove most of the spells, and we will see how he reacts. The brain is a complicated thing, and he's worn that for nearly a decade now."

Wizard Milsa was drumming her fingers on the arm of her chair. "This is a callous thing to say," she spoke up. "But might breaking those spells do more harm than good? Might it cause distress, even make his condition worse, even kill him?"

Craduticus nodded slowly. "It might, yes, but if we don't try, he lingers on in this not-life. He hasn't now the wits to understand the question, so there is no point in asking him if he wants it removed, but I recall his screams and how he fought. He did not want it then, and I believe that if there is any part of him still aware, he would want us to try to take it off, to try to free him, even if he does die from it."

Colby made a dismissive gesture. "Do as you like."

"I'll help," Giri volunteered at once.

"And I," Ylanzo said, surprising Vor. She hadn't expected the stiff-necked man to lift a finger for anyone's benefit.

"I would," Strafa spoke up, "but that girl needs my help more. There might not be much left of her to save, but as it is, she'll shortly be a drooling invalid, and I have a good touch for the kinds of mind magic I sense upon her."

"Very well then," Colby said, slightly gritty. "When we conclude let us separate as we will into two groups and do what we can for the king and girl. Nothing that Weldom would object to can come from that."

"Even if we renew Northnest's king, who hates us?" Craduticus pointed out.

Colby's gaze fell fully onto Jessika. "Which brings us to the discussion of the role, if any, the Northnest royals will play in this region."

Vor did not envy the girl the attention that now focused onto her. To her credit, she kept her back straight and her expression steady.

"It is my kingdom," Jessika said softly.

"You were conquered," Colby refuted. "If you want it back you'll have to conquer the new owners, and you don't have the military might to defeat Weldom unless there are thousands of your griffin friends willing to fight and die for you. The sooner you accept that, the better. You must be grateful that we are allowing this conversation at all."

Jessika's brow had firmed. "My family—my ancestors—built this kingdom, with the griffins: an alliance between races."

Colby had his gaze constant on her. Vor wondered what he was thinking. At last he looked slightly away.

"We do not wish to see the slaughter that was the invasion ever again," the State Wizard said. "Are you aware that your father rebuffed Weldom when overtures were made for a trade alliance between our two countries?"

"No," Jessika confessed. "He must have had a good reason."

"His reasons were not explicitly outlined to the Ministers," Colby said, folding his hands. "When we could not get what we wanted by cooperative methods, we turned to violent methods. I say we, although none of us present were involved in the decision."

"And have you gotten what you wanted?" Hawkwind growled.

"Yes," Colby confirmed, seeming unimpressed by the griffin's anger. "The mage-stone lode under the castle—nearly all of it has been mined and distributed back to Weldom. So have several other small mines in the country been exhausted."

"If you have what you want, then give Northnest back to me," Jessika commanded.

"It is not in the nature of the Ministers to abandon conquered territory," Ylanzo explained.

"There is the possibility of you having a role to play in this region," Colby stated, "but I, we, cannot grant that to you. We are not the decision-makers, only the servants who carry out the decisions."

"These Ministers you speak of," Hawkwind said, "they make the rules?"

"That is one way to put it," Colby confirmed.

"Where are they?"

"Back in the capital."

The griffin nodded sharply. "Then to get a decision from them?"

Colby nodded back. "The princess would need to go to them, and plead her case." He transferred his gaze back to Jessika. "If you ask them for Northnest back, they will laugh at you. If you build your argument, however, for why you should be a part of the governing of this area, you might yet find a place to be content. They might agree for you to live here, in the palace you were born in, to watch over your people and advocate for them to the Ministers—or something along those lines."

"Go to the capital of Weldom?" Jessika echoed, looking pale. "Is it far?"

There were some politely smothered chuckles from the wizards.

"By horse, you could expect a journey of a month if travelling in the summer," Colby described. "We teleport ourselves by magic. One or more of us could take you along, and you'd be there almost at once."

"Or in a few days," Milsa added softly. "Going such a distance in one jump is rather difficult, so sometimes we do it in legs, staying over at inns between jumps."

"I think we could get you there in about a week, flying," Hawkwind muttered to Jessika, "depending on the weather. The average griffin is around five times faster than a horse, unburdened."

"And that is the other reason it might be profitable to go," Colby interjected, "for some of you feathered folks to go. You had an alliance between griffins and humans here in Northnest. Why not expand that to all of Weldom?"

"You wizards understand," spoke up Snowdark from the outer circle, "the difference between the words alliance and slavery?"

"I am coming to understand that griffins are not simple animals, as drakes are, but people as much as humans are people," Colby affirmed. "My messages to the Ministers will convey that, and you will be treated as guests as much as the princess and whatever human escort she brings. Like her, it will be up to you to discuss the possibilities with the Ministers for what place griffins might find in Weldom, and likewise you would have the choice to accept or reject it."

Hawkwind had clenched her bill, and Vor had the sudden impression that she was holding something back. The feathers on her head and shoulders fluffed up, likewise her tail, and every other griffin made a curious subtle movement—shifting their posture as their own feathers settled flatter. Vor couldn't begin to guess what Hawkwind had just told them, but she had no doubt that something had been communicated.

"That is good information to take under advisement," Thornfire murmured.

Jessika was biting her lip, brows creased. Rikah reached over and put a hand on her tense shoulder.

"If any of us should decide to go visit the Weldom capital and the Ministers—" the blacksmith's son spoke up.

"Simply come and inform us," Colby provided. "We'll send a message ahead of you. The Ministry schedule is always overbooked; there will probably be a reply of when is best to come, and if you go then, you'll avoid having to wait around for days or even weeks to be seen."

Jessika had her hands clenched tightly in her lap. One thing the young woman was not good at was hiding her feelings. Vor thought she had better work on that if she was ever to venture into politics. When for a few moments the princess said nothing, Colby sat back.

"Perhaps we should adjourn for now," the State Wizard suggested. "The king and poor girl there can be tended to, and maybe we might all share a meal this evening, as friends?"

Still Jessika said nothing, staring a hole in the floor. Colby folded his hands.

"Or at least," he revised, "as something other than outright enemies?"

"Let it be as you say," Hawkwind concurred.

The group went into motion then. The griffins at the back gathered together, now attempting to drink their tea by lifting their bills skyward and pouring the drink into their open mouths. A couple of them immediately coughed and spluttered. With the help of the four men who had been mine slaves, the king and the false princess were guided away. Jessika, Thornfire, and Karolan all followed the group with the king.

"I'd best go, too," Craduticus said from beside Vor. "Will you give me a hand?"

She helped him to his feet and fetched his fire-scarred staff for him to lean on.

"Why don't you come also?" the old mage encouraged. "It won't be pleasant, but you could learn a lot from this."

Vor hesitated. Karolan and Giri both were with the group, plus the griffin and Jessika—all people she felt uneasy around, for different reasons.

"Come along, Vor," Craduticus all but ordered.

Firming her jaw, she took his free arm to support him, and walked with Craduticus to the workroom where they would attempt to help the Northnest king.

Chapter 26
New Ventures

It was one of the larger workrooms that Altare had used extensively. Someone had moved a table into the center, cushioned with blankets, and the king was being led to it. Giri and Lissian were drawing the circle of runes. Other mages were bringing in a few other small tables and supplies like water, towels, metalworking tools, candles, chalk, wands of various woods—and more. It looked like this was potentially going to be a complicated task.

"Vor," Milsa caught her sleeve. "I understand you are an accomplished potion-maker. Do you have anything soothing, to help keep the king relaxed, even asleep, while we do this?"

She was a little surprised to be asked, but she nodded. "I'll be back shortly."

Vor walked quickly down to her stillroom and fetched a few different potions that might be suitable from her cold storage, as well as some of the skin-numbing salve and another pat of burn cream for Craduticus. When she returned, the king was sitting calmly on the table. Jessika was holding his hand. Thornfire and Karolan were standing with the wizards, talking about the procedure.

Milsa came to Vor right away, and the latter held out the potions.

"Here are three different ones," she explained, and went on to tell Milsa briefly the effects of each.

The lady wizard nodded, taking all three, and went back to the gathering long enough to interrupt, get an answer, and go to dose the king. Vor edged closer to the group. Craduticus noticed her and waved her in.

"Vor, I want you and Hawkrain watching only," he said. "Giri and Lissian, too, and our honored guest Thornfire, will be mainly here to observe. This is advanced, delicate work—nasty work, really. I am relieved to have the chance to try to undo it. Let's begin."

Jessika and the two former slaves were guiding the king to lie down on his front. Milsa caught his forehead in her hands, for his head was beyond the edge of the table. Lissian dragged a stool over, and with a towel padding it, helped to rest the king's head on it. Jessika dragged over another stool and sat herself down beside the table, holding her father's limp hand. Thornfire sat to watch from behind Jessika, next to the lower part of the table, and Vor saw him briefly nibble at the princess's hair. Odd as that was, tension left Jessika's shoulders when he did it.

Milsa and Ylanzo stood on either side of the king's head with Craduticus facing his crown. Lissian stood behind his master. Giri stood across the table from where Jessika sat. Karolan stood between Jessika and Milsa, and Vor ended up sort of behind and between Craduticus and Milsa. The old master mage eyed them all.

"We're going to begin by breaking the simplest spells first," he explained. "Wizard Giri, you will be monitoring the king's heart and breathing, and alert us at any irregularity. As long as he is stable, we will continue on to spells that have deeper hooks into his mind and body. We will go as far as we can without risking his life," he frowned, "or perhaps other consequences."

"And the metal cap?" Jessika spoke up again. "Will you be able to take it off?"

"This piece of metal is just metal once the spells are removed from it," Craduticus said. "We can remove the gems imbedded in it, once we eliminate the spells they are connected to."

"But it's so," she muttered.

"Ugly?" Craduticus provided. He made his voice gentler but completely clear. "Hawkwings, listen. This cap has not been applied over his skin."

Their gazes met over the king's sleeping body, and Vor guessed the meaning of the master mage's words, but Jessika didn't seem to understand—or was avoiding understanding.

"It was fused to his skull," Craduticus murmured, "directly onto the bone."

Jessika flinched and looked away. He said nothing more about it, and the princess did not ask again for it to be removed.

"Vor, Hawkrain, Lissian, and Giri, too, if we run short of energy, may we depend upon you?" Craduticus asked politely.

"Of course," Karolan muttered.

"Yes, sir," answered both Giri and Lissian.

Vor nodded. No one asked the griffin, and he didn't offer.

"Thank you," Craduticus said. "I'll guide us. Master Ylanzo, Wizard Milsa, follow my lead and cushion my actions."

The two indicated their agreement, and the process began. Vor engaged her magical senses carefully, expecting the magical cap to be a complicated, dizzying collection of spells—and indeed it was. She had nothing to compare it to in the physical world, but tried to invent an analogy. Perhaps it was like coming upon a huge room decorated with multicolored tapestries and vases of flowers, stuffed with bookcases and furniture, full of different colored candles and lamps and lanterns, chandeliers and banners hanging from the ceiling, crowded with dancers in a multitude of costumes both wild and mundane, with each group of dancers—large or small—moving to the music from one of a few dozen bands of musicians or soloists also crammed into the room, all somehow without getting in each other's way.

The wizards would have to go to each musician and tell him to stop playing, and then remove the suddenly befuddled dancer or group of dancers without tripping up any of the other dancers. If they were to try to silence and still everything in that crowded room all at once, the people would come crashing to a halt and probably knock over all the other contents in the room, breaking important items, and maybe even setting the room on fire when lanterns shattered and spilled their oil. Once all the musicians and dancers had been removed one by careful one, however, the king's own musicians and dancers—who were now bound and gagged and stuffed into corners and under tables—could be freed to stand up again and try to remember how to play and dance.

Vor put her attention back on the actual task. The analogy wasn't perfect, but it was something like that. Craduticus used a wand to touch the first gem, a small clear one set in the metal by the king's left ear. Vor sensed the spell did have something to do with hearing, and after it was released and Ylanzo pried out the gem, Craduticus moved to an identical one on the other side of the king's head.

He continued on, going for the smallest gems first and working up to paired gems and larger gems, and Vor tried to follow, but the spells connected to each of them got progressively more intricate. She thought she detected more spells that altered hearing, others that linked in with sight, and even scent. Three were actually power sucking, draining the king's own life energy to keep him weak. One even affected his balance, probably making it difficult for him to walk without help.

So far, the king had only twitched once or twice—Vor's potion keeping him unconscious. But then Craduticus moved on to some of the biggest gems and progress slowed. Vor sensed that these were the ones that blocked his memories and impaired his conscious thinking. Craduticus was able to remove one, a large red stone the size of his thumb, and then stepped back, hands shaking.

"These are difficult," Milsa breathed.

"Indeed it is no small thing to lock a man's mind away while keeping him alive and functioning in some aspects," Craduticus agreed. "Hawkwings, we've removed the spells that kept him numb to his surroundings, hearing only Altare's voice and simple commands. This red one impaired his comprehension and logical thinking. If we wake him now, he will be able to listen and see and respond to anyone. He will probably be better able to care for himself. He should be able to interact and respond to many situations. To most people he would appear then to be a normal human being."

Milsa and Ylanzo were nodding in agreement. Jessika was staring at Craduticus expectantly.

"And the rest?" she prompted. "He's still breathing and everything, right? You can keep going."

Craduticus wiped his face free of sweat with a towel, and took a sip of water.

"The rest," he sighed. "The rest imprison his memories, skills, experiences—all the things that would make him able to argue, invent, laugh at things that are funny, and make critical decisions."

"And remember me," Jessika interjected.

"And remember the invasion, the deaths of the rest of his family, the fall of his kingdom, and the tortures we put him through," Craduticus added.

Jessika stared at him and Vor read the conflict on her face.

"The shock of all these spells coming off, combined with the resurgence of all his memories, could upset him profoundly," Milsa contributed. "That's what I have been worried about."

"It could drive him insane," Ylanzo grunted.

Vor opened her mouth, and shut it again, but Giri had seen her.

"What, Vor?" he prodded. "You had a thought?"

Now she had everyone's attention and glared a little at Giri, but half his mouth curled in a smile in reply. He didn't look sorry.

"Once these permanent spells are off," Vor began hesitantly, "if you do decide to remove them, put a calming spell on him, a temporary one, that will wear off on its own, slowly, over a few days, to give him time to adjust, so it's not a shock."

Craduticus grimaced. "Spells this deep will take more than a few days to recover from."

"Then make it longer," Vor said, "but you can't leave him like this."

Jessika's gaze snapped to her, and Vor figured the princess must be surprised to find her on her side.

"This is a vast improvement already," Ylanzo started to say.

"You haven't brought him back if you don't free his memories," Vor pressed. "You've done nothing but make him a more capable phantom. Who we are comes from our memories and experiences. Leaving him at this point leaves his personality locked away, leaves an empty shell that, sure, can walk and talk, eat and bathe itself, but isn't the king, and more importantly isn't Jessika's father. He still won't know his daughter, even if he acknowledges her identity and speaks freely to her. If that's where you intend to leave him, you might as well not be doing this at all."

Karolan was staring down at the table, but Jessika's face had pinched, suggesting she was edging towards tears.

"She makes a point," Thornfire rumbled.

All eyes turned to the griffin.

"The late and unlamented Altare stabbed me with a dark dagger last year," he went on, "nearly severing my soul from my body, and thereby damaging my brain's ability to attain a conscious state. For some time I had great difficulty communicating, and it was a long healing process to fully recover. However, I had family and friends around me who cared for me and helped me to come back."

He nodded his great hooked bill toward Vor. "As she says, employ a sedative spell on him so it is not a shock, to allow him to adapt slowly. It might take a year, as it has for me, and yes there will painful memories returning with the good, but it is not life without these things.

"I, too, have a daughter. She helped me return to myself." Now the griffin looked at Jessika. "If you will allow Hawkwings to remain here, and give some magical aid in the king's recovery—even if it takes a year—I believe he will overcome all these challenges you speak of, because he will have something, someone, to live for."

Tears streamed down Jessika's face but she did not sob aloud. Karolan put his arms around her and Thornfire surrounded them both with a wing, nibbling at her hair again.

Craduticus sighed. "I am at your service, Hawkwings." He glanced at Ylanzo and Milsa. "Let us proceed, but first let's apply a generalized spell of sedation."

"I can do that," Giri offered. "Save your energies for what's ahead."

"He can," Milsa confirmed.

"If you would then," Craduticus agreed.

Vor watched Giri's spell float out as gently as a leaf on a pond and settle over the king. He had quite a delicate touch. As he finished, he glanced up at Vor, and she thought she read approval in his gaze. She kept her expression impassive—but it was suddenly difficult not to appreciate his regard, or admire his magical skill in return.

"As we were then," Craduticus grunted once the spell was in place.

The trio of lead mages went back to work, fingers or wands touching lightly on one large gem after the next, carefully extracting them once the binding spells were dispersed. They passed noon and worked into the afternoon until with a final clank, Ylanzo dropped the last gem into the bowl with the others. Craduticus stepped back, swaying, and Vor steadied him. Milsa immediately sought a stool. Ylanzo remained staring down at the metal cap on the king's head, frowning.

"Well, it's done," he said. "I hope this works out as best as it may."

Vor spoke up. "I can fetch the men who helped bring the king in here, and we can move him to a bed."

"If you would," Craduticus consented.

Vor went out, finding the four men after asking a servant for their whereabouts. At the same time she found Amlee and asked for a new set of rooms—not the ones Altare had been keeping the king in—be made ready to receive him, but Amlee had thought of that already.

The two women watched as the still unconscious king was carried out of the workroom. Craduticus, Ylanzo, and Milsa went out leaning a little on each other, but Vor could tell with a quick survey that their energies would recover fine with food and rest. Thornfire gave Vor a grateful nod as he passed her, and Giri gave her a smile. Jessika, however, stopped—and Karolan slipped by behind her without so much as a glance at Vor.

"Mistress Vor," the princess began softly, pulling Vor's gaze from the retreating Karolan—or was she watching Giri?

"What?" Vor uttered, not trying to be rude but also seeing no point in conversation between them.

"Thank you," Jessika said, "for taking my side."

"I wasn't taking your side," Vor clarified. "I was taking the side of what was right."

Jessika's brows puckered, as if Vor's words had confused her mightily, but she continued to gaze at Vor with kindness in her eyes.

"I hope your father recovers," Vor told her sincerely. "Mine is dead. So is my mother. The only other father figure I had saved me from the streets, taught me magic, and hurt me on a regular basis. I killed him a few days ago. I hope yours turns out to be a good one, and if he is, I hope you appreciate him."

Since Jessika didn't seem about to leave, Vor turned to go instead.

"Wait," the princess called out, "we could—"

"No," Vor denied, pausing to look back. "I don't think we could ever be friends. Don't expect anything more from me."

She caught a glimpse of Amlee's sad face, but disallowed herself any reaction to it. Jessika displayed only fear and shock now.

"You should grow a tougher skin," Vor suggested as she resumed her escape. "You'll need it in Weldom."

She turned a corner, getting out of range, and used her complete knowledge of the halls to get herself quickly far away from the workroom. She wanted nothing more to do with the Princess Jessika.

***

"Can I get you something else, Mistress?" Marklin the cook asked with concern. "It's not to your taste?"

"It's not your cooking Master Marklin," Vor told him. "I'm too upset to eat well."

"Pie?" he suggested. "Pie cures all."

The idea of sweets turned her stomach. The vegetable stew was perfectly adequate, and normally she'd have eaten it without trouble and had seconds, but Vor had to force herself to finish the one bowl of it.

She stood. "Thank you for all your efforts. I am a difficult customer today."

Marklin took no offense. "All the disturbances lately are enough to put anyone off their feed. You've had some of the hardest of it, Mistress. I know you'll bring your healthy appetite back again. Just give it a few days."

"I shall," she promised. "If you'll excuse me."

Vor took her leave, needing to move. A walk in the garden would not be enough. She knew better than to engage in strenuous physical activity immediately after eating, but the bowl of stew had been small, and she was too impatient. Her feet took her to the training salle.

Only a few soldiers were about, and they made way for her without her even having to glare at them. She hadn't dressed for a work out, but shucked out of her jacket, leaving her in a short sleeved shirt and vest, and fetched her fingerless gloves anyway. At least this time she'd remember to wear them, so she wouldn't scrape the skin off her knuckles.

Vor went at the hanging bag methodically, slowly building up her tempo and strength, instead of unleashing all her frustration at once. Her strikes hit with satisfying thwaps, as hard as her slender body could make them without damage to her own self. Soon the world narrowed to just her breath and the bag and each strike: jab, reverse punch, inner elbow, outer elbow, back hand, reverse punch, knee, roundhouse kick, and on and on, letting the blows flow from one to the next. Eventually the repeated impacts started to sting, but she didn't bother thinking about it.

Time passed without her realizing it, until she was drenched in sweat. She didn't even know someone was calling her name until that someone grabbed her wrist with a quick dart of his hand. She hadn't known he was there—so focused and inward turned had she become.

"Vor," he insisted, and she managed not to punch him in the face.

She staggered, panting, only now noticing that her muscles were trembling. It was past time to stop, but she didn't feel much better than before she'd started.

"Look what you've done to yourself. You're dripping blood on the floor and getting it on the bag, too."

"Giri?" she puzzled.

He had her wrist still, and she saw that her bandages covering the burn-bites from the salamander had started to loosen. Further, it seemed the scabs had cracked, so blood had soaked them and indeed there were some speckles on the floor and bag.

"Drat it all," she huffed.

"Go bathe," Giri said. "I'll clean this up and come help you bandage your arm."

He let her go, but she stood there staring at him: perplexed by his presence, his offer—and him in general.

"Get going before you drip more blood. I won't be long."

Bemused, Vor turned and did as suggested, trying to keep the blood from dripping as she went. She used the showering mechanism in the bathing room, not wanting to wait for a tub to fill. After, she wrapped her arm in a towel—having now loosened most of the scabs with the water, and disposed of the bloody bandage. Like her arm, she wrapped her body in a robe, tossing her sweaty clothes in the hamper. She toweled her hair as dry as she could get it, and left it down to finish drying on its own. A little heat spell would have fixed it, but it was summertime, and she didn't mind the cool weight of it against her neck. Vor headed up to her room. She had spare bandages there, and burn cream.

What she hadn't expected to find there was another person.

"You look surprised. I told you I'd help you bandage your arm."

Vor half turned to look at her doorway. "I put up wards."

"You need better wards. I'll teach you some."

"Giri," she said firmly. "Men aren't allowed in—"

"Oh stop that," he scoffed. "We're mages."

As though that explained something. He'd shed most of his robes, leaving him in just trousers and shirtsleeves, so he looked strangely informal and younger. Without the flourishes and drama, she could see how lean he was—

and forced herself to stop looking. He was at the table in her sitting room, everything set out to tend to her burn-bite.

But then he straightened as if realizing something. "I will leave," he offered, "if that's what you want. I don't mean to—"

Vor shut the door, and he shut up, but only for a moment.

"Sit, then. Show me your arm."

"I don't need your help," she tried again. "Besides, this is a bite from a—"

Giri pulled up his own sleeve. "Greater salamander? Yes, I know a bit about them."

Vor blinked. Pale, slightly puckered points of scar tissue wrapped his arm from wrist to elbow, vanishing up under his bunched up sleeve. He let the fabric fall and picked up the jar of salve Vor had sitting on the table. He unscrewed the lid and took a sniff.

"You've got some good burn cream, though," he commented. "Yours might not scar as badly as mine. Lucky for you you're such an accomplished herbalist. Now come here, before you bleed through the towel."

"It's not that bad," she muttered.

Giri just raised an eyebrow at her. Vor sat and unwrapped her arm, extending it across the table towards him, leaving the towel below it to catch any drips of blood.

"How were you planning on tending this one handed?" he teased gently. "And what were you thinking, abusing yourself like that in the salle in the first place?"

She almost told him to shut up, but a little voice said that would be ungracious. "It's none of your concern," she muttered instead.

He gave her that half smile as his quick hands went to work smearing on the salve and then binding it on with the gauzy inner bandage before finishing with the tougher outer layer. It was a better job than Eriducus or Amlee had done, and far better than Vor would have been able to do alone. Jesine might have been able to do better, but Vor hadn't asked her.

"How'd you get your bites?" she asked him, as he was finishing up.

"Long story," Giri shrugged. "I can tell you about it sometime, but it's nothing like yours. Yours is," he frowned, "admirable, and unfortunate."

"Unfortunate?" she echoed curiously.

He shook his head and set aside the remaining bandages in the bowl. "What Altare was up to here wasn't right. What happened to you—and his other victims—wasn't right."

"He came from Weldom," Vor challenged. "Craduticus did some of the same things. Even Ulver, Eriducus, and Chirolen, and you and your fellows—"

"We from Weldom aren't against sex for power or a bit of bloodletting in times of need, but only ever willing," he interrupted. "What happened here, without oversight, snowballing to greater and greater depravity, without mutual consent—" Giri grimaced. "Start forcing people and it causes problems. Altare is a perfect example. His practices eventually got him dead."

He gave her a little nod: a salute to the woman who had murdered her master. Vor looked down and ran her fingers lightly across her bandages.

Giri shook his head again and folded up the bloody towel with the stains on the inside. "Weldom should have done something, for the sake of keeping a contented populace if nothing else. The Ministers should have had someone check in here long before, or sent someone more powerful than him to keep his excesses at the minimum." He winced. "That it all fell on you—although you did have some help—was more than you should have had to endure. I'm sorry I—we—couldn't help."

"Well, it is what it is, and it's over now," she remarked softly.

She stood, taking the towel and going to toss it in her hamper.

"That part is over, yes, but there's the future to consider. You could be a great wizard, Vor," Giri said eagerly. "You're skilled enough now, we could even grant you the title if you want it. You could stay on with us, return to Weldom. Milsa has even expressed some interest in taking you on as an apprentice."

That gave Vor a bad taste in her mouth. "Another master? You saw how well that worked for me the first time."

"Most Weldom wizards are with a master until middle age. They say power settles at twenty, and wisdom at forty. There is always more to learn and most of us like the company, and ready help in times of trouble."

Vor turned to look out her window, away from Giri and his fervency. "I see," she uttered.

"You don't have to accept Milsa, of course. There are more in Weldom."

She licked her lips nervously. "Not you?"

At last, he didn't have a quick reply, and she thought she might have embarrassed him. Of course, she hadn't been serious—had she? Vor was a little unnerved to realize that she wasn't sure.

"I'm too young," he deflected eventually. "I'll stay with Colby a while longer yet."

She nodded idly, but didn't turn to look at him, although the urge to do so was suddenly making her heartbeat quicken. He was really quite nice-looking. Looking at him again would also be—nice.

"Besides," Giri murmured a few moments later, "my interest in you is of a different nature."

A hot shock went through her. Her mouth had gone dry. Now she couldn't stop herself from looking over at him. He was gazing calmly back at her, expression suddenly vulnerable. Vor guessed what he meant: the same thing he'd meant that evening the first day they'd met. This time—she was a little surprised to realize—the idea was not so unpleasant.

Giri looked away first. "Not that masters and apprentices don't, hmm, make use of each other, if they want to. It varies from pair to pair. But I don't want to be your master. Magic is not what I want to teach you."

She saw his cheeks color, and a breath later felt her own do the same. Vor looked back out the window as if she'd find an answer there. The day was reaching late afternoon and the shadows were lengthening. A pair of ravens flew from the neighboring roof and off towards the forest. She shut her eyes for a moment. The view could not distract her from her acute awareness of Giri in her room, and her wearing only a bathrobe of all things, and she didn't know what to do about it.

"How old are you, anyway?" she asked in an embarrassed breath.

He didn't answer right away and she stole a glance at him from the corner of her eye. He looked nervous.

"Twenty-seven," he admitted hesitantly. "Too old?"

She shook her head in the negative, going back to staring out the window without seeing anything. Vor didn't really care how old he was; she'd just been curious. She clamped her jaws shut on other questions that came up to her.

Giri passed the question back to her. "How about you? How—?"

"Twenty-one," she provided.

He didn't say anything, and Vor knew that he—just like she—was calculating the difference in their ages, and wondering if it meant anything, good or bad. In the end, she had to throw out the contemplation. It wasn't anything they could change, and she decided it didn't matter. Other things might matter, but not numbers, at least not between them.

"Is it the topic," Giri asked eventually, and softly, "or the teacher?"

Vor hadn't the slightest idea how to answer that. Somehow it was both and neither.

"Everyone knows by now how you got the power to break through all those doors and destroy the stone," he went on. "You summoned a greater salamander, and that takes a lot. Of course you would have made use of every resource available to you, but seeing as how you two aren't snuggled up like courting black-breasted geese, I was assuming it was only practical, not enjoyable."

Everyone knew, did they? Vor gritted her teeth. "Only practical for me," she simplified, "but I think he might have enjoyed it, some of it."

"Do you love him?"

How was she having this conversation with him? "I hardly know him."

"Point," Giri allowed. "Were you using him?"

"Perhaps," she had to admit—although it hadn't really felt that way at the time.

"Don't forget that he and his friends were using you, too." He kept his voice steady and gentle, without adding drama or emotion. Vor thought it was only that which kept her able to answer his questions at all.

"Do you want to be in love with him?"

"He's in love with the nymph, who died," she said.

"That could be, but it's for him to say. Are you in love with him? Do you want him?"

"I don't know," Vor breathed, and then immediately revised. "No, I, he was something to hold onto in a difficult time: exciting, distracting."

"But now you don't need him?"

Since the battle, Karolan hadn't acknowledged her, hadn't sought her. It didn't hurt that they were apart, and in fact her reluctance to go find him was greater than her desire to. Maybe that was all the answer she needed. Vor managed a glance back at the wizard, cheeks no longer flaming. "Perhaps not."

Giri made a slight nod, his calm gaze steady on her. "No promises were made?"

"Nothing in words, nothing by me." She took a breath. "Besides, it's not enough. I mean," she made a frustrated gesture. "It's a lot of hassle, for little reward."

"Ah." Giri leaned forward, folding his hands on the tabletop.

He stared at them for a while. Vor watched him do it, but her thoughts were hard at work. She'd stepped between Karolan and Altare, abandoning her circle of defense, trying to save his life. Karolan hadn't run out to try to defend Vor from her master; he'd run out to try to defend Kassandra. The nymph had still died. Karolan hadn't said anything to Vor, hadn't come to her—either in anger or gratitude. Vor couldn't deny the awkwardness of their act of intimacy the day before that; she knew they'd both been unsatisfied, although in different ways.

Their courtship had been passionate and desperate, but perhaps there had been more desperation than passion. Perhaps now there was not enough left to sustain it, not with the memories of the inadequate first bedding, and the scar of the nymph's death. It might be a gulf too great for either of them to bridge, especially if neither of them wanted to try. Even if they did, perhaps there would be no improvement: little enjoyment of significant measure, and she didn't want to be burdened with that.

Enough. Her thoughts were running around in circles. Karolan was gone. She didn't miss him. Giri was in her room, and that signified—potential. Perhaps, yes, perhaps she would see what might come of this.

"I'd like," Giri began, and then shook his head. "You know what I'd like, but as I said before, I'll not take that which is not willingly given."

"I know what you'd like," Vor confirmed, cheeks flushing again.

It was flattering, somehow, and warmed her, but Giri also didn't seem to be that discriminating—after all, he'd bedded Pella within hours if not minutes of meeting her, just to replenish his energies. Of course, it was hypocritical of her to judge him for that, when she had taken Karolan almost purely for the power it brought, too. Perhaps she'd known Karolan better, and there had been some emotions involved, but she'd discarded her one-time lover almost as quickly as Giri had.

Vor frowned a little. "I ask you, what are you offering, exactly?"

"A good question," he approved, although he still looked a bit nervous. "It's important to be clear. May I join you at the window?"

He waited calmly for her answer. Vor took a moment to ask herself if she'd like him to come stand by her, and discovered a promptly affirmative response. "Yes."

Giri stood, slowly, watching Vor appraisingly, as if paying close attention to any signs of displeasure. She let him approach until he stood within arms reach. She noted clearly now that he was only slightly taller than her; she hardly had to look up to meet his gaze. She found she liked that: liked feeling that she was looking at an equal. She'd had enough of being loomed over and made to feel small.

Giri let them take some time for them to look at each other. His eyes were golden brown: pretty. She found herself examining his face and measuring the breadth of his shoulders. Vor's heart was pounding harder. Why was this, when she knew well enough that a man's embrace provided little reward? Why did her body respond to his nearness and his intent regard with heat and urgency?

"I offer my company," he answered in a murmur, "that you may do with me what you will, as time allows, while we are here." A slight shadow crossed his face and he spoke a bit quicker, glancing down. "I tell you true, so you know, I have no intention of pairing permanently with anyone, in which I expect you are the same—or you'd be running after that boy."

Vor could not deny it—at least insofar as Karolan was concerned. "Your company," she echoed softly.

It wasn't that she didn't know what he meant: more that she was trying the words out on her own tongue. Vor lifted a hand and extended it towards him. Giri glanced back up and she held his gaze as she reached out. He didn't evade her or stop her; she set her palm against his sternum, fingertips touching his clavicles: bare skin above the collar of his shirt. It was the first time she'd intentionally and consciously reached out to touch him, and she noted particularly the heat of his body and the quick pulse of his heart under her thumb.

She pressed a little firmer, and he took a speculative step back. Vor glanced to check his expression and realized he thought she might be trying to push him away, and was complying. Her lips quirked with a hint of a sheepish smile, and instead she caught his shirt in her fingers, and tugged him back. He came willingly.

Hesitantly, as if afraid he might offend her, Giri brushed his hands lightly over her shoulders and down her arms, barely touching the thick fabric of the robe she still wore. Though she could hardly feel it, still his gesture made her shiver pleasantly. She caught herself watching his slender, agile fingers. At the same time, she was becoming more and more aware of his aura of mage energies touching on hers—and hers reaching out to his without her consciously doing it.

"And if you're not going to make a pair with him," Giri went on, "and you found no enjoyment in having him, you might let that discourage you from ever considering another attempt, which would be a shame, in my opinion."

His eyes flicked up to hers, as if to check for confirmation.

Vor's jaw muscles clenched, but she forced herself to reply. "I was never given the impression, nor found myself, that there was much to enjoy, at least for the female involved."

A faint expression of pain struck Giri's face. He moved closer, making her elbow bend, stretched in, and kissed her forehead, slowly, for a few breaths. A burning as strong as and sweeter than the salamander's bite spread from where his lips touched her skin. It wasn't something magical—no, this was pure physical sensation that her body was producing in reaction. It melted some remaining resistance. Tremulous warmth suffused her and she leaned towards him: suddenly needing. His hands came back to her shoulders, holding her slightly away.

"I offer not to leave you unsatisfied," he whispered near her ear. "I promise."

Vor pressed in and this time he let her, so her hands touched his sides and her cheek brushed his hair. He smelled good, like books and cinnamon.

His arms went carefully around her, so she slipped hers around him, too, and there was no fear.

Mouth beside his ear now, she whispered back, "yes."

Chapter 27
New Magic

"We'll fly out now," Hawkwind told Jessika and the others.

They were alone in the hallway finally, and could talk without worrying what the Weldom wizards would think. The former griffin mine slaves had already left, trying to get back to the ruins in the forest where they were temporarily staying before nightfall. Going on foot, it was going to be a hard run. Hawkwind, Thornfire, and Thornwing, however, could fly back, and so had lingered with Jessika, Rikah, and Karolan.

"You're staying?" Hawkwind confirmed.

"I'll return to my parents' house," Rikah explained.

"And I want to tell Chika what's been going on," Jessika said. "I can sleep there tonight."

"Should we pick any of you up tomorrow?" Hawkwind continued. Even though she considered all three of her remaining human chicks to be adults now, she still had the instinct to protect them—especially since she'd just lost one.

"I can walk home," Jessika said.

"You're not moving in here, to be with your father?" Hawkwind wondered.

"They're saying he won't start regaining consciousness for about a week," she explained, "because of the tranquilization spells they put on him, to help him transition. Amlee can take care of him for now, and I'll be back by the time he starts to wake, but I need to go home first and tell Koki."

The young woman's face creased with apprehension. Hawkwind didn't press her, but she was worried. Jessika had seemed happy with the faun for several months after the rescue of Hawkjoy—through the winter and into spring—but when the discussion had begun of how to remove Altare, and when Jessika had resumed her talk of reclaiming the Northnest throne, Koki had started to withdraw. The griffin could only wonder how he would take these new developments.

"Use the contact stone then," Thornfire directed, "if you need anything."

The male griffin pointed his bill expectantly at Rikah and Karolan.

"I'm going to keep living with my parents," Rikah said on cue. "I'll see

Jessika all the time, once she comes back. I can help with the king and the false princess, too."

Jessika added, "I hope she'll be able to tell us her name soon, so we can stop calling her that."

"She might not ever remember," Karolan contributed suddenly.

His voice was low, almost disinterested, and he was staring away from them all, as if trying to shut them out. Hawkwind snorted. He'd slipped back into the worst of his moody sulks from his younger years. She didn't appreciate the reversion. Thornfire poked his apprentice with the wrist of his wing.

"You should stay here," the griffin mage admonished. "You will, right? These human wizards can teach you much."

"And Vor is here," Rikah muttered.

Karolan's gaze stabbed over at him. Hawkwind tried not to show how puzzled she was about the exchange. As far as she could tell, that female human had only scarcely left the outright-enemy category and approached the no-longer-likely-to-immediately-attack category. It was undeniable that the woman had been central to the defeat of Altare, and it seemed to Hawkwind that Karolan had clearly swayed her to their side for it—somehow—but she had seen no evidence that Vor was now a true ally or lasting friend.

"Her life is nothing to do with mine," Karolan declared.

"Then you will return to South-scree?" Thornfire asked. "There's also this Weldom place they keep speaking of. There are other human mages there, it seems."

"He's going to go sit at Kassie's tree and feel sorry for himself," Rikah muttered again.

Karolan whirled on the shorter, stockier man, hands balling into fists and tears standing in his eyes. Thornfire flipped out a wing between them, but Rikah tried to push it down—and had about as much success as he would have in trying to push an oak tree down. Griffin pectoral muscles were no trifling things.

"No, let him hit me," Rikah urged, raising his voice. "Maybe it'll help him feel better."

"You shut up," Karolan hissed.

"Rain," Jessika winced.

"Enough," Hawkwind ordered. "This kind of a scene would not help Wings' position here."

Karolan spun away, swiping at his face and Thornfire folding his wing again.

"We all carry the wound of her absence," Hawkwind went on, feeling the

pinch in her own throat and chest. "We all loved her, and miss her."

Rikah opened his mouth to say something else at Karolan, but Hawkwind cowed him with a fierce raptorial glare. In the sign language of the Snow-in-lee griffins, so Karolan wouldn't hear, she said, "leave it, Dare. He's hurting."

"We're all hurting," Rikah signed back, "just like you said."

Thornfire joined the conversation the same way. "Different people have different ways of mourning. Her loss is still fresh. If weeks and months pass, and he does not begin to recover, then perhaps your approach will help, but not now."

Rikah just shook his head, but did not argue.

"Don't worry about me," Karolan interrupted, back still towards them. "I'll take care of myself."

"As you like, Hawkrain," Thornfire said mildly. "You have my contact stone if you need anything. You have only to call, and I—or another perhaps, as my wings are feeling their age—will come to you."

"And you are always welcome in South-scree," Hawkwind added.

Thornfire bobbed his head her way. "We should get going. Never mind my wings, these old eyes of mine don't do as well with night flying, and I'll need to apply the levitation spell again, so this burned wing will support me."

Jessika threw her arms around Hawkwind's neck for a hug. "I'll be back to visit," she promised. "I'll need to call for a ride, though."

"That can be arranged," Thornfire told the young woman as she turned to give him a hug, too, and then Thornwing, who had been thoughtfully silent for some time.

"Don't let it be too long," Hawkwind urged. "I want to be updated on what's happening with Northnest, and if you decide to go to Weldom, some of us will be coming with you," she shrugged, "probably, after I convince the matriarchs."

"Alright," Jessika agreed, sounding rather noncommittal.

Rikah got his hugs next. Karolan hadn't turned around yet, but Hawkwind wasn't about to leave without an equivalent farewell. She nudged him with her head, nibbled his short hair, and stepped up to embrace him with one arm and opposite wing. He stood stiffly for a moment, until she trilled to him, softly, as she would to a frightened chick, as she had many times when he was a scared little boy, and he crumpled.

Hidden from the others by her massive, encompassing wing, Karolan clung to her chest and leaked silent tears into her fur for a few moments. His body shook, but he stifled all his sobs. Quickly enough he straightened again, wiping his face with his sleeve, and Hawkwind loosened her grip, but kept her shielding wing in place.

Karolan didn't look up at her, but his fingers made a few brief gestures. "I loved her. I always loved her. Now she's gone."

Hawkwind set a gentle hand on his head, but there was nothing she could say. Kassandra Hawksky, the quiet, careful, little girl had left them years ago, vanishing into the forest and returning wreathed in leaves and flowers. What had happened to her, Hawkwind still didn't know, though she didn't doubt that it had something to do with the unicorns. She'd never seen any sign of courtship between Kassie and Karo. Kassie had changed to that leafy form before maturing, even. Whatever love it was that Karolan spoke of, it was love from afar only.

Still, it seemed his feelings had been strong. Maybe he'd known he could never meet her as equals. Maybe he'd known his feelings would forever be one sided. Regardless, his wound went deep and Hawkwind expected he'd be long in recovering.

"I think she would want you to love and honor her memory," Hawkwind offered awkwardly, one handed, "but it would grieve her to see you mourn overlong."

Karolan didn't reply, and she couldn't know if her words had helped or hurt, but she gave him another hug.

"If you need anything, do not hesitate," she said aloud. "You are my Hawkchick, and there will always be a place for you in the Hawk Line."

He nodded, and she let him go.

***

Giri had Vor tucked close against his chest, her head under his chin, where she could hear his heartbeat, calm and easy now. Their legs were still tangled up with the bed sheets, but neither was making a move to rectify the situation. Vor drifted in a deep pool of contentment, awash with new memories of greater sensations than she'd ever known before.

"I knew love existed," she mumbled, "because my mom chose my dad, even though it meant she lost everything else, but I didn't think—"

Giri's arm tightened for a moment around her. "An art like any other," he murmured back.

"Of which you're a master?" she half-teased.

He huffed a bit of a laugh. "Just a practitioner. Someone had to teach me, you know. We all start knowing nothing. You shouldn't blame Karolan for being unable to show you this on the first attempt."

Vor nodded a little and ignored his mention of Karolan, tracing her fingertips over the smooth skin of his pectorals. Giri turned his face into her hair, so his breath stirred it.

"I should warn you. Too much of this and you might find yourself with strong feelings for me, if you don't armor your heart against it."

She didn't reply.

"Vor?"

She shut her eyes.

"Vor? You're not already—," he stuttered, "I told you I don't intend to pair with anyone. I told you before so—"

"Is that why you didn't make use of Pella again, when you came back?" she interrupted.

Now she'd caught him without words. "Yes," he confirmed eventually, "I suppose. And I wasn't exhausted. And," he hesitated, "I didn't want her."

"Why don't you want to pair?"

"Why don't you want to pair?" he countered.

Vor hid her face against his neck. Giri's arms went around her and he pulled her onto him, soothing her back muscles in firm strokes.

"Can we not speak of this?" he requested timidly.

"Alright," she agreed.

She lay quietly on him for a time, feeling his breaths and his heart beating just below hers. Eyes open again she lifted a hand to touch a peculiar scar on his shoulder that she'd noticed earlier.

"That?" he asked in a much more cheerful voice. "That makes me a wizard."

It was like a five petalled flower, with each petal about the size and shape of a thumbprint: some a bit larger or smaller than others. Vor set her own thumb against the nearest petal—and pulled it away, surprised at a faint tingle that felt much like—

"Colby," Giri chuckled. "I knew you'd do that. As you sensed, that one is from Colby."

"What do you mean?"

"The five thumbprints, each from a different senior wizard marking their recognition of me as a wizard, too. Any other mage can touch them and sense the identity of the wizards who left them."

"That's odd," she commented, "to have that mark left on your body."

"It creates accountability," he explained. "If I ever do something magical that gets me in trouble, of course I'll be punished for it, but those five who approved me will also hear of it. My actions might damage their reputations, and they might punish me further. Altare had no mark like this, did he? It's another reason he reached the state that he did."

Giri adjusted himself so he could look Vor in the face and she lifted her head obligingly.

"Do you want to be a wizard?" he asked again as he'd encouraged earlier in the day, only gentler. "I'll give you your first mark, and then you'll just need to find four more. I'm sure Colby and Milsa will contribute."

"I'm still not sure what I want," she demurred, laying her head back down on his chest.

"The offer stands," he told her, petting her hair. "You just let me know."

Vor nodded against him, closing her eyes again and letting herself sink into the sensation of being held. It had been so long since she'd been held with such gentleness, and without fear, without shields, in a state of complete vulnerability. It hadn't been easy to relax so much, but now it not only didn't bother her—she liked how it felt. She supposed it should have scared her, but in the moment, it did not. Of course with Giri there were some additional, different emotions involved, but she could only liken it to being held by her parents: with complete trust that she wouldn't be hurt.

She thought of her mother: dark of hair, skin, and eye: upright in stature and refined in movement: a true noble of Brasson. Juleena had been so kind, always holding Vor gently—if she was frightened or sad or woke up from a nightmare. And yet for all her apparent timidity, Juleena had not been scared of her husband's warlike ways, for Vor's father had never turned any but a tender hand, word, and gaze upon her and Vor, despite his occupation.

Her father: stocky and strong, skin browned only by the sun, and nut-brown hair cut short in military style. Vor could remember riding him like a horse, and he swinging her swiftly through the air until she was breathless with laughing, trusting instinctively that he would never let her fall. When she looked in the mirror she saw his eyes, for hers were the same red-brown mahogany color, as though painted by an artist with the same pigment. And Vor's hair: just like her mother's, and her skin at the midpoint in tone between that of her two parents.

The war for Northnest had eaten them both.

"House Mrandis might welcome you back," Giri said suddenly, surprising her and making her think he was somehow following her thoughts. "Especially if you come back a wizard."

Ah, so he was just continuing his line of persuasion.

"I've never met any of them," Vor told him. "My mother was disowned before I was born."

"Well, it's a thought anyway," he subsided. "Wizards have status in

Weldom."

"If they did welcome me, they'd probably try to marry me off."

Giri chuckled. "I can only imagine how well that would go. My parents try to do the same thing to me."

Vor had to laugh a little, too. Giri shifted her against him and drifted his fingers down her spine, pausing to make little circles here and there.

"Do you feel better now?" he murmured.

"I do," she admitted, finding it to be true. "Do you?"

"I do, very much."

Vor could hear a smile in his voice, and couldn't stop her mouth from curving into one, too. She hadn't planned to ever take him up on the offer he'd first given within an hour of meeting, but somehow her feelings had changed, and she didn't regret it.

"Have you eaten? It's late now, but want to go for dinner?"

She groaned. "It wasn't supposed to be another group meal, was it?"

"It might have been," he shrugged.

"Is that why you were coming to find me, to drag me off to the dinner?"

He kissed her forehead. "It might have been."

"And then neither of us showed up."

"This was more important."

She had to agree. Now that she had the experience to compare them, she'd take a tumble with Giri over a formal dinner anytime. Still, she pushed herself up so she could see his eyes. "But now everyone will suspect—"

"So what?" He was grinning. "Besides, there will be no suspecting about it, at least for the other mages. One glance will show we've been sharing personal energies on a rather intimate level, and the list of activities that can cause that sort of thing is one item long."

"Then Karolan will know," Vor breathed.

His expression turned more serious. "If that truly bothered you, wouldn't you have turned me down again?"

She hugged his shoulders and nodded. "I think, in a few days, I will leave the castle."

Giri's alarm—and even dismay—was clearly detectable. His energies vibrated with it, and with all their shields down, energies so intermingled, she felt it acutely. His arms wrapped her, as if that would keep her from going.

"Where will you go?" he asked.

"I don't know."

"Won't you stay? Or at least go to Weldom?"

Vor again hid her face against his neck, and he must have sensed her distress, too, for his own emotions calmed and he stroked back her hair.

"I'm sorry. You have to do what is right for you. I just—"

He cut off his own words, and said nothing more.

"You what?" Vor prodded.

His breath escaped him but his voice was tight. "We'll just have to enjoy each other's company for what time we have, and maybe someday we'll meet again."

Vor knew as well as she knew her own name that he'd not said what he'd been going to say. That was his choice; she wouldn't push. After all, they were just sharing company—not deep confidances. She would let him keep his secrets. Still, now that he'd said that, some new sensation—fear or dread mixed with pain—moved in her throat and chest.

"Yes, we shall," Vor concurred, trying for a happy tone. "Now, about that dinner?"

"I suppose we should, but we'll need to clean up first."

Vor almost chuckled. "I suppose we do. My bathing room can fit two, if we get close."

She sensed his smile.

"Yes," he concurred. "Let's get close."

***

They did eventually make it down to dinner, but the servants were already cleaning up the used place settings and the diners had departed.

"They're in the conservatory," Edgard informed with a bow.

"All of them?" Vor clarified.

"Not the griffins," he explained, "but most of the wizards, the princess, young master Karolan, and young Rikah. The three guests will not be staying the night; it seems they have other lodging arrangements."

"Thank you," Vor told him.

The thought of facing all of them made the discomfort that Giri's lovemaking had banished begin to return, but at least Karolan wouldn't be sleeping in the castle. That would prevent—possible complications.

"Would Mistress Vor and Wizard Giri prefer to dine in the kitchen?" Edgard offered. "There are some light foods in the conservatory, otherwise."

"I'll join my master," Giri said easily.

"I think I'll take you up on the kitchen," Vor opted, with a glance at Giri to see how he took that.

"I'll make your excuses," he winked. "And I'll see you tomorrow, to teach you those wards I mentioned, and basic teleportation, if you still want to learn

330

it?"

"You're allowed to, even though you're not a master?" Vor asked to cover her slight disappointment that he might not want to sleep through the night with her. After all, they hadn't talked about anything like that, and it might cross that line between keeping company and pairing up.

"It's good practice for when I am," he shrugged, "and you don't have a master, so I'm not stepping on anyone's toes. I'll check with Colby first."

"Alright," Vor nodded. "Goodnight then."

Giri's soft smile warmed his eyes and lingered on her gaze. "Goodnight, Vor."

He exited swiftly then, and Vor made to imitate him, heading for the kitchen before anyone else could wander into the dining room and encounter her. This time, when Marklin set down a bowl of his fantastic vegetable stew, Vor dug in hungrily, so a hunk of brown bread soon joined it. When she was nearly finished with that, some seed crackers and cheese with slices of apple appeared at her elbow.

Nearly full, but not stuffed, Vor sighed with contentment—and then a dish of strawberry pie replaced the empty cracker plate. She raised her eyebrows up at Berthana and Marklin, standing arm in arm in the emptying kitchen and grinning at her.

"Pie solves all problems," Marklin said.

"Does it?" Vor asked curiously.

"Of the spirit," Berthana clarified. She touched Vor lightly on the shoulder. "But not the heart."

"Good thing I don't have any of those then," she said.

Vor dug into the pie. It was delicious.

***

Giri caught up with her the next morning as she was taking down the last cage from the last empty flower room. Vor had expected it to be at least slightly disturbing to walk through her late master's quarters, but it seemed wizards must have passed through already, deleting and dispersing any and all of the remaining spells, wards, and shields Altare had left behind. Even now a small army of servants was removing furniture and furnishings, opening windows to let in the summer breezes, and deeply scrubbing every surface. All evidence of her master's presence and deeds was being scoured away—from the physical world anyway. Memories in people's minds—Vor's not least—would unavoidably linger.

"Altare told me he bled out the girls he kept in here," Vor said clearly as she sensed Giri's approach. "The wizards didn't stop him?"

"We didn't know what he was up to," he replied after a moment, sounding ashamed. "He just came to us, a few hours after we'd all returned, brimming with both power and rage, in a fury about you."

"I see," she conceded, setting down the cage in the hallway beside the others.

No one had thought to feed the birds, apparently, but the seed and water trays in their cages were not yet completely empty, and the bright little creatures were healthy enough. Each time she set down another cage next to the other ones, the bird inside would start twittering nonstop, fluttering about at the side of the cage nearest to the other ones, and the other birds would do likewise. Vor assumed it was because they were happy to see each other, though if it was because they wanted to fight, she admitted she probably wouldn't be able to tell the difference.

"We didn't know what he'd done until he told you during the battle," Giri explained softly. "When we got back, and you were unconscious, we searched the workrooms, and put the young ladies to rest."

"They're not the only ones he's killed," she said flatly.

"I do not doubt it. He will kill no more, thanks to you."

Vor found she couldn't yet respond to that. "Will you carry a few of these?" she asked instead.

He complied at once, hefting a trio of cages with their chirping, fluttering captives. "What are you going to do with them?"

"I've never seen wild birds that look like these," Vor said, taking the remaining cages. "I doubt they'd survive if I set them free, and they obviously don't belong in this region."

"I think you're right."

"But they shouldn't be in such small cages, kept separately from each other."

"We'll think of a solution," Giri assured her.

Since the weather was warm, they put the cages in the garden, in a tight cluster, so the birds could at least see and hear each other, if not touch yet. They fetched more seed and fresh water for them, and then Vor stood back and watched as they flitted about, chortling and chirping.

"I wonder if the blacksmith could make one large cage big enough for all of them," she mused. "I'll go talk to him about it."

"A good idea," Giri agreed. "Now?"

She felt the urge to smile, and gave in to it. A flush of warmth went through her when Giri matched her grin. "Later."

"Great. I wanted to show you those wards I was talking about."

***

They practiced through the morning in one of the larger workrooms. Giri was a thorough teacher, but kind, patient—far different from what Vor had been used to with Altare. How different his life must have been, learning from Colby, for although the State Wizard did seem stern, Giri's good nature was enough to prove that his master was not cruel.

"You catch on so quick," Giri praised at one point.

"I had to," Vor said, "to avoid my master's anger."

"There's something I don't understand," he went on a while later. "Why didn't you leave?"

"And what would I have done?" Vor scoffed.

He shrugged. "Mages can make their way with their skills," he said.

Vor shook her head. "He would not let me go. I tried to run, once, but he had his power in my body. I could venture only as far as the length of my leash."

Giri was staring thoughtfully at her, and she paused before her next application of one of the new wards.

"What?" she prodded.

"You won't be tied down again," he observed, "now that you've broken his hold."

"I suppose."

"Your freedom is long overdue. I see why you relish it."

Her brows puckered. "You are just as free."

"Ah, no," he smiled. "I am employed, and loyal to my master. No magical bonds hold me, but bonds of duty. I would not be an honorable man if I broke them."

Vor's frown deepened somewhat. "I have never had such bonds."

He shrugged again and turned away from her to face the wall and closed door they were practicing on. "Perhaps you will someday. Perhaps you won't. Bonds of duty you choose to enter into when the opportunity presents itself. They can't be forced on you. Now, there are a few more variations to these wards."

He drew his utility blade, clearly transitioning back into lecture mode. Vor didn't dispute it, and drew her own knife.

"They require a drop of blood," Giri said, glancing at her to gauge her reaction. "Your own, of course."

She nodded briskly. "I am accustomed to that."

"I'm not surprised," he remarked dryly. "It also requires getting a bit of blood on the door, which some people find gruesome. On the other hand, there are wizards in Weldom who have little ceramic tiles affixed to the inside of their doors, specifically for the blood anchors."

He shook back his sleeve, going for a spot on the outside of his arm where the bone was close to the skin, where she'd noticed yesterday he had a series of tiny old scars and fresh scabs. He took his blood on the tip of his knife to tap the door and Vor followed his actions with her magical sight, watching as he put up a variation of a ward he'd shown her earlier. The blood energy in it made it larger and stronger, with a wider range of detection.

"Most spells are stronger if you work a bit of your blood into them," he muttered, "except of course any that summon creatures averse to blood, or ones where you're tracking something by an outside blood source. In that case you'd just muddy it."

Vor nodded idly. He told her nothing she didn't already know. She pricked her own arm—not the one that was still bandaged from the salamander bite-burn—and placed a ward of her own, one of the new ones he'd taught her.

"I wonder if my master never showed me these wards because he didn't want me able to keep him out of my rooms," she mused, "in case he ever decided to come after me."

Giri scowled, but not at her.

"He didn't teach me many locks, either," she went on.

"He ruled you with fear and by keeping you ignorant—as ignorant as he could, although it seems to me he largely failed at that," Giri said, "and with pain and magical leashes." He grimaced. "That is not how it should be. We must trust and respect each other. That is how loyalty is gained—and how masters can avoid having an apprentice so angry that she kills him."

He said this last with a half smile. "If you'd come to Weldom, you'd see it for yourself."

Vor swallowed a hiss and turned away. "So-honorable Weldom that invaded this country and killed the people and griffins at this castle? That war killed my parents, too, and left me alone in the streets, and—"

"It's not perfect," Giri interrupted, a trifle loudly. "There are those of us trying to make it better."

"How? You're not a Minister."

"I'm not," he agreed, "and I was hardly older than you when the invasion happened, too young to get sent along, too young to understand enough to have a good perspective on what was happening."

"I'm not blaming you," Vor said carefully.

"I know. I'm not trying to say that the invasion was good, or that Weldom did nothing wrong in it. I just want you to know that there is potential there, that there are good people, and possibilities, and power: power that can do great evil, or great good."

Vor worked to keep her calm. They weren't arguing, not exactly, at least not yet.

"We come from different positions on the matter," she tried to soothe.

"Indeed," he agreed at once, some of his intensity fading. He went to perch on the edge of a table near the back of the room. "I never saw the war. I was safe, protected, the pampered mage-son of a minor noble house. I can't imagine what you went through."

Vor took his words graciously and tried to put her own feelings into perspective as well as he was doing it. "I don't remember Weldom much. I lived with my father's family. They weren't dreadfully poor, but it was a simple life. I was happy enough. The war took it all away. It's hard not to blame Weldom for it."

"And then you were here." He made a gesture to encompass the workroom, the castle. "I imagine you must have a lot of bad memories here, too."

Vor didn't want to think about it. Most of the time she managed by not recalling all her master made her watch and do. Those events still appeared in her dreams—nightmares—but she hoped they'd fade in time. "I got used to it."

"So you feel like you have no home anywhere? You don't want to go find your grandparents, your father's family, if not your mother's? They probably think you're dead, too."

"Another attempt to get me to go to Weldom," she sighed.

When Giri didn't reply, she looked over at him. He was watching her with an intent stare, but without a sign of anger. Rather, there was a hint of pain in his eyes and she had to look away. It made her chest hurt.

She heard his feet hit the floor.

"How about putting some of these wards on your own door, now?" he suggested, sounding buoyant again.

Vor complied, placing her hand on the workroom door to reabsorb the spells she'd placed there. Beside her, Giri did the same, and then they exited, taking the halls and stairs to her own suite of rooms. In the sitting room, she pricked her arm again. It was easier applying the wards to her door than it had been to the workroom door. Only her own energies had ever been in her door before, and the new, more complex wards settled there with little resistance.

"Beautiful," Giri praised from behind her. "Now I'll have much more difficulty sneaking into your rooms."

A blush shocked her cheeks, and she stayed facing the door, not wanting him to see. It seemed the lesson was over, and they'd both used up some energy, and now he was conveniently in her rooms with her. Vor's desire for him surprised her—and embarrassed her. This must be what the Skire had meant when she'd spoken of mating urges, but Vor had the fear that she would somehow lose something if she desired him but he didn't desire her and he became aware of it.

Giri stepped up beside her. "May I?"

It took her a moment to realize he was asking to look at her knife, which she still held frozen in her hand. Weakly and without protest she handed it over.

"Pine," he said gradually, as though that had told him something; Vor had to suppose it had.

After all, she'd purposefully chosen pine for the handle because of its soothing, dispassionate nature. It helped keep her mind clear and sharp. Pine also had the quality of being able to survive in harsh conditions, which she figured she had lots of. She took it for granted that Giri would have studied the same topics as her, including the magical qualities of herbs, woods, crystals—all of it. He probably had access to a much more extensive library than she did, so he probably knew far more.

"Mine's hazel," he muttered before she could even start to glance towards the knife at his belt.

She laughed breathlessly. "Of course it is."

"You think me arrogant for choosing hazel?" he replied, not sounding offended.

"No."

"Shall I tell you how I chose it? Master Colby had me blindfolded and put my hand into a box full of pieces of wood. He told me to pick the one I liked the most. When I touched this one, it sang to me."

Vor couldn't argue with that. "Hazel isn't arrogant, and neither are you," she said.

No indeed, hazel was not an arrogant wood. It did judge and seek justice, but only after fair and balanced perception from a position of unruffled calm, viewing all sides. Hazel sought truth and brought balance. She supposed, that should tell her something about the man who had naturally been drawn to it.

Giri's eyes flicked lightly up to hers. Deliberately he put the tip of Vor's blade into his mouth and licked off what vestiges of her drying blood remained. Her breath stopped and urgent pressure materialized in her belly. He stepped closer and slid the blade back into the sheath at her hip, leaving his hand on her waist.

"If I'm going to teach you teleportation this afternoon, we'll need all the energy we can get," he whispered.

"Yes," Vor nodded without hesitation. "Good idea."

Chapter 28
Uncharted Territory

Rikan the blacksmith was hard at work. His son Rikah was in the shop, too, with several chunks of wood on a new-looking workbench—not the table anymore—which he seemed to be examining.

"Mistress Vor," Rikan greeted at once, with a larger smile than she'd ever seen on him.

"Good blacksmith," she replied with a nod.

"You're looking well," he went on, surprising her again. "One moment if you can wait, and I'll be with you. I'm almost finished here."

She noticed Rikah glance her way. He didn't look nearly as happy as his father, but nor was he throwing any visual daggers at her. He set down the piece of wood he'd hefted, and came over to her while the strikes of Rikan's hammer filled the air.

"What is it?" Vor asked him coldly as he got close enough.

"I just wanted to tell you," he flinched. "Karolan left the city. He wouldn't tell me where he was going, and I don't know when he'll be back."

Vor made little reaction. So he'd left without saying goodbye? Honestly, she couldn't blame him. She hadn't made any more of an effort than to try to catch his eye since the battle. If she'd really wanted to she could have cornered him, confronted him. It just hadn't seemed worth it. Apparently he'd felt the same. There was no pain from it, just a little hollowness, but Vor expected even that wouldn't last long. Their flame of passion had burned out and the embers were cold.

"I thought, if you were friends now," Rikah went on, squirming a little, "you'd want to know."

"I wish him well," Vor settled on.

"He's really sad because Kassandra died, the girl who turned into the tree."

"I know," she said as gently as she could.

"I don't think he's acting very mature by just running off like that," Rikah continued huskily, "but everyone's telling me to let him go for now."

Rikan came walking over then, pulling off his thick gloves. "What can I do for you, Mistress?"

"Have you ever made a birdcage?"

He nodded. "Several small ones, some years ago."

"I expect those are the ones I've gathered up," Vor supposed. "The birds in them, I'd like to be able to put them together in a larger cage, so they have more room, and company."

"Certainly," Rikan said. "How large would you like? Have you considered where it will be put?"

They discussed it for a while, with Rikah, too, contributing thoughts. Vor had already decided she wouldn't be staying, so she wouldn't be the one caring for the birds. She had the thought that the large conservatory in the private wing—the one with the piano and loom and other diversionary equipment— might be a nice place. There were large windows there that could be opened to the air in summer, and gave a view of the garden year round. Once they had a plan in place, she went back to see Amlee, worried that the woman would resent the new duty Vor was going to ask of her.

"Lovely," the castellan said instead, "I'd be happy to care for the little dears."

Vor let a breath go, relieved. "Rikan and his son Rikah will come here for the installation in a few days. I've already paid them."

"I'll make sure they have everything they need, but you'll be here to guide them as well?"

She had to shake her head. "I'm leaving."

Amlee reached for her hands, then seemed to think better of it, and didn't. "Where will you go?"

"I don't know, but I can't stay here."

"Why not? We are happy to have you here. You're not happy to be here?"

Vor turned away. "I just need space, air. I'm too unsettled."

"How soon will you go? I'll have Marklin make you some travel rations."

"I don't know. Tomorrow, or the next day," she huffed.

"Vor," Amlee begged, now touching her arm lightly. "You should stay. These wizards, some are a little rough around the edges, but they're of a decent sort, really. You could do well with them, and Wizard Giri—"

Vor jerked away. "Enough."

She sped off at a fast walk, leaving Amlee alone behind her.

"I sent some food to your room," the castellan called after her. "You have to eat, Mistress."

When Vor reached her rooms she saw indeed that there was a tray on her table. Someone had made her bed, too. She'd left her door unlocked, with the wards in a passive state, so there would have been nothing telling the servants to stay out. Servants went where they were sent all over the castle, where Amlee and Edgard told them to go, getting into everything, knowing everything, and gossiping about everything. Altare's locks, wards, and reputation had kept them away from the workrooms and his quarters, but they took their liberties everywhere else.

They all probably knew Vor was bedding Giri by now. That meant that practically everyone at the castle must know. She snarled silently but restrained herself from removing the lid of the food tray violently—or throwing it all across the room. The meal below was meant to be served cold and indeed it was, but that was fine. Vor sat and ate with as good grace as she could manage.

So what if everyone knew? Giri apparently was not discriminating. He'd bedded Pella, and Vor supposed he and Milsa, both being apprentices of Colby and thus frequently together, were probably regular bedmates. But if that was true, why had he needed Pella? Because she'd been a virgin and so provided more energy? Because Milsa had instead gone to her master's bed?

Vor stabbed viciously at a piece of fruit on her plate and berated herself. Why did it matter? She was having fun with Giri and both of them had clearly established that they were not going to attempt a long-term exclusive relationship—like marriage or some such nonsense.

It didn't matter if everyone knew. No one had the authority to tell Vor what to do, and so far it seemed that Colby wasn't ordering Giri to stay away from her. Since they were being careful to gather all the energy being produced, there was no chance of conception. There was no reason for Vor to feel scared or ashamed or anything else. Besides, this was a temporary liaison that would be over in a day or two.

She tried to spear a small tomato but it dodged out from under her fork and went flying across the room. Vor fought back a scream of frustration.

***

Vor met Giri that afternoon for teleportation training, as they'd planned, in the largest workroom. What hadn't been planned was that Colby and Milsa were there, too, also brimming with power. Vor hesitated at the threshold.

"Come in, Vor," Colby said, with a hint of command.

She stepped inside but came no further. "I'm not your apprentice," she said softly, and cautiously.

The stately mage chuckled. "No, I know that, but teleportation is tricky, and I thought my overeager apprentice could use some guidance in his instruction."

Giri looked up sheepishly. He was on his knees, drawing out a circle—it seemed to Vor that a great deal of life as Colby's apprentice seemed to involve drawing magic circles. To reinforce that observation, at the other end of the room Milsa was in the same position, doing the same task. She didn't look up, and she wore a deep scowl.

"I don't want to impose on your time or energy, sir," Vor said. "On anyone's time or energy."

"You're not," Colby waved. "Come in and take a look here. There are written charts for making these circles, of course, and these copies are for you, so there's no need for you to memorize them now."

He walked around the circle Giri was drawing, pointing out critical runes and explaining why they were used.

"This is your departure circle," he said. "Over there, Milsa is working on an arrival circle. They have different runes and purposes, and it's always easier to teleport if you have proper circles to work with."

"My m—Altare—could teleport without them," Vor mentioned.

"Of course it can be done," Colby nodded. "I can do that, too, and Milsa has managed it a few times as well, but it's exhausting." He shrugged and muttered darkly. "If you're powering yourself with slaughter and rape, though, as he was, I suppose you'd have energy to spare."

He guided her over to a table. "You're going to start with teleporting inanimate objects. It's how all mages start to learn this skill."

There was an array of objects on the table: several lumps of coal, bits of wood, beads, a cup, a glass of water, and then a couple potted plants.

"Exactly how teleportation works is difficult to explain, as no one understands it fully," Colby said. "The best I can say, is that you must convince the world that this place," he pointed to the departure circle, "is the same as that place." He pointed to the arrival circle. "Then you tell the world, wait, no they're not, but you leave behind in the arrival circle what was originally in the departure circle, as you let them separate again."

"And magic can do this?" Vor remarked.

"Yes, but it requires power and concentration. Lacking either, you won't be able to make the connection, or when you separate the connection, the object you want to move gets separated, too."

Milsa and Giri had both gotten up by then and were checking each other's work.

"Here, Giri," Colby summoned. "Show off for your lady friend and teleport something."

He tossed a lump of coal at his apprentice, who caught it without expression or comment, but then surrendered to an embarrassed smile. Giri went to set the coal in the middle of the departure circle, turning his back to them.

"Watch what he does," Colby instructed as Milsa stepped out of the way.

Vor focused, observing the energy of both Giri and the world, paying close attention to the areas inside the circles, as she figured that would be where most of the action would happen. She thought Giri must have been doing it slowly, for it took him a minute or two to execute the spell. Then with a blink the coal was sitting in the arrival circle and he took a deep and steadying breath.

"Very good," Colby praised mildly. "Can you do that, Vor?"

"I think I understand the process," she answered. "I don't expect I can do it on the first try."

"No one does it on the first try," Colby said. He held out another lump of coal to her. "Give it a go. We'll stand here watching and make you nervous."

Vor took the coal with as much comment as Giri had made and went to take the position he vacated for her, while Milsa fetched the other coal out of the arrival circle. She set her piece in the center of the circle, put herself down in a light trance, and made the attempt.

It was like forcing fire and water to occupy the same space, or trying to shove a block of wood through a tabletop, getting the world to accept that the interiors of these two circles were the same place. Vor tried and failed several times, resetting herself and taking calming breaths between each attempt. She knew she was getting better at it, and the wizards behind her made no sounds that might have distracted her as she practiced.

At last she felt her stomach drop out from underneath her as for a brief moment the two circles merged to her magical sight. Then she lost her grip and crumbled bits of coal were sitting in both circles.

"Ah, excellent," Colby applauded from behind her.

He went and picked up the bits of coal from the arrival circle.

"Here you see why we start with nonliving items."

Vor had to catch her breath, but she, too, was pleased. Colby walked up to her and handed her another lump of coal.

He nodded encouragingly. "Do it again. This time, don't leave anything behind."

Vor set her jaw and cleaned out the remains of the first coal from her circle. She placed the new lump and went to work. She destroyed two more lumps before she finally got a whole lump to teleport without breaking.

Colby moved her on to wood. "Softer, easier to leave behind," he warned.

It only took her two tries. Next he gave her three beads. She only got one transferred on her first try, but got the rest of them over on her next one. The cup she didn't break. The glass of water arrived in the second circle as separate glass and water, leaving a puddle. She had to try that one three times before the water remained in the glass through the transfer.

Then Colby handed her a potted plant. "The head gardener assures me these are extras," he said.

By that time, Vor was getting low on energy, but she took it with a nod.

"You'll need to practice a lot before you advance to animals," Colby warned. "Expect to accidentally kill a few before you learn the gentle touch that keeps them healthy and alive through the process, so you might consider using lower animals like worms, slugs, and such, and gradually working up."

"Yes, sir," she said.

He sought and caught her gaze. "Advance to big things, like horses and cows, and achieve consistent success before trying it on a human." His expression turned mortally serious. "It's best to try it on another mage, an experienced one, who can help you, and has a chance of saving himself if you mess up. Only after years of successful teleportations should you consider trying to teleport yourself. Do you understand? Many a mage has killed himself with a failed teleportation spell."

"I understand," Vor assured him.

He shook his head a little. "Everyone wants to learn how to blink in and out here and there, but it takes a great deal of skill and power. Speaking of power, I see you're running low. Try sending the plant, but then you should stop. You can practice more tomorrow if you want."

Vor just nodded, not sure yet if she might not even be at the castle tomorrow. She prepared and executed the spell, thought she'd done well, but was shocked to see that half the plant arrived crisp and withered.

"No," she uttered. "I thought I did it right."

"This is what I mean by a gentle touch," Colby said. "You teleported it, true, but you also scorched it without meaning to. Practice."

She went and fetched the plant. "I think it will live," she diagnosed.

Vor took it back to the table and poured the water from the glass into its soil. When she looked up, she found both Colby and Giri smiling at her. Milsa still wore a scowl, however.

"You should rest, recover your energy," Colby suggested. "You'll have dinner with us tonight? Nothing formal, just common fellows breaking bread together."

Vor hesitated as Giri gazed at her hopefully.

"I know Giri has invited you to join us. Come back with us to Weldom when we go, or go on ahead yourself and join our ranks there," Colby said abruptly. "I wish to extend my invitation also. You are skilled and disciplined, Vor. You would be welcome."

She gritted her teeth and looked away. "I appreciate your time in teaching me," she began.

"I'll give you my mark, Vor," Colby interrupted. "You are already as skilled as many Weldom wizards, and I trust your judgment."

Vor put her hands on her own shoulders defensively. "I don't know what I want yet," she objected. "I need some time to sort myself out."

Colby nodded. "As you like. Perhaps you are correct in what you need. If you decide it's what you want, ask it of me at any time."

"Thank you, sir," she said grudgingly.

"Let us go then. Let's leave the circles and you can practice more tomorrow."

Colby led the way out of the room. Milsa followed while Giri lingered beside Vor, but the lady wizard sent a glance at Vor as she exited. In it, Vor saw more than a hint of loathing, and it took her aback. Giri didn't notice, his eyes also on Vor. Giri had told her Milsa was interested in possibly taking her as an apprentice, but he must have been wrong, or something must have drastically changed in the past day.

***

Both Vor and Giri were tired, and had been together only a few hours before, so their time before the dinner was gentle, slow, but still they clung to each other, and still Giri's promise held—that he did not leave her unsatisfied. Afterwards, they snuggled together under the blankets, to no discernable magical benefit, but Vor had never felt so warm or so content, at least on the surface.

Below that was a place she dared not examine too closely. It was a place that whispered of the future, of pain and solitude, of aching loss, and she would not listen. There was only now. Giri was in her arms now, making her feel so good. Now was all that mattered.

He stirred and kissed her forehead.

"Will you come to dinner?" he murmured.

"Alright," she agreed.

His arms tightened around her and Vor thought for a moment they quivered, but she must have imagined it. Giri was untangling himself from her,

344

smiling easily.

"Ready to go?" he asked.

Vor nodded and got up. They had a quick wash, dressed, and went down to the dining room together. Two seats had been left for them, side by side, and the servants were only now placing dishes on the table. Colby greeted them, waving them in. Ulver, Chirolen, and Eriducus were there, and so was Craduticus, all at ease among the new come Weldom wizards. They sat to partake.

Vor had expected some ribbing or teasing about her and Giri keeping company, but no one made so much as a single insinuation—although Ulver did look at her and wink once. By the time the meal was halfway over, Vor had even started to relax and participate a little in the conversations. It was a new sensation, not having to be always on guard, although she still couldn't relax completely. It was too strange; she kept waiting for a threat that never came.

The group broke up a little as the meal concluded. Lissian and Rossilla went off together, and Ylanzo pled fatigue and muttered something about meditating. The rest, however, moved as a group into one of the sitting rooms. Eriducus produced a pack of cards and tempted Strafa, Chirolen, and Colby to join him at a table. Strafa pulled out a dainty pipe and began smoking something that thankfully produced only a little smoke and of a scent that was not too objectionable.

Ulver sat down with Craduticus, apparently continuing a conversation, leaving Milsa, Giri, and Vor in awkward silence. Milsa raised an eyebrow in Vor's direction and took herself over to the corner where sat a neglected harpsichord. Ignoring the rest of the room, she took her place at it and began to play softly, apparently from memory, unless she was improvising beautifully.

"Sit with me?" Giri invited.

He picked a book off one of the shelves, seemingly at random, and plopped down onto a couch. He patted the cushion beside him and Vor moved hesitantly in his direction. Giri smiled and reached up to tug at her sleeve.

"Oh, come here," he chided, and she gave in to his pull, taking a seat on the edge of the cushion.

"Closer," he urged, "or you won't be able to see."

Vor fought the instinct to flee as Giri drew her tight beside him, slung his arm around her shoulders, and opened the book in front of both of them. Her heart was pounding with anxiety, and he must have seen something of that when she looked nervously at him, body stiff with self-consciousness.

"Does it bother you," he whispered, "that everyone knows we're, ah, what we're doing?"

A humiliating blush burned her face, but she tried to ignore it, especially since Giri sounded serious and unsteady.

"I'm getting used to it," she told him softly, trying to keep the conversation private.

Luckily, between the carousing of the four playing cards and Milsa's music, the room was loud enough that no one would hear them if they spoke quietly.

"You'd prefer I didn't touch you in public?" he asked next, his expression slightly closed. "It's fine, if you want. I don't want to make you uncomfortable."

Vor felt like half a dozen attacks were coming at her while she tried to balance dishware on her head and navigate down some steep stairs—so many thoughts and emotions. Foremost: she wanted to touch Giri; she always wanted to touch Giri, ever since they'd become intimate. She'd thought, however, that their touching would not extend beyond the privacy of a bedroom. Now he was trying to carry it on into public—and it wasn't that she didn't want him to, but she wondered why he was doing so.

And now, Milsa was giving evidence of disapproval of their association, and others—like Colby and Ulver—seemed to be encouraging it, when it was only supposed to have been a bit of private bedding for amusement and power purposes, wasn't it? Vor was feeling like she was getting more than what she'd bargained for, and Giri's words and behavior weren't exactly being consistent, and she wasn't sure if she wanted to get more than she'd bargained for—or what it was she was getting. And she definitely did not want to examine how she felt about it all—or even acknowledge that she didn't want to examine it.

But, "I do want you to touch me," she confessed: face burning again, and not giving in to the urge to hide it with her hands.

"It's alright," Giri soothed, bending his head over to kiss her hair. "Read with me."

No one seemed to object to them sitting together, or gave reaction to that little kiss. Even Milsa was focusing on her music, not looking in their direction. As Vor let Giri draw her closer, she tried to recall the last time she'd made any display of affection before others. Surely not since she'd been with her mother had she allowed any such evidence of public vulnerability. She fixed her eyes to the open book. She nodded whenever Giri asked if she was ready for him to turn the page, and thought the book was some sort of biography about some long dead lord or other, but was far too distracted and anxious to really read anything.

Gradually, as no one made comment—although Ulver, Craduticus, and a couple of the others looked over with little smiles—Vor began to relax again. She let herself lean more fully against Giri. He responded by adjusting his arm tighter around her. Eventually, she let her head come to rest on his shoulder. Some time after that, her eyes closed of their own accord. Milsa's music, the bickering of the card players, the murmurs of Ulver and Craduticus' conversation, and the rhythm of Giri's heart and breath lulled her to sleep: a sleep without nightmares.

***

"That's what I get for playing with you crooks."

Vor blinked awake. Chirolen was standing up from the card table. Colby was chuckling and Strafa was grinning victoriously. Eriducus patted Chirolen's arm in conciliatory fashion as he rose.

"Luck of the cards, my friend," Colby told him. "This was not your night."

"Crooks, all of you," Chirolen repeated, but as he stumped away in defeat, he saw Vor watching him and gave her a grin. "Good night, all," he called as he made his way to the door.

"It's a night for me, too," Eriducus announced, gathering up his cards and following Chirolen out.

"Us old folks need our beauty sleep," Ulver concurred, exchanging a nod with Craduticus.

Milsa's music came to a graceful conclusion as the three oldest of the mages exited. Strafa's pipe had gone out, but she sat back in her chair, still holding it in her teeth and stared across at Giri and Vor on the couch with a pensive look on her face.

"I guess that's it for me, too," Colby sighed, standing up and stretching his back. "Giri, Milsa, I'll need you tomorrow morning for the communication to Weldom."

"Yes, Master," the two chorused.

Milsa stood stiffly and followed her master out, managing to give Vor a little glare from the corner of her eye as she went. If Giri noticed, he made no reaction. That left Craduticus, Strafa, Giri, and Vor, the latter of who sat up on her own. Giri removed his arm from around her and quietly closed the book.

"It looks like bed time," Craduticus remarked, "unless anyone wants another game of cards?"

"Eriducus took the cards with him," Strafa denied.

"Ah, well, that's that, then. A pleasant evening to you all."

Craduticus left and Strafa sat up, tapping out her pipe and stowing it. She eyed Giri and Vor one more time, but then shook her head, as if to herself, and left without a word.

"Time for bed, as they say," Giri muttered.

He got to his feet and shelved the book, then turned to smile gently at Vor, but his actions were slightly wooden, and he looked away too soon.

"You'll be practicing teleportation again tomorrow?" he prompted.

"I suppose I may," Vor shrugged.

She was also thinking of leaving, although she still didn't know where she'd go, but she found her throat tight if she thought of telling Giri that.

"You heard my master, I'll be busy in the morning, but I'll find you in the afternoon?" he hoped.

Vor nodded. "Alright."

Swiftly, he bent down and kissed her forehead. "Goodnight."

"Goodnight," she replied.

Giri hesitated a moment, as if waiting or pondering something, but when she didn't stand up or speak, he left. Vor sat alone on the couch. For years she'd been without a friend in the castle, subject to the whims of her master, but she'd never felt the ache of being alone in a room. Now, as she sat, the warmth of Giri's body fading from where she'd been pressed against him, thinking of going back to her empty suite, suddenly she was lonely.

But nothing had changed, she told herself, nothing of any importance. There was no reason to be lonely; she was as she had always been, only minus a manipulative, abusive master. Vor got up and blew out the lights. Then she turned her feet towards her suite, planning to bathe in her own little bathroom instead of using the communal one, not wanting to see anybody. As she approached her door, she sensed a presence, and adrenaline leapt as she thought it might be Giri—but no, the aura was completely wrong.

"Finally," Milsa growled from where she stood in the center of Vor's doorway, obviously blocking her path. "I won't ask what kept you."

"Excuse me?" Vor retorted.

"I was waiting for you," she said, as though implying Vor should have known.

Vor regained her mental footing. Milsa was older, wiser, and more powerful than Vor, but this was Vor's home, and Vor's room, and she wasn't going to just submit to her.

"Why?" she asked. "What do you have to say to me that couldn't have been said anywhere, anytime?"

"Stay away from Giri," Milsa said flatly.

Vor tried to keep a handle on her emotions, and consciously act, not react—not throw a firebolt at the woman, for example.

"Can't Giri make his own choices?" she suggested.

Milsa's expression suggested she'd bit into something bitter.

"Are you jealous?" Vor tried. "I—"

"Jealous?" Milsa spat, and then barked a laugh. "You think Giri and I are a pair?"

"No," Vor replied calmly. "He told me he doesn't pair."

Milsa eyed her again, as if trying to figure her out. "I'm with Colby," she whispered finally.

"Oh," Vor uttered in genuine surprise.

"Yes, he's older than me, and he's my master, but it's just what happened, and we like it," Milsa said, sounding a trifle defensive.

Vor swallowed, tried to think. "Then, if," she stuttered, "why does it matter if Giri and—"

"You're distracting him," Milsa accused.

"I can't be anything that unusual. I was under the impression that Giri is hardly celibate," Vor offered.

"He's not as promiscuous as you seem to assume," the older mage went on, starting to show her teeth.

But Vor was thinking back now. "If you're with Colby, why did you suggest that you wanted to bed Karolan?"

Milsa scoffed. "You're such an idiot."

"Pardon me?" Vor drew herself up, reconsidering the firebolt.

She made an exasperated gesture. "You thought I was serious? You may be quick when it comes to magic, but you're a dunce when it comes to people."

Vor's surprised look must have been answer enough. Milsa took a step closer, her expression somewhere between indignation and sincerity.

"Look," the wizard began, "Giri is not my partner, but he is special to me. I've spent years with him, learning from Colby together. He's like, like a little brother perhaps, and a friend, and I did teach him about sex, years ago, before my bond with Colby developed. Giri is," she paused as if searching for words, "he's, he's good, you know?"

Vor, forehead well creased with discomfort, struggled to understand. "Good?" she repeated. "In what way, exactly, are you referring to?"

Milsa threw out her hands. "He's a good man," she emphasized. "Yes, he has tumbled women in the past, but not to excess, and he's honest about it, and he never promises anything, and he tries not to hurt them." She glared daggers at Vor. "A couple of them hurt him, and that's why he decided he won't pair up, that he won't go beyond a little physical pleasure. Do you understand me?"

Vor was still trying to take it all in. What struck her most strongly was that Milsa was saying Giri never promised anything. He'd made a promise to Vor, though. It was just about sex, nothing else—or so she supposed—but was that important?

"Lately he hasn't even been seeking that much—I had to bully him into renewing himself with that servant girl—and he never does more than one time, except with you," Milsa was going on. "And now he's parading you around in front of Colby and the others. Don't you see what's happening?"

Vor could only stare, face pinched with confusion against all the new information the lady wizard was pouring onto her. Milsa huffed again and grabbed the lapels of Vor's jacket. She leaned in to hiss her words directly into Vor's face.

"One of the reasons we came back, and followed Altare when he went after you, was because Giri argued for it. I'll bet he hasn't told you that. We could have let your master run off to finish you without repercussions, but instead we went to observe. Giri even wanted to help you fight him, but Colby stopped him because of all the political complications it could have created. If Giri had stepped into the fight—and a few times we thought he might, even against Colby's orders—Altare wouldn't have stood a chance, especially not while you and Craduticus and everyone were distracting him. Giri is a talented mage, and only getting stronger, smarter, more skilled," Milsa said, "and he's a good man."

Vor managed a nod and two words amidst the windstorm of Milsa's tirade. "I agree."

Milsa shook her once, an anguished snarl on her face. "Then, don't you ruin him."

Vor stepped back as the wizard released her, a hand going reflexively to her chest. "I don't understand," she confessed. "But I'm leaving tomorrow, so I won't be seeing any of you anymore."

"Good," Milsa spat. "Get out of here before, before it's too late. Go in the morning, while we're doing our report. I'll draw it out it as long as I can."

The older woman swept by Vor and walked swiftly away. Befuddled, Vor opened her wards and went into her rooms. She bathed and got in bed, still going over the things Milsa had said, and still not understanding most of it, but feeling a pulsing, pervasive warmth to know that Giri had argued for going to watch the fight, and had wanted to help her fight. She thought if it had looked like she might truly die, he would have disobeyed his master and stepped in. Vor felt it like the certainty of gravity, and wondered why she believed it so strongly.

What Milsa had said about ruining him Vor still couldn't understand, but she knew the thought of hurting Giri caused her pain. She clenched her hands in the sheets, hoping nothing she did or said would cause any harm to the young wizard. Eventually, thoughts and emotions hopelessly jumbled, she fell into sleep.

Chapter 29
Vor's Decision

Vor woke up, aware that she wasn't alone, but not alarmed; the other's presence was familiar, safe. The room was still totally dark, without a hint of dawn. A cautious hand touched her shoulder. She reached up and put her hand over his.

"I couldn't sleep. You left your wards down."

"Mm," she accepted, brain already descending back towards slumber.

"I put them back up."

"Mm," she grunted again.

"Can I sleep with you?"

"Mm," for a third time.

The mattress shifted as Giri got in bed with her. He didn't touch her, but gradually she felt his body heat permeating the blankets. She fell back to sleep, and recalled nothing of Milsa's threats or warnings until sunrise lit up her curtains. Then Vor found herself on her side with Giri curled around her back, head tucked against the nape of her neck, knees bent behind hers.

Something tight twisted in her chest, something that burned more painfully than the greater salamander's bite. She was going to leave, to sneak out while Giri was with his master, without saying goodbye, without telling him where she was going. But if she told him, she knew he wouldn't let her go, and she'd let him convince her to stay.

Would staying be so bad?

Vor winced and bit the insides of her cheeks. No. One day, a few, would turn into weeks, months, years of living in this castle, this place that had been something of a prison, something of a sanctuary—something too complicated for her to sort out now. She needed distance from it, a place without distractions, without reminders: a place where she could get some perspective. At least for now, she had to leave. She couldn't let him talk her into staying.

But now, she sensed him waking. This was her last chance to hold him, so she took him into her arms. He wrapped his arms around her and pulled her tight against his chest. The hard, burning feeling compounded and Vor clamped her jaws shut to prevent some primal, heretofore unknown sound from breaking free.

She took him fiercely, desperately, for she knew it would be the last time. When at last he kissed her forehead and gathered up his clothes, he indeed seemed pleased, for he didn't know. She managed to smile at him as he left, keeping the tears back until she heard the door shut.

***

Vor didn't cry long. She knew there was no use in it. It wouldn't make the pain go away, and she had things to do. She collected what she thought she wanted to bring with her, and realized it was far too much for her to carry. Quickly, she began trying to pare it down; she didn't know how long Giri would be occupied. She was in the midst of this when Craduticus walked in through her carelessly unlatched door.

"Going to Weldom?" he asked, making her jump.

Vor scowled at him and went back to packing. "You, too? Everyone wants me to go there."

"Maybe everyone is right," the old mage suggested. "Sometimes they are."

"No," she grunted back.

"Running away instead?"

"I'm not running," she refuted. "I just need some distance, some perspective, to know what I want."

He shrugged. "Fair enough. Are you planning to carry all that?"

"I can't. I'm trying to reduce it."

"Buy some goats."

She raised an eyebrow at him. "Goats, sir?"

"You need a place to go for peace and reflection," he summed up. "Unless you want to wander around aimlessly, I have a suggestion."

"It involves goats?"

He held out a rolled parchment to her, and Vor took it gingerly.

"What's this?"

"I made some houses," he explained. "Follow this map to them. There's quite a good one out at the end of the road. I suggest a pair of goats to help carry your baggage. There will be one difficult cliff to climb, but I'm sure you'll find a way."

Vor regarded the parchment, and found herself considering the offer.

"Someone should know where you are," Craduticus said seriously. "I won't tell, if that's what you'd like."

That hard, hot pain in her chest burned again.

"I won't even tell Giri," the old mage added softly.

Her chest nearly exploded. Vor spun away, hiding a traitorous tear that spilled down her cheek.

"You might consider leaving a note," the old man added.

"A note?" she grunted.

"Or you could just up and leave, like Hawkrain did, leaving everybody wondering."

That struck her, that sense of abandonment: that she wasn't even worth saying goodbye to. She wouldn't do that to Giri. Vor fumbled for paper and a writing stick, sat down, and stared at the page. Time was short; she couldn't spend hours composing exactly the right words.

She wrote, "I'm going away for a while to clear my head and decide on my next course." Her hand hesitated, shaking. "I hope I will see you again" –the tip of the stick was suspended, hovering, like a hawk that might stoop, or might abort the attempt and go glide off somewhere else. She stooped, adding, "soon," and her name.

Vor folded it, and glanced up when Craduticus held his hand out for it.

"Shall I give it to him?" he asked, barely audible.

Her jaw trembled, but she set the note in his hand. The mage tucked it inside his robes. Vor had to turn away again as a few more traitorous tears fell.

"Goats?" she croaked finally.

"Goats. I'll help you pick out a likely pair."

***

Craduticus showed her how to situate the packs. The goats were skittish, but Vor did her best to soothe them.

"They'll get used to it. That way," Craduticus said at last. "Follow the map: out of the city, bear left past the first fork of the main road. It's the path back to the house where you found the princess."

She recalled that well: the house where she'd first seen Karolan, where she and her master's soldiers had done such violence. It was a week by carriage, much longer by foot, then into the wilderness.

"Thank you," Vor told Craduticus.

"You are sure about this?"

The pain in her chest was throbbing now, in time with her heart. She could hardly speak, so she nodded.

"I'm old," he told her, "and my years left are few, but I hope to see you again, Vor. You might be right that some time is what you need; you went through a lot here. I hope you will return. There are people waiting for you."

She nodded again, although not necessarily in agreement, and started to

go.

"Wait," Craduticus croaked out. "Wait. One thing, Vor, please."

Starting to feel exasperated, she turned back obediently.

"I am a wizard," he said, "recognized by Weldom," and he tugged down the collar of his robes, showing a five petalled mark like Giri had on the front of his shoulder. "In case I am gone when you return, let me give you a mark now."

Vor scowled.

"Just one won't make you a wizard," he emphasized. "I did nothing for you all those years ago. I can do something for you now."

"How will this help me?" she managed to ask.

Craduticus paused to consider that seriously. "If you never choose to become a wizard, perhaps it won't," he said. "Perhaps, actually, it will only help me, to make me feel like I've helped you, because I have faith you will pursue that path, so I will feel some of my guilt ease."

No argument he could have made that it would help her could have convinced her to let him do it, but whether he knew it or not, the possibility that she could help him reached a part of her that swayed.

"Alright," Vor agreed. "Over here."

They moved into a shadow between two buildings. Vor took off her pack and adjusted her clothes until she could expose her left shoulder.

"It hurts," Craduticus warned her.

"I never thought it wouldn't," she replied.

He touched his thumb to her skin. "In my eyes, Vor Hearthsraven, you are a wizard," he declared.

Then the spot he touched burst afire with pain and Vor stood her ground against it. A few moments later Craduticus was withdrawing his hand and there was a shiny patch of scar on her skin, still red. The pain began to fade, which was good because the strap of her pack would rub right at the edge of the spot. Vor put her clothes in order and prepared again to depart.

"On your way then," Craduticus nodded. "Safe journey to you."

"Thank you," Vor mumbled, "for everything."

"You're very welcome."

She looked once more at his wrinkled, sadly smiling face, and turned to set out on her road.

***

It was afternoon. Vor had left the city behind her and was entering the fringes of a forest, when Giri caught up to her. She stepped off the road when she heard the pounding of hooves behind her, but was surprised when horse and rider pulled up and stopped beside her. Then she realized the rider's identity. Giri swung down from the saddle while the goats bleated in perturbation, and grabbed her in an anguished hug.

"You left without saying goodbye," he accused. "Why?"

The burning pain, which she thought she'd walked off, returned full force and she hid her face against his neck. Her arms gripped him. He was repeating her name over and over, nearly breathless.

"I need," she choked out, "I need some time to think."

"That's fine," Giri declared, stepping back and holding her at arm's length. "That's fine, but tell me when you're going. Don't leave Craduticus to—"

Then he seemed to notice something and pulled back his right hand.

"Craduticus," he uttered. "Craduticus gave you a mark. He did, didn't he? I can sense it. It's fresh."

Vor winced and confessed. "Yes."

Giri stood there, staring at her with a hint of pain at her betrayal in his eyes, and after a moment she let her pack fall to the ground and shifted her clothing. Then he was staring at the mark, still red and livid on her skin, and moved closer. She knew what he was going to do. He didn't ask her if she wanted it, and she said not a word to stop him.

He held her close with his other arm as his thumb pressed into her skin and again she braced against the pain. It was good; it helped to lessen the other pain, the one in her chest. When he was done, he brushed her clothing back into place. Then they stood there, inches apart, each waiting for the other to do or say something. Around them the released goats grazed eagerly and the tired horse moved to do the same.

"Vor," he breathed at last, "don't go."

She almost couldn't stand it; it hurt so much.

"I'm sorry," Giri revised. "If you need to go," he swallowed, and it sounded like he was forcing the words out, "you can go."

He spun about and like the strike of a spear the pain nearly overcame her, but he was back in a moment, having only fetched something from the horse's saddlebag.

"In case you really did leave, I made something. I made it last night, and then when I was finished, I couldn't sleep, and had to go to you," he babbled.

He handed over a thin bound book and a tiny sack. Vor immediately went to open the sack. A silvery ring of mage-stone dropped into her palm. Giri opened his other hand, revealing a twin of it.

"They're like contact stones," he explained. "So we can send messages, while you're away."

Like lancing a boil, pain drained from Vor, although an ache remained.

"If you want," he muttered on. "You don't have to wear it. It's just, if you're going to be alone, that's good for sorting out your thoughts, but there might be times you get lonely, too."

Vor put the ring on, finding the finger it fit best on. Seeing that, Giri did, too, and then they looked at each other for a while. Both realized something had changed, or was changing between them. There was more now than their original agreement—perhaps there had always been more, but neither had admitted it.

"The book has some communication codes I made up," Giri murmured, cheeks coloring. "It's not much, but it's something. At least we can let each other know that we're doing alright."

Vor nodded reassuringly. "Yes," she said. "I'll use them."

"And you can tell me when you're coming back."

His tone was still uncertain, as though he doubted if she would really return, but now—

"I will come back," she promised. "It won't be long."

"How long?"

She pursed her lips, thinking. "By spring."

He flinched. "That long."

"I just don't know if I'll be able to get back once the snow comes."

"Yes," he nodded. "Of course, I didn't think of that. The winters must be harsh up here."

Silence fell between them again. Vor didn't know how to say goodbye. How could she leave him now? In a couple weeks, everything had changed. She'd ended her innocence, betrayed and killed her master, lost Karolan, discovered Giri, and with him pleasure, passion, and—and what? What was it that had brought him all this way out to her, and that kept her now from walking away?

His hands came up to touch her cheeks. Ah, yes, so now he would kiss her on the forehead, as he always did, and let her go, but he wasn't tipping his chin up. He wasn't much taller than her, so he always had to stretch a little to reach her brow. Instead, he was hunching slightly, bending down.

When Vor felt his breath on her lips, her eyes flew wide open. He was trembling, and she had the sudden thought that he'd never done this before. As gently as she could, Vor stepped a little closer and slid her hands to his jaw and the back of his neck, guiding and encouraging.

Their mouths met lightly at first, and he even twitched a little at the sensation, but Vor drew him in. As Giri surrendered, the last of the pain in her bloomed into joy that ran all the way out to her fingers and toes in waves of wildflowers. They stood on the side of the road in each other's arms for several long moments, feeling their way through their first kiss together.

"I'll come back," Vor told him again after recovering her breath. "I need to get myself centered. I don't think it's fair to you if I'm not ready to—"

She broke off: to what? No, she knew what: to be with him, fully and wholly, for more than a few tumbles—for a long time. A long time: she'd never expected such a thing to be part of her life, and she had no idea how to navigate it. He kissed her again, saving her the need to try to express it.

"It's alright," Giri assured her. "I'll be waiting for you. I promise. Then, we'll work everything out."

Vor nodded.

"You should get going," he managed after a few more moments. His voice was thick.

A tear spilled out of each of her eyes. "I will come back. I promise."

Giri brushed away the tears with his fingers, kissed her once more, and stepped back. He gathered up his horse's reins, and she fetched her goats. They stood on the road then, facing each other, until Giri mounted up. He raised his hand with the mage-stone ring.

"Send me messages whenever you want," he urged.

"I will. You, too," Vor replied.

"Be careful."

"You, too."

Words burned in her mouth, on her tongue, against the inside of her teeth. Giri gazed down at her as if memorizing her, and then clucked to the horse, turning it, and began to ride away. Vor stared at his back. He turned his head, looking at her again, but didn't stop. He smiled and made a little shooing gesture, telling her to get along.

Vor turned, tugging the goats to follow, every few steps looking back over her shoulder, to see Giri looking back over his shoulder at her, until at last the road turned, and he was out of sight.

Epilogue
Long Distance Call 

Vor reached the first place Craduticus had marked on the map. It was not one of the houses he'd built, but an ordinary inn, still only a day's walk from the capital. Vor hadn't yet gone very far, but to her it was a world away from her old life. She had coin enough to lodge the goats in the inn's livestock yard, and to get herself a meal and a tiny cupboard of a room with a narrow pallet and a lamp with a chipped chimney.

There she opened the book Giri had given her, ring still on her finger. The first notation in the book was a simple single pulse indicating "hello." It also served as "yes" and was basically for reaching out to see if the other person holding the ring wanted to talk. Despite their affectionate farewell on the road, she was suddenly anxious.

Perhaps Giri had gone right back to the castle and tumbled poor infatuated Pella? Even if not, maybe he'd come to his senses once he'd spent the evening without Vor, and realized how much freer he felt not having her around?

Vor grimaced. Well, she'd never know if she didn't try. If he didn't respond, then she'd know he was either busy with something important, or disinterested. If he didn't respond for several nights running, she'd have a definitive answer. She focused on the ring, and sent one quick pulse of energy into it. Now she just had to wait—

The response was all but immediate and Vor nearly laughed and cried at the same time. A series of pulses came, and Vor flipped through the book to try to decode them.

"Are you safe?" he was asking.

"Yes," she sent back.

There weren't that many pages in the book, and not that many phrases that could be encoded with a series of pulses until the codes got unmanageably long. She wanted to talk, but wasn't sure what to send, but since she'd found the one page, she just replied with the same question.

"Are you safe?" she asked.

"Yes," he replied. "Do you have food?"

"Yes."

"Are you warm?"

"Yes."

He sent another series she had to look up, but found it quickly enough. He'd said, "me, too."

Vor wanted to tell him she missed him, and looked deeper into the book, wondering if he'd included the phrase. There, near the back she found it. It took few a few moments, however, to find her courage.

"I miss you," she sent.

A breath later, he replied the same.

Vor held her hand with the ring against her chest, trying to stay calm, trying not to cry. Just as she'd gotten herself under control, he sent another message, and she had to go flipping through the book to find it.

There, on the last page.

For a second she thought her heart stopped. She stared at the words written by his own hand, as peace and resolve settled over her. Now not trembling at all, she brought the ring back up to her chest again, and sent back the same pulses Giri had just sent her, whispering them under her breath.

"I love you."

Second Epilogue
Jessika and Koki

Where was he? Jessika scrubbed at her dishes. She'd been back at the little house in the trees for two days. Although she'd lived there with Koki, and sometimes Karolan, for a year, seeing the faun everyday, now he was nowhere to be found. He hadn't left a note, either.

"What is it with men just vanishing without saying anything?" she growled at her dishwater.

She couldn't stay much longer. The trip back to the castle would take a whole day moving quickly, and she worried her father would wake up soon, or start to. She wanted to be there when he did. Jessika didn't figure he would recognize her right away, or be able to respond to her fully, but she wanted him to get used to her being around. She wanted to take care of him, to show him that she cared about him. She hoped that eventually they would build a relationship, and love each other as father and daughter.

Well, she would leave tomorrow, whether Koki came home or not. When they'd started to plan the overthrow of Altare, in the early spring once Cray had awakened and regained some strength, the faun had flatly refused to be involved in anything having to do with the castle or the people in it. He hadn't told them they shouldn't do it—and he admitted that he thought the world would be a better place without Altare—but whenever the conversation turned to it, he'd just get up and leave without a word.

Jessika bit her lip, wondering how he would react to her telling him she wanted to go and live there. Of course, now Altare was dead: killed by Vor and burned to ashes by State Wizard Colby. Maybe Koki's attitude would be different knowing that. There were still wizards at the castle though, and it didn't seem like Weldom would be turning it back over to the rightful owners. She snarled and twisted the dishrag.

"It's my home," she hissed between clenched teeth.

But then she tossed down the rag and took a breath. The wizards had a point, too. The strong conquered. Griffins hunted prey. If the prey wasn't strong enough to defend itself, it deserved to be eaten. That left the most competent, the strongest and smartest, to carry on, to lead, to govern.

She still thought Weldom should not have invaded Northnest and killed almost everyone at the capital. She still thought—now that they'd gotten the mage-stone they wanted—that they should give Northnest back to her. She understood, though, why they wouldn't. There was no reason they had to, other than the questionable goodness of their hearts.

A sound outside alerted Jessika, and she stepped to the doorway.

"Koki?" she called.

Still a ways away, walking under the trees, the faun lifted his head. Then he was bounding towards her. She came out in the little clearing in front of the house to meet him with relief spreading across her face. He skidded to a stop in front of her with excitement stamped across his features.

Jessika grabbed him in a hug, but was surprised at the state of him. He was bare-chested, wearing only a wrap around his waist. She'd never seen it before: it was leather, and finely beaded with shells, quartz, and agate, so it sparkled. He had bits of leaves and twigs in his hair, which was tousled and loose, and somehow looked longer than she remembered from when she'd left only a week ago. He had an armband, too, of braided cord dyed red and black. Where had he gotten that? Had he made it?

Koki hugged her back, and she heard him laugh.

"He's dead," she blurted out. "Altare: he's dead, overthrown. There's wizards from Weldom there in the castle, different ones, but they aren't going to hurt us, and my father, they're helping him recover."

They parted, Koki still holding her shoulders, and merriment dancing in his eyes.

"That's excellent," he smiled. "I'm so relieved. That's so much better than it was."

Jessika beamed back, so happy that he was happy for her. "Now we can go—"

"I have news, too," he interrupted eagerly. "I found them."

She blinked at him a little, but still happy, not bothering to be upset that he'd talked over her. "Who?" she asked.

"My clan," he gushed. "I went out as soon as you left, looking for signs, trying to remember. It took me days, but they're still alive. I found them. I met them. I have an aunt and uncle, and a cousin there still. They welcomed me. They cried. I cried."

He looked like he was about to cry again, and grabbed her up in a hug so tight it knocked some air out of her.

"Slow down," she begged when he let her go. "Whom did you find?"

A hint of irritation entered his face.

"My clan," he repeated, a bit slower. "Fauns, other fauns, the ones my family lived with before we were caught."

Jessika felt her eyes widen. The information wormed into her. A cold chill began to spread in her chest, and she didn't want to hear it, didn't want to know it. Her happy mood deflated like clouds covering the sun.

"You have to meet them," Koki smiled. "They're wonderful."

Her skin tingled, starting to feel numb. Her tongue was like wood. Koki's mirth slowly faded.

"Don't you want to meet them?" he asked eventually.

"Well, yes, but I thought," she stuttered, "now we could go live in the castle, now that Altare is gone and the wizards are cleaning everything up. My father is going to wake up, and—" Her fingers gripped the seams of her trousers, aching. She stared at the ground. "I wanted to be there, to be like a family."

They stood, not looking at each other, both having plummeted from the heights of excitement into the rocky chasm of dread. The silence between them stretched on and on. Finally, Koki lifted a hand and touched her arm.

"That's fine," he said with what sounded like forced cheer. "You go visit your father for a while, and I'll go visit my clan, and then—"

"It wouldn't just be a while," she broke in. "The wizards say it could take a year for him to heal to be like himself again. He's going to need help. I want to help."

Koki's hand slowly dropped. Pain opened in Jessika's chest: a huge, gaping hole. Only the greatest force of will stopped her from crumpling into sobs. As it was, a tear streamed down her cheek.

Her throat went tight so she could hardly talk. "You won't come with me?"

She heard him suck a breath. "I," he began, "I can't go back to that castle."

Jessika nodded blindly, staring at the ground. "I understand."

"I'm sorry."

"No. You should be with your family," she whispered through a tight throat. "You should be—"

"With my own kind," he finished for her.

Jessika looked up at him through her tears, at his horns poking through his curly hair. They'd gotten about a quarter inch longer since she'd known him. The pelt on his legs was short now, his summer coat, and rich and brown, close to the color of his hair. When he'd shed his dull winter undercoat it had gotten all over the house, and made him itch for days. He'd even confessed that Chika used to collect it and use it in her knitting. Jessika hadn't known whether to be amused, disgusted, or appreciative of Chika's practicality. She couldn't see his short little tail from this angle, but if she glanced down she'd see his hooves. He was every inch a faun.

"Maybe you're right," Koki admitted.

She shook as the hole in her chest yawned wider, aching through her whole body. They were parting. That's what this was. They'd said when they'd gotten together a year ago, that they'd be together while they were happy being together, and if they stopped being happy together, they'd stop being together. Only, this—it wasn't that they weren't happy together. Jessika hadn't thought that there would be other things that might part them. She'd thought happiness was all that mattered.

"No," she croaked. "No, it doesn't have to be like this."

"Jessika," he whispered, reaching out to touch her arm.

"No, we can figure it out. We can."

"What do you suggest?" His voice was soft, but he didn't sound optimistic.

She tried to think, but her brain wasn't working very well. After a minute or two, Koki spoke again.

"I think I want to know my people. They want to know me. It isn't that I don't like living with you; I do. But somehow I'm still lonely. I thought maybe we could live between the two worlds, yours and mine, and get to have both, but if you want to live in the castle, with your father, and stone and wizards all around you—that's no place for a faun. It was hard enough living with Chika in the city, where I could sneak off into the forest whenever I wanted."

"I have to go to Weldom, too," she announced. "I'm going to argue for Northnest to have its sovereignty restored."

"Weldom." Koki raised his hands again and cupped her face. "I wish I could go with you."

"You can," she said.

"No," he refused after a moment. "I can't."

It was really happening. She couldn't believe it. No, it was true. How could it be? He put a hand over her heart.

"I'll go with you in here," he whispered.

A sob broke from her.

"No. Don't cry, Hawkwings. This is better," he went on.

"No," she refuted.

"It's better for you."

"No."

Koki took her back in his arms. "What we've had, I'll never forget."

The collapse came and she fell apart. He held her up, her tears running down the bare skin of his back.

"You're the most special person in the world to me," he told her, voice husky.

From a great distance, she felt him fumbling in her pockets, and a little bit of her mind that was still working realized he'd found the contact stone Thornfire had given her. Koki went on holding her as the pain left her with nothing but raw tears, and she felt him shaking, too: felt the warmth and then coolness of his tears soaking her shirt.

"Come," he encouraged, and led her into their little house.

Koki took her into bed with him and held her, just held her as the crying went over her in waves, until she was exhausted by it. The day stretched into afternoon, but still he stayed, not talking, just keeping her warm and close, every now and then stroking her hair or gently kissing her.

Jessika knew little but the pain and the fact that he was leaving, would be gone, that this might be the last time she held him, or saw him. A little of what he'd said reached her. It might be better. Surely they would both take time to heal, but at least they were parting while still friends. There would be no lingering bitterness. He'd rejoin his clan. Probably he'd someday be able to pick a mate, and have children. She? She didn't know what she'd do. At the moment she had no desire for the affections of any other, or for the far off hypothetical possibility of children: more distant than the stars.

The sound of wings came to her ears. Koki stirred.

"I'm going now," he murmured.

Letting go of him was the hardest thing she'd ever done. He bent over her and kissed her. Their eyes met and held for a long moment.

"You must take care of yourself," he told her.

"I want you to be happy," she told him, voice breaking.

Koki drew away, holding her hand for a few precious seconds, before he stepped back, and their fingers slipped apart. He backed towards the door, and then he was through it, and then he was gone.

***

Hawkwind watched as Koki came stumbling out of the house, almost blind with tears. Her feathers lifted with alarm as he staggered up to her, grabbing onto the front strap of her harness.

"I'm sorry," he wept, face twisted with sobs. "I'm sorry. Take care of her,

Hawkwind. Take care of her."

"What's happened?" the griffin demanded.

Koki shook his head. "I'm leaving," he rasped. "I'm sorry. Please. Take care of her."

So that was it. Well, she couldn't say she hadn't expected it would come someday. Hawkwind patted his back.

"I will," she promised. "And you? You have someone to take care of you?"

"I found my people," he said.

And that explained it all. "You've treated my chick with nothing but care and kindness," she told him. "It is sad that this is the way it ends, but I can feel no other wind that would allow you to fly together. Go, and be glad of your time together. Let it strengthen you for your future."

Griffins couldn't understand the romantic love that humans felt, for they didn't normally pair bond, but Hawkwind knew it existed, and had seen it between Jessika and Koki. Sometimes, it had even made her wistfully envious, but not now: not when she saw the pain it inevitably brought. Jessika must be suffering.

"Perhaps," she offered, "we will meet again. May you find many warm thermals, to carry you high."

Koki hugged her hard, and then dashed away, swiping at his face, agile legs carrying him speedily into the trees. Hawkwind watched him until he disappeared into the thick summer greenery. Then she turned and went to comfort her chick.

Third Epilogue
Northborn Year 12: Winter

In the deep of winter, two unicorns huddled together in a hidden grove far back in the mountains. Here, below dense towering trees, the snow did not reach the ground. Hot springs bubbled continually, filling the air with steam. All around them were breathing mounds of color on the moss and grass, occasionally flicking bright tails or shaking prismatic, jewel-like horns. This was where the unicorns came when the cold bit hard and the trees slept.

The male of the pair, called Glacier, nuzzled his mate, Violet, who rumbled reassuringly at him. The winter was cold, and beyond the vale the snow lay in blankets thick enough to come up to a unicorn's chest, but here they were safe, and all would be well. Her belly was growing large now, and come late spring, or early summer, it would be her time, but not yet. There was no need to think that far ahead just yet.

Then her ears pricked up, and she opened her eyes from her light doze. "What is it?" Glacier asked.

Violet curved her neck around to look at her abdomen. She felt it again, just slightly, the first hint of movement.

"Did you feel something?" he pressed.

"Yes," Violet replied. "I think so."

The male bent down and laid his horn across her back, nose touching gently to his mate's belly. He rumbled softly to their unborn foal.

"Patience, Sky. Patience."

Addendum: Giri's Memories
The Engagement Banquet

Giri staggered a little as they arrived. Colby was the only one of them to have ever visited the Northborn castle, so he had controlled the teleporting, with Milsa and Giri just tagging along and contributing energy. Giri had only teleported himself once before, with Colby's help, and never this far. He nearly passed out from the energy drain, and Milsa caught his arm.

"Pull yourself together, Giri," Colby ordered. "We must appear strong."

Milsa gave him an encouraging pat, and he focused, dragging up the remains of his energy. After a moment, he was able to stand tall again.

"Good man," Colby praised. "Just hang on a little while, and then we'll see what can be done about energy renewal. It's a celebration; at the least they should feed us. Are you both ready?"

They gave affirmatives, and Colby sent a blast of air to knock the great doors open. The party inside jerked to a halt, and Giri followed his master in, paralleling Milsa. He scanned the room: six mages: all weaker than Colby, some very weak, and only one strong enough to approach Giri's strength. That one was sitting nearly at the center of the high table, and his power was laced with the energies of blood, pain, and sex. There was nothing wrong with that, as long as it had all been consensual, but Giri's instincts declared that it had not been.

The three weakest mages were old men, of hardly any magical consequence, although they might be wise and experienced. Then Giri's scan caught on the second most powerful of the mages. The only woman among them, she was sitting near one end of the high table, beside the third most powerful mage. As Altare stood, so did she and so did the boy beside her. The boy had his full height—and plenty of it—but Giri could easily scent the immaturity of his energies, even without touching them. The young woman, however, was a completely different matter.

He had to pay attention, following the prompts of his master, but every bit of focus he could spare fixed covertly on her. She was tightly controlled, and he didn't dare yet probe her aura, for he knew she'd catch him at it, but the sense of power about her was profound. Her attitude spoke of strength and deliberation—and caution. She was also physically lovely. Just a bit shorter than Giri himself, slender, with skin a shade darker than his, black hair held artfully up away from her face, and a wary, observant gaze: she piqued his interest at once. He couldn't imagine anyone not being impressed and intrigued by her.

Through the introductions, Giri learned her name was Vor Hearthsraven. By her looks, she likely was from western Weldom, although he didn't recognize her surname as having come from a noble house. His seat at the table did not put him beside her. Colby's subtle cues had directed Milsa to take that seat—perhaps because he thought this Vor Hearthsraven would be more willing to speak with another woman. Giri was aware of her all through the dinner, as he ate heartily in an effort to restore his energies. He listened to Milsa bantering with her and hid his amusement. So she was witty as well as strong, poised, and lovely—but she was also guarded, so very guarded. If she'd had a dozen loyal bulldogs surrounding her she couldn't have been more guarded.

Based on Giri's initial assessment of her master, he could guess what—or rather whom—she was guarded against. He didn't sense that she was depraved, like Altare, which meant she had a difficult position to endure. Intriguing indeed: Giri felt a growing urge to know more. How had someone like her come to be the apprentice of a man like Altare? When finally the dinner was over and Altare began to lead them off, Giri made sure to fall in next to Vor. She was edgy, defensive, and clearly worried, although she tried to hide it.

It only intrigued him more.

<u>The First Night in Northborn</u>

Giri had collapsed on the divan in his sitting room, so exhausted now he could barely stand. The food had helped—had allowed him to at least make it as far as the guest quarters—but he needed more. It wasn't unheard of for a seriously depleted mage to go catatonic if he didn't replenish his energy reserves after heavy magical work. Giri's situation wasn't quite at that point, but it scared him a little to think how close he was, and he didn't think there was much chance of help coming.

His thoughts lingered on Vor, on her ultimately unspoken but undeniably clear refusal of his offer to share company. When Colby had given him that nod, confirmation that Vor's master had no problem with her joining them, he hadn't known, hadn't realized at all that the permission had been given without Vor's consent. He should have been more cautious, considering the depravity he'd sensed in her master but which was absent in her.

But he hadn't known until her confused hesitancy, until he'd touched her energies, that she was a virgin. Giri stifled a groan. A virgin would replenish his depleted reserves like nothing else—except that she was a mage, too, and he'd feel honor-bound to allow her the energy of it. However, her master had offered her up like a sacrificial lamb, without a flinch, as though a person's first sexual experience were not a life-altering standard-setting event to be approached with deliberation and trust. It set Giri contrarily against the man: forcing him to take the opposite position, and not nonchalantly try to coax Vor into bed.

Still, the thought of showing her, of teaching her about intimacy—Giri grimaced in frustration. He wanted her, but if she didn't want him in return, he would not act on his desire, even though his body wasn't getting the message to stand down.

His mind replayed their encounter. Shortly after his discovery, she'd touched him back, tasting his energy with what must have been the most delicate probe she could muster; she'd been trying to be as subtle as him. That was somehow flattering, and he'd loved that she'd touched him back. It spoke of considerable bravery, especially considering that he was the more talented of the two of them, and indicated a willingness to do what—for mages—was something of an intimate act.

Giri put a hand over his eyes. He was pretty sure she didn't think him loathsome or ugly. That hadn't been why she'd refused, and she had to have sensed his soul-deep depletion in that wary touch: his urgent hunger. No, he sensed she had a general reluctance for physical intimacy, widespread distrust of others—especially her master—anxiety with the whole situation, and an unconsummated infatuation with the boy, Karolan Freyaliv. Giri huffed. He thought Vor deserved better. They were both virgins, and if they tried sex on their own, it was going to be awkward and probably unpleasant.

It would have been perfect, actually, if they'd both consented to join him. If they had allowed him to guide them, they could have probably had a remarkably good first time. It would have taken patience and sensitivity on Giri's part, and trust on theirs—but the power: the power it would have released. He nearly whimpered aloud. Two virgins: there would definitely have been enough extra energy for Giri to reasonably recharge himself, even if the pair claimed a plentiful amount. And perhaps afterwards, when the boy was sated and sleepy—

She would likely have remained unsatisfied, even with Giri's advice and guidance to Karolan. For any couple to have full pleasure together the first time could be a challenge, and for two virgins? But perhaps she would have lost her shyness by then, and been envious of Karolan's satiation, and if she'd come to trust that Giri's intent was simply for everyone to enjoy themselves—maybe Vor would have consented to Giri's embrace as well. He could have gotten her past any lingering pain. He could have brought her to her own completion, and of course attained his own.

He sighed. Well, there was nothing to be done now, even if his body was still prepared for an event that wasn't coming. He could take care of his need on his own, but the little bathing chamber attached to his bedroom seemed so far away. It would give him a bit of energy, if he could just get there—but nothing like the amount of energy he needed. He supposed he could blood let a little. He was young, healthy; he could handle it. That would help, too.

They were going to have to teleport in the luggage in the morning, and he'd need some energy for that. Nothing else for it, he'd have to drag himself back there and take his frustration into his own hands. As he was considering the first step—getting himself off the divan—the adjoining door between his room and Milsa's opened, and Milsa strode in wearing nothing but a short shift.

Of course, she would be passing through on her way to Colby. Giri gave her a little resigned wave. There was no nudity taboo among the three, and besides Milsa had been the one to introduce Giri to the pleasure of female company, over a decade ago, and had taught him much. That had been before her bond with Colby had developed. So although he didn't see her unclothed as often anymore, it wasn't like either of them had a reason to be shy about their bodies.

But Milsa didn't pass through. She went straight to the divan where he lay and poked his shoulder.

"Come on," she urged. "I got her ready for you."

"What?" he uttered. "Her, who?"

"The maidservant they assigned to me: she's a virgin; her name is Pella. She's ready."

Giri blinked at Milsa, mouth falling open a little as he realized what she was suggesting. "I don't want her," he managed.

Milsa scowled. "I know. You want that Vor, but she turned you down, and you're going to be worthless tomorrow if you don't replenish yourself. Come on, just do it, before she cools."

She grabbed Giri's wrist and pulled, but he gave her no help in getting him off the divan and Milsa was too petite to shift him by brute strength alone.

"No. I don't want to," he said firmly.

Milsa looked pointedly at his lap. "It's clear you want something. Come along. You need this, and she's willing. You'll feel better after." She pulled on him again, flat out commanding him. "Get up, Giri. Get up."

He was accustomed to obeying her, since she was older and more experienced, even though she was technically not his master. She had established her dominance as soon as Colby had taken him in as a second apprentice. Scared and unsettled, he slid his legs off the divan and sat up.

"Milsa," he objected weakly.

"None of that," she scolded. "Get up. Come on."

She took his arm, and he stood on shaking legs as she led him towards her rooms. He tried to resist again at the adjoining door, but she glared at him, shoved him, and then again at the door to her bedroom from the sitting room.

"Get in," she ordered softly, pushing him inside and shutting the door.

The girl was on the bed. What had Milsa named her? Pella. She indeed seemed as ready as Milsa had said, but did not seem aware yet that they were in the room. At least he detected no spells on her, but it was obvious that Milsa had seduced the girl and brought her to this state.

"No," Giri refused, turning to go.

Milsa caught him, stepping close, reaching low, until he winced. She didn't relent, and easily foiled his weak attempts to get away. Gradually, his reason began to fade as his blood heated.

"Pretend she's Vor," Milsa purred. "Come on, she's ready for you and you're ready for her. Let yourself have what you need."

Milsa drew him to the foot of the bed, undressing him as much as was necessary, and then joined Pella on the mattress.

"I brought young lord Giri to join us," she murmured to Pella.

Milsa gave Giri a stare that brooked no argument, and now that he was here, his resistance was eroding. He wouldn't have to do anything but the critical act, it wouldn't take long, and if he didn't take this opportunity, Colby would want to know why not in the morning, and he'd be useless to them magically the rest of the day.

Milsa reached down to adjust Pella's position—and the last of Giri's resistance gave up. He got on the bed, but first he had to be sure. He always had to be sure. He sought Pella's feverish gaze.

"Is this alright?" he asked intently. "Are you certain?"

He noticed Milsa roll her eyes a little bit, off to the side.

Pella lifted her arms to encircle Giri's shoulders. "Yes, milord," she whispered, without a tremor, and gave a hopeful smile.

Milord: of course. She was a servant, accustomed to obeying her masters as much as Giri was accustomed to obeying Milsa and Colby, which had surely allowed Milsa to get her started on this course, until her own instincts kicked in. Now at this state, she had no nerve to deny someone she saw as a man to be served and pleased. Giri sat back, and Pella's arms fell away as he moved out of her range and grip.

"Don't worry, Pella," Milsa crooned, "Giri's good at this."

He shot a glare at her. Of course he would satisfy her, even though he hadn't wanted to do this at all. Now, well, he'd finish it, take the energy, and try to please Pella. He turned off his mind, tried not to think. There was nothing to do but do it.

Pella flinched at first, but didn't cry out. Arms shaking, Giri drew in the energy bloom, as thirsty for it as for a drink of water after working all day under a hot sun. Now he'd make sure Pella got some satisfaction before the end. She deserved that at least. She wasn't even looking at him, though, and he was glad of it. First times could be difficult, and it took some experimentation, but soon enough Pella arched up, gasping and trembling. The surge of energy confirmed her climax, and Giri siphoned it away dispassionately.

Enough.

He left her, completing what his body demanded onto her belly. It had lacked any hint of the usual euphoria, and he was just glad to be done. He sat back on his knees. Milsa set a hand on Pella's forehead, and Giri sensed her apply a harmless sleep charm. It would last perhaps a quarter of an hour.

Then she gestured at him with disgust. "What was that?"

"I don't want her to think she might kindle, and I don't want to explain to her why she won't," he excused himself.

But it wasn't just that. Pella wasn't ugly or distasteful, but he hadn't wanted her, and leaving that evidence of himself in her had felt too intimate.

"What is wrong with you?" Milsa muttered, sounding genuinely perplexed.

Giri got up, leaving the girl and the mess he'd made, so when she awoke she'd see and hopefully understand. The last thing he needed was for her to go bed a fellow servant the next day, get pregnant, and accuse him of fathering it. He snatched up his clothes, turning his back to Milsa.

"Look at yourself," she demanded. "You're no longer staggering about on the verge of collapse. You're full. Don't you feel better?"

"I didn't want to do this," he declared. He turned to glare at her, holding his clothes self-consciously in front of his hips. "Don't ever try to make me do this again. Ask me what I want first."

Milsa got up, pointing down at the sleeping girl. "She was willing. She got a good climax. We gave her the best first time she could ever hope to have."

"Did we really?" Giri challenged. "You seduced her, didn't you?" He waved his free hand in exasperation. "She didn't approach you and request it, did she? She had to be manipulated into wanting it. She might regret it. She doesn't love you or me."

Milsa stared at him, face cold and accusative. "When has that ever mattered to you?"

He flinched as if she'd slapped him.

"You think love makes a first time good?" she went on angrily. "I can tell you it guarantees nothing."

He had to look down. Indeed, he'd been thinking how—if Vor and Karolan tried it, they'd probably have a difficult first time, even if they loved each other.

"I've never heard you say such things," Milsa observed. She stepped menacingly close to him. "If Vor had consented, you would have taken her tonight, for her first time. Don't tell me you and she fell in love at first sight."

Giri winced sharply, a hint of thickness in his throat, and turned away.

"Perhaps you should consider bedecking yourself in mage-stone jewelry," Milsa taunted, "if this is your new policy. Of course, you'd still have to charge the stones with power from somewhere, so you could take it out later when you need it. Will you switch to animal sacrifice?"

"Maybe I should," he retorted, feeling more and more combative.

He did have a mage-stone statue back in his room in Weldom, and he did sink extra energy into it whenever he had it to spare, but it was too heavy to cart around with him when he travelled, leaving him without that handy power reservoir to draw on in a time of need like this one. And he wasn't bedding women every night; rarely was he so depleted that he considered finding some stranger open to a one-time tumble. He hadn't even done so in—how long had it been? Not since before his grandfather had given him that statue for his twenty-fifth birthday: so that Milsa would suggest some kind of policy change rankled him.

"Let's get out of here," he grunted. "She'll wake up soon."

Without waiting for Milsa's consent, he strode out of her bedroom, through the little sitting room, and back into his own. Milsa followed him all the way back to his tiny bathroom, where he threw down his clothes and began to rinse off. She leaned in the doorway, watching.

"What are you thinking?" she asked, sounding truly curious.

He glared at her. "Turn around and give me some privacy."

Her eyebrows danced up, but she obeyed.

"I don't like this place," he said eventually. "I don't like Altare."

"No, you like Vor," she retorted at once.

After a moment, he confessed softly. "I do like Vor. She intrigues me."

He finished washing and wrapped a towel around his waist. Milsa was shaking her head.

"I'm going to Colby now," she muttered. "You have a good night."

"You ruined my chances of that," he accused.

Milsa spun around. "You're full of surprises tonight, aren't you? No, apparently, Vor ruined your chances of that."

His lip began to curl, and Milsa surged forward, right up towards his face, although he was half a head taller than her.

"You remember that last time," she hissed, "when that bitch broke your heart? And the one before that? You remember how you cried on my shoulder? You vowed to never get involved again, to shield yourself apart. Are you going back on that, Giri?"

His anger melted a little and he swallowed hard. Those memories still hurt sometimes.

"No," he managed, "I just like her, maybe. I don't know her much yet."

"Yet?" Milsa challenged.

He nodded. "Yet."

She shook her head again, but slowly. "Don't get your hopes up. I think her master is going to ruin or kill her pretty soon."

Milsa again turned to go.

"I won't let that happen," Giri said softly to her back.

She froze, and then whirled back. She stuck a finger in his face. "You will do what is best for Weldom, and what Colby says."

Giri hadn't flinched. "Vor is best for Weldom, far better than Altare."

"That's not your choice to make," Milsa said clearly, and with a hint of calm now. "I happen to agree, but it's not your choice or mine."

Giri bit down on whatever else he might have said. Seeing that she'd get not another word from him, Milsa finally left. He heard the door between his sitting room and Colby's open and shut. She would tell Colby every detail of what they'd done and spoken of. Giri turned out the lights in his rooms, shut his own bedroom door and put a strong ward on it, enough to indicate to Colby and Milsa that he didn't want to be disturbed, and enough to keep Pella out, should she come searching for him.

Then he threw himself onto his bed, wretched and disgusted with himself. Pella had wanted it, true, but only because Milsa had seduced her and helped heat up her body. She hadn't necessarily wanted Giri. She didn't even know him. They were strangers, and he'd taken her first experience from her. Yes, he'd been sure to give her pleasure, and it probably had been better than a lot of other possible ways it could have gone for her—but still.

Nor was it the first time he had done such a thing. Giri never made an effort to get to know the women he'd bedded, not since the couple times early on, in his late teens, when he'd gotten smitten with a woman, only to have her drop him as soon as she found out he wanted more than adventures between the sheets. As Milsa had just reminded him, those experiences had cut deep. Now, he just made sure it was one time only, and that the woman understood that, and that she was willing.

At first, he'd been able to go to Milsa, for neither of them had developed strong feelings for the other that would have made them want more, but then she'd started turning him down. Eventually he'd realized she had developed strong feelings—but for their master, for Colby, and he returned them. That had ended that.

Giri curled up in a ball. Sex was both a power source and something he enjoyed, and craved via his primal instincts, but it was also complicated somehow—maybe only in his own head? He supposed, he could lie to the women, let them become enamored of him, take advantage of that, and use them until they became inconvenient—but that was wrong. Having had it done to him, he knew it was wrong.

Now, however, he was feeling acutely that what he'd just done to Pella was wrong, too. If Vor had consented, and he'd done it to her, would it have been wrong? His body roused a little at the thought, trying to tell him that it wasn't wrong at all, that it would have been glorious. Of course, he would have done far more with her than he'd done with Pella. Plus, he would have asked her to stay the whole night with him, to sleep beside him, and he would have talked to her and—

Giri frowned. That was odd. He wanted her, of course, but he also wanted to know her—not just know her body, but know her as a person, too—and that was different from all his more recent dalliances. In addition to that, she was a mage. They could share power. They could learn from each other and merge power in magical works. Vor could be an ally, a friend, a—a what?

This line of thought was bringing up uneasiness, even fear that killed whatever arousal he had left. He curled up a little tighter and covered his face with his arms. Vor had rejected him once—although not necessarily because she thought him repulsive; there was more going on than just two unmarried adults considering if they found each other attractive. The situation was complicated. He could try again, but what if she still said no? Or what if she said yes? Now Giri wasn't sure which answer he wanted.

The Inspection of Northborn

Colby looked with concern at Giri the next morning. They were up early, preparing to help their distant comrades teleport over their luggage. Giri was silent. He hadn't slept well and was still sore at Milsa. He supposed Milsa had told Colby all about Giri's resistance and combativeness. He didn't care. Let them see that he was maturing, that he wasn't going to be pushed around anymore. He was far removed from the boy he'd once been and he felt now that it was time Milsa started acting like it.

Thanks to what Milsa had made him do, however, Giri was able to help out with the teleportation, and the luggage landed with satisfying thumps.

"There's almost no point in bringing it over," Colby remarked. "I expect we'll depart tomorrow, taking Altare with us."

"You've decided that already?" Giri asked.

Milsa didn't look surprised. He figured Colby had told her all that the previous night, too.

"We'll give a fiction of letting him show us around," Colby shrugged, "and it might be informative, but I learned all I really needed to know last night."

"You know that although he indicated his apprentices were free to join us for," Giri struggled, "helping us replenish ourselves, they both refused."

"I am aware," Colby nodded.

"They're both virgins," Giri went on. "They didn't understand the situation, or what their master had decided was expected of them."

"I am aware," his master repeated. "It is one more thing that makes me want to bring Altare back to Weldom for further discussion. Prepare for your day now."

Giri dressed in fresh robes, and when he saw Vor again, she had restored her calm and composed behavior. He didn't get any chance to talk to her, though, for Colby sent him off with General Krant to tour the castle military. He wondered if that separation of them was deliberate. Two of the old mages accompanied him, and they seemed like decent folk, if reserved and nervous. He let the others do most of the talking.

When they joined back up for lunch, Colby took both Milsa and Giri to go talk privately with Altare—although the apprentices said little. Giri hadn't gotten a chance to have any interaction with Vor, again.

The Second Night in Northborn

"Vor is planning to betray and kill Altare," Giri announced as he strode into Colby's room.

His master and Milsa were snuggled together on the couch. The latter raised her head briefly. He felt the brush of her energy, and then she put her head back down with a snort.

"What?" he bristled.

Colby just smiled. "I was suspecting that, too. She told you?"

"Not outright, but I think part of her wanted to."

Milsa snorted again. Giri went and took a seat on the chair across from the couch. He folded his arms and tried not to glare. It was late. He'd borrowed a staff and practiced a series of martial exercises until his back ached, come back and bathed, and dressed for bed in a loose shirt and shorts. He'd found Colby and Milsa here, enjoying staring at the little decorative fire in the sitting room fireplace. As it was summer, there was really no need for heat, although Northborn was much colder than Weldom in general.

His companions were already recharged with energy—much more than his practice session had gotten him. They must have come straight back from the after dinner drinks in the conservatory and made love. Giri firmed his jaw.

"Should have brought her back here with you," Milsa muttered, sounding smug and sleepy.

"Now, now," Colby soothed, "leave the boy alone."

Giri shoved to his feet, tempted to retort that he was no boy, except that it was something a juvenile would do, thereby reinforcing the label. He walked over to stand in front of the fire, the rising heat waves lifting strands of his drying hair.

"We're going to help her," he said, making it more of a statement than a question.

"Well," Colby drawled, "I don't think we have any reason to get in her way. I'm not pleased with Altare, and I doubt the Ministers will be either. The lack of him would not be upsetting."

"She doesn't have enough power to do it," Milsa observed, sounding a little more awake.

"That's what I'm worried about," Giri said.

"Even if they were equal in potential," Colby expounded, "he is steeped in blood and sex magic, and she," he sighed, "she isn't. She needs a few more years before she'll equal him."

"I want to help her."

"It's not our place to interfere with someone else's master-apprentice relationship," Colby said patiently. "Altare has performed no crimes against Weldom."

"He's abused the people here," Milsa put in. "You've seen the king and that girl he calls the princess, wrapped up in spells. He keeps political prisoners as slaves. And the stench of blood is so thick in his power, he must be spilling it on a regular basis, and not his own."

"It could be consensual," Colby offered.

Both Giri and Milsa huffed without humor.

"I doubt it, too."

Giri could hear the wry smile in his master's voice but it didn't comfort him. "That's not enough reason for us to move against him?"

"With the blessing of the Ministers, I'd be ready," Colby affirmed.

"They aren't going to give such a thing purely on our speculation," Giri scoffed. "You know that, Master."

"Of course I do."

He turned to look back at the pair on the couch. "So?"

"So, we can watch, and withhold any assistance from Altare," Colby explained.

Giri's gaze did not waver. "I won't let her die."

Colby winced only a little.

"Altare isn't a wizard, is he? He's not confirmed," he pressed.

"You are correct," Colby nodded.

"Then we are under no obligation to protect him."

"That's why I have been saying that we won't," his master reaffirmed, starting to sound slightly impatient. "But nor do we have the freedom to kill off anyone we want."

"And if he strikes at Vor first, we can't protect her, to stop him from killing off anyone he wants?"

Milsa narrowed her eyes. "Won't the girl be trying to kill him right back? Whom do you suggest we protect? Or would you have us just stop the fight?"

Giri turned back to the fire with a groan of frustration.

"If you just want the girl," Milsa raised her voice, "I can help you—"

"I don't," he retorted angrily. "Stop suggesting—"

"Giri," Colby scolded, sitting up taller, and the apprentice flinched. "Control yourself."

Milsa had a satisfied look on her face. "He's smitten."

"I am not," Giri breathed back.

Colby stood up and approached his youngest apprentice. Gently, he drew him into his arms. After only a moment, Giri gave in, leaning against his master's strength.

"Milsa, will you please leave us for a moment?" Colby asked.

Giri heard the sound of her getting up, and a door opening and closing.

"You do have feelings for this young woman," Colby prompted.

"I admire her," Giri corrected, pulling away. "Yes, of course I have some desire for her—"

Colby chuckled. "If it weren't for Milsa, I would, too. I could list Vor Hearthsraven's qualities, but I'll not lecture the expert."

Giri closed his eyes in embarrassment. "I hardly know her."

"She's enough to make you reject all others, at the least. Giri, you know I care for you as though you were my own son. I've seen you hurt before. Are you sure you want to take this path?"

"No," he replied at once. "I'm not taking any path. I just don't want to see her killed."

"Nor do I."

"But you would stand back and let it happen," Giri accused. "You wouldn't want to see it, but you wouldn't risk your position to stop it. What's so bad about slapping down Altare?"

Colby raised an eyebrow at him. "I haven't become a State Wizard by getting involved in quarrels I'm not authorized to get involved in."

Giri gathered himself and took a steadying breath. "Master, I have great respect for you, but when we come back—"

"You assume we will be reassigned here?"

A chill shot down his spine. He hadn't thought of that, that Altare might be sent back alone, with new orders, or that different wizards might get the assignment to return with him.

Colby patted his shoulder. "Don't worry. It's likely we'll be sent back to finish what we started, and if for some reason there are complications, I'll argue our case for returning."

Giri nodded. "Thank you, Master. As I was saying, when we come back, if there's a fight, if it looks like she's going to die," he braced himself, "I'm stepping in. I won't raise my hand against Altare until he raises his against me, but I'll protect her."

"And you think she'll thank you for that?" Colby asked softly.

Giri was caught without a reply.

The older man's face was lined with solemnity. "This conflict runs deep. She must face her master, and she must win. Dying or being rescued by you might equate to the same thing for her: failure. If she's ever to be rid of his influence, she must kill him herself, or at least have a decisive victory—but I doubt he will surrender to her—and even if he does, I doubt she will accept it. Their battle can only end in death."

Colby hugged him again, and Giri did not resist.

"You have always had a noble spirit, my apprentice. I honor your values and your feelings and I wish for you to be free to live them."

He released him.

"Will you tell Milsa to lay off me?" Giri muttered.

Colby grinned. "She has your best interests at heart, too, in her own way."

Giri just glared at the inoffensive fire, and didn't reply.

"Get some sleep. We have to teleport in the morning."

He nodded. "Thank you, Master, for your wisdom."

"Thank you," Colby corrected, "for your spirit. You keep this old man on his toes."

Giri nodded, and sought his solitary bed. He stood in the dim light, looking at it. They'd been given fine rooms and the bed was large, plenty large enough for two. Vor, however, had again turned down his subtle invitation. Had he really expected otherwise? No. It was a foolish hope, but maybe, somehow, if she and her master fought, and she won, maybe—

No, there was that boy, Karolan. Perhaps it would be best if he gave up on any thought of ever being more to her than an acquaintance. Maybe he could hope to be a comrade in arms, if she became a wizard? Then again, he revised, even if she and that boy had a mutual infatuation, relationships did not always last. Not that he'd intentionally sabotage it, but if they did part ways, well, maybe. Or maybe they'd be open to multiple partners?

Maybe. There were too many maybes, nothing concrete, leaving the ground beneath his feet as unsteady as swampland. There was no point in this speculation, and it was keeping Giri from his rest. He moved to go get in bed but had to stop and sigh. Speculation wasn't the only thing that would keep him from sleeping. Thinking of Vor and what he wanted to do with her had elicited a predictable reaction.

Well, there was a solution to that, and it would give him a little extra energy, too. He turned back to his bathing chamber, not bothering with a light, but then he leaned against the wall, covering his face with a hand. His body's needs were perfectly natural—he knew that. He was trapped in this male human body that regularly acted this way, and there was no reason to be ashamed of it. He'd never indulged in letting himself feel ashamed before, especially since Milsa had taught him to embrace instead of judge himself.

Then why?

Giri came to an answer shortly. It was because he'd been about to let himself fantasize about Vor and that—his eyes flew open in the darkness. Somehow he felt that would dirty her. Of course it wouldn't: except in Giri's own mind. All right, then there would be none of that. He didn't need to indulge in such mental drama, but—but—she kept intruding.

Fine. If he couldn't keep her out of the black space behind his closed eyes, he could at least try to give her dignity in his own mind. So, he would recall only standing outside the salle with her, just meeting her gaze, nothing more: which turned out to be plenty. After only a few moments he found his release with a throttled exclamation and took a calming breath as he incorporated the generated energy into his core. As he took stock of himself he realized that had felt better than what he'd done to Pella the previous evening, and caught himself in a miserable chuckle.

"What a sorry state I'm in," he laughed.

But as he finally got to bed, he had to admit that it wasn't actually very funny.

The Return to Weldom

Giri almost fell to his knees when the four of them with their luggage landed in the teleportation arrival circle in Weldom. Only his fierce need to hide any hint of weakness in front of Altare kept him on his feet. At least he was at the back of the group, so no one saw him swaying except for the trio of wizards who were there to meet them.

Colby stepped forward with open arms, giving introductions and greetings with flamboyant enthusiasm, and Giri wondered if he was doing that to take attention off of his youngest apprentice passing out at the back of the circle. The greeting wizards handled the baggage and Colby walked off with Altare firmly in hand.

"You're an idiot," Milsa hissed to him as soon as everyone else was out of hearing range.

"I'm well aware," he muttered back.

"Are you going to collapse on your way to your room?" she asked.

"I can make it."

She made a sound of pure exasperation. "Here, you stupid moron: take this."

Giri didn't have the strength to pull back as she grabbed his arm in both her hands. She herself was depleted by the teleporting, but at once he felt some of her energy flowing into his.

"Stop that," he objected, trying to shake her off.

"I have Colby," she murmured.

"I'll be fine. Let go."

Milsa reluctantly obeyed, but she eyed him firmly. "You'd better get yourself in shape. We're probably going back in a couple days. It's a lot of teleporting in a short time, and it's being hard on all of us. Do you have anyone you can call on for help?"

"Oh, stop," Giri growled. "Just leave me alone."

With an expression of deep doubt, Milsa obeyed. Giri forced himself to take steady, careful steps out of the room. Luckily, the teleportation rooms at the Wizard Citadel were on the top floors, since air was such a vital element in teleportation spells—there were even a few open platforms on the roof. He could go down stairs, but didn't think he'd be climbing up any for a while. When he got down to his hallway, his luggage was waiting for him outside his warded door.

The Weldom wizards employed by the state were generally a trustworthy bunch, but not always. Everyone warded and locked their doors with magic, trying to use unique, inventive spells that would discourage others from snooping—or stealing. Many of them, Giri included, used mundane methods as well; he pulled a metal key from his pocket. Of course, it also had a spell on it, one that matched the spell on the metal lock. Not only did the key have to fit the lock, the spell on the key had to fit the spell on the lock.

Giri also had to unlock the magical locks, but his wards recognized him and parted for his entry. He kicked his luggage bag inside, managed to shut the door, and stumbled the two steps he needed to be able to fall face first onto his bed. He groaned unintelligibly and fumbled his hand up onto the mage-stone statue on his nightstand. It had been a gift from his grandfather: a beautiful piece, more than a foot tall and carved in the shape of a rearing horse. It was mostly full, and within a few moments the power was flooding into him, until he was mostly full, and it was empty.

"Took me weeks to get it that full," he mumbled into his pillow, but with a deep sense of relief.

The rooms granted to ordinary wizards were small and sufficient, not luxurious. Colby, as a State Wizard, got a suite. Giri's room contained only his bed—although it was big enough for two if they were friendly—a nightstand, a desk and chair, wardrobe, and a dresser. And bookshelves: he'd covered every bit of spare wall with bookshelves, and there were boxes of books and scrolls under his bed. That left little floor space, but he didn't much mind that. He also had a window above the head of the bed, which was just as well. If it had been a window in any other location he'd have covered it with bookshelves, but shelves above the bed would mean a head-bonking hazard, so the window stayed unobstructed.

It was home: more his home than his room back at his family house. Now, lying on his own bed, surrounded by his books and all the layers of his energy he'd put in the walls, floor, ceiling, and door, he felt home. The smells were right, the sounds were right, and he was recharged from his horse statue.

Giri sat up, pushed open his window for air, and put away his unused clothes. He changed into lighter, less decorative clothing since Weldom was far hotter than Northborn and he was now off-duty, and then took his dirty clothes to the laundry and got a meal in the mess. Dining facilities were shared, although wizards were permitted to bring food back to their rooms, as long as they cleaned up after. Since they all warded and locked their doors, there were no servants for tidying up. Bathing facilities were communal, too, separated for men and women.

Wizards who were not employed by the state could also have a room at the Citadel, but they had to do work exchange for it. Those wizards were the ones who cleaned the bathing chambers, made the food, did the laundry, and cleaned the other shared areas. In that way, there were no servants: no non-wizards living in the Citadel.

If Giri's family had owned a house in the capital, he could have lived there instead of in the Citadel itself. Most wizards came from the nobility, and if their House was rich enough, they would have an outpost here. The Holstor House was minor nobility, known well only in Croun. If any of the heads of the House ever visited the capital, richer nobility they were friendly with, who did have a house in the city, accommodated them.

Giri knew Milsa's family was one such. She was from southern Weldom, where the Thauket House was one of the major powers. Only her large facial birthmark, stubborn personality, and now her resolute devotion to Colby had prevented her family from using her in one of their never ending marriage alliances. She had a place in their massive house in the capital—Giri had been there once—but these days she lived in the Citadel with Colby. Giri figured they should just marry each other and be done with it.

Meal finished, he returned to his room. There were a few dozen workrooms in the Citadel for use by the wizards, but they had to be reserved—except for State Wizards, who got a small private workroom along with their suite. Giri often made use of any of the four extensive libraries, but just now he found himself preferring some solitude. Besides, he anticipated a summons from Colby at any time. The Ministers would probably hear out Altare in the afternoon, and he expected to be called to attend, although not likely to speak.

Giri shed most of his clothes and flopped himself back down on his bed, stretched out, hands behind his head with his unbound hair scattered across his pillows. He let the breeze from his open window blow across his skin on its way out the ventilation grate above the door, cooling him. He smiled wistfully, recalling his farewell with Vor. He'd been a little forward, more than necessary—he knew that—but he'd wanted to warn her and try to imply she had an ally in him. And he'd craved getting close to her. She'd smelled like herbs and fruit.

His smile grew. Her surprise when she'd realized she'd been holding his hand ever since he'd lifted it to kiss had delighted him. Of course, he'd alarmed her with his closeness and warning. Of course she hadn't known she was doing it. No, her body had done it without her conscious mind directing it to. That said something, didn't it? On some level at least she did not reject him, and didn't mind holding his hand. If she'd truly disliked him, she would have made a point of letting go, even—or especially—when alarmed. Instead, she'd held on. It had felt good.

And he'd made bold to touch her shoulder, and she hadn't recoiled, hadn't even flinched. And she'd asked him for teaching, to be taught how to teleport. He wished he could have taught her, but there was truly no time; teleportation was a challenging skill. He wished she'd asked something he could have given her. He hoped she would be safe until he saw her again. He hoped she would be ready for Altare's return.

Giri chuckled at himself. How his focus had changed. A week ago he'd had not a thought in his head for Northborn or any of its people. He hadn't had any idea Vor existed. He'd just returned from a visit home to his family in Croun—wizards employed by the state all got a certain amount of leave time.

His little sister had birthed twin baby girls, product of a marriage that was convenient, advantageous, and—a rarity among noble marriages—for love. That had been a joyous meeting, although the babies were still too small to appreciate his little tricks of magery. He'd also done his sister and her husband the favor of giving the girls a professional assessment, and had been able to report that he sensed no magical potential in either of them.

The couple had been both happy and sad at that. They had no other children, at least not yet, and so had been glad the girls wouldn't have to leave for apprenticeships, but somehow every parent was disappointed when the seeds of magery did not germinate in their offspring. It wasn't even guaranteed when mages bred with each other—although it was much more likely.

Giri was not the only mage in his family. His grandfather on his father's side was a powerful wizard, retired now and living higher up in the mountains, but had even been a State Wizard for a while. There had been wizardly great grandparents, too, and a few cousins with magical inclinations. His aunt on his mother's side was also talented, although not very strongly and had never gone off to be apprenticed, instead training as an herbalist healer and midwife.

A pounding knock came at his door, interrupting his reminiscing.

"Giri, oma, you're back?"

He smiled, recognizing that voice, and the colloquial greeting of eastern Weldom "Dello, oma, it's open."

The door swung wide, and the tallest, skinniest, blondest man among the wizards strutted into the room. He threw his hands forward in mock horror, blocking his sight of Giri.

"Heart of my mother, man, put some clothes on," he exclaimed.

"Everything important is covered," Giri retorted. "Besides, I was alone until you barged in."

Giri sat up, extending a hand to bump fists with his grinning friend. Dello—whose full name was Dellostrikata Traskitandi; there was a long tra-dition of tongue tripping names in his House—took the chair from the desk, spun it around, and sat backwards on it.

"It's been weeks, man," Dello said.

"It has," Giri agreed. "I'm glad to see you."

"You're telling me? You're not an easy man to track down. I got back a couple days ago to hear you were assigned to go to Northborn."

"You heard right, and I'm probably going back in a day or two."

"What can possibly be of interest out in those sticks?"

Giri nodded significantly. "Go watch the session this afternoon and you'll see for yourself."

Dello raised an eyebrow. "You brought someone back?"

"Nasty piece of work mage who's been running the place," Giri grimaced, rubbing the back of his neck. "He's into it all: murder, torture, rape, mind manipulation, slavery, all kinds of abuse."

"They're going to execute him then?"

Giri shrugged. "Well, we know he's doing it, but we don't have hard evi-dence of all the stuff."

"So he'll get off?"

"Well, yes and no."

Dello eyed him with suspicion. "There's going to be wizards going back with him, and now they'll watch him, so he won't be able to do any of it anymore? Is that what you mean?"

Giri lay back and hesitated. Dello was his best friend at the Citadel, excepting Colby and Milsa, who were friends but also his superiors. He'd entered the Citadel at the same time as Dello. They'd had their initial group classes together, before being taken by masters. Although Dello came from a prestigious House in the east, he hadn't looked down on Giri at all—except literally, because of his height—and somehow they'd just naturally become pals.

How much did he want to tell him? Dello wouldn't be able to affect any of it, no matter what he knew, unless for some reason he was assigned to go to Northborn, too, which would be great, but unlikely. Dello's master was an expert in Lackland politics and culture, and was always getting sent there, perforce making Dello go, too. Since Dello happened to have the Lackland sort of body type, he was a good one to go there also, as he could blend in. Giri thought it was unlikely that pattern would be changed when there were plenty of other wizards who weren't such specialists.

"You quit talking, man," Dello prompted.

"It's complicated," Giri deflected.

"Is it now? All right then, how about your trip home? Anything you want to share about that? Did your father try to marry you off again?"

Giri chuckled. "Of course he did."

"I'm guessing you declined."

"My mom and dad offered plenty of pretty women, all from acceptable Houses," Giri shrugged, "and said I could pick the one I got along the best with."

Dello snorted. "Any mages?"

"A couple."

"But you're still not biting."

He couldn't help but frown. "No."

"You're going to end up old and alone, man."

"That's what they keep telling me. They're nice about it, but it's still pressure."

"You're their only son," Dello grunted. "And you only have one sibling."

Giri nodded. "I haven't forgotten that. They've got grandkids now, though: two of them." He paused to think. "I guess that makes me an uncle."

"That is the generally accepted term," Dello ribbed. "Boys or girls?"

"Two girls, twins: no mage talent, I checked, but looking healthy. My aunt won't let them die of any childhood illnesses. I'd hoped my mom and dad would be satisfied with that and leave me alone, especially since my sister might have more. I've got cousins, too, and they have kids. House Holstor isn't in danger of vanishing."

"So you're telling me you're still totally against the marrying thing," Dello said, "even a perfunctory one where you visit the bride enough times to make some babies and spend the rest of your time here?"

From his angle lying on the bed, Giri could look out his window, up at the perfect blue sky. It sounded like a simple thing, but— "That's not fair to the woman, to have a husband that doesn't love her, who isn't around to help raise the kids."

Dello scoffed. "That's marriage when you're born to a House. The men and women both know that."

"So how is your wife?"

"Pregnant again, and happy about it."

Giri swore under his breath. "That makes it your fourth. Take a break, Dello."

"We get on well. Maybe it's not love, but we like each other." He shrugged. "The sex is good. She likes babies. Maybe this time we'll get a kid with some mage talent, but whatever. The governesses and nursemaids raise the kids anyway. That's who raised you, right?"

It was true, although being from a smaller House, there had been fewer servants than Dello would have had, and Giri had known his parents better than most noble children.

"Dello, I don't want that," Giri mumbled.

His friend was silent for a long while. "I know you don't, but it's not so bad as you make it out to be."

Giri sighed, closing his eyes against the blue of the sky. Dello didn't speak for a couple minutes.

Finally, "What's going on, Giri?"

Giri opened his eyes, but didn't reply at first. He felt Dello lightly touch his energy and didn't object to it: although it wasn't something they did to each other often.

"Yeah, you've got something going on," Dello muttered. "Are you going to tell me about it, or should I just leave you to lie here all tormented?"

"I'm not tormented," Giri denied.

Dello snorted. "If you say so. Did whatever it is happen at home, or in Northborn?"

Giri draped an arm over his eyes. "Northborn," he confessed.

"Does it have to do with this piece of work mage you brought back?"

"Somewhat."

"Uh huh. And tell me how."

Giri cringed. It was like pulling a fresh scab off a wound, trying to admit it to Dello. "His apprentice."

"What about him?"

"Her."

He heard the creak of the chair as Dello sat back. "Ah."

It was just one utterance, and yet his friend had put a number of flavors into the sound.

"I didn't bed her," Giri blurted, wanting to head that off right away.

"Oh, but you want to. She doesn't want you?"

"It's, her master is probably going to, I mean, she's planning to betray him, and he'll probably try to kill her, and Colby is saying I can't get involved and—"

"You're afraid she'll be killed before you get a taste of her?" Dello taunted. "Man, there's plenty of ladies around here enchanted by your pretty face and prodigious power who would love to find themselves in—"

"I do not want them," Giri declared. "Any of them."

Dello was silent so long that Giri finally lifted his head to look at him. His friend was gazing at him with a serious expression in his green eyes.

"Sit up here, and talk to me," Dello requested, patting the foot of the bed, and Giri reluctantly obeyed. At least when he leaned forward to rest his elbows on his knees, his long deep brown hair fell down around his face, hiding the flushing of his skin.

"You're telling me this girl from the sticks is the one you want," Dello said clearly. "The only one."

"She's from Weldom, from Mount Brasson originally," Giri informed. "Her surname is Hearthsraven."

Dello shook his head. "Never heard of it."

"Me, either, but I don't care about that."

"She has power?"

"Yes, considerable. Her power's settling."

"Settling? Hang on. She's not a little kid, is she?"

"No," Giri grunted. "She's younger than me, I'm pretty sure, but she's an adult, about my height, um, slender, long dark hair—

"I get it," Dello interrupted. "And her master is this sack of slime?"

"Yes."

"So he's probably been a nightmare to live with."

"I imagine so."

"But she's somehow not gotten all corrupted and nasty herself?"

"Right."

"But he's probably been raping her and such?"

"No, she's a virgin."

Dello paused to blink rapidly in surprise. "And she's going to throw down against him?"

Giri nodded. "That's what it sounds like."

Dello grinned and crossed his arms over his chest. "Damn, I think I like her, too."

That got a smile out of Giri. "You're married."

He lifted a hand helplessly. "Alas. I'll have to leave her for you." He rocked forward in the chair again. "So tell me true: you think she'll win?"

Giri shook his head. "I don't know, but Colby says I can't help."

Dello grimaced. "Damn, my friend. No wonder you're all a mess."

Giri spread his hands. "Even if she wins, that doesn't mean," he gestured helplessly at himself.

"She might not want you," Dello provided.

"I think she's," he searched for a word, "intimidated. And there's a boy, a teenager, also a bit of a mage."

"And?"

"I think they have a mutual infatuation," Giri sighed.

Dello eyed him in disbelief. "You're letting some kid—who's probably just following the lead of whatever he's got in his pants—get in your way?"

Giri huffed. "We're both ones to talk about what leads us around."

Dello stuck his finger at him. "Hey now, just because I can hear what my magic wand has to say doesn't mean I follow its orders, and I know neither do you, especially not lately. But a teenage boy? You remember what that was like. And this fine young lady being as impressive as you're saying she is? No wonder he's infatuated, but why in the wonderful world is she? If she's not smart enough to recognize that you have far more to offer than that horny little puppy maybe she's not worth your time."

"She is smart; I can tell she's smart," Giri refuted, and made a helpless gesture. "The kid was there first."

Dello scoffed. "Whip his ass and send him home to his mama. Then your way is clear."

Giri shoved to his feet and started trying to pace in the confines of his limited floor space. "It's not, I mean, it has to be, argh," he growled in frustration.

"What do you want out of this, Giri?" Dello demanded. "You want to marry this girl, or just pluck her flower and bang her a bunch?"

"Hey," he scolded with a glare.

"Alright," Dello drawled, spreading his hands. "I guess that means marry her then."

Giri slumped down to a seat on the bed, covering his face with his hands and rubbing his forehead. "I don't know what I want," he confessed. "I know I don't want her to die."

He snuck a look between his fingers at his friend. Dello had sat back again, with a pensive look on his face. "Well, you've certainly got it bad," he muttered.

"What?"

"A serious case, I'd say."

"What are you talking about?" Giri demanded.

Dello grinned and leaned in. "You are in so much trouble, my man." He slapped him on the back, making Giri flinch from the skin-to-skin sting. "You make all those vows, and then you let some young virgin lady-mage break them all to pieces for you. So you're going back to Northborn?"

"Yes, probably," Giri answered, still befuddled.

"Just one thing then," Dello said, holding up a finger. "If she wants you, too—provided she wins the mage-duel and all—especially if she wins the mage-duel—women who win mage-duels are totally top shelf—don't let her get away, man." He held Giri's gaze for a long ponderous moment. "I mean it. You'll regret it if you don't take this one seriously."

Dello stood up then. "So, do you have time for a little workout? I haven't slung a staff around in weeks."

"Yeah," Giri accepted softly, still struggling with everything his friend had said. "I need to pay you back for those defeats."

Dello laughed and held his arms out wide. "Look at these freaky monkey arms of mine. I have the reach, man. What can I say?"

"How about: if we could use magic, I'd mop the floor with your face?"

He laughed again. "Alright, yeah, you've got me there. You're all buff when it comes to magic. I get it."

Giri managed a little smile. Dello punched him lightly on the shoulder.

"Put some clothes on and let's go."

***

Colby never summoned him. After several bouts with the staves—all but two of which Giri lost—and dinner with Dello, a concerned Giri went seeking his master. He presented himself at his master's door and knocked. Milsa opened it.

She smirked. "Well, surprise, surprise."

Giri blinked at her tone.

"We figured you'd show up, asking about the hearing," she explained.

"Yes," he answered. "Is it tomorrow?"

Colby called out from inside. "Come in, Giri."

Milsa let him in, and he found his master with a book, spectacles perched on his nose, sitting by a lamp, in his favorite reading chair.

"I must apologize to you, Giri," he began. "The hearing was today. I didn't summon you because I didn't want you there."

"Pardon?" Giri retorted.

"See," Milsa muttered, going to her own favorite chair, at a table where she had a stack of papers, ink, and quill. "I told you he'd be upset."

"I was concerned you'd get too agitated," Colby explained, "and speak out of turn, thereby compromising my dispassionate conveyance of just the facts."

Giri stood staring at his master.

"You're too emotionally involved in this situation," Colby concluded.

A complex combination of feelings and thoughts went through him, but he tried to sort them out before speaking. It was a talent that had been hard to pick up, but it kept him from saying things he'd regret later.

"I think I could have kept myself handled, Master," he said eventually. "I'm sorry I have been behaving a manner that has eroded your trust in me."

"You wouldn't have been called on to speak anyway," Milsa offered. "Nor was I."

"I can tell you that the Ministers will be debating and discussing the situation. They'll have an answer in the next day or two."

"And will we be sent back with Altare?" Giri asked.

"That is one of the things they'll tell us," Colby reiterated patiently.

Giri stood, clenching his hands and not sure whom to be angry at.

"Get some rest, Giri," his master encouraged softly. "I will summon you as soon as I know anything. Until then, or until I tell you otherwise, pursue your own studies as you see fit."

He sighed in frustration. "Alright. Thank you."

"You may join us if you like," Colby offered, gesturing at his collection of books and comfortable chairs.

"It's kind of you to offer, but I think I'll take my leave," Giri replied.

"Rest well."

Giri nodded. "Goodnight."

***

The next day, Giri went straight to one of the libraries. Dello found him there in late morning. The tall, spindly wizard sat down on the table beside Giri's stack of books and picked up the top one.

"Oma," he muttered.

"Oma, Dello," Giri replied absently.

"These are records of troop movements," Dello observed, "from around ten or eleven years ago."

"Correct."

Dello flipped through a few pages, and then rolled his eyes and shut the book. "Alright, tell me. Why are you looking through old military records?"

"How would a ten year old girl get to Northnest eleven years ago?" Giri prompted.

Dello stared for a while. Giri kept turning pages, looking down lists of names.

"This is about that apprentice in Northborn, the one you're all twisted up over."

Giri nodded silently.

"You said you didn't care about her origins."

"I don't," Giri mumbled.

Dello sighed enormously and opened the book he'd moments ago shut. "Tell me her surname again."

"You don't have to help," Giri said.

"Tell me."

"Hearthsraven."

"Do you want to trust me with her first name?"

Giri scowled at the page in front of him. "Vor."

"That's it? Vor? At least her surname makes up for her first name."

Giri gritted his teeth. "Not everyone has a name as long as yours."

The pair read silently for perhaps another half an hour before Giri found it. He almost skated right past it, and did a double take.

"I found one, a Hearthsraven," he announced.

Dello hopped down from the tabletop and looked over his shoulder. "Stratus Hearthsraven. Infantry, fifth division," he read.

"And two dependants," Giri added, pointing to the number beside the name.

"It doesn't give names."

"No, but most likely a wife and child."

"Could be younger brothers or cousins come to help out," Dello mentioned. "I think that's more likely. Most soldiers don't bring their wives and babies."

"Alright, give me the infantry records. That one."

Dello handed it over and hovered behind him. Giri turned to the section for the fifth division. It was organized alphabetically, and contained the brief statistics of each soldier's stay in the military. The pair scanned silently until they found the entry for Stratus.

"Hah," Giri crowed in victory. "He was married."

"It still doesn't say who the wife and child were, or that they're the ones who went with him, and there could be other Hearthsravens. This isn't necessarily her father."

"It says he died in battle. That's consistent."

"But it's also a dead end, pun intended."

Giri kept scanning the page. "Not quite. Look, it has his hometown: Trivale. I need an atlas; I don't recognize it."

"Me, either," Dello grunted. "Where do they keep the atlases?"

"Seriously, you could do with spending a little more time in a library."

Giri got up and strode down a few aisles, coming back a minute later with an atlas of Weldom. Dello had cleared the military records to one end of the table, and Giri put the massive book down in the created space. He flipped to the alphabetized index in the back and ran his eyes down the listings. Having found Trivale, he flipped to the page indicated, and used the provided coordinates to locate it on the map.

"It's on Mount Brasson," he gulped. "There. It's a little village on the outskirts of a city: Lenali. Vor came from Mount Brasson, she said."

"Provided she was telling the truth," Dello pointed out.

"I don't think she'd lie."

"Alright," Dello shrugged. "You know there was a man with the surname Hearthsraven, who had a wife and maybe a kid, who came from Trivale. There's still nothing telling you the kid was Vor."

"Marriage records for Trivale, and birth records: she would have been born there before the invasion of Northnest," Giri pounced.

"Look at the data on this town. It has a couple hundred people. What are the chances there would be decent records kept? And that they'd be here in the capital?"

"The census," Giri insisted. "There's a census every ten years. The people would have been counted. If the kid was Vor, she lived there until she was ten, and based off the year of the invasion, let's see, the census was four years before. She would have been old enough to be counted for sure. I need the census records for Mount Brasson."

Dello waved a sarcastic hand. "You'll have to fetch it. As we've established, I don't know where anything is."

Giri scoffed only a little. He was far too excited to get upset at Dello. He only hoped that the end of this trail would indeed lead him to Vor's origin. If it got to a truly dead end, or if it turned out the child indicated was male, for example, he'd have to go back to the military records and keep going. He'd gone through two books before finding the first Hearthsraven. There might not even be another, and then maybe he'd never know—unless she told him someday.

The census from Mount Brasson landed on the table with a satisfying whump. Giri flicked it open and found Trivale in the contents, as a subentry below Lenali. He paged to the section, heart pounding, and began reading down the list of people. Each name had an age and sex, and a note of who was married to whom, but usually little else. Only if the person hadn't been in that location for the previous census was there a note of where they'd come from. Birthdates for new children were also noted.

He reached the Hearthsravens. There were several. First came the oldest family members. Then there was Stratus Hearthsraven, as expected. Directly below him was a wife: Juleena Hearthsraven. There was a note by her, but Giri's eyes skipped right over it. There, below her mother's name, was Vorella Hearthsraven.

Giri flopped down into his seat, body tingling. Dello leaned over the book.

"Is that her?"

Giri shook his head weakly. "How could it not be? How could it be a coincidence that there was some other girl of the proper age born to a Hearthsraven family on Mount Brasson with a name that starts with Vor?"

"Looks like she's about twenty-one these days."

Giri shrugged. "If they got it right. Sometimes the census people don't really listen when they're counting peasants."

"Giri."

"What?" he grunted, rubbing at his eyes.

"Giri, look at this."

"What is it?" he muttered.

"She wasn't a peasant."

Giri slowly raised his head. When Dello fixed him with a serious look, he got back to his feet to lean over the book again.

"You didn't read this note, by her mother," Dello instructed.

"Juleena Hearthsraven, female, twenty-six—" His mouth went dry. "Formerly of Lenali, House Mrandis."

Dello nodded. "Her mother was from a Noble House."

All the Houses had genealogy records in the capital libraries. One of their duties was to update them yearly. Giri fetched the one for House Mrandis and opened it to his estimated year of Juleena's supposed birth—and there she was. He followed the years forward, until when Juleena was about nineteen or twenty she vanished from the book. There was no more mention of her.

"Something happened," Dello mused. "She was expelled from the family."

"Consider the timing. How much do you want to bet she got pregnant with Vor, by Stratus Hearthsraven, a peasant?" Giri said grimly.

Dello nodded his head. "I'd say that's a sure bet."

***

Giri found his master in his study, going over some kind of documents or other. Colby had only just looked up, registering his apprentice's hurried entrance, when Giri slapped down his summarized notes of Vor's origin. He'd cited his every reference.

"She's nobility," he said flatly. "Look, her mother was from House Mrandis."

Colby glanced down at the page, and then back up. "This wasn't what I meant when I said you should pursue your own studies until I call you."

"You should have been more specific," Giri replied, "Master."

Colby eyed him for a moment, and then perused the notes fully. "Yes, it would seem you've found her. Well done."

Giri couldn't stop his grin. Colby gave a little chuckle.

"You'll not be distracted, will you?" he muttered.

"She's a wizard and nobility," Giri declared. "Or, well, she has the potential to be a wizard."

"House Mrandis disowned her mother," Colby reminded him. "They won't have recognized the marriage, and they won't recognize Vor."

"They should," Giri stated. "Vor's incredible. So what if Juleena married below her station?"

"Keep in mind that even if they would allow it," Colby said, handing Giri back his paper, "Vor might not want it. She didn't tell you her ancestry. I wonder if her master even knows, or if she's told anyone. She uses her father's surname after all."

Surnames did not automatically pass down either the male or the female line. When a pair married, whose surname would persist was a part of the negotiation—especially among the Noble Houses where marriages were usually made for gaining political or economic advantage. Marriage arrangements were sometimes abandoned if neither side could be convinced, bought, or manipulated into letting go of their surname. Once it was settled, however, any children of the union received the surname that had won.

In this case, it was clear that Juleena had given up Mrandis and taken on Hearthsraven because her family had expelled her—rejecting along with her, her chosen husband and unborn child. She must have gone to live with her husband's family then. When she'd found out she was with child, she could have chosen to terminate the pregnancy, hide it, and stay with her House, but she obviously hadn't. Perhaps she'd hoped her family would accept it. She must have lived in her House for at least the first part of the pregnancy, or the mage-stone in the metal the peasants use would have blocked Vor's mage potential from arising. She must have loved Stratus very much to leave behind her luxurious home for a simple soldier's house.

"Do you think it's possible Vor doesn't even know her mother was nobility?" Colby asked.

Giri furrowed his brow. "That hadn't occurred to me," he admitted.

Colby gave a one-shouldered shrug, dismissing it. "Thank you for the information. There is no news yet of our return. You may go back to your so-called studies."

Giri bowed and turned to leave—spying Milsa in the doorway, where she'd obviously been listening with a shield up so he wouldn't sense her. The woman just arched an eyebrow at him, and stood aside, so he could leave.

***

Giri packed hurriedly, hardly paying attention to what he was throwing in his bag.

"Oma, I heard you're leaving."

He took a precious second to glance up at Dello, who had come to the open door he hadn't shut.

"Yes," Giri answered quickly.

"Pack the umber robe; you look good in it."

Giri froze for a second, head cocked dubiously up at Dello.

"I'm serious. It brings out the highlights in your hair and darker flecks in your eyes."

He snatched up the indicated robe, rolled it swiftly, and added it to his bag. "How do you know these things?" he muttered.

Dello just shrugged. "I guess you're leaving right now."

"My master said to get ready and get to platform three, and then we'd go."

"Three?" Dello echoed.

"Yeah. I'll bet we're bringing drakes."

"Dang," he winced.

"Yeah."

Platform three was the largest teleportation platform, taking up nearly the whole of the actual flat roof of the Citadel. They wouldn't be using it if a whole bunch of people—or things—weren't being sent.

"Anyone else going?" Dello asked.

"Strafa and Ylanzo their apprentices," Giri answered idly as he stood and hefted the bag.

Dello extended a hand. Giri gripped it without hesitation, but then his eyes widened as he felt Dello donating some energy to him.

"You're going to have to teleport—with a bunch of drakes—and then who knows what," his tall friend explained.

"Thank you," Giri accepted.

"Go get her, man," Dello whispered next. "Get her and don't let go."

Giri almost smiled, and nodded a little.

"I mean, unless she asks you to let go," Dello amended, as though explaining something to a naughty child. "Holding onto ladies when they tell you to let go is not nice."

Now Giri cracked a smile. "I'll remember."

Dello sobered, dropping his teasing tone. "But your problem is that you never hold on, even when they want you to."

"I need to go," Giri grunted, starting to feel embarrassed.

"Right. Good luck, Giri."

Dello slapped him on the shoulder, released his hand, and let him exit. Giri turned around and put up his wards and locks as quickly as he could. Then, with a last wave to his friend, he headed off for teleportation platform three at a fast walk.

The Wizards Return to Northborn

It was clear almost immediately that something had happened in their absence. The only people who came out to greet them when their massive teleportation shook the sky were Amlee and Edgard, the two heads of the servant corps. The drakes landed in ranks in the courtyard, angry and upset about the teleporting dizziness. Strafa and Ylanzo, the two additional State Wizards who had been assigned to straighten out Northborn, moved to calm the drakes at once.

No one else came running, although Giri thought he detected a multitude of people hiding behind curtained windows. Altare strode directly to the pair of servants, only staggering slightly from the power drain.

"Where are they?" the mage demanded. "Eriducus and the others, Vor and Karolan?"

Edgard stepped slightly in front of Amlee, as though to shield her.

"They vanished, Lord Altare," he said.

"Vanished?"

Edgard shrugged as if perplexed. "No one can locate them. They aren't in the palace."

"All of them?" Altare growled.

"And the king, the princess, and the mine slaves," Edgard added.

The mage's shout made everyone flinch. "What?"

"Please forgive us, Lord," Edgard begged. "We didn't see them escaping, and we don't know how to find them. General Krant has sent out scouts with dogs, but they haven't reported back yet."

"Is there a problem?" Colby called, coming up behind him, although everyone in the courtyard had heard the conversation clearly.

Giri hung back with Milsa, ostensibly helping with the luggage, but sharing a knowing glance. Altare whirled at Colby, his teeth showing.

"I will find them," he declared. "I will find them and bring them back, and—" He broke off. Then Altare sprinted for the door into the palace.

Giri came up beside his master.

"So it begins," Colby muttered. "Get the carry baskets ready."

Giri nodded grimly. "Yes, Master."

***

When they came in sight of the meadow, Giri could see Vor and Karolan at one end, each standing in a simple circle they'd cut into the ground. Although no one else was in sight, Giri doubted very much that they were alone. He could sense that they both had shields up, and pretty good ones, but Altare was charged to overflowing with power—where he'd suddenly gotten it, Giri dreaded to contemplate—and had a lot more experience slinging magic around than his apprentices. Vor seemed to have two fire elementals with her, and Giri thought he sensed a hint of earth about her, too, but was too far away to tell any details.

Colby directed the drakes down for a landing, and Altare was up and out of his carry basket almost before it touched the grass. Giri fumbled his way out of his own basket as Altare began throwing his first attacks. As he screamed out his intent to kill his apprentice, he made the conflict clear, and Giri felt his own power begin to throb.

"Giri," Colby ordered. "Come here."

He obeyed—for now—going to join his master and Milsa. Colby put up shields around them all. Altare was shouting again, sending more attacks. Neither Vor nor Karolan had yet retaliated, only defended. Altare summoned shadow elementals, which bounded into the trees, starting a ruckus with whoever was hiding there. But then someone he hadn't suspected, someone he hadn't sensed in the least, showed himself.

"That's Craduticus," Colby gasped. "The old man is still alive?"

"And moving against his former apprentice," Milsa marveled.

Giri didn't know the man, had never seen or sensed him before, but he'd been hiding under a shield until just this moment, and none of them had known he was there.

"He was a State Wizard, one of the heads of the expedition to Northnest," Colby explained as the old man and his apprentice began exchanging blows in earnest. "He was always sharp, although a little too dark in my opinion. With him here, there might be a chance, if he hasn't lost his edge."

Altare, however, began demonstrating the impressive ability to block Craduticus' attacks and keep strikes raining on Vor at the same time. The latter was buckling down, repeatedly reinforcing her shields, and none of the blows were getting through. Then Altare exposed a critical error, for he claimed that Colby and the others were going to step in on his side.

Giri hid a smile as Colby denied it. "We said we would accompany you," his master enunciated. "We did not say we'd help you kill your apprentices, or your former master. As they have done nothing against us, that is a personal matter you had best settle on your own."

And as Altare stood, dismayed and stunned, Vor released her salamanders. Craduticus called lightning onto Altare. Then Vor began throwing lances of fire at her master. Altare looked to be in trouble. Giri had trouble hiding his eager grin this time.

"Don't look so happy," Milsa chided. "There's still a good chance she's going to die."

But then, just as things were looking up, the allies under the trees began emerging, flushed out by the shadow elementals. Vor took her attention off her master, and began aiding the humans—and griffins. Giri had never seen griffins before, but he didn't have the luxury of getting too excited about it now. Vor was diverting precious energy to helping them, and he clenched his jaw. She could have stayed focused on her main target, and with Craduticus' help overwhelmed him, but now Altare had only the old wizard to deal with.

"The boy hasn't moved," Milsa muttered, referring to Karolan.

"He's working on something," Colby whispered.

"Look at the drakes," Giri interrupted, for they were flexing and hissing, watching the griffins on the field.

Colby made a gesture, and the swarm quieted: magically sedated. As more humans and griffins began fleeing the trees, Vor shouted out.

"Only Altare," she ordered her allies. "Leave the drakes and the others. Don't attack them."

Colby chuckled. "She's taking someone's advice, I expect." He winked at Giri.

Just as Altare finished off Vor's second salamander, he staggered.

"That's what the boy was doing," Colby went on. "He's made a lovely swamp: creative, but not the most effective use of his energy."

Altare, however, seemed pleased, and when he plunged his hands into the morass and began chanting, Colby stiffened.

"What's he doing?" Giri asked, for he, too, felt an unpleasant, squirming magical sensation.

"He's calling a demon," the State Wizard hissed.

"How does he know how to do that?" Milsa demanded.

"It's forbidden," Giri concurred, "isn't it?"

"We don't teach it, but there are those that find the texts, and learn how to do it," Colby lamented darkly. "It will be good that he dies this day."

Giri felt himself tensing, eager now that his master had strongly implied that Altare would be defeated—if not by Vor and her allies, then by him. The demon erupted from the morass in a boiling wave of stench and rushed forward. It impacted Vor and Karolan's shields and began eating away at them, while Craduticus reengaged Altare.

Then the griffin mage came out of the forest. Colby, Milsa, and Giri all gasped. Giri had seen only drawings and sculptures of the beasts, so even the ones thrashing around with the shadow elementals drew his interest—but this one wore a coat of flames, flew high, and began raining magical strikes onto the demon.

"I didn't know griffins could be mages," Milsa said weakly.

"It seems they can," Colby shrugged. "Amazing. Look at it. The flames aren't real; it's just magical overflow materializing visually. The creature has so much energy—far more than a human mage—and it's airborne, with no circle of any kind to anchor itself."

It was indeed impressive. Unfortunately, its attacks on the demon did next to nothing: nor did the physical attacks of a big, brave brown griffin or the falcon-like strikes of a black and white one. The demon, undaunted, fought on, tearing at the two apprentices' shields until they were nearly gone. All the while, the one-on-one fight between Altare and his former master was becoming literally more heated.

Karolan's shield shattered and the boy had to retreat, leaving only Vor and her griffin allies to face the demon. Although they were well coordinated, their best efforts did little against the creature. Giri sensed Vor release the hint of earth magic he'd detected earlier, and quickly he spied a pair of earth toads on their way to distract Altare. Vor rebuilt her shields, and Karolan arrived to shield Craduticus just as Altare was getting the upper hand. The earth toads pounced then, too, altogether giving Craduticus a chance to get back to his feet.

The trio of wizards flinched as Vor called a brilliant strike of lightning onto the six-legged demon, but Colby was shaking his head.

"Altare made a strategic choice by calling that demon," he bemoaned. "Ordinary magic will have little effect on it. Craduticus might know what it is, but he's too occupied to act against it, and I doubt Vor or Karolan have the slightest idea that it's even a demon."

"What would get rid of it?" Giri asked intently.

Colby eyed him. "You'll not be helping her."

"For educational purposes, Master," he coaxed.

Colby sighed, still watching as the battle raged. "There are things that could discourage it, but the best way to get rid of it would be for the summoner to send it back. Baring that, you counter it with a different sort of creature."

"An elemental?" Giri asked.

"As much an elemental as this demon is. There are creatures which exist, whose purpose in the universe is to combat such creatures, and vanquish them," Colby said, just loud enough to be heard over the clamor of the fighting.

"What are they?"

"I shall set this to you as an assignment," Colby smirked. "I'd like to hear your short list of possible beings tomorrow, and then I will tell you if you are correct."

"We might need one or two of those beings today," Milsa grumbled, "if this thing doesn't get sent back."

While Altare seemed again to be gaining the upper hand over Craduticus and Karolan, the demon was having little trouble dealing with the dozen griffins, two men, and one mage confronting it. All three wizards winced when a man was snatched up and severed in two. Giri winced again when Vor's retaliation used up far more of her remaining power than he thought wise, although it did make an impact on the demon due to sheer force.

"She needs to leave the demon and go after her master," Milsa scolded.

"I agree," Colby muttered.

Then the three wizards recoiled as an explosion of flame went up at the edge of the clearing near them. They'd been focused on Vor and the demon, and not paying attention to Altare's fight with Karolan and Craduticus. The two avengers were down: Craduticus scorched and unmoving, half buried in dirt, and Karolan absent—probably having fled into the trees.

"Damn," Colby breathed.

Now Altare turned his attention fully onto Vor.

"It will start now," the State Wizard went on.

It started with taunting. Altare advanced on his apprentice, throwing distracting attacks at her, and making her have to defend against both him and the occasional attacks of the demon. The griffin mage was still trying to help her, but Giri doubted he'd last much longer with all the powerful blows he was generating—not that they had much effect on the demon except to distract it. He would have been better off going after Altare.

Giri had a moment of shock when Altare declared that Vor had bedded Karolan. Something hurt for a moment in his chest, and when he took a critical look at her energies, he saw it, too. They'd altered their shape, as he'd seen several times before, both in himself and in the virgins he'd bedded or Milsa had bedded before Colby.

He felt his master pat his shoulder in sympathy, but Giri told himself it didn't matter. He himself was no virgin anymore, but he still considered himself to have worth, to be desirable, and the same was true for Vor. Giri also wondered if she had enjoyed a good experience with the boy. He privately doubted it, but now wasn't the time to ponder it.

Altare took down the griffin mage—although not fatally—and the demon had the remaining griffins exhausted and wary. Vor spent more energy protecting one from Altare when it seemed to be getting a good grip on the demon. Giri could understand her feelings, but again it was energy that should have been spent directly against her master instead. The last shadow elemental entered the fray, the demon got a grip on the griffin Vor had been protecting, and Altare continued to rain blows onto his apprentice.

Giri saw Vor's shield taking the hits, eroding away, and start to buckle. She was fighting admirably, but she had too many focuses, and too little power. Beside him, Colby sighed regretfully.

"No," Giri growled.

He took a step forward, and his master's grip came down on his arm, almost hard enough to bruise.

"Let me go," Giri requested.

"I can't do that," Colby apologized.

He started to draw himself up, torn between needing to help Vor before it was too late and obeying his master. Then swift movement caught everyone's eye as a slender figure bedecked in greenery ran out onto the field.

"A nymph," Milsa identified first.

The plant-person dropped to her knees and summoned vines to entwine the demon, and Vor threw another shield to protect her as Altare retaliated. The effort had Vor down to the dregs of her power. She dropped to one knee, and Giri saw her pull in the ambient blood energy from all the fighting. He nodded: a practical choice. She wasn't quick enough, though. Altare soon had a magical lash around the nymph's neck. Karolan burst from concealment then, running to the nymph's aid even though he was seriously wounded and out of power, too.

Milsa groaned. "This is going to be a right mess."

Altare struck at the boy. Vor tried to stop it and only partly succeeded. Karolan was back on his knees almost at once, still trying to remove the lash from the nymph. At least the nymph's vines were holding; the demon was restrained for the moment. The griffin mage stepped up, threatening Altare— and then Altare pulled the lash. Milsa whimpered and looked away, and Giri flinched, too. Colby sighed, shaking his head. The boy started screaming, and then Altare made the critical error of threatening him.

Vor stepped out of her protective circle.

Giri cursed, starting forward again, and this time both Milsa and Colby held him back.

"It's the final lap," Colby muttered. "Hold on. Now it's just her and him, and we shall see."

Altare had energy left, although not a lot, and Vor hardly had any. As he rained blows on her, she began to close on him, a step at a time, but all she could manage was to keep a bit of shielding up, and deflect parts of the strikes. It seemed obvious from his comments that he considered her no threat.

Giri found himself snarling at the things Altare was saying to her, and everyone gasped when he revealed that he'd bled out some unspecified number of women to supply himself with power for the battle. Vor finally got within touching distance.

"She has nothing left," Giri pled. "Please, Master."

Colby's face was as expressionless as stone. "Wizards must earn their place."

Vor fell.

Giri cried out in denial, sucking up power and preparing to launch a shield between Altare and Vor, to stop the fatal strike that must come next.

But then she was back up—and in her hands was a spear, dropped by one of the human fighters early in the battle. She drove it into her master's chest, drove him to the ground, and kept pushing. As he tried to steal her life force, she stole his right back, until he was too weak to fight. Even as he cried out and begged, she pushed with silent, stalwart, implacable focus, until the spearhead sunk all the way into his chest, until blood pulsed out around it, until it pierced his heart, until he died.

Giri Returns Vor to the Castle

With relief that staggered him, Giri thought that would be the end, but there was still the tangled demon.

"She won. We can get rid of it now," he begged his master. "Right? Altare is dead."

Colby started to respond, but then the screaming in the forest made them all slap their hands over their ears. Giri had never seen a unicorn. He could hardly see it now. It was so bright it made tears run from his eyes, although Colby and Milsa both covered their eyes entirely. A second scream came, and a second unicorn. Giri fell to his knees, trying to watch, suspecting that he would never have the chance again to see unicorns.

They circled the dying nymph, and when they left, slowly and together, there stood a small tree in her place. Only then did his companions recover, but no one had any words of understanding or wisdom for what had just happened. The demon, however, was dissolving into muck, flesh falling off its bones like half-cooked cake batter.

"And that is one thing that can defeat a demon," Colby panted, "unicorns."

Karolan began screaming again, clearly mourning the nymph girl's death—or whatever had happened to her. Vor had made an attempt to crawl to him, but stopped in exhaustion or a sense of futility, or both.

"Now," Giri asked intently but politely, "now may I go to her?"

Colby gave him a slight, pained smile, and nodded. "Go."

Giri walked as well as he could across the buckled, swampy, torn up meadow, past Altare's cooling body, to where Vor was trembling, trying to support herself on all fours. When he attracted her attention, she didn't ask why he hadn't helped. Instead, she let him help her now. She accepted the watered tea he offered, she accepted his hand to pull her up. He wanted to embrace her, to tell her everything was alright now, but he held himself back: afraid she wouldn't have the strength to push him off if she didn't want it. As he walked her from Craduticus to his master to the griffin leader, he could only admire her tenacity, her ability to speak and care and continue to do all she could.

It could not last forever. When she fell again to the ground, when he touched her energies and saw for himself that she had but seconds of consciousness left, he was not surprised—and only more impressed. After she collapsed, he rolled her onto her back, so she wouldn't be breathing into the bloody soil, and petted her tangled hair off her face. She would recover, but she desperately needed rest and warmth, and perhaps a little infusion of energy from a willing fellow mage.

Giri heard squelching footsteps and the sway of mage robes and looked up. His master had crossed over to him. He crouched down and touched Vor's forehead with a finger.

"I guess you'd better take her back then," he said.

"Master, would you? I just promised I'd help with the healing."

Colby shook his head slowly as a wry smile bloomed on his face. "You take her. I'll help with the healing."

"Master, are you sure?" Giri confirmed.

Colby stood. "I'm all entangled in your romance now, so I might as well accept it."

"It's not a—"

"Oh don't tell me lies, Giri. Go. I'll send the drakes off with you and teleport back."

Giri stood in alarm. "Twice in one day, Master?"

"I'm a big wizard," he quipped. "I can handle it. Go. It's an order."

Giri took him at his word. As Colby moved off, Giri crouched back down, and as gently as he could, tried to stand up with Vor in his arms. He could get his arms under her knees and back, but she weighed almost as much as he did, and he, too, was weary.

A huge shape moved up beside him. "Here, silly human," said one of the griffins. "Put her on my back. I'll carry her to the basket. That's how you intend to take her back, correct?"

"It is," Giri uttered, staring up in fascination. "You're not too hurt?"

The griffin, one in colors of red-brown and rust, fluffed up its crest. "I can handle it," it said, echoing Colby even in tone.

It crouched down now, and Giri managed to get Vor lying on her front between its wings, with her legs dangling down its sides by its belly.

"Good enough. Steady her as I stand."

Giri obeyed, and walked beside the griffin as it approached the baskets. "You don't mind the drakes?"

"These ones don't seem to be violent," the griffin said lightly.

"Not at the moment," Giri allowed.

The drakes let the griffin pass with only a little hissing, and then it crouched down again and Giri rolled Vor into the carry basket. The griffin stood back up, still looking down at the unconscious mage.

"She has done a great deed today," it said, "and much benefited the humans and griffins I call friends. We will remember this."

"Thank you," Giri uttered, not sure what else to say.

"Last summer she led an attack of soldiers against me, my brother, my Linesister, my niece, the three human chicks of my dear friend Hawkwind, and another griffin of my home," the griffin went on. "A few of us nearly died from it, and she kidnapped the princess Jessika from us, whom we call Hawkwings."

Giri raised his eyebrows, filing away the information with some surprise, but not prepared to condemn Vor for her actions just yet, without hearing her side first. The griffin ruffled up the fur feathers on its chest, exposing wide white spots of tissue where no fur grew.

"These scars came from the spears of the soldiers she brought." It looked over to where Colby had burned Altare's body. "But today, she put a spear to its proper use, and I thank her."

The griffin bent down and gently mouthed a bit of Vor's hair. "I forgive her."

"Thank you," Giri said again, softly, finding himself moved by the griffin's sincerity. "May I ask your name?"

"Thornwing, and if you do not know, I am male. That mage, Thornfire, is the brother I speak of. This woman, Vor, protected him today, and Hawkwind, and others."

"I am pleased to meet you, Thornwing. My name is Giri Holstor."

The griffin bowed its head. "Perhaps someday you could have speech with my brother. Mages often have much to say to each other, and you two of such different origins."

"I would like that," Giri told him, finding it to be true.

"I will take my leave now," Thornwing said. "My companions need what help I can give them."

"Yes, good flying to you," he managed, trying to think of a way to say farewell to a griffin.

He thought maybe Thornwing smiled, but it was difficult to tell. The griffin moved off, and Giri began strapping down Vor for her flight back to the castle. She stirred once, groaning, but he paused to murmur reassurance and stroke her forehead until she quieted. Prepared at last, he went to the other basket and got in, sending a quick energy pulse at his master to indicate his readiness.

The drakes took off on an unspoken magical signal from Colby. Giri rode with them, watching the smooth progress of the basket holding Vor, until they again landed in the courtyard. Servants were milling about, and he quickly had a half dozen jabbering around him. Then the older woman, Amlee, came striding through their ranks like a general, and took Vor completely out of his hands, with a few other women assisting.

He tried to follow, but Amlee gave him a glare as they went into the bathing chamber, and he relented. He waited outside, however, until they came out again, carrying Vor—still unconscious, but clean, bandaged, and wrapped in a robe—up to her room. He started to follow them inside, and one of them, a slender girl with a tremulous stubborn chin turned to stop him.

"No men in the lady's chamber," she declared.

"I just want to donate some energy to her," he said. "It's a mage thing. You can watch me the whole time."

"Let him in, Kari," Amlee called. "I'll keep an eye on him."

The young woman got out of his way with a dubious look, and he tried to be as professional and proper as possible as he moved through the servants, into Vor's bedroom, where she'd been put to bed.

"What, exactly, are you going to do to her?" Amlee demanded outright.

"I will put my hand on her hand," he explained clearly, "and transfer some of my own personal energy into her. She's depleted from the battle. You know she killed Altare?"

"We know, and we are glad, and we have every interest in her safe recovery," the castellan all but threatened.

"Giving her some energy will help her recover," Giri assured her. "It won't hurt her."

Reluctantly, Amlee moved a step aside, still looking at him as though he were a seemingly friendly dog she expected to suddenly turn rabid. "Go ahead then."

She hadn't given him much space, but Giri moved slowly into it, knelt down by the bed, and let his hand rest on top of Vor's where it lay on the coverlet. He didn't have much energy to spare, but she had far less. He was dizzy by the time he finished. While he was kneeling, he let his other hand drop and touch the floor. He placed an extremely simple ward, one that would break as soon as Vor touched it, but would alert him to her getting up. With her aura so close at hand, he could even structure the ward so it would alert only on her footstep, not Amlee or the servants.

"Her color is better," Kari observed timidly.

"It is," Amlee agreed. "Out, all of you."

The servants scattered like frightened geese as Giri fought his way up to his feet.

"Thank you," he told Amlee.

"I'm keeping Pella away from you," the woman said without preamble.

"Good. Please do," he admitted. "Is she alright?"

Amlee sniffed. "She's a bit silly about you."

Giri winced. "I'm sorry."

"You must have treated her well."

He hid his face in his hand. "It's complicated. I didn't really want to do what I did. I won't touch any of your servants again."

"As I would expect," she retorted. "Do you intend to touch Mistress Vor?"

He felt like his stomach had just plummeted out of his body, and he took a moment to gather himself.

"I will speak honestly with you," he said. "I am interested in her, and if she returns that interest, I will not stop it from developing, but I will not touch her if she refuses me."

Amlee seemed to take that in. "I'm guessing Pella didn't refuse you."

"I asked. She did not."

"I see."

Giri lifted his head and met Amlee's gaze. "I am trying to be a better man."

She snorted at him. "That's what they all say. Now get out."

Giri nodded his head in a little bow, and obeyed.

While Vor Sleeps

"So I suggested she summon a greater salamander," the mage Chirolen went on.

Eriducus, Ulver, and Chirolen had returned almost immediately to the castle when the griffins had carried them word that no retribution would befall them. They'd shown up on griffin mounts who immediately left again, and explained that they were too old to try living in a forest. Now they were recounting what had happened at the castle while Colby and his apprentices were in Weldom with Altare. All the wizards looked with surprise on Chirolen at his latest statement.

"But surely she couldn't do it," Wizard Ylanzo dismissed.

"Oh, she did it alright, our Vor," Ulver beamed, his two companions confirming with chuckles and nods.

Giri felt his lips curving up into a smile. He covered his mouth with a hand, trying to look contemplative.

"What are you grinning about?" Milsa grumbled.

"I'm not grinning," he denied, but unable to keep a straight face.

"That's impressive," Wizard Strafa praised.

"It seemed almost happy to serve her," Eriducus contributed.

Chirolen nodded eagerly in agreement. "Hardly chewed her up at all."

"So the salamander destroyed the mage-stone," Colby prompted.

"Quite right," Ulver contributed. "Then we put Vor to bed, and went and freed the slaves."

"That's right," Eriducus nodded, "and then got some rest ourselves. We'd all burned up quite a bit of energy."

"And today she fought her master and killed him," Milsa spoke up, "after having depleted herself just yesterday. No wonder it was such a close fight; she started out handicapped."

"Altare did teleport the same day, too," Lissian spoke up timidly.

"But he bled out all those young women," Ylanzo growled. "He was charged up."

"He certainly was," Colby agreed darkly, sitting back. "He hardly contributed to the teleporting, either: just nudged himself along."

Strafa nodded. "He didn't help with the luggage or drakes at all; I was watching."

They were gathered in one of the conservatories with tea kindly provided by the servants: trying to get their bearings on how to settle in and handle the various situations at the capital. Strafa set down her teacup with thoughtful deliberation.

"I look forward to meeting this young woman," she said softly into the silence. "She sounds like wizard material."

A rustle ran through the room. Giri was gratified to see Colby nodding with no hesitation. Milsa sat up a bit straighter.

"My apprenticeship may soon come to an end," she offered. "I might be willing to take her on, with the approval of the Citadel, of course."

Excitement stirred in Giri's chest. If Vor could be accepted by the Wizard Citadel, she could begin training in earnest, far better training than what she got from Altare. His only concern remained how to stay close to her, but if Milsa took her as an apprentice, she would be around all the time, since Giri was Colby's apprentice still, and Milsa was Colby's devoted mate. He even wondered if the two might marry—then they would have to be sent on assignments together; married wizards were not split up unless they volunteered for it.

"It is a good possibility," Colby agreed, but he seemed to want to move on. "Well, let me tell you of the battle with Altare then."

He went on to describe what had happened, but Giri had no need to pay close attention, for he already knew everything, having seen it himself. Instead, he daydreamed about potential four-wizard assignments while appreciating the delicate flavors of the tea, and thanked Amlee with a nod when she came in to refill his cup. The talk had moved on to future Northborn objectives when he felt the ward he'd put beside Vor's bed snap.

Giri sat up, almost spilling his tea. "She's awake," he blurted.

Everyone looked over at him, and in the abrupt silence he felt the shameful rush of blood to his face.

"Vor, she just got out of bed," he admitted in a tiny voice. "I put a detection ward in her room."

Colby smiled and shook his head. Milsa narrowed her eyes. The others just blinked at him with faint amusement. Still blushing, Giri turned to Amlee, who was standing by now with a confused look on her face.

"She might need help," he muttered weakly, and then looked to the other wizards. "And if she's up already, she might want to come to the dinner later. She's invited, right?"

"Of course she's invited," Colby said at once.

Giri glanced hopefully back at Amlee. The castellan gazed at him with a complex mix of emotions—although disapproval seemed to be upmost—but then she pivoted without even a sigh and left the room, handing off the teapot to the page standing by the door. The young man looked perplexed as to what he was supposed to do with it, until a few seconds later when a different maidservant came and relieved him of it.

The Dinner and a Moment in the Garden

She was wearing the dress again. Above and beyond that, she must have had the servants braid her hair, and told them how to do it in the western style. Giri gazed at her, feeling no need for food if he had Vor to look upon. That dress was modest in that it covered her well, but it hugged her, too. The grey suits she usually wore fit her nicely, but this was different. Plus, he didn't get the impression that Vor was normally anything other than practical. He appreciated that about her, actually, but her showing up like this indicated that she had intentionally gone to some effort and purposefully stepped out of her comfort area.

Was it for his benefit?

Giri dismissed that immediately. She'd shown little indication that she had interest in him. She'd certainly become less wary of him, and she was polite, but there had been no secret looks, no non-accidental accidental touching, no teasing phrases slyly slipped into conversation: nothing. Why did he hope, then? He was firm on not pressuring women into bed; he required outright and clear consent. Vor had to want him before he'd proceed, and she wasn't giving any clear signals that she did—unless braiding her hair like his and dressing up to show herself off was a subconscious signal she didn't even know she was intending to send.

Or maybe she was just trying to make a good impression on the new wizards? As he sat, he tuned out the conservation while he pondered—until he heard his master introduce Vor with a description of her parentage: half of it outright, and half of it implied. Then he saw the flash of distress on Vor's face, and wished he'd never told Colby what he'd discovered. What good did it do to reveal it now? Did his master think the other wizards would respect her more, knowing she had noble blood like them?

Vor recovered quickly, but didn't join into the conversation much as the dinner went on. He tried to give her an encouraging smile, and though he was sure she noticed, she didn't make any visible reply. She didn't linger after the meal either, and everyone seemed to accept her departure as a sign of her need for rest to recover from the battle with Altare. Indeed, Giri, too, thought she must still be convalescing, but he had a feeling that her exit was more an effort to get away from people in general than a retreat to bed-rest. To follow her, however, would be—

"Giri," his master muttered to him behind his teacup, as they sat in the conservatory listening to Milsa play the harpsichord.

"Yes, Master?" Giri replied, a little startled.

"Vor didn't say much during the dinner."

"No, she didn't." Giri thought for a moment and decided to be honest. "I don't think she liked everyone knowing her parentage. It put her more on the defensive than she already was."

Colby raised an eyebrow, setting his cup into its saucer with the slightest click of porcelain on porcelain. "I didn't get the opportunity to ask her about these people and griffins who will be joining us in a couple days. I was hoping Vor would consent to telling us what she knows about them. Would you ask her for me?"

Giri wanted to tell his master to go ask her himself, but he kept that comment behind his teeth. This wouldn't be the first time Colby had asked him or Milsa to go make contact with someone on his behalf, especially when the person might be less intimidated by a younger, less powerful—or female, in Milsa's case—wizard.

"If she hasn't gone to bed already, and I can find her," Giri muttered back, "yes, I'll ask her."

"Thank you, my boy. One other thing, if possible, do you think you could find out a bit more about what she's thinking? I mean, related to us being here and our plans for Northborn, and her plans."

Giri eyed his master. "Is there a particular manner in which you wish me to do this?"

"Just talk to her." He gave a little shrug. "She likes you; she might tell you things."

He swallowed his automatic retort of denial and tempered it a little. "She doesn't like me, Master."

Colby's eyebrow made another upward venture, this time approaching his hairline. "Well, she likes you more than any of the rest of us."

Giri looked away. He supposed he couldn't deny that, but that still didn't mean she'd tell him anything of importance.

"And then you want me to come tell you what she told me?" he asked.

Colby made a little wince. "I don't mean that you're to convey anything told to you in confidence."

Giri firmed his jaw. "Are you sure? Because that's what it sounded like, Master."

The older wizard sighed softly. "Forget I asked, Giri. I can see where your alliances lie."

That sent a chill through him. "Master—"

Colby set a hand on his. "I know. I know you are still my loyal apprentice." He turned to look at him, and his expression was both tender and worried. "I am glad you are the man you are. I hope, if you do learn anything of concern to us, that you will encourage Vor to share it with me."

Giri nodded slowly. "I think I can agree to that."

Colby patted his hand once and released him. "Have a good evening, Giri."

***

A servant told Giri where Vor was, and he didn't try to hide his approach.

He even reached out to brush her energy from afar: a bold move; usually only mages who knew each other well, and were friends, did such things uninvited. Vor had a formidable set of shields up considering her low power state, but gave no detectable evidence of displeasure at his magical contact—but nor did she give much sign of welcome. At least she consented to his presence, and was willing to talk to him.

He watched her covertly, with all his senses, all through the conversation. Her shields indicated her anxiety about the potential for magical attack. In word and behavior, too, she was guarded, closed off, and he couldn't tell if a harvest celebration or a mourning procession was going on behind those high walls she had around herself. Still, she had wit and spirit—he already knew that much—although both seemed a little subdued this night.

The fight with her master and the demon, seeing people die, killing her master herself, witnessing the grief of that boy Karolan, the damage done to her own self, and now returning to a home so changed, without her master in it, and instead peopled with a half dozen new mages, all strangers and possibly dangerous, couldn't have been easy for her. Even though her master had been cruel, abusive, manipulative, a rapist and murderer however many times over—that had been her normal. Giri could only assume that she was feeling terribly unsettled now with all the sudden changes: hence the cold emotional walls against everyone around her.

Like after the battle, he again wanted to go take her in his arms: not for any seductive purpose, but to give her comfort. He wanted to tell her everything would be fine now, that she was safe. If she needed to cry, he'd let her cry on him and not judge her for it. If she needed to talk, he'd listen for as long as she needed, and never breathe a word of it to anyone.

And as he watched her, and wanted desperately to offer all of those things to her, he was afraid that if he made any move, any gesture at all, rather than helping it would only cause her to bolt further away. She would slam shut the few doors in her walls that remained open, lower all the portcullises, and bar every gate. She would pull her trebuchets up to the inside of her walls and man the battlements with archers.

Giri knew, if he tried anything now—platonic or not—he might never be able to approach her again. She wouldn't allow it. So instead he kept his hands to himself and tried to make his words kind and simple. She did agree to consider talking with him again—keeping the lines of negotiation open. She also agreed to talk with all the wizards tomorrow about the princess and her companions. Colby at least would be happy.

And when she said goodnight, and he had no substantive reason to call her back or follow her, he let her go. He took her place at the pond, in the warm summer air, and watched the stars come out, thinking of all the things he wished he could have done and said. Only when the night started to cool did he go back to his rooms and seek his lonely bed.

The Day Before the Delegation

Giri paid close attention to Vor as she spoke about the princess, griffins, and others who might come visiting. It did not escape him that she was particularly circumspect when she spoke of Karolan. She was dispassionate through the entire interrogation, but maintained that stance even when what must have been a sensitive subject came up. There was not a stammer, not a blush, and she said nothing about what she might feel towards the boy—or towards any of the others. Yet there was no doubt that she'd bedded him.

The evidence was undeniable in the configuration of her aura. The lowest power node in the human body was linked to the reproductive organs—there were several others: heart, belly, and head being some of the other main ones. It tended to open most strongly after the first sexual encounter, although other events could affect it also. A traumatic sexual event could even partly close it. Through that node, and the others, mages could generate power.

Giri could detect the alteration clearly. Although it was not as complete as it had the potential to become, it gave Vor access to more power—especially if she chose to make use of it. Since she and Karolan had apparently parted ways, Giri didn't suppose she'd be doing any of that with him. Then again, separated people could and did reunite. Or she could choose someone else— or no one at all, which would really be a shame.

He resisted the urge to shift in his chair and tried to focus more on what she was saying, and less on her altered aura and what it meant or could mean. He still wanted her. It didn't matter that she wasn't a virgin anymore; he didn't want her for that one-time ultra-power generation event—though any sex would generate some power that would naturally be an extra benefit to the enjoyment of the act. Her wanted her for—for—well, what exactly did he want her for?

Giri wasn't doing a very good job listening to the conversation, and rested his face in his hand to hide the coloring of his cheeks. Other parts of him were following along with his train of thought, too, and he crossed his legs. He wanted to see her impassioned, wanted to show her, to help her find the pleasure that could be had. Vor was walled off, and probably burdened with a number of distressing memories related to sex or intimacy and possibly the blemish of a less than satisfactory first experience.

Beyond all that, Giri doubted she trusted anyone or anything not to hurt her, take advantage of her, or dismiss her. How could he get through to her that he—Giri paused his thoughts. What did he want to do to her? How would he be any different than those she didn't trust if he was just trying to get her in bed, even if he considered that his motivation of wanting to teach her about intimacy in a positive and useful light was doing her a service? Was he not simply justifying his lust?

No, he would have to be clear: completely clear. He didn't just need her consent. He needed her agreement that bedding him would be only for educational and mutually enjoyable temporary purposes. If she didn't agree, that would be the end of it. There would be no forcing, no manipulation, and no seduction: just sex: trusting, kind sex between equals, but just sex. Just like Milsa had done with him a decade ago. Because that was all he wanted, wasn't it?

"Giri," Colby snapped.

He looked up, his blush having long ago faded, to his relief.

"Were you sleeping?" his master scolded.

"Even with an empty bed, he gets no rest," Milsa taunted under her breath.

Beside her, Rossilla tittered, and Giri's face flushed two-fold. At least Vor was already gone. He hadn't noticed her leave, and worried that she might have thought he was ignoring her, or thought her boring, because he had been lost in contemplation and not listening to her. She didn't know he was actually obsessing over her in the most personal way possible, even though he hadn't been looking at her.

"Pay attention," his master sighed. "Come here. We're discussing how we might implement this third order."

Giri scooted his chair closer and looked over the document with the others. He really did try to keep his mind on topic.

****

Once his master let him go, his first thought was to find Vor—not necessarily to spring his plan of friendly, show-and-tell intimacy on her, but just to—to what? Giri leaned against the nearest wall and rubbed his forehead. To what? To talk to her about ordinary things, he realized, or unordinary things, about anything. He just wanted to see her, to hear her, and find out how she was doing on getting used to not having a sadistic master tormenting her in various physical, mental, and emotional ways. Of course mixed in with those wishes was the desire to hold her eager, trembling body against his, and to watch the waves of pleasure move across her face—

He smacked the side of his fist against the wall, wincing at the pain. Would he never be free of this? Did he even trust himself to be around her? Lust could overcome good sense; he knew that first hand. If she showed him any vulnerability at all, he might act without due diligence. He might try to talk her into bed, seduce her, and if she was accustomed to that sort of manipulative behavior from her master—because of the consequences should she not comply—she might respond to Giri the same way she'd responded to Altare.

That was the absolute last thing he wanted.

Giri clenched his jaw and pushed off the wall. He could control himself. What kind of a wizard was he if he couldn't exert his will to have mastery over his more primal instincts? A little voice whispered that he was making a snap decision perhaps because he wanted to see Vor so much, and was underestimating his questionable willpower.

"Of course, if she does respond to me like she did to her master, she might ram a spear through my chest," he muttered to himself. "And if it's because I'm trying to pressure her into sex when she doesn't want it, well, then I suppose I'll deserve it."

Giri had discovered that asking a servant was a nearly guaranteed way to find anyone in the castle. It was almost like they were a hive mind: knowing everything their fellows knew. He was aware that it was actually just the truism of servants everywhere—they gossiped almost continually, so that information flowed and spread like water, or fire. It held true this time, too.

Vor was in the stillroom. He had to ask directions as well, and knew that the word would spread that he was seeking her—twice now, for he'd asked about her the previous evening as well. As Giri moved off following the directions he'd been given, his self-doubt resurged. Looking at it from someone else's point of view—perhaps Castellan Amlee's—it was like he was stalking her, the way a predator would plot and plan its ambush of a prey animal. So as he approached the stillroom he found his steps slowing, until he came to a complete halt.

He didn't know how fast to go, how hard to push. If he never left her alone she was sure to get annoyed with him—and he definitely did not want her to feel persecuted. Perhaps she didn't want company? There were times Giri desperately craved being alone. Vor had just spent the morning getting interrogated by a half dozen wizards. Perhaps she had gone to the stillroom for the solitude, and that he should not interfere with.

Giri wrought a few shields around him, sealing in his aura, and bending light around him. It wouldn't make him invisible—true invisibility was a high level spell that even the best wizards struggled with. If he moved slowly and silently, however, he could probably get a look at Vor without her noticing him. She was skilled, yes, but he was better. Consistent, kind, and effective training would naturally have that result. Plus, he was older, and his powers had already settled in full.

Another little spell muffled any sounds he might make. Thus equipped, Giri approached the open door to the stillroom. He listened first, hearing only the faintest of sounds of slight objects being moved, and the tiny rustle of clothing from minor movements. Then he heard the sound of chopping, like any cook might make in slicing vegetables. Thinking that cutting something up would take Vor's total concentration he snuck a peak around the doorjamb.

She was sitting on a tall stool at the long, deep tabletop built into the wall of one half of the stillroom. There were several capped jars, a couple small sacks, and a bowl in front of her, along with a few different cutting and mixing utensils. Her sleeves were rolled up above her elbows—exposing a lengthy section of bandaging on one arm—and she was indeed slicing up some fresh mallow flowers with her utility knife. She had her feet hooked through the legs of the stool, and every now and then she rubbed her insteps up and down on them. There were shiny spots on the wood that revealed this was a regular habit of hers. She must go through shoes.

Her mass of hair was twisted up into a bun and contained under a knit cap. Her eyes were intent on her task, but her face was relaxed, if not happy. Vor finished her cutting and scraped up the minced flowers, dropping them into the bowl with whatever else she had in it. Giri had only basic knowledge of herbs and their uses, but he guessed she was making some kind of stomach soothing medicine. She certainly seemed confident in her motions, not even needing to refer to a book. It must have been a recipe she'd made many times before.

After a few more moments, Giri started feeling like a sneak, peeking in on her when she thought she was alone, and withdrew from the doorway. He turned his feet towards the salle. Once he got a couple rooms away, he dispelled the extra shields. Vor was obviously in her element, doing tasks that she knew well and that gave her comfort. As much as he wished he could be what gave her comfort, he couldn't bring himself to disturb her now.

Instead, he shed most of his robes, borrowed a staff again, and put himself through his paces, practicing the movement patterns over and over. With that physical exertion came his own serenity. Once he was sweaty and tired, he went for a bath, hoping he would see Vor at dinner.

Vor didn't come to dinner. Her absence was noticed, but the other wizards didn't seem overly concerned. Master Eriducus even mentioned that Vor tended to like her own company best, and his two fellows concurred. Giri, however, was wishing she wouldn't isolate herself. Maybe she didn't trust the other wizards, but how could she ever come to realize that they were trustworthy—at least mostly, which was as much as could be expected of anyone in Giri's opinion—if she never made an effort to know them?

As the dinner concluded, Giri excused himself. He wanted to at least be sure she'd eaten. Her door was closed when he reached it, and she had some simple wards on it. They'd be enough to give an unwelcome visitor a little shock if he tried to force the handle. If another mage tried to take them down, Vor would at least sense it, giving her a few moments to prepare to face him.

Giri could definitely get in if he wanted to—and he did want to—but he wasn't going to. The wards wouldn't react to someone just touching the door, so he knocked. He thought he saw some faint light through the cracks between door and frame, so hoped she might be awake, but there was no response to his knock.

Vor couldn't know who was knocking. He thought about announcing himself verbally, but then he felt anxious about raising his voice in the hallway. He couldn't extend a magical probe through the wards without setting them off or defusing them first—and Vor had put up wards for a reason. Along with her shut, locked door, it was a signal that she was closed for the day, and didn't want company. He knocked one more time.

"Vor," he murmured to the door.

There was no reply. After waiting another few moments, Giri left, going—again—to his solitary bed.

The Conference, Mending Magic, and Thornwing

Giri got to see Vor again the next day. She stayed close to Craduticus during the meeting with the princess and her companions, and said little. Griffins came to the meeting, too, which pleased Giri. The more he saw of them, the more fascinated he was by them. Of course, Karolan came to the meeting as well, which pleased him less.

Giri attended closely to any interaction between the boy and Vor. Although they did glance at each other a few times, it was never with longing, and never did they meet each other's gaze. They didn't seek each other out or attempt to talk together, either. Karolan looked distinctly depressed; Giri supposed it was because of the death of the nymph. He didn't seek out Vor for comfort, though. Death of a loved one was never easy to bear, but the warm arms of another loved one would help ease the pain. Karolan was not seeking that powerful balm from Vor. To Giri, that was telling of emotional immaturity on the boy's part, or lack of strong feelings for Vor.

As time passed and the glancing subsided into apparent indifference, Giri was able to relax more and more. He concluded that, whatever might have once been between them, it didn't seem to be there anymore. While on the one hand, bonds of affection fading could be sad, for Giri this particular situation only relieved him. If Vor was not fixated on Karolan, she might be open to other options. It was no guarantee of anything—but he could court her now without feeling like he was trying to interfere with her feelings for the boy.

Giri would have smiled sardonically if he'd been alone. Never before had anyone captured his attention so. In the past, if he'd wanted a woman, he'd bluntly asked her. If she said no, that was it. He'd apologize for bothering her and take himself elsewhere. It hadn't really mattered. Never had he gone so carefully, analyzing his every move and word, trying to be sure he did not offend, holding himself back while waiting for signs—either of welcome or rejection: and Vor was giving neither. Perhaps she was unsure, or perhaps she didn't want anyone now, but at the least she didn't want Karolan and the boy didn't want her. Might she want Giri? He realized to his chagrin that this time it mattered to him. Milsa was right; he was smitten.

Giri tried to put that aside for the moment, and turned his attention to the informative conversation. He did not contribute, but the idea of an alliance between griffins and all of Weldom intrigued him, and he hoped the idea might be explored further in Weldom, if the griffins chose to go. The so-called princess Jessika—whom the griffins called Hawkwings—he was not much impressed by, although he could dredge up some sympathy for her situation. He certainly did see a pressing need to try to help the old king, her father, and volunteered to join that task force at once. What Altare and his cohorts had done to the man was, in Giri's opinion, an inexcusable breach of morality.

When the gathering broke up, and Craduticus made Vor join the group going to help the king, Giri was pleased. Again, that Karolan was also going along made him less pleased, but the two were still treating each other with indifference. They weren't purposely ignoring each other, or pouting, and nor were they trying to get closer, or flirt; it was as if, to each of them, that the other was present did not really matter, or perhaps was just a slight annoyance.

The magic in the mage-stone-metal cap was nasty, advanced mind-magic—not something Giri had ever worked with—and it was no doubt beyond Vor's experience—and worlds beyond Karolan's—but observing the unraveling of it would be educational. Giri was also gratified when Vor was called upon to provide some soothing potions for the king, and that he himself was detailed to monitoring the king's unconscious status as the older mages worked on the cap.

Then when Giri prodded Vor to speak, having seen her suddenly burdened with a thought, he was quite proud of himself. If Vor had been a book she would have a thousand pages, and he thus far had only been able to skim the first few—but he knew enough to be certain that if she had something to say, it would be relevant and as wise as her two decades had made her. She did not prove him wrong, and it was partly her argument that swayed the senior mages into going on with the procedure.

He was even happier when his offer of applying the sedative spell was seconded by Milsa and approved by Craduticus. Giri exerted all his skill—while trying to do so without looking like he was exerting all his skill—to make the spell as gentle as possible. After, he met Vor's gaze, trying to make his admiration of her plain in his expression. She didn't look away, but her face was tightly controlled. Whatever was going on behind it she was not about to share with the world: if she was even allowing herself to examine any emotions her body and mind might be proffering up.

Once the procedure was complete and Vor had fetched the men to take the king to his rooms to begin the long recovery process, everyone began to vacate the workroom. Giri contemplated lingering, to try to talk to Vor, but Milsa gave him a look and a jerk of her head, indicating that he should go with her. Still, he dawdled, until Milsa muttered at him to come along and report to Colby. With a sigh of regret, he obeyed. Once he met up with his master and received any orders he might have, he would go seek Vor. He promised himself that—even though the idea of finding her somewhere, and being alone with her, made his stomach flop and roll over with nerves.

***

It wasn't only his master who was waiting for him. Colby was seated again in the throne room turned conference room, with Strafa and the other two apprentices, as well as the young man Rikah and most of the griffins. One of those griffins, the brown and rust colored one who had helped carry Vor after the mage duel, looked up at Giri as he entered. The gorgeous creature puffed out the feathers on his head, and shifted his body such that Giri got the impression he was inviting him over.

Since his master was deep in conversation, Giri left tired Milsa to shuffle over with Craduticus and Ylanzo, and cautiously approached the griffin.

"Thornwing," Giri greeted, "it's nice to see you again."

"Likewise, Giri Holstor," the griffin smiled—Giri was pretty sure it was a smile.

Although the shape of his bill could not much be altered, the feathers under his eyes lifted the way a human's cheeks lifted when smiling, and he inclined his head and flicked his crest a little.

"What do you think of all this?" Giri asked softly, trying for a casual tone of voice.

"Many changes in the castle of Northnest, or Northborn," Thornwing responded lightly. "I'm not of this country, but my dear friend Hawkwind and her human chicks are, originally."

"Are you worried for them?"

"Hawkwind has a home with us, with the other Aerie griffins, and bonds there that are now likely stronger than those to her birthplace. It concerns me that she might get involved, however."

"I don't think," Giri began hesitantly, "that anyone would try to hurt her now, not unless she did something violent first."

Thornwing nodded. "But she might leave us. If Hawkwings goes to Weldom, Hawkwind might follow."

Giri had a thought, but wasn't sure how to articulate it. After a moment of pondering, he decided on bluntness. "Is she your wife, or your mate, or? I'm sorry, I don't know how it is with griffins."

Thornwing made a dip of his head that Giri interpreted to mean no offense was taken. "Griffins almost never pair bond. The romantic love humans speak of is something of a puzzle to us, for we don't experience it as far as I can tell. Our society is much different from that of humans," he informed. "It would take me some time to explain it."

"I have time," Giri offered.

Although his emotions were tugging him to go find Vor, he really should check in with Colby, and his new fascination with griffins and the chance to talk to Thornwing held him. Vor wasn't going anywhere—at least not yet, he hoped—but the griffin might depart at any time. Besides, after all that time in company, Vor might be seeking solitude again, and his nervousness at the thought of being alone with her redoubled at the possibility of trying to do so when she wanted her own space. Perhaps a little chat with the griffin wouldn't hurt.

"Very well then. When Hawkwind escaped the killing here at the castle, she was the last of her Line," Thornwing complied. "We live in Lines—that is, with the mother we are born to, with our siblings, aunts, and uncles. Our fathers come from different Lines and we rarely know who they are. There is only ever one breeding female in a Line. It passes from mother to daughter, or to sister or niece, each female becoming fertile for a time: as short as a year, as long as several. During that time, she may have chicks.

"As Hawkwind was the last of the Hawk Line, she became fertile—we call it awakening—but she was not an Aerie griffin; she was from Northnest and she had to earn a place among us. She also brought with her four human chicks, these three among them. The fourth died two days ago."

"The nymph," Giri provided gently.

"Yes. Kassandra: we called her Hawksky."

Thornwing's voice was soft, and Giri assumed he must have mourned her death, but his expression remained difficult to read.

"And you say now that Hawkwind has earned a place among you?" Giri prompted.

"She has," Thornwing confirmed. "The tale is a long one, and I'll not tell it now, but it ends with her being accepted by the Aerie I live in. She re-founded the Hawk Line there with the birth of twin chicks, one of which I am fairly certain is my daughter."

"Ah," Giri absorbed.

"You understand, I tell you this in confidence," Thornwing confided. "The sires of chicks are not normally discussed, and I ask you not to speak of it, though I don't expect you'll have occasion to meet her."

"I understand. So then, you didn't get to take care of her, or know her?" Giri wondered.

"Normally, I would not spend much time with any chicks I happen to sire, if I even knew they were mine. The matriarchs—that is, the female griffins currently fertile—choose the males they want when they are in heat. They might mate with more than one during a heat, and if that produces a chick, no one will be able to tell who the father was, although sometimes chicks do resemble their parents' colorations."

"Normally," Giri prompted again.

"Yes, normally," the griffin nodded. "Males normally care for the chicks of their own Line: those chicks being their nieces and nephews and so on, but this case was not normal. Hawkwind came without any other Linemembers to support her. She did encounter two other Hawks later—part of the long story—but there are normally dozens of other griffins in a Line, able to help with raising chicks, and she had twins."

Giri was a little surprised to see the exposed skin of Thornwing's nares blush pink.

"I found her a pleasant companion, and she needed help, and my matriarchs—that is, of the Thorn Line—have been indulgent in allowing me and another, Thornsoft, to assist Hawkwind in raising her chicks—our chicks."

"Thornfire said he knows his daughter, too," Giri mentioned after a moment.

"Yes. My brother is a mage, as you've observed, and so is his daughter. He took her as his apprentice, but for much of that time she did not know he was her sire as well as her master. She's a competent mage in her own right now, and currently the matriarch of the Star Line. Just a couple months ago my grandnephew was born."

Giri nodded, trying to understand and organize it all in his thoughts.

"My daughter does not know I'm her sire, unless she has guessed," Thornwing went on. "Sometimes they do. I have been able to be a part of her life more than any sire could hope to be, just as my brother has been with his daughter." He looked across the room to where Hawkwind was sitting behind Jessika and the two young men. "I remain quite fond of her mother, and her half-siblings, and indeed all of the Hawk Line."

The griffin put a serious gaze onto Giri. "I fear the changes that might come, if griffins go out into the human world again. I have been accused of being reckless and bold and even careless, but as I have aged I have come to have a care: a care for the balance not only of predator and prey, but between humans and griffins as well. We have been happily ignoring each other and staying out of each other's ways for a long time now.

"Let me tell you a bit of history I assume you might not know. Many hundreds, perhaps thousands of years ago, there was a great war between humans and griffins in this area. It ended when several griffin Lines allied with the humans. They founded Northnest. The rest of the Lines, my ancestors included, retreated into the mountains and became isolationist. Northnest stood for some time, but the alliance could not protect it from Weldom's invasion. Many of my people and yours died. I fear griffins and humans becoming entangled again. Hawkwind escaped the slaughter the first time. Will she do so a second time?"

Thornwing's great dark golden eyes bored into Giri, and he didn't know how to reply, but made his best effort.

"I hear your concern," he acknowledged. "You give me much to think on. I confess that you griffins fascinate me. I don't want harm to befall any of you. I find myself wishing to know more of you, to be friends with you, and whatever else might come of that."

Thornwing chuckled. "Do not be too impressed. We have as many faults as humans do."

"That is good to hear," Giri smiled back. "Otherwise I might think you are as exalted as unicorns."

The griffin snorted and looked away again. "They have their faults, too, if fewer."

Giri went on. "I don't really have any power to make policy—"

"I'm not asking you to," Thornwing said quickly. He resettled his wings. "I suppose, I just wanted to speak with you. You seem a reasonable human."

Giri shrugged. "Perhaps I am sometimes."

"Perhaps I seek an advocate. When you return to Weldom, when the topic of griffins comes up, you might speak with some competence and compassion about us. Although you might not make policy, perhaps the policymakers will hear you."

"That might be," Giri allowed. "If there is discussion of griffins, I will try to bring my voice to it."

Thornwing partially extended a wing and touched his shoulder lightly with the edge of it. "If Hawkwind does go to Weldom, perhaps you might keep an eye on her. She is stubborn," Thornwing laughed softly. "She might not listen to you, but maybe if you have the chance, you could try."

Giri agreed. "If any griffins come to Weldom, and I can put myself in position to help them, I will do what I can."

"I thank you for that," he said, folding his wing.

They stood together in silence for a few moments, until Giri ventured a question.

"I've been wondering, when you mouth people's hair, what does it mean?"

"We preen our feathers, like any bird," Thornwing explained promptly. "We preen each other's feathers, too, if we like each other. It can be a sign of affection and give comfort. Humans don't have feathers, but hair is something of a substitute. We are careful not to pull too hard."

"That makes sense."

"You humans touch each other with your hands," Thornwing said, "but our hands are also our feet, and not always clean, and we have claws, although we can retract them. Skin on skin touching must feel nice, but we have fur and feathers almost everywhere—although I must say that a good scratching from a human feels great."

He fluffed up his feathers and chuckled. Giri grinned, but talk of touching was making him think of Vor again.

"You have a mate," the griffin whispered, as though reading his mind.

"Not really," Giri denied quickly.

"Vor," he went on. "She is your mate."

"No."

Giri couldn't tell if Thornwing was looking at him directly or not. Griffins seemed to move their heads to change where they were looking, instead of rolling their eyes in their sockets, as far as he'd noticed, but the placement of their eyes suggested a wide field of vision. He suspected Thornwing was giving him a sly look, or would have been were he capable of it.

"You act the way young griffin males do, when they start to sense a matriarch they like coming into heat: excited, but uncertain. Are you afraid she will not choose you?"

Giri clenched his jaw.

"I am delaying you from going to her, aren't I?"

He let his breath go. "Could you not say things like that?"

Thornwing chuckled again. "Go on. I'll not keep you from her longer."

"I should speak with my master first," Giri muttered.

"No," he grunted, loosening and tucking his wings. "No, you shouldn't. You should just go. Present yourself and let her choose. She might refuse you, but then you will know. If she does, go gracefully."

Giri found himself nodding slowly.

"But she won't refuse you."

"How do you know?" Giri challenged in a whisper.

"Because she turns toward you the way matriarchs turn toward their chosen males," he replied frankly. "It is in the arch of her neck and the spread of her shoulders. It is in the way she is always looking at you, even when she's not—just as you are always looking at her. I have only seen you two in the same room some short time, and easily have I discerned it."

Giri felt his skin starting to heat. "You really think so?"

"That is my interpretation. Of course," he shrugged a wing, "she might deny herself, and refuse you anyway. Females are not always rational—especially humans."

He said that last with a layer of disdain, and looked over at Jessika as he did. Giri wondered at it, but did not voice any question. Thornwing poked him with a wing wrist.

"Go then," the griffin urged. "Let your master wait. Mating takes precedence."

Now Giri did nearly blush, but he complied.

"If I don't see you again for a while, best of luck, and good flying, and thank you," he said in farewell.

"And to you as well, Giri Holstor, except the flying. Do not attempt it.

You will fall."

Giri thought Thornwing was making a joke, and smiled. Without talking to his master, he left the room, and went to find Vor—and present himself.

Giri and Vor

She had agreed: verbally, magically—though she might not be totally in charge of her energies that were starting to interlace with his—and even with a physical gesture of reaching out to touch and draw him near. Most of her shields were down. She was looking at him steadily, waiting for him to make the next move. Giri had no idea what to do, but he should know what to do; he'd done it before. He knew what to do with a woman—

No.

Vor was not any other woman, and he couldn't—wouldn't—treat her that way. This wasn't like his usual, casual tumbles; there was something more here. Her face, usually so composed, controlled through all that happened, now revealed emotions. There was desire there, but like thin veils trepidation and uncertainty obscured it. She might have taken that boy—technically— but she hadn't enjoyed it, so not only was intimacy still new to her, she had very low expectations.

If he let his hunger rule him, he could easily get what his body was demanding he get, and she might not stop him. He could still make her feel good, but there was more to satisfy than just bodies. He'd promised, but even without a promise, he wanted to share with her the deeper connection that two people could share.

He wanted to share true intimacy with her: not just circumvent her fear but dispel it entirely so that she would participate in the experience fully: both learn and teach. He sought not just a tumble, but synergy. He'd yearned after that before, in his late teens, with two other women, but they— Giri shied away from those memories. Could the same thing happen here, as he'd worried days ago when he'd first seen the chance of this coming?

Vor was waiting for him, searching his face. He gazed back at her, really looked, and saw only what he'd seen before—no hint of any intent to lure him into an emotional attachment and then abandon him. No, what had happened before with those women would not happen with Vor, but Giri had the sudden fear that what might happen instead was something worse.

There might come to be more than tumbles between them. Already he was thinking about synergy and deeper connections. Already they gave each other respect and admiration; they had a mutual attraction; they were both mages; they shared a common culture—that sounded like a foundation upon which one built a house. There might be no abandonment, because neither would want to abandon the other. Long term: he'd vowed never to consider that again.

Giri's mouth had gone dry, his palms sweating. Dello had been right; he was in so much trouble. He shut his eyes for a breath: suddenly terrified. After a moment, rationality reasserted itself. He couldn't predict the future; why borrow trouble until it happened? He'd deal with it then. Vor was here now and he could not turn away from her. Plus, if he abruptly rejected her after reaching this point, what would it do to her emotionally? The thought of hurting her because of his fear could not be countenanced.

When Giri opened his eyes he knew he needed to do or say something. They'd stood facing each other for a few minutes now while he wrestled with internal debates. So do something, fool. What he wanted to do was kiss her. He'd never kissed anyone on the mouth, although he'd come close a few times, years ago. It had been Milsa's policy and he'd adopted it, too: he did not kiss on the mouth because it was too personal and too promising.

Despite that, he wanted to kiss Vor. It felt like the best idea he'd ever had. He almost did it. Instead, he kissed her on the forehead again. Her hands tightened on his shirt, tugging a little.

"Take it off me," he encouraged, as quietly as ever he could, "if you want."

"Can I touch you, a little?" she whispered.

"Yes. Yes, touch me as much as you want," he breathed back emphatically.

She did so with surprising confidence. It felt wonderful. Then Vor huddled up against him and held him. He put his arms around her, and just holding her felt so good.

"Touch my skin," he requested, "please."

She complied again. He was supposed to lead, but at the moment he could hardly think. Belatedly, he tried to reciprocate. He lifted a hand and ran his fingers through her hair, swept it to one side, exposing her neck. When he settled his mouth she trembled and her hands stilled their exploration. After another moment, she gasped, and then made a little sound—but she cut the utterance off and stiffened.

"You don't like that?" he checked.

She hid her face against his hair, her voice barely audible. "I like it."

"Are you scared?" he murmured, as gently as he could.

She didn't reply, which to him meant yes.

"Did it hurt, your first time?"

"Inconsequentially," she breathed.

"It'll be easier this time," he said.

The continuing tension of her body told him she didn't believe him, or that he was off the mark. Perhaps that wasn't what she was afraid of, and why would she be? Pain was something she knew: something all mages knew. But if she'd had no evidence, ever, that intimacy felt good—if in fact it had only ever been unpleasant—these new sensations she was feeling with him—and based on the state of her aura he could be confident he was making her feel good, not bad—might be frightening.

He wrapped her in his arms again and held her tight. At that, she melded to him, not resisting at all. The comfort of an embrace she would take, so that must have been why she kept seeking it from him, but when he touched her in a lover-like way—

"It will be alright," he breathed to her.

"How?" Vor murmured tremulously. "How do I—?"

He lifted her head, found her gaze: her remarkable red-brown eyes. Again surged the desire to kiss her. Again he fought it down. Giri stroked her face with his thumbs.

"As long as you're still sure this is what you want, try to embrace everything you're feeling. Give in to it," he told her softly. "Trust me."

Her eyes widened a little, and he realized he was asking something of her she'd never done before.

"It might take practice," he murmured, bringing his face close, so their foreheads touched. "Let yourself feel everything. Don't fight it."

She made a tiny sound and shut her eyes. How could he help her? He needed to; he didn't want her to be scared. New experiences of any kind could be scary, but as long as she did want it, there was actually nothing to be scared of.

"I don't know what you saw or felt before, but this is how it's supposed to be. What you're feeling is right. It's normal. It's what we get to have when we're together," he said. "Whatever you feel, don't judge it. Don't hold back."

He wrapped his hands behind her head, needing to kiss her almost more than any other objective of their tryst.

"Be with me," he begged.

For a second he thought she was the one about to kiss him, but instead she seized him, pressing fiercely against him, tormenting him. Giri found her skin with his mouth, and this time she did not stiffen or hold back her voice. The outermost of her remaining shields disintegrated and he could sense her more closely.

Never had he spoken with a woman like that. The feeling was delicate, but strong. He wasn't sure what it was, so for now, he ignored it. As he'd just told her, what was important was focusing on being together, on trusting, on letting everything be. Vor had to have all his attention; she deserved it.

Giri leaned back. As he found and held her gaze, he still saw the uncertainty of someone in a brand new situation, not sure what to expect, but he thought some courage now mingled with the fear in her. He took the hem of his shirt in his hands.

"Do you mind if I take this off?" he breathed.

He waited for an answer, and saw restrained hunger enter her eyes.

"Help me?" he offered, feeling his mouth start to curve in a smile.

"Yes," she nodded, and it was out of his hands.

Giri didn't stop her, but he was shocked to feel himself blush. Suddenly he was shy in front of Vor—but the reason came immediately. It was his first time with her, and he was scared she'd be somehow disappointed. He was lean, a scholar not a warrior, but Vor gave no indication that she minded he wasn't bulging with sculptural muscles, and when she met his gaze with the beginnings of a tentative smile, he felt relieved.

She leaned in with a hint of mischief in her eyes. "You're pretty," she murmured.

Another blush, this one of delight, surprised him. Yes, this was going well. Never before had he been so patient, so careful and thoughtful in intimacy, but the delay did not upset him. In fact he was enjoying it immensely, and in more than just the physical sense.

As they stood in gentle, mutual exploration, another of Vor's shields faded away, and he worried he would just sense another below; she carried around so many. Giri had already dismissed all of his but the last. As his energies touched around hers, however, he saw that now they were equal. Except for the innermost, which a mage almost never lowered, they had both abandoned all magical defenses.

At last, Vor gave a little push, and he let her draw back. She didn't flinch, didn't look away from his eyes, as her fingers went swift and sure to the knot at her hip. In a moment, she let the robe land in a puddle around her feet. Well, he'd known she was brave, but she'd managed to surprise him.

Vor's hands went to his hips next, to the waist of his trousers. He nodded at her. Her fingers went to the clasp and soon he was kicking them off. He had also made the realization that her bed was all the way in a different room, and he had no intention of trying to manage on the floor.

Vor rescued the situation, taking his hand and leading him off with a shy smile at him over her shoulder. He followed her, admired her form as she walked, and noticed some pale freckling in the middle of the soft brown of her back, near her spine. It didn't look like a scar. He guessed it was a birthmark, and wondered if she knew it was there, or if now only he did.

She paused at her bed for a breath, and then seized and threw back the covers until they spilled off the foot. Then she turned to him, apprehensively. Giri guessed she knew that as soon as they got down there together, restraint would weaken. He went to her as gently as he could, cautiously reaching out to touch while watching her face for any sign of distress, but she held his gaze without a hint of it. Encouraged, he leaned in further, monitoring her reactions to try to learn what pleased her the most.

When Vor grabbed for him, trying to bring them closer together, he decided that more learning would have to wait for another time. They went down to the bed and though he was still holding back she seemed to move instinctively, making it obvious what should come next.

"Giri," Vor breathed in a mix of hunger and confusion, and he lifted himself up to find her eyes. "I need you."

His every exhalation was shaking, but he tried to talk. "Yes. I need you, too."

She nodded at him. He nodded back.

Giri lowered his hips, but met resistance and after a few moments of trying sought out Vor's gaze again, unwilling to force it. He saw a hint of frustrated dismay, and embarrassment.

"Are you scared?" he whispered.

"Maybe," she confessed.

He bent down and kissed her, as close to her mouth as he could without actually being on her mouth. She responded to it, kissing him at the same time, and he had the thought, if they just slid a little to the side, they'd meet. One of his vows would break. Would that be such a bad thing? But she didn't do it, and he didn't do it.

"I'm with you," he told her, "and it will be alright."

Vor nodded wordlessly, but he could still see and feel her tension. Giri stroked her hair back off her forehead, waiting for her.

"Look at me, Vor," he urged.

She did, eyes fixed on his. He didn't blink, and didn't look away.

"I'm with you," he murmured on. "It'll be alright. I won't leave you until it's over, until you're ready. Just stay here and be with me."

This surrendering, this faith that he wouldn't hurt her, it seemed the hardest thing for her to find. In a deep corner pocket in Giri's mind surged a rage at all the people who had taught this fine young woman that all she could expect from others was mistreatment. It had locked away her ability to be vulnerable. No wonder her experience with Karolan had been a failure. Giri had the perception to understand some of what was going on for Vor—and to figure out how to respond to it—but an overeager teenage boy wouldn't have had a chance, and neither he nor Vor would have been able to understand why it didn't work.

"Listen to me," Giri summoned. "I won't hurt you, Vor." He couldn't truly promise that; there might still be a little pain, but the type of hurt he meant was not physical. "Whatever you need," he continued, "I'll give it to you, and I ask nothing in return except the hardest thing you have to give: your trust."

Her eyes widened a trifle.

"If you can't give me that, we might as well stop," he said, "because I am not going to force this." Giri's voice quavered. He realized again that he was saying things he'd never said before, and yet the words came forth easily and urgently, needing to be said. Even as they scared him, he refused to stop them. "I would rather not have you, than have you without your trust."

Giri saw his words sink into her like stones plunging into a well. He sensed a shift in her energies: something subtle, like a violin suddenly joining the rest of the orchestra, almost unheard, and yet completing the music. And then her innermost shield, the one she wore like a second skin, as all mages did, thinned and vanished: reabsorbed. That left her completely unguarded, left her soul exposed and free to touch his—if only he trusted her enough to do the same.

There was no question. In a moment, it was done: his last shield, which he had not lowered for years and years, not since he'd first learned to put it up, melted back into his core energy. Giri sensed Vor more acutely than he ever had anyone. If he hadn't been so close to her, their energies already mingling, it could have blinded him magically. If his brain had been working a bit better, he might have had the luxury of being terrified, but instead all he did was go to her: auras drawn together like undeniable forces.

She couldn't not have felt it, sensed him as deeply as he sensed her. Vor's throat tightened, and he felt her chest shudder. All the while she stared at him, and he waited, letting her look with both eyes and mage senses, hiding nothing, hoping she would see his sincerity. Vor blinked, and a tear ran out of one eye, soaking into the hair above her ear. Then she gasped, let go her breath—and relaxed.

Giri rushed into her and she cried out, but not in distress, and her hands on his hips held him near. He trembled, and it was all he could do not to release immediately—like some untried boy. After a steadying breath or two, he took control, murmuring soothing nonsense, and trying to show her the rhythm. Quickly enough Vor caught on.

"Does it hurt?" he needed to know.

"No," she breathed back.

"Can I—?"

"Yes," she declared, "yes," not even having heard the whole question.

So he gave himself a freer rein, all the while listening and feeling for her reactions: learning her. Vor's first climax seemed to surprise her, but Giri had felt it coming, and reassured her, gathering up the energy it released. The second she embraced, taking the energy herself, and by then Giri could no longer hold back his own. It gripped him deeply, and he worried he might be going beyond her tolerance, but he couldn't stop, and had no thought of leaving her before the end.

When the echoes of his cries had faded and his quivering muscles began to relax, he looked down at Vor, to her flushed face and mussed hair, and the naked vulnerability in her eyes. She'd given him her trust.

Giri wanted to collapse, but a sensation like terror and bliss was flooding him now, holding him suspended by his shaking arms. There was something as helpless and precious as a newborn kitten, soft and paralyzing, stirring in his chest. It was as though he cradled it in his hands—and he had the power to dash it to the floor and break it, or to draw it in close against his own warmth and nurture it. Giri took a careful, measured breath, and another. Gradually, the feeling faded, and a little sense returned.

He did a quick assessment and realized he hadn't grabbed any of the energy from his climax—but there, Vor had it; he could see it swirling, mixing with her own personal power, and he didn't begrudge her it. There was even something satisfying about seeing it in her. Now Giri collapsed half on, half beside her, and took her into his arms. She held him in return, stroked back the strands of hair that clung to his face and neck, and nuzzled against him.

Giri pulled her closer, partly onto his chest. He made no move to get up, and neither did she, so he let himself relax and catch his breath. This had landed among the best encounters of his life, and more than that—the most intimate of his life. He'd never before felt so close to his partner. Now he hugged her, unable to let her go.

Vor snuggled closer against him in response. Such affection from her: he'd hoped and believed she was capable of such, but she really hadn't looked or acted like it when he'd first met her—or when she'd been busy impaling her master with a spear. Somehow, Giri had brought it out of her; she was sharing that side of herself, which she might not have ever thought was there, with him. Certainly she'd seemed surprised at her own reactions to the things he did to her, and he strongly suspected she'd never had an orgasm before.

He stroked her hair and she made a soft sound. Again arose that trembling, struggling sensation inside him. It scared him a little, and his mind shied away from examining it. No, whatever it was, it must have just been some side effect of the sex. He took some more calming breaths, willing it gently away. After a time, it subsided, and his head felt clearer again. Vor was tight against him, showing every evidence of being as sated as he was.

Silently, Giri congratulated himself on a job well done.

Giri's Evening in the Conservatory

When Giri walked into the conservatory after parting from Vor in the dining room, every head swung to him like needles to the North Star. He managed not to grin too widely, but he was still floating in residual bliss from bedding Vor, and it was hard not to look like the fruit drake that had emptied out a whole bowl of mumfruits while no one was watching.

Reactions varied, flickering across faces. Milsa scowled, but Colby's mouth quirked in a hint of a smile. Ulver, Chirolen, Eriducus, and Craduticus took a moment to catch on, but then they showed signs of concern in creased foreheads and frowning mouths. Giri looked to them pointedly and bowed his head a fraction of an inch, and with it his eyes, inviting their judgment or retribution. After a moment, he looked back up. Now, they seemed satisfied, or willing to accept the situation for the moment.

"Nice of you to join us, Giri," his master grunted.

"Have you seen Mistress Vor?" Master Strafa asked clearly.

"I have," Giri answered. "She is still recovering from the battle and wishes solitude this evening."

Well, she was recovering from something, perhaps including the battle. A few people nodded. Giri tried to observe Karolan without alerting the boy—and sensed almost nothing. Had he not realized? Did he not detect the threads of Vor's energies that had seeped into Giri's own?

Giri took a seat near his master, and conversation resumed. Jessika was talking with Rossilla, and didn't seem to be aware of what had happened. Rikah and Karolan were sitting with Lissian, but Karolan wasn't talking, and Rikah, too, seemed oblivious. Giri didn't make an effort to enter any conversation either, and after a little while decided to force the issue.

He turned enough to purposefully meet Karolan's gaze.

The boy knew—oh, he knew. His jaw tightened as Giri stared at him and he stared back. For a moment, Giri wondered if Karolan was about to call him out, if they were going to throw down right there—not that the boy would stand any chance. But then all the tension ran out of him and he suddenly looked sad. His gaze dropped, and he nodded submissively.

Giri could read that clearly enough. He'd just renounced any claim he had on Vor: the four-pointer buck had yielded to the six-pointer, allowing him to take the doe he'd formerly coveted, and without a fight. He'd accepted that she was with Giri now. Only—she wasn't really with Giri. They'd had fun, yes, but—Giri looked away and wondered. He had no claim on her, either. She was free to choose whatever bed partners she liked—wasn't she? She could start bedding Karolan, too, and Giri wouldn't have the right to stop her—right?

Perhaps—perhaps he could interest Milsa in Karolan. Perhaps she could teach the boy, the same way she'd taught Giri. Maybe then, if there were genuine affection between Vor and the boy, she would find pleasure with him, and overcome the past bitterness of their first attempt.

Giri glanced towards Milsa. She had her arm draped over Colby's broad shoulders—property of the eight-pointer buck on the field. No. Milsa was devoted to Colby now, and he to her. She wouldn't undertake a project like that. And besides—Giri steeled himself to face the squirming emotion in his chest—he didn't want to see Vor go back to Karolan.

Giri wanted to keep her all to himself. Besides, if that boy would give her up so easily, he didn't deserve her. Had Giri been in his place, he would never have let her go. Giri tried to act natural, to smile and laugh at the conversations around him. He tried to hide how joyful and terrified that thought made him, but he suspected Colby at least, knew.

State Wizard Colby's Blessing

The next noon, after spending the morning with Vor, Giri took lunch back to his room. Vor was gone off somewhere—asking the blacksmith about a big birdcage, he thought. She acted so tough, but she was concerned about the health and happiness of a half dozen little birds. It made him smile. Of course part of the reason for her wanting to care for the birds was because she blamed herself for Altare's killing of the girls who had previously accompanied those birds. Indeed, Vor was tender inside, and he'd seen that first hand, both in the most intimate way possible and in her public actions. Giri wondered though if anyone else had noticed: if they saw her as anything other than a cold bitch tainted with dark magic.

Giri settled down at his little table in front of the window, food all but forgotten as he replayed some choice moments from a short while ago in Vor's bed, after the warding lesson concluded conveniently in her room. This time he hadn't needed to talk her through her nervousness, and she'd been much more confident—and even a little aggressive, which he had not disliked.

But there'd been one moment, one thing that remained, like a rock in his shoe, troubling. She'd been on top of him, holding him down, taking what she wanted. He'd liked it: liked the sensations she was causing, and liked watching her causing them, but then he'd said some stupid nonsense.

"See, you can do it all on your own. You don't even need my help."

Vor's focus had snapped down to him instantly. "I need you," she'd insisted.

She'd lowered herself then, face to his face, and he'd thought she was going to kiss him. Her eyes even darted down to his mouth, and back up to his eyes, giving the cue, asking him if she could, if he wanted to.

Giri in the now winced and bit his knuckle. He hadn't responded to her cue; he'd been too surprised, and too afraid. His stupid vow, his dumb policy: why did he still cling to them? After a moment, Vor had bent down further, so his lips met her forehead instead: the usual way he kissed her. She'd trembled, but after a couple seconds resumed what he'd interrupted as though he'd never spoken.

Afterwards, as he'd held her in bed, body curled around her, she'd hidden her face in a pillow and pretended she wasn't crying. Not a tremor had escaped her, not the slightest sound of a sob, but with their energies merging and their shields down, he'd sensed her distress. Giri hadn't known what to do about it, so he'd done nothing but hold her. He wasn't exactly sure of the cause, but something told him it was his fault. After a minute, she'd stopped, and her aura had calmed.

Giri shook his head and tried again to forget it. That ought to teach him to say stupid nonsense. Aside from that bit, it had been intensely pleasurable. Despite her inexperience, Vor was picking things up from him rapidly and inventing her own techniques, which she experimented on him, to his amusement and often delight. If they had time to continue this development, soon enough they'd know each other so well—

A knock disturbed him. He sensed the questioning touch of his master's energy and sat back, trying to calm himself down.

"Yes?" he called.

The door opened and Colby came in with a little smile. "Please pardon the intrusion."

He shut the door and went to take the chair across from his apprentice at the table. Giri bent to his food and for a minute Colby just watched him obliquely, pretending to admire the view out the window.

"So, my apprentice," Colby began. "You have gotten what you wanted?"

"Pardon me, Master. What do you mean?"

He began to tick off items on his fingers. "Us back here at Northborn castle; Altare dead by his apprentice's own hand; Vor alive and well," he paused. "Vor in your bed."

"I'm in hers," Giri corrected immediately.

Colby stared at him. "And in her heart as well?"

Giri looked down at his plate, slowly chewing a piece of apple. He swallowed. All he had to do was say no. That was all. "I don't know," he muttered.

"You want to be?"

"I don't know," he repeated, more strongly. "This sounds like a conversation I had with her, asking her about that boy, Karolan."

Colby let it pass. "Have you convinced her to stay here, or go to Weldom, and become a wizard?"

He shook his head. "She says she wants to go away for a while."

"And how do you feel about that?"

"It's her choice."

Colby made an exasperated sound. "Of course it is, but I asked how you feel about it."

Giri paused and glanced up at his master. He'd never kept secrets from Colby, partly because it was impossible. The man was sharper than a knife for one thing, when it came to observation of other people's behavior and words— and what lay behind them. For another, Giri lived so closely with Milsa and Colby both, that they all three of them eventually ended up with their fingers in each other's business, whether they liked it or not. They meshed energies for magic so often that they were frequently sensing each other's feelings, and by that means knew more about what the others were going through than any non-mages ever could.

So there was no point in trying to keep anything from Colby.

"I don't want her to go," he confessed.

His master stared at him flatly. "Giri, are you in love with her?"

But despite all the rational that had just ran through his head for being honest with his master—now Giri found himself looking away.

"No, of course not. Besides, I told her I don't pair, and she says she's not interested in pairing, either."

"Hmm," Colby muttered, his ongoing stare heavy on Giri's bowed head. "You're just enjoying her, and when you get tired of her you'll move on without a care? There's nothing wrong with that, if she's good with it, too, but if there's more than that happening?"

Colby went on staring, as though trying to bore a hole through his apprentice and see what was inside. Giri continued working through his lunch, avoiding his master's eyes, pretending he hadn't heard, and squirming internally at his disobedience in not answering. He couldn't answer, because no matter what he answered—

"I was planning to teach her some teleportation this afternoon," Giri said in an attempt to alter the subject.

"That's ambitious."

"I think she can handle it."

Colby smiled broadly. "I've no doubt she can. I think it's ambitious for you to try to teach it."

Giri shrugged a little, trying to make himself smaller and still feeling acutely uncomfortable. "She wants to learn. She asked me. I want to show her."

"I'll give you a hand. I think Milsa will come, too."

He finally looked up at his master. "Are you sure?"

"If I don't help you, I'm afraid of the consequences of fouled up teleporting," Colby explained.

Giri smiled sheepishly. "You might be right."

"I'm right about a lot of things." Colby got up. "Enjoy your lunch. I'll get a workroom set up."

"Thank you, Master."

The older wizard headed back for the door, and paused with his hand on the latch. "Giri," he summoned, and his apprentice looked over meekly. "You should seriously face the possibility that you are in love with Vor, and what you want to do about it, before it's too late."

Giri stared. His eyes glazed. Some part of Giri's mind ran and hid from those words. Some other part erected a shield of denial. He looked right down at his plate. No, he was not going to fall in love again—or infatuation, stupid juvenile puppy love, or whatever it had been that had allowed those women to jerk him around and make him wonder if death would be less painful. He would not go through that again.

"Or maybe I am wrong," Colby went on softly. "But you'll have to forgive me, my son, if I am fervently hoping I'm not."

His master made a smooth exit, giving stunned Giri no time to reply. Awkwardly, he lifted another piece of apple and tried to chew it, but found he could not swallow.

After the Teleportation Lesson

Giri had been impressed at how quickly Vor had caught on to teleporting—but he had to admit that she'd done so well because of how his master had structured the lesson. Giri wondered if his own teaching would have been as good, or if his teaching would ever be as good. He hadn't yet considered that someday he could have apprentices of his own. Most of the time he still felt painfully awkward and young.

Without talking about it, Giri and Vor had started walking back towards her rooms. The instruction to rest did not automatically mean amorous behavior, and Giri was no longer a teenager with inexhaustible stamina. He hadn't been holding back with Vor at all, and wasn't sure he could perform a third time in less than a day. Still, he wanted to be around her, whether in bed together or not. He didn't examine that desire closely, even as he obeyed it.

Vor took down her wards and entered without any indication that she wanted privacy. Giri followed her in, shutting the door while she walked straight towards her bedroom, kicking off her shoes and shucking out of her jacket as she went. A few moments later, as Giri reached the doorway to her bedroom, he saw that she had flopped down on her bed—which the servants must have made up since the previous episode—with the rest of her clothes still on.

He approached slowly, removing his own outer robes, and sat on the edge of the bed. Vor was on her belly, eyes shut, but he could detect easily that, though tired, she was not sleeping.

"Do you want company?" he enquired.

In answer, her eyes cracked open a little and she tossed a hand over, grabbing his wrist. Her mouth quirked up just slightly. Some kind of worry melted; she still liked him, still wanted him around. Perhaps because when she'd wanted to kiss him earlier and he'd refused, or when she'd cried after, he'd been carrying a lump of fear that he'd done something inexcusable.

Vor didn't speak, closed her eyes again, and tugged on his wrist. Giri moved onto the bed and tucked himself behind her, hooking a leg between hers and wrapping an arm around her waist. She wiggled back into him, and for some time they stayed that way. It felt remarkably good. She didn't ask anything more of him, but as Giri continued monitoring her depleted energy levels—after all, she'd done several times more teleporting than he had—he began to feel like he should do something for her, although he wasn't sure he could.

Gradually, he nuzzled into her neck, kissing her behind her ear. Vor made a pleased sound and tried to roll over, so he pushed himself up, letting her position herself below him.

"Are you sore?" he murmured. "We did a lot in a short time, and you're not used to it."

She shook her head. "I don't think so. Are you?"

A smile surprised him at her concern. "No, but I'm somewhat low on," he trailed off. Staring into her eyes and lying on her body was belying his words, at least a little. "Sometimes men need time to recharge. The time needed usually gets longer as they get older."

Vor took that in with what seemed to be genuine interest. "How much time do you need?"

She rocked her hips and he flinched, but with a sheepish smile. "Apparently not as much as I thought."

"Would it help if I—?"

Vor slipped a hand down him and Giri groaned. "Yes," he admitted.

He didn't have to give her much direction. Her patent inexperience and curious exploration was more appealing than he'd expected. They shed clothing slowly, neither feeling the need to rush. Vor pushed him down, continuing her conquest, and if he wouldn't let her kiss him on the mouth—well, she apparently decided to put her mouth to work on him everywhere else. It was an experience Giri had rarely enjoyed, and not for the past several years. He returned the favor—glad now that Milsa had included the technique as part of his education, although he hadn't used it since—and was even able to conclude in full measure.

Afterwards, they lay close together, and though his body was beyond sated, his thoughts were troubled. Vor had her eyes closed, apparently contented, but he stared at her. She kept saying she was going to go away. She kept refusing to become a wizard. How could he make her stay? He needed her to stay.

Imagining her leaving, not having her in his arms, not being with her to talk to, to admire—not being able to feel her energies pulsing in time with his—prompted that strange, helpless feeling to begin swelling inside him again. Only by distracting himself with some other thought could he stop it. He knew that if he let it grow something terrible would happen. Or if Vor stayed, that terrible thing wouldn't happen.

Giri held her close, and tried not to think.

The Making of the Rings

"Well, it's out now, isn't it?"

Giri startled as Milsa walked uninvited into his sitting room. It was getting late, but he was still up, at his table, going through a small collection of mage-stone items: some his own, some donated by Wizard Ulver when he'd asked after leaving the conservatory. The lady-wizard leaned against the back of his couch, crossing her arms over her chest.

"What are you talking about?" Giri dismissed her.

"I'm talking about the mess you're in with Vor," Milsa retorted, "which you know perfectly well, and which you've now proclaimed to everyone by, by—" she made a frustrated gesture "—by cuddling with her in public."

"It's none of your business," he muttered back.

"It is completely my business," Milsa spat. "You and Colby are my business. What exactly do you think you're doing?"

Giri looked up. "Your relationship with Colby is not my business," he said. "My relationship with Vor is not yours."

Milsa was immediately on the defensive. "My relationship with Colby does not compromise him or me, or you."

"I'm not compromising anyone, either."

She strode across and took the chair opposite him with unnecessary force. "You're telling me you can't see what's happening?"

Giri ignored her. He'd narrowed his options down to four different items. Idly, he picked up each one, waiting to see which felt the best in his hand. He closed his eyes as he did so to help focus his magical senses.

"Or are you actually refusing to acknowledge it? Are you denying what you feel?"

Giri blinked up at her. "I'm in the middle of something, Milsa. Can we talk tomorrow?"

She sat back with a thump. For several moments she stared at him, but he didn't look at her. Whatever she was thinking, he let her think it.

"What are you doing?" she asked begrudgingly, now referring to his item selection process.

"This is also none of your business," he said softly.

He'd eliminated one option, and with that, there was really no more difficulty in choosing. He set one more aside, and placed the two mage-stone rings in front of him. Ulver had provided them with a smile. They were similar and simple, one slightly larger than the other. Giri picked up his quick reference book and opened it to a certain page. He set the book on the table, laid out flat—he'd bound the book himself so that he could open it completely and it would stay that way. Milsa was eyeing the page, and the magic circle inked on it.

Giri had built up this book over time, drawing perfect circles for a variety of spells that used small items—small enough to fit inside a circle drawn on the page of a book. It allowed him not to have to redraw a circle every time he had to use a common spell. It was a shortcut, and some mages scoffed at shortcuts, but he'd spent a lot of time getting the circles exactly right, and had used ink with his own blood mixed in, so the circles worked especially well for him. Giri had no irrational pride to keep him from using something with no downside. There were still plenty of large circles that had to be chalked out anew every time, and those were impetus enough to keep his knowledge of runes sharp.

From the circle alone, Milsa could surely tell what spell he was about to use. A glance at her showed a complicated emotion on her face. She was obviously still angry about something, but she also looked achingly sad. Abruptly, she got up, walked around the table and hugged him from the side, his shoulder against her sternum and her head tucked against the back of his neck. Giri startled a little, but didn't pull away.

Milsa kissed the top of his head. "I'm sorry," she whispered.

Then she rushed straight out of his room, probably headed for Colby's, before he could gather his wits to respond.

"About what?" he breathed.

***

A few hours later, both rings were done, and he'd also written out instructions into two identical slim journals. His eyes were blurring with fatigue and he knew he needed to get to bed. Giri set the rings and journals aside and fumbled his way to his bedroom. He shed his clothes and crawled under the covers, but the sheets were cold. He rolled over. His arms felt empty. He hugged a spare pillow. That wasn't good enough.

Stubbornly he lay there anyway, hoping sleep would sneak up on him, but after what felt like another hour or two, he was still awake, despite the weariness in him. Muttering to himself, he tossed back the covers, got up, and staggered to the wardrobe. He pulled out the first robe that came to hand and wrapped himself in it.

The halls were dark, with only a few night candles burning, but he made his way unerringly to Vor's rooms. As he reached out to touch the door, his tired mind alerted him that she'd have her wards up—and they were good ones now. He wouldn't be able to sneak in. Muttering some more, he checked anyway—and saw that her wards were all in passive mode, allowing anyone to enter. Giri opened the door, went in, shut it, and with a half conscious wave of his hand, set all the wards to active. Halfway to her bedroom, he dropped his robe on the floor.

Vor stirred as he approached, apparently sensing him. He touched her shoulder, murmured something, and knew only that he sensed welcome. Now his body began relaxing. Now he knew sleep was coming. Giri managed to get into her bed before it hit him, but as soon as he was flat, he was drifting off. With Vor's warmth beside him, and her aura interlacing gently with his—even though they were just sleeping and not touching—all was well enough that he could rest.

The Last Morning

She must have been waiting to sense him coming awake. As soon as Giri was conscious enough to recognize where he was and remember how he'd gotten there, Vor was sliding over to him, wrapping him in arms and legs, her mouth seeking out the warm, soft spot under his earlobe. He wanted her at once, and she did not deny him. No, she took control right out of his hands, gave him everything he wanted and more, and left him lost and drowning in shuddering ecstasy—until her hand slipped into his, her lips kissed his forehead, and she murmured to him.

"It's alright. I'm here."

Giri clasped her to him, never wanting to let go. What was this? This power that held him to her was unlike anything he'd known before. It was more than the lust for her body and the release he found in it. It was different, too, from the bonds he felt with Colby and Milsa, and yet there was something of that in it also. There was even a hint of the jolly camaraderie he had with Dello. But it was more, more than all those things.

"Vor," he breathed.

"Mm?"

He needed to tell her about it, about this feeling. If he told her, he thought it might be less scary. Yet the words wouldn't come. They boiled behind his tongue, in his throat and chest as he had the sudden fear that they were a spell and if he uttered them, something would happen. Would it be something good, or bad? Maybe he shouldn't.

Giri rolled them so he was atop her, hands holding her face, forehead against hers, and breaths mingling. He knew he should kiss her now. This was long gone beyond whatever foolish vows he'd made years ago. They were like old winter ice, and Vor the spring sun. They were never made to stand up to her, only to keep his heart safe through the season of cold, until she came and melted it. He just hadn't known it at the time he was making them. Giri would be lying to himself if he continued to pretend otherwise, and he knew it.

Then he felt a tug, faint but undeniable.

"What was that?" Vor murmured.

"My master," he confessed, "calling me."

"You shouldn't let him put his energy in your body," she advised, suddenly serious.

"It's not that," he was quick to assure her. "He's just strong enough to reach out and find me, if I'm not too far away, the same way I could reach out and touch your energy across the room."

"Oh." Her voice calmed a little. "Does this mean you have to go now?"

Giri swallowed, licked his lips, and drew his head back enough that he could bring her eyes into focus. "It does."

Vor was staring intently at him, her forehead tense, but then she seemed to relax and let herself smile a little. He'd seen so few smiles on her. Lightly, he traced a fingertip over her lips. That made her smile more and she opened her mouth a bit and caught his finger, but after only a moment, she released him.

"Then you should go," she said.

He knew he should, but he felt now a weight between them—all the words, all the gestures, everything that was remaining unsaid and undone. It had been building and building over the few days they'd spent together—or perhaps it had started building from the moment they first met? Giri knew as well as he knew his own name, that those things needed to be addressed, and would be. He had to tell her all he felt, and he had to take her in his arms and kiss her, thoroughly and repeatedly, and he could only hope she'd kiss him back.

Colby tugged again, a bit harder, and Giri winced. It would have to wait a few more hours. Vor gave his shoulder a little push.

"Go on," she smiled.

"I'm sorry," he apologized, bending to kiss her forehead.

Giri untangled himself from Vor and the blankets, staggered out of the bed, and fetched his nightclothes from between the sheets. Vor was lying back, stretched out like a contented housecat, watching him. He found the robe he'd worn to her room last night and bundled himself up in it, hoping Colby's summons wouldn't grow too urgent while he ran back to his room to clean up and dress properly. He'd fool no one showing up to the workroom in bare feet with just an outer robe hiding his nightclothes.

Before he ran out, he went back to Vor, kissing her forehead, cheek, and coming perilously close to her mouth.

"See you later," he told her.

"Bye," she smiled.

Giri dashed out without a single thought, or a single worry, not making the connection that bye was short for goodbye. Nor had he noticed the tears brimming in her eyes.

The Pursuit

"Where is she?"

Craduticus looked up from his book to Giri in his doorway.

"The servants said they saw her going out with you," he went on. "Where did she go next?"

The old mage pushed himself to his feet and reached into a pocket of his robe. For one wary moment Giri thought he might be reaching for a wand, but he brought out only a folded square of paper. Giri stared at it, suddenly broken with cold dread.

"It's for you," Craduticus said, waving the paper a little.

Giri didn't reach for it. He looked instead at the old man's lined and weathered face, still showing the red puckering of burns on one side. Craduticus was somber.

"She's gone," Giri admitted, "isn't she?"

"It is good you're not hiding from yourself about that. You knew she'd go. She told you often enough."

But he was shaking his head, hand covering his mouth and chin, just staring at the folded letter.

"It's not your fault," Craduticus told him. "Romantics want to think that love overcomes anything, but it doesn't. Otherwise we'd all be falling in love with each other all the time and the world would be a right mess, with too much love in it: easy love, love of superhuman strength and no consideration for other things that are just as important as love."

Giri was hardly listening.

"Love has to struggle," he continued. "Love has to fight and overcome."

Giri shook his head: gaze still transfixed. "It's not—"

"Oh hush, boy," Craduticus scolded. "Don't talk nonsense. I thought you were being honest with yourself."

There was a buzzing in his head, and the cold dread that had hit him was spreading now.

"Don't blame yourself that your love couldn't keep her here," the old mage went on. "Vor has far too much going on in her head right now. Your love is in there, too, fighting for all its worth—and it's worth a lot, I have no doubt—but it has a lot of enemies. In this place, where her master spent a decade trying to break her down into something like himself, those enemies are strong."

Craduticus approached and put the letter into Giri's hand. He went on holding his hand with all of his gnarled, scarred, swollen-knuckled fingers.

"Your love can't hold her to you right now, young Giri," he imparted, "but give her some time to face her battles. She won the battle against her master, but the battles in her mind continue. She'll win, and then your love will hold sway, and bring her back to you."

Giri met the old man's eyes as a hint of hope tried to hold off the dread from swallowing him. "How do you know?" he whispered.

Craduticus gripped his hand harder. "Trust her."

***

Somehow Giri made it back to his room. He fell into the nearest seat: the couch in front of the little fireplace. He held Vor's note in his hand as carefully as he would hold a cup of tea full to the brim, fearful of spilling, but it was a different liquid that was on the verge of spilling.

Craduticus wouldn't tell him where Vor was going. He said he'd promised not to. She'd gone without saying goodbye—but Giri had to be honest with himself. If she'd tried to say goodbye, he would have done everything short of physically restraining her to try to make her stay. At least she'd left a note, and though it wasn't addressed to anyone, that Craduticus had been holding it, waiting for Giri to come get it made it clear that she'd written it for him.

"I'm going away for a while to clear my head and decide on my next course. I hope I will see you again soon. Vor."

Something broke open inside him and the tears made tracks down his cheeks. Anguish welled up and he had to throttle down a moan. Then the adjoining door to Colby's suite opened. As his master swept in without asking, Giri hastily wiped his face and tried to compose himself. He hid the note in his hand. Colby went directly to him and stood over him, arms folded, looking down at the top of his head.

"She's gone then?"

"Who do you mean, Master?"

"Vor," he declared impatiently. "As you know very well."

"Oh, yes." Giri shrugged. "It's her choice."

Colby made a huff of exasperation. "Don't try to pretend. I felt your pain through the wall."

He shook his head. "It's fine. She needs some time by herself. I can understand that. It's fine."

"She left you a note?"

He gritted his teeth.

"I can see it in your hand, Giri. Show it to me?"

Wordlessly, he lifted it up, letting his master take it.

"You told her how you feel, before she left?"

"There's nothing to tell," he all but snarled.

"So she still thinks you're not planning to pair permanently with her, and spend your days merging magic and doing works together to the point that you can't tell whose energy is whose anymore, and marry her, and maybe even have some babies with her someday?"

Giri gaped, still staring at the floor. "Master," he scolded softly.

Colby's voice was rising. "That's what you want, isn't it?"

"No," he uttered.

"Stop lying to me, Giri," Colby ordered, as angry as Giri had ever heard him.

He flinched, hunching himself down.

"Giri, look at me," Colby commanded.

Reluctantly, he obeyed. His master's face was serious and yet tender at the same time. Colby put his hands on Giri's shoulders, pushing and making him sit up straighter.

"Listen to me. If you let her go, you will regret it forever. What you have had with Vor, these past few days, you will never be able to get back. I have seen you more passionate, more alive, than ever before. I would not see you die again."

The tears poured and he couldn't stop them, but he at least kept his sobs silent. Colby got down to one knee in front of the couch and pulled his apprentice into his arms. Giri clung to him, hiding his face against his master's shoulder.

"Go after her," he instructed. "If she won't come back right now, as she says she needs to think through some things—and it doesn't surprise me—and she needs to be alone for it, alright then. But you must not let her leave without telling her you want her to come back, and why."

Colby released him and held him out at arms length again. "Do you understand me?"

"Yes, Master," Giri whispered.

"I can't permit you emergency leave to go with her right now, but I can give you today, and I'll try to push through a request, so you can join her for a while, if you want."

One thought after another piled in on his overburdened brain and Giri scrubbed at his forehead. "I don't know if I should—or if she'd want—but thank you, Master—don't I need to stay here? Can I go? I don't know where she's going. Craduticus wouldn't tell me."

"He's protective of her because he left her behind with Altare when he escaped years ago," Colby explained. "He feels guilty."

Giri nodded absently.

"There are not that many roads leaving the capital, and she hasn't got much of a head start. Borrow a horse. You still have traces of her energy in you; use it to track her."

He nodded again, but with consolidating focus.

"Milsa told me you made a pair of contact rings last night," Colby added.

"Yes," Giri admitted.

"Now is the time to give her one."

Some of the pain had faded. Now was creeping in an icy anxiety; he was going to have to tell her, confess his feelings.

Colby put a hand on his head. "You'll be fine, my son. I believe she will answer you."

"What if she doesn't?" he managed to ask.

His master was silent for a few moments. "I truly do not think that will come to pass, but if it does, you will return here, and Milsa and I will be waiting for you. You will not grieve alone. After that, we will see, but do not think of that, for that will not be the future. You may have some weeks or even months without her, but when she returns to you, she will be prepared to meet you as the partner you need and deserve, and you will rise to be the partner worthy of her, too."

He smiled into Giri's eyes. "I see this future clearly, my son. Do not be afraid."

"I'll try not to be, Master."

"But none of this will happen," he said more firmly, "if you do not get up off you arse and go catch her."

Giri almost smiled. "Then take your hand off my head, so I can get up, Master."

***

There she was. Her aura shone out to him like a fire in the night. She must have heard the hoof beats, for she stepped to the verge to let him pass, without looking back. When he pulled up and dismounted, when she glanced at him, recognized him, and let him grab her up into a hug far rougher than he should have done, her powers surged, energies crashing into his, and they wrapped together as urgently as their arms wrapped each other.

Giri was babbling; he knew it but couldn't stop it. Over the hour-long ride so many things had gone through his head, so many words he'd thought he'd say to her. He'd revised over and over the right things to tell her. None of that remained. He was finally knocked out of his stupor a little when he sensed the mark she'd accepted from Craduticus.

He, Giri, had offered that to her and she'd declined. Part of him was instantly, irrationally jealous, and another part howled in victory from a mountaintop. Vor had accepted the first step along the path to being recognized as a Weldom wizard. Why she'd taken it from Craduticus and not from him, Giri couldn't know yet, but now she wouldn't put him off, and she didn't try as he picked the spot for his own thumb.

He held her close, knowing it would hurt her, as it had hurt him, five times, getting his recognition from five senior wizards. The last one to award a mark, one of Colby's contemporaries, had taught him as he did it how to bestow marks on others. Giri had never given anyone else a mark until now. Vor didn't flinch. If anything, she held him closer, but let him go when he was done and had tugged the shoulder of her clothing back into place.

The rings: he was scared she'd refuse it, or wouldn't wear it. When she put it on, and he put his on, he felt the sudden weight of the moment. In some parts of Weldom, rings were used as a symbol for marriage. Of course, this wasn't a marriage; marriages were done before witnesses, usually with an official that would write it into a book somewhere, and often after months of planning.

In arranged marriages between nobles, it was quite common that the two people being married would have spent not much more time in each other's company than Giri and Vor had done, and they wouldn't likely have been intimate, and they wouldn't know each other as well, and wouldn't feel as strongly for each other as Giri and Vor did. But still, Giri told himself the rings did not mean anything symbolic like a vow of matrimony.

These were just practical communication devices, and so he told Vor. Rings were easy to carry around—not like something loose that must be kept in a pocket. The hands could still be free to do other things while using the ring for communicating. It was a perfectly mundane choice. Still, when they had them on, when they'd agreed to use them to send messages to each other, he felt the firmness of the promise to each other.

"I will come back," she pledged. "It won't be long."

"How long?"

"By spring."

Summer was on in full, but that meant autumn and winter without her. "That long."

"I just don't know if I'll be able to get back once the snow comes."

"Yes," he nodded. "Of course, I didn't think of that. The winters must be harsh up here."

Northborn was indeed much farther north than most of Weldom, only abutting it on one small edge, about a tenth of the total length of the larger country's border. He didn't ask where she was going. If she wanted it kept secret, he would allow that, now that he could at least keep in contact with her—if she'd continue wearing the ring and responding. There was always the chance that distance would make the heart forgetful.

Now, however, his heart pounded with strength and rightness. They had the agreement of the contact rings, but he hadn't really told her anything to confirm that they were more than bed friends. After all, he'd started the relationship by emphasizing that he was just going to teach her about sex, have some fun together, not pair up permanently. She'd agreed to those conditions, but he'd suspected even as soon as in the aftermath of their first coupling, that more was happening, that she was enamored—and likewise he.

Giri thought, they both knew how they themselves and each other felt, but they hadn't said anything aloud because of that agreement. He hadn't kissed her because of that agreement, even when it was plain she wanted him to. They stood close now, not touching. If he were just her friend, now was the time he'd say farewell and fetch the wandering horse, but he couldn't say goodbye yet.

He couldn't say anything. His throat was tight, fear holding back any words—clever, tender, or otherwise—that he might have uttered. Well, if he couldn't tell her, he could show her. He could do with Vor what he'd never done with anyone, and there was no better time than now—except perhaps two days ago, or yesterday, or this morning.

Giri lifted his hands to touch her face and started to lean in. For a moment, hope and anticipation flared in her eyes, but she damped it quickly, dropping her gaze—ah, she was expecting him to kiss her on the forehead, as he usually did. Well, he would surprise her, then. Instead of lifting up, he bent down, tilting his head as he had seen done.

When his breath hit her lips, he sensed her burst of realization through the surge of her aura. She didn't pull back, didn't stop him—she reached out to him with surety. Vor's gentle touch made him tremble, and when their mouths met, all was lost. Any resistance, any so-called vow, or any self-denial that remained crumbled: dashed aside by the swelling glow of synergy.

Giri didn't really know what he was doing, but Vor seemed to have some idea, and so he let her lead, let her teach, until he started to catch on. More than pleasant, kissing her was arousing, too, and the thought crossed his mind of trying to find some private place off the road for some more extended intimacy. But then again, she was headed somewhere, and he had no idea if she needed to reach a certain place by dark. He was already delaying her.

"I'll come back," Vor told him again after recovering her breath. "I need to get myself centered. I don't think it's fair to you if I'm not ready to—"

That was all he needed to hear. Even if she couldn't express it anymore than he could, he knew what she was saying, and she didn't need to say anymore. He kissed her again, saving her the need to try to express it.

"It's alright," Giri assured her. "I'll be waiting for you. I promise. Then, we'll work everything out."

Saying goodbye was still nearly impossible to do. He tried to be strong. She cried, and he almost swept her up, told her she would not go, and put her on the horse. But no, he would be a part of her life where he fit in; he didn't fit right now. He would fit, soon, but if he forced her path to change, she would never grow into the woman she needed to be. He wouldn't be left with the woman he loved, but rather the warped and stunted possession he coveted with memories of how she'd once been and frustration at why she wasn't that anymore.

So he wiped her tears, got on his borrowed horse, and they said their farewells. He thought for a moment Vor was about to speak, but he waited, and her words did not come. Perhaps it was not yet time for them.

Watching her go, trusting the horse would take care of itself and stay on the road, until Vor was out of sight, until he turned to face the way back to the capital, only the hope of seeing her again and the tentative promise of a future together could keep the pain of parting from overwhelming him.

Long Distance Call

Giri was walking the horse back into the palace stables. He was no great horseman, but had learned to ride as all nobility did, and it had come in useful a few times in his assignments with Colby. A stable boy came out to take the gelding, and Giri started to protest that he would take care of it, but the boy was not to be put off, and Giri didn't really have the determination to stop him.

He much rather wanted to go find a quiet place in the garden and think of Vor. He was tempted to call her on the ring already, but held himself back; she was probably still walking to her destination. He would at least wait for nightfall. Maybe he should even wait for her to call first, so he could be sure he wasn't bothering her? But then if he didn't call, would she think he was ignoring her? His master found him in the garden, sitting by the pond where he'd talked to Vor that one evening.

"Well?" Colby asked softly, taking a seat beside his apprentice.

Giri couldn't hold back a shy smile. He felt his master lightly touch his aura.

"I would venture a guess that things went well."

Giri nodded slowly. "I think so."

"You think so? You told her you love her, right?"

He made a weak, uncomfortable gesture. He opened his mouth to speak, closed it, and opened it again. "We kissed," he confessed in the end.

"Ah." Colby surely recalled all those angry, wounded, juvenile vows Giri had made. "Does she understand the significance of that?"

Giri nodded. "I never kissed her before. I wouldn't, even when I knew she wanted it. And I told her I didn't want her to go, that I wanted her to come back, and other things. I think we have an understanding."

Colby sighed. "You should have told her outright."

Giri licked his lips. "I still could."

He pulled out the slim journal with the ring codes he'd made up. There were some codes used commonly among the wizards of Weldom—for contact items were common things—but Giri had added additional codes that were not normally used to convey business-like information. He flipped to the back of the book and showed Colby one in particular.

"And you gave her a book identical to this?" his master clarified.

"Yes."

"Well, then you have told her already, once she reads it, but you should send her that code before she does."

Giri looked at the sky. It was late afternoon.

"She hasn't contacted you?"

"Not yet."

Colby patted him on the shoulder. "Well, get some dinner then. If she doesn't call you by nightfall, you should call her, at least to find out that she's safe somewhere."

Giri didn't argue. His master giving him direction was a relief, taking some of the agony of indecision off his mind.

"And tomorrow we're doing the assessment of the mine," Colby went on. "We'll need you for that."

"Yes, Master," he agreed at once.

Vor was on her path now, and moping about wouldn't help her or him. Giri had work to do; he wouldn't impress Vor by neglecting it.

***

Dusk had just fallen. Giri sat with Colby, Milsa, Strafa, and her apprentice Rossilla in Colby's suite. Strafa was perfuming the air with her pipe again as they all sat around playing Magic and Manticores: a childish game that was nevertheless entertaining and even addicting. Giri was having trouble concentrating, and his pride of manticores was in danger of being wiped out by Milsa's band of wizards. He normally performed well at the game—although there was an element of chance, so success was never guaranteed—but tonight, his mind was elsewhere.

Then he felt the ring pulse.

"I forfeit," he declared, standing so quickly he almost upset his chair.

Immediately, he focused and sent back a single pulse of his own: confirmation of contact established. Colby grinned widely and nodded. Ever the opportunist, he quickly absorbed the remnants of Giri's manticore pride into his own.

"Have a nice night," his master bade.

"Thanks, goodnight everyone," Giri said quickly.

"What was that?" Rossilla muttered as he left. "He could have recovered if he'd just—"

Giri didn't hear what else she had to say. He shut his door as he sent the message he'd memorized to send first.

"Are you safe?"

He drew the codebook from his pocket as he went to his couch. Too impatient to light a lamp, he just touched the metal of it and spelled it to glow. Vor replied in the affirmative and asked if he was safe, too, which made him smile. He went on enquiring if she was warm and had food, and then came a brief pause.

And then a longer pattern of pulses from Vor, and Giri had to look it up to confirm it.

"I miss you," she'd said.

Giri shut his eyes for a moment, cherishing the message. He sent it back to her.

Now.

He knew it needed to be now, if it was going to be anytime. If she'd flipped that far back in the book to find that phrase, then she was only one page turn away from the bigger, brighter phrase.

He turned to it, braced himself, and told her he loved her. There was only a breath or two of waiting. Then her next message arrived.

Giri leapt to his feet with a laugh of joy. He punched the air, spun about, leapt the couch, dashed across his room, and flung open his door. Still grinning wide enough to split his cheeks, he ran down the hall, slid down the banister, ran into Amlee at the foot of it and swept her up into a hug, spinning her around.

He set the flustered castellan down and capered down the main corridor, out through the doors, and skipped through the garden until he emerged into the soft summer air of the nighttime courtyard. Giri spread his arms wide and reached up to embrace the sparkled sky.

Through it all he was sending pulses into the ring in time with his clamoring heartbeat. He brought his clasped hands in against his chest, sending her the message again, and again. She replied the same again, and again. The stars got a little blurry as he stared up at them: head tipped back, long hair stirring in the cool breeze coming down off the mountains.

"Vor," he whispered to the heavens, "Vor Hearthsraven, I love you."

Spring still felt like a lifetime away, but for Vor, he would wait.

To be continued...

Thank you for reading!

Did you enjoy the journey?

Please leave a rating or review on Goodreads, Amazon, or
wherever you talk about books. Reviews help books get
to readers who might enjoy them.

You can find more information about me and my books,
and updates on future books, at my website or on my
Facebook or Goodreads page.

www.elucidationimages.com
Kasmith Art & Books